CORTÉZ:

FOR GOD AND SPAIN

CORTÉZ:

FOR GOD AND SPAIN

An Historical Novel

by

S. FOWLER WRIGHT

THE BORGO PRESS

MMX

FOREWORD

Sydney Fowler Wright wrote this 237,500-word tale of the extraordinary achievements of Hernando Cortéz, after visiting México, whilst in California (1932) assisting with the filming of his first novel *Deluge*, in 1933—the final chapter being written in December 1934.

It is likely that his original interest was awakened by the turn-of-the-century discovery of the Spanish friars' eyewitness accounts.

Of the only known (carbon) copy of the manuscript, pages 1-4, 708 and 816 are missing.

As with the majority of Sydney's writing, it was not intended to be commercial. It was written to tell a story that both entertained and made the reader think.

—Gus Fowler Wright

CHAPTER ONE: FORTUNE'S SMILE

[missing pages 1-4 of the manuscript]

...both for distance and storms by the little sailing vessels they were. They took in water. They waited for a friendly wind and a placid sea, that they might, at least, make a fresh start on a lengthy way.

Quintero thought that, if he could arrive first and alone, there would be a better market for the cargo that bulged his hold. There came a night when he slipped cable, and in the morning his place was bare.

The comrades he had left smelled the wind: they looked at the sky: they thought their anchorage good. They were soon content to be watching a storm that raged on the outer sea. Quintero struggled back with a broken mast, which was a better fate than they had thought him likely to have. They met him with oaths and gibes, but consented to wait while his ship mended her wounds.

As they neared the Indies, he tried the same trick again, putting on a press of sail in the night, but the winds were unkind once more. They seemed to keep storms for his special bane. He was buffeted from his course with a perversity of weather the rest of the squadron did not observe, and when he sailed into San Domingo, his comrades had already cleared their cargoes and made their trade, so that he must deal with those whose purses were lean, and their warehouses well-supplied.

Hernando may have observed again that Fortune will refuse a too-impatient attack. She is best wooed by those who are alert to watch for her smile. But, beyond that, Quintero's doings were nothing to him. He sought Ovando, Governor here, and with powers of which a king may come short, his royal master being so remote, and with brief leisure for thoughts of his Indian realm, so long as the treasure-galleons it sent home were frequent and richly filled.

Ovando had been absent in a distant part of the island when Hernando arrived, but his secretary was kind, and when he returned he received his young kinsman in a liberal way, giving him a wide grant of land, and solid advice therewith, which was accepted with some demur.

The young Cortéz had come with dreams of golden fortunes that could be won by the sword's device, in strange and difficult lands. He found strangeness enough; but he was pointed to fruitful ground, and told that it was there that his fortune lay, where rents were none, and Indian labour forced, and needed no gold to pay. The Governor gave him slaves (as they were in all but name) sufficient to work his land; he made him Notary also for the Acua District, in recognition of the slender legal education that he could claim, which may have been more than could be shown by any other of the adventurers among whom Ovando must make his choice.

Hernando accepted legal office, land and advice, in his smiling way, waiting his chance of a more spirited life, and quickly finding that that to which he had come would be better than dull.

Ovando had a lieutenant, Diego Velásquez, whose part it was to keep order in the land where the Indians, though of an indolent docile kind, had not yet learned that insurrection was no more than a futile invitation to their new masters to scourge them with heavier whips. Cortéz joined his expeditions. He gained knowledge of the conditions of Indian warfare, and confidence in the powers of Spanish weapons and tactics to overcome far more numerous native foes. Confidence in himself he could not gain, for that he had never lacked. He would have joined Nicuessa's disastrous expedition, which would have been his probable end, had not Fortune smiled upon him with an illness for which he must have given belated thanks, when he saw what it had caused him to miss.

But when he had been eight or nine years in Hispaniola, Velásquez was appointed to command an expedition for the conquest of the neighbouring island of Cuba, and Cortéz had been quick to leave his plantation to join in that successful adventure. That was a year ago. Cortéz, at this time, was known as a man of a ready sword and a ready jest, whose constitution had proved equal to endure a climate where many died, and who had worked his plantations with judgement and energy sufficient to fill his pockets with easy gold. In the conquest of Cuba, he had been popular with the troops and approved by Velásquez, to whom he gave valiant aid. When it had been brought to subjection, and Velásquez was appointed its governor, Cortéz may have considered the secretaryship which came to himself to have been no more than his deeds deserved.

Don Diego was a man who had come to his present power without adversity's test. He had been born to wealth, and to a high name in his own land. He had served in the European wars for nearly twenty years in posts of some importance, if not separate command, and had avoided discredit, though he had not established a shining fame.

He had seemed a safe choice for Ovando's lieutenant, and had proved equal to the task of reducing the natives of Hispaniola to the docile labour their new rulers required. He had seemed a safe choice again as a commander of the Cuban expedition, and for its subsequent government. It was the constant difficulty of this expansion of Spanish power in a distant world that men must be found of a temper and ability that hardy ventures required, and who could yet be trusted to continue an allegiance at a later time when subordination might become hard to enforce.

Diego Velásquez had been successful in Hispaniola and Cuba, in such wars (if they can be dignified with that word) as had been easy to win. As a governor, he had not been tested at all. He proved to be of a restlessly suspicious temperament, cautious to hesitation in all he did, not remarkable for sound judgement of others, nor oversure of himself; yet with a vanity which much extolled the importance of the position which he had gained, and his services to the Spanish Crown.

He was reputed to be avaricious, which was not a failing to make him conspicuous among those who crowded to plunder a golden world, unless it were a vice of robust growth. It is certain that he was soon surrounded by the discontent of those to whom he had become the patron by which they lived, being the power that could allot land and apportion slaves; and it is equally sure that these men were of a most lively greed, which it would not be easy for him to sate.

He had for lieutenant a Spanish hidalgo, Narváez, who was no more capable than himself, or perhaps less, but with a more buoyant self-belief, which was to end in shame on a later day. Narváez may have thought the easy subjugation of Cuba to be a greater deed than it was, and exalted himself as the active instrument of the event. But, in fact, there had been no stubbornness of resistance from men who had neither love for war nor practise in its pursuit; except only from a chief, Hatua by name, who had fled from Hispaniola before rather than bend his neck to a foreign yoke. He fought hard, and, being captured at last, Velásquez condemned him to be burned alive for the 'rebellion' of resisting the Christian power. If we call him cruel for that, which is a moderate word, we must still observe that it was no more than would have been done by most of his time and race who were of the disposition to come to places and power; and few excepting some of the priests would have called it an evil deed. The priests were earnest to save Hatua's soul, beside which, as they were firm in belief, his body's fate was a trifling chance; but he said that if Heaven were a place to which Spaniards went, he would prefer to set off on another road.

Cortéz looked on, seeing him burn, and if the smile left his eyes, he did not protest. He may have done more than Narváez to bring Hatua to the stake, and Cuba to the possession of Spain, but, unlike him, he did not think them to be very noble deeds.

That was a year ago, and Velásquez had been his friend for some further months, which would be too much to say now. The governor had come to look on him with suspicious eyes, as one who was too disposed to take the part of the malcontents in a jesting way; and now there was a difference of a more personal kind.

Hernando Cortéz stood in a frowning doubt on the steps on the flower-clad porch of the house he had built, but three months before, to overlook the wide grant of fertile land that was now his for his slaves to till; and as he did so, Juan Xuárez rode up, and alighted before the door.

CHAPTER TWO: MISTRESS OR WIFE?

Juan Xuárez deserves such pity as is due to a weak man who is thrust by the malice of events into a position calling for strength which is not his. Yet we must allow that it was by his own will that he came to Cuba from his Granada home, unless we say that his four sisters were not merely of the same mind, but controlled him wholly in that.

Being there, with them on his hands, it was an easy guess that there would be trouble for him. The girls were beautiful in the Spanish style. They were poor by the standards of those among whom they must make the only acquaintances that were possible here. They were of gentle birth, but of an obscurity that held them off by no more than the flimsiest fence from the plebeian crowd, in the country from which they came. They may have had dreams that they would arrive at more splendid wedlocks than would be likely at home, in a colony to which some noble and wealthy Spaniards went out (though there were far more of baser degrees), and where women of equal rank would be hard to find.

But they overlooked an essential factor in the social problem with which they dealt. The morality of the island settlement was simple and unashamed. Gentlemen of Spain took all the mistresses they required from the docile population they had subdued. It was a condescension, and if sin at all by the Church's rule, it was one of a most venial kind. Nay, it might be meritorious, if it should bring these heathen women into the Church's fold, as it was almost certain to do.

It would be a misconception to attribute this attitude to the hypocrisy of the priests, in oblivion of the hard logic from which it came. The priests were honest in their belief that they could save those whom they baptized from the horrors of endless hell. Some of them had shown the true spirit of Christ in the boldness of their protests against the oppression of the natives of these West Indian isles, and of the cruelties of which many of the invaders had been guilty in their lust for wealth without toil. They had even resisted the system of forced labour by which the whole economic structure of prosperity was sustained. They had been so loud in their protests to the Spanish court that a royal commission had been sent out with full power to decide the issues that they had raised. The commission had consisted of three friars with a chairman of legal training. Their investigation was thorough, and their sympathy with the natives beyond denial. They recommended many reforms for their protection. But they could not honestly approve the freedom for which petition had been made by the local priests, for they encountered one objection beside which all others shrank to dwarfish size. If the natives were not forced to labour on the plantations, they would not come under Christian influence. They would be saved from aching muscles at an enormous cost. So the Indian maiden went, happily enough as it often was, to the oppressor's bed, that she might be taught to kneel to the crucifix he revered. The Spanish official or planter was content with a mistress now, and would look for a wife of good social rank, such as his own name would deserve, or his opulence would secure, when he should return to Grenada or Castile. He had no mind to burden himself before that with a wife of humble degree.

Juan's sisters found that they were of an immediate popularity. They were quickly and warmly wooed. But they discovered that it was as super-mistresses, not as wives, that there would be a ready market for what they were. Isabella took the best prize that the traffic showed, or what would be commonly so esteemed. She became the Governor's mistress. Catalina, the second, found that she had drawn the eyes of a younger, and much handsomer man, whom it was very easy to love. Her surrender had been from passion, and not for price, and that to one who was skilful to woo in a bold and yet tender way.

Juan learned from a sister's lips, in words that were barbed to wound, that Catalina was heading privily for the same path that Isabella had taken a month before in an open way. He was a much-worried young man. Isabella's conduct had vexed his pride, but he had recognized it to be a matter far beyond his control. She neither required, nor would have endured interference, from him. Nor could he have brought the issue, had he so desired, to a duel's test, the Governor being too high for his sword to reach.

But this matter of Catalina was of another colour. She was not content to parade what she would have considered shame, nor yet to be kissed and left in a private way, such as (it might be hoped) would be unknown outside the doors of her own home. Having given all in one passionate hour, she asked to be paid to the same sum, or (as Cortéz would be likely to think) very much higher than that.

Isabella was on her side. She thought that Cortéz presumed, making that which she had done herself look a cheaper thing, a family failing, rather than an individual choice. She said with indignant eloquence that Catalina was worthy in every way to be Hernando Cortéz's wife. If he loved her, why should the event pause? It was clear that it was not she who was seeking delay. If he did not, he had done her insult indeed.

Isabella said these things also in the Governor's ears, making it clear that she looked to him to protect her sister from being held at Hernando's price. Velásquez spoke to his secretary thereon, doing Catalina no good, but deepening a growing breach between Cortéz and himself.

Cortéz was not pleased that the Governor should intrude into his private affairs. He would not be likely to agree that Velásquez should expect to obtain a Señorita of the Xuárez on easier terms than himself, humility not being a virtue which he cultivated to any vigorous growth. He declined to admit that there had been such intimacy with Catalina as had been implicit in the Governor's words. Velásquez replied that he had Isabella's warrant for what he said.

"Then," Hernando was curt to say, "she should be practised to curb her tongue." After which he left the Governor's presence with less courtesy than his position required.

He would have preferred to continue his relations with the girl without the obligations of a permanent bond, and in a discreet way, thinking it to be a matter for himself alone, and for her. Catalina's cause was being urged by worse advocates that she should have used, which were those of her own lips, and her own tears. Hernando might be quick to smile, but was not therefore easy to drive.

Isabella, finding her lover unable to help, gave her brother a jibing word, which moved him less than the sight of his sister's grief. Doubly spurred, he got out his horse, and rode to Cortéz's hacienda, ten miles away.

Cortéz, as he saw him ride up, had been half resolved to go to Catalina, and make accord at her own price, if she were not to be brought to smiles at a lighter fee. He saw Juan appear, and the intention was put aside.

Now he came down the steps in a smiling confident way, very sure of himself, and of his ability to control the position. He might have his doubting moods, but he would always be confident and cool when the moment for action came.

He held out a ready hand, which was taken in a more hesitant grasp. He was quick to call one who would take charge of a steaming horse. He led the way hospitably in from the sun's heat.

Juan was not a coward. He was young, and diffident among louder men. He knew the reputation that Cortéz had, he having fought half-a-dozen duels since he had made his home on the Indian Isles, and they had left him without a scar. That only one of his opponents had died was attributed more to his own will than any boast of theirs. He had trained himself to great skill with the sword.

Men did not give him the name of one who was of quarrelsome moods. The duels had been the choice of those who thought that he made too free where he should not have looked. All but one had had a woman for cause, as most duels would. And in that he had done no ill, nor had it in thought. But he was not quick to explain; he drew his sword in an easy way, as though a bout of such strife were a trivial thing.

"I would know," Juan said, when they were seated at ease, and he could no longer defer the subject on which he had come, "when you would wed Catalina, as Isabel tells me you have a purpose to do; and to say you are one whom it will be an honour to call our kin."

Cortéz looked at him with eyes that had ceased to smile. "The Señorita Isabella," he said, "intrudes where a man would have discretion to keep away. Would you cheapen your sister's price by offering her thus, before petition is made?"

Juan was confused by a point of view which he had not considered before. But he saw that it ignored facts, and that Cortéz played with words in a skilful way.

"That," he said shrewdly enough, "would be true, if you were a stranger to her."

Cortéz struck straight, as his way was if a feint should fail. "What," he asked, "will you say that I am to her?"

"You are one," Juan replied, holding his point with a timid courage which would not yield, "who was in her room for two hours during the night, having climbed the vines after you left, when the house was barred."

Cortéz frowned, "Does she say that?"

"It is not she—"

"Then there is no other who should. If you will give me the name he bears, I will silence that in a quiet grave, though it be Don Diego himself."

"It is not a man. It was María who watched you descend."

"Women again! If you knew of aught that could silence them! But a brother should do more than another may."

Juan was confused again, but he had an obstinacy that replaced wit. "It is not that which I seek, but my sister's peace."

"Which you accuse that I too lightly regard? It is of that I will talk with her."

The boy was silenced at least, not knowing how much that promise might prove to mean. He sought, as he said, his sister's peace, though it was jeopard of honour which had been the urgence to bring him here. He had sense to see that he would bring her no joy by violent path, though it were to Cortéz's death, or else his, which was the more probable end.

Hernando had leisure for thoughts which he did not like. He had implacable moods, for all the laughter that filled his eyes, but he would be generous too, at times, in a large way, so that they did not utterly lie. He had a love of justice also, which he may have learned from when he read the books of the law; he added to this a sense of what was due to himself, and also to God. He did not care overmuch for the opinions that others held, but he would consider his own deeds in a frank way, and he was annoyed if they could not be called by a knightly name.

There was a time when he had clambered a rotten wall. He was too wise for that now. He had been sure of the vines that had exalted him to the soft warmth of a woman's arms in the night, but he was not sure that he might not be slipping here in a worse way.

He had no will to wed; and bullied to such an end he was resolved he would never be. He looked on the fortune he had made in the last years (which would be called wealth in his own land) as no more than the foundation on which he had still to build. He had dreams at times of returning home to a great name, and to alliance to some noble house of Castile. At others, he thought he would be content to make himself strong and secure in lands that were still only dropping the first jewels from fists that were tightly clenched, but were overfull.

"Juan," he said, after the silence of thought, "you are one whom I would not harm, and I will not cheat, either for yourself, or for Catalina, to whom I would be a friend, and perhaps something beyond. I will talk to her as I have said, and if it lead to her peace or no, well, I suppose she will be equal to tell you that.

"But I will ask you to look at this in a fair way; and you will see that you shall put the blame on those who meddle in matters which they would do better to leave. For, if I wed Catalina now, what will be said? That I have done so under threats which I lacked manhood to turn aside. That will be shame to me; but will it be honour to her? It will be said on all sides. But I will not say that. I will say only, that if we wed, it is my honour on which she must found her pride, and I should not be untarnished in that, if it came to be said (as you may see that it will) that I have danced to the tune that Don Diego or Isabella had played. You should tell Isabella to hold her peace, and I may bring all to a good end on a later day."

Juan did not know what to answer to this. As a promise, it was not much. As an excuse, it might be called good or bad; but excuses were not what he had come there to get. Yet he had an instinct that more might be gained by goodwill than by the show of a naked sword.

Seeing him to be silent, Cortéz went on: "You may say more than that. You may give her warning that Don Diego would do better to look to his own defaults than what he considers mine, or else there may soon come a day (as I think there must) when there will be a governor here with another name. He has given you a wide portion of land, and I suppose that Isabella could tell you why; and for myself, I do not complain. But have you thought how large and fertile this island is, besides the wealth of the mines? And of how much of the fairest parts he will not allot, keeping them for those who will follow us (who have had the burden and heat of the day), and we might rightly suppose that they will not be favoured thus, except they augment the wealth of him by whom they will look to be richly fed?"

Juan rode back with the doubt which had caused Cortéz to frown transferred to his own mind. He was not exactly sure of what he had done, or whether it were little or much. He felt it to be more than he could put into easy words, the fact being that he had been overborne by a stronger and more resolute will.

But if he had come to doubt, he had left Cortéz better content than before, for he had avoided a quarrel he did not wish, which had not been easy to do, and had asserted himself against what he regarded as insolent interference by Velásquez in his private affairs, which his official position did not excuse.

Juan told Isabella the warning he had received, which she repeated to him for whom it was meant, putting it in a worse way than it had been said. It did not cause Velásquez to conciliate discontent, but it made the breach between him and Cortéz wider than it had been before.

Cortéz came to see Catalina, as he had promised, and as it was his pleasure to do. If he thought to continue the intimacy he had commenced, with some whispered promise of a more legal bond at a later day, he had a disappointment to meet, for Catalina had taken counsel which she preferred from the lips of Las Casas, her own priest, by whose gentle wisdom she gave her lover her lips, but no more from that day till the Church should sanction a closer bond.

CHAPTER THREE: HAZARD OF TREASON

In the months that followed, Hernando Cortéz showed that a bold man may be very cautious, and a cautious man very bold.

It became known, from the Governor's own querulous words, that Cortéz was out of favour with him. Malcontents began to make a rendezvous of his house. He received them well, and the plans that he nursed in his secret mind may have looked to a time when he would sit in Don Diego's place, and the Governor be a ruined man. But the advice he gave to those who grumbled was such as might be shouted for all to hear. If they had grievances, they must seek legal redress in an orderly way. They must lay complaints before the higher power at St. Domingo. The advice seemed futile, however good. Ships did not frequently sail, nor ever without the knowledge of Velásquez, who would be sure to prevent the departure of any emissary of his foes. He was, in fact, keeping a close watch, with better spies than even Cortéz observed.

Yet with this cautious propriety of advice, Cortéz showed himself willing to take a risk, for when suggestion was made that one might slip away in an open boat across the fifty miles of treacherous sea that divided Cuba from the more easterly isle, he was ready to venture himself, as was rightly agreed, for he was the best spokesman that discontent would be likely to find, being of good repute in Hispaniola, and standing well with the government there.

Had he put off, and escaped the seas, he might have changed the course of the island's history, for it is certain that he was not one to take such a chance without plans having been formed in a mind that was as subtle as it was bold. But Velásquez was more widely awake than he had judged him to be. Before the night when it had been planned that the boat should leave, Hernando Cortéz found himself a shackled prisoner in the common jail, with a charge of treason against his name.

In the quiet hours of the night, he had to adjust his mind to a position that he had not expected to meet. He had spoken treason to none; and there was no treason in what he had purposed to do. He was lawyer enough to see that, but he also saw that if he were promptly hanged, the irregularity of what the Governor did would be no satisfaction to him. Velásquez had the power of life and death over as turbulent a band of adventurers as might be found at that day in the world's breadth. He could make his own tale, and it was unlikely that it would be closely surveyed. There may be little urged on behalf of a man who is dead, and whose friends are quiet in the fear of a kindred fate. He considered what he would do in Don Diego's place, having gone so far, and was sure that he would be speedy to use the rope. He judged Velásquez to be less resolute, perhaps more scrupulous, than himself; but even so there was a doubt in his mind that he did not like.

While he thought, a file came through the open window, and fell at his feet. He knew that he was not without friends, but he had not expected that, and by whose hand it was thrown he would never know. He did not seize it at first, which was not his way. He liked to think first. What could he do, should he get free? Would it be better to show the file as that which he had had, but declined to use, having a conscience so clear of wrong?

On the whole, he thought not. The doubts which had been on his mind before became active again. When he picked up the file, he had formed a clear plan. He worked till the fetters fell. When he was free of them he had little to fear. He was but one floor from the ground, and the window was wide in a month of heat. He watched till the sentry passed, and dropped unharmed to the ground. Then he ran for the church.

In the morning Velásquez learned what he had done, and was a wroth man. But sanctuary was a sacred thing. In the church, Cortéz was safe; but to stay there was a dull life. After a few days he ventured out at times when the pavement was quiet and bare, or seeing those with whom he was anxious to talk, for he had things to say that he wished should reach the Governor's ears. There came a time when, as he did so, men sprang upon him, and he was captive again.

This time, he was not placed in the same jail; he was taken aboard a ship that lay in the harbour, being ready to sail for St. Domingo, where Velásquez now designed to send him in irons, to be judged by those who would not be likely to favour him.

Having done this, Velásquez could feel that he had acted in the resolute manner that his position required. He could put the incident from his mind, and give Cortéz's estates to a more pliable man. He had no reason to fear anything that Cortéz could do, now that he would be sent back in chains, as a turbulent and dangerous man. Even if appeal should be made to the Spanish Court, he had higher friends, and could bribe if need were great, with more gold than Cortéz's family could command. But in the morning he waked with the quick coming of tropic dawn, and there was Cortéz beside his bed. He was dishevelled and drenched, having again escaped in the night, and in a boat that he could not control, so that he had been forced to swim against the current, which was not easy to overcome; but he was quiet in manner, and self-possessed.

"You have nothing to fear from me," he was quick to say. "I have watched you for the last hour, but I was content to wait till your sleep was done. I have come to talk sense, for you injure me with no cause, and so may oblige me to work you injury in my own defence, which is what I am not anxious to do. We were friends before, and you had good service from me. If you will be friends as we were, you may have good service again."

He was sincere in this, for he had resolved, while the file lay on the floor, that he would abandon plans that would not go as he had first meant that they should, and make peace if he could bring Velásquez to the same mind, as he thought he could.

He asked now what his offence had been from the first, and in such a way that Velásquez was led to mention the trouble over Isabella's sister, as he had meant that he should. He replied to that, that it was his purpose to wed Catalina when he was free, as he would have done before, had it been put in a different way.

In the end, they made peace. Cortéz was not to be a secretary again, which he did not ask, but he was to wed Catalina and settle down on his estates, to which Velásquez would add some mining rights he had not had before, and which would prove to be of a solid worth. He undertook to leave discords alone; and he kept his word.

He settled down for the next five years to draw wealth from the land. He imported cattle, being the first man to have the foresight to do that which was costly and hard to bring to success. He married one to whom he was faithful and kind, though she proved to have little wit, and bore no children to their bond.

So the years passed, moving on to their incredible end.

CHAPTER FOUR: THE UNKNOWN CALLS

It was something more than two years after Cortéz's reconciliation with the Cuban Governor, that a Spanish captain, Hernández de Córdova, sailed with a little squadron of three vessels for the Bahamas on a slave-hunting quest, and he was met with such a storm as drove him headlong to unknown seas.

It was some months later he struggled back, sailing into St. Jago with no more than half the crews he had taken out, and himself dying of wounds.

He said he had been driven far to the west and had come to an unknown coast, where the inhabitants were fiercely hostile, and appeared to be of a more formidable kind than any whom the Spaniards had encountered before.

Their buildings were massive and high. They did not live in huts of rushes; they quarried stone. They were richly and gaily dressed. Their ornaments (and this was the point of all) were of solid gold. Of these he brought some specimens, wrought in barbaric style, which he had bought at his life's cost. He had, in fact, encountered the northern corner of Yucatán, and had skirted its northern coast.

Velásquez determined to know more of this golden land. He fitted out four ships, which he strongly armed. He looked round for a man to be trusted for their command, and chose his own nephew, Juan de Grijalva, on whose attachment he could depend. They left St. Jago on May 1st, 1517.

Three months later, one of the ships came back. Its captain, Pedro de Alvarado, brought a great treasure of jewels and gold, which had been bought with barter of scissors and glass beads. De Grijalva had sent him back to make report on the rich harvest which he had found, while he continued to explore a new and wonderful land.

St. Jago stirred to the news like a roused hive. There were many eyes and thoughts turned to the still undiscovered west, with bold avaricious dreams.

Don Diego Velásquez felt that the moment for fame and fortune had come. He despatched a ship homeward to Spain, sending a royal share of the gold, and a letter petitioning that he should be granted a commission for the colonising of this new, vaguely-outlined land. He despatched another, having Christóval de Olid in command, with supplies for Grijalva, and an order for the conduct of his return. He began to consider the fitting out of a larger expedition, more commensurate with the extent and wealth of the territory of which Pedro da Alvarado told, and was quickly surrounded by the clamour of those who thought themselves to be equal to its command.

At this time, it was not the custom for such expeditions to be fitted out at a public charge, neither was Velásquez in a position of unregulated control, being circumscribed by the terms of the commission he held from the superior authority at St. Domingo, and in some ways less free than a private citizen would have been.

But a limited authority his commission explicitly gave, with more power to veto than permit; and it was a fact that this great discovery had been made by an expedition that had sailed from St. Jago with his authority, and with his own nephew in command. It is not surprising if he considered that the fame and wealth (and extended rule, if conquests should follow in these unknown lands) which would result, should be his primary right.

The commission he held empowered him to send out an expedition to this extent, that he could either give or refuse permission for it to sail, and, if he should give such an authority it became his duty to issue a licence defining what it could do under the authority of the Spanish King. Also he could equip it, if he would, and if he were possessed with sufficient wealth, at his private charge; but not at that of the public treasury which he controlled.

But he was restricted, even within these bounds, by the terms of his own appointment, and was explicitly without authority to authorise the establishment of any settlement outside the limits of his Cuban territory.

It appears that while he was naturally anxious to take full credit with the Spanish Crown for the great discovery which had been made, and to bring it into subordination to his own governorship, he lacked the will or the means (or perhaps, both) to equip an expedition at his own cost, of the size which he recognized as necessary for such an occasion.

He had, therefore, to look round for a leader who would be likely to remain loyal to him, even when far beyond any physical control; and who must yet be one of a resolution and temper both to rule his own turbulent crews, and to confront the perils of the unknown seas and unfriendly lands with the combination of boldness and prudence which such expeditions required. Beyond that, he must also be of private wealth enough to finance such an expedition from his single purse, (which was beyond reason to expect), or else one of such character and public esteem that others would invest their substance in an expedition over the precarious profits of which they would have so distant and limited a control.

Velásquez considered various claimants for a position which was not easy to fill from the half-piratical adventurers among whom he must make his choice. He would not have overlooked Hernando Cortéz, but he must have weighed his name in a doubtful mind. Other possibilities must be sifted first.

But there was one in whom there had been neither hesitation nor doubt from the moment when he had sat opposite Pedro de Alvarado at a tavern board, and listened to what he told; and that was Cortéz himself. From that hour, he showed the energy of a man who works on a sure plan to settled goal.

He counted the gold he had, which had grown to a large sum during several industrious years. He sold all he had of valuable kind by which that sum could be swelled. He mortgaged his estate. He borrowed all that he could. He bribed those who had the Governor's trust to suggest his name.

He interviewed men who had wealth at command, and found that his persuasions prevailed. He had gained the name of a capable, dependable man. It was recalled that he had shown both courage and diplomatic resource in the way in which he had resisted the Governor some years before, and had then extracted himself from the difficult circumstance into which he fell.

Since his marriage, he had lived a blameless domestic life. Catalina might be of slender education, and not overburdened with wit, but she worshipped him, and he was kind and patient to her in his generous, smiling way. The priest, Las Casas, who did not like him in other ways, was a witness to the happiness that was theirs. He recorded that Cortéz said that had he wed a duchess, he could have had no fuller content.

All these things weighed with those who must venture gold in the purchase of cargo or ships which would disappear from the harbour-mouth on a quest so dangerous and so vague.

It became common talk that Hernando Cortéz was planning to go, and that there was no better choice.

It could be seen, even now, that he was in many ways an ideal leader for such a venture as this was likely to be. He had a bold, confident, smiling mien, which made dangers seem less than they were. He had a habit of legal caution in all he did which the merchants approved. He offered generous terms to those who would invest either gold or their lives, but when a bargain was made, he would have the terms drawn with scrupulous care.

It was observed that he was minute in his enquiries as to what such an expedition might need. He was exact and detailed in all that he planned and estimated. He was one who would leave nothing to chance for which pre-thought could provide.

Even before the Governor was aware that his own mind was resolved, men were talking of Cortéz's leadership as of a settled, evident thing. Velásquez, aware of more doubt than it might be wisdom to show, took counsel with those on whom, at this time, he most surely relied.

They replied with Cortéz's promises in their ears, and some of his gold already in their hands, that they could not imagine a better choice. A bold man, and yet cautious in all he did. One who had been successful in war, a popular captain, whom others followed on easy feet. Yet one who would be able to rule at need in a ruthless way.

His plantations also—were there many in the breadth of the isle that were as well-ordered, as well-equipped, as well-reputed for heavy crops? He was one who would woo success with the many-detailed care to which the fickle deity is most apt to yield.

The day came when the Governor's seal was affixed to a commission bearing Hernando Cortéz's name.

CHAPTER FIVE: THE TEST OF FAITH

Hernando kissed his wife in a buoyant mood. He said she must expect that he would remain in St. Jago for three days if not four, when she would see him again. She was not to see him for three years (or more nearly four), when she would be near to death in another land.

He had said no more than he meant. It was the 15th of November 1518, and though he had already assembled six ships, being more than could lie at once alongside St. Jago's quay, and they had taken much cargo aboard, he did not think to be ready to sail for some weeks. He would not have an hour lost, but, even so, he thought to have Christmas at his own hearth.

He got lightly to horse, his mind busy with many affairs of recruiting, equipment, organisation, and financial bargaining, any of which he might now omit without censure of other men, but on which success or failure might depend on a later day.

Twenty thousand ducats were already staked on this wild venture across strange seas to an unknown land. It was an enormous sum in those times for one man to own or control.

Velásquez had not had such a fleet to command when he had been commissioned for the conquest of Cuba; Córdova's first expedition, which had ended at Yucatán, had been of three vessels; even Grijalva had commanded no more than four.

But Hernando was still less than content. Six were well enough, but eight were to be preferred; and four hundred men would be much better than three.

But he would not delay, even for the advantage of greater strength. Expenses were heavy while the ships were moored, and men idled, along the quay. He would bustle all, and sail early in the New Year. There would be flourish of trumpets then, and half of Cuba would see them sail.

When he reached the city, he put up at the tavern of the True Cross, where he transacted his affairs, so that, in these days, it had become like a private hostel for him, and those nearest to his designs.

On the third morning, Velásquez's secretary, Andrés de Duero, called upon him and requested a private interview, as their personal friendship and Duero's office made it natural for him to do.

Duero was a man of peace, though he wore a sword, as did all of rank in those days. He was in dark blue velvet, richly but soberly clad. He was discreet and frugal of speech, and if the Governor gave him trust, it was a confidence which he had had no cause to regret.

It is said (but unproved) that de Duero, like the treasurer de Lares (perhaps a more wily man) had taken Hernando's gold; but, if that were so he may yet have been sure, in an honest mind, that the best Captain-Commander had been chosen that the island contained; and his own stake in the venture had not been small.

He found Cortéz surrounded by many who came and went in a busy way, but he was not slow to put them aside, and take de Duero into his private room. He called for wine, and asked what he might do, either for His Excellency or his friend.

"His Excellency," de Duero said, "has sent me to let you know that he has twenty bullocks that he can spare you from his own herd to provision the fleet. You are to have them at your own price."

Cortéz knew the secretary as one whom he had good reason to trust, and who had the reputation of a discreet man, but he was careful to meet this with an expressionless face.

Everyone on the island knew how the Governor sold his stock. It was always 'at your own price', and he would be riding for his own fall who did not overvalue that which he was directed to buy.

"You are more expert in such values," he answered smoothly, "than I can be. You will thank His Excellency for so gracious a thought, and put on them such price as will match their worth."

Andrés smiled slightly. "You were ever discreet, as few are who are as bold as we know you to be; which is why I am in your venture with every ducat that I can spare, or beyond that."

He became silent, but looked as though he had more to say, and Hernando waited, with a caution as great as his.

At length, the secretary asked: "If I should speak as a friend, would you give me a friend's reply?"

Cortéz said: "Do I not know whom I can trust?" His eyes smiled. "Or would you call me a fool?"

"Well, it is no more than this: Do you know why His Excellency should wish you ill?"

"I can answer that with neither guile nor reserve. He has no reason at all but a fool's word."

"And what word was that?"

"It was two days ago, when I rode in, and waited upon him, as it is my first duty to do. He was desirous of inspecting the ships, and we walked together in this direction. On the way, we saw his fool in the street, and the rogue cried out, from the other side of the way, that he who sends such a captain to hunt may come to a day when he will be hunting him.

"I said, hastily, that he should be whipped for so lewd a word, to which His Excellency did not respond, for a fool's license must leave him free.

"There is nothing other than that. But he was cool thereafter, who had not been of embracing mood from our first word."

"Well, be that as it may, if you will take the quiet word of a friend, you will be wary of speech and speedy to leave the quay."

"I thank that which is kindly said. But can I make more haste than I do? I must be well furnished for that in which I am resolved that I shall not fail. And what have I to doubt or dread? Is it to be a knife in the dark? I have the commission signed; and its wording is all I would."

The secretary did not deny that, for he had drawn it himself, with good feeling in what he did. But he said, as one merely stating a fact: "A commission may be revoked."

This remark was met by an instant's uncomprehending or incredulous stare, which turned to one of black wrath; and more of fear than Hernando's eyes may have shown to any until that hour.

Beyond the wrecking of all his hopes, the revocation of his commission now would be utter financial ruin to him.

It would be impossible to put things back as they were. It would be injustice, gross and intolerable, to cancel his authority now.

And it would be without justification of any kind!

Yet—if it were done? Would he have redress that would be of any avail?

He thought that he could read the Governor's mind like an open book. Jealousy of the success that he would be likely to have had grown as he added ship to ship, and the potentiality of the expedition increased; jealousy of his efficiency, of his popularity—of all that justified his selection, and should have proved to be to the Governor's praise.

It was the jealousy of a smaller man, who might see logical reason to fear that, while the failure of the expedition would be detriment both to his reputation and purse, its success in a far land, in these insecure times, might take Cortéz beyond his credit or his control. Commissions could not be revoked only in St. Jago; they could be revoked in Madrid.

But while Hernando thought thus, his face had regained its expression of sanguine energy and resolve. He said lightly: "You have been to me as a friend, which I shall be very slow to forget, though we may see more than the balance weighs. His Excellency will ever have moody hours. Yet I will assemble no more. I will be content with the ships I have."

Andrés said: "It is a most prudent resolve." He turned the conversation in other ways.

After a short time he rose, saying that he must not keep the Captain-General from more urgent affairs. They parted cordially, and the secretary, walking away, and seeing the ships which were no more than half loaded as yet, and which would scarcely be ready to put to sea for some weeks at the shortest count, had more than a doubt of whose flag they would fly when that day should be.

Hernando, being alone, unlocked a chest in which were his private concerns, and took out the commission on which all his hopes must depend. He studied it with care, and a lawyer's mind, which it would always be his fortune to have.

It required him first to seek Grijalva, and to make consort with him. Second, to probe a tale which Córdova had heard on his first landing in Yucatán, that six Spaniards, supposed to be survivors of a previous disaster, were in captivity there; and to buy their freedom if that might be. Third, and central of all, he was to open trade with the people of Yucatán, doing them nothing of fraud or harm, but acquainting them both of the gracious clemency of the Spanish Crown, and of its invincible might. He was to advise them of the expediency of sending presents to a monarch of such potency and goodwill—presents of gold, and precious stones, of little value to them, but which he would be gracious to accept as evidence of their regard. And he was to bear in mind the importance of saving heathen lives from the flames of a waiting hell.

He was also to survey the coast, and gather information of the civilisation, customs and resources of the new land, seeking ever the glory of God and Spain.

There was no instruction to establish settlements, of which Cortéz had no cause for complaint, for he knew that to be beyond the Governor's authority. He must act on his own, if he would do that and be condemned or justified by the event.

Actually, such authority was being conferred on Velásquez at the time, but St. Jago was not yet aware of what was being done in Madrid.

Finally, and of a potential importance difficult to assess, it was endorsed by the Governor of Hispaniola, by whom the appointment was thereby approved.

Cortéz put back the parchment, with a mind resolved on that which he had been debating before.

He did what he could during the day to advance the loading of the ships, but only so far as might be without his secret purpose being disclosed.

When night came, he summoned his principal officers, and told them that he had resolved to sail without a moment's delay. Much that was unsaid must have been easy to guess, unless they were duller than those of such positions should be.

When he was roused to face a critical hour, there were few who could be more persuasive than he.

There was none making objection now, none who took the tale to where it must have been ruin for him.

Velásquez slept, and there was bustle along the quay, and in the streets of the town.

Should they sail without meat? Cortéz knocked up the chief butcher, who controlled the abattoir which provided for the needs of the town. He would take all he had, not counting the cost. The man was dubious about that. Should all the townsmen go short on the next day?

Cortéz had a heavy chain of gold round his neck. He threw it down, and there was no answer to that. The meat was paid for a dozen times.

Before dawn, the crews were aboard. Hawsers were loosed, and ships were warped clear of the quay.

It was no later than sunrise when the tale of their movement was brought to the Governor, who leapt from his bed, very actively for his weight, for he was unwieldy now, and would become grossly fat as the years passed.

He got to horseback in haste, and galloped to the quay at such a pace as he had not tried for five years, or perhaps ten.

He saw Cortéz on the deck of a ship that lay within hailing distance, its sails half-dropped from the yards, but still riding on a bower-anchor, which the capstan was manned to raise.

The other ships were moving. Two were clear of the bay.

Cortéz waved in greeting, before the Governor had found words, or perhaps breath. He shouted that there was a fair wind, which he could not miss.

So it might be, when they should be clear of the lands. It was fair in another way, that it brought the words of Cortéz clearly across the water, while those of Velásquez, less coherent in themselves, were blown away, and Cortéz shouted with real truth, and with feigned regret, that he could not hear.

Then the anchor rose, the sails filled, and the ship made a tack for the harbour mouth.

CHAPTER SIX: GATHERING STRENGTH

It had not been Hernando's true reason for setting out, but it had been a true word that the wind was fair.

It bore his armada fifteen leagues along Cuba's coast. So he reached Macaca, which was a small settlement, but having some farms that belonged to the Spanish Crown.

Here he helped himself to as much meat as he could usefully carry away. He made no payment for this, but—always careful in his accounts—he valued the beasts at a fair price, and booked it to the credit of the Spanish King.

He sailed on to Trinidad, and went boldly ashore. Velásquez had calculated that he must make harbour there, and had despatched a letter to Verdugo, its commander, requiring him to take Cortéz into custody, and to send him back as a prisoner to St. Jago, he having been deposed from his command.

But this letter had not arrived.

Cortéz showed Verdugo his commission. He received permission not only to purchase stores, but to set up his standard on the shore, inviting recruits; and here fortune became his friend.

There were scores of men in the town who had taken part in Grijalva's expedition, and been disbanded by him. They included several of the best officers that Grijalva had had. They were eager to join this new venture, and Cortéz was generous in the offers he made to them.

Soon he had added more than a hundred men to his little fleet, including some of the noblest and most influential residents in the Trinidad settlement. He had gained in numbers and prestige; and he now had officers who could give him valuable accounts of what had happened before.

When Velásquez's letter arrived, the commander consulted with his subordinates, including those who were joining the expedition, and they decided that the arrest of Cortéz was not only beyond their power (and perhaps their will), but that any such attempt would lead to the shedding of blood, which would be most probably theirs. He replied that Velásquez had required him to do something beyond his power.

And meanwhile the six ships had become seven.

For there had come a day when a Spanish gentleman adventurer, Señor Sedeño, sat in Hernando's cabin in a state of anger for which he had cause enough, as he was not timid to say.

He had sailed from Spain, bringing a cargo of wheat in his own ship, for which he expected to get a good price in the New World, where wheat was scarcer than gold.

What he had come to was an armed caraval flying the standard of Spain, and a private flag which he had not known, which had required him, by the argument of the cannons mouth, to surrender cargo and ship.

He had insufficient force to resist, and he was brought to Cortéz in a confused mood of anger, wonder, and fear.

He said: "I did not think to be treated with violence under our country's flag. Are you pirates or loyal men?"

"The fact is," Cortéz replied, in his friendliest tone, "that I need the wheat. I have men to feed."

"So it may be. But I must still ask by what right you make violent spoil of one who should expect protection from those who fly the holy colours of Spain."

"It is by the right of my armada of ships, that have many guns, and crews that are trained for war. But I would do you no wrong. I will buy ship and cargo at prices of which you will not complain. And when that is done, I will ask you to come with me to where gold can be lightly won."

In the end, he talked Sedeño round to a willing mind. They agreed a price, and Cortéz signed a bill of exchange by which payment must be made on a later day, and Sedeño agreed to join the expedition. The six ships had become seven, and all been done at the last in a legal way.

So the six ships became seven and the three hundred men became more than four, and much had been added (besides the cargo of wheat) to weapons and stores from the resources of Trinidad and the surrounding country.

Cortéz begged or borrowed, bargained or bought.

Much was secured by the sale of shares in ultimate profits, if such there should ever be. Men gambled on the hope of a great gain, as they are ever willing to do.

But Cortéz was not content. He decided to sail round the island to Havana, and continue recruiting. He chose one of Grijalva's lieutenants, Pedro de Alvarado, to march across the island and meet him there, taking a small party of such men as would talk in the right way, and so obtain recruits who would not otherwise have been reached.

The choice of Alvarado showed Cortéz's appreciation of the qualities of those who served him. Able, handsome, sanguine, loyal, unscrupulous, recklessly brave, he had the aspect of the successful adventurer. He could make men believe, even when he spoke boastful words. He was to do much, and go far, at the side of a greater man.

When his party reached Havana, it had been joined by those who would do good service in future days.

At Havana Cortéz displayed his standard again. He was active in all he did, but showed no haste to sail till he had obtained the last persuadable recruit, the last item of the munitions and other stores which might be of use in a hostile land.

Not that he proposed war. He was on a mission of peaceful trading. But he would be prepared for the worst that might be encountered in a land that was great and strange. He had vague dreams, of which it was too early to speak.

He found that supplies of cotton were available and he had the coats of all his men quilted thickly, so that they would be protected from arrows, by which many Spanish lives had been lost in the New World.

And while this was being done he landed not only the small arms, but the heavy artillery, and had them cleaned and repaired.

He raised his armada to eleven ships, and though some were small—there was a sloop among them, which could hardly be dignified by the name of ship—it was the largest fleet which had assembled in Western seas under the standard of Spain. And to each vessel, large or small, he allocated its share of soldiers, each with a separate commander, to be drilled into a trained unit while the fleet delayed.

There were more letters from the Governor while these preparations went on.

The Commander, Don Barba, had one. He was to arrest Cortéz and seize his ships.

He replied temperately that it was an impracticable request. He said, also, with plain politeness, that it appeared to him to be a foolish idea. Cortéz was a good man for the job, and he was sure that he would be loyal to Velásquez, if the Governor would treat him in a different way.

Cortéz also had a letter, in which Velásquez fatuously suggested that he should delay his departure until a personal interview could be arranged, which was acknowledged in courteous words, and with assurances of devotion to the Governor's interests, as to the sincerity of which we may think as we will, and observe what the course of events would be.

On the 10th of February, 1519, the fleet moved to its final point of departure, St. Antonio's Cape. They were tiny vessels by any standard. That of Cortéz, the largest, was of no more than a hundred tons. There were two other square-rigged ships of seventy or eighty tons, and the other small craft were of sundry sorts—caravals and open-decked brigantines, and a one-masted sloop.

No one appears to have made complaint of the loads they bore, but the careful records of their commander show that they would have had no use for a Plimsoll line.

In addition to huge quantities of provisions, weapons, ammunition, trading stores, and miscellaneous requisites, they had on board:

Crossbow men—32
Arquebusiers—13
Other Soldiers—508
Sailors—110
Indians—about 200
Heavy guns—10
Falconets—4

Horses—16

The horses should not really come last, for they had been brought from Europe at heavy cost in small wind-tossed vessels; and, for the service to which they were destined now, each of them would prove to be of more value than many men.

The weight of cargo and men might be much for the ships to bear, but from another angle they were so feeble and few that the mission on which they sailed might seem to be a fitting cause for the laughter of sober men.

Had it been for no more than a trading venture in a strange land, with barter on open sands, it would have been well enough, or might even be said to have been prepared with more elaboration than the occasion required. But that Cortéz had larger dreams became apparent when he arrayed all those who had enlisted under his banner, before they embarked for the unknown land, and addressed them with the eloquence which his father would have preferred him to have used in the law-courts of Spain.

"Comrades," he said, "we are about to start on such a voyage as will give us fame till the setting of the last sun that this earth shall know." (The marvel was that he spoke no more than the truth when he said that). "Men do not come to such heights by ways of safety and ease. I offer you danger, and wounds, and death. I offer hardship and toil.

"If there be any here for whom that be too hard a bargain to make, let him speak now. He may go without a reproaching word, and with return of any stakes he may have entrusted to me. But if he be silent now, let him be so also in later days, for I have told him my purpose without disguise.

"I would have you do all for the glory of God and Spain; but if there be any here who is incited by lust of gold, let him be true to me, and he shall not lack. I will give him riches beyond his dreams. For we go where gold is like the pebbles of the sea shore. Men will give us that which is of little value to them, and, if you be guided by me, they may do it with goodwill, and the extending of peaceful hands. And for their gold we will give them a better thing, being the gospel of Christ, and salvation from the hell to which they are otherwise doomed.

"We are few in numbers, but if we have resolute minds, knowing that no infidels can prevail against God and Spain, we shall bring all to so fair an end as shall be to their glory, which we shall be blessed to share."

The short speech was answered by deepening cheers. They had a leader whom they knew to be courageous, confident, and yet very cautious in all he did. He was one whom they had good reason to trust, and by his spirit he made them one.

It was the 18th of February 1519 when the little fleet weighed anchor to cross the channel of Yucatán.

CHAPTER SEVEN: COZUMEL

It is not easy to hold a fleet of small sailing vessels together on stormy seas in the dark hours.

Cortéz had a simple plan, probably the best there could have been, but it went wrong.

He hung a lantern at his own stern, and gave orders that no other lights should be shown during the night. They must follow, or search for him. There would be no wandering after one which was going astray, and so splitting the fleet.

Beyond that, they were all to meet at the island of Cozumel on the coast of Yucatán, where Grijalva had landed before.

It was well that they had that destination agreed, for nine of the eleven lost touch with the guiding beacon, when they were struck by storm in the night. One by one, they arrived at the rendezvous, with leaking hulls, or damage of masts and spars. But it was several days before the commander's vessel appeared, in company with the other missing ship, which had been disabled in the storm. It was explained that Cortéz had observed its distress, and remained beside it till repairs had enabled it to proceed.

He was not less popular for that, nor for the days of doubt which had taught men to realise how great a loss his absence would be, but he quickly heard of that which would test his fitness to lead in another way.

Alvarado, whom he had trusted to lead the recruiting party to Havana, and who had the advantage of having been in Grijalva's expedition, was one of the best captains he had.

But he had disobeyed orders during that leaderless week in a characteristic way.

He had landed, and plundered some public buildings, frightening the defenceless native population, so that they fled into the interior. He had brought two captives aboard.

Cortéz had these men brought before him. For intercourse with those with whom he sought to traffic, he had to rely upon a native of Yucatán who had been brought back by Grijalva, either as a guest or slave, and had been taught some Spanish in Cuba during the intervening months. By this medium, Cortéz explained that the violence of Alvarado had been without his authority and against his will. He gave generous presents, as a convincing proof of his sincerity.

This policy succeeded. The fugitives returned, and a brisk barter began. Each party gave that which they regarded as of little value, for that which they more highly esteemed, and were well content.

But Cortéz did more than that. He gave Alvarado scathing rebuke in a public way. If any thought he could do his own will under his present leader, he had much to learn.

Next, he turned his thoughts to the tale of Spanish prisoners upon the opposite mainland.

He sent two brigantines to that coast, with letters for the captives, if such there were, and an offer of rich reward for their release. The ships were to remain as long as eight days, if necessary; and the time of their absence to be used in exploring the island.

Cortéz found that its inhabitants were few, its resources poor. But there were ancient, substantial buildings, and other evidences that greater days had gone by.

So they had. It was destined to be entirely uninhabited in the next century, and choked by growth of jungle from shore to shore.

Cortéz had more than one object in what he did, the glory of God not being least in his mind. But he had with him two missionary priests who had one object alone—the conversion of heathen men. Their belief, however crude, was sincere and simple: a man baptized was a recruit for the ranks of Christ. He was one less to be consigned to the endless torture of hell.

With such a creed, any method, any violence, could be excused, if it should bring men to the font.

Cortéz did not doubt that this efficacy of baptism was literal truth, and gave the priests his support. He would not use violence for trading gain, or for the conquest of peaceful men. God forbid that he should do such a wrong! But he would use violence to save their souls.

During the ten days the brigantines were away, he challenged the loyalty of the inhabitants of Cozumel to their peculiar gods, by rolling their symbols and images in the dust.

The outraged natives had no heart to resist, but they pleaded with tearful eyes.

The priests replied through the interpreter. Let them see what their gods would do, which would be nothing at all.

So it proved. In the end, the bewildered people were baptised into a faith of which the interpreter could not have told them much, or in very luminous words.

The bold course had been a success. There had been a saving of many souls. Give the glory to God!

Having spent their eight days on the Yucatán coast, the brigantines returned. Their captain, a young Spaniard of noble family, Diego de Ordaz, reported that he had heard vague tales of men who were said to be enslaved. The letters which had been written to them had been sent inland by Indian hands. He had offered rewards, far beyond what their slave-value was likely to be; but there had been no response.

Cortéz had done all he could, at the cost of ten days' delay, and the gain of some men baptised. He could wait no more. He sailed northward, skirting the Yucatán coast.

Then he was stayed by the fact that one of his ships reported a leak that its pumps could not control. It had been strained by the recent storm, and must have repair.

This meant more delay. Cortéz would not abandon one of his ships. He decided that it must be careened, and that this could be more safely done at Cozumel than on a mainland he did not know.

He put back.

It seemed a matter of minor importance, though it meant some delay.

In fact, it was a leak that changed the history of the New World.

CHAPTER EIGHT: JERÓNIMO

The fleet was anchored at Cozumel again when a canoe came rapidly over the water from the Yucatán coast. There were four men who paddled on either side, and there was one who sat in the stern, doing nothing.

The canoe came to the side of Cortéz's ship, probably because it was the largest, and the sailors crowded to look down upon it.

The man in the stern rose. He had an Indian look, and was clothed (or unclothed) in the Indian mode. He called out, in Castilian, ill-pronounced: "Am I indeed among Christian men?"

One of the paddlers spoke to him, and he added: "He says there is a price fixed, at which I am sold to you."

Cortéz looked down from the stern deck. He ordered that the interpreter should be called. He learned that this man was one of the shipwrecked six, and he ordered that the price should be paid in measure of bells and beads, and that the man should be brought to him. He said: "He is not a beast to be shown. I will see him in my cabin, and only he."

When the man was brought, he bent at Cortéz's feet, his hand touching first the ground and then his own head, which was the Indian salutation.

Cortéz pulled him to his feet. He said: "You are now among Christian men." He unbuttoned his own cloak, and cast it round the shoulders of one who was nearly naked and unconcerned.

He asked: "What is your name?"

"Jerónimo de Aguilar."

"Where are the rest of the six?"

"The six?" The man looked vaguely puzzled, and then intelligence came to his eyes.

"Some of us," he said, "died in the boat. We had been long adrift. Some were...killed. I was not ready for the right day. Not for the feast. We took a long time to fatten. We had been very thin. That was how I had time to escape. A woman helped me to get away."

He stopped, as though there were no more to be said. Cortéz wondered what he had been eight years ago. He must have been young. He did not look like a seamen. He had a thin ascetic face.

He asked: "What were you before this happened?"

"I was a priest—in my second year."

"And after you got away?"

"I went inland. Hiding. Some people were kind. Then I got caught when I was asleep. I was bought by a rich man. A cacique. He kept me alive. But he was hard. Then he found I was useful, and didn't lie. After that he was kind."

"Then he told me I must marry. There was trouble about that."

"Why trouble?"

"I couldn't. I am a priest. There were the vows."

"But why trouble?"

"He wouldn't understand. He thought I was obstinate not to obey. He didn't believe in my vows. He used to put girls in my bed."

"But you kept your vows?"

"Of course. When he understood, he was kind again. He gave me charge of his house, and all his wives. He didn't want me to come to you, but he gave way after a time. He was a good man."

Cortéz thought: "This man will be a great gain to me. He knows the people of these parts. He knows their customs. Best of all, he will know their language, as he knows ours. He will be a better interpreter than an Indian who does not understand half I say."

He ordered that Jerónimo should be put into a cabin near to his own, and, in the following days, they talked much.

So it was that he heard of a continent on which a civilisation had developed, great and strange: of a dominant race, the Aztecs, hated and feared by other nations that they had conquered, to reach whose territory he must sail much further along the coast. He was on the doorstep of a rich and wonderful land, inhabited by millions of men alien in customs and faith. Could he make friendship with them?

Could he be more than a jest as their possible foe?

His mind leapt forward to vague impossible dreams. He became eager to reach the far land which was only hearsay, even to this man who could tell so much.

But this eagerness did not overcome his self-control: his cautious thoroughness of approach.

The next item of his programme had been to put in at the mouth of the Tabasco River, where Grijalva had found a friendly reception, and most lucrative trade. If the Tabascans had been friendly to Spaniards before, they would be so now. There was reason in that.

He sailed northward along the coast till it fell away, and he must steer due west to keep it in sight on his left hand.

Richly wooded, too distant for visible signs of life, if any there were, he watched it till he came to the river mouth that he sought, and entered, and anchored there.

CHAPTER NINE: SKIRMISH

The fleet anchored at the river mouth, and waited for traders who did not come.

Grijalva had had a friendly reception from Tabascans whom he had left in the same mood. He had done lucrative trade. What should be different now?

Something was. Cortéz must either find it out, or sail blindly away. He could not take his ships up the river. There was so much silt at its mouth that even the little sloop drew too much water for that. He ordered that boats should be launched. These were many and large, which is a measure of prudence in lonely seas.

They were soon loaded with men and arms, and with goods for trade. They pulled up the stream.

It was wide and shallow. Mangroves grew thickly on either side, and the water spread among their roots.

As the boats pulled up the centre of the stream, dark forms were seen moving among the trees, forms of men who were plainly observing them, though keeping more than a bow-shot away.

After a time they came to where a large island divided the river, and, above that there was a stretch of open land on the right bank, where many Tabascans were assembled, who greeted them with defiant shouts, and the bending of bows.

Cortéz summoned the boat in which was the Indian interpreter. "Go forward," he said, "to the bank. They will not think that we have any hostile aim when we advance one boat alone. Tell them that we come in peace. And ask why they meet us in this way, who had been friendly before."

This was done, and the Tabascans, while maintaining their hostile front, made no overt attack on the boat. When it was within hailing distance, the Indian interpreter talked with them for some time.

No one could tell what was really said. It must remain no more than a guess.

He returned to Cortéz to report that they said that they had been blamed by the whole country for the friendly reception they had given Grijalva, and he must choose between destruction and swift retreat.

That may have been all that was said, but next day he was gone. He left his Christian clothes as evidence that he had abandoned what he may have judged to be a hopeless cause, for he had learned by then that Cortéz would not retreat.

It was well indeed that Jerónimo was there to take his place, and with far better qualifications than he.

Cortéz decided to do nothing till the next day. The island in mid-river was large enough to serve for a camping-ground for the night.

Landed there, he called around him for consultation those of his officers who had been with Grijalva's expedition.

They agreed that the town of Tabasco was not more than a few miles up the river. Perhaps five. It was a town of considerable size. Alonso de Ávila said that there was a road from the town to the river mouth. They had passed a byroad that came from it to the river bank half a mile below. He had himself been to the town. Could he find the road again? Yes, he could do that.

Cortéz said: "It is a great hazard to land, and if we are beaten here, we lose all. But we do if we go back to the ships, for the news would spread, and we should be held in contempt."

He said to Ávila: "I will give you a hundred men. You will go down the stream when the dawn is near, and land by the road you know.

"We will land here, on the right bank, and if they join battle with us, you may take them upon the rear."

It seemed a good plan, for the land was not inhabited there, being mangroves and swamp. A quick march might secure a decisive surprise.

So it was done. Ávila was gone before dawn, and, as the light grew, Cortéz ordered the rest of the men to the boats.

They saw that more Indians had arrived during the night. They were thick on both banks, which were also lined with canoes, crowded with men.

Cortéz made one more effort for peace. He approached the bank with all his remaining boats, prepared to force a landing if it should be in his power, but he first told Jerónimo to make a last declaration of his desire for peace, and to threaten what he would otherwise do.

If the Tabascans understood what was said, it had no effect. Arrows began to fly. The next moment the boats clashed with the canoes, which had neither advanced nor fled.

There was a confused turmoil of strife, fierce and short. Some of the canoes overturned. The Spaniards leapt from their boats, seeking to wade to the bank. Men fought waist-deep in the muddy stream.

Cortéz, with the advantage of body-armour, which few had, was of the first who won to the bank. His sword was active for the aid of others, as well as for his own defence. But he was caught in the mud. He lost a sandal. He must go on with a bare foot. There was a shout among the Tabascans that he was the leader. If they could get him down— He became the centre of crowding foes.

Loyal comrades were also there. A flurry of bitter strife saw the Indians thrust somewhat back. With firm ground beneath them, some of the arquebusiers got their clumsy weapons to fire. It was a sound of terror, never heard before in that land.

Crossbow bolts were also beginning to fly. The quilted coats of the Spaniards were some defence against the Indians arrows; but the Indians had no protection that would resist the force of a crossbow bolt.

They had made a wooden barrier across the way to the town. They retired to that. But the Spaniards were too closely upon their heels for them to rally resistance there.

They went over the barrier together in a confused riot of strife—and then Ávila's men were at the Indian rear, and they broke and fled.

Cortéz led the way to an empty town.

CHAPTER TEN: BATTLE

The town was a small matter, compared with those the Spaniards were to see in the coming days, but it was enough to show them that the new continent was a civilised land. There were mud huts there, but there were also houses of stone. As for their contents, they were mostly gone. The Indians had stripped the place, in anticipation that it might not be held. There was some food, but little else. Gold, in particular, had been taken away.

Cortéz did not return to the boats. He did not suppose that the morning skirmish was more than a curtain-raiser for greater things; but he saw that he must stand his ground.

None of his men was dead, but there were numerous wounds. He sent those with the worst injuries back to the ships, and the boats that took them brought every whole man that could be spared from the crews. They brought the horses also, stiff from long confinement, but quick to regain mobility on the welcome land.

They brought up some of the cannon also. It was a busy day, during which they were not molested at all.

But Cortéz was never one to await his foes. He sent out two parties to ascertain in what force and how near the Indians might be.

Alvarado led one, and encountered nothing.

Francisco de Lujo led the other, and had a different experience. He became surrounded by Indians, in such force that he felt it hopeless to fight his way back. He took refuge in a large stone barn, where he was closely besieged.

Fortunately for him, his enemies' cries of triumph came to Alvarado's ears. If Alvarado had found himself at the gates of hell, he would have challenged the devil there. He was not one to count numbers at such a need. He was swift to come to his comrade's aid. Together, they fought their way back, to be met midway by Cortéz, coming to their relief.

It was a warning of what there was soon to be.

They had taken a few prisoners at the last, and these talked to Jerónimo freely enough. He said the whole country was in arms. Tomorrow they would be attacked with a great force.

Cortéz said: "Do they think that? They will find that they are wrong. We shall attack them."

If that decision were bold, it was prudent too.

It showed confidence, on which much might depend.

Besides that, the Indian strength might increase, but that of Cortéz would not. He had his horses. He had his guns. He had every man that the ships could spare. He said: "They shall not come to us in these streets. We march out at dawn."

There was an engineer, Mesa, among the soldiers, who had had experience in the Italian wars, to whom he gave command of the artillery. He gave a general command of the infantry to Diego de Ordaz, taking the little force of cavalry under his own direction, for his favourite operation of an attack on the rear of his foes.

He chose fifteen with care, captains and cavaliers who had armour of plate and were accustomed to ride, and to use of the knightly lance.

They rode out at the first hint of dawn, intending to make a wide detour, and find the rear of their thronging foes.

Alvarado and Ávila were among these. And there were Velásquez de León, Olid, Sandoval, Montejo—names that would become famous in days to be.

The horsemen rode away, and de Ordaz led out his little army, to advance over three miles of difficult ground—maize-fields, intersected with ditches for irrigation, brimming with water, through which men must splash and flounder, while the guns were hauled, one after one, along a narrow causeway that ran through the fields.

They came to an open plain, and to sight of a great army of Indians, which they would afterwards say to have consisted of five divisions, each of eight thousand men, which we may believe if we will. It was certainly a great host.

But the nearly-naked bodies of the Indians had no protection, and their offensive weapons were arrows and stones, fishbone lances, and swords of brittle kind, that would be blunted by many blows.

Now the Spaniards tried to deploy upon open ground, and were met by volleys of arrows that caused many wounds, in spite of the quilted coats for which Cortéz had delayed his ships in Havana Bay. But for his prudence in that, his hopes must have ended in the next hour.

For there was an hour during which the battle swayed. There was no sign of the sixteen cavaliers, who were to have made havoc upon that numerous rear. With hard fighting, sufficient space was made to enable the guns to be swung round, and ranged in line.

Ammunition was brought up. With explosions that were new and dreadful to the New World, balls of iron or stone tore through crowded ranks, having a front which was not many paces away.

Arquebusiers and crossbowmen got to work also, having a wide mark that they could not miss. There was fearful slaughter in crowded ranks, but they did not fly. They closed and came on.

It seemed, as the minutes passed, that the hard-pressed line of struggling pikes, and straight-thrusting swords, must be overwhelmed, or driven back upon dyke and maize, although the dead were becoming a breastwork around their front—and then hope came, at the sound of a distant cry.

Cortéz, with the caution of method by which his audacities were always controlled, had decided that he must make a wide detour to avoid the number of his confronting foes. He would not modify this determination when he found that the ground was so difficult that rapid progress could not be made.

More than an hour after he had proposed to be there, he looked on the far-stretched ranks of those who were too intent upon what was going on in front to become aware of the menace upon their rear.

Sixteen against thousands—Cortéz had been endeavouring to visualise what would happen when they rode into so dense a throng. To be separated would be surely to die. But how should there be instant recovery of a lance that transfixed a foe?

"Comrades," he said, "you will aim at their faces, as though they had heads alone. That is an order to be obeyed. When I cry St. Pedro! It will be a signal to charge. But keep together. We shall not be running a race. We must hold our ranks, and ride as one, till we reach our friends."

It was good counsel, for which as it proved, there was little need.

At the cry of "St. Pedro" the squadron charged, some taking up the same cry, and some preferring St. Jago, who was the patron of Spain. With two such saints to aid, who could doubt what the end would be?

But, in fact, there was no resistance at all. Horses had not been seen in that land. Man and horse were regarded as one, a monstrous, murderous apparition which no man could be expected to face.

With deafening cries of terror, the Indians broke and fled. The horsemen would not have reddened their lances but that men cannot run at a horse's pace, and that they were impeded by their own density.

"Shall we pursue?" Diego asked, as Cortéz came to his side.

"No. We have done enough. Let them go."

It was a decision as wise as it was humane. There would have been no further reduction in morale from a few hundred additional deaths, nor material alteration in the number of those who had been their foes.

And, besides, the Spanish were weary men.

But a few prisoners had been taken, and, among them two officers of rank, as their clothing showed.

"I will eat first," Cortéz said, "and after that I will talk to them. Treat them fairly; and let Jerónimo be here."

When he had dined, he had the two prisoners brought before him. He looked at them with the friendly smile which would bring most men to serve his will.

He said to Jerónimo: "Tell them they are free to go. Let them tell their countrymen that we have no quarrel with them. We came in friendship, and desire no less at this hour. But, should further violence be tried, we will slay till there be none who still lives, neither man, nor woman, nor child. Let them think well, and then say which it shall be."

The captives went, with bewilderment and relief, and Cortéz was quick to ask what the Spanish losses had been. There were many wounded, but only two dead—two of unregarded names, though it was important to them.

Of the Indians, estimates varied. Some said a thousand lay dead on Ceutla plain. Some said many thousands. We may have it which way we will. No one counted the slain.

There was a deputation from the Tabascans on the next day. They desired peace. They could have that, Cortéz said, but it must be entreated by the heads of the state themselves.

At that word, they were quick to come, bringing many gifts. Among these gifts there were twenty well-chosen girls with whom the Spaniards might do as they would (in return for baptism, of course, which outweighs all).

This may seem to be of minor account. But it was not. It had consequences which cannot be told in a short word. He who looked for St. Pedro's aid could not complain that he had a negligent saint.

CHAPTER ELEVEN: MARINA

About sixteen years before the day of the Tabasco battle, and about the time when Hernando was falling from a treacherous

Medellín wall, far away, in the south-eastern corner of México, a rich cacique died.

He left a wife, and a young girl child.

He lived in a highly civilised state, though it was outside the knowledge of Europeans, and itself knew nothing of them. According to its laws of inheritance, the widow had certain rights in the property which he left, but, at her death, the girl must inherit all.

The widow married again. She had a son, whom she loved more dearly than the girl, as some women do. Should the boy have nothing, and she all?

She nursed this bitter feeling as the boy grew, till she hated the girl. She began to plot ways in which she might foil the law.

She had one plan which involved procuring the dead body of another girl, which was no more easily arranged in México than elsewhere. But she had patience, and there was a day in the spring of 1519 when the chance came.

She heard that a girl of her daughter's age was ill, and likely to die. She sought her parents secretly, and said, if their child should not recover, she would give a large sum for the dead body, if it could be delivered to her unobserved.

The bargain was made. The girl died. The body was delivered secretly. The woman announced that her own daughter had died suddenly. The dead body was buried with the usual rites, and the boy inherited all.

But the daughter had waked from a drugged sleep to find that she was in the hands of slave-dealers, far from her home, and being hurriedly borne to a distant land.

The merchants, who, instead of paying for her, had been paid to take her away, carried out an evil bargain as honest men. They took her across the breadth of Southern México and through Yucatán, till they were near the Atlantic coast. They sold her to a Tabascan cacique, as the ships of Cortéz appeared at the river mouth.

She was beautiful, gently-nurtured, well-educated, intelligent. The conditions of slavery were not severe, according to the laws which prevailed before the Spaniards came. She was one who would be likely to make the best of whatever circumstance she might have to face.

But what happened was beyond her wildest dream, or her sharpest fear.

Almost immediately after she had been bought, her owner was required to contribute to the presentation which must be made to those who were to become friends. The slave he had just bought was naturally to be preferred for such a purpose to those who were established in his household. She found herself herded with nineteen other young women of sundry sorts who were to pass to the control of the strange and terrible white invaders, who had come with thunder and fearful beasts from the unknown sea.

To be transformed in a single day from a life of secure luxury in an honoured home to the condition of precarious slavery, was an experience which falls to few, and which few indeed could face with the outward serenity which she had continued to show. But to pass from that condition almost instantly into the power of these white barbarians, alien in language, and religion, and in the habits of daily life, whose existence she could not have imagined the week before, was a development which might have excused her deciding that it was beyond belief—that she was in the spell of a dreadful dream.

The twenty girls, having been assembled at the house of a chieftain some miles away, and provided with better clothing than many of them may have worn before (for should not costly gifts be presented in such a way that their value is not in doubt?) were led by foot—vehicles were not a feature of Maya civilisation—to the Spanish camp.

The dress in which she had been sold by her mother had a collar of feather-work, very beautifully wrought, such as only noble-women in México were allowed to wear.

The merchants into whose hands she passed had produced it as evidence of her gentle birth, and it had been included in her sale, but taken from her by her new owner, as obviously unsuitable for a slave to wear.

Now it had been returned; but the elaborate feather-work, surpassing anything which could have been procured in the markets of Europe or Asia, could mean nothing to the Spaniards, beyond the fact that it was lovely, intricate work, its brilliant iridescent colours being attractive setting to a cream-brown neck.

She must get what satisfaction she could from the beauty of what she wore. There was little else of beauty the way she went, which was across the plain where Indian burial parties were digging trenches into which they were tumbling dead bodies too numerous to be identified in their deaths.

The cannonballs which had bounced along the plain, mowing them down, had not been reticent in what they did.

The girl looked on the shot-torn bodies with eyes that saddened, but did not flinch. They came at last to the large stone house in Tabasco which Cortéz had made his headquarters. They were herded into a room on the ground floor, while Cortéz, with the interpreter in an upper room, was interviewing those who till yesterday had been the lords of the land.

The girls were not given seats. Should a slave tire? Some sat on the ground. This one stood, declining either to meet or avoid the glances of the cavaliers who came crowding into the room.

There was Montejo, with penetrating eyes, but in mirthful mood. He looked less a warrior than a business man. He passed a jest to Alvarado, taller bolder, more gaily confident, at his side.

Morrales entered alone. An old man, somewhat lamed by an ill-healed wound. Hard-featured, but one to trust, either for a fair bargain, or the thrust of a friend's sword at a time of need.

Christóval de Olid, a red-faced, hawk-nosed man of robust strength, but somewhat bow-legged through the long years during which he had cared less for the solid ground than a horse's back, came in at the side of a younger comrade, Diego de Ordaz, lover of adventure of any kind, or strife of wits, be it war or chess, or who would turn to a merry mood with a fiddle beneath his chin.

There also came Ávila, for whom a fiddle would have no tune, but who would be cool and competent either to command in the field or to administer more peaceful affairs.

Now he listened with restrained impatience while Ircio, vainer than he, boasted of the part he had played (well enough) when the Spaniards had been near defeat through Cortéz's delay.

Even though they spoke in a foreign tongue, those whom they came to inspect, of whom some wept, and some giggled, some looked on the ground, and some looked up with inviting eyes, could not doubt what their fate would be.

"Twenty female slaves?" Cortéz was saying in the room over-head. "They have been brought here on foot? Have they been refreshed?"

He gave order that a meal should be promptly served.

He thought that his officers would find pleasure with these. But there would be jealousies as to whose they should be. That must be handled with care. There would be those who must be placated with a smiling word of regret, such as he knew how to speak. For himself, he would not compete. There would be wisdom in that.

But he must cast an eye on the tribute that he received. There can be wide differences in the quality of female slaves. Were they of the kind to sit at the board, or to clean the floor—or perhaps both?

When the conferences ended, and the humbled chieftains of Tabasco withdrew, he went down to the lower room.

He passed Bernal Díaz as he went in—a young, blunt-mannered captain whose special duty—and privilege—it was to care for the horses, on which the success of the expedition would so largely depend. An illiterate man, perhaps, but thorough, efficient, of some knowledge, and one to trust. He was doubtless hoping to get one of the girls; and was one who would have to be denied, with smiling words of regret, and a future hope.

He paused a moment, to enquire whether any of the horses had suffered hurt in the battle of the last day, and while he did so was unaware that a girl's eyes were on him with a straight glance, very different from the way in which she had looked past the other officers who had been filling the room.

She saw a man of thirty-five years—nearly double her own age—but in whom there was no reduction in the light vigour of youth and health. He was of somewhat more than average height, slender and strong, dark of hair and eye. Alert in movement and glance. Smiling with eyes and lips as he talked to one who was plainly of lower rank than himself.

He was strange, but not repellent, to one who had never seen a white man till the last hour, and seldom any as tall as he.

He was dressed soberly enough, in indigo velvet, but it was of a quality she had wit to perceive, and the ostrich feathers that curled round his broad-brimmed hat, which he had adopted when he received his commission as a distinguishing sign, were strange to her, but their significance was emphasised by the fact that, among her own countrymen, feathers were the insignia of rank, which it was an offence to wear without legal right.

As he advanced into the room, her eyes sought his, without boldness, but yet in an intimate, equal way, which he did not miss.

"Oh," she prayed silently to the gods she knew, *"if it could—if it could be he."*

He stopped short, while, for a long moment, they regarded each other, and were regarded by all around.

Then he turned to where Jerónimo stood a few paces behind. "Tell her," he said, "that she will be conducted to my own ship; that she will have nothing to fear."

He turned to Montejo to say: "Will you order this, that it be done with courtesy and regard?"

Alvarado was at his side. He said, in his jesting way, but not as being free from chagrin: "You said you would have none. You should have said none but the best."

Cortéz was short in his reply, as he would seldom be, unless in angered rebuke: "Have I said I will have any now? I have said she is not for you."

He went on to nominate those to whom the remaining nineteen would fall. Olid asked: "Is that the order in which we choose? Or how is it to be?"

His own name had come late.

Cortéz knew the jealousies of those he controlled too well to fall into that trap. Was he to make one man content, and eighteen wrathful to the degree that others were esteemed to be more than they?

He said: "Not at all. If you differ, are there not dice?"

He went, without giving her a second glance, and became busy with other affairs.

CHAPTER TWELVE: SHADOW OF POWER

The landing at Tabasco had not been as disastrous as it had threatened, but it had not been evidently fortunate in its results. There had been hard fighting, and little gold. That might be the view which soldiers, and even Cortéz, would take, but Father Olmedo thought differently. The Tabascans were in a mood of subjection, and if swift action were taken, might they not find themselves in the Christian fold before normal independence of mind should be resumed?

Cortéz, though he might have other matters upon his mind, was never loth to listen when such suggestions were made. It need mean no more than a day's delay.

The essentials of Christianity (according to Spanish Catholicism) were very briefly explained to very pliable minds. Jerónimo, having a thorough knowledge of their language, and a training for priesthood that could not be wholly forgotten, was doubtless an excellent medium for such a mission.

The temple images were cast down. One of Virgin and Child was set up. Mass was celebrated before a vast concourse of wondering Indians, with all available pomp.

Cortéz, as he was rowed back to the waiting fleet, could feel that he had come through the second ordeal of his adventure without discredit, and that the approval of Heaven was very sure.

When he climbed the side of his own ship, horses and cannon, all the impediments of the invasion, and all of presents or plunder that had been collected, had been hoisted aboard, and the fleet was ready to spread its sails to the friendly wind for a further goal.

Hour by hour, with Alvarado at his side, he leaned on the counter-rail, watching a coast along which his companion had sailed before.

Alvarado could point out the river which Grijalva had named after himself; another, where they had done a lucrative trade; a third, where they had been horrified to find evidence, if not of cannibalism, of human sacrifices to heathen gods.

But Cortéz was not willing to stop at any of these places. He did not wish his voyage to be a mere repetition of what Grijalva had done before. And he had stopped once, to come away with honour, but little else. He sailed on.

The weather was pleasant, the wind fair. The scenery along which they sailed had luxuriant beauty which asserted a gracious land.

Cortéz anchored at last, finding good shelter in the lee of the island of St. Juan de Ulna.

He had already passed the limit of Grijalva's venture, but might have continued further along the Mexican shore, had not a large canoe almost immediately appeared from the mainland and steered for his own vessel. It contained Indians of a different aspect and dress from the Tabascans he had met before, and of an evident friendship. They brought welcome presents of fruit: gracious offerings of flowers. They had trinkets of gold, which they would gladly barter for the glass beads and other articles which were stranger to them than was the gold to European cupidity.

Cortéz called upon Jerónimo to interpret for him, and found a difficulty he had not foreseen.

He spoke Tabascan only, and these people conversed in another tongue. But he said there was a way by which this difficulty could be overcome. The girl whom Cortéz had brought aboard knew this and other languages of the New World. She knew the Tabascan tongue. He could translate to her, and she to the visiting Indians.

Cortéz said: "Ask her to enquire of who they are, and of the lord of their land, whom I am anxious to meet."

"So I will, and so, I am sure, she will do. But it will be no more than she knows without enquiry from them. She has told me of much, during the last two days, of the Aztec land, including matters of which I had known little before."

"Then let her say no more than I will come ashore tomorrow, and I will hear first what she can tell."

They returned with many presents, having expressed pleasure at the intimation that Spaniards would land.

Cortéz ordered Jerónimo to bring the Aztec girl to his own cabin, where they would dine together that evening, a cavalier, Puerto-Carrero, who was in his confidence, making a fourth.

It was intended that she should give an account of the Aztec people and land, which Jerónimo would translate, but, in fact, she said little during the first hour, for the priest had learned so much from her already that he could compose his own narrative, only turning to her from time to time for elucidation or further detail, when some incisive question from Cortéz would require more explanation than he could give.

In the cabin of the sea-house, which was the best name she could give the ship in the Aztec tongue (it must have been an almost incredible marvel to her), she sat silently and self-possessed, listening to the rapid Spanish of Jerónimo (which she was already beginning slightly to understand), and answered in low musical Tabascan, if any question were addressed to her.

She knew that the commander's eyes were upon her continually, but avoided showing consciousness of that, only looking at him when she spoke, when she seemed to be addressing him personally, as it was surely courteous to do, though she might be speaking in a strange tongue, which must be translated to him.

Jerónimo said: "There is a great Emperor, Montezuma, who rules over the whole land, from a city that is in the midst of a lake (a kind of inland Venice, if I understand rightly what I am told). It is about two hundred miles from here. But his dominions extend much further than that, for, it may be, a thousand miles; and his rule includes nations of different languages, some of whom would rebel, if they had courage enough, but he is stronger than they."

Cortéz asked: "Are these reluctant vassals nearer to us, or further away?"

Jerónimo turned to the girl, and for a minute or two they spoke rapidly together, she drawing outlines at times with a pink nail on the damask cloth.

Then he turned to Cortéz. "Marina says—"

"Marina?"

"Yes. Did I not tell you that she has accepted the faith? She was baptised yesterday in that name. She said that she would take our faith, she having become one of us."

Cortéz said: "It was most wisely resolved." He wondered what measure of persuasion there might have been from one through whom she must speak (if at all), and who was so earnest in his own faith. "Well," he asked, "what does Marina say?" To which

Jerónimo gave a detailed reply, showing the central position of the Aztec power, and how strong the subordinate nations were.

Cortéz listened with more care than he allowed to appear, and there was little that he forgot. Then he began to question Marina, through the priest, concerning the social customs of this strange empire, its laws, its religion, its military strength, and, not least, as to its stores of gold and of costly stones, and from where they came, and finally as to herself, as it became evident that she was educated and informed, as a slave was unlikely to be; and so heard a tale which would have been hard to believe, had she not been such as to make its wonder less by her own evident fitness for the rank and its background she claimed to have.

And he noticed at times that she had the look of one who is not entirely baffled by what is said in another tongue. And once she spoke a few words of Spanish, in a halting way. He thought: "Is she learning our language already?" And then: "But she is hearing it all the time. Except when Jerónimo speaks Tabascan to her." And then: "But, if she will learn Spanish well, what a boon she will be! It seems that she can talk in all the tongues of this land, having been so taught in her school days, with no time to forget. Our landing at Tabasco was of more avail than I had seen. As was my putting back to Cozumel for the leak I cursed. Surely it is the overriding mercy of God."

He dreamed of Marina during a restless night. Once he rose, remembering that her cabin was very near to his own in the high poop of the ship, as he had ordered that it should be. He thought: "She is my slave. Shall I not have what I will?"

Surely she would be glad—but perhaps not.

She was not of a kind with whom a hidalgo of Spain should deal in a rough way.

He lay down. He would talk to her when the morning should come, which would not be long.

But that was just what he could not do.

He told Jerónimo, when morning came, that it was important for her to learn Spanish with speed, for she could then interpret direct, and the priest said that that was true, and he would do what he could. She was one who was easy to teach.

CHAPTER THIRTEEN: ENVOY OF MONTEZUMA

Cortéz considered the friendly reception which he had had, he considered also that Marina had said that if he were resolved to see the Emperor he could not land at a much nearer point. He decided to go ashore.

But, after the experience he had had, he would do all in a cautious way.

The shore was barren and flat, with a ridge of sandhills, in which he saw advantage if he should be met, after all, in a hostile mood.

The next morning, being Good Friday, he began by sending his guns ashore. Mounted among the sandhills, they commanded a wide range. When this was done, he started the building of what had the appearance of a permanent camp. In this, he had the help of many of the natives. They shared the labour of building huts. They did not object to the felling of trees, on the edge of the sandy plain. They brought cotton cloth for the tents.

The work was willingly, even merrily done; but they gave the Spaniards an impression of being under orders in what they did.

There was much trading also, with ease and goodwill, though it must be conducted by signs alone, for both parties were sure that they got more than value for what they gave.

Marina watched from a quiet deck, for there had been an order that no woman should go ashore. There were a few of a menial kind among the two hundred Cuban Indians who had been shipped to do the services which Spanish cavaliers would require, whether on water or land. They were of little account, and, besides them, there were only the twenty slave girls who had been acquired a few days before.

After the way in which the interpreter had disappeared, it was mere prudence not to allow them a similar opportunity. Marina might observe that, but she had reason for discontent.

She asked Jerónimo, who was with her, teaching her his language, as he had been told to do: "Should we not be on shore? I might find out much which it would be important for the captain to know."

"He would fear lest you should rejoin your own people. You are important to him."

"So I wish to be. But—my own people? These are not of my race. I suppose all of this land are alike to him. I do not wonder at that. If I should come to your world, I might go from country to country saying, 'they are all pink. How can you tell them apart?' But these people are not mine. They are not of the Aztec race. They are men conquered by Montezuma."

"Even so, you might go through them, and return to your own home."

"How could I do that? I have told you what was done. If it were known, it would bring my mother to death. Do you think I would do that?"

"It would be an act from which a daughter might shrink, even though she had been hostile to you. But you cannot be sure that it was by her act that you were carried away." (Marina did not reply to that.) "And you could surely do other things, without returning to your own home."

"They might be of little comfort to me. But that is what we need not discuss, for it will not be. You can tell your captain that I came here without many things of which I have need, and which it is important for me to buy now. And if I talk to these people here, it may be useful to him."

The priest went ashore, and put the matter to Cortéz, as she had put it to him. Cortéz thought: "It is a great risk, for she is beyond price for me to have, knowing, as she does, so much that I could learn in no other way; and as interpreter also. But if I go inland (as I aim to do) I must take her with me, and she could not be guarded against escape night and day unless she were held in chains. Besides that I desire her myself for a better use. If she be trusted, she may stay with us, as she would otherwise be unwilling to do. It is a risk I will take."

Showing no sign of these thoughts, he said to Jerónimo: "You have talked with her. You know her better than I. Will she keep her word?"

"I know little of women. But she is one whom I would trust before most."

"So I will. She must have needs, as she says. Give her the means to buy what she will."

The priest returned with the permission. He said: "The boat waits. You may go now, if you will, I have brought you these."

He gave her twenty small diamond-shaped beads of glass, at which she laughed, taking four, and handing the others back. "Did you think I would buy a house? These are jewels enough. But no, give me two more. There are others who will have needs which are like to mine."

She went ashore in a gayer mood than she had known since she had walked among the flowers of her own garth. She found men who would serve her needs (and those of the other slaves, who could not come ashore, and whom she did not forget), though she must wait for her requirements to be brought to her from a nearby town on the next day, for those who had come to barter had not thought that there would be such a market to meet, And she talked to those who were glad to find one with whom they need not converse by grimace and gesture, and they talked freely with her.

When sunset was near, she returned to the ship, to which Cortéz also retired, though he planned to lie ashore on the next night.

Marina sought Jerónimo. "I must see the Commander," she said. "I have learned that which he should hear."

There was no delay about that. Cortéz knew that a decisive moment had come. He could remain at this spot for sufficient time to barter the cargoes which he had brought, for as much of gold, or stones of value to the Old World, as he could contrive to get, hoping that the amount would cover the heavy expenses of the expedition; and return, knowing that others would come afterwards, who would go further than he. His part would be one of doubtful profit and little fame.

Or he could go boldly into the interior, seeking this fabulous emperor in his city of solid gold, and find fame and wealth; or defeat and death by a much likelier guess. Well, the girl had come back. She had not judged him a sinking wreck, as the interpreter had. There might be a good omen in that. He said: "I will see them now."

Marina and Jerónimo entered the room.

Cortéz asked: "What has she heard?"

The priest answered: "She has told me nothing. She has said it is first for you."

Cortéz was pleased at that. It was how he had hoped it would be. He preferred to digest tidings before it became necessary to discuss them with others. That was why he had postponed a social meal with his captains (of which he was aware of a sharp need) so that he might see them entirely alone.

Marina said: "You may think it is not much I have learned, but it is what you should know. The viceroy will visit you at tomorrow noon, having had orders from the Emperor as to what he shall say and do."

She looked directly at Cortéz as she said this, as though he could understand; and he replied in the same way. Jerónimo interpreted for both with a quick ease, and they must both have been listening to him, but their eyes were not turned his way.

Cortéz asked: "The viceroy? Who is he? Is he one of a great name?"

"Our lord Montezuma," she explained, "took this people into his empire only a few months ago. He appointed Teuhtlile governor in his name. In his province, none will question his will. But he is still a dog that barks as his master bids."

"Has his master bid that we be well received? Or is it too soon for him to know?"

"The Emperor knows all. Every hour you have been watched since you anchored, and his runners have carried word of what has occurred."

"Then it has been by his will that we have been received here in a friendly way?"

"The orders are that nothing shall be done to give you offence before Teuhtlile shall talk with you himself. It is from him you will hear the Emperor's will."

"If the people here only lost their freedom three months ago, could he depend upon them to carry out commands that they might not like?"

"They have always been of a docile kind. As they are told, they will do. They will do anything except fight."

"But they fought before?"

"As a wren will fight the snake that invades her nest. Our army went through them as a sickle goes through the corn."

The use of the possessive pronoun reminded him that it was an Aztec who spoke. But he did not doubt either her loyalty or her candour for that. Indeed, it was evidence that she did not trim her words to make them welcome to him.

He said: "You have done me good service in warning me of what I have to expect. But I do not think to be turned by a viceroy's word. I am the envoy of a great king, and it is with this emperor himself that I must make occasion to speak."

She said simply, as though stating a fact too certain for argument or offence: "You could not do that without his consent."

Cortéz showed no resentment at this. He asked: "Why should you think me so feeble? You have seen the battlefield where the best of Tabasco died."

"But you have not seen Montezuma extend his power. Your king may be greater than he. How can I judge? But what avail can there be in a distant throne? Would you put a thousand to flight with each man you have? And you would still be victim to him, could you do that?"

"I believe what you say, that he is one of a great power. But there is One who is more than he. God is over all; and my own saint is not weak."

He looked at her with a confident smile, as he said this, and he knew, as their glances met, that she had no less courage than he, though it were of a gentler kind. He knew that he could count on her, whatever chanced, though she had warned him of what he faced in a clear way.

She said: "Well if you are so sure! It is how I would have it be."

He rose, saying: "We will go to the large cabin, where supper is laid, and we have been delaying some hungry men. You will dine with me tonight."

She could not have declined that, had she wished. She was his slave, as she did not forget. But she was not unwilling to go.

Asking her, he must ask Jerónimo also, through whom the invitation was said.

He went on less willing feet, being one who had little longing for wine, or for such conversation as he would be likely to hear. But it enabled her to ask him at times what was said, and she listened, and learned more of the Spanish tongue.

She watched the captains, and learnt more of some of them than they would have chosen that she should know.

She watched Cortéz also, and saw that he was in a very confident mood, or, rather, that he wished that it should be so thought, which was not quite the same thing.

She thought: "Here are men of valour and wits, and they may have gods who are watchful for their relief, but there is none but he who would steer a resolute course. Were he down, they would fall apart like a bundle of staves if the cord be cut."

They did not sit late, for Cortéz would be fresh of body and mind for the next day.

He had talked of what might be done if they should be constant in purpose, and yet adroit to put causes of quarrel aside. *Suaviter in modo*—he had quoted, to some who understood, though not all.

They were to be restrained and patient, that a great wealth should be theirs.

He spoke as one who looks out on a harvest that ripens beneath his eyes, and brought them to a more confident mind than he was able to feel when he was alone in the dark hours.

"Mary aid me," he prayed, "for our need may be beyond the limits of earthly man."

But the virgin of his thoughts had an Aztec's eyes.

CHAPTER FOURTEEN: PAUSE OF DOUBT

Cortéz prepared for the reception of the Aztec envoy by the erection of a large tent, so that he could receive him in the presence of his principal officers, and that there would be protection from a pitiless sun.

When he was advised that Teuhtlile was approaching on foot, with a large train, he went a short distance to meet him, with a few of his captains, whom he selected for their appearances rather than any attributes which it would be harder for an envoy to see.

Their meeting was with a restrained and formal courtesy, limited by mutual ignorance of the etiquette of an unknown land, and a jealous anxiety to avoid anything which might appear either deliberately rude, or as an admission of the inferiority of their own king.

Having no common language, Cortéz motioned his guest towards the pavilion, and when he and his retinue had been seated on his right hand, and the Spanish cavaliers opposite to them, mass was celebrated by Father Olmedo, with a ritual appropriate to the day (it was Easter Sunday), and intended to impress their heathen visitors, who observed it with a polite silence, giving no indication of what they thought.

A banquet followed, at which the best of the wines and delicacies that the ships contained were served and received with the same gravity and politeness; and then, when this had been cleared away, the interpreters were called in, and the serious business of the momentous meeting began.

Teuhtlile spoke rapidly to Marina, and there was some show of animation both in his questions and her replies, but as the conversation had been mainly about herself—who she was, and how she came to be there—she was able to speak to Jerónimo with much greater brevity.

The priest turned to Cortéz, to say only: "He enquires from what country you come, and what purpose your visit has."

"Then it must have taken much longer to say in the Aztec tongue! Tell him that I come from a king who is very distant and very great, desiring friendship and trade. I bring gifts, which I am to deliver to his Emperor's hands, with a message which is only for him. I would know how soon such an interview can be arranged."

Jerónimo gave this reply to Marina literally enough, and she had discretion to transform it somewhat, if not in substance, in the courtesy of its form; but it was easy to see that it was not well received.

The viceroy's answer was curt and brief. When it reached Cortéz's ears, it was no more than: "Does a stranger who comes from a nameless land demand to see the greatest Emperor of the world on his second day?"

But, before Cortéz had decided upon his reply, it was seen that the viceroy was speaking again, and at greater length. What he now said was: "The Emperor has sent gifts, which I am about to present. I will send back those which are intended for him, and we will put forward the request which has been made, so that his pleasure will be known."

Without waiting for Cortéz to assent to this, he ordered that the gifts should be brought forward.

His attendants then entered, bearing thirty rolls of cotton cloth, a basket containing many golden ornaments of fine workmanship, and, most beautiful in themselves, and most costly to make, a number of dresses of featherwork, in which the plumage of México's brilliant birds had been stripped from their quills, and woven, thread by thread, on a background of cotton cloth, by a process which was to be forgotten in future years, into patterns of loveliness, both of colours and of design.

Challenged in this concrete manner, Cortéz saw that he must respond. Could he reject the gifts? They might not be proffered a second time! Should he say, I will accept them, but I will give nothing myself unless I have the interview I demand? It would hardly be a politic method by which to seek to persuade a proud and reluctant king!

He said: "Tell the envoy that he shall send to the Emperor the gifts I bring, with a petition that I be allowed to wait upon him; should I fail in this, my sovereign's displeasure would be a heavy burden for me to bear."

With these words he had the gifts brought forward, which, by European standards, were of little comparative worth, but were of a different valuation to Aztec eyes, as a quantity of cut glass articles were included.

The equity of such exchanges, and of the daily bartering which went on, may easily be misapprehended, and unjustly condemned. The defence of *caveat emptor* is not required. The fact is that both parties to these exchanges were satisfied with good reason that they were making very profitable deals.

In México, gold was plentiful, and easily procured. It had been found to be of very limited uses.

In Europe, it was very highly valued, and had been hard to obtain.

In Europe, cut glass, while of sparkling beauty, was not difficult, nor very expensive to make.

In México, where the process of making glass was unknown, such articles could not be obtained at all.

The balance of advantage appears to have been on the Aztec side.

The envoy showed no sign of discontent at what he beheld, but his attention wandered.

He had noticed a soldier who had on a helmet which appeared to him to be made of gold. He said it reminded him of the headdress of a Mexican god. He thought the Emperor would be particularly interested to see it. Would Cortéz lend it for that purpose?

Cortéz assented readily. He suggested that it would be a courtesy which would be appreciated if it were filled with gold-dust on its return.

The helmet, which was not gold, but gilt, the vanity of the soldier having put his own gold to the use which he preferred, was handed over.

Cortéz went on to explain that there was a serious disease in his country, for which gold was the only cure.

While the interview proceeded, he had noticed that one of the envoy's suite was busy with pen or brush upon a sheet of canvas, and enquired what it might be.

Soon the cavaliers were crowding around a vividly painted representation of themselves, which was being prepared for the Emperor's sight.

Cortéz said there should be additional material for the artist's skill.

Horses were saddled in haste. Sixteen cavaliers armed, and were soon displaying their skill on the incredible monsters that they controlled

The guns were loaded, and a salvo of shots tore through the woods on the landward side.

The Aztecs looked on, trying to appear indifferent to the strange centaurs, and the deafening noise of the guns; and the artist drew.

After that, he was invited to draw the ships.

The palace of the Emperor of this unknown world was two hundred miles away, but the envoy, coldly courteous at the last, assured Cortéz that the Emperor's decision would be communicated to him within ten days' time, and he had it in less than that.

The Aztec had no method of transit speedier than their own legs, but they used them well.

Relays of runners had laid the pictures, and the envoy's hierographic reports, at the Emperor's feet before the close of the next day.

A week later, Teuhtlile came again, accompanied by two Aztec nobles, and many scores of slaves bearing presents of such beauty and profusion as must make any return which Cortéz would be willing, or even able to make of a very paltry comparison. The gilt helmet was returned, filled with the gold dust for which he had asked.

The nobles bent in gestures of humility at the Spanish leader's feet. They looked with expressionless faces at the gilt goblet and Holland shirts which were to be his gifts in return for the munificence of their Emperor to him.

The message which they gave to the interpreters was full of flattery and regard. But it was a clear refusal to allow the Spaniards to approach the capital.

Here was the gold which they valued so highly beyond its worth. Let them take it, and return to their own land. The journey to the capital would be too long and arduous for them to undertake.

Cortéz made a final effort to gain his will in an amicable way. He said, with apparent reason, that, having come three thousand miles for the honour of greeting the Aztec Emperor in his King's name, he was not likely to consider the last seventy leagues too hard an exertion to undertake. Would they not repeat his request?

They replied that they would report what he said, but he must not expect that it would be of any avail. Their manners had become cool and aloof.

Ten days later they came again. They brought further gifts, but their message was the same, and with more emphatic finality, than before. The Emperor desired only that the Spaniards would go.

They had arrived at a later hour than before. Vespers was about to be sung. Courtesy or (more probably) curiosity induced them to remain, and to watch the Spanish soldiers kneeling around a wooden cross which had been set up on the sands.

Father Olmedo took the opportunity to expound, through the interpreters, the dogma of Catholic faith. He gave them a small sacred image—Mother and Child—with a suggestion that they should place it in the temple of their own gods.

They took it with expressionless faces, and in that manner they went.

On the next day there was silence around the camp. Ominously, the native population had been ordered to keep away.

CHAPTER FIFTEEN: DECISION

On the next morning, Cortéz called a counsel of his chief officers, to decide what should be done.

Or rather—for he usually had a decided mind on these occasions—to leave the responsibility of decision to them if it should agree with his own resolve, or to persuade, divide, cajole, or command, as it might otherwise be necessary to enforce his will.

On this occasion, he knew that he would have no easy task, for the camp was seething with discordant counsels and discontents.

During the fortnight of waiting, matters had not gone well.

The natives who visited them came through the woods, from higher, cultivated ground, but in other directions beyond the sands there were swamps that bred strange noxious insects. They bit the men, and the men sickened. Already, at the wood's edge, there were the wooden crosses of thirty graves.

Here was serious loss, which would be disastrous, if it should become worse. There was little pleasure in doing nothing for fourteen days under a sultry sun, watching comrades sicken, and wondering when your own turn would come.

There was one thing, it was a safe guess, on which all would agree. They would not stay there for another day. But what were they to do?

There was another reason for leaving. Cortéz had been fortunate to engage the best pilot he could have had. Alaminos had sailed with Columbus, and with most subsequent explorations. He knew all that was known of the tides and tempests and winds of these Western seas.

He had said that the channel where they had anchored was not a safe position in which to remain. At the moment when they had anchored—yes. They had lain windless, in the lee of the land. But how if the wind should change? If it should come from the north?

In these seas the north wind was the one to dread, and they would have no protection at all.

Cortéz had dealt with this warning by sending Alaminos, with two ships, of which Montejo had chief command, to sail northward exploring the coast, but they had not returned.

It was of the nature of Cortéz that his spirits rose to the height of the danger with which they might have to deal. He might have hours of depression after defeat, or when there was a stagnation of circumstance which he could not stir, but at the moment when battle joined he would be alert and confident, to the measure of his confronting foes.

Now he was rowed ashore from his own ship, which he had visited in the early hours of the day with sufficient pretexts, among which was the importance of maintaining his daily practice with Marina in the use of the Spanish tongue. It was of an obvious advantage to eliminate the awkwardness and delay of having to use two interpreters, and Marina was learning fast. Indeed, as, when Cortéz was absent, Jerónimo took on the task, she was talking more often than not. It is a method by which a language may soon be learned.

Cortéz had gone to the ship, because he had issued an order that no woman should come ashore. There had been reason for that, apart from that which he gave, which had been that they might escape. It had been made after a duel between Ávila and a gentleman of Havana, which had left the latter without the use of his right arm for some weeks to come.

To have made Marina an exception would have been a kind of folly which Cortéz did not commit.

And it was certainly natural that he should wish to teach his interpreter how to talk to him. There would be no wonder for that. There was wonder, and some grumbling, that he appeared to make no more use of her in other ways. Why should he keep from others that which he did not take for himself?

But most men remembered his curt word to Alvarado: "She is not for you," and had discretion to leave her alone.

Only one of Alvarado's brothers, who was an officer of the ship, and of more hazardous moods than Alvarado himself, tested her growing knowledge of Spanish by asking: "What would happen to me if I should mistake your cabin for mine at the end of the second watch? "

Perhaps it was not easy to find the right words in a foreign tongue. There was a pause of silence, during which she looked at him with amused eyes, after which she said slowly, selecting words: "You might live till the next time you should sleep; but not longer than that."

"That," he asked boldly, "being the custom of slaves in your land?"

"But I am not yours."

"You are his by whom you are not desired. Are you so content?"

She made no answer to that, but the laughter had left her eyes.

Now Cortéz went, with a half jesting but promising word: "You will not be bored longer here. We shall sail or march. I go now to be told which I shall do."

There was intimacy and understanding in the mockery of her reply: "*Sir*. You are one to be told! Do I grumble? It is better to be bored than to die."

There was reason in that. There had been no sickness among those who had stayed in the ships.

She watched Cortéz's boat pull to the shore. She saw him make his way to the great pavilion upon the sands. The beach was crowded by those who argued or quarrelled, groups joining or breaking apart. There was excitement and animation among those who were still in health, which might endure till the sun gained height in the sky. But there were others stretched on the sands who were too fevered to care for more than their present ill.

She watched Cortéz (for he was taller than most) till he entered the tent, and then turned her eyes to a quiet sea, the blue reflection of a heaven that had no cloud, and that shone with the bright light of the mounting sun.

She was not looking for anything to appear on waters which, till they came, may have been crossed by no keel in ten thousand years, but on the northern horizon now she saw what might have been two small white birds, that grew larger the while she gazed. She thought: "Montejo returns. Does he come at the right hour?"

Meanwhile Cortéz looked round on a score of those on whom he must most depend to carry on to success whatever might be decided to do.

Voices, as he entered, had been bitter in criticism, or in dispute. He knew that he had sure friends, and that others were less than that. He knew that most thought first of themselves, and might not have blamed them for that. He knew that some were most concerned that they should now speak and act so that they would have the approval of Velásquez on their return. There was most danger from them.

He said: "Señors, I have called you here because we are all partners in this venture, and I would decide nothing alone. We have done much. We have come further in the New World than any European has come before. We have obtained much treasure, though the holds of our ships are still heavy with goods which we could barter for more. You have heard the refusal of the lord of this land to let us enter it in a peaceful way. We have to decide what next we will do, both for ourselves, and for those others who, though they are not here, were joint venturers with ourselves; and for the glory of God and Spain.

"I will not say first what I may think. I would have all freely discussed. Diego is the youngest among us. Let him speak first."

Diego said: "It is not I should decide. I will do as is resolved, whether to stay or to go, with a light hand. Yet what have we left to discuss? We are refused admission to this land, which we are too few to compel to our own will.

"If we stay here, we may die of disease, for which it seems that none may have long to wait; or we may be attacked by these Aztecs in such force that many would perish before we could scramble back to our ships.

"Or if we be spared both by God and man—by disease and our human foes—what can we do here but to starve? We have scarcely food in our holds to sustain life till we shall be able to get supplies at Cozumel, which I take to be the nearest place at which we can safely call. It is plain that there should be orders to get back to the ships in the next hour."

Cortéz said quietly: "It has a reasonable sound as you put it thus. But should we not wait Montejo's return, and hear what his report will be?"

Velásquez de León, who was nearly related to the Cuban Governor, added: "That's what we all think who have our feet on the ground. There's really nothing more to be said. I don't see what difference Montejo's return will make, but you'll find, when he does come, he'll say the same."

Cortéz did not doubt that. Montejo was one of the Cuban Governor's closest friends. He had had that in mind when he had chosen him for a purpose which would silence him for a few days at the least.

But before he could reply there was a disturbance at the entrance of the pavilion, where men with excited voices were pushing in.

Someone shouted that Montejo was back. His ships were in sight now.

Cortéz called for order in a voice which few men would disregard. "Must we have disorder for that?" He had a moment's doubt of what it might mean. Had he an organised conspiracy to face. Had they only been waiting for Montejo's return?

But in the next moment he learned that the interruption came from another cause.

A deputation of Indians, of an obvious importance, had appeared, speaking a language which no one could understand.

He said: "Bring them in. Give them seats, and let the interpreters be summoned in haste."

The five Indians who now entered the pavilion were of a different aspect from any who had been previously. They were not ill-dressed, but, by European standards, if compared to the Aztecs, they would appear to be of a more barbarous kind. Gold gem-studded rings hanging from nostrils and ears, and gilded chins, were alien to anything which had been seen before in the New World, and unattractive to Christian eyes.

Jerónimo and Marina quickly arrived, and she began to talk to the most prominent of the five, but it was evident at once that there was a new difficulty to be faced.

Marina turned towards Cortéz to say: "They are Totonacs by the way they dress. I can tell you that. But it is a language I do not know."

Talking to Jerónimo now, in the Tabascan tongue, she gave more details of whom they were, while they listened blankly to tongues that were strange to them.

It was only when she tried them with Aztec that she found that it could be understood, more or less, by two of the five, although not by the chief.

She had already explained that they came from a nation of some importance, which occupied coastal plains to the north. They had been there for several centuries of independence, but had recently been overcome by the Aztecs, and their country included in the Empire of Montezuma. Beyond that, she knew little of them, and their language had not been taught in the Aztec schools.

So the chief envoy of the Totonacs must state his business through the medium of three interpreters, but it was of sufficient importance to render this a matter of no impediment, though the process of communication was exasperatingly slow.

They said that the weight of Aztec oppression was becoming intolerable, and having heard of the rout of the Tabascan army, and of the strange and terrible weapons that the Spaniards possessed, they had come to solicit their help in a war of liberation, for which they would be generous in reward.

Cortéz, despite the difficulty of interpretation, was patient and detailed in enquiries as to their resources, population, and strategic position, and then answered them with diplomatic vagueness, though with avoidance of discouraging words.

Their proposal, he said, could not be answered without deliberation, but they could expect to hear further from him.

Would he not visit them, they asked, in their own capital, and see how resolute, how united, and how well-munitioned they were?

Yes, he replied, he might do that. They might expect that he would be there on a near day.

He gave them many presents, and they went away without certainty, but with good hopes.

Meanwhile Montejo had arrived, and had his report to make.

For several days, keeping the coast in sight, he had contended with adverse winds, until, coming to the headland which was named

Panoco in later days, he had vainly attempted to round it, and had abandoned the effort after narrowly avoiding wreck on a lee shore.

On returning, with helpful winds, he had surveyed the coast thoroughly, and, on the pilot's advice, there was one place, and one only, where they could find anchorage protected from the fury of northern winds. It was much superior to their present location, being surrounded by fertile, well-watered land.

"Well, gentlemen," their commander said, at the conclusion of this report, "you have heard what the Totonac envoys say, you have heard that there is good anchorage further west in a pleasant land. There is one thing on which I think we are all agreed. We cannot stay here, now that food is no longer brought to the camp. Shall we go forward or back? And if we go on; in which direction is it to be?"

He looked round a crowded tent, in which many stood behind the seats and around the door, for none who obtained entrance by any means had been willing to leave. He had still expressed no opinion himself. He left it to them.

Pedro de Alvarado sprang to his feet. He said: "We have heard counsel, I will not say of cowards, but of timid men. And, after that, we have heard of opportunities such as men of courage are quick to seize. I say, let us found a new state here for the glory of Spain. We know that you have no commission for that. The Cuban Governor could not give you more than his own charter allowed. But we have our duties to Church and State; and that which we do now may be confirmed by Madrid on a later day."

Puerto-Carrero said, more quietly: "There is reason in that. Why should not the fleet sail to this better anchorage of which we have heard, while we march to the city of these men who would be our friends—which is, more or less, to go the same way—and leave further decision till we have seen what reception we may have there?"

As he ended, several voices broke in at once in a discordant clamour which only ceased as Cortéz rose.

"Gentlemen," he said, "we waste words, for I have resolved that we sail home, and I will tell you why it must be.

"It is a decision to which I am reluctant to come, because it will end in little profit for us. When the treasure has been set aside which must go to our Lord the King, and de Velásquez has had his share (and who would wish him to go short?), there will be little for us.

"But there are three things which I must observe.

"First, it has been rightly said that, if I should found a colony here, I should go beyond my commission, which I do not propose to do.

"Second, although we may go back having done little, and with little profit in our own hands, and although, as I do not doubt, my commission will not be renewed, we have blazed the trail. What do we matter, if the end will be, as Don Pedro has said, to the glory of God and Spain?

"And the third reason is this: We could not go forward with a fair prospect of fruitful days unless we were alike in purpose and hope.

"I am not deaf to the arguments of those who consider that to go forward is a duty which we owe to Heaven and our King. I will tell you this: however anxious I may be not to go beyond the letter of the Commission I hold, if you had been united in your demand that we should go on, I should have had a most anxious decision to make. But, as it is, there is no occasion for doubt at all. We sail home at tomorrow's dawn."

He looked round on those who had become silent, and among whom there was none who had a face of content.

Among those who had wished to pursue the adventure further, and who had supposed that they were supporting him, what hope could there be, if he himself should pronounce against them?

That they should be disconcerted and dumb may have been natural enough, but it was more curious to observe that there was no elation among those who had obtained their demand with such singular ease.

They had supposed that Cortéz would be resolved to go on, at whatever price. If that were so, those who made vocal protests might lose nothing thereby, and be sure of the Cuban Governor's approval on their return. They would be freed from any share of responsibility in the very likely event of the expedition ending disastrously.

They may not have analysed their motives or intentions to such a point, but, had they done so, preference would have been that the expedition should go forward under protest from them.

They had invested in it; many to the limit of all they had. If it should end without profit, it would be bitter consolation that Velásquez might fit out another, under a different captain, which would have a success which they might not share.

And, so far as they had been actuated by personal enmity to Cortéz, their protests had failed by their success. His decision had been prompt, and its propriety was beyond dispute.

He would be clear of rebuke, while his statement that their attitude had forced his decision would put the blame of failure upon themselves. There were many who had invested in the venture, but had not joined it. When the reason for its partial failure should be discussed, would they be praised or contemned? No one could prove that, but for their opposition, it might not have gone have on to a great success.

But Cortéz was already issuing orders in accordance with the decision he had announced.

"Mesa," he said, "you should get the guns aboard. And you, Bernal, should have the horses loaded with care. There must be no haste about that. And I will have census of the food in each ship, that it may be equally shared. We may be near to starve before we see the shores of Havana Bay."

Puerto-Carrero, quiet of manner and voice, but knowing his commander as few did, thought silently: "Why does he remind them of that? He might decide to return; but would he do it in so cheerful a way?"

But Cortéz went back to his own ship. He strode down the beach, whistling a tune, as one whose troubles were over now.

Afterwards, while he continued to improve Marina's Spanish, for which it might be thought that he would have less use than before, he watched a beach where men were less busy in striking tents than in arguing in little groups on the sand. He showed no sign of vexation at that.

CHAPTER SIXTEEN: VICTORY BY DEFEAT

Velásquez de León commanded the sloop, a position that had been given to him rather because of his relationship to his namesake, the Cuban commander, than from any skill he had in controlling an hour of storm. He was not short of courage or enterprise, but he was of a scrupulous honour, and that relationship came near to being ruin to him. His second in command was one, Escobar, who had been his page, and remained with him after the years of such a position would generally have been past.

Escobar now acted as his lieutenant upon the sloop, and he being the only other officer on so small a boat, they were alone in their cabin at the last meal of the day, which had been little trouble to cook, and could be eaten in little time.

Escobar looked at a platter he could not praise. He was one who valued his food. He said: "We shall be thinner men in a week's space. Why could he not have foraged first, before he sent us aboard?"

Velásquez made a poor joke. He said: "He will be sick at heart for this day. He will be too sick to eat. We shall profit by that."

Escobar gave a literal reply. "How can that be, when we are not on his ship? But is it he who should fret?"

"Well, he must go home with his tail low. He will have a poor boast."

Escobar was a doubtful man. He said that which was being said by others of Velásquez's party throughout the fleet, and, if they did not say it, those of Cortéz part would say it to them. "Are you sure of that? It is we who will take the blame. Men will say that we held him back from a great gain. He would have gone on to we know not what of defeat and loss, with no warrant for what he did. We may have done evil or good for ourselves, which is hard to guess, but we have assured that he will come clear, while they will have names for us of a scoffing kind."

"Why did you not say this before?"

"Could I foretell what he would do? Did we not suppose that we should be met with a stiff neck. That is done now. But I say we should forage first."

On the sloop, there was no more than these grumbling words, but others were more alert for their own relief.

Montejo took a boat to the Commander's vessel, and was received by Cortéz in his most genial mood.

"You say that larders are bare? So it is. But as to calling at Cozumel, can we be sure of how much we could get there? We have failed, and it cannot be too soon that the tale is done. I will for home while the wind is fair."

"Is there nothing that can first be taken aboard? As you know, I have not been here, but some who know more—"

"Have you not heard that there was none yesterday who came to our camp? They must have been ordered to keep away."

"Can you not go to them?"

Cortéz considered this with a friendly smile. "It is an idea.... We might have little opposition, if we should forage with speed. There need not be more than a day's delay, at most, two. Because we have ended our quest for gold, is there reason that we should starve? But you will see how I stand. I called counsel, and must abide by that which was resolved.

"Yet you are one whose opinions I must respect. If there should be others of the same mind.... My captains have not found me to be one who will not listen to them."

Montejo replied: "That is fairly said. I should forecast that you will have mandate for this."

He did not go back to his own ship. He rowed to another. During the night there was passage of other boats under the stars of a still night.

Before dawn, it was known by most that they would not sail until provisions had been obtained. In any case, they could not have hoisted sails at that hour. All had not been brought aboard by men who had argued and quarrelled rather than toiled during the previous day.

Cortéz thought: "It will be easier than I could have guessed. I shall be driven by those who would not be led."

Alvarado rode out while the sun was still low, with three other steel-clad cavaliers, and forty men on foot who had swords with which to argue, and beads for barter, and sacks to fill.

But they found that there would be no occasion for use of swords. The natives were glad to deal, having compulsion for their defence. More than that they were willing, for little payment, to offer their own backs for burden on the return to the camp.

They came back before set of sun with good store of food, and some golden trinkets that they had been no less eager to buy.

Alvarado, who had been fluent before in contempt of those who had advocated return, would not have been surprised had he seen the guns landed and the tents erected again, but there was no change of that kind. The beach still lay bare, and it was not till he was in Cortéz's cabin, making report, that he had any indication of what had been happening during the day.

Cortéz said, almost as soon as he had commenced. "That is well. I will not ask for the details now. You should go to the *Santa Anna* with speed. There is a meeting there which I have not been asked to attend."

Pedro stared at that: "They have had their way! What more do they plot now?"

"Well, you will learn that, if you go. And you have a voice that they will be likely to heed. But you must not suppose that there will be quarrel to make. You may find they will come to me in a begging way. Christóval and our two Alonsos are there; and you will find Montejo may deserve to be heard. Where are the cavaliers who rode out with you?"

"De León and his page have gone back to their own sloop, and I left de Ordaz marshalling and dividing the stores."

"You have done well. Leave them thus. The *Santa Anna's* cabin must be crowded enough."

Alvarado rowed to the *Santa Anna* with lively speculation of what would be happening there. He saw that the three cavaliers who had ridden out with him had been chosen so that they should be out of the way. He had learnt that Christóval de Olid, and the two Alonsos—Puerto-Carrero and de Ávila —were at a counsel which Cortéz did not attend; and that Montejo—the Cuban Governor's most dangerous adherent, except perhaps de Ordaz—was to be regarded as a possible friend.

He entered a cabin where those of most account sat round a centre table, with Puerto-Carrero at its head, and others stood, to the most that it would contain, or looked in through an open door.

They made way for him to enter. Someone gave him a seat. Puerto-Carrero said: "Pedro, you have come at a good hour. You shall hear that on which we have come near to agree.

"We all know that our Commander feels that he can do no more on the commission he holds. We do not say he is wrong in that. He had from Cuba all the authority which it could give, which was not much.

"But we have to think how we now stand. The commission is not ours, either to limit or to allow. We have only our duty to God and Spain. We ask ourselves, why should we not plant a colony here."

Montejo said: "As I see it, we can decide that, and we are too strong to be overruled. But our Commander cannot be one with us, unless he shall first resign the commission which he holds in a public way. If he do that, Velásquez must be free from blame for what may be done in the next hour, and we shall have been faithful to him, and still free to make profit for all who have trusted us, before we make our return."

Alvarado was not of a subtle mind. He was rather one to go a straight way, and trust to a naked sword, but he saw that Montejo had shifted ground in a way that Velásquez might find it hard to condemn. He asked: "What would you do now?"

"We would found a colony here, in our King's name, and for the glory of Spain. Cuba has no portion in this, but those who have wealth at stake shall have their share in a private way."

Alvarado saw that they were united in what they did. Cortéz was not to be asked. He was to be told. He could resign his present commission, and join them, or stand out, if he would. He knew that Puerto-Carrero was the Commander's friend. So were others who were most prominent there. It was more likely that Montejo had been won over than that they had gone over to him.

He said: "It has the sound of a good plan, if our Commander agree thereto."

"That," Puerto-Carrero replied, "will be for himself to say. But we are herein of a settled mind."

"Then, "Alvarado agreed, "it should be put straightly to him."

They spent no more time in debate, but agreed on eight of their number, of which Montejo was the only one who had been of Cortéz party, rather than that of the Cuban Governor, who should go forward to the Commander's ship, and tell him the resolve to which they had come; and they elected Montejo to speak for all, which was shrewdly done.

When they were seated in Cortéz's cabin, Montejo said: "It is true that there were some (I do not speak of myself; I was not here) who thought that it would not comply with the terms of the authority which you hold for us to have invaded the land, as they thought it to be your purpose to do. Their duty to His Excellency appeared to constrain them in this, and it quickly became clear that you were of the same mind. But there were others who looked further, so that they became aware that Cuba is less than Madrid.

"From our Lord the King you have no mandate herein (neither have we) either to go forward or turn aside. That being so, we must put his honour and welfare first, lest we be traitors to him—lest we be traitors to God and Spain."

Cortéz listened to this in a quiet way. He said: "I would be clear as to what you mean. Do you call my commission naught? Do you depose me from my command?"

"We say no more than that our duty to Spain does not allow us to retire from a work half-done. We would found a colony here, claiming the greatest land that hath yet been found in the Western World for our Lord the King. We think most will be with us in this. Would you sail eleven ships back with your single hand? It could be done. But we have not said that we are disloyal to you. It is the common hope that you may decide in the same way."

"It is a matter which must be looked at from every side. I will give you answer at prime of day."

He rose at this, and the deputation understood that there was no more to be said at that time. They scattered to their own ships, in each of which men of all ranks, whether of land or sea, were debating in eager groups, but with less of discord, and more of enthusiasm, than they had shown on the previous day.

CHAPTER SEVENTEEN: DECISION AGAIN

Marina's cabin was small, and though its neatness made the most of what space there was, Cortéz was conscious that he over-crowded it, as he bent his head so that the wide-plumed hat might come through the door.

As he did so, Marina rose from its single seat, as a slave should. She had been alone, for even Jerónimo could not talk all the time, and her thoughts had been such as would be natural to one who was about to sail, in the hands of alien men, to an unknown land. But she was one who accepted life with serene eyes, facing whatever came in a quiet way, and having learnt to conceal her thoughts through a girlhood in which the narrow restraints and inhibitions of her education had not been modified by the warm affections which prevailed in most Aztec homes.

Cortéz threw his hat on to her bunk, and then picked it up again, as he said: "I do not want your stool—no, we cannot talk here. I have that to say to which you should answer with care. You shall come with me."

She did not understand every word of his rapid Spanish, but the last ones, and his meaning, were clear. She followed him into his own spacious cabin, which was near to the whole ship's breadth, and watched him thrust the bolt with expressionless eyes.

"Now," he said, "if you will sit, we can talk at ease."

He sat down in his great carved oaken chair, throwing his hat onto the table before him, and motioning her to a seat at his right hand.

He wondered what went on in her mind. She was looking less at him than at a porthole through which a brilliant star in the low sky of the tropic night would come and go, as the ship lifted upon the tide. He saw that she did his will without arguing words, as a slave should. But he must know more than that—it had become vital to him to know.

He came straight to the point. "Marina, will you look at me? I have not known you to lie. If the choice should be yours to make, would you be true to me, or to those of your own land?"

She had to ask him to repeat this, but when its meaning was clear she only said: "Does it matter now?"

"Should I ask, if it did not?"

She had a moment's thought—did it feel like a hope? She was not sure—that he was offering her the choice of freedom, or of going a Spaniard's way. Now that he was leaving the land, she saw that her value as an interpreter was done. He might think to repay her with freedom for the service which she had rendered to him.

She said: "I meant that you will not need me now—now that you are going away."

"But suppose that we do not go?"

She was silent at this. What other course could there be? He could not think to defy the Aztec empire with the little strength that he had. It would be insane.

He went on, repeating or altering his words when he saw that he was not understood: "I will tell you all I intend, so that, when you reply, there will be nothing you do not know.

"I will plant the flag of Spain in this land, and will spread our faith for the salvation of men.

"Your Aztec emperor may be friend or foe as he will, but he will find that he is facing a tide which will not retreat.

"In three day's time, if not less, you will see these ships take the northward way which has been already explored, to find better anchorage than there is here; while I shall march overland to the Totonac city, and may gain potent allies. "When I do this, I shall need you as interpreter, for which Father Jerónimo will be no use at all.

"I do not wish to hold you in bonds, or set a watch in a trustless way.

"But you will see that we may be at strife with those of your own blood; we may be allied with your own country's foes."

She did not know all the words he used, but she understood enough. Indeed, it was only necessary to learn that he was not sailing away for her dilemma—and his—to become clear.

She had become essential to him, and she must either be most closely guarded by night or day, or she would, sooner or later, escape to her own people, if she should be so inclined.

Also, she could hold converse with those whom she interpreted, the purport of which he could not know. She could betray in a score of ways.

She thought: "I was sold to slavery by my mother, as I believe. I can have no certain proof, but I am sure I was drugged while still in my own home, and how else should it have been? But that was a private wrong. I do not blame my nation for that.

"But, after that, I was sent to these men by orders which came from the Aztec viceroy of Tabasco. I was given to them as a slave, to serve them in what qualities may be mine, as a slave is expected to do.

"If I should escape to my own people again, it might be said that I should be defying the Emperor's will. They might even send me back, if they should make treaty of peace, to be paid with stripes, as is the custom with slaves who flee.

"It is a choice I would avoid, if I could, but it must be made. I must choose, and must then be faithful in what I do, which means that—"

She saw that she was inclining to stay, or the question of faith would not arise. But, if she said she could not be faithful to him, would he let her go?

She approached obliquely to that which was in both their minds when she said: "The Totonacs are a barbarous folk. I suppose we are savages in your eyes, and there are ways in which you seem no better to us; but the Totonacs would be so called both by us and you. It is not only for their nose-rings and painted chins."

She had difficulty in expressing this, but was sufficiently understood. He replied: "I have made no alliance with them. I go to hear and to see. But the judgement must be mine, and those who are of my part must not refuse any road where I lead the way."

"Yes," she said, in her own tongue, so that it had no more meaning to him than a tone will give, "that is plain to see. It must be nothing or all."

They looked at each other in a silence during which understanding grew. He had considered her in two ways from the first day—as a woman to be possessed, and as an interpreter to be used for essential ends; and he had put the advantage of the expedition before his own—or, perhaps we should say, the good of the expedition had seemed to be of more urgency, if not of more importance to him.

And while he had acted thus she had practised his speech, until it had become possible for them to be of a unity which need not be of the body alone.

He broke the silence with: "If we go by land, would you lie bare on the ground, as most will? There will be few tents. Will you share mine?"

She looked puzzled, as though his words were not easy to understand, which might well be; but in fact she understood well enough, though being unwilling to risk misunderstanding.

But when he repeated his words in a simpler form, and with clearer meaning for that, there was a sudden glow in her eyes, and she laughed in a way which it was a pleasure to him to hear, as she said: "The nights may be cold on these shores, though the days are hot. Shall I choose the ground, when I am offered better than that?"

He knew little of the customs of her land, and she little of his, and it was of the mingled caution and boldness by which he would gain his ends that he made no further approach at that time, and it was from the same quality which recognised equity rather than law (as when he had seized the grain-ship, and then agreed to buy at a full price) that he said, as he rose to unbar the door for her to leave: "I have a wife in Cuba. You know that?"

"I have heard," she answered gravely. And then laughed: "Should a slave protest? Who can alter the past? And every day you will be further away. Men have more than one in my own land."

It was a betrothal of a strange kind between those of alien races: between master and slave—but a slave who could do a service which could be obtained from no other source.

And they were both largely content. She had that for which she had hoped, from the moment when she had seen him first at the slave-room door. She thought of it through a wakeful night, with confidence both in him and herself that they would go far, though she could not guess to what end it would be.

He was doubly content, foreseeing a mistress for himself whom he was urgent to have, and one who would be of large service to the plans which were exciting his mind. He also lay long awake, but she left his thoughts. He had much to resolve and design for the coming day.

CHAPTER EIGHTEEN: A CITY WITHOUT A SITE

Having thought in the night, Cortéz was ready to act when the day came.

He had an early conference with Puerto-Carrero, on whom he could entirely depend, after which that discreet cavalier went off to attend another meeting on the *Santa Anna*, to which again Cortéz was not invited.

He was back within an hour, in company with Montejo, the two saying that they had been delegated to hear his decision.

Cortéz asked: "Are you still resolved that you will go on, or have you listened to more prudent advice?"

Puerto-Carrero replied: "We are resolved that we will go on."

"But does none dissent?"

"There is de León, and he has the support of his page. There is none other of any name."

"Then how will you proceed?"

"We will found a city here, on the barren coast, to the glory of Spain, no man being ousted or wronged thereby. We must have officials chosen for that, and we have agreed, to avert dispute, that they shall be nominated by you, and we will abide by the choice you make."

"I cannot do that. I have no license therefor, either from Cuba or from Madrid."

"But you can advise, which is all we ask. If we resolve that we will accept such advice, you have usurped nothing which is not yours."

With these words he produced a sheet of parchment on which a list of offices had been written, with a blank column where the names of those who would hold them could be filled in.

Cortéz examined it with an expressionless face. He noticed that the non-existent city had received a name: *Villa Rica de Vera Crux*. He thought well of that.

He looked up to ask: "You will have two *alcaldes*? There are spaces for two names."

"Yes. Their first duty will be to convene a meeting for the election of a governor, who will be answerable to none but the Spanish Crown."

"It is well designed."

He picked up a pen, and wrote with a rapidity which suggested that the matter had had some previous thought. When he handed the parchment back, the two who received it may not have been greatly surprised to observe that their own names headed the list. Montejo had been bought (if that word be fair) at a high price.

The names that followed were selected from those who had been loyal to Cortéz throughout, but that does not say that they were not the most worthy choices. Most of the best men were among those who had been loyal to him.

The council of the city-to-be met at a later hour. They were very formal in all they did.

They had been elected at a meeting held on the sands, from which few of the adventurers had been absent. General acclamations had drowned the protests of a few who had been resolved that their opposition should come to the Cuban Governor's ears.

Now the council debated gravely as to who should be elected Governor of the proposed Colony, and did not surprise themselves when they agreed unanimously that Cortéz was the best choice.

It is equally unlikely that he was surprised when the now formally elected *alcaldes* waited upon him again, and entreated him to accept the office. But he was still scrupulous in procedure. He said that it would be an impropriety for him to accept it until he had re-signed the commission which he had received from Velásquez. How was that to be done?

There was only one possible way for it to have definite and chronological proof. He must hand it over to the heads of the new colony, and then, after it had been accepted by them, he would be free to take what other office he would.

So it was done, with public ceremony enough, and so he became absolute ruler, subject only to the distant control of the Spanish King, of those he led, and of all the land he could acquire by bargain or spoil in the new land.

With the carefulness which he always applied to all questions of property, he arranged, as a condition of his acceptance of the appointment, that his remuneration should be one fifth of the precious metals that might be acquired either by violent or peaceful means.

His first act of authority was to order the immediate arrest of those who had been most vocal in protest against what had been done. De León and Escobar were soon sitting in chains in the cabin of their own sloop.

The whole proceedings had an element of unreality, even of farce. Can men create authority by electing themselves? Under some conditions they certainly can. And, it may be asked, how could it have been done better?

The essential fact was that these men were determined to continue their wild adventure, and that they were loyal to Spain—which was thousands of miles away.

Cortéz may be said to have self-created his own exalted office, through the loyalty of those he led, but he had also created an obligation of loyalty in the new land to the Spanish Crown.

It remained to be seen how he would deal with those whom he had arrested, which would be the first, and perhaps the decisive test of his fitness for the office which he assumed.

CHAPTER NINETEEN: TOTONAC

The arrested men had not muttered treason and clanked their chains for more than two hours when they heard a boat's hail, and the running of feet overhead, following which the Governor himself was in their cabin, looking at them with speculate humorous eyes, but not removing his white-plumed hat, as he had done when he had intruded into Marina's cabin on the previous night.

"Gentlemen," he said, "I would have preferred to see you in greater comfort than you are now."

"Then why—?" Escobar began angrily.

"That is what I came to explain.

"I have no quarrel with you. You are good men, whom I need. But we are going into unknown dangers, which require that we shall be united in all we do. I cannot take those who will either differ or doubt.

"But if I send you to Hispaniola—"

León interrupted him quickly: "Why do you say that? It is to Cuba that we belong."

"So you do. But I am now Governor here, and accountable only to Spain. Besides that, how can Cuba's Governor be judge in his own cause? It is Hispaniola's Governor who must decide your case, or send you to Madrid, as he may think well.

"But you should know that it is not of my will that I do this. I would rather that you were loyal to me, and to the great adventure on which we go. It is still for yourselves to decide, either to sail or to stay."

He went without giving time for reply, and was not surprised to hear at a later hour that they had professed their willingness to accept that which they could not change, and to swear loyalty to him. He thought that he had done well, and that his clemency would be regarded with more respect than if he had not first put them in chains. He supposed that there would be no more trouble from them.

Having all now under his own control, with far greater authority than before, he was swift in action, as the position required.

He left his heavier guns on the ships, for they would have been too great a labour to drag. He sent the falconets back to land.

He gave the fleet orders to sail to the new anchorage which had been found, leaving it with only seamen enough for its safe handling. All others, including the Indians, who would be most useful as beasts of burden, were to march overland to Cempoalla, the capital city (if it should prove to be worthy of such a name) of the Totonacs, to a total of nearly seven hundred men, and about thirty women, including the Tabascan slaves, most of whom had now attached themselves to their new masters in preference to those who had treated them as suitable gifts for an alien foe.

They set out with the caution which their commander always applied to his wildest risks. Ten cavaliers rode ahead, at the walking pace which the march required. The footmen advanced on a wide front over open land. Cortéz rode in the midst. The most precious of the baggage was immediately behind him. Then the women. Then more footmen. Then the Cuban Indians, burdened with many things. Then the four falconets, drawn by Indians, and with their gunners beside them. Then five mounted cavaliers to protect the rear.

Cortéz had come with his utmost force, which was intended to give confidence to those who might be doubtful allies.

When they came to more fertile, cultivated ground, they must advance on a narrower front. But Indian scouts were now sent ahead, and widely to left and right, though they had no cause to suppose that they would be met in a hostile way.

Nor were they; but rather it appeared that they were not being met at all. They came to houses and huts, but there was no sign of human life, and orders were strict that they should not break ranks to explore what might lie under those silent roofs.

"If any man," Cortéz had said as they set out, "shall do violence to any, or take a spoil without orders from me, he shall hang, though it were but a string of beads, and he the best friend I have.... So be warned, for I have none to spare, and it is what it would be no pleasure for me to do."

Following directions which had been given to them, after the first few miles they took a leftward road, and were soon out of sight of the sea, and in a country that was brilliant with butterflies and tropic flowers.

In wooded places they saw wild turkeys, and many smaller birds of more brilliant hues.

At noon, when a halt had become imperative, they came to a deserted village, where they camped and dined.

The village was not very large. It consisted of a number of stone houses and mud huts, surrounded by luxuriant gardens, and intersected by narrow paths (the absence of vehicular traffic tended to limit the width of all Mexican streets). It was built round a large central space, which would be used as a market on the last day of their five-day weeks, for which ample accommodation was required, as they had no shops. At one side of this square a stone temple was overshadowing all.

It was evident that the village had been evacuated in great haste, and the contents of its residences were open for all to take. For the nations of the New World were alike in this, that their doors were not provided with lock or bar. They had a simple law that he who steals dies. It applied equally to a manual thief or a defaulting trustee; and its result was not so much that victims were provided for sacrifice at religious feasts as that the fear of being robbed rarely entered a Mexican mind.

Cortéz's orders were quickly issued, and exactly obeyed.

The horses were taken into the temple courtyard. The dismounted cavaliers, and about two hundred other Spanish gentlemen, were to join him in the marketplace for rest and food. All others were to camp outside the village. No one was to enter the deserted houses on any pretext whatever.

It was a decision of honour and prudence, and most fortunate in its results.

Far more rapidly than the Spaniards moved, the news went forward to Cempoalla of what they did, and influenced the reception which would be theirs.

Having arranged this, and sent out watchful pickets on every side, Cortéz could turn his thoughts to his own affairs.

He called to Díaz, who came out of the temple courtyard, where he had been assuring himself that the horses would have good care. "Bernal," he said, "will you ask Doña Marina that she shall join me here?"

Díaz stared for a moment at the title of courtesy that the Governor used, but there could be no doubt of who was meant, and he obeyed without reluctance. For Doña Marina, as her name would be from that day, was liked by all, and her essential value was understood.

Those who had ridden or walked for long hours in increasing heat were glad to stretch themselves at ease on cloaks which had been spread on the dusty ground. The cavaliers of most account sat with Cortéz thus, and when Marina appeared he made a place for her at his right hand.

He drew her into the discussion which went on as to the nature of this new land. Was it everywhere as beautiful, as prolific, as that which was round them now? Was this a typical example of its villages, or its towns? Was the fact that it had been so completely vacated to be taken as a sign of timidity only, or in a more ominous way?

Her replies, in tentative, halting Spanish, had the attention not only of those in that circle, but of other cavaliers who crowded around in increasing numbers.

She did not understand all that was asked, nor could she always make her own meaning clear. But they understood that there were cities yet to be seen beside which this was no more than a paltry slum, that the country was of varied luxuriance of which they had not yet seen either best or worst, and that they need have little fear of anything that the Totonacs thought or did. They would be more than equal to them. What they had to dread was the remoter shadow of Aztec power.

"For what you have done this morning," she said, "the Emperor will know tonight."

They thought they must have misunderstood her in that. Was not the Aztec capital two hundred miles away? Jerónimo was called to make interpretation sure. But they found that there had been no mistake. A news runner would be trained to go at a high speed for a few miles, and he would then pass word or a pictured scroll to another, who would continue at the same pace.

Even burdened, these speeds would be maintained. If the Emperor should desire saltwater fish, or fruit from a distant province, must it not be on his table on the day on which it was caught or plucked?

Cortéz saw that this was not a picture to raise the confidence of those who heard, however vital it might be that he should be truly informed. He said: "Señors, I have said that the houses of this village shall not be entered, but I have a mind to explore the temple myself, and those who will, to a short count, may come with me, though we shall touch nothing, even to cast down the idols that we may see."

He went into the temple, with Marina, and eight or nine of the most intimate of his cavaliers, and they saw little that had not been similar, though on a larger scale, in the temple of Tabasco, which they had cleansed of its heathen gods.

There was the same cold stone of pavement and walls, the same images, which seemed grotesque to their eyes, besides being of Satanic wickedness, as they believed.

There was the same profusion of flowers, hanging in brilliant garlands, cunningly woven in colour patterns that were unrivalled in the countries from which they came. They were so fresh that it was evident that they must have been woven that day, showing how recent the desertion of the village had been.

Nothing of novelty or surprise would have been seen, had not Cortéz's curiosity led him to penetrate to rooms in the rear of the temple, where its priests dwelt.

Here again the furnishings, though they might be strange to European eyes, were little different from others which they had seen before. Until they entered the kitchen, they were no more than casually intrigued by the beauty of a silver ewer, or the quaint carving of knife-handle or pipe. But here they saw that which stirred them to exclamations of horror, which Marina heard at first with a puzzled frown, and then with an expressionless face, as she realised the inexplicable depth of a feeling she could not share.

It was no more nor less than a joint that hung from a hook of the ceiling—obviously a human ham.

Why, she wondered, should they be excited by that? It could not have belonged to any relation or friend of theirs. Its cream-brown skin was obvious proof of that.

Yet excited they were, to a degree which might, as she was able to realise, have led them to make unprovoked attack upon the priests, or indeed any of the inhabitants of the village, had they appeared at that moment—or, at least, if provocation there were, it was something she was unable to understand. It was plainly absurd!

And yet, the feeling that they expressed was so violent, and so sincere, that she realised that nothing she would be likely to say or do would alienate her from these friends, who were strangers still, so much as to let them understand that it was causeless to her.

It gave her a cold fear of what hidden perils there might be in the alliance she was about to make. Would she dare to discuss this outburst with the one to whom she should in future be so closely united? Dare to challenge him to give a reasoned reply?

Perhaps it would be better to talk it over first with Jerónimo. She could express herself so much more freely in the Tabascan tongue, which they both knew.

While she was agitated by these thoughts, they left the temple, and she soon had a more immediate ordeal to face, of terror to be concealed and be overcome.

Cortéz said to her kindly: "You have walked all morning. You must be weary. You shall ride behind me, as I should have said before now."

As he spoke, the black monster he was accustomed to ride was brought out from the courtyard.

It jerked its head in an impatient way. It pulled at the leading-rein. It opened a huge mouth, showing teeth such as even the deadly puma could not display. And how small was a puma beside this monster of shining jet! A loud unearthly sound came from its throat.

All morning it had been restrained to a walking pace. Now it reared on its hind legs, rising to a most menacing height. What would happen should it break loose from that slender cord?

Now it was almost on them. But Cortéz showed no sign of fear. He stepped forward, stroking its neck. She half forgot her own fear in admiration of what he did. He was more like a god than a man!

She knew that well-bred girls did not show fear. But what girl had ever had such a test as this?

She said: "I have only walked. I am not tired at all."

That was sense. She had not run a yard. She could walk all day. Anyone could.

But he did not seem to understand. He had gained the saddle now, in one springing motion, though he was in full armour except for his unhelmeted head.

He stooped toward her, stretching out an inviting arm. He said, with sudden realisation: "Help her up, Díaz. She has never ridden before."

Soon she was mounted behind him, sitting sideways, her arm round the cold corselet, her heart beating in a way that she hoped that he did not hear.

He said: "I should have thought of it before." He looked ahead to the coming night. Who would wish to have a weary bride, who had toiled for the whole day in the heat of a dusty road?

But walking meant little to those who had been born to a land where no beasts were tamed.

It was good fortune that the charger was not allowed to move faster than men will do on a burdened way.

CHAPTER TWENTY: CEMPOALLA

The sun was low when they came to a river over which there was no bridge, and which was too deep to wade.

Its crossing must evidently be left to the next day.

Cortéz ordered that a camp should be made. He was busy with many details, for he was one who would leave nothing to chance, and few things to the discretion of other men.

There was to be search up and down the river bank for boats, or for a possible ford which would not be too deep for the horses to splash across.

There was to be felling of trees for rafts, for which there would be almost certain need.

Marina found opportunity to talk to Jerónimo, and determined to clear the enigma that vexed her mind.

She said: "There was part of a woman's leg hanging in the priest's kitchen. Why did they mind that? You might have thought it was their own mother's by the fuss they made. I almost thought they were mad."

Her words were less puzzling to him than they would have been to any other Spaniard there, he having lived for eight years in a land where such uses prevailed; but they were still shocking to hear: He said: "Do you not feel that the killing of men for food is a very horrible thing?"

She answered: "But of course you know that it isn't done! She wasn't killed to eat, she was being eaten because she had had to be killed, which is an utterly different thing. She may have been a thief, or even an adulteress, for all we know! We know that everyone dies sooner or later. We can't make a fuss about those we didn't know when they were alive. And most ways of dying are worse than that."

He said: "They would have killed and eaten me when I was wrecked eight years ago, if I hadn't escaped. Do you defend that?"

"I'm glad you got away. But I don't see what complaint you would have had. You can't say that if you come to a strange land the people there are *obliged* to keep you alive as a slave. They're under no obligation to you."

"You should put such ideas out of your mind, now that you have accepted the Christian faith."

"I don't see that. Your God—no, I'll say our God; I know I'm a Christian now—cooks people forever, after they are dead. I should think if He finished them off, and ate them, they'd be *grateful* for that."

"But you forget that there is a way of salvation open to all."

She did not pursue that argument, having found on other issues, that it was best to accept what she was told of the Christian creed. She opened attack on another front. She said: "Do you remember the battle at Tabasco? I walked through the men that were killed while they were burying them. It was a horrible sight. I've seen men sacrificed several times, but never saw anything like that before. Your cannon balls had knocked them to pieces. Some of their insides were half out. They must have died horribly, and some of them may have lived for hours. What do you say about that?"

"It is inevitable when a battle is fought."

"But you know that, though a lot of you got hurt, there were only two killed. You know why that was, and you can't say it isn't the better way."

He was almost silenced by that. He knew that the Spaniards thought that it had been their own prowess, and their defensive armour, that had protected their lives, or they might say that it was the overruling mercy of God, but he knew that none of these explanations was entirely true.

Throughout all México it was the custom of warfare to capture rather than to kill. Captured men must expect to be killed and eaten, which could be done at future dates. Men fought to obtain captives, and to defend themselves from the same fate.

This difference of objective had been very disadvantageous to the Tabascans, and had contributed materially to their defeat.

Men who died in battle were not eaten; those who met that fate were ceremoniously killed by the priests—with some qualifications, applying to private feasts.

Every year of her life, from early childhood, Marina had been present at the annual religious festival in México, at which human sacrifice always occurred. But her dominant recollections were not of horror and blood, they were of music, and the colours and fragrance of many flowers.

These half-civilised Spaniards looked at things in perverse ways. They distorted facts.

Not that the facts were beyond reproach. The many wars that the Aztecs had waged upon weaker neighbours, by which they had established an empire similar to, though not of the extent of, that of Rome at its greatest day, had brought them many prisoners, so that there had been no lack of victims for festival days; and there had been some, even among the Aztecs themselves, who had said that the prospect of securing such victims had been the purpose for which such quarrels had been provoked.

But this did not alter the basic fact that it was a better method of warfare—more civilised and more humane—to capture your enemy alive, give him the enjoyment of being fattened, and then kill him in an almost instantaneous manner, than to smash him in ugly random ways with great balls of lead, and leave him lying about for his friends to shovel him into a ditch on the next day.

She faced the fact that the Spaniards were not of her standard of civilisation. In their daily habits there were some things that were coarse and repellent to her, as they would never be likely to guess. They were so arrogantly sure of themselves—and of their religion—that they would thrust on all.

And that religion was like themselves. It was better than that of her own people. She recognised that. But it was also worse. There was discordant beauty and ugliness, and the Spaniards appeared to accept both with equal certainty and satisfaction. Yet, if you shut your eyes to its darker side, it was a very beautiful thing. Jerónimo had taught her half the Spanish she knew in eulogies of his own faith, and his earnestness had not been without influence. But it was growing dusk, and there was another adventure to face before midnight came.

There have been numberless unions in the world's history of men and women of alien lands; there have been fewer in which the difference has been of a racial width, as when European weds with

Chinese, or either with one of pure Negro blood; and it is unlikely that such, even when they have endured, have resulted in harmony of the closest kind.

But it may be doubted whether, in the whole history of the human race, there had been a union to compare with this. It was not merely that the two had come together from two separate civilisations. Each was almost entirely ignorant of what the other's civilisation was. It was not only that their codes of conduct, their conception of honour and dishonour, of right and wrong, were fundamentally different. They did not even know what those differences were.

Cortéz knew no more of what life was like in the Aztec capital than Marina could imagine of the domestic life of Madrid.

Even in the relationship which was now established between them, there were mutual misconceptions as to what its status was understood to be.

Cortéz considered that he had taken an attractive mistress from the native population, as Spaniards who did not intend to marry until they should return with rich profits of adventure to their ancestral homes, or who had left wives behind, thought it natural to do. Certainly, it was a sin; but it was a venial one, which a light penance would condone, particularly if the concubine should thereby be brought into the Christian fold.

Cortéz honestly believed that by mentioning that he had a wife, he had made the nature of the contract clear, and that he was dealing with a slave (of whatever status) in a way which custom allowed. A man could not have more than one wife. That was obvious. When he had mentioned her existence, he had made the remaining possibility clear.

But to Marina it was not clear at all. She did not regard it as inevitable that a man should have only one wife. On the contrary, though polygamy was not common among the Aztecs, for the obvious reason that men and women were about equally numerous, it was legal, and it involved no dishonour at all, either to the first wife, or those who might subsequently join the home.

But the obligations of marriage were very strictly observed, and the penalty of deviation was death. Divorce, under any circumstances, was very difficult to obtain. Irregular unions with certain definite exceptions were not recognised or condoned.

Aztec marriage was preceded by public elaborate ceremony. Cortéz did not know that. Neither did Marina know that Spanish marriage involved any ceremony at all. She did not know that she had not acquired an equal position to that of the absent wife. She did not know that the absent wife would have any cause for resentment against herself.

In fact, what these two did not know of each other's customs, or social laws, was a much longer catalogue than that which they did.

Even if those of Cortéz had been explained to his new partner, they would have been puzzling to her. She was not familiar with the idea of venial sins, or laws which were not obeyed.

Her people had civil laws, which differed in many details from those of Western Europe; but they were generally obeyed.

They were administered by judges independent of priest and king, with impartial justice, but pitiless severity. Those who broke them must expect to be handed over to the priests, to be sacrificed on the next appropriate day. Had such criminals been numerous, there would have been less need to seek other victims by means of war.

But a God who made laws which his followers were not expected to keep, who could be coaxed to condone or forgive at an easy price! Why should such laws be made, if they were to be derided thus?

Knowing little of each other's civilisation, and repelled or puzzled by what they did, almost equally confident that their own was the higher form—but Cortéz excelled here, having no moment of doubt at all—they joined in the most intimate of human bonds in the wildest adventure which is recorded in human history—an adventure the results of which would be incredible, if they were not certainly true.

It was noon of the next day before the little army was assembled on the further bank of the river, some having been rafted across, and some ferried in canoes which had been found, waterlogged and derelict, on the river bank, and hurriedly but skilfully repaired under the direction of one, Martín López, who had been a shipbuilder in earlier years.

They struck due northward now, taking a beaten road through rich woodlands and fertile plains.

The woods were alive with game, prodigal of purple grapes, and brilliant with great butterflies, and bright-plumaged birds, and profusion of flowers.

The heathen Mexicans might be doomed to a final hell, but it seemed that indulgent Heaven gave brief paradise first, with an inconsistency which did not appear to puzzle the Christian invaders' minds.

As they advanced, they came to enclosed orchards, and fields, and human dwellings, and nose-ringed Indians who were timid, but did not flee.

Then they were met by the cacique of Cempoalla himself, with twelve of his subordinate officials, to be their escort and guides.

These were men in loose graceful cotton garments of many colours, belted waists, and nose and earrings of patterned gold, who greeted them with courtesy and respect, but delayed the slow ordeal of translated negotiations till they should come to their journey's end.

They camped that night under open sky, but advanced next day into a more thickly populated country, where they became surrounded by increasing, friendly, curious crowds.

Women were among them now—well-dressed women, some of them, gaily bright with rich clothing, jewels, and brilliant flowers.

They carried long chains of roses, which they threw round the necks of the leading cavaliers, and some, greatly daring, draped the neck of Cortéz slow-pacing charger in the same way.

Some of them attempted speech with Marina, but their words had no meaning for her, and they made no response when she spoke to them in Aztec tongue.

So they came to Cempoalla, the houses of which were stuccoed in such a way that they shone silver-bright in the noonday sun, causing the foremost cavaliers to ride back through a scattering crowd, with excited cries that the whole city was solid silver.

The town was not, in fact, large. It had substantial stone-built houses, and a large central temple, and which was common with these edifices, a wide courtyard, with surrounding buildings, spacious enough to accommodate the whole of the little Spanish army, and which was surrendered to their occupation, its religious character not being regarded as an obstacle to secular uses.

Here, with military precautions that would have been considered needless by a less wary leader—sleepless sentinels patrolling the outer walls and loaded cannon blocking the courtyard entrance—the little army slept.

Chapter Twenty-One: Doubtful Allies

The lord of Cempoalla was a large man, burdened with fat.

He came down the terrace of his mansion to meet the Spanish leader with an outstretched hand, having learnt that that was the form of greeting the strangers used.

Cortéz had brought fifty men with him, who had fallen in, twenty-five a side, as he rode up to the steps. There he had dismounted, given his charger to the care of Bernal Díaz, and advanced to meet the Indian chieftain accompanied only by Puerto-Carrero, and the two interpreters.

Seated in the comparative coolness of an inner room, fragrant with honeysuckle that twined round its open casements, the slow course of a negotiation proceeded in which Cortéz strove with confident and sometimes boastful assurances to secure Totonac support, and their ruler, showing himself to be already frightened of what had been done, hesitated, temporised, and spoke with awe of the Aztec power.

"Tell him," Cortéz said to Jerónimo, "that I come from the mightiest king that the earth contains, and that these Aztecs of whom he talks can have peace or war as they will. The difference will be to them, not to us. But tell him we come in peace, excepting only that we are the servants of a God who must be obeyed, and we must plant His worship here, even though it be by the argument of the sword. For the gods of the Aztecs are demons, which we are sworn to destroy."

This speech must be repeated to Marina, and by her translated to the Aztec interpreter, and by him conveyed to his chief in the Totonac tongue.

The answer came by the same devious route: "That is beyond reason to ask. The gods of the Aztecs are ours also. They send sunlight and rain. To offend them would be our death."

Before a reply could be made to this protest, it became evident that Marina was being pressed with questions to which she was giving her own replies. Exchanges became animated and swift before Jerónimo heard anything which he could understand.

Cortéz was content for this to proceed, making a true guess that Marina would say nothing to diminish respect for the Spanish power, and that some assertions might have more weight if they should come spontaneously from her than if she should appear to be a mere channel of conversation.

But it was not long before she turned to Jerónimo to say, partly in Spanish, which Cortéz could understand, but more often in Tabascan, as her limitations required: "He says that he is afraid that when the Emperor hears that he has entertained you, after you had been ordered to leave the land, he will send such an army as will seize the best of their young men, and their girls also, to be sacrificed in the usual manner."

"Tell him," Cortéz replied, "that we will not allow that to happen. It is to prevent such evils that I am here. Ask him what number of warriors his own nation has, who can join us to save themselves."

The question was more easily asked than answered. The Aztec knowledge of mathematics was in some respects actually superior to that of Europe, and the Totonacs may not have been too ignorant to comprehend such calculations with ease, but their methods of notation were naturally different from those of Europe, and may be said to have been superior to that of the Romans, but inferior to the Arabic which the Spaniards used.

Cortéz was led to understand that they could raise a hundred thousand men. A neighbouring nation of Tlascala, which had never submitted to the Aztecs, was far stronger than they. He knew already from Marina that this was true. What he did not know was whether the Tlascalans would be any friendlier than the Aztecs to him.

But he replied boldly that these matters were of no importance. It was for their own sakes that he must know who desired the friendship of Spain.

He had a rendezvous with his ships, which he must first keep, and after that he would know how to protect those who looked to him, and the Christian God.

For the moment, boldness prevailed. Totonac professions of friendship were confirmed by the supply of abundant provisions and costly gifts.

Returning to the temple camp, Cortéz asked his interpreters how far he could rely upon the assurances he had received.

Marina said: "I told them that you would require four hundred bearers by when you will march tomorrow. If they are here, it will mean that they are more anxious for your goodwill than afraid of what Montezuma will do."

"Four hundred! Do we require so many, having our own Indians?"

"Yes. It is strange to these people, as it would be to ours, that you all carry as much as you do. All burdens with us are borne by porters trained for the work. If you continue to do that, you will be regarded with less respect."

"Then you have done well."

The next morning, four hundred porters were there. Even the Cuban Indians were loaded lightly from that day. The Spaniards marched with essential weapons alone. It increased the comfort and the military efficiency of the little army, and conformed to the etiquette of the land. They had good reason to thank Marina for that.

They set out to cover the twelve miles that separated them from the sea, and the waiting ships.

CHAPTER TWENTY-TWO: CHALLENGE

The fleet lay in its new anchorage, protected by a cape that projected from the northward coastline, forming a barrier from the dreaded northerly gales.

On the eminence above them was a second Totonac town, to which its inhabitants, who had fled in fear, were returning timidly. They found their possessions undisturbed, and confidence grew.

The army had not long arrived when a litter appeared, bearing the Cempoalla cacique, who had decided that the nearer he could keep to his new allies, the greater his safety would be.

With its new retinue of bearers, the army had become a total of more than a thousand men. There was no accommodation for them in the little town, apart from its central market place, where many must camp, as they had done elsewhere.

The square was crowded with Spaniards and Indians, among whom Cortéz stood, with Marina at his side, giving orders and receiving reports, when there was commotion at its western approach.

They saw five men advancing, before whom the Totonacs gave way with frightened respect, while the Spaniards themselves were contemptuously disregarded. The five halted in the centre of the square, with a group of attendants behind them.

They called out, in a tone in which men might order dogs, and the cacique of Cempoalla, and some officials of the town, hastened obsequiously forward.

Cortéz, standing in apparent indifference, but warily watchful, noticed that these newcomers were different from the Totonacs in aspect and garb. They made no show of force. They were richly dressed. They were garlanded with flowers. They were cooled by the fans of attendant slaves.

Their aspects were those of masters, too assured of themselves to need demonstration of strength.

Cortéz asked: "Who are they?"

"They are Aztecs," Marina replied. "They will have come to collect the tribute for Montezuma."

So they might have done, but their errand was more than that. It had been true that everything which occurred had been observed by the distant Aztec emperor, and he sent these men to proclaim his will and impose the penalty that insubordination required.

"We had better go nearer," Cortéz said, "you can tell me what it is that is being said, which is making our fat friend tremble with fear."

So they did, Marina said: "Montezuma is displeased that they have shown hospitality to you, after he had issued orders that you should leave. He requires twenty young men or women to be surrendered for sacrifice, as a condition of his overlooking the offence."

"They have the insolence to say that? Where is Jerónimo? There must be other things said and done."

It is a disadvantage to have to be angry in a strange tongue, but he made his demeanour clear.

"You must have these men," he told the frightened cacique, "laid by the heels at once. You say you cannot do that? Do you mean to send twenty of your own people to death because you have been friendly to us? You would lose our friendship forever. You will either arrest these impudent men, or I will leave you without protection. If you are my friends, you must resent an insult to me."

The astonished envoys partly understood, but their confidence did not abate. They were too aware of the Aztec power. They looked at the Spanish leader with contempt, and found their glances returned in the same way.

And, in the end, the one who was sure of himself prevailed over those of doubtful minds.

The astonished Aztecs were seized. They felt the indignity of cords. Bound at wrist and ankle, they were confined in one of the rooms that opened out from the courtyard of the temple which was beside the marketplace, as was the common feature of all towns in this land.

There they remained till night, at which time Cortéz, thinking that they would be in a less truculent mood, ordered that two of them should be brought before him.

Marina, having been told before what should be said, did the talking now to men of her own race, who looked humbler than they had done before.

"The Commander," she said, "who represents a greater king than Montezuma himself, has decided, in his clemency, that you shall be released, and take a message from him.

"You will say that he regrets that you should have suffered so great an indignity, but it is the natural result of your insult to himself and to his King, who sent him here, on a mission to Montezuma of friendship and peace. Did he not order that we should be left without food in a barren place? But we are still willing to resolve all in a peaceful way. For this end, the Commander will talk to Montezuma himself, as he has always purposed to do.

"When the Emperor sees that he has let you live, he will understand that there can be friendship and peace. Will you take this message to him?"

"We will report all that has happened, and that we have heard, as it will be our duty to do."

"Then there is no more to be said."

Before dawn the two Aztecs were taken on board the sloop, which sailed up the coast, and landed them at a spot of their choice, from which they would be able to return safely to their own land.

But when morning came, angry Totonac chieftains were at the gates of the temple court, demanding speech with Cortéz at once.

They encountered firm though polite refusal. No one could enter without his authority. He should be informed. An attempt to pass the guard was met with crossed halberds, and the sight of Christóval de Olid's sword leaving its sheath.

Common language was meagre, but bare steel could be understood. They waited while de Olid crossed the courtyard to where Cortéz breakfasted with Marina in a chamber he had reserved for his own use.

He said to her: "*Amada*, will you find out what the trouble is? I am no lackey to them, to be bustled before I feed."

She thought she could have told him with one guess, but she went without words, and was soon back, bringing Jerónimo with her, for there might be more explanation to give than her Spanish could undertake.

She said: "They are wroth because you have let two of the five escape."

"You allowed that I had done that?"

"Yes. They had heard. Was I wrong?"

"Not at all. It could not have been long denied. But why do they fret for that? Yesterday, there were chattering jaws because I would have them seized."

"So it was, but, it having been done, they think they should have been sacrificed in the usual way. Montezuma will not forgive what has been done. It is certain war. And even their short triumph is spoiled if their captives go."

"Well, they are gone. They cannot change that. Do they seek to quarrel both with Montezuma and me? They will have full days."

"They know that the two are gone too far for recall. They would have the other three slaughtered at once, so that their end be sure."

"Then they have much to learn. Tell them I will see them. Or, at least, three. Tell them I am in a small room, and will not be crushed."

Marina went back with this word, and brought in three of the caciques, who were inpatient to make complaint, but found that Cortéz was not docile to be rebuked.

He said: "Ask them this: was it they or I who proposed that these men should be seized? Is it I who ask them to be my shield, or have they pleaded to me? If I should give them these men to slay and eat, and then sail away in the next hour, would they be content? Or would they think they might be about to fill their bellies at a price they would not be willing to pay?

"But having asked them those questions, you must be plain to add that they should not sacrifice these men by any bargain with me of whatever kind, either to stay or to go; for it is a thing which my God will not endure."

After that, Cortéz must be content for some minutes to listen to words that had no meaning for him. The three could talk Aztec, having perhaps been preferred for that reason, so that Marina could speak directly to them, and it seemed that she had more to say than they had to reply; but Cortéz was content, for he saw that they had become frightened men.

Marina turned to Jerónimo at last, but not to tell him that which he would translate. Now she asked him for any Spanish word she might lack, and so spoke to Cortéz direct, as he would prefer it to be. She said: "You will have no more trouble with them. I have made them fear that you will cast them off like a worn shoe. And I have told them that when you do things which it is not easy to understand, it is then that you have the wisdom that sees ahead."

Cortéz was pleased at that. He said: "You are strength to me. I know not whether you please me better by night or day."

He would have kissed her then, had she been of his own race, but he had learned already that she had a reticence far greater than his.

She was not cold of blood, and what they did together when none was near was their own affair, but before others— There were many points of manners in which she thought the Spaniards uncouth; but she excused them, as being of a lower culture than hers. Could they help that?

It remained that they were finer, bolder men than those of her own race. And, for life or death, she had chosen her part with them, which she would not change.

When the envoys had gone in a subdued way, Cortéz said: "I will have no risk. They might sneak them from us, if we continue to keep them here. That would spoil the plan I have; and it would force me to a quarrel here which I do not want. They shall be put on to one of the ships."

That was done in the next hour. Alvarado marched them down to the beach, with forty Spanish swords nakedly displayed around them. They may have wondered why, being gyved as they were, there could be need for as large a guard. Or their minds may have been fuller of unpleasant doubts, as to the fate to which they were being led.

But, as to that, they had no occasion for fear. Cortéz saw them on the next day, and released them in the same manner as he had done the others, sending further messages to their emperor that he desired friendship with him, though he had no occasion to fear his power, and he was releasing them as further evidence of his good-will.

He did not expect that such friendship could ever be. The Aztec power, by all that he could learn, was too great, too arrogant, too intolerant, for that to be a probable thing, and his own belief that he had Heaven's mandate to force salvation upon them gave aggressive complexion to all his plans. But he thought that he was taking a course which would produce hesitation, and hence delay. And on that anticipation he was correct, as he would so frequently be.

CHAPTER TWENTY-THREE: THE CITY OF VERA CRUZ

As the days passed and there was no sign of retaliation from the outraged Aztec power, the Totonac chieftains' confidence in Spanish support naturally increased. And in that confidence, or the courage of desperation—for they could not hope that México would forgive, if it should have the power to enforce its will—they resolved to accept the pledges that Cortéz gave, and to rely upon the protection of Spain.

When they were committed to this course, he announced that there was a simple condition. They must swear allegiance to Spain, and they would have no reason to fear. Soon all the caciques of the little nation had taken the required oath. Spain had acquired a legalised footing in the new continent.

And Cortéz made it clear at once that she had come to stay.

He said he proposed to build a city beside the harbour where his fleet lay. Would they help him with materials and labour?

They made no objection to that. How could they? They may have seen that they would only be changing one tyranny for another. But they did not want Cortéz to go, leaving them naked to the vengeance of Aztec power.

So the council which had elected itself further down the coast was to have the town which it had been appointed to rule. Its boundaries were marked out on a wide waste plain overlooking the harbour. Its public buildings rose with a magic speed. Cortéz could not have built it in those few weeks by the hands of the thousand men, more or less, white and brown, who obeyed his will. But the Totonacs gave a more numerous help. And all men laboured alike on the task which might be decisive for their own prosperity, their own lives. His own hands became rough with the handling of stone and beam.

Private houses might not be numerous within the girth of its barricades, but there were strong storehouses in a central fort, a meeting-hall and other buildings for public use, and a church of somewhat heathen design (could that be avoided?) for the worship of Europe's God.

It was while this building proceeded that Cortéz was gratified to hear of the approach of a deputation from the Aztec Emperor.

Marina, having to interpret again, found herself listening to those whom she had seen at a distance before, but had not expected to encounter at closer range.

It was in the cacique's residence at Cempoalla that he had received them, they having halted in that city, in evident anticipation that he would meet them there, which he thought it prudent to do—and the more so because the reception hall of his new city was incomplete.

He met them accompanied only by Puerto-Carrero and Montejo and the interpreters. He saw two young men, very richly attired, and of a haughtiness of demeanour which appeared to be normal to them, rather than directed against himself. They took the foremost of the offered seats, four older men giving them that precedence.

Marina said, in a toneless way, before the conversation began: "Do not show surprise, for they notice all, but the two younger men are nephews of Montezuma, and the others are among the greatest noblemen in the land. It is a condescension to send them here, such as has never happened before, and is almost beyond belief. I suppose they may have come not only to do honour to you, but to take back reports which the Emperor will not hesitate to believe."

While she spoke, slaves entered the room, and spread out an array of presents more numerous, various, and costly than Montezuma had sent before.

Were they sent in a spirit of real friendship, or in expectation of an equivalent munificence? It would have been hard to believe.

Were they an evidence of fear? Did weakness seek to propitiate strength with tributary gifts? To credit that would have been to disbelieve all the evidences of those who trembled at the Aztec name.

Or was Aztec wealth so great that these garments of jewelled featherwork, exquisite in workmanship and design, these wheels of silver, these bucklers of beaten gold, were mere trifles of no account, to be thrown contemptuously at the feet of a begging knave?

Cortéz received them with courteous indifference, which concealed a thought that they might be sufficient in themselves to pay the whole cost of the expedition, and to justify all that he had done. Tomorrow they would be catalogued, valued, weighed, and entered in the complicated books of account which he so carefully, so scrupulously, had continued to keep.

Now he gave the word that some presents which he had had in readiness should be brought forward in courteous response. Some of these may have been of workmanship or materials new to Aztec eyes, but nothing could disguise their relative paltriness. Five of the envoys regarded them with coldly appreciate eyes, but in those of the sixth, a lean old man in the rear, Cortéz caught an expression of sardonic contempt which had been unmistakable, though it was as brief as an eyelid's wink. Then the elder of the two younger men began to speak.

He ignored Marina, looking straight at Cortéz, and speaking as one who has no doubt he is understood. But afterwards he remained silent while she translated what she had heard, and he must turn to her after that, in a cold way, to hear Cortéz's reply.

Marina translated: "The prince says that his uncle, Montezuma, the greatest Emperor in the world, has sent him and his companions to demonstrate his regard for you master, the Spanish King, for whom these trifling presents are meant.

"And he thanks you for rescuing his messengers when they were in danger of death from local vermin, with whom he will know how to deal on a future day.

"But he is divided between distress and surprise that you have countenanced their rebellion against their acknowledged lord, which your king surely would not approve.

"At the same time, he recognises that you are not plebeian men. Your coming was foretold by his own gods, and that you would be of the same blood as himself.

"For these reasons he will delay, until your departure, the chastisement that his rebellious vassals must feel; but after that they may be sure that it will heavy and swift."

There was a short silence before Cortéz replied. His audacities were never randomly planned, and there had been some things said—and some left in silence—with implications not easy to read. Then he said, speaking directly to Marina, a difference of procedure which might be insult, or have no significance at all: "You can tell them on my own monarch's behalf, that I value their emperor's friendship highly, and appreciate the munificence of the gifts he sends. But, as I shall shortly be paying him the visit which is the purpose for which I came, I will say no more at this time. When we shall meet, he may be confident that all misunderstandings will be removed."

Marina required some repetition, and some aid from Jerónimo, before she had every word of this clear for translation into the Aztec tongue, but when she addressed him at last, the Aztec prince must turn his eyes upon her, which he did with an aloof curiosity which he did not conceal.

He heard the reply with a cold disapproval. "I have not said that the Emperor will receive you," he said, turning his glance directly upon Cortéz, as he had done before. "He has twice declined."

Marina did not wait to translate this. She replied at once: "But that is the purpose for which my lord Cortéz came, and it is one which he cannot change."

"What is that?" Cortéz asked.

"He says you have been refused permission to go, and I have told him it is a purpose you will not change."

"That is well. You will hold to that."

The eyes of the Aztec prince were now on Marina with a cold hostility which few of her race would have been equal to meet. He asked: "Who are you?"

"I am the interpreter."

"You are Aztec born?"

"Yes."

"I would have your name, and your place of birth."

There was a moment's silence while their wills fought. She did not know what tale her mother had told to account for her disappearance, but she made a sure guess that it had all been contrived to give the inheritance to her brother, and that would have been impossible without legal proof of her own death.

She wished no ill to her mother (and certainly none to her half-brother) whatever might have been done or intended to her.

She said: "I cannot tell you that."

She was aware of the blank amazement that she had roused in the minds not only of him to whom she spoke, but of his companions, who had certainly never heard such a reply given before to a prince of the royal blood.

The prince controlled his wrath, as one who would not be vexed by an insect's bite.

He said: "When you come to the knife, as you soon will, you may expect that your death will be very slow."

Marina received this with no sign of response, for in such controls she was as well practised as he.

CHAPTER TWENTY-FOUR: TRIUMPH OF THE TRUE FAITH

The Aztec embassy withdrew in an attitude of cool aloofness, which certainly gave no assurance of future friendship, but, whatever its purpose may have been, and whatever might be the subsequent action of the Emperor whose wishes were so boldly defied, its effect upon the Totonacs was almost incredulous amazement, with an increase of confidence in their new protectors, which Cortéz encouraged by making an armed progress through the country, in the course of which he reconciled an internal quarrel which had weakened the national unity, and increased his popularity by the strict discipline with which he restrained his troops in their relations with the native population.

There had been difficulties in such control, even while they had been occupied in the exhausting toil of the building of Vera Crux. To maintain order in idleness might have been beyond his power.

The realisation of this difficulty caused him to have an unwelcome doubt of whether the Aztec policy might be even subtler than his own. Did they leave him unattacked that he might have time to alienate his allies by the excesses into which idle troops are so likely to fall? Or did they hold back, so that he might be induced to march inland to his own destruction, leaving the barricades of the city that he had built, and the refuge of the waiting ships?

His procession through the Totonac country was intended both to occupy the troops, to gain surer knowledge of the numbers and qualities of his native allies, and to provide a demonstration which might induce the Aztecs to attack him if such should be their disposition, for he saw that, if a trial of strength were inevitable, it might be better for them to come to him.

It roused no sign of hostility. He had been forbidden to enter the Aztec territory, and had replied that he intended to do so. Were they waiting to see what he would do, in caution or in contempt?

He had encouraged their vassals to revolt, and to refuse the tribute they were required to pay, and the Aztecs had taken it lying down. But here again they had made it plain that they did not accept the position as permanent. They would deal vengeance upon the rebels when he had gone.

It was a position which could not last.

And the necessity to enforce discipline had become acute. An example must be made. He had given out several weeks before that the penalty would be death for theft or rape, and when, after he had made camp on the second day, a complaint reached him that a soldier had taken a couple of pheasants forcibly from a nearby villager, which the man could not deny, he gave a reluctant order to de Olid that he should hang.

Alvarado dined with him, and others in his tent that night, and he asked: "Did any murmur that Morla was hanged?"

"Not so that it would be easy to hear," Alvarado replied, "Christóval told them that there would be room for more than one on the tree. At least, so I heard, for the man was strung up before I happened to pass."

"It was an order I was most reluctant to give. There is not a man we can spare."

Alvarado laughed. "It might have been worse. I was just in time."

"In time for what?"

"Why to cut him down, as I had no doubt that you would wish me to do."

There was a blaze of anger in his commander's eyes which even Alvarado did not find it easy to meet. But next moment it was gone. Cortéz said quietly: "You may have been right in that. But should I give such an order again, I shall mean it to be fully obeyed."

He reflected that Morla would be a living warning to others. He hoped he had been hanged long enough for his throat to be very sore. He, at least, would be likely to be an honest man from that day.

They got back to Cempoalla on the following afternoon, and were met by its cacique, with an Aztec-speaking companion at his side, by which medium he explained that he had a presentation to make which would demonstrate the sincerity of Totonac friendship, and increase its intimacy for future days.

"He says," Marina interpreted, "that it is evident that some of your officers who have no women at all must be needing wives. To achieve this need, the daughters of eight of the noblest caciques of the land have volunteered, and will be given to you for distribution at your discretion. They will be richly endowed, and each will have a retinue of three female slaves who have been chosen with care."

Cortéz answered: "It is nobly intended, and cannot fail to draw us more closely together. Our marriage customs are not precisely yours, but I am sure that there will be those of my officers who will be both free and willing to take advantage of such a gift. But there is one thing I must say: they cannot wed any who have not first adopted the Christian faith."

He saw that the cacique was not pleased by the translation of this reply. After some short exchanges, Marina said: "He thinks that there may be no difficulty about that, though they should not be coerced. But he says that there is a general feeling that the gods of this land should not be disturbed by the God of yours. He is supreme in Spain, and with that He should be content.

It was a challenge Cortéz was in no mood to decline. He had already resolved to make immediate preparations to march into the interior to whatever fate he might meet, and, for this desperate venture to have a fair prospect, the blessing of Heaven was a necessity.

How could it be better secured than by the conversion of heathen men?

"Tell him," he said, "that our God is not only God of Spain. He is supreme and universal, and others, if they exist at all, are evil demons whose images should be broken. If he would be relieved from the terror of Montezuma, he must abandon the Mexican gods for One Who is much stronger than they."

But the exhortation was ill received. Spanish fanaticism met with a superstition equally sincere, equally stubborn, equally terrified of the unseen powers that its imagination conceived.

Marina did what she could, using the argument of her own conversion, and the conviction to which she had come that Christianity was the better faith. But she said that she could make no progress at all.

Cortéz said: "There is more eloquence needed than mine. Let Father Olmedo be called."

So he was, and Marina did her best to convey the substance of the priest's exhortations from the Spanish that she imperfectly followed to the Aztec tongue. But whatever it became when it had been rendered again into Totonac had no potency to convince the obstinate heathen mind.

And by now the knowledge that the issue had been so acutely raised had spread to the soldiers, who thronged the marketplace, and the temple courtyard.

They looked at the images, grotesque to them, which were sacred to native eyes; and at the bloodstained altars, which roused a natural horror impossible for the Totonacs to comprehend. A cry rose to put an end to this demon-worship, and to establish the purer faith.

Against this threat a hostile crowd was gathering with loud outcries, and the menace of swords and bows.

It had not been Cortéz's intention to bring such a crisis at this moment, but, they all being as they were, it was bound to come, and he made no effort to still the storm.

The disputants had left the cacique's residence for the marketplace as the quarrel developed, and there he suddenly found, that, though priest and interpreter were still at his side, he was surrounded by Spanish swords.

Marina was not talking religion now. She said: "If you cannot control the crowd, if but one blow be struck, or one arrow shot, you and your companions will be slain without mercy or delay. Can you not see that it is a matter for the gods to determine between themselves? If the Spaniards cast them down, it is not on you that their vengeance will fall.

"The Spaniards are resolved now. They will break the altars or die, and if you should be able to kill them (which you would not, it would be your own people who would bleed), where would you be on the next day? You would have the Aztecs here. Would your gods save you from them? Are they not Aztec gods? Cannot you see which god is most likely to be useful to you? The Governor says that you can address the crowd. You are to tell them to keep still, and to watch how little your gods can do for themselves, and your life will be forfeit if you shall fail."

So he did, and with such final success that a sullen, appalled crowd watched without intervention while their sacred images were shattered, and their altars were broken down.

Father Olmedo took possession of the temple. He exorcised its demons. He consecrated it to a better use.

After that, could not the Spaniards go forward, whether to conquest or martyrdom, with the certain blessing of God?

CHAPTER TWENTY-FIVE: APPEAL TO SPAIN

As Cortéz approached the new harbour, he saw that the eleven ships had become twelve. A cavalier of Spain, Sanceda by name, in a tiny vessel, smaller even than the sloop that de León commanded, had sailed after him, seeking to join whatever his fortunes might prove to be.

He had followed the coast until he had seen the sails of the fleet he sought, and the Spanish flag. He brought two chargers, and eleven companions, all of whom were content to swear fealty to the Governor of the new land, and augment his power.

It was not a large reinforcement, but it was welcome in itself, especially in its two horses, and to Totonac eyes it may have been significant of the fact that they had not yet seen the extent of the strangers' strength.

To Cortéz, the time of decisive action had come. He had converted a whole nation to God. He had won a new realm for Spain. And he had done it all with no more than a few hundred men—and a great faith in God, in Spain, and, perhaps not least, in himself.

And now it was clearly time to ignore Velásquez, and report what he had done directly to Madrid, which was the unlifting shadow upon his rear. Madrid could ruin him. Jealousy or greedful intrigue at the Royal Court might obtain the signature which no Spaniard would disobey.

Now he chose the most seaworthy ship of his little fleet for the long Atlantic voyage. He wrote an account of the rich new land which he was acquiring for God and Spain. He was not too modest concerning his own exploits, or what he intended to do; but he wrote in the humble language which the etiquette of the occasion required, and which his education and legal training had made him adroit to do. He chose the two on whom he had already bestowed the greatest honours—Puerto-Carrero and Montejo—to be his representatives at the Spanish Court.

This was a most discreet selection. One was his personal friend, a man of moderation, and discretion; the other had been an adherent of the Cuban Governor, whom he had won over to loyalty to himself. Both of them were men of rank in their own land, who would have no difficulty in gaining hearing at the Spanish Court, even to the ear of the King.

With scrupulous equity, he assessed the value of the treasure which had been gathered, and set aside a full fifth, which was the usual tribute paid by the adventurers of the New World to the Spanish Crown.

But he was not content with that, he called a general assemblage, and told them that he was adding the whole of his own share of the spoil, as an evidence of his loyalty; and he invited others to do the same.

"Comrades," he went on, "we are about to set out to secure a new dominion for God and Spain. What we have acquired now may be almost naught beside that which will be ours in the later days. But there is one thing on which all will depend at last. We must have the King's license for what we do. We must be sure that others will not be sent to reap that which our hazards and toils have won.

"Now the shares that should go to each of you are not much, when they are considered apart, but if they should be in one pile they would be such as a monarch would not despise.

"I am sending the whole of my own share in humble loyalty to the King, and I ask you to do the same.

"But you will understand that I only ask, I do not command. Those who do not approve will have their shares set scrupulously aside, and they will have no censure from me."

He ended here, being one who would not continue words when he had finished that which he had to say, and was answered by an acclamation of assent, in which those who were silent were overlooked.

After that, a document was prepared which all must sign if they were willing to relinquish in this manner the gains already won, for the prospect of a more prosperous future, and it may be considered evidence of their confidence both in themselves and in their leader's advice that there was not a single soldier whose name was not signed upon it.

But it may be considered also that, when the proposal had once been made, it would have been a gesture of disloyalty both to King and Governor to have refused to accept it. That all men did not sign willingly may be conclusively inferred from an occurrence of the next week.

But, for the moment, there was no dissenting voice, there was no evidence of dissatisfaction on any ground, as preparations went on for the ship to sail, and for the inland march on which Cortéz was resolved.

To his own letter to the King, a petition from his officers and from the officials of the new 'city' was added, begging humbly that the authority of their Governor should be confirmed; and the envoys went aboard with a last injunction that they should not call at any intervening port, till they should drop anchor in Cadiz bay.

Unfortunately, though they intended to obey the spirit, they did not observe the letter of this instruction, or important subsequent events would have gone differently.

Montejo did not wish to visit Velásquez, being now committed to Cortéz's interests, and the vessel steered its course along Cuba's northern coast, in accordance with the instructions it had received; but that brought it past Marien, near to which Montejo owned a plantation, which he wished to visit, and so they anchored there for a few hours, and during this time a sailor deserted, and made his way overland to St. Jago, where his talk brought him into the presence of the Governor, who thus had his first news of the expedition.

Enraged at learning that a vessel had been sent direct to Spain, in contempt of his own authority, he despatched his best two available ships, to double the island at its eastern end, and arrest, by force if necessary, the rebel vessel, as he considered it to be.

CHAPTER TWENTY-SIX: TREASON

Those who had volunteered for this wildly hazardous invasion of the New World were of varied virtues and vices, but there was one quality, that of stubborn courage, which all might claim, or they would not have been there. All of them—except the priests.

They had brought more than a dozen priests, whom they considered to be more important than their swords, and as necessary as they.

Men of boldly adventurous dispositions do not supply the church with its most numerous recruits. They may have other enthusiasms, such as cause them to imperil life for the conversion of heathen men. Father Olmedo was of this kind, and so were others who were ministering to the spiritual needs of the little army; but there was at least one among them who was of less resolute mind.

Father Juan Díaz told himself that he was not a coward. To act as chaplain upon a ship which set out on exploration or trading ventures in unknown seas had not been beyond his choice. But to march into the interior of a hostile land which could marshal a million foes, being no more than a thousand in all, including about forty women, and several hundred of bearers and sundry slaves, he considered to go beyond the bounds of sanity; and it is a conclusion with which many prudent minds would be disposed to agree.

Priests hear confessions, which are of a sacred privacy. But, even if he would, a priest cannot keep his own mind naked of the knowledge which comes to him in that way.

Father Juan heard the confessions of Escudero, a cavalier of the lower rank, who had been a paid retainer of the Cuban Governor.

In the old days, when Velásquez had arrested Cortéz, and he had escaped and fled to sanctuary, it will be remembered that he had been rearrested when he had incautiously strolled a short distance from the shadow of the protecting church. At that time, it had been Escudero who had been the first to leap out upon him. It had been he whose dagger had touched his throat, while others had grasped his arms, and loosed the sword from his side.

Cortéz had never alluded to this incident afterwards. He had accepted Escudero as a volunteer, as though it were a stranger whose name he took. But the man had the type of mind which will retain grudges until the opportunity of retribution will come, and he could not conceive of others being of different temper. He supposed that, at the best, Cortéz would never show any favour to him. But would he not be advanced by his former lord, if he should return to him with a report of what Cortéz had done, and of the mission that he had sent to Spain?

It was an idea which the priest put into his mind, at a time when he was already nursing an inward wrath which he must not show at having been obliged to sign his treasure away to the distant king.

Father Juan saw opportunity, which might be the last, to escape from the very shadow of death. He said: "He has lost his wits. He has become insane with success. It is not a small state, it is an empire he will invade. They will be thousands to one. But to steal away with a few friends in one of the smaller ships?"

Escudero saw that, without occasion for further words. But he saw difficulties. It must be secretly done. A crew must be assembled of like mind to himself. Others must not be on the vessel. It must be provisioned for a voyage of uncertain length, which would be ruled by capricious winds.

Having considered these matters, which appeared to him to be of a daunting total, he went to Father Juan again, and when they had been talked over they became less.

Father Juan had an agile mind, which a priest requires. He pointed out that the ships were to be left with no more than skeleton crews, which were all that would be required while they rode at anchor. And even these limited numbers were not easily to be made up without direct orders and bitter grumbling. They themselves, being sensible men, might see the wild gamble to be what it was, but most, under their leader's mesmeric influence, saw it differently.

Father Juan said that the selection of a sufficient number of companions to work the ship could be left to him. He knew who would be glad to go.

The provisioning also was not a matter of extreme difficulty. Many boats were plying backwards and forwards, as everything was removed from the ships which men would require to take with them on so complete a severance from their base, and which was to be joined by a majority of the seamen, who had previously had all their effects on board.

So it was contrived, and all went well up to the evening on which the vessel was to slip away when the darkness came. A sufficient minimum crew had been recruited. Sufficient water and stores had been taken aboard for their small muster, on a voyage that should not be long.

The sun was low in the sky when Escudero, who had been aboard during the day, took a boat for the shore. He asked for Father Juan, telling those who would listen that he had a man sick, who had confession to make.

That had been the procedure arranged, to enable the priest to join the ship, without causing enquiry to which it might have been hard to reply.

Father Juan showed some timidity now that the decisive moment had come. He asked: "You are sure you are not suspect?"

"Yes. That is sure. I have had no doubts of any except Paulo Redes, and I have not allowed him ashore since doubt came."

"He has wanted to come?"

"He was urgent about noon, and fertile of reasons, which may have been false or true. But I told him that we had necks which we would not risk. He became quiet after that. He protested his faith, but he is in a cabin with two good men seated between him and the door."

"Well, let us go."

They walked down to the waterside together, and were about to enter the waiting boat when the priest, whose eyes had been nervously alert to the significance of surrounding things, drew back with an exclamation of fear.

"There are too many there!" He said sharply, "Do you see?"

He was interrupted by a voice behind him: "Father, the Governor requests that you should attend him without delay."

Though he was a fearful man, he was one of alert wits. He said: "So I should be pleased to do, but I am called to one who is sick. It is a call that is the most sacred of all."

He had turned now to confront Bernal Díaz, with three others behind him as well armed as himself. Díaz answered with respect, but no change of will: "My orders are that you come with me. I am not to use force if fair words will avail."

Father Juan made no further reply. He turned and went with them. He would have had no inclination to enter the boat had his will been free, for he had seen that there were more on the deck of Escudero's ship than the total of the crew who should have been there, and he was afraid of what it might mean.

Escudero had now seen the same thing, but he was not required to change what he had intended to do. Bernal took no notice of him.

He could condemn himself, if he would, by running away. But where to? And he could not yet be certain of the meaning of what he saw, though he had a cold doubt.

He got into the boat, in which two men sat await, and they pulled toward the ship.

The fleet lay in a long line in the channel, with anchors out, bow and stern, riding the tides. He had contrived that he should be put in charge of the vessel at the leeward end of the line, that he might slip cables in the darkness, and have a wind that would take him quickly away.

He had a panic thought that if he could get those men—but why could they be there—on some pretext to leave the ship—or would force avail? He would not wait for Father Juan, he would hoist sail at once. Would unready ships be as quick as he? Like his own, they had only skeleton crews. They would have no orders to make instant pursuit.

But what of the guns ashore? They could soon be swung round from how they were pointing now. Would he—or how long would he—be in danger from them?

It might be that the Governor had a suspicion—a mere doubt—which he had summoned Father Juan to probe. If that were so, his one hope was in instant flight, for which there might yet be time, if he were bold. He could say that he had orders for what he did.

The boat passed under the bow of the ship. It left its sunlit side for that which was in shadow, where a rope-ladder hung to the water's edge. He went up it with a show of confidence which he did not feel.

As he gained the deck, his hand reached for a sword-hilt it did not grip. They were too quick for that.

Chapter Twenty-Seven: The Burning of the Fleet

Cortéz said: "They shall have fair trial, however their guilt be clear. They are traitors to Spain, and they would have broken their oaths to me. I will hold court on the ship."

So it was done.

Ten men stood before him on the ship's deck, all being shackled, except the priest.

Cortéz said: "There are too many here." He looked them over shrewdly, and told four to stand out.

He said: "Take off their irons," and then to them, when that had been done: "Do not let me hear of you again until it be a good word. You can go your ways."

So they did, with eyes of bewildered relief.

He looked next at the priest. "Will you own your guilt, speaking truthful words, as a man of God should, or will you say that you were ignorant of what was designed?"

"I was called to my priestly office," he began, in the tone of one who did not expect belief, when Cortéz interrupted him with a sharp contempt: "Then will you say why your chest, and all your garments, were here?"

There was no answer to that. He said: "I claim benefit of clergy, if I have erred."

So he could. He could claim the protection of the church against the secular law. Father Olmedo must deal with him, giving such penance as severity could devise.

Cortéz looked at the remaining five. He said: "I will tell you this. I have known all, within an hour of when you thought that you had won Redes to share the treason that you designed. Your caution was two days late. You may confess or deny, but you will lose nothing if you admit your guilt, and there are those among you who may gain, for I am a busy man."

There was a moment's silence, and then Escudero said boldly: "What have we to deny? It was Cuba's Governor who sent me here, and whose servant I am. It was to him I would have returned with a true tale. We are in your hands, and you may do what you will, but a day of justice may come. He was clement once, but I should say that he will treat you at the last as you treat us now."

Cortéz looked at him with cold eyes, but his lips smiled. He said: "It is a shrewd threat, but it will not avail. I do not think to come again into Velásquez's hands.

"You would say you designed no wrong? Would you not have sailed on a stolen ship? Do you forget the oath of fealty that you took to me?

"You have not only broken that oath, you have persuaded others to the same crime. There can be no mercy for you. Nor for Sancho, who was as active as you. You two must hang on the yard of my own ship."

He paused to regard the other three, to whose eyes a flicker of hope had come, thinking that their lives might be spared.

Two were soldiers of fortune, of small account, but the third was an experienced navigator, without whom the ship could not have been sailed.

Cortéz said: "You are too useful to hang. But it is your head, not your heels, which may be useful to me. Your feet have led you astray. They shall be cut off."

He disregarded the look of frantic horror which had come to the man's eyes. He spoke to the other two: "You have been misled. You must feel the lash. But after that you will be reinstated to what you were."

He rose and went with some haste, having many matters upon his mind, for he planned to march on the next day.

There was general agreement that he had shown a singular moderation toward the criminals, giving the minimum penalties by which his authority could be sustained.

But, being alone with Marina, he spoke with bitterness of the necessity for the death penalties which he had felt it had been inevitable to pronounce, about which he was so far right that it would have been a cause of astonishment had he failed to do so.

Indeed, by the laws of that time, civil, naval, or military, the execution of the culprits was a matter of mere routine.

So it would have been, without question, by Aztec law, which, not having developed the wasteful expedient of prolonged imprisonments, considered essential to Eastern civilisations, regarded the elimination of unsatisfactory members of the community as a hygienic necessity.

Marina asked: "You do not like to lose men, having few?"

"I do not like to order a man's death, who is less than foe."

"Yet you would cut off his feet?"

That was the horror to her.

Cortéz looked at her with the smiling eyes which so often concealed subtleties of far-reaching design. "They are not off yet."

Marina said: "So?" Understanding, without further words, that they were to remain at the ends of their own legs.

At a later hour, the man stood before Cortéz, who was alone, except for Alvarado, who was in his confidence in a matter on which their thoughts went by the same road.

Cortéz asked: "You can tell whether a ship be fit for a long voyage? If it be likely to spring a leak when the winds are high? If it be rotten of cordage, or mast, or spar? These are no more than it is your business to know."

The man was silent. He was trembling between hope and fear of what this examination might mean for him, and he could not to see what the question would lead. He suspected a trap.

Cortéz said sharply: "Speak, man! Unless you would have your tongue follow your feet."

"Yes, I know that."

"Some of our ships are old. If we should load them with men for a long voyage, might we not be sending them to death in the first gale?"

"You would have them overhauled and repaired? It could be done."

"It would require that many men should be left behind?"

"It would need some."

"I have none to spare. Might it not be found that there are some ships that are past repair?"

"So it might be."

"So I think it would. If you should go over the ships with care, could you make report in three days from now?"

"Yes. I could do that."

"And it will be fixed in your mind that I would not risk the lives of men in a rough sea?"

"Yes."

"You will need your feet for this work? Then they shall stay where they are for the next week. I will think again when I have read your report."

Alvarado laughed when the man was gone. "Will he leave them a sound spar, or any cordage which will not snap?"

"He will be shrewder, if he do less than that."

Next day, the bulk of the army, with Pedro de Alvarado in command, moved forward to Cempoalla, Cortéz remaining behind to make final dispositions regarding 'city' and fleet.

The despatch to Spain of the two to whom Cortéz had given the highest offices had cleared the way for the advancement of Alvarado, a man without the diplomatic abilities or social standing of those who had gone, but with some superior qualities for the arduous hazards of war.

He was handsome, strong, agile, highly reputed for skill both with lance and sword, recklessly courageous at any critical need, bold in decision and swift in tactical action, though incapable of the far-reaching strategic conceptions or the patient subtleties of his chief. He would have been temperamentally incapable of conducting to a successful issue the enterprise which was now beginning; but as its lieutenant he was of a value which it would have been difficult to exceed.

Had their positions been reversed, it is unlikely that either would have made the name which in fact he did.

Three days after Alvarado entered Cempoalla, Cortéz arrived, and took over control. He immediately called a council of his principal officers, as it was his habit to do when, by an attitude of deference to the opinions of others, he would endeavour to sway them to approval of a course on which he had already resolved.

He said that while he had remained behind he had had an inspection made of the fleet, with disconcerting results. He laid before them the report which had been made. He said it would be a poor end, if, when the time should come when they would seek to return in triumph to Spain, with their gathered treasure aboard, they should founder in the first storm.

They agreed on that. They were not seamen. They all inwardly dreaded the perils of wind and wave, which, in those days of small sailing vessels, were not light at the best.

The enquiry seemed to some of them a fresh evidence of the vigilance with which their commander regarded the welfare of those he led.

The report was discussed in detail, and it was agreed that at least five of the ships were in such condition that they were unfit for sea, and beyond their resources to repair. It would be prudent economy to strip them thoroughly of everything which could be useful ashore, and then burn the worm-eaten hulks.

It would give useful occupation to those who must be left behind, and, when it had been done, it would release some of them to augment the strength of the little army, that must contend with unnumbered foes.

"It was more lightly agreed," Alvarado said, when they were alone, "than I had expected to see."

"So it was," his commander said, "I would have proposed that we burn all, had I thought they would be in so complaisant a mood."

"They might have taken that in another way."

"So they would. Yet we might have prevailed. Pedro, it can be done."

"There are some who would be most hard to convince."

"Then they must be taught. I will have no more plots to take news to Velásquez's ears. It might ruin all. Nor will I have men looking back to a safety that lies in flight. You shall talk to those you can trust, but yet not as coming from me. Suggest that they should urge me to fire the fleet."

"Would Escalante do that?"

"He will do that, and more, if he have orders from me."

Escalante was the officer whom Cortéz had left in full authority over fort and fleet. He was of a loyal mind, and with that quality of courage which gives hazard a friendly smile.

It was only two days later that he received a letter from Cortéz which said: "The remaining ships must be stripped and burnt, they being unfit for sea. You will spare only that in which Sanceda came, for it is not mine. When you have done this, you will send to me forty of the men, who will then be released from their present charge, retaining any beyond that number to augment your strength on the land."

Escalante read this letter with a clear appreciation of what it meant. He knew that the ships were not in so bad a condition as to justify their destruction. Some of them were no worse than the one which had been sent on the long voyage to Madrid—with orders to avoid any intermediate port. He knew that some, at least, of those to whom the orders of destruction must be given would know this as well as he. He observed, incidentally, that if, while the army were far away, he should be heavily attacked in his fort or 'city' of Vera Cruz, he would not have the safe refuge of the ships to which to retire.

He considered the reaction which might be expected from his men—especially of those seamen who had been left on board—at the giving of such an order. Protests were certain; insubordination was probable. He decided to commence the work without explanation, and in a casual manner. He gave orders for various details of dismantling, and for stores to be brought ashore. They were not orders that could be questioned. The work was well advanced before its significance had become plain; and meanwhile he had talked to those on whose spirit and loyalty he could rely.

Three days later the condemned hulks were fired during the night, the one small ship that was to remain being anchored safely to windward.

A red pillar of crackling fire rose into a sky that was brilliant with tropic stars, and thick smoke drifted toward the land. Startled men ran out from Vera Cruz, to what appeared catastrophe of an inexplicable kind, and heard with astonished ears that the general's orders had been obeyed.

The next day the forty recruits joined the army at Cempoalla. Some of them came in a mood of bitter wrath for the destruction of ships which had been homes to them, and because they, who were bred to the sea, had now been isolated without retreat in a hostile land; others were resentful of the destruction of their only visible means of ever returning to Spanish lands; and these feelings were the stronger because the men concerned were not the most resolute of seamen or troops, for Cortéz had used discrimination in leaving such men, rather than those of a better sort.

They talked to those they met, some of whom were of the same mind. Murmurs grew. Fellow-adventurers felt, with reason, that Cortéz had gone beyond the bounds of the wide authority which, as Governor, they had conferred upon him. Open mutiny was only delayed by the fact that those who would most naturally have led it had been won over beforehand in private talks.

Cortéz stood amidst a group of loyal officers at the raised portico of his house. He looked on street and marketplace crowded with angry, gesticulating, shouting, arguing men.

Olid said: "In half an hour, if we let them gather thus, they will be a howling mob around us on every side. Shall we break them up?"

Few men in the world's history can have been more adroit to avert a crisis than Hernando Cortéz; few to meet it with readier coolness when (probably by his own planning) it was to be squarely faced.

"On the contrary," he said, "there should be more here. Tell them that I will speak to them in ten minutes from now, and that it is my order that all be in the marketplace at that time." Having said this, he went back into the house.

Ten minutes later, he came out, and walked indifferently through a crowd which had become comparatively silent in expectation of what they would hear, and careless of the fact that his best officers were an anxious retinue at his heels.

He mounted one of the temple pedestals, and looked down on a sea of faces which showed bold and sullen anger, with an almost entire absence of loyal support. He had had difficulties with these men before, but nothing comparable to this.

He looked at them with the smiling eyes with which his moments of danger were always met. He spoke quietly, but his voice had a penetrating quality which carried it, without apparent effort, to the limit of the marketplace, which was now filled, beyond the rebellious mob of his own men, with a Totonac crowd, curious of what they saw to be of a turbulent kind, though they had no key to the problem of what was wrong.

"Comrades," he began, "I have called you together here, because things have happened of which you should all know, together with the good reasons for what I did.

"I have had the ships burned. Most of them were my own property, and, unless we succeed in what we are about to do, I am no more than a ruined man.

"Men do not burn that which is theirs without having cause. Had I so willed, could I not have ordered their crews to sail them to Cuba or Hispaniola, and sold them there at a great price?

"But when ships are eaten by worms, and their seams gape, when they have sails that the winds will slit, and masts and cordage that will snap at the hour of need, would you have me gamble thus with the lives of men? There were ships among them that wallowed here with their holds awash, through the storm you will not forget.

"Now, when you think, you will see what I have done has brought us forty men to augment our strength, besides adding as many to that with which Vera Cruz is held. That may be less than the differences that will turn the scale of the worst hazard before us now.

"But I will have none with me who would prefer the safety of Spanish land. There is one ship that remains. Will those who would return raise an arm now, and they shall sail the first hour they will?"

He paused to look down on a crowd from which no arm rose. These were men who looked at their neighbours, as those in hope that they would be first to give the signal of flight, but it went no further than that; and now Cortéz spoke in a higher tone: "Do you fear even to raise an arm? I tell you to speak now, for we would have none with us who is of a doubtful mind. We go forward to win this country for God and Spain, and if we fail we shall surely die, and if we succeed we shall have no use for vessels in which to flee.

"Let those speak now who would fly, and watch for our return with the golden treasure that we shall bear.

"Is there none? I will give you a further chance, for I would weed out those of a cowardly sort, who will have no comfort the way we go."

He paused, and looked down on a silent crowd.

"Then," he said, "will those speak who are constant to come with me."

He was answered by a shout of assent that rose again and again in added volume, with the rising temper that sways a crowd. The watching Totonacs could not understand what was said, but they knew that they looked up to one who was a leader of men.

CHAPTER TWENTY-EIGHT: DIVERSION UPON THE REAR

Having so literally burnt his boats, in a manner to which there may be no comparable event in the whole history of civilisation, and having sent his mission to Spain, Cortéz could now address himself, with no backward glance, to the wild adventure on which his heart was set, and to which he had been able to inspire his followers, whose faith was in himself, rather than in the logic of what they did.

Or, at least, so he may have thought; but next morning there was an urgent letter from Escalante: "Your ships," he wrote, "were scarcely burnt down to the water's edge when there came four others from seaward that hoved alongside, but would not answer my signals, and did not stay.

"They are now moving, with wind abeam, slowly northward along the coast.

"They fly the flag of Spain, with one beneath which I do not know."

He showed it to Alvarado and Sandoval.

The younger officer laughed. "If it be Cuba's Governor, he will be too late by a day."

"You counsel that we should march the more quickly for this?"

"Yes, in the next hour."

"But I would deal with it in a different way. I will have no hornets buzzing upon my rear."

He sent for Bernal Díaz, to whom he said: "You will have my horse and yours, and two others, saddled within an hour. We will take two cavaliers and there will be a company who are to follow on foot, and all lightly armed, for it is pace I desire, and there should be no occasion for guard of shield."

So it was done. The four horsemen arrived at Vera Cruz when the high sun was hot in the August sky, and Escalante told what he knew of the four ships, which was not much.

He had sent scouts to watch their movements, which as they sailed nearly to the land, it had been easy to do. The last news was that they had anchored, close in shore, about ten miles to the north.

"Then there are ten more miles," Cortéz said, "that our steeds must take us."

"You will stay to eat?"

"Are we babes? We had meat two hours after dawn. We can last at need till the light fails."

He spurred on.

They made good speed, for both he and his companions rode without body-armour; but they had not covered more than four miles when they met three men on foot, who had been landed from the ships, and who stood their ground in a peaceful but resolute way.

Cortéz hailed them in Spanish, and, being answered in the same tongue, he came down from his horse. They met the smiling glance by which he gained more than could have been won by a single sword, though it were the best in the land. He said: "The Spanish tongue has a good sound for those who wander in heathen lands. But will you tell me what you do here?"

There was one dressed in a lawyer's garb who answered in a very firm though courteous tone: "That should rather be asked of you. I have landed here to survey the land on behalf of Señor de Garay who discovered it during last year; and to take possession of it in the name of the Spanish Crown, in accordance with a warrant which has been granted to him, and I bring two witnesses, before whom you should speak with care."

Francis de Garay was Governor of Jamaica. There was something here of which Cortéz had not known until now, and that it must be handled with care was a certain thing. But he did not think it to be as menacing as an expedition from Cuba, with authority to supersede him, would have been. He thought he could turn its assault aside; and his thoughts went further than that. With the mental agility which would so often give birth to audacious deeds his mind became active in contrivance of how these men could be won to augment his strength.

He said: "We must all obey the word of our Lord the King. Will you show me the authority that you have?"

The lawyer did not object to that. He said: "It is not a document to be carried about by me. But I have an attested copy here, which you will not scorn."

Cortéz read it, and had no doubt that it was a genuine copy of an authority which he could not resist. But he read it with a lawyer's mind, and he saw that which brought laughter into his eyes.

He said: "This is a document to which obedience is due. It gives De Garay a noble power. But do you know where you are?"

"We are on the land which he discovered a year ago."

"But I should say you are not."

"If you will read with care, you will see that it gives him power not only on that, but adjacent lands."

"So it does. But should you call it adjacent here? Should you call Italy thus? Should you call Cathay? Do you know the longitude or latitude here? It is you who should look with care."

The lawyer considered the licence again, and stood in doubt, rubbing his chin. The fact was that de Garay had landed upon the Florida coast, and this second expedition had turned westward too soon, seeking a coast which was not there, and had sailed into the depth of México's bay. The very precision with which de Garay had made his observations, and the care which was taken in Madrid to define these distant authorities, issued to adventurers over whom it had only vague control, had left the position of Cortéz secure.

Seeing the lawyer's hesitation, he went on to tell of what he had done, and what he now intended to do. At the end, he asked: "Does de Garay make a large boast of the gold which he saw, or he brought away?"

"So far, there has been no mention of gold."

"Then you may suppose there is none there. You will plough in a barren land with no payment to come. With me, every man has a written bond, and his share of gold will be weighed in very scrupulous scales."

The lawyer hesitated. He looked at his companions, and saw them to be of the same mood. They were landsmen, who hated the sea, where they had met storms. He asked: "You have good licence for what you do?"

"I have that of Cuba's Governor, who has staked much on our success, though much less than I. I have sent a great treasure to Spain."

There was more debate after this, but not much. In the end, Cortéz had gained three recruits, to his partial content. He was as hungry for men as his followers were for gold. He wanted not three but all.

They went on together till they came to sight of the anchored ships. But he met a caution here which was hard to foil. The commander of the expedition saw the horsemen, by which he was more puzzled than he had been by the burning ships, for he had not heard of horses being taken to these unexplored lands. He saw the three men he had sent ashore consorting with them. Being puzzled, he remained passively watchful, not allowing a boat to put off for the shore.

Next morning, Cortéz tried stratagem. He disguised three of his men in the clothes of those who had become his. They went down to the shore, making signals that they desired to be fetched aboard, which surely would not be refused.

Now a boat came to the land, from which men landed to meet those whom they supposed to be friends.

Finding their error, they would have run back, but they were already being surrounded by those who had been ambushed for their detention.

Four were seized and persuaded to join their captors as easily as the first three. Indeed, they had little choice, for the boat, at the first sign of trouble, had pulled back to the ships, which were soon raising anchors and spreading sails.

Having gained seven men by a day's delay, and disposed of what might otherwise have continued an anxious doubt, Cortéz returned to Cempoalla.

On the 16th of August 1519, the assembly bugles blew, and the little army, with a group of steelclad cavaliers at its head, and a long procession of porters and camp-followers in the rear, took the road which wound through the tropical luxuriance of the plain to the heights of the Aztec land.

After deducting the garrison at Vera Cruz, there remained sixteen horsemen, and four hundred Spaniards on foot. They took seven of the more mobile cannon. They were joined by thirteen hundred armed Totonacs, with some of their principal men. They had the services of over a thousand native porters to bear ammunition and stores, and to drag the guns.

There had been no sign during the last weeks of hostility from the Aztec Emperor, or that he took any notice of what they did.

CHAPTER TWENTY-NINE: THE LONG MARCH

For five days the little army took an uphill road through a prosperous peaceful land. They did harm to none, and no one offered violence to them. The Totonacs were friendly with the people who dwelt on these fertile slopes. They spoke the same language. They could explain that there was no occasion to fight or flee. But though all was peaceful, the army moved in the guise of war, with weapons in ready hands, and scouts far out aflank and ahead.

Always, the road climbed. They left behind the tropic luxuriance of the plains, and the lower slopes. Not only the wild flora, but the crops were different in the fields which the cactus hedged. The banana was left behind. Maize-crops ripened under the August sun. The nights had become cold, and even in summer daylight some winds were chill. So far, the Spaniards, bred in a temperate climate, did well enough. But to Indians who had never climbed to these heights before, and were lightly clad, the climate threatened to be a worse foe than the hand of man.

They had passed at times through narrow defiles when they could have been stayed, if not destroyed, by a hostile force, but the scouts had always sent back reports that the way was clear, and the army, with its numerous train, had narrowed its front, and stretched, a two-mile-long ascending serpent, to emerge again to wide prospects, but always taking an upward way, and looking down upon the rich fertility of the coastal plain, now seven thousand feet below.

It had been of essential assistance to the advance that they had come through a land where food was abundant, and friendly inhabitants had been ready to barter it in large quantities for a handful of fragile beads, or other trinkets of little worth; but the last two days of this toilsome week were through more desolate scenes. They climbed by wild and barren ways, and were additionally vexed by cold gusts of wind, and sharp showers of hail, and drenching rain.

From these discomforts, they emerged to a wide prospect of level land. They had ascended to the great central Mexican tableland. The sun shone again. The air was mild. Maize-fields were ripening round them.

Before them were the suburbs of a town of twenty thousand inhabitants, stronger and better built than Cempoalla.

Cortéz halted, and made camp with all the precautions of military science, but he met with no hostile reception. In fact, he met with no reception at all. The country was receiving him with a vast indifference. His little army was like a tiny ant that crawls on a sleeping man.

Faced by this aspect of unconcern, he decided to ride into the town. With half his little force of cavalry, his interpreters, and an escort of fifty footmen, he marched through the narrow streets, and called on the cacique.

He was received with a cold politeness, of which, in this land of measured speech, he had learnt to beware.

The cacique spoke the Aztec tongue, and Marina could translate quickly, with only occasional resort to Jerónimo for a Spanish phrase. The conversation went thus.

"Do you obey Montezuma here?"

"All men do."

"That is not so. I come from an Emperor who is far greater than he."

"There is none such in the world. You will know this when you see the city in which he dwells, if he should allow you to go so far."

"In my land, there are a score of cities to match with his."

"How can you say that of one which you have not seen? It is in the centre of a great lake: an island of temples, and palaces, and of the houses where princes dwell. Every year he sacrifices twenty thousand victims taken in his victorious wars, which still extend his domains, as they will continue to do till the ends of the earth are reached.

"The causeways by which the city may be approached over the lake are each several miles in length, and when the bridges are raised he is in unapproachable power.

"He has thirty lords at his feet, each of whom has an army of a hundred thousand most valiant men."

There was difficulty about the rendering of these numbers, and as Marina's translation paused for consultation with Jerónimo, Cortéz said: "I had not thought your people to be of so boastful a kind. How much is truth in his tale?"

"He is not," Marina answered, "of our people, though he can speak Aztec. They are a subject race, and there is (as you may have observed) an Aztec garrison in the town.

"He speaks in a boastful way, of a place which as I suppose, he has not seen (as I have), but it is largely true. Shall I tell him how much greater you are?"

"Yes. You may do that."

She turned to the cacique to say: "I am speaking to you myself, telling what I know, for I am Aztec born, and would save you from peril, if prudent counsel can win regard.

"The Spaniards are so great, and have the support of such mighty Gods, that they could possess this land without a pause in their own routine.

"Montezuma knows this, though he may not have been careful to share his knowledge with you.

"Do you know that he sent two Princes of the Royal Blood, with four others of the highest in all the land, to lay rich gifts at my lord's feet? Will you ask yourself why he should do that, if he thought as you?"

The cacique, who had been little impressed by her previous boasts, was visibly shaken by this last assertion, for he had heard a rumour of it, which he had refused to believe; and, seeing the effect of what she had said, Marina went on; "And do you know that a great army of all the Tabascan nation attacked my lord, and he slaughtered them, with no loss to himself, till the dead were so many that they must be cast in a common grave?"

The cacique had heard something of this also, though as it had come through Tabascan mouths, it had been somewhat more favourable to themselves, but their defeat was beyond disguise.

He said, in a somewhat altered tone: "All these things are for our Lord Montezuma to overrule. What is your lord asking of me?"

"He would pass on in friendship and peace, having had the refreshment his troops require."

"How will he pay for that?"

"He will give things of a more excellent kind. And if you make some presents of gold you will do well, for these Spaniards value it more highly than we. They say they have a disease which it alone is potent to cure."

Cortéz watched a conversation which he could not understand, but he saw the change in the cacique's manner, and he told himself (which he had not doubted before) that when he met Marina it had been his fortunate day.

She told him briefly what the conversation had been, and went on to arrange, at his suggestion, that the wearied army should camp for a few days outside the town.

In the end, the cacique not only supplied the provisions which had become an imperative need, but gave some golden trinkets of small account, and a more valuable present of female slaves, expert in making the maize-bread which must become the Spaniards' staple food, now that they had left behind the lowlands where bananas grew.

The days of rest would have been less ominous had not Bernal Díaz, a quietly observant man, come upon a storehouse which was stacked with human skulls in a very orderly manner. Writing many years afterwards, he said that there were a hundred thousand of them, which may have exceeded fact; but there were certainly more than could have been obtained from the living population of the little town.

There was no attempt to conceal the fact that they were the skulls of those whom the priests had slaughtered. To the Indians, it was an obvious thing. What else should they be?

It roused Cortéz to an anger of indignation which caused him to approach the cacique with a proposal that the people should be converted to Christianity, either by persuasion or force, and when he showed no disposition to entertain this audacious proposal, violence would have followed, with dubious results, had not Father Olmedo showed a sounder judgement than his secular chief. "If we set up the Cross," he said, "against their will, it will be pulled down when we are gone, with degradations which we need not imagine, but can reasonably foresee. Would you expose it to that?"

His words restrained, though they did not entirely convince, one in whom the missionary spirit might be more dominant than that of the Master he served with sincere if sometime imprudent zeal.

CHAPTER THIRTY: THE MORE DANGEROUS ROAD

The long march was resumed on a road shadowed by great woods that followed the course of a broad river, which provided, what would become at times, their most critical need on this arid height.

It was thickly populated by a curious, friendly people, who readily provided their needs, but were otherwise negative in their attitude, cowering under the shadow of Aztec power.

So the march went on, until it came to the dividing of roads, one of which led to the far-off Aztec city of Cholula, through a province the inhabitants of which were said to be of a peaceful kind, and subject to Aztec rule.

The other went through the land of the Tlascalans, a people few but fierce, who had maintained a precarious independence by their reputation for an uncalculating courage which did not yield while their lives remained. If a man should crush a hornet in a bare hand, it would be worse for the hornet than for him, but his damage would be no less sure, and one which a sane man would prefer to avoid.

So the Aztecs had been disposed to look elsewhere for the victims their rites required. Could they overcome the Tlascalans, if they should come against them with all their might? No one could doubt that. Did they? They were often busy in other ways.

The friendly people through whom Cortéz passed advised him to prefer Cholula. It seemed obvious. There would be no fear of hostile reception there.

His Totonac allies thought differently. They said that the people of Cholula were mean and treacherous in their ways. Men to avoid. They, at least, had no friendship for them, and desired no intercourse.

But the Tlascalans were honourable, fair-dealing men, and very friendly to them. So they thought and said.

Cortéz listened, and his mind fastened on what to him was the vital fact. The Tlascalans were not vassals of México. They were actual or potential foes. He would go through their land.

But he was never rash in procedure, though he was always bold in design. He sent an embassage of Totonac chiefs, asking permission to pass that way, with a present of a kind which would be likely to please—a crossbow, with a few steel-headed bolts, and instructions for its use.

After resting for three further days, the army moved forward in a leisurely manner, allowing ample time for the return of envoys who did not come.

Several days having been spent in this dilatory way, in a pleasant land, Cortéz resolved to go forward, whatever his reception might prove to be.

Coming to a more barren rockier land, the army approached a gap, about six miles in breadth, between defensible heights, and then paused before such a barrier as has seldom been raised by the hand of man.

A wall, of large, smooth, unmorticed stone, was nine feet high and twenty feet thick, with a parapeted platform for its defenders to man. It stretched for over six miles, the whole distance from hill to hill.

There was only one entrance in all its length, and this was a passage, ten yards wide, and curving for forty yards between wall and wall.

Had it been manned, it must have been difficult, if not impossible, for the little army either to storm or turn, but it lay solitary and silent for all its length.

The scouts penetrated the curving passage, and reported that the wild country beyond was entirely deserted.

In the counsel by which the Tlascalan republic was ruled, there was assumption that the strangers would await their envoys' return, and they were now engaged in fierce debate as to how they should be received.

Meanwhile the invaders had entered a land which consisted of a wide fertile plain surrounded by inaccessible hills, excepting only by the walled approach through which they had come.

Here, for several centuries, the Tlascalans had maintained themselves in a condition of almost constant warfare with the more numerous peoples outside their pale.

As the power of the Aztecs had grown, the major menace had come from them. Attempts to penetrate into the republic had met with repeated and disastrous defeat, which had delivered many Aztec warriors to the sacrificial altars of the Tlascalan deity. But the Tlascalans remained in a state of loose but perpetual siege. For many years they had existed without salt, without fish, without the fruits of the lower plains. But they had abundance of such crops as their valley grew. They had timber and stone, and they kept themselves fit by constant athletic exercise for the ever-waiting menace of war.

CHAPTER THIRTY-ONE: WITHIN THE TRAP

Xicotencatl was an old man. He had lived more than a hundred years. It was his habit to remain silent in the assembly, listening to the views of others, before, if at all, he would intervene.

He had a son of his own name, one of youthful energy, who spoke more. He was speaking now.

He was saying: "How do we know that they are enemies of Montezuma? They have received embassies. They have taken gifts. How do we know they would not be treacherous to us? They throw down the Gods of the land, putting up their own. Is there any friendship in that? Shall we allow them to do it here?

"They have strange weapons of war. The crossbow they have sent us is a wonderful, deadly thing. But they are few. If we slay them, their weapons will become ours. We could make more of the same kinds, and should conquer the whole land.

"It is with this thought that I have withdrawn my men from the wall. If they enter, they will be ours.

"When they are routed, can they escape through one narrow gap? Will they get their baggage away?

"We are not Tabascans, to be put to flight by a four-legged beast, or a long pole.

"I see no friendship in their coming here, or in what they do."

The elder was too blinded by age to see his son, but he heard his voice, and nodded approval of what was said by the younger man, who commanded the garrison that defended the gap. He would have spoken assenting words, which would have been decisive, for he was one of the four elders whose voices were final for peace or war; but the discussion was taken up by one of more cautious mood. He said: "We hear the rash counsel of youth, which we should not heed.

"Is it not foretold that white men will come out of the west, who will themselves be of the blood of the gods? I say, let them pass in peace, and their friendship will be our strength.

"If they be foes to Montezuma, as is the common report, so are we. Shall we destroy each other, to make Montezuma's mirth?"

There was a murmur of assent as he ceased, for it was true that there was a legend that white men would come from the west with the blood of México's God in their veins. It was known in México, and had confused counsel there. But it might not be true, or these men might not be they. There was no legend that such men would come bringing violence and death, and overthrowing gods who would be kindred to them.

As he ceased, the elder Xicotencatl spoke, and the council became silent, feeling that the moment of decision had come.

"I have heard you all," he said, "and there is none with whom I wholly agree.

"I do not think that these men can be those who have been foretold; but I am not sure.

"That Montezuma would make peace with them cannot be known. But we know this: if he meet them in wrath they will quickly die.

"But if he make concord with them, they will become foes to us, and we have enough without them.

"It were better than that to destroy them now, which my son must be very sure that he will be able to do, or he would not have let them enter the wall; for, as you know, he is wise in war.

"My counsel is that he be allowed to attack them, as he wishes to do.

"If he succeed, their weapons will be ours, and much else that we shall be glad to have.

"If he fail, we will say that he did it against our will, and we may still make allies of those who will have proved themselves to be of invincible power, and we may even join them in putting the Aztecs down."

It was a subtle counsel, which might have obvious difficulties of application, but it compromised opposing views, and was almost unanimously approved.

The young general, having no doubt that the intruders would be destroyed, hurried back to his troops.

CHAPTER THIRTY-TWO: A DESPERATE STRAIT

The little army moved forward for several miles, through a barren, deserted land. They had not arrived at the cultivated thickly inhabited plain. But they passed hundreds of barrack huts, where the garrison was normally housed, and there was no man moving among them.

Cortéz rode ahead, closely on the heels of the probing scouts, questioning what it might mean.

Alvarado was at his side. He said: "It seems that we have come by a quiet way."

"It is that I do not like. It is an unnatural thing."

"Had they meant to receive us in a hostile mood, would they not have guarded the wall? It might have been held, with the armies we know to be theirs, even against our resolved assault, the walls being too thick to breach with the guns we have."

"But have you thought that it would obstruct a quick retreat? Do they lure us on? You must regard that our envoys have not returned."

"They may be feasting them too well for them to hasten away."

"Or they may have been themselves the feast for a guileful foe."

Alvarado did not dispute that, but it did not disquiet a mood which at times broke into song. He thought the army equal to anything it was likely to meet, and he had been inactive too long for his own peace.

"If," he said, "they have a force in the field, which is retiring as we advance till we come to its chosen place, it might be gainful to know. Let us ride ahead, at a better pace than the scouts can move, and we may resolve the doubt which I see you have."

Cortéz agreed to that, though with some doubt in his mind. He said: "Then we will do it in greater force."

He called up six other cavaliers, making half the horse that he had, and they rode forward briskly, their steeds being fresh, having been only walking before. They rode fully armed, their long lances ready to drop into the rests at any sign of a lurking foe. But how could footmen, lightly armed and lightly clad, be any menace to them?

He took Marina also, whom he was teaching to ride, in case occasion for speech should come.

They rode in a single file, on a path that was well-defined, but narrow, as were all the roads in this land. It was open, bushy country, level enough for men who did not deliberately conceal themselves to be seen afar.

So they observed a little band of Indians while they were some distance away. They were not more than twelve, armed with bucklers and obsidian swords, and otherwise dressed in a uniform way. When they saw the horsemen, they ran.

Cortéz shouted to them to halt, which they did not heed. Then he used spurs.

The Indians had friends ahead, with whom they would be safe, or as safe as any, in times of war, can expect to be. With life at stake, as their fears advised, they ran well.

But they could not run well enough. They were ridden down. Seeing that they could not escape by speed, they turned on their pursuers with naked swords. But they had no common language, and naked swords can be met in only one way. They fought like cornered rats, but would have been quickly slain, if a regiment of their companions had not been seen running forward for their relief.

Cortéz looked back for support which was not in sight. He said to Marina, who had reined her horse a few paces backward, to watch the bicker: "We may be hard pressed. Will you ride back, and hurry the footmen on?"

Marina turned her horse, and he watched her go with approving eyes. She was a light weight to a charger accustomed to the burden of an armoured man, and was able to make speed at which she had never attempted to ride before. He thought: "They will not be long," and turned to his more immediate concern.

A few weeks before, a great host of Tabascans had fled incontinently from the lances of sixteen armoured and mounted men. It was true that a smaller number were here; smaller also was the number of the Tlascalan regiment which confronted them, but the great difference was in the spirit that ruled its ranks.

Actually, the regiment was not comprised of Tlascalans, but of Otombi warriors, the Otombis being a race which had long occupied a part of the height-surrounded plain, and had become politically so closely allied to the Tlascalans as to be practically one nation, but they maintained a separate identity, and a spirit of emulation between regiments raised in the two territories was encouraged by those who ruled. It was the especial honour of the Otombis that they had the duty, under the command of the younger Xicotencatl, of defending the six-mile gap by which invasion of their country could be most easily made.

Now they came forward too eagerly to allow of a prolonged discharge of arrows, which might have had little effect upon the steel-clad cavaliers, but would have fallen more disastrously on horses less fully protected.

They came on with a rush to their comrades' aid, and the Spaniards spurred to meet them, that they might gain the impetus of a charge. The long lances, aimed always at the face, would not have been met by less resolute men.

Many died, but their numbers were too great for that to avail, so long as the spirit of conflict lived in those who remained.

The lances were caught in many hands. Obsidian is not steel, but it is hard enough to cut through a horses' neck. They hacked with their serrated swords, and the horses took many wounds. They swarmed round the cavaliers, striving to drag them, with bare hands, to the ground. The Spaniards' swords were out now, and they were in a close group, with the Otombis swarming upon them from every side.

The struggle, short or long, must have resulted in the destruction of the cavaliers had not their supporting infantry, roused by Marina's urgent summons, come up at a run.

Arquebuses sounded, and crossbow bolts fell in the Otombis' ranks. They did not await this major attack, but retired, rather as under orders than in a condition of rout; and Cortéz gave no signal for their pursuit.

They were soon beyond sight, and the cavaliers could have leisure to lick their wounds.

They raised a sword-hacked man from the ground, who would soon die.

They looked on two dead horses—a greater loss. Others bled, and would give Bernal Díaz much to do before they would be fit for service again. That most, both of horses and men, were free from mortal wounds was due to the fact that the Indians use of the sword was to hack rather than thrust, owing to their desire to take captives rather than to kill.

Cortéz bandaged a bleeding wrist which the gauntlet had failed to guard. He looked at Marina, quietly ready to help, and, for a moment, his eyes smiled. He said: "You were quick. You saved all." But she saw his eyes become grim again, his mouth hard.

Delicately, she rubbed a sandal upon the grass which had trodden blood when she had dismounted beside him. With undisturbed serenity, she answered his mood, rather than his words: "There are many dead."

So there were. Over thirty dead bodies around them were being stripped of weapons and clothes. The Otombis had retired with sufficient deliberation to bear their wounded away.

Cortéz replied, with equal truth: "There are more who live."

For the first time, he saw with clear eyes the wild folly of what he did. If they did not fear the horses—if they did not run from them in panic, as the first who saw them had done—he had lost an advantage on which he largely relied. And two were already dead. Resolutely, he thrust the vision of failure away; but it would be with him in sleepless hours.

"Sandoval," he said, "You shall ride ahead with two others, whose horses are fresh. Ahead, but not far. And you will fall back at once at the sight of foes."

The little army dressed its ranks again, and moved on until evening came, through a land which was well cultivated, and with many cottages scattered about, but they saw no men moving.

They came at dusk to the bank of a stream, where they camped, glad of the water it gave; but the need of food had become acute. There were nearly three thousand including the porters, and some hundreds of additional Indian warriors who had been recruited as they had passed through the friendly lands, who must be fed.

They plundered deserted cottages on the river bank. They gathered wild figs. For most of them there was no more than a spare meal.

When they advanced again on the next day, it became difficult to avoid straggling, as the sight of deserted homesteads offered prospects of food. Behind the ordered array, and the ranks of the loaded porters, the camp-followers spread over the land.

Before noon, they were met by two of their own envoys, with two Tlascalan officials. The latter said that they had come to make apology for the skirmish of the previous day, which had been contrary to the instructions the troops had received. That was why they had been withdrawn as soon as a responsible officer came on the scene. The Spaniards could now be sure of friendly and peaceful passage.

Cortéz replied with equal courtesy, but with a doubt in his mind. Why, he asked, had not *all* his envoys returned? They awaited him in the Tlascalan capital. Would he be supplied with much-needed food? It would await him at a place not far ahead, where he could make camp.

So they went, and an hour later the three horsemen who rode ahead met two men who panted and ran.

They were the two remaining envoys, who said that after their comrades left, they had been handed over to the priests, to be slaughtered in the usual way at an appropriate time; but they had escaped, and, as they ran, seeking covered ways, they had seen a large army moving forward to block the road which the Spaniards would take.

The meaning of this was unmistakably plain, the fact being that the skirmish of the previous day had confirmed the opinion of the younger Xicotencatl that the Spaniards could be destroyed. The deaths of the two horses had been considered decisive. The embassy had put the previous plan to a different use, its intention now being to lure the Spaniards on in a careless mood.

But, being warned, they advanced with caution, though not enough, for there was a further lesson of their enemies' craft yet to be learned.

They came to a place where the maize-fields were interrupted by hilly and broken ground, but before this barrier, clear in sight, was a regiment of about a thousand men.

They held their ground as the Spaniards came on, uttering defiant whistles.

Their number was not formidable. The Spaniards halted, extending their front, while Cortéz made a final effort for peace. He caused Indian interpreters to shout pacific assurances. He desired only to pass through their country without offence. He ordered his notary to record that this had been done, for his justification in future days.

The Indian reply was a shower of arrows, and the slinging of stones. Their bows were too weak for the shafts to do much damage at so long a range. They rebounded from steel, or did little more than penetrate the thickness of the quilted coats. But they roused the Spaniards to charge.

With a volley of bullets and crossbow bolts, far deadlier than they had received, horse and foot, Spaniard, and Totonac, swept forward. Out-weaponed and outnumbered, what could the Tlascalans do but retreat? So they did; but it was only slowly and sullenly, with a fighting front that drew the Spaniards on for a time, and when at last they accepted defeat, and fled at a swift pace, they had lured them into a narrow gorge, where it was no safety to be.

Cortéz looked up to walls of sheer rock that were near both to right and left; he looked down upon ground that was broken and hard to tread. Horses could move on it at no more than a walking pace, and even then must be guided, and step with care. The guns would need extra men on the ropes, and their progress would yet be slow. He could not see far ahead, for the gorge bent. He could not tell how long it might be, or if it were clear of foes, for its bend was abrupt, and only a short distance ahead. He said: "Forward, comrades. Let us hasten to open land."

He feared that they had been trapped, which was nearly true.

A struggling, straggling front scrambled onward to take the bend, and, when they did so, they saw the open country before them for which they had wished, but they saw it covered with men. They saw a marshalled army, such as they had not met nor imagined, until that hour. This being how Tlascala arrayed its strength, what was that of the Aztec likely to be? That must be a question for later days—if such they were destined to see.

Now the narrow vanguard of the Spaniards looked on marshalled regiments which massed beyond its limits of sight. They saw plumaged helmets, and the white uniforms, banded with gold, which were the sign of Titcala's house. They saw many regimental banners, but, over all, that of the heron upon a rock, white on gold, which was the symbol borne by all those whom Xicotencatl led.

Here were no half-hearted levies, thinking of flight, but an army confident of its numbers, and that the invaders would be their spoil.

The first appearance of the Spaniards was greeted in what to Mexican ears would have been no more than an expected way. A loud derisive whistle burst from thirty thousand mouths, in one deafening blast of sound, followed by the throbbing of many drums.

Then the host surged forward to the mouth of the pass, and the Spaniards found themselves engaged on their narrow front before they had space to deploy, or time to array their ranks.

Cortéz himself, with other steelclad cavaliers, fought hardly with lance and sword against foes whose weapons were not of steel, and whose defensive armour was less than theirs, but they had now no advantage beyond that actual superiority, for superstitious terror was gone.

There were minutes during which it seemed that the Spaniards would be forced backward and overcome without ever being able to use the advantage their weapons gave. They were saved by the method of warfare that sought to capture, rather than kill, and which regarded it as a point of honour to immediately remove a dead or wounded man. Gradually, the little army forced its way outward in an extending arc until the crossbows could be got to work, and arquebuses discharged their heavy bullets with a noise that was new to Tlascalan ears.

But, before that, a horse had been brought to ground bleeding from fatal wounds, and its rider, Moran, a cavalier of repute, was seized by eager capturing hands.

There was a rush for his rescue, which was so far successful that it dragged him out of Tlascalan custody, but he was no more than a dying man, and the horse was lost.

Many fearless hands, gripping mane and legs, hauled its bleeding bulk out of the Spaniards' reach. And next day it would be hacked to pieces, and the joints sent to every city in the land, in convincing evidence that these quadrupeds were not of a godlike kind.

Marina, coming to ground that she might give her horse to one who could use it to more avail, found herself at the side of a Totonac cacique, who was glad to speak to one who could understand. He said: "We are no better than dead. It is beyond our power to contend with so great a host."

"But you will see them fly, as others have done before," she answered confidently.

"That is vain talk," he replied in a hopeless tone. "All men know that the Tlascalans do not fly from a field of war."

His glance fell before confident eyes. "They have not," she answered, "met the Christian God until now. They will find He is very great, and St. Jago is little less. You should rather think that, when the fight is done, my lord will ask himself: were the Totonacs any use to me? And much of evil or good for you may depend upon what his answer will be."

They looked on that which confirmed her words, for the Christian front pressed forward somewhat and extended to right and left, and the cacique, in better heart for her words, answered: "We have no choice but to do our best for our lives," and turned to direct his men as they pressed forward out of the pass.

Some ground was being gained, but not much, and it would have been a sanguine hope that the enemy could be overcome, had not the cannon now been hauled to the front. Here was not only more dreadful noise than the other firearms were making, there was a hundred times more dreadful effect.

The nearness of the Tlascalan ranks, and their close array, made them a mark that required no aim. The cannonballs tore lanes of death, and military etiquette required that each dead or wounded man should be lifted at once, and borne to a safe rear.

Xicotencatl, looking on with bitter anger, but yet with the cool judgement of a competent general, reluctantly gave an order for his regiments to withdraw, which they did in a sullen, orderly way.

There was no strength for pursuit. Few were dead, but the wounded were very many. Cortéz, looking ahead, saw a flattened hill which could be made the site of a strong camp. He pushed on to secure this before night should come. They passed through villages which had been abandoned so hastily that they still contained abundance of food. They gained the hill, and camped, licking wounds.

The soldiers, in spite of many hurts, were in buoyant mood, boasting of the great army they had repulsed. Had they not shown themselves to be of invincible strength?

The Totonacs also were inclined to exult to the degree of their previous fear. Actually, they had fought well.

So Cortéz said to Marina, who told him her conversation with the cacique. "You did well, you are a regiment to me. But have you thought that if we could win these stubborn foes to be friends to us, we need not fear Montezuma himself?"

"So you might. But I should say they will not be easy to win."

He agreed on that. He was of an anxiety which he was reluctant to show. He gave an order that the white men who had been killed should be very secretly buried. They might be few, but his whole force was not large. It must not be thought that they were easy to kill. He went to where Bernal Díaz and his assistants ministered to the horses. They were only thirteen now; and all with wounds to dress, though most of these were not deep.

Cortéz knew that it was not customary in this land to attack by night. Marina had told him that. But he set his pickets with no less care. He would run no risk of surprise. And he ordered that every man should sleep with his weapon beside his hand, as it was, indeed, their custom to do.

But the night was quiet, as Marina had told him that it would be.

CHAPTER THIRTY-THREE:
TLASCALA ROUSES ITS STRENGTH

The next day was quiet, and the next night. The idea of making peace, and winning allies, persisted, and, on the second day, Cortéz sent for two Tlascalans who had been captured during the battle, and who had expected nothing better than to be handed over to the Totonacs to afford them nourishment in the usual ceremonial way. He released them, with a message expressing his continued wish for peace, and a friendly passage.

Having seen them go, he organized a raiding party, which took spoil from the surrounding country, and captured a number of villagers. He took them with no other purpose than to treat them kindly, and let them go. He wished to show at once his clemency and his power.

It was shrewdly tried, but it did not succeed.

The two Tlascalans appeared again. They had seen Xicotencatl himself. He was at the head of a great army, not far away. He had told them to return with a message that the Spaniards would be welcome at the Tlascalan capital, where they would provide an exceptionally good feast; or, if they preferred to stay where they were, he would come to fetch them without delay.

Marina asked them: "Why should he talk so, having been beaten before? You may tell me all, and you have my word that you shall go free."

"Can you promise that?"

"So I can, for I know the mind of my lord. Also, he would do much for me, if I should ask."

"Then you should warn him that a host will come such as will make all resistance vain. It will not be only Otombis and the house of Titcala now. The Eagle regiments are with him: five tens of thousands in all."

"Do you think so?" She laughed. "The more who come, the more the fame of my lord will be."

She spoke to Cortéz, who let them go. When they got back, they would talk in the right way.

"Hernán," she said, when they were gone, "I do not doubt; but you should know that their army will be much more than has yet been seen."

"Those who plant the Cross have no cause to be frightened of heathen men."

"So I supposed you would say."

She answered with her usual serenity, and none would know how far she guessed the doubt that he sought to conceal from all, and which led him to the characteristically bold decision of the next day.

Then he broke camp, left the high ground, and marched on, seeking his foes. "For I must rely," he thought, "beyond all, on the fear which our successes have spread; and to advance, as holding their strongest force in contempt, will give confidence to my own men, and breed doubts with those who must bar their way."

So he arrayed his ranks with a front of war, and marched boldly onward, with outrunners on either flank, and a blare of trumpets along the line.

But he had moved no more than a short way, and the rearguard, delayed by some straggling among the porters, was still not half a mile from the eyrie they had left, when the Tlascalan army appeared—fifty regiments of a thousand each—spread over an open plain that was six miles in breadth, and sufficiently below the Spanish position for them to view it in all its strength.

As a spectacle, it was superb, and far surpassed that of any European army of the time. But the Spaniards could not be expected to derive much satisfaction from the fact that each army they encountered was more splendid than the last they had put to flight.

Elaborate feather-work of brilliant colours, and intricate patterns, distinguished its leaders, as did defensive armour of gold and silver, quilted embroidered coats, and gilded helmets designed to represent the heads of ferocious beasts. Above all the innumerable banners of the chieftains rose, and, in the rear, the great eagle-standard of Tlascala, always present, but never captured, in its major battles: wide-winged, a marvel of intricate featherwork, with egg-sized emeralds for its eyes.

The regiments were uniformed in quilted coats, or even with painted stripes on their bare bodies, coloured according to the arms of their various chieftains.

The whole scene was one of formidable barbaric splendour, rendered more brilliant and more menacing by the fact that the points of their weapons were of a copper alloy which sparkled redly with the reflected light of the morning sun.

They were armed with weapons similar to those of European traditions, though with differences, and more primitive in character than were those on which the Spaniards depended to adjust the disadvantage of numbers.

Their obsidian swords had a very keen edge, but without the endurance of steel. Their novelty was a serrated blade. They were good archers, their bows being curiously adapted to the discharge of two, or even three, arrows at once. They had throwing-spears of various kinds, the deadliest being a short javelin which was attached to the wrist by a leather cord, so that it could be pulled back from a vain throw, to be cast again.

At the sight of the advancing Spaniards, the wardrums to which they marched were deadened by the screeching whistle that burst from fifty thousand throats, followed by volleys of stones, arrows, and darts, that, as Bernal Díaz would afterwards say, "hid the sun from sight."

Many of them fell short, and the little army, stubbornly enduring the scourge, lengthened its front, and was soon replying with cannonball and bullet, shaft and bolt, in a louder and far deadlier way.

The havoc wrought by the cannon in crowded ranks was, indeed, more than the most disciplined troops could be expected to endure, and, had they been resolute to do so, their habit of instantly bearing away both dead and wounded might have employed those who were uninjured until, in course of time, their whole force would have removed itself in that abortive but most orderly way.

Cortéz, in the front rank, seated on his white charger, that stood immobile amid the uproar, though watching all with alert intelligent eyes, felt assured that they would not stand.

"They must break," he thought, "and the longer that stubborn courage endure, the greater will be the loss they must count in a cooler hour."

His greatest fear was of an outflanking movement, against which danger he had so placed some of his guns that they could be swung to bear on such a movement from either side. Behind the Spanish ranks, the porters rested, having piled their loads as a protecting wall. The issue of the strife meant very little to them. They were a caste apart. It was simply a question of whose burdens they would have to bear on the next day.

But, to the army, their loads were the essentials of safety and life itself. Around them, and the women, the Totonac warriors were a protective girdle.

Cortéz was right when he thought that the Tlascalans could not long endure the volleys which tore their ranks. They must soon break, he supposed; as they did. But he was wrong when he thought that they would be forced to fly. They came on.

With their wild whistling warcry, they surged forward, racing over the deadly fire-swept space between, and hurled themselves in overwhelming numbers upon their foes. The next moments were pregnant with the fate of México, and the future dominions of Spain. In the short interval before the impact came, Cortéz had ridden along the short Spanish front, shouting to his trusted lieutenants repetition of instructions already known, and then joining his little squadron of cavalry where it was drawn up somewhat behind, that it might be prepared for a flanking charge.

The Spanish infantry knew what it had to do, on which its existence must depend. It must maintain an unbroken front, closely and firmly knit. It must not use the sword's edge, but the deadlier point. It must give no ground, lest it be borne back in a movement it could not stay.

So it had been trained, and so it struggled to do. But the weight of the wave that broke upon it was too heavy to be sustained. It was borne backward. Striving to maintain its array, still facing its foes, with the out-thrusting of many swords, yard by yard the swaying line yielded reluctant ground.

It was when it seemed that it must break into the confusion which would have brought swift destruction or capture to individual Spaniards, surrounded by thronging foes, that the position was saved by a charge of the cavaliers which Cortéz led. Emerging from the left Spanish flank, and riding forward, they swerved to the right, and rode through the Tlascalan ranks, their long lances, always aimed at the face, doing execution to which there was no sufficient defence or reply.

The broken ranks closed behind them as they went through, but the pressure upon the footmen had been relieved. They thrust forward with new heart, in a rallied line, and it was now the Tlascalans who gave ground, shunning to meet the thrusts of the steel swords that they could not match, and that their defensive armour was unequal to stay.

The Tlascalans broke contact at last, retiring somewhat from those who did not pursue. They did not flee. They had carried off their dead to the last man. But their effort had failed.

Yet they were in no mood to accept defeat. The more distant regiments were moved to the front, and another charge was made against a Spanish line which, if more exhausted, was more confident than before. The attack failed in the same way, and in shorter time.

But Xicotencatl was resolved on the destruction of the Spaniards, at whatever cost to his own army, and though a third assault was repulsed with an even shorter struggle, Cortéz looked with bitter doubt at the huge host of his foes. If these tactics should be continued, the end could be delayed, but no more than that. Could they throw back forever fresh waves of assault, while their own arms were becoming too weary to slay?

He looked at the sky, but he had broken camp soon after dawn, and the sun was not yet at its highest point. There was no hope of night.

Had all in the Tlascalan army been of its leader's temper, there would have been an end of the little Spanish army, and it might have passed from the records and memories of men.

But Xicotencatl, watching the third charge, and what he thought to be its too easy repulse, was moved to anger against the commanding officer of the regiments concerned, and he was not one to restrain speech when his wrath was stirred.

"Is all," he asked, "to be done by my own troops? Is all the loss to be theirs?"

"That I drew them off when I did," the cacique replied, "was according to the sound science of war, which you will not heed. Do you know what our losses have been already?"

"I know that there are some who yet live who would be no loss at all."

They were words of angry contempt, which may have been quickly regretted, but were not withdrawn. In all that he said and did, Xicotencatl was guided by a conviction that the Spaniards were a deadly menace to his people and land, which would not be lessened by regarding them as friends, or accepting them as allies.

Now he faced an angry man who challenged him to immediate duel for the insult he had received.

"You know," he replied, "that it is a challenge I cannot accept while I am in command here, but were you to repeat—"

"As to that, I will reduce your difficulty at once, for I am one whom you will no longer command. And I should say that the time is near (if you shall still live) when you will have leisure to spare."

What he meant by that was partly shown in the next hour, when he not only withdrew his own regiments, but persuaded other commanders to the same course. The astonished Spaniards saw twenty thousand men, most of whom were still in reserve, making an orderly withdrawal. They saw that the Eagle standard had gone, and only those who fought under the sign of the white heron remained, and these, while they held their ground, made no further attack.

Cortéz was content to do nothing more of a provocative kind. He ordered the guns to remain still, and reflected that St. Jago is a most powerful saint.

As the sun declined, the Tlascalans withdrew to their own camps, and Cortéz ordered that the army should return to the hill they had left at dawn; and be very vigilant during the night.

There was debate among the soldiers in the camp next morning as to what Cortéz would do. To advance again, perhaps to meet another army as strong or stronger than the one with which they had had so hard a bout was not a programme to be lightly approved: to stay where they were would be abortive in itself, a confession of weakness to their foes, and a road to almost immediate starvation that no one would wish to take.

What he did was to send a new embassage to Tlascala, with a renewed assertion that he desired only friendship and peace.

He chose prisoners for this, as he had done before. To Marina's suggestion that some of his own officers might be of greater avail, as they would answer argument and discuss terms, he replied that they would be useless without her, and she could not be risked among those whom he had come to regard as of a very treacherous kind.

The envoys reached Tlascala in the afternoon, where the senate was already in session. There was bitter debate which the message they bore did nothing to reduce.

Those who advocated coming to a friendly understanding with the strangers had now found powerful support from one, Maxixcatzin, who, like the elder Xicotencatl, was a member of the Council of Four, who were the ultimate rulers of the republic.

"Are we infatuated," he asked, "that we must insist upon incurring loss after loss from those who still seek our friendship, and who treat the prisoners they capture with a clemency which this land has not known in its five centuries of remorseless war?"

"Are you so infatuated," his opponents replied, "that you cannot see that these men are no more than the first of those who will destroy us utterly, if we allow them the footing they seek to gain? Let them learn that they come here to a certain death."

The deadlock was resolved by the customary method of asking the advice of the priests, who would not be likely to feel amity towards those who brought alien gods into the land, but still had their reputation for wisdom to sustain.

Their reply showed the subtlety that bends superstition to politic ends. The strangers, they said, were powerfully protected, but not by the ultimate gods to whom the Tlascalans bowed. They were servants of the Sun, who can protect his own during the day, but is powerless in the dark hours. They must therefore be destroyed by a night attack.

It was shrewd advice, shrewdly conveyed. A night attack was certainly the most hopeful that remained. It allowed of approach without the destruction that the Spaniards' weapons wrought during the day. But it was utterly contrary to the military habits and traditions of the land, and nothing less than this fantastic reason might have been sufficient for its adoption now.

What they could not know was that there was no such inhibition of custom among the Spaniards, and that the caution of method with which Cortéz would proceed, even in his wildest audacities, had directed that vigilance should not be relaxed in the dark hours, whatever report might say.

So it happened that when a large Tlascalan army made cautious approach during the night-hours to the hill on which the Spaniards were camped, they were perceived at a very early stage by an outlying sentry post, which fell back silently, and roused the sleeping host.

The Indians were not quick to attack. With cautious thoroughness they crawled forward on every side, awaiting the time when they should be near enough for the final rush. But this very caution was fatal to their design. It gave time for Cortéz to silently rouse and array his ranks; and, having done this, he did not wait till the enemy whistles should give signal for attack, but charged out on the crawling foe.

There was no battle here: the astonished Tlascalans leapt to their feet and fled.

A full moon gave Spaniards and Totonacs light enough to strike at the backs of a flying foe, whom there was no reluctance to slay.

For once, the Tlascalans did not remove their dead, nor even bear their wounded away.

Cortéz followed this new success by a further embassage, offering peace and alliance. It was a reasonable hope that Tlascala would now be glad to make terms to end a conflict for which it was entirely responsible, and which was so inglorious in its results.

But the envoys did not return.

CHAPTER THIRTY-FOUR: PEACE

Cortéz rode into the camp at the head of half a dozen cavaliers, threescore foot soldiers lightly armed for quick marching, and several hundreds of Indian soldiers and porters, who were now burdened with the spoil of a swift and successful raid.

But he was a sick man, ill with malaria, and tortured by anxieties which he must not show. He grasped the saddle as he came to earth, that men might not see him to be unsteady upon his feet.

The raid had been successful in its object, but it had not been carried through without difficulty.

The weather had been bleak: the winds fierce and cold. For some reason half the horses with which he had started out had fallen sick, and it had been necessary to send them back. The cavaliers who remained with him—six of the best companions he had—had begged him to return. He had been obviously too ill to stand, and he swayed in the saddle, though the horses moved at no more than a walking pace, as the presence of the footmen required.

But he answered only "God is stronger than Nature," and sustained himself by the inexorable purpose he had to save the nation from hell (which he did not doubt that only baptism could do), and to gain a new empire for Spain.

Now, as he alighted, he was greeted by Sandoval, whom he had good reason to trust.

Sandoval saw that he was a sick man, and the fact was an added weight to the good sense of what he had been chosen by his comrades to say.

"In your absence," he said, "there has been much talk in the camp of what it will be prudent to do, which has gathered strength as the envoys do not return, for we have learnt to know the meaning of that. There is a general agreement that to attempt to go deeper into this hostile land would be to throw our lives away, and to lose all that has been already won."

"Cannot I be away for two days but there must be new mutinies in the ranks?"

"I would not call it that. All—or almost all—are most loyal to you. But they look at facts. Each time we repulse attack, a larger army confronts our path, and each time we lose those, many or few, whom we have no hope to replace. And the Aztecs whom, we are told by all, are the greatest power in this land, we have not encountered at all. If we go back now, we bear a great tale. We may say we have done much. We may return with a greater force. If we perish here, none of our own land will even know what our fate has been. It will make abortion of all the valiant actions already done."

Cortéz looked at him in considering silence. "*Et tu, Brute?*" he quoted; and then, in a voice that had become stronger, he said: "Summon all men, for there is that here on which all should be agreed."

He walked on with a firmer step, as though indeed there were some inward force before which the infirmities of the body must be subdued.

He gave direction that all men of Spanish blood should assemble in the open air before the pavilions which he occupied with his secretaries and other personal confidants, and in which, besides his own possessions, the books of account of the expedition, and such small stock of treasure as had been accumulated since the departure of Montejo and Puerto-Carrero was guarded well.

And while this was being done, Sandoval explained in very plausible detail, the plans on which the whole camp were agreed, and for which they asked the assent which responsible leadership surely required.

Of the little army which had marched boldly from Vera Cruz, more than fifty had already died of sickness or wounds, or were so far incapacitated as to be a burden to better men. There was hardly one who could not show the scar of a wound from a hacking sword or of javelin or arrow which their quilted coats had been insufficient to stay. That they would fight through these stubborn Tlascalan hordes, and then defy the mysterious but certainly far greater Aztec power, was not sane to suppose.

Did not the Aztec Emperor watch them ever, as a cat watches a mouse that ventures too far from its hole?

To go further was certain, profitless death. But they did not propose to throw away all that had been so hardly won. They did not propose unconditioned flight. They would fall back on Vera Cruz in an orderly way, and fortify themselves there, while the remaining ship should return to Cuba, or Spain, with the great tale of all they had done, and a plea for reinforcements, which would surely not be denied.

Cortéz faced a crowd of men whom he had come to know well, and he saw many who looked at him in anxious expectation of what he would say, and more who looked on the ground.

He began weakly, being conscious of bodily pain, but his voice gained strength and confidence as he went on.

"Comrades," he said, "I hear that you are well agreed as to what we should do, and it only remains for me to assent to the wish of all.

"You are agreed that we shall go back. Well, so you may. I will blame none. I will not remind you of oaths you have sworn. I will not tell you the difference which lies between honour and shame. But I will tell you this: as for myself, I go on.

"I would go on though there were fewer of you of the same mind than the horses would bear. I would go on if there were not ten.

"And I will tell you why. I prefer hazard to certain loss, which you do not see.

"You have won victories which have brought you a great name. You have a prestige which is more than swords. It is through that name for unfaltering strength that you have lain in peace while I have been away; through it that I have obtained the ample stocks of provisions which the porters are unloading now; through it that the envoys of Tlascala may be here at any moment with words of peace.

"If you turn back, you will admit a defeat that you have not had. All mens' hands will be lifted against you in the next hour. Some of you may reach Vera Cruz, but I should say not. If you should, it would be through the better heart of those who will go on with me, whose advance may disguise the motive of what you do.

"Have you thought that you would leave our Totonac friends to the vengeance of most merciless foes? What would it be natural, and even right, for them to do? Would they not seek forgiveness and favour from those who would be their masters in the next week, by betraying you?

"If you should regain Vera Cruz, and despatch your ship, and they should summon others to do that for which you would have proved too weak—as I do not think you to be—would they make alliances here again? Could they hope to gain one confident friend?

"And do you think that they who would come would hazard their treasure or blood for you? You would be those who had failed:

to be praised, perhaps, with fair words, and be thrown aside, or to fall in at the tail of those who would flaunt in fresher attire.

"I tell you, you would betray yourselves seeking safety, you would find dishonour and death. You would betray your faith in the God Who has led you here, and Who would have to look for others to work His will.

"Death may lie ahead, but it will have the consolations of honour and faith; death would lie more surely behind, and shame would be the companion to share your graves."

He paused here, having spoken as he would seldom do, with the passion that weakness breeds.

He looked round on ranks of men who had become very still, and his eyes changed to the smiling regard which was usual with him when moments of crisis came.

"Friends," he said, "I have told you where, as I suppose, the path of greater honour and safety lies. I will say no more, beyond this: I have never told you that which I did not myself believe, nor asked you for toil or hazard I did not share. You will each do as you will, but those who think as I will not fall below the old song that our fathers sang:

"*Better the way of honoured death to go*
Than life and shame as lasting comrades know.

"Those who are returning to Vera Cruz will now fall out, and make a backward rank; but those who stand their ground will remain with me."

His eyes were on them now, smiling, challenging, almost mocking, as no man moved. For who would be first in that, with no certainty that he would not also be last?

His words had been few, and been quickly said. He was never one for long orations, though he might have a lawyers' verbosity with his pen; but he had appealed to every tradition, to which his audience would respond; and though much might have been said (and had been said in the last two days) of a contrary kind, it had actually become doubtful whether they had not gone too far for retreat to be a less desperate hazard than to continue into the unknown. The greatest difference was that the perils of retreat could be approximately assessed, while those which lay ahead were of an unpredictable kind.

Next morning it seemed that there was added reason for reliance upon Cortéz judgement, for envoys came, as he had foretold they would do.

They were not those he had sent out, but they gave a plausible reason for that. And the nature of their mission was shown by the white badges they wore. The civilisation of the New World was a separate growth from those of the Old, but it had many natural resemblances, among which was the use of white as an emblem of peace. The nature of their mission was guessed before Marina had interpreted what they said.

They announced that Tlascala was weary of a war which, from the first, its elder statesmen had not approved. If the Spaniards should be willing for such a peace as would be honourable to all, Xicotencatl himself would visit them to arrange its terms. In evidence of goodwill they brought a retinue of nearly fifty men, loaded with provisions and other gifts.

Cortéz replied that he would be pleased to end a strife he had never sought. Their general would be welcomed, and terms of peace would be fairly made.

The envoys left at once, having this message to bear, but the most of their followers remained, consorting with the Totonacs, and the porters of various nationalities, in a friendly way.

They talked to Marina also, or rather she talked to them, for a doubt came to her mind which she was slow to speak, but quick to probe.

She watched the Tlascalans who lingered about the camp. She spoke to some of them; she spoke more to Totonacs who had been talking with them.

When she was alone with Cortéz at the evening meal (for he was too ill at the day's end to have comrades there, as had been his custom), she said: "Hernán, you should beware of those men whom the envoys have left behind."

"You doubt that they are here in good faith?"

"I do not doubt; I am sure. They are here to spy."

"Could we prove that?"

"If you examine them one by one. It is a method that should not fail."

So it shall be. So you say they are all in this?"

"It is likely, though less than sure. There are five in charge. You could begin with them."

"So we will." He ordered that the five should be seized, which was soon done, they being in one tent, and with them a Totonac chief who showed terror when they were disturbed by the Spanish guard.

They let him go, as one to whom their orders did not apply, but they took notice of who he was.

The five were brought, one by one, to where Cortéz now sat with four of his officers, and Marina to interpret the inquisition, and a scrivener to take down what was said.

The first three were stubborn in assertion of honesty and good-will, though it was clear that one, at least, was a frightened man.

Before the fourth was brought in, Cortéz asked Marina: "Are you still sure? I would not have them abused without cause."

"I am more sure than before. They deny all, but they do not speak as men would being falsely charged."

He saw that all must depend on her, for he relied entirely upon what she reported that she had asked them, and they replied; but her own faith was beyond doubt, and her wits were not lightly foiled. He said: "As you are so assured, we will proceed in another way. You shall talk to the next as though all has been already betrayed, and tell him, if he confess, he shall not die (as he surely should), but we will do no more than slice off his hands, which is much less than a spy's wages should be."

"I am to say that?" Marina exclaimed, her eyes dark with sur-prise—or was it consternation?—or horror?—or simply inability to comprehend? Her glance met that of Cortéz, and they were aware, as they must often, suddenly unforeseeably be, of the gulf that sepa-rated the civilisations from which they came.

And then he thought that he understood. "There can be no treachery in that," he said, "by which innocence could be brought to ground. For if he be conscious of no offence, he will not confess to that which would be against the instructions on which he came, and being constrained to invent."

"I have had no such thought," she said. "But is it well to threaten that which he will not believe? Or can we think he would prefer to live in so maimed a way?"

It was a new idea to Cortéz that there could be a doubt about that. The punishment of cutting off hands was common in the Europe from which he came, and was regarded as incomparably milder than that of death. Besides, reason was on its side. If you let a rogue live, must you not mark him in some way which would ex-pose him to honest men?

On the other hand, the idea that criminals should be fattened and killed for the feast-day board was a horror to him, to a degree that Marina did not find it easy to understand. It was not, of course, a matter for detailed discussion now.

He answered: "You can assure him that it will be well to be-lieve, for he will find it exactly true; except that he can die, if he prefer that."

"I do your will," she said, and those who watched heard her talk to the man in a language that meant nothing to them, to which at first she had short replies, but they became longer after a time, and his face became grey with fear. They saw him look at his hands in a shuddering way, but when Marina spoke in the Spanish tongue they found that death was not the easy choice that he made.

"He asks: will you be content with one hand, if he tell all? He asks me to say that he has a hand which is soft and plump, and would roast well."

"Then there is a tale to be told?"

"There is much, unless I guess wrong."

"Tell him he need lose neither hand nor foot. If he tells all, he may go free. But if there be anything left unknown, I will lop off both feet and hands, nose and ears, and aught else that good shears may find. He will have no further mercy from me."

Then there was talk again in the strange tongue, and it could be observed that the man was doing the more now, with a question from Marina at times, to which he would be voluble in reply, with gesticulations of the threatened hands, after which she told what she had learned, with reference to Jerónimo at times, who sat beside for her to consult should her Spanish fail.

"When our envoys went to Tlascala," she said, "they were well received. The High Council met, and resolved that they had suffered much, in a war they themselves provoked, and which you have always been willing to end. Also, the advice of their gods had failed, proving that your gods are stronger than they. So they decided to send your envoys back with such gifts as can be found in a poor land, and high nobles with them, empowered to make a good peace, and to invite you to visit Tlascala in friendship, and pass onward. This was proposed in good faith, and would have been fairly performed.

"But they had been told to visit Xicotencatl upon their way, ordering him to cease hostilities, and to send provisions to your camp, which he passionately refused to do."

"For, with clearer sight than that of his compatriots, he had seen that the invaders introduced an incompatible element which would not blend with their civilisation. It was not a matter of primary importance that they professed enmity or friendship to either México or Tlascala. If either Tlascala or México were to endure, they must be expelled or destroyed.

He had detained the envoys of Cortéz. He had persuaded the Tlascala nobles to his own policy. He had sent these men as spies to the Spanish camp, with instructions to observe their routines, to ascertain at what point they would be most vulnerable to attack, and, if possible, to persuade the Totonacs, and the miscellaneous army of porters, who increased their strength and supplied their mobility, to desert or betray them.

Cortéz said: "It is enough. Let him go free. Let the hands of the other nine be cut off, but let them be sent back in one bag, that it will be clear that they will not be eaten by us."

So it was done, being regarded as a most merciful decision by those who heard, for the whole fifty merited death by the customs of war both of the Old World and the New.

CHAPTER THIRTY-FIVE: ALLIANCE

The fifty spies, including their mutilated leaders, were expelled from the Spanish camp amid the ribald japes and laughter of its European occupants, and the whistles and jeers of the Totonacs, whom it had been their purpose to suborn.

With their return from this ignominious expulsion, Tlascalan resistance ended. The envoys who had remained with Xicotencatl declined to disregard their orders further at his entreaty and proceeded to the Spanish camp to make peace with Cortéz. Finding them to be inflexible in this resolution, he realised the impracticability of further resistance, and told them that he would follow to make his own surrender.

The next day the envoys arrived at the Spanish camp with words of peace on their lips, and assurances that the Tlascalan general was about to follow. To the soldiers, it was a climax of triumph, which gave them lordship of the New World; to Cortéz it was no more than a height surmounted which showed the way to more difficult heights ahead; but even he felt some elation when he saw a well-ordered troop approach under Titcala's banner, and showing the uniforms, white and gold, of the chieftain who had been his most formidable and determined foe. None knew better than he how near to the edge of ruin he had been brought in that desperate struggle; and who could be more adroit to gain full value of the position that faced him now?

Xicotencatl approached the seat where Cortéz awaited him under an awning which gave relief from the heat of September sun, surrounded by his officers in such arrogance of steel and silk as they could still provide. They saw a man more nearly of their own statues than most of the Tlascalans were. Bold-featured, upright in carriage, having an aspect of one who ruled, which did not abate as he looked around, or even when, with the courtesy which the meeting required—by the custom of his own land, and the purpose for which he came—he bent to reach the ground with a hand which then touched his head.

Cortéz did not rise. He met the bold Tlascalan eyes with a cool, smiling, inscrutable glance. He said to Marina, who sat at his right hand, consort or interpreter as men might think her to be: "Tell him I will hear what he has to say."

The Tlascalan general spoke at some length. His tone was courteous in a fearless way. It was observed that Marina asked one or two questions, as though she would elucidate what was meant before rendering it in the Spanish tongue—they were brief questions, which had somewhat longer replies.

Then she said: "He offers more than you have asked, that by such means there may be the real peace and concord on which the future of his country would depend. He is very frank about that.

"He has no claim to speak for more than himself, the Otombis, and the great house of Titcala. He is no more than the leader of the army which has been defeated by you. Tlascala's envoys are here, and its voice is theirs.

"But, for himself—and he thinks it a policy which will prevail—he is prepared to accept the overlordship of your distant mostmighty King, if only Tlascala may remain free in its internal affairs, and a bond of friendship be woven thus, which would be sincere on Tlascala's side.

"He would join you in war against the Aztecs, who have been Tlascala's continual foes, if such be your purpose, which is an enigma that none who watch what you do has been equal to solve; but he would warn you, in all courtesy and respect, that the Aztec armies are very great, their power extending across the world to the further sea. Tlascala has held them back from its mountain walls, but only because it is fortressed thus, and perhaps, because weaker victims have been elsewhere. But had its armies ventured out to the open country beyond, Montezuma would have eaten them at one meal.

"He says that he does not doubt that your King could make Montezuma bend, if he could send his ultimate power, but, your present force being what it is, he would warn you in friendly words of that which you may not entirely know.

"He said more as to the Aztec power which I need not repeat, for they were things you have heard already from me."

Cortéz listened to this with an aspect which did not change, for he would not show his thoughts while he was surrounded by watchful eyes. He said: "Tell him that his words are good, and that the Tlascalans will find our King to be a most gracious lord to those who are loyal in heart to him. But, should they be less than that, they will find him to be a raging and fatal fire.

"As to the Aztecs, I will deal with them as they deal with me. But I dread them not at all, be they weak or strong, for it will be found that my God is more strong than their armies are.

"Beyond that, say that we end a war which I did not seek nor begin. We will forget what we cannot change, and look forward to fairer days."

Xicotencatl listened to this with a face as sphinx-like as that which Cortéz had shown to him. At its conclusion, his expression changed to one of frank acceptance of that which he had himself proposed. He said: "It is well. I have brought presents of little worth from a poor land. They are not much of themselves, but they are given with willing hands."

Cortéz heard this, and saw the gifts which were now brought forward by waiting slaves. It was true that they were of little worth. But he ignored that. He said: "Be they what they may, they are of great value to me, for I consider only from whom they come."

A large proportion of the little Spanish army had been marshalled for the reception of the Tlascalan chieftain, and others, to the limits which discipline allowed, had crowded to see their reputed enemy, and witness his submission. It followed that the approaches to the hillside camp were lightly guarded. Even the ceaseless vigilance of the outpost sentinels, which Cortéz had never permitted to be relaxed, either by night or day, had not been fully maintained at this moment of triumph, and there was no alarm raised at the arrival of a very numerous troop until it was close at hand, and then its presence was known by a burst of music, which one of the five Aztec nobles who formed its centre ordered to be played in ceremonial announcement of their approach.

After short parley with those who had no common language, and neither a firm front of force nor a decisive authority to hold them back, the Aztec deputation moved on toward the centre of the camp, where they were halted by an array of opposing swords while word was taken to Cortéz of whom they were.

On learning this, he ordered that they should be allowed to advance into his presence, saying to Marina: "Ask the Tlascalans to stand aside, but not to withdraw. Tell them that, as they are now friends, they shall hear all that is said."

It was adroitly worded, for the situation was not without potential difficulties, hard to assess in advance of knowledge of the errand on which the deputation came, which the Tlascalans must learn even before it could come clear to Cortéz's knowledge, they being familiar with the Aztec language.

The five nobles approached with courtesy. They spoke flattering words. Beyond that, it was an occasion for further gifts, and for repetition of that which had been said and rejected before.

Marina translated: "The great Emperor has watched your progress through Tlascala with interest and admiration. He congratulates you on your victories. He would invite you to his capital, but that the populace is so great, and so unruly of character, that he could not guarantee that your safety would be assured. Could he risk that harm should come to his guests, who represent his brother of the Far Land?

"Rather than that, he sends gifts of such quantity and kind as will be proof of his goodwill and esteem."

While she spoke, the gifts were brought forward and unloaded from the backs of two hundred slaves. Of their munificence there could be no doubt. They were sufficient in themselves to have enabled Cortéz to return to Madrid with the triumph of a great spoil. There were three thousand ounces of gold. There were hundreds of dresses, both of embroidered cotton, and of the intricately woven feather work which was the finest art of the land.

Cortéz said, with smiling courtesy in his eyes: "Tell them that I am grateful for gifts beyond my present power to repay, which my sovereign will esteem in the spirit from which they come.

"But I regret that I cannot return until I have thanked the Emperor himself, for I must do the will of my own King; yet I am grateful for the warning I have received, and have no doubt that my men, while in the great city, will be equal to protect themselves, and all that is mine."

The envoys received this blandly defiant reply with a consternation they could not wholly conceal, even though they were acutely aware of the watchful unfriendly eyes of the Tlascalan general and his retinue, so few paces away.

They whispered among themselves.

Then their spokesman said: "It is not a reply which we can lightly take; for Montezuma has spoken, and this is a land where all men bend to his will.

"If it be gold that you seek (as it seems that it is), we will promise you that there shall be a yearly gift to your King to a weight at which he will be content, and we ask nothing for this beyond your promise not to advance further into the Mexican land."

It was an offer of tribute which the Tlascalans heard with incredulous ears, and to which Cortéz was not quick to reply.

He said to Marina: "It seems that they fear us much."

She bent puzzled brows. She said: "Montezuma has a name for having an open hand. His wealth is vast, and he is said to love the pleasure of those who give. But he will have his will, and having said that you shall not visit México, and wishing for peace— But, even so, they may be offering more than he would approve. It is hard to judge."

Cortéz saw that he had a decision to make which was even more difficult than that which had confronted him a few hours before. He had the opportunity now of returning to Vera Cruz, not as a discredited fugitive, but in triumph and treatied peace; and with promise of an annual tribute of vast amount, to be offered to his sovereign, from a great state, which he had secured by the mere demonstration of a few hundred men, who had fought only with weaker tribes!

It would be an astonishing, almost incredible, tale.

But his inflexible purpose held. He had said that he would visit the Aztec capital, and he was resolved that nothing but superior violence should turn him back.

He noticed also the restless enmity between Aztec and Tlascalan, which was so great that the formality of the occasion could scarcely restrain them to stand quietly a few paces apart. There might be much gain in that.

He said: "Tell them, with my profound respect to him, that I would gladly do that which their Emperor is liberal to propose, were I not too straightly constrained by obligation to my own monarch. Propose that some of them should return to explain to their Emperor that I have no choice but to go on, while the others remain with me till I have his further reply. I will not move in haste, for I would have all arranged in a friendly consenting way."

So it was agreed, for he had come to a resolution he would not change.

When a separate opportunity came, he asked Xicotencatl, through Marina, what he thought of the attitude of the Aztec Emperor. He answered: "It was strange to hear. But Montezuma is a most affluent monarch, who ever gives with a generous hand, and you would err greatly if you should doubt that he has a very great power, or that his gentleness will endure toward those who oppose his will."

Marina agreed to that. She added: "I cannot tell what it may mean. It would seem that he watches ever, and would turn you, if he could, in a peaceful way, or else he will draw you deeper into his own land before he displays his power."

CHAPTER THIRTY-SIX: TLASCALA

The forward road led through the city of Tlascala, at which its lords entreated Cortéz to make such a halt as would enable them to make demonstration of their hospitality and goodwill.

To this he agreed—it would not have been easy to refuse without giving offence—but he was slow to move, the circumspection which alternated his audacities controlling his mood. He had been three weeks in the hill camp when he marched out with the little group of horsemen in the van, the marshalled ranks of Spanish soldiers around them, the numerous armies of laden porters—increased now by an addition of five hundred which the Tlascalans had provided to deal with the recent gifts of Montezuma, and other spoils which had accumulated during the three weeks' halt—and the now-confident array of his Totonac allies.

They marched for twenty miles through a populous land, to which they were welcomed with smiles and flowers. It was high, irregular country, with hilly ridges, and stretches of barren rock, but diligently cultivated where ever fertility could be obtained. So they came to sight of Tlascala's walls.

Being developed by entirely separate civilisations, it was not surprising that Mexican towns differed from those of Europe. The wonder was rather in an astonishing similarity. But it was natural that the attention of the invaders should be drawn to features that differed, rather than those which agreed.

Tlascala was not only surrounded by a high wall, after the manner of most cities both of European and Asian civilisations. It was internally divided by similar barriers into four quarters, each self-contained, and ruled by one of the four lords of the Great Council, each having his own palace, and separate administration.

Leaving the main body of the little European army to camp outside, with the native allies and porters, Cortéz entered through the gate which led into the elder Xicotencatl's part of the city. He rode at the head of his principal captains, and a sufficient bodyguard for his own dignity, through cheering, flower-throwing crowds which made progress slow.

The streets were narrow, as was natural in a land in which there was no vehicular traffic. The houses had flat, terraced roofs. Most of them had neither windows nor doors, but the latticework which broke the wall-spaces admitted light while securing privacy, and no one could enter or leave unheard, owing to the tinkling metal attached to the hanging reeds. There were no shops, retail trade being mainly carried on in an open market, held every fifth day (there were seventy-three weeks in a Mexican year); but more personal needs, which should not wait for a set day, were not neglected. There was convenience of barbers and public baths.

Slowly, with the help of an efficient police force—better organised than any similar body (if it could be said that there was any similar body) in the Europe of those days—the Spaniards advanced under festoons of sweet-scented flowers, stretched over the narrow streets. They looked up to see flat, terraced roofs crowded with those who cheered and wondered at the sight of the white strangers from an unknown world—strange in themselves, stranger in the terrible outlandish weapons which had enabled them to force irresistible way so far through a hostile land, strangest of all in the dozen of great beasts on which their leaders rode, and which obeyed them in ways which it was mystery and marvel to see. Surely such men must have a most great and terrible God!

Wary, but well-content, Cortéz heard the wild strains of welcoming music: he looked round on the cheering crowds. He had taken a bold risk, entering thus, leaving the bulk of his forces, his artillery, his stores, his treasure, outside the walls. But when he had decided to take a risk, who could do it with more assurance than he? And he saw that it went well. He thought himself to be on the way to gaining loyal and powerful allies. *Divide and rule*. It is a maxim that seldom fails. He had not precisely done that. He had found division. But he might prove adroit enough to gain by that which was already there. Here was a wide courtyard, and a great house. The police held back the people on either side. He advanced to dismount before a flight of steps down which the elder Xicotencatl came, a girl whose dark hair was wreathed in honeysuckle guiding his steps.

Garlands of roses were thrown over his neck as he grasped the hand of the aged ruler, whose own was then lifted to pass lightly over the features of one whom his dim eyes could not see sufficiently.

Marina, alighting at his side, and garlanded with the same profusion of scented flowers, was quick to translate the words of greeting and invitation which introduced them, and a dozen of the principal Spanish officers, to a banquet where none others were present except the younger Xicotencatl, and the girl—his daughter—who was accustomed to guide her grandfather's steps on the few occasions of state for which he would leave the security of the rooms he knew.

Marina said to Cortéz: "I am to ask your pardon that there will be a woman at the table, which is not the custom, but our host's infirmity of sight requires that his granddaughter should be near at hand, and I am also free to be there, so that you may converse during the meal. For the same convenience I am to ask your pardon that I shall be placed between you and him, so that I may translate that which may not be spoken loudly for all to hear."

She said this as they washed faces and hands in the silver ewers at the side of the hall, which was the strict etiquette of all meals in these lands, even in humble homes. Teeth also must be cleansed, both before and after, lest the Spaniards be regarded as greater barbarians than was already assumed.

Marina went on, as they took their seats at a board now piled with turkey and other game, and variety of supporting dishes, bright with cup and platter of silver and gold, and vases of such pottery as few European tables could equal in any land, and decorated with the invariable profusion of scented flowers: "I am to apologise to you for the fact that there is an absence of human meat. It would have been no more than routine courtesy to kill a prisoner of war, or a slave of no better use, on such an occasion, that you might be fed in the best way. But it is known that you do not favour such food, and it was held the higher courtesy to consider your customs before their own."

"Will you say I am grateful for that? And will you tell me if I do anything unmannerly by the standards which are recognised here?"

"You will do little wrong if you observe what I do. But if you have any doubt you can ask, for who but ourselves can understand what is said?"

She turned, as she spoke, to their aged host, who was now requiring her services for a conversation on which the future course of events might largely depend.

"Will you tell your lord," he said, "that it was I who advised resistance to his invasion of a land to which he had not been invited to come; and, but for that, there would have been general agreement to let him through. That being so, and the one who led the attack being my own son, and we having come to another mind, he will understand that he will have nothing further to fear—I should say to doubt, for I suppose that fear to him is no frequent mood.

"You may say further that, if he deal with us as a friend should, he will find us to be straight of speech, and of deed alike. If I ask him with what purpose he would go on to the Mexican land, and by what route, it is that I may give friendly counsel concerning that which I know well."

Marina translated this. Cortéz asked: "Is he one to trust?"

"He has that repute. I should say, yes."

"Tell him that I go to visit the Aztec Emperor, as my duty to my own sovereign requires. I go in peace, for my part. But I care not, be it peace or war. As to the route I choose, I am not yet settled of mind. I would welcome counsel from him. But I am told that there is a city, Cholula, upon the way, which is a wonder to see."

"Yes," she smiled. "You had that from me. But he will tell you that it is a great risk, which you need not have, and that it is not on the route at all."

She turned to the aged ruler again, and there was a long period during which the Spaniards could only watch the animation of a conversation they could not share. They judged by gesture and tone that Marina was receiving a warning message to which she did not assent, with some contrary argument, to which he gave patient reply.

Then she gave the shortened substance of what had been said in Spanish which she had become fluent to speak.

"As to what you would do, he says, he has not been asked to advise, and you have so far seemed to be of invincible power. Also, the men of his race regard the Aztecs as mortal foes, and they would aid you against them with willing swords, if such occasion should come. But that is not to say that they would advance their armies far beyond the great mountains which are their girdle of strength. For the Aztecs are too many to be encountered on level land. He would have you warned with a friend's voice of the extent of their power, which is beyond anything you have yet seen.

"He tells you also that, if you depend upon the presents you have received, as proof of either friendship or fear, you may guess wrong, for the whole land (knowing Montezuma as you would not say that you do) is watching a riddle it cannot read.

"They know that, from the day you landed, there is nothing that you have done which has not been spied, and carried by swift runners to him, so that he knows all that happens from hour to hour.

"They know that he does not wish you to approach his city (which has no like in the whole world), and that there is amazement there that you should continue to flout his will. It is the conclusion of most that you will end as sacrifices at the next ritual feast, and, if he means you to come to that end, he may think that you do better to go to him on your own legs than to be carried so great a way.

"But, however that may be, you will reflect that his armies are very great, and that he has not used them at all. There must be a meaning in that.

"As to the way you take (should no warning avail), he would have you know that the city of México is to the east, but Cholula twenty miles to the southward of where we are. It is far from the direct way. It is not a warlike city, but one of ancient religions and many arts. Its inhabitants are expert in treasons and cunning wiles. They are foes to us, and will not welcome our friends. They may not be friends to the Aztecs, but they are too shrewd to offend them, having maintained some measure of independence by the wealth and prestige that their city has, and by ever agreeing to that which the Aztecs will. They would welcome you with fair words and massacre you in the night if they thought that Montezuma would give them thanks. If you go that way, you will ask for dangers you need not have.

"But if you approach the city of México by the straight road, you may be foiled in the end, even without strife, for it is set in the midst of a great lake, and its causeways could be barred, or else cut.

"Or else, should you be permitted to go in, you might find that you had entered that which you could not leave. It might be no better to you than a baited trap."

Cortéz listened to these friendly warnings (as he took them to be) with no change in the smiling courtesy of his eyes. They told him little that he had not heard in the privacy of their own tent, and in greater detail, from Marina before.

But this was not private. It was heard by his officers also, and half his thoughts were given to what its impact on them would be.

He looked at Alvarado, who, if not the most reliable, was the most adventurous of a most venturesome band. Did he take it with the gay courage which threat of danger was so constant to rouse? But Alvarado was not listening at all.

His eyes were on the girl who was seated on her grandfather's further side, and it was evident that his attention was fixed on her, and characteristically, oblivious of what others might think or see.

He saw one whose black hair was piled high on either side of her head, and wreathed in honeysuckle, with a white rose in the depression between. He saw a complexion of golden brown, lighter than that of those who dwelt in the lower lands, her cheeks slightly stained by the cochineal which was the only cosmetic that was used by those of patrician birth in her land. But this was obscured now by a natural colour which had risen as she had become conscious of the bold regard which had challenged her own dark eyes, till they had been hidden by fallen lids.

Every civilisation has its own modesties (which are but the following of the mode), and those which had surrounded her had been stricter, and yet given more freedoms, than were known at that day in Spain.

Her childhood, princess though she might be, had been very straightly controlled. Then, as adolescence passed, she had become free to do most things as she would, in the assurance that the conventions which she had been taught would be fully observed. They were things which everyone did, and the penalties for transgression, which it was seldom necessary to invoke, were too severe to be lightly incurred. It was as though there were a large domain with absolute freedom to wander therein, but surrounded by a pale which was death to climb.

She would marry in due time, with the necessity of her father's assent, which would not be capriciously withheld. Her husband might have other wives (though few did). What could be wrong in that? But the breaking of marriage vows was something so exceptional that it might be said that it did not occur. If it did, its very locality would be cursed of god, and the punishment of the criminals would be of such a kind as would discourage disloyal thoughts from rising in other minds.

It was an ordeal for her, even with all the prestige of her high rank, and the assurance it gave, to be eating thus amidst a concourse of men. Men of her own race would have recognised that, and been careful not to embarrass her with a direct glance, or a needless word. And this golden-haired, godlike stranger from a land which none had imagined to exist even a year ago. She cast down her eyes and hoped that none could perceive the beating of a heart which she could not control.

Her grandfather's feeble sight made it improbable that he could have seen anything of this, but he was speaking to Marina again, and, when she translated his words, they had a very positive sound.

"He says that it is misfortunate that you are here without women of your own race and degree, for it is the custom in every land that such alliance as they have now made with you should be secured by the mutual giving of brides.

"But, even so, they would not fail of their side, and they have maidens enough to content your men of rank, which they will not be backward to do."

"Thank him for that which is nobly meant, and which you will not say that we decline; but you will remind him that some of them, if not all, may have wives which they have left in their own land."

He was conscious next moment that this might have been differently said, for did she not know this to be his position? And if it were a bar to them, what was her status with him? But she gave no sign of such thought as she translated what he had said, and then gave him the Tlascalan ruler's reply: "He says it is natural that that should be, but a wife the more should be no burden to them, and should be welcomed by those who are lonely now."

"You will say that it is an offer we most highly regard, and there may be those who will lightly agree, but they cannot wed except they have Christian wives, and it would be necessary for them to be baptized."

"He says that there would be no dissent about that. A wife should be of her husband's faith, that they may be together in all that they do. Doubtless, had you had women here, they would have been wedded to their own nobles with a like transit of faith. I know what you would answer to that, but it should be left unsaid."

Even Cortéz, zealot for his faith though he was, could see the wisdom of that advice.

CHAPTER THIRTY-SEVEN: PAUSE

The Spaniards stayed for three autumn weeks, enjoying Tlascalan hospitality, and making closer a friendship which survived more than one difference which might have led to an opposite end.

They were feasted in the other quarters of the city, by their various lords.

They were offered wives with more of formality than there had been in the first suggestion, and five Spanish officers married Tlascalan girls of good families, who were baptised, and took Christian names.

Among these was the granddaughter of Xicotencatl, whom, to her equal satisfaction, Alvarado acquired, as he would most things on which his eyes fell, and his heart was set. Knowing no word of each other's language, of such alien civilisations as may never have come together in the world's history before, there is no evidence that these marriages did not succeed, and that of Doña Louise (her new baptismal name) was of a happiness none could doubt.

Meanwhile, the main part of the little army, with its porters and camp followers, remained outside the city, so severely restrained, by

Cortéz orders, from consorting with the townspeople as to rouse the resentful protests not only of his own officers, but of the Tlascalan rulers, whom he placated with assurances that it was the military custom of Spain, which was a diplomatic rather than a truthful reply.

It would not have been in accordance with his character to let the weeks pass without an attempt to force redemption upon his allies, but here he found argument in vain, and urgent persuasion badly received, and it may have been only the wisdom of Father Olmedo which averted disaster.

He urged restraint upon one who was not easy to rule, even on a matter of faith, and when it was the voice of the Church that spoke.

"Father," he protested, "how can we expect the blessing of God upon what we do, if we are faint of heart to bring the people to him, whether by violent or peaceful ways?"

"You will not call me," the priest replied, "lacking in zeal for the conversion of heathen men. But will you give thought to this— that, if you provoke these people to anger now it may mean disaster such as will end the hope that you might lead them to the feet of Christ on a later day? Or have you thought that, if you constrain them to yield with resentful hearts, you will pass on, and they will return to their own gods the next week?"

"Father, had they a less loathsome faith! Who could endure the foul images of their blood-smeared gods? Are we to take men whose bellies are heavy with human flesh as our companions in this crusade for the glory of God and Spain?"

"Son," Father Olmedo replied patiently, "have I asked you to make them companions in what you do? But I tell you that you have a people to deal with here with whom violence will not avail. We must persuade and teach, or else fail, with the wreckage of all you dream. If you snap at the shadow, do I need to say you will drop the bone?"

He turned to Marina, who had been listening with silent gravity to this debate, to ask: "Cannot you persuade him that I am right, knowing these people's ways better than we?"

Marina said: "They are not my people. They have ruder ways. But I would talk to Doña Louise of this. Her grandfather listens to her, and she will aid us the most she may. Father, would you join me in this?"

Father Olmedo had already learned much of the tongues of the New World, on which the success of his teaching must depend, but he knew that he could not talk or understand as Marina would, nor would his influence with Louise be of the same kind.

Louise had given herself to her new lord and her new faith with the fervour of a great passion, and the docility which was natural to the women of her race, and any influence, across the difficult bridge of language, that Alvarado might have with her would be on the right side. He wore his religion as easily as an old cloak, and had nothing of his commander's proselytizing zeal.

A quick friendship had developed between the two girls, who had been mutually helpful. Marina told Louise much of the ways of the white men, which it was useful to her to know. Louise had provided gay clothes which Marina had been eager to have. Cortéz did not know enough of the fashions of the land to judge whether she dressed as his consort should; and the hundreds of costly garments that the munificence of Montezuma had sent would have been more useful if they had not all been for masculine wear. Feather work and embroidery, however richly wrought, could not be easily altered to the purpose that she required.

Louise was willing to help, but not sanguine of much result. She took them to her grandfather, and Father Olmedo listened to much conversation which he only partially understood.

The aged Xicotencatl was courteous but definite in rejection of any proposal that there should be a national acceptance of the Christian God. "Why," he asked Marina, "should we do that?"

"It is the better faith, which I can say, as few could, having known both."

"It may be better for them. To each nation its own gods, who will be of the pattern which it requires. Will you tell me how you come to be wedded to your lord, being plainly of Aztec blood, and from a country where he has not been?"

"You ask that which I must not say."

Xicotencatl turned his dim eyes searching upon her at this reply, but made no protest at its refusal of information of so apparently innocent a kind. He said: "We will go far to render our Spanish brothers content, but this is beyond reason to ask."

Father Olmedo said: "It is what I expected to hear; but, perhaps, if we ask less, we may get more."

So it proved to be. When they left, they had the promise that (subject to confirmation by the Council) the Spanish priests should be free both to practise and teach the faith. They were to have permission to erect a Cross in one of the public squares, where they could celebrate Mass in the sight of all men who should be drawn by devotion or curiosity.

Beyond this, as a gesture of courtesy to their guests, the Tlascalans would release the captives who had been intended for current slaughter. It is improbable that these could have been numerous, and certain that the practice of ritual cannibalism was resumed after the Spaniards left, but the concessions were substantial, and exhibited a spirit of tolerance far beyond anything which would have been shown either by the ecclesiastical or civil authorities of Seville or Madrid.

Meanwhile a further embassy to Cortéz arrived from the Mexican Emperor. Protected by the immunity which their mission gave, they entered the capital city of the hated Tlascalans, and, having secured a private audience, they informed him that their monarch had now decided, in recognition of their earnest prayers, to receive them as they desired. He sent gifts with the same princely generosity as before. He warned against making alliance with the savage Tlascalans, which would be too base a connection for those whom he would call his friends. He recommended that they should travel by way of Cholula, where he assured them that they would be well received.

Promising little, except that he would do that which he had previously resolved, Cortéz answered them with friendly assurances and protestations of high regard for Montezuma, and appreciation of the invitation he had now received. He said that the warning they had given him regarding the Tlascalans would be remembered, and pondered well.

But he was in no doubt either of Tlascalan good faith, or of the advantage that the alliance would be. What he pondered most, in a dubious mind, was Montezuma's intention toward himself, and how he might be able to break through any snare into which he might be cunningly led.

He had further light on the confused politics of the land to which he had come when another Aztec deputation appeared, with implications for which the facts which Marina had already told him had not wholly prepared his mind.

He knew that Montezuma claimed supremacy over a neighbouring kingdom of Tezcuco, which had been ruled by Nezahualpilli, probably the greatest and wisest monarch that the land had known, who had died three or four years earlier. The right to the Tezcuco throne had then been contested by two brothers of whom one, Cacama, had had Montezuma's support, through which he had obtained the city and fertile province of Tezcuco itself, while his brother, Ixtlilxochitl, had been allotted an outlying province, mountainous and sterile, with which he was ill content. He did not know whether there were now a spirit of concord or animosity between the two.

But the deputation left him in no doubt about that. It brought a blunt request that Cortéz would join Ixtlilxochitl to assist him to seize a throne which was rightly his. He might ask much for that, and the terms would not be considered too high.

To this astonishing offer, Cortéz gave an encouraging though indecisive reply. He had come to a land where all things were strange and new. He desired friendship with all. But he would give much to see justice done. He must hear more of Ixtlilxochitl's claim at another time.

There was one fact that emerged clearly from this—it must be the prevailing belief throughout Tezcuco that he was of a very formidable power.

Marina confirmed this inference. Ixtlilxochitl had no force to contend with the armies that Montezuma controlled. His closest friends would be unlikely to support him in so wild and hopeless a claim. He must regard the Spaniards as having an almost invincible power.

This deputation went, and another came. They were men from Cholula now. They said that they had come to invite the Spaniards to visit their city on the way to México. They could be sure of good hospitality, and to visit the ancient city of Many Faiths would be a contrast to what they must have endured in this barbarous land.

Cortéz looked at them with more doubt than he had felt before. They were mean men, meanly clad. He said they should have an answer on the next day. Meanwhile he arranged for them to have lodging among his own officers, for when they looked at Tlascalans they shook with fear.

He said to Marina, when they had withdrawn: "I was told that Cholula is a rich city, of wealth and temples and ancient arts, but they are beggarly men."

She answered: "So they are. I do not understand it at all."

Louise came at a later hour. She said: "My grandfather and father have been talking to others who are friendly to you, and I come from them with cautioning words.

"They say that the deputation from Cholula is an insult in itself. The men they have sent are the very scum of the town.

"Besides that, there is certain report that an Aztec army has moved to the southward of the city (where it would not be seen by you till after you had entered its walls), and they regard it as certain that some treachery is resolved. Why else should you be urged to go to a place which is not on your direct way? If you would take counsel from them, you would remain here, where you are secure."

Cortéz said: "I must go on. But I am not deaf to a friend's voice."

He sent for the deputation. He told them: "You will go back with this word: if I visit Cholula, I must know that it is at the wish of those who are in control, and not only those who may sweep its streets."

The men cringed, and went. Being alone, Marina asked: "What shall you do now?" They had come to a level at which he confided in her, as in no other, woman or man, and would heed her advice at times. But he was now in a very confident mood. He said: "If I go that way, it will be with the caution that warning breeds."

Two days later another deputation arrived. There could be no question now of the status of those who came. They were men of rank by their known names, their manner, and their attire.

They had an excuse for the meanness of the first embassy, which might have been true. They had feared to come themselves, knowing how they were hated by the Tlascalans. It had seemed prudent to send men who would not have been missed, even had they gone to the cooking-pots of the priests.

Cortéz accepted this. He said to Marina, in the tone of one who is polite to inferior men: "Tell them that I have decided that I will visit Cholula on a near day."

CHAPTER THIRTY-EIGHT: CHOLULA

"I hear from Father Olmedo," Cortéz said, "that you do not wish the circumstances under which you left your home, or even where it may be, to be widely told. Is there a good reason for that?"

"So I think there is. But you must consider that I must guess more than I know.

"I went to rest at night in my own room, in a great house that was mine, in a peaceful land, and I waked on the next day (unless it were later than that) in a litter that traversed a mountain road, in the hands of those who had bound me both foot and hand. I must have been drugged, and sold or given to those who had bargained to bear me far. I ask myself: who would have done that? And there is only one reply.

"My stepfather would not. He was a man without guile. My half-brother was a young child, with whom I had bonds of love. My mother ruled all, and if she did not hate me (which I would not say), she hated the law by which all was mine, and my half-brother could inherit nothing unless I died.

"Now he will have all, if she can make me dead by the law, which she must contrive, though I know not how.

"But you must see that, if I should return, and my guess be true, it might be hard to conceal so much that my mother would not die by the law, as most would call a just doom. But can you think that I wish that?

"She has brought me to no ill, but the joy of love. And my brother is welcome to that which was mine by law, but could have been his by my will.

"I will stir nothing of my own choice."

"Should not those be dealt with by law who had kidnapped you in so foul a way?"

Marina lifted astonished brows. "But they were merchants! You could do nothing to them."

Explanations followed. The merchants were a caste apart, overreaching the frontiers of many lands. They had their own customs, their own laws. They were not specifically above the laws of the lands about which they moved. Rather they stood aside, and even the Aztecs would think more than once before challenging their untested power.

Without vehicles, without beasts of burden, the long lines of laden pedestrians toiled in single file, perhaps a thousand strong, up the mountain paths, an occasional litter being the most conspicuous feature of the slow-moving file. They bore no arms. They had no military support. But they had little reason for fear.

Once, in past years, such a caravan had been scattered, slaughtered, plundered, in a southern land; but the vengeance which had fallen upon the robbers was still a tale of terror to all who heard.

No one knew what their wealth might be, or entirely how their influence worked; but their power to stop all trade with a city or race which incurred their wrath was alone sufficient to give them a menacing power.

Apart from them there were no financial interests in the whole subcontinent to challenge those of the civil power. There were no industrial magnates, for there were no organised industries. Featherwork, jewellery, pottery, weapons and tools—they were all made by skilled hand-labour behind the reed-curtains of private rooms.

Whatever trick Marina's mother might have used, whatever bargain with the merchants she might have made, the Aztec law would not be invoked against them, but only against herself. And no one who knew their ways would doubt that the merchants, with an exact honour, had fulfilled whatever bargain they might have made.

The explanation of this curious international power of the merchants' guild led to further understanding of the status of the city to which they were preparing to go.

So far as the merchants had any known central organisation, it was seated there. Cholula was not the largest city in the land, but it was probably wealthier even than México itself, and it certainly produced merchandise of unrivalled value. Its bulk might not be greatest, but its artistic quality was incomparably highest. Almost every one of its twenty thousand houses contained craftsmen whose work was in demand as far as civilisation extended to north or south.

The men of Cholula were not warriors, and its wealth must have been tempting to poorer neighbours, but, though internally independent, it was loosely under the domination of the Aztecs, whose policies it would always support. And its pre-eminence in trade, with the support of the merchants' guild, was not its sole, nor even its major, claim to the immunity which it enjoyed. It was the centre of religious worship throughout the known civilised world.

It was a very ancient city. It had been ancient—of unknown antiquity—when, centuries before, the Aztecs had come out of the North, and founded the lake-surrounded city, which, from ocean to ocean, had become the centre of secular power.

All the religions of the land had a temple here.

It contained the greatest wonder of human building known to the Western World—a flattened pyramid the base of which covered a hundred and forty-four acres, and of which the top platform was crowned with a splendid temple draining pilgrims to view it from many lands. For it was a wonder that all men must wish to see.

It also had been built by a past civilisation, in the dim days before the Aztecs entered the land. It proclaimed the worship of Zuetzalcoatl, who, in remote time, had been a God Incarnate, clothed in human form. For twenty years he had dwelt there, teaching man the good conduct of life, and, that, if they must sacrifice to the Unseen, their offerings should be fruit and flowers. But his worship was debased now, his teaching largely contemned. His altars, like those of his Aztec rivals, were foul with the blood of men.

It may have been Marina's explanation of Cholula's wonders, and its curious eminence and immunity, which had finally caused Cortéz to resolve that he would not pass it unseen, for the benefit of a shorter road. The thought of seeing it brought some pleasurable excitement to her own mind. And its qualities did not appear to be of an aggressive sort.

Even the information they had from the Tlascalans at the last moment, that spies reported recent activity in strengthening the gates of the city, and repairing neglected walls, did not change his mind, but when, having found his resolution fixed, the Tlascalans offered that their army should go with him until he had passed through the ancient city, he compromised to the extent that he agreed that they should strengthen his ranks with a force of six thousand men.

"To take more," he said to León, who had argued consistently for the direct route, "would be to suggest hostile intent. It would be excuse—it might be the actual occasion—of attack upon ourselves which we need not have."

So, as October waned, he marched out of Tlascala while the rising sun was still low, and moved slowly on the mountain roads, the little band of horsemen leading a mile-long snake of artillery, and marshalled warriors, and baggage porters, and the miscellaneous camp followers that joined such movements, as jackals follow the lion that rises to seek a prey.

While the sun was still high, they left the Tlascalan hills. They looked down on a great plain, itself six thousand feet above the ocean they had left two months before, and yet surrounded by distant mountains on every side, of such height as made little of that commencing eminence, and towered through tropic sunlight to cold heights of unchanging snow.

Ahead, they saw the walled girth of the ancient city, its huge central pyramid crowned with a gleaming temple, and surrounded by an incredible number—said to be four hundred—of temple towers.

Between was a level fertile plain, thickly wooded in places, irrigated by canals, intensively cultivated, and showing fields of ripening maize, of aloes, pepper and other crops, indicating a prosperous and peaceful land.

They marched on till the sun was low, and they were near to Cholula's walls, and then halted in a woodland space, where a small natural river supplied their most urgent need, Cortéz recognising that his force was too numerous to attempt to enter the city abruptly at such an hour.

Soon there came an official deputation. They welcomed the Spaniards, but protested against the presence of their Tlascalan allies. Those who might be friends to Cortéz were foes to them. To allow such numbers to enter the city would be to invite riots, which they would not be responsible to restrain.

The difficulty was overcome by a compromise. Cortéz was to enter the city next morning with his Spanish soldiers and a few camp-followers only, while the Tlascalans, with the bulk of the porters, were to remain camped outside, and to rejoin him when he should go on to the Aztec capital.

Next morning he rode through the city gates, amid welcoming crowds. He thought their greeting to be less ardent than had been those which had met him when he had entered Tlascala. But he had no cause for complaint. They cheered; they threw flowers.

He looked round on finer buildings, he looked down on wider, cleaner streets than he had seen before in this land. He noticed that the Cholulans were more gaily and richly dressed. He said to Marina: "Since I landed on your coasts, each city to which I come is finer than I have seen before."

"Yes?" She said, unimpressed. "But you have not seen México yet."

They rode on to one of the numberless temple buildings, which had been prepared for their reception. It had many rooms, and a spacious courtyard, sufficient for all to camp who could not be accommodated within the building. They were supplied with ample and varied food. The weather was fine. The visit had started well.

Next morning they were visited by some of the governing caciques of the city. They offered additional lodging accommodation, which Cortéz declined, preferring to keep his men together, and to be with them. They offered to show their visitors the sights of the city, but gave a warning against wandering without escort, there being unruly elements of which to beware. That might be meant well, or in another way.

Taking a bold risk, Cortéz accepted an invitation next day for him and his principal officers to be shown the city.

They went through busy, crowded, prosperous streets. There were priests everywhere, usually white-robed, some with faces grotesquely blackened. There were many professional beggars. There were pilgrims, variously attired, from every country of the civilised Western World. The scent of incense was everywhere. There were tower-crowned temples in every street.

They climbed the huge central pyramid. They entered a temple erected to the great Teacher who had been deified after his death for his wisdom and gentle ways; but now his altars were stained by the shedding of human blood.

His image, in the midst, was grotesque and black, but its jewels, of sceptre and mitred crown, would have bought a kingdom in the Old World.

The next day there was another of the incessant embassies from Montezuma. Unlike the last, it made it clear that the Aztec Emperor did not wish his city to be more nearly approached. When Cortéz replied that he was acting on the invitation he had already had, they became openly resentful. They went abruptly, with less of courtesy than any previous embassy had shown. And there had been no gifts.

Cortéz asked, when they had left: "What is the meaning of that? Does Montezuma wish to pick a quarrel with me?"

Marina asked: "But why should he wish for that?"

It was shrewdly thought. If violence or treachery were the design, he would gain nothing by showing a warning hand.

After a short silence, she said: "Hernán, have you thought that it may have been a last effort to turn us back in a peaceful way? Before he give the word for another course that he is reluctant to take?"

"Yes. I was thinking of that."

"I will find out what I can."

Cortéz had another invitation to go abroad on the next day, which he declined.

Marina, protected by her colour and dress, wandered about the city, and visited the wife of one of the caciques, who had shown a friendly disposition to her. She suggested to her a remedy for a sick child, which was efficacious, and won thanks. But she learned little. When she came back she said: "They seem guarded in what they say. Most of them know who I am, or I might learn more. They are curious to find out exactly when we shall leave."

"Which shall not be known till the last hour," Cortéz replied. He planned to remain still for a time, and then to move suddenly.

He sent out three porters as spies. They slipped out in the night. He thought that they were not likely to be observed in the cosmopolitan crowds of that pilgrim city. They came back with a tale which was not pleasant to hear.

"As you go on toward the northern gate, at which it will be natural to leave the town, you come to places where pits have been dug across the width of the streets. They are well covered now, but they could be so lightly boarded that a man would pass in safety, but a loaded horse would fall through. And the lesser streets are barricaded on either side. Also, there are large stones on the terraced platforms of many roofs, so shaped that they could be heaved over with ease." They added that the streets were less crowded than had been the case on the previous day, so that it had not been as easy as they had expected to return unobserved.

Alvarado, riding out alone to the Tlascalan camp, in his gallant, insolent way, heard further tales of the same kind, which he took in a laughing mood.

"Hernando," he said, on his return, "the rats think they have trapped the cat. There is net here to be broken through! They say the army of Montezuma, which lay five miles south of the city, is moving close up to its walls. There have been many leaving the city, merchants and pilgrims, and few come. Women and children have been leaving during the night. The pits are a fact, and there are great stakes within them, on to which the horses are meant to fall. They will wait till we are marching out, and then assault us by every means, and from every side. Shall we endure that?"

It was gravely asked. But his eyes danced with the excitement of strife to be. Cortéz said: "I am well served. Being warned, we shall find away."

But what was it to be? He could stay there as long as he would, while they dug more pits, and put more stones on the roof. And perhaps while six thousand Tlascalan allies fought against twenty thousand of Montezuma's best troops. Would there be profit in that? And how long could even that possibility be? This was the first day that no provisions had come.

Marina entered. She said: "I have the wife of one of the city's lords in my own room. She is a good friend. I have been packing to leave you, and she is finishing what I began."

Cortéz looked at her with bewildered eyes. She was one who would often smile, but would seldom jest. He asked: "What do you mean by that?"

"What I say. I am to leave after dark, and she will stay to help me, for I have much that I wish to carry away. It is to save my life. Surely you would wish that!"

"Will you tell me more?"

"I will tell you more. But I must have your word that no harm shall be hers."

"It is as you will. Should you doubt that? But I think you have that to tell which should not be delayed."

"There is time enough. She is a good friend. I saved her child. She asked me to spend this night in her house, and was too persistent for it to have been for a light cause. I said little, and she made a wrong guess that I was not loyal to you. When I began to pack as one who would not return, she said enough to show that she would save me from a mean death."

Cortéz called the guard. He ordered that the woman should be fetched from Marina's room. When she had been brought, he said: "Tell her that she has nothing to fear, but we must know all."

In the end they did. She had, in fact, said too much to become dumb.

Montezuma had sent rich gifts, as his way was, but this time they had been for Cholula's caciques. He had required their co-operation in the elimination of these pestilent invaders, which they had not refused. The hour of massacre was now near, and she had been anxious to save a friend. "Am I?" she asked Marina, "to die because I would have saved you?"

"Tell her," Cortéz said, "that what she would have done for you, we will do for her. She will stay here, which may be a safer place than she would be likely to think. And I will save her husband also, if it can be done by looking another way."

CHAPTER THIRTY-NINE: MASSACRE

The two priests had been attached to the temple which had been cleared to make room for its present guests. They had been transferred to a nearby shrine, and Cortéz had had them fetched, on an excuse which had been easy to make.

They sat opposite to him, entirely at ease, waiting for Marina to explain why they had been asked to come.

Cortéz said: "The priests always know. Tell them that they must confess all, or they will be dead men in the next hour."

"But they will not flinch from that. They will think only of what their gods would wish them to do."

"Then what can be said?"

"Shall I tell them you will cut off their hands? They will have heard that you do that."

Cortéz smiled in a way that the watchful priests, who were no fools, did not like. He said: "I can do better. Tell them that I will peel the skin from their legs, from the knees down, and that they shall walk back on the bare flesh to escape what worse punishment I should otherwise be certain to do. Promise gifts, and what else you will."

She talked to the priests for a time, and Cortéz saw that they were frightened men, but that their faces cleared as she went on.

Then she said: "I told them about skinning their legs, which they did not like. I told them also that they can have a gift of gold, and go back as they are, if they will tell what they know; and that none can guess what they will have said, for it will remain private to us. They agree that that will be the much better way."

After that, she talked to them again, and then said: "It is much as you supposed, but they say that Montezuma has really been in a great doubt as to what he shall do, which is hard to believe. He first said that you were to be treated well; but after that there was a consultation of the gods, and it was revealed that there would be a great massacre in this city, leading to peace. It would have been strange if he had not taken advantage of that."

"Did you say that we have no fear of their gods?"

"I told them that your God is so much greater than any of theirs that he keeps many scores of such shut up in a palace of fire, because they were disrespectful to Him. They did not like that at all, for all men already know that we have a God who is potent to have His way. It made them more ready to talk than they were before.

"They say it is true that Montezuma has sent great gifts to their rulers here. He has also sent poles and thongs by which those who are captured alive (which they will seek to contrive) will be sent to México for ceremonial sacrifice there. But they are to keep one in five of you, and one in twenty of the Tlascalans, for their own altars, that they also may have cause to rejoice."

"Then there is no doubt that all we have heard is true. Tell them that we shall leave the city before noon tomorrow. They need have no fear when they say that, for it is how I intend it to be. They will ask that the city's lords, or some of them, shall be here at prime of day, when I shall have thanks to give them, and a last favour to ask. If they can spare me five hundred porters for the short march to México I will thank them and pay them well. They must not fail here, for till I have seen them I cannot leave."

The priests went, thinking that they had done little harm, or even that the information they had obtained might be of advantage to those of their own part. Also, they had a present of gold, which they did not despise, for its dust was currency there, as it was in the Old World.

They gave the message to those for whom it was meant, and were prudently careful to say nothing of the betrayal that they had made.

When they were gone, Cortéz called his officers to Council, and listened first to those of faint heart, who thought that, caught in such a trap, and surrounded by so strong a body of foes, both within and without, they would do well to attempt escape during the night, rejoining the Tlascalans, and retiring with them to the mountain strength which was theirs.

But when they had spent their words, bolder voices prevailed, and so, when they were in the right mood, Cortéz told them of what he planned to do when the morning should come.

After that, there was sharpening of weapons, and repairing of armour for breast and back; and Bernal Díaz had horses groomed and well fed, that they should be equal to any need.

It was not yet fully light when Cortéz requested that the Mexican ambassadors, who were lodged in the next street, should come to take their farewells, which they were ready to do. The victims were about to march forth to their doom, and nothing must be done or omitted to cause suspicion which was not supposed to exist.

They came prepared with words which would have been false and fair, but they had their first doubt when they found that they were not received by Cortéz and Marina alone, but were quickly surrounded by armed men of a hostile mien. And the doubt became something worse when Cortéz said: "Tell them that we know, that we may hear what they can do for the saving of their own lives," which Marina did, in words which were straight and few, as her way was.

But the accusation was met by exclamations of blank astonishment. Montezuma knew nothing of any plot, which he would neither approve nor condone. It was the false Cholulans who must be blamed.

Had there been the faintest reason to regard these protests as genuine, it might have been expedient to enlist their aid to bring Cholula to a more peaceful mood. But, however little they might be believed, Cortéz saw that there might be advantages in avoiding an open quarrel with México. He said: "Tell them that we had heard before that Cholula is a city where treason breeds, and it is pleasant to hear that their Emperor is not so base a sort. For the time, they shall remain here, which will be safest for them, and will be proof that they will have no part in that which is about to occur."

They were led away under a strong guard, as three of the city's rulers were shown in.

They came confidently. It was to be the final act of ceremonial courtesy which would satisfy the Spaniards of their goodwill as they marched out to the waiting trap.

One of them said, before Marina started to speak: "We had your message, and have brought the porters which you require. It was a pleasure to do."

Cortéz could believe that, for, as it was said, Alvarado entered the door of the crowded room, and gave a nod which told him all he needed to know. The five hundred men were not porters at all, but soldiers in porters' garb, and with concealed knives, such as no porter should bear. They were crowding into the courtyard now, which might be unhealthy for them. For Cortéz had made his own preparations during the night. Having made it known that he was to leave, what could be more natural than that he should be sending messengers to the Tlascalan camp, or that there should be noise in the courtyard of artillery being dragged about? The Cholulans were less watchful of him than fearful lest their own movements should be suspect.

Marina was translating now: "We know what the porters are. We know all your plots. You will do well to confess."

Their complacency suddenly gone, their dusky faces pallid with fear, they muttered among themselves. Then their spokesman said: "Whatever may have been proposed was against our will. It is Montezuma's order that you must blame, and not us."

"But Montezuma's envoys say that you had no orders from him. You can go back to your porters. Take them away—if you can."

Not understanding the meaning of this, the bewildered men went out to the courtyard, none staying them; but, as they appeared there, a shot was fired, which was the signal to wake it to dreadful life.

The five hundred had been marshalled in the centre of the crowded yard, and now the Spanish soldiers attacked them with every weapon they had, and from every side. Their knives were no match for the Spanish swords. It was slaughter rather than strife. The gods of México were to have the massacre which they had foretold.

Those who struggled to reach the gates (of which there were three) were met by a line of pikes.

Comrades from without, roused by the shots, who tried to rush for their rescue, were met by the blasts of cannon—a form of thunder of which they had heard marvellous tales, but which had not come to their ears until it sounded a death-knell now. A few escaped by lying quietly under the slain. One athlete clambered over the wall.

But almost all of the five hundred died, and no one troubled to search for the Cholulan rulers among the slain.

By now, the Tlascalans, not waiting for the Aztec army to appear, had forced a way through the city gates, and were attacking the rear of those who were trying to force their way into the courtyard, and already having trouble enough from the heavy Spanish fire that poured forth from the narrow width of the gate.

In the end, their abortive losses being beyond further endurance, they turned, and fled through the streets, with the outbreaking Spaniards upon their heels, and six thousand Tlascalans, and more of Totonacs and promiscuous recruits than anyone had been careful to count, following closely behind.

The main body of fugitives made for the great central mound and the crowning temple, impelled by thought of its defendable strength, or a blind instinct to seek the protection of their peculiar gods, Spaniards and Tlascalans (the latter distinguished, through Cortéz's prudent foresight, by wreaths of sedge round their heads) slaying industriously on their rear.

The havoc and confusion were increased by the Tlascalans (waging war in the fashion they understood) firing such buildings as were of wood, or of which the walls were hanging reeds, as was common to the private houses, so that the narrow streets filled with smoke, and their sides became raging flame.

The great central temple, which could only be reached by the climbing of six score steps, offered prospect of successful resistance, but the Spaniards stormed upward against volleys of shafts and stones. The building was largely of stone, but its towers were of gilded wood, and were soon sheets of flame and ascending smoke to a windless sky.

The army of Montezuma, camped to the southward of the city wall, could not doubt the significance of that pillar of smoke and flame. But it did not move. It maintained the enigmatic character of the Aztec attitude by remaining quiescent throughout the day, and so gave apparent support to the protestations that the envoys had made, and support for the attitude Cortéz adopted when he released them on the next day.

It is possible that the detention of these envoys was the direct cause of the inactivity of the Aztec host. They may have been entrusted by Montezuma with authority to direct its movements according to the developments within the city, so that it was immobilised when the critical moment came and no orders arrived.

But within the city panic and plunder ruled. Fires burned unchecked, and Spaniard, Tlascalan, and Totonac, chased and slew; or turned to looting a city rich with the choicest wealth of the Western World.

Resistance soon became slight from a people who were not naturally warlike, who had depended upon treachery and surprise, whose plans had failed, and whose essential leaders were seized or dead.

The blocks of stone on the terraced roofs, now hidden in rising smoke, were not cast down on the confusion of friends and foes that raged and shouted below. The exultant whistles of the Tlascalans shrilled through the din.

Wholesale massacre and outrage might have been the fate of a city that had ceased to offer any organised resistance, and cowered in terror before its triumphant foes. But, in that moment of excited victory, Cortéz achieved a miracle of control both over his own men, and allies with whom he could only communicate by translated eloquence, with Marina's aid.

The soldiers were brought back to their ordered ranks. Further promiscuous looting of the unwalled houses was forbidden. It was announced that any violence to women would incur prompt and merciless punishment.

The head cacique, and other leading officials, had died on the temple hill, but one was found to whom Cortéz delegated authority to proclaim that those who went about their peaceful affairs would have nothing to further to fear.

In the two hours of wild confusion and massacre, the losses of the Spaniards had been negligible, and that of their allies had been very light. Even the Cholulan dead, including those who had been trapped in the courtyard did not exceed three thousand—a moderate total which may be largely explained by the fact that the Tlascalans, as resistance slackened, had sought to capture rather than kill, as their method of warfare was.

Father Olmedo, active in the mission of Christ, as the occasion required, saw their captives being led away to the Tlascalan camp—hundreds of every rank, women and children among them, walking with bound hands, to be sent back to Tlascala, put into the fattening pens of the priests, and slaughtered as their condition suggested, or provision for a festival might require.

He went to Cortéz, whom he found, with Marina inseparably at his side, busy with many urgent affairs, but with time to listen to him.

"Hernán", he said, with the familiarity of address that friendship and his position allowed, "you must stop this. Can we retain the blessing of God, if we hold alliance with those who blaspheme his image in such unspeakable ways?"

"I would stop it with glad mind. Marina, will they listen to me in this?"

There was doubt in Marina's eyes as she replied: "You would ask much. It is the universal custom of war. And you cannot expect them to understand of what you complain. When you fight, you kill men in many barbarous ways. When they fight, they capture them to be killed on a later day in a more civilised manner.

"You do not like to eat human flesh, and they will say that they respect your custom, and do not serve it to you. Why should you not respect theirs?"

There was a moment's silence when she had said this. They knew that, if they should quarrel with the Tlascalans, they might be equal to that, though the difference would be ten to one.

And, in fact, the worst that would be likely to happen would be that they would refuse to surrender their captives, and go home in a sulky way.

But there were twenty thousand Aztecs on the further side of the city wall, not three miles away.

Cortéz said: "I am held here. I must talk to the Mexican envoys at once, for which there may now be additional cause.

"You will ride yourself to the Tlascalan camp. Bernal will be your guard. You will say that the voice is yours, but the words mine. The captives will be released in the next hour. It is an order from me, which my God requires, and it will not change though the skies fall. You will put it in the best way, as you ever do."

Marina said: "I will go at once." She looked undisturbed, as her way was.

Father Olmedo said: "God will bless you, my son, for this, though we should all die."

Cortéz was unconcerned. He smiled: "We shall all die at our own time; but we live now."

He sent for the Mexican envoys, to whom he said: "I have observed that your army has not broken camp while I have dealt with the treason here, and I can the better accept your assurances that your Emperor was not concerned. But I do not know why they are so near. Will it please you to move them further away?"

They promised that this should be done at once, and painted an order to that effect, which Cortéz, as he could not read it, kept back for Marina to see.

But, on her return, she said it was a plain direction for them to march back to México, and next morning their camp was empty, and the mystery of the Mexican attitude still unsolved, though Cortéz thought it policy to accept the assurances he received.

Regarding her mission to the Tlascalan camp, Marina said: "There were angry words from all, and some would have defied you in a bold way. But I made it plain that it was a matter on which you would neither bargain nor yield. I asked them, would they have fired Cholula without your aid? Would they have taken captives except for you? So they let them go free, though with sullen looks; and, after that, I made a bargain about the spoil."

Cortéz looked grave when she said this, and there was as instant silence and anxious looks from those standing around.

It was good news indeed that the Tlascalans had given way to a request which must have seemed perverse to them, and sacrificed that which was regarded as the main spoil of war, and evidence of its success. But the question of the division of the spoil was also serious in another way, and while she was absent it had been the subject of hot debate. Cortéz had seen, with inward dismay, that it might be necessary to make a further demand on their allies, which, after what had just happened, they might be most loth to concede.

The Tlascalans, apart from their living captures, had taken a far richer spoil than had fallen into Spanish hands. They were far more numerous, and they had taken no part in the most serious fighting, which had occurred in the storming of the great mound, and the destruction of the temple upon its summit. They had followed the rear of the Spaniards, taking captives and other spoils, as was their habit of war, which had been an almost unobstructed process, owing to the hanging reeds of the unwalled houses offering no obstacle to their intrusions.

Now that order was being restored, and stern directions given that there should be no further looting, the Spanish soldiers had become aware that they had made little profit, unless there should be distribution of the spoil on a different basis.

Cortéz had actually been debating how far he could go in this matter, if Marina should have succeeded in securing the release of what the Tlascalans would regard as the most valuable part of the prey. At the best, it could not be expected that it would leave them in good temper to hear a further demand. Now it seemed that Marina had used it, without authority, as a bargaining point of a reverse kind. It had an ominous sound.

But she looked equably at the anxious or scowling faces around her. She said "It is what I had no license to do, but I think you may be content. The gold and silver and precious stones, of which there is much spoil, are to be surrendered to you, for they hold them in light esteem, but of garments and provisions they are to have not less than four parts in five, and, in particular, they are to take all they will of a store of salt over which they have placed a guard, for they value that at a great price, having none, for their way to the sea is through hostile lands."

There was no murmur at that. She saw approval in the eyes of him from whom she esteemed it most.

"Hernán," she said, "that rent in your doublet sleeve will be ill to mend."

She went in to their own room, knowing that she had won praise, which she may have thought she deserved. She twisted fresh flowers in her hair.

Chapter Forty: The March to México

Cortéz remained at Cholula during fourteen eventful days.

The Tlascalan army remained encamped without. They sent a long train of porters, laden with salt and many other desirable things, back to their own land, in evidence that those who allied themselves with the Spaniards throve well.

The threat of the Aztec army had moved away.

Cortéz remained in the quarters which had first been placed at his disposal, but he was lord of a city now which feared him with a great dread, and was grateful for a clemency which had so quickly followed the chastisement which it had deserved and received. Its rulers were now of his own appointment. Commercial activities were quickly resumed.

The temples of its many religions were allowed (after some argument between the zealous commander and the more Judicious Father Olmedo) to reopen, but release of the Tlascalans' captives was made the basis of a demand for similar freedom for all who were in the pens of Cholula's priests, which could not be denied.

It was announced that the ruins of the great central temple which, from the height of its flattened pyramid, could be seen far over the surrounding country, would be restored in the altered form of a Christian church, and the impetuous energy of Cortéz was such that, before he left, a huge wooden cross had already been erected, making Christianity the most assertive among the many creeds and deities of that city of ancient faiths; and Father Jerónimo, whose services as an interpreter were no longer essential, and whose knowledge of some at least of the languages of the New World rendered him particularly fit for the office, was installed as the bishop of a diocese which was yet to be.

There was gratifying evidence of the reputation which the Spaniards had gained in the visits, during the fortnight's pause, of caciques from neighbouring towns, with offers of friendship, and aid if need should be, and gifts which were little in comparison with those that came from the Mexican court, but substantial in relation to the resources of those who gave. There was nothing in these visits necessarily treasonable to Montezuma, for he was still professedly at peace with the invading strangers, but Marina, talking to them with the freedom that only one of her birth and native understanding could have done, reported that the purpose of these visits was not in doubt. They had shown resentment of the tyranny and exactions of the central power. They wished it to be understood that hostility to it would have their sympathy if not their open support.

There was only one warning, though it was of an emphatic kind, of the formidable nature of the enterprise on which Cortéz was inflexibly resolved. The leaders of the Totonacs came to him to announce a decision to go no further on a road which had become too perilous. It was a sinister incident, both in itself and its implications.

The Totonacs had done good service. Although not very numerous, they had been an important addition to the little army he led. Individually, they were of the elite of the peoples of these new lands: taller, handsomer, though not tougher than the Tlascalans, and equal in aspect and manners, though not in attire, to most of the Aztecs who had so far appeared.

Now they made it clear that, even after all they had seen and shared, they regarded further advance as an almost insane adventure. They suggested that Cortéz had even yet no adequate conception of Aztec power. And further advance to the capital must be by roads where the destruction of the invaders could easily be arranged.

México, like Cholula, like Tlascala, was the centre of its own plain. But the plains were not on the same level. The road to México was a hard climb: there were defiles where those who entered could be destroyed by rocks flung from above, while their assailants remained secure. It was true that Montezuma might intend to give the Christians a peaceful reception. No one knew what his final intentions might be. From ocean to ocean, all watched, and wondered, and waited for what would be. But there was a tale that the shorter road was being blocked by the felling of great trees, which had been cast across it. There was no evidence of goodwill in that. And even if Montezuma should offer friendship to the Spaniards, through caution lest he offend their God (who had shown His power), it was certain that such clemency would not be extended to them.

Cortéz accepted with apparent readiness a decision which he saw that he would be unlikely to change. He thanked the Totonacs for good service done. He made gifts. He asked only that they should take back a letter to his captain at Vera Cruz.

His thoughts turned from the unknown perils that lay ahead to those which were ominous on his rear. He had not yet heard anything of how Puerto-Carrero and his colleague had fared. If they had obeyed his instructions, and avoided landing in Cuba, they should be in Madrid before now. The die which would allow potential success or be certain ruin to him, might have been cast. But it was too soon for the result of his mission to be known in the New World. What was sure, in the meantime, was that the Cuban Governor would be doing all the harm he could.

He wrote to Escalante:

"My dear Juan,

Our Totonac friends, who bear this letter, have done me good service. They dread the Aztecs. What ever else may happen, they must not have cause to regret that they have been loyal to us.

Continue to strengthen your defences. Build—build—build. Never cease to watch the seas. Do not hesitate to resist whoever would seize our right, unless they have direct authority from Madrid.

I enclose a full account of all that has happened since I left Vera Cruz, both for your information, and that there may be record if we should be destroyed—which I do not fear. We have the protection of God, bearing His faith among idolatrous men.

Your governor and friend,

Hernando Cortéz"

Two days after the Totonacs left, the little Spanish army, led by its group of horsemen, and followed by its artillery, the long train of laden porters, and the more numerous Tlascalan army, marched out, between crowds of flower-throwing civilians, on the road to México.

Uncertain whether they were captives or honoured guests, and too circumspect to test the doubt, the Aztec envoys continued with them. Having no wheeled vehicles, or beasts of burden, they were accustomed to use their legs, but, even so, there were differences of physique between politicians and priests and porters, and these envoys were weary men when, after the long march had wound its slow way for many miles through land that was luxuriant with ripened crops, and the sun was descending the autumn sky, they came to a place where the road forked, and the signal to halt was called and whistled back to the distant rear.

A man of their own race came to them, where they walked in the midst of the long processions, where the gold and the women were. He said, with respect, but as one who brings an order that must be quickly obeyed: "The General desires speech."

They followed him to the front, where a dozen horses moved restlessly, as their riders debated the meaning of what they saw.

Cortéz was there, Marina, on a bay stallion (the lightest of the heavy cavalry horses) at his side.

He pointed to the right-hand way, which was barricaded with fallen trees. "Ask them," he said, as their eyes followed the direction he indicated, "what is the meaning of that?"

He must wait for minutes during which there were rapid exchanges in the unknown tongue with an interpreter who knew more of the topography of the land than they would have supposed they would have to face.

Then she said: "They allow that this block has been made by the Emperor's orders, and that its intention is to cause you to take the left-hand road, but they say that it is meant in kindness to you. The road they have closed may be the more direct way (as I know it is), but they say it is narrow and bad, and of steepness, at its worst, which the horses would be unable to overcome."

"Do you believe that?"

"It may have some truth, though not much. But it could have been said in a better way."

"So I think. Tell them it is our habit to go by the shorter road."

He ordered that camp should be made, and that porters should be called up to clear the obstacles from the path.

They moved forward next morning upon a road which was certainly becoming steep, though not yet of extreme difficulty either for horses or laden men. The air grew colder as they advanced. They knew that they were at a great height, having done so much upward marching since they had left the shore two months earlier; but as they looked right or left the impression was of being at a great depth, for they were entering a pass between two of the highest mountains of the New World.

"That," Marina said, looking northward, "is our greatest mountain: The Hill that Smokes. Have you any such in your land?"

They gazed at Popocatepetl, exceeding by two thousand feet the greatest of Alpine heights. A black plume of smoke rose from its volcanic crest to the autumn sky.

"There is none such in my own land," he answered cautiously, "but there are great mountains beyond, which I have not seen."

They looked southward to a mountain of kindred bulk, but a quieter kind—the White Woman, Marina called it—showing bright smooth flanks of eternal snow.

There was one side, she said, from which it really had a vague resemblance to a woman's form, though of course the whiteness—

and then stopped, aware that she had been near to unmannerly speech. The Spaniards couldn't help their queer colour, and in any case, it wasn't white like *that*. It even turned to a quite decent brown when it was exposed to the sun. All the Tlascalan brides agreed that, though it had been repellent at first, they were getting used to it now. For herself, she had loved too greatly to care. (And what difference did it make in the dark?) But she had a doubt of sickening horror at times as to what colour her child might be.

Her thoughts were interrupted by the voice of Diego de Ordaz, the cavalier who was riding at her left hand. "Doña, has it been climbed?"

"No. I suppose that none could, and it is likely that none would dare the cold slippery sides, and the heat above.

"Besides, men believe that demons dwell in such torment there as causes them to cast fire abroad, as they often do. They are said to be the spirits of rulers who did evil before they died."

"You believe that?"

"How should I know?" She gave him one of her quiet smiles. "You can go to look, if you will."

"So I shall, if I have leave."

Cortéz spoke, from her other side: "It may be tried, if you will. You are young. Your feet may hold and your breath last. But I should not like you to fail."

There was a halt on the next day for the laden porters to rest. They were in the midst of dense forests; but the volcanic mountain looked very near.

Diego's idea had become a plan. Nine Spaniards had volunteered to join him, and four Tlascalans had said they would make the attempt in such company, though they would not have done it alone.

They set out at dawn with store of food and such aids to climbing or protection from frozen heights as their foresight suggested, and their resources supplied. They had valour, but little skill for the attempt. At sunset the four Tlascalans returned.

They said that at first the forest had been so dense that their progress had been slow, but, as they went on and up, it had changed its character. There had been no more undergrowth. The straight boles of great pines had been round them, and there had been a soft carpet of pine needles beneath their feet.

Then they had left the pinewoods beneath them. They had gained heights where vegetation failed. Still they had gone upward, although they could now hear the demons bellowing beneath their feet. Soon the bare precipitous slopes became white with hard-frozen snow. They breathed with difficulty in a thin air. The wind was bitter against their backs.

Exhausted by the hazardous, slippery, hard ascent, they had camped under the sheltering side of a great rock, and debated whether more could be done. Around them was bitter cold. Far above was black smoke, lit at times by quick-flickering flame. They looked upward to treacherous heights where a snowslide, a single footslip, would cast them to inescapable death.

The Tlascalans said that they decided to go no farther, not that they were cowards, but because they were sensible men. What was there more to see, or to where should they hope to go?

Would they penetrate the region of fire where the demons howled? Would they swallow the burning cinders on which they fed? No. They came back because they could gain nothing further by going on.

But the Spaniards had decided to continue the climb—and nothing more, they supposed, would be heard of them.

Cortéz listened, and was well content. He did not wish to lose ten of his best men, and he saw danger of that. But he knew that his present security (precarious at the best) was founded on the admission of European superiority, the prestige of the men he led. He praised the courage of those who spoke, and approved what they had done.

As the next day waned, and the adventurers did not return, he asked Marina what was being said about them in the camp, in the strange tongues he was only beginning to understand. She said: "It will mean much that they return. It is said that your God challenges those of this land, even in their stronghold of fire. There will be many at Father Olmedo's font on the next day."

"You do not doubt that they will return?"

"Diego will. He has your eyes. They are eyes that win."

"I should have said that his are darker than mine."

"So they may be. I did not mean that. They are eyes that laugh in a very resolute way."

"Have they skill to see in the dark? It is that they will soon need, for the night is near."

So it was; but in the next hour they came. They were ten sound-limbed, but most weary men. Two of them brought a quaint evidence that they had climbed to the frozen heights—a huge dripping icicle, slung on a pole.

Diego said he had failed. They had climbed to a point where the air was hot, the smoke dense, and falling cinders had burned their clothes, as was plain to see. But they had been turned back by that fiery shower. They might have been near the summit. But he thought not.

However that might be, Cortéz said that they had done boldly and well. He wrote a generous account of the incident for the Court of Spain, to be sent on when the next opportunity should come. As a result, the House of Ordaz quarters a flaming volcano on its coat-of-arms to this day.

The march resumed. The road twisted upward toward a curtain of rock, far lower than the two mountains, but yet at a great height, an unavoidable barrier intervening between them. The air became bitter cold, and the slowly ascending column encountered tempests of sleet and rain.

The hardships of the march were partially mitigated by the fact that the Mexican government had provided shelters at regular intervals. They were solid buildings, substantial and commodious. They sheltered the women, and those who were hurt or sick; and the horses, which Bernal regarded as far more important than they—a preference to which the facts gave some support.

Cortéz looked at these buildings with thoughtful eyes. Their provision was an indication of the settled civilisation of the people on whom he was thrusting his obviously unwelcome presence. Their substantial character was ominous of its most formidable power.

The day came when they ceased to climb. As the little group of horsemen led the advance on the winding rock-walled road they came to a sudden bend, and next moment were looking down on the wide expanse of the Aztec plain.

CHAPTER FORTY-ONE: MONTEZUMA'S LAND

In the clear sunlit air, eight thousand feet above the level of the ocean which they had left less than three months before, the cavaliers looked down on a wide plain which stretched to the limit of vision, where it was bounded by rocky hills as red as those upon which they stood.

They saw green forests, and fields in which rich crops ripened, still unmown (for the season was later in this high plain than in those they had passed before). They saw still lakes, in the midst of the largest of which a great city stood, with palaces and temples that shone in the morning sun.

They saw other cities, gardens and orchards, woodlands, and fields of ripe grain and abundant flowers, that stretched to the far limit of the great plain, the whole of which, from ruin to ruin, resembled an enormous opulent palace garden—the affluent centre of Aztec power.

The band of steelclad cavaliers—formidable, but so few!—gazed down in silence upon a scene of cultured luxuriance, which outdid all that had been forecast by cold doubts or audacious dreams. They had imagined much, but not this.

Beside these palatial cities, these mile-wide garden grounds, Tlascala was a place of hovels, Cholula a vulgar slum.

Cortéz said: "That is plainly México, in the midst of the central lake. There are woods on the further shore, and white towers beyond. What are they?"

"Yes. That is México," Marina replied. "It is the lake of Tezcuco; and it is the city of Tezcuco that lies beyond. It was the ancient capital, before México was built, and its splendour remains today. The prince of Tezcuco is young, but he one of our greatest kings."

"And that city, also in its own lake, that is nearer to us?"

"That is Cuitlahuco. The Lake is Chalco. You can see the causeway which crosses the lake, and the low ground (which is flooded at times, so that the two lakes become one), for several miles. It is a fine city, but, compared with México, it is of little account."

Those around listened to what was said, but they said little themselves.

They saw that they were at the climax of the high folly of that which some of them had been eager, and some persuaded, to do.

And they felt differently now. They were alike in recognising that they were confronted by a magnificence of civilisation, and formidable confidence of unchallenged power, beyond anything that they hoped or feared or expected to meet. But they reacted variously to this entrancing, menacing scene which was spread out beneath them. To some, it was a final warning of the destruction which must be theirs, if they should make further advance: to others a richer lure than they had expected to see.

Perhaps only Cortéz was mentally comprehensive of these conflicting attitudes, the extremity of the risks he took being as clearly seen, as accurately weighed, as was the vastness of the prize which success might bring.

Perhaps Marina alone was entirely, serenely, confident that there was no occasion to doubt at all.

Diego de Ordaz showed the puzzled doubt that lay behind the sanguine audacity of his disposition, as he exclaimed: "Had they meant to stay us, would it not have been done before we had come free of the mountain roads?"

And Pedro de Alvarado, sanguine and bold as he, but of longer practice in the warfare of the New World, touched the weak point of that argument when he replied: "Yes. But they did not mean us to come this way. What should we have met had we come by the southern road?"

Cortéz had the same thought. But he was inclined to the view that vigorous direction would have found time to adjust itself. He wondered, as he had done many times, what the explanation of Montezuma's enigmatic attitude might be. Was it possible that it was the weakness of irresolution? That his own inflexible determination had encountered a wavering will? There was much to support that interpretation, but, against it, was the Emperor's established reputation throughout the land. Surely all men could not be wrong! Surely they were not sternly, if justly, ruled, or brought to reluctant subordination by one who could not, during many weeks, resolve what his course should be.

Wary, doubtful, alert of mind, with smiling eyes that looked right and left in ceaseless vigilance and enquiry, with frequent questions to Marina as to the meanings of what he saw, Cortéz led the little cavalcade on a road that now sloped so sharply downward that their chargers must tread with care, and be held on a steady rein; while behind them came the long procession that still stretched backward for more than two miles in the narrow twisting defile.

They moved slowly, a contingent of steel-capped spearmen being followed by the artillery, with the drag-ropes pulling no longer, but holding back the guns on the falling way. Behind them came a body of laden porters, with the treasure, ammunition, records, and the officer's personal effects; then the women; then the main force of the Spaniards; then the more numerous Tlascalan ranks; then the main body of the porters bearing food and baggage for seven thousand men; and last a rearguard, not large, but selected with care, arquebus and crossbow showing amidst a ring of protecting spears.

As the day passed, they came to a land of hamlets and fertile farms. The inhabitants, at some points, lined the road thickly, curious, friendly, offering not swords but flowers.

Marina talked to them, as Cortéz would have her do, and said they praised the Emperor's rule, if at all, with most grudging words: their young men were conscripted for ceaseless wars, from which many did not return; their young women were required to become the consorts of Aztec nobles.

The exact nature of the second grievance was not simple to understand, under a social system which did not regard polygamy as a derogation of womanhood, did not recognise any status but that of wife, and in which infidelity was a most exceptional vice. But Cortéz said that they should be met with vaguely comforting words: "Do not say that we are hostile to Montezuma. But assure them that a new time has come, and that all grievances will be smoothed away. Tell them they will be under the protection of a most potent God."

The sun was still high when they were met with another embassy from the Aztec ruler. It brought the usual munificent gifts; it made the usual request that the Spaniards would return home. It offered astonishing bribes: four loads of gold for Cortéz himself, and one each for his cavaliers, with the promise of a yearly tribute of gold for his distant King, if only he would return without penetrating into the centre of Aztec power.

But the embassy had come too late. It had lost its point. The Spaniards were already there. The fact was that it had been sent to meet them on the other road. It had not turned back till it had learned that Cortéz had forced his way along the shorter, steeper route.

Now it came in belated, literal obedience to its instructions, doing no more than give further indication of the very subtle or very timorous policy of the Aztec throne.

Cortéz took the gifts. He sent back a courteous, but uncompromising reply. It was too late to turn back. The subjects raised by the envoys could be dealt with best at a personal interview. If his presence should prove unwelcome, perhaps his visit would not be long.

In fact, whatever had been the impulse under which the mission had been dispatched, its effect was only to give greater confidence to those whom it sought to turn. Even if full allowance were made for the fact that gold was abundant and its limited utilities understood among the Aztecs sufficiently to lead them to give it with indifference for the satisfaction of Spanish greed, it remained that the continual efforts at bribery, and suggestions of future tribute (however insincere they might be) could only spring from diffidence or actual fear. Or was there some unguessable reason why Montezuma should be desperately anxious that the strangers should go without sight of the treasures that palace or capital might contain?

Cortéz asked this of Marina, but, when she had told him all she knew, the problem remained unsolved.

CHAPTER FORTY-TWO: COUNSEL IN MÉXICO

Montezuma took counsel with those of his own house whom he trusted most, and who were nearest of blood to him—his brother, Cuitlahua, and his nephew, Cacama, who ruled in the older city of Tezcuco, beyond the lake.

They sat together in his private audience chamber—a small room compared with the vastness of the main reception hall, but with a rich magnificence in its carved cedar-wood ceiling, its gorgeous matting, the priceless tapestries of glowing featherwork which concealed its walls.

They sat or reclined on deep soft cushions around a table which was little more than a foot in height, that being the custom of the land. They had been served with chocolate by an attendant who wore a flowing garment embroidered in gold and green, which indicated that he was a noble of royal blood, for Montezuma disliked any less exalted attendance, and such servitors as the palace held (which is to say hundreds) who were nobles of lower birth, were required to wear coarse garments of unadorned cotton, that all might know how deep was the gulf which lay between them and those they served. The empty cups in which the chocolate had been served were still on the table. They were delicately, beautifully, but plainly made. Their quality, good though it might be, was ruled by the fact that they would never appear again. They would be given away. Fresh plate and pottery must appear at every public banquet or private meal at which the Emperor ate.

His clothing, rich of texture, and richly wrought though it might be, was subject to the same rule. It looked new, as it was, for he never wore a garment twice, and might change as much as three or four times a day.

He was tall, thin, dignified in appearance, remote in manner, restrained in speech, magnanimous if his pride were not touched, carelessly, lavishly generous with the wealth which hard taxation brought to his door from all parts of the World as he had known it up to three months ago.

Three months ago, he had not doubted that he had been the first man in the World, both as king and priest. He would have put priest first. He had been priest for a longer time. When he had been told that he had become the greatest Emperor in the world, he had been found sweeping the temple steps.

He had succeeded to the throne of a great conqueror, whose work had been well-nigh done. He had been the greatest prince in his world at that hour, and from that hour every year had seen his power more absolute, his dominions extended.

Not that he had been an active warrior on many occasions himself. His brother, and other generals, took the field. But the honours had come to him. And each year he had grown more exact in observance of the religion of which he was the earthly head, and more exacting in the deferences which he required, both from noble and common men.

Now he had been disturbed by these swarthy or pink-skinned invaders, who had landed from the sea, with talk—indeed, themselves the proof—of the existence of a land of which he had known nothing before.

They were absurdly few, but they brought strange weapons, strange beasts, and strange thunders that killed those who were far away.

But these were terrors of which brave men should not be too greatly afraid. At sufficient expense of life, they could be wiped out. He had been advised of that from the first. His best generals were agreed upon it, and had urged him to give them a freer hand.

He had not denied that their counsel was good, but he had been deterred by a great doubt. There was an old prophecy about a white God who would come from the Western Sea. He had doubted whether Cortéz were he. He was doubting still. If it were so, should he be opposed by the Chief Priest of the Faith? Would it be possible to oppose him successfully?

Having the doubt, was it not an obvious precaution to do only that which the priestly oracles might advise?

So he had aimed to do, and his resultant difficulty had been that the oracles had been far from clear, or, where they had been definite, as in advising the treachery of Cholula, their advice had not been fortunate in its results.

After that failure, he had reverted to his intermittent attempts to bribe Cortéz to return to the sea with ever more sumptuous gifts, to which he had at last added an offer of perpetual tribute of the gold which the Spaniards showed such an incomprehensible passion to get. It would be a cheap bargain, if their absence could be bought with nothing of more value than that.

Neither brother nor nephew had approved. The first said that it was a position which should be met not with gifts but swords; the second had merely said that it would only encourage the Spaniards to come on.

He, at least, had been right. But Montezuma had intended that the final offer should be made before Cortéz could see the wealth of the Mexican plain. This intention had been frustrated by the forcing of the upper road, and the offer had been abortively, foolishly made when it was almost certain to be put aside, as they had just heard that it had been.

It was a result which left Cuitlahua unmoved, or even something better than that, for he did not approve of these tributes of Mexican gold, and far more valuable things. He said: "First or last, you will find my advice good. It is what you will be obliged to do. Let me set on them with every sword that we have. They will be dead to the last man—to the last horse—in a day, or at most two. Be the cost to us heavy or light, we shall survive that, and all the gold they drag about with them with so much labour (but what else can they do with it? It is useless to eat or wear) will come back to us, with much better things, including the weapons that we have some reason to dread, but which yet can be overcome."

Montezuma looked at him with troubled, irresolute eyes. In this private conference he allowed his emotions to appear as he would not otherwise have done. A stranger might have thought that they would all have been affected by the heavily scented air, which was that of a hundred rose gardens closed in one, but it was too natural to them for any influence to be felt.

He said: "It all fails: violence or craft! If it be a God against whom we contend—"

Cacama replied: "So I have said from the first. Let them come in peace. If we restrain, we do not thereby lessen our power. Let them come in peace, and if we decide that they should be destroyed, it can be on the way back. By your leave, I will meet them, even now, with consenting words, such as will bring all to a good end."

Montezuma looked as though it were counsel he would be ready to take. But then he asked: "Can we do that, with a Spaniard's head in the next room?"

There was certainly a snag there. It was a matter of which he supposed that Cortéz must know, as indeed he did, though no one else in the Spanish camp had been told or guessed, except Marina, who had a vaguely accurate idea of what the truth was likely to be. A messenger had come to Cholula from Vera Cruz, and had seen Cortéz alone, only a few hours after he had given his letter for Escalante to Totonac hands. He had gone back next day, having been confidential with none, in company with others whose orders were not disclosed.

Marina had seen that Cortéz had had news which had put him into a black mood. She saw that he did not mean to tell what it was, even to her. It was easy to guess of what kind it was likely to be.

Cortéz had thought: "They are half of them of a mind to go back: they could be turned by as light a wind as a feather needs. Shall I tell them this? I can spare few men to send to relieve those who are pressed. Will it do good if I say: 'There has been treachery at Vera Cruz, by which two of our men were slain. I suppose that the Aztecs have picked their bones. After that, there was desperate fighting; Escalante, on whom I relied, is dead. Vera Cruz may still stand, or it may not.' Would it do good to say that?"

He thought not.

The head of one of the Spaniards had been sent to Montezuma. He had been a very large man, and those who had killed him were boastful of what they did. The head was huge, swarthy, scowlingly formidable even in death. Montezuma had considered it with less satisfaction for one decease than concern that there should be some hundreds alive of a like kind, who advanced inexorably upon him, with deadly thunders in their control.

Cacama did not dispute that it was a complication to be deplored. He said: "You can assure them that it was done without orders from you."

He thought: "They must be used to hearing that now." But he was a young man of exceptional discretion, and it was not spoken aloud. He did not resist adding: "You will allow that it was against the advice I gave."

"It was," Montezuma said, "by the advice of the gods."

There was no answer to that.

Cacama saw how it would be. He said: "I will set out at once."

Cuitlahua thought: "It is two to one. They will have their way now. But my time will come."

He went out, saying nothing at all. But, after that, he made some military dispositions of those under his control, on which he was more content.

CHAPTER FORTY-THREE: PEACE?

Three days had passed since the Spaniards had first gazed down on the far-spread vista of the Mexican plain, rich with palaces and temples, with fair cities, placid islanded lakes, woodlands, corn lands, and fields of flowers.

They had advanced in a leisurely manner, increasingly astonished at the numbers of the inhabitants, the style of the houses, and the evidences of wealth and culture around them. They were now at Agotzinco, a considerable town on the edge of the lake of Chalco.

For the first time they saw houses built on piles, spreading far out into the water, with intervening canals, and many canoes moving upon the lake. They saw also, for the first time, the floating artificial islands with which they would become familiar in later days. Some were covered with flowers; there were others on which vegetables were grown.

The people through whom they passed had been friendly, curious, generous. Even the Tlascalans, traditional enemies though they were, had had no cause for complaint. There had been much bartering, with difficulties of language to be overcome. Everywhere there had been profusion of given flowers.

But there had been an unhappy incident during the night. The untimely curiosity of some Aztecs, and the alert watchfulness of the Spanish sentries, had resulted in shots being fired. Some wounds, possibly some fatalities, had resulted, which had been exaggerated by report.

With the dawn, Cortéz had sent apology by Marina for an incident which should not have occurred, yet for which he did not feel that his sentries should be blamed. But it showed how little of real cordiality, of confidence, lay beneath the surface of this contact of alien civilisations.

When Marina came back, she said: "I have laid the blame on them, as you would have it to be. You will hear no more about that. But there is an envoy from Montezuma here. I have brought him through the lines, but he will speak only with you."

"Are we to have gifts, and a fresh admonition not to advance?"

"There are no gifts. It is one man alone. He brings a written letter which I must read."

So it was. It was a scroll of picture-writing, the interpretation of which was a mystery that would never be mastered by Cortéz, or any Spaniard he led.

Marina gave it a glance. She said: "The Emperor asks you, of your courtesy, to await an embassy which will meet you here. The Prince of Tezcuco himself is on his way, and will arrive two hours before noon."

"That is not long to wait. Who is he?"

"He is a great prince in his own right. He is next to Montezuma himself. He is young, and is liked by all. You would find it hard to quarrel with him." She added: "It is a great honour to you, which all men will understand."

"He is one to trust?"

"I should say he is one to trust well. But there may be more than I know."

"Well, say I will meet him here."

He ordered that a chain of glass crystals should be unpacked, that he might have a gift in readiness of the right kind.

At the stated hour, he rode out a short way to meet the Prince of Tezcuco, taking with him only Marina, and the four captains, to whom he was now accustomed to give the most confidence that he allowed to any—Alvarado, Sandoval, Velásquez, and Ordaz.

He rode unarmoured, wearing only his sword, and the girl beside him was evidence of his peaceful mood, but the four cavaliers were in complete steel, bearing lance and shield. The heavy chargers wore frontlets of steel, and silk housings that fell nearly to the ground, making mystery both of man and beast. Even the steel itself was strange and formidable to Aztec eyes.

"I come in peace," the strange invader seemed to say, by the manner of the approach, "but you see what the alternative might have been."

But there was no fear in the eyes of the young prince who descended from a closed litter that flashed with jewels and shone with gold.

The road was hard and dry, but obsequious attendants swept it before his feet, in what was evidently a ritual way.

Cortéz, descending from his own horse, with Marina beside him, saw a man about ten years younger than himself, spare, but athletic of form, who advanced lightly toward him, and met him with frank, fearless, and friendly eyes.

Great prince though he was, he gave the Aztec greeting appropriate to those of high rank, bending to touch the ground with one hand, and then raising it to his head; but it was done in an easy natural way, and he took embrace which the unbending Cortéz bestowed upon him with the same ease, as though that method of greeting were not alien to all he had been taught or experienced.

He said: "I have come to welcome you to México in the Emperor's name. If there be anything of necessity or comfort that you require, you have only to let it be known, for he would receive you as honoured guests, both for yourselves and your distant King."

It was a greeting of greater sincerity, and more adroitly worded than the previous messages of Montezuma had been, and it was followed by a well-chosen present, of a more portable kind than were those which Montezuma had given—three large and lustrous pearls, the value of which would have been agreed by the peoples of every land. But the glass necklace which Cortéz gave in return was of even greater value, in a land where the secret of glass-making was unknown, and Cacama's appreciation was not in doubt.

Though doing all in a leisurely and most courteous manner, the young prince did not prolong the interview. Having said what the occasion required, he returned to his stately green-plumed litter, and his numerous retinue of Aztec nobles fell in behind it, as it was borne away.

Cortéz rode back to where his troops were already arranging themselves to resume their march. He may have been more content in mind than at any time since he had left the rising fortifications of Vera Cruz. He thought that the Prince of Tezcuco had spoken with sincerity, and that, whatever might have been intended earlier, the Emperor had now reconciled himself to the audience which had been pressed upon him, and decided to give it a peaceful reception.

Marina agreed. She could see no other possible explanation of the Prince of Tezcuco's condescension. He would not, she said, have done it for anyone in the Western World.

Father Olmedo's hopes, though scarcely his expectations, looked the same way.

"My son," he said, when the evening came, and he had an opportunity of talking to Cortéz apart, "may we not seek now for a path of peace, and avoid violent debate?"

"Father, so I would. Have I sought strife? Yet I am the servant of God and Spain. Am I not called of God to establish Faith in a heathen land?"

"So I think that you are. But it is that which should be done in such ways as will be pleased by a God of Love."

He went off to his own tent, where he lived in a plain way, unsure of the wisdom of what he had said, or of much more which he did not say.

He was a man without fear, but also without pugnacity. He understood the spirit of his religion far better than did many of the zealous laymen who did violence with devout wills.

Hearing the confessions of his Commander, he knew him as none other, even Marina, did. He knew that this wild expedition of exploration, conversion and conquest, might have been in far worse, but could not have been in more capable hands. He knew that Cortéz considered that almost any violence or slaughter would be well-pleasing to God if it should result in the baptism even of reluctant ignorant men. Did he himself deny that? Rigid dogma fought with the spirit of Christ in a mental conflict which would never be lost or won, *I came not bringing concord, but division.* Those were the words of the Prince of Peace. Was there explanation in that?

CHAPTER FORTY-FOUR:
THE PALACE OF MANY FLOWERS

With the lake of Chalco upon its right, and deep woodlands on its other hand, the lengthened procession continued westward through scenes of beauty and settled peace, until it came to a great causeway which had been built out into the water for several miles, the direct northward road to the palace-city of Montezuma's brother, Iztepalapan, which was only a few miles from México.

Cortéz reined up as this huge causeway came in view. At its southern end, though its substance was solid stone, its upper surface was not more than eight yards in breadth. How long would be the train of horses, hand-dragged cannon, more than six thousand soldiers, and further thousands of burden men? What would be its front of defence, if it should be attacked from the lake, which was thronged with boats? Or if, when most of its strength should be moving forward upon the dyke, a hostile force should assault those who were still to come?

The danger was plain. But he had better expectation of good faith being meant since he had been met by Tezcuco's prince, and hesitation would have been foolish now. The die was cast, though it might yet lie beneath an unlifted cup.

"Alvarado," he said, "you will go ahead, taking four of the cavaliers. Do not halt till the dyke is passed. Marina, you stay with me."

He remained at the head of the dyke, somewhat aside, directing a new order of march, so that there would be no long train of women, or baggage of price, which could be assailed from the water and not swiftly relieved. The cannon were divided into twos, which were widely apart, and drawn by their own crews, who had them shotted, and ready to be swung round at an instant need. The parties of women, and the treasure bearers, were broken up in the same way, with spearmen before and behind, and the mounted captains dispersed among them.

He did not move forward himself until the whole of the Spaniards, and such baggage as he would have been most troubled to miss, had gone ahead, and only the Tlascalans and the main body of porters remained.

Alvarado rode on till, in the very midst of the lake, they came to a city of some extent, built entirely on piles (for the lake, though of wide extent, was not of a great depth). And here his orders not to halt became hard to observe, for Aztec hospitality had provided refreshments for the whole host, which no one would choose to miss.

He observed the spirit, though not the letter of his orders, by spreading out, as space allowed here, so that there was no halt for those coming behind, until Cortéz himself appeared, by which time, being refreshed in a quick way, the head of the column was moving forward again.

North of this water-city, the dyke was much wider, so that advance could be made with ease on a broad front, and so the whole army, unmolested except by curious folk in the canoes (who had clambered up, and been a crowding nuisance at times, as curiosity led them to do), they came to the greatest, loveliest place that they had yet seen, the garden city of Iztepalapan.

They had learnt from the first that the New World was a land of flowers, and of brilliant birds, making a jest of those which Europe could show. Now they saw gardens which had no rivals in the Old World, and aviaries the limits of which were beyond sight, and their contents, brilliant with parrots and pheasants, and varied from hummingbirds to mountain eagles, were beyond the previous imagination of those who gazed.

Cuitlahua had not changed his belief that the Spaniards should be destroyed, but that did not affect the hospitality with which he received them.

A ceremonial reception, to which other princes of royal blood had been invited to meet the strangers, and at which lavish presents were bestowed upon them, was followed by a palace banquet for Cortéz and his cavaliers, of a magnificence which led him to ask himself, what had the Old World to compare with this? And—of more immediate concern to him—what of military power did it imply?

He was approaching the citadel of a civilisation which he had challenged, if not defied; and he could already see that it was of a more settled and menacing strength than his most anxious doubt had thought it to be.

Not that any display of force was before him now. The absence of such a show, the apparent indifference with which his armed intrusion appeared to be received, might be variously interpreted; but was not its most probable interpretation that Montezuma was too assured of overwhelming power to be troubled by any threat it could be to him? Or perhaps he might regard it as no more than the peaceful mission which it professed? That might be. But against it was the fact that six thousand Tlascalans were in his train. What were they doing there, in the very citadel of their country's foes? And why did Montezuma accept their presence without remark?

So he thought, the while he showed a front of smiling courtesy to his Aztec hosts. Among his captains he was quick to laugh, or to respond to another's jest. But Marina, unwinding flowers from her hair, as they prepared for their common couch, and twisting fresh ones to greet the night, saw that he was an anxious man.

And while the banquet had taken its lavish course, the Emperor of the New World, sitting alone at his evening meal, as his custom was, had shown as serene a front to the waiting nobles who brought in a score of various dishes, that he might eat what he would without the need to order, or have a moment's delay.

He was as serene to the observation of the jugglers who performed before him at the next hour. He listened with inscrutable eyes when his jester made a remark concerning the Spaniards which could be taken in more ways than one. But when the girls of his zenana, who were on the list for the (five-day) week, sent in the names of those who were ready and fit to obey the royal command, they waited through an unprecedented, impatient hour to know which he would have, and were told at last that no one would be required.

So he lay alone, and slept ill.

CHAPTER FORTY-FIVE: ENTRANCE TO MÉXICO

In these days, before the great woods were felled, and the rainfall lessened, the two lakes were so nearly one that they would often unite their waters in time of flood. The band of horsemen who led the van arrived at the southern shore of Tezcuco's lake before the last porters had fallen in at the distant rear.

Yesterday they had been astonished by the length and substance of Chalco's dyke. Now they were doubly amazed at the sight of a causeway in comparison with which it was no more than a trivial thing.

Straight and far, across a lake which was still half hidden in morning mist, stretched a causeway of concrete and solid stone, of such width that the cavaliers, eight of whom had been riding, two by two, behind their Commander and Doña Marina, now spread out in a single rank.

The problem of array might be similar to those of the previous morning, but their solution was simpler, for non-combatants and precious baggage could now be protected by a file of spearmen on either side.

Mile after mile, the great causeway struck its straight way through the lake; sometimes giving a wide view of waters which were deserted except for a passing canoe, or a floating island of flowers; sometimes passing through villages built on piles, the inhabitants of which occupied themselves in abstracting salt from the waters of the lake.

The leading cavaliers were approaching the centre of the lake, and were less than two miles from the lake-city which was their final goal, when they were confronted by a twelve-foot-high barrier of stone, very solidly built, with a central gateway and flanking towers. It was an obstacle which they might have found hard to surmount, had they come in a hostile way, but now the gate swung open at their approach, and the wide causeway beyond was bright with the gay apparel of some hundreds of Aztec nobles who had assembled from courtesy, curiosity, or their Emperor's command, to welcome the outlandish invaders.

Here there was long delay, for each must be introduced separately to Cortéz, and give his country's salute, but he endured the ordeal with a smiling courtesy which did not lessen, and Marina gave him their names in an untiring way, while the two-mile train behind them relaxed, and rested upon the dyke.

But the last noble, gay with jewels and featherwork as a tropic bird, had touched the ground, and been cordially embraced at last, and as he climbed into the litter which would take him back to his city home, Cortéz gave the signal for the slow march to resume.

The final obstacle they encountered was a drawbridge, which was lowered to enable them to pass a wide gap in the dyke, and when this was crossed, they saw that the causeway had become a long straight street, continuing for as far as their eyes could follow it, with buildings on either side.

Most of these were of red stone sometimes elaborately carved, but seldom of more than one or two stories, though there were high temples with summits on which fires never ceased to burn.

But their eyes were drawn from all other sights when a glittering procession turned into the street and advanced toward them, in the centre of which the Emperor's palanquin was bright with gold, and brilliant with featherwork. Barefooted nobles bore it. Others supported a canopy, shining with silver, and plumed highly in royal green.

The palanquin came to rest, and the man who had been undisputed lord of the known world, until this strange oversea shadow had darkened before him, descended from it.

The Spaniards were aware of barefooted nobles spreading cloth on the ground for him to tread on as he advanced. They were aware that the watching crowds were bending humbly with downcast eyes, or stretched in adoration upon the ground. But their attention was not for them.

They saw a monarch who was taller than most of those he ruled, graceful in movement, and with an air of dignity, serene and benign, which it might be thought by those who worshipped around him that nothing could overcome.

He wore a white, girdled cloak, embroidered, and studded with emeralds and other jewels of the same colour. His headdress was a high plume of green feathers, curving downward behind his back.

Cortéz, with Marina, and the four captains who were immediately behind him, dismounted, and advanced with equal deliberation.

Marina translated the words of courteous greeting with which the Aztec monarch welcomed his uninvited guest, and rendered the equally conventional, and perhaps almost equally insincere, reply.

Then Cortéz stepped forward. He placed a chain of coloured crystals around the neck of the impassive Emperor. Never lacking in the cool assurance which he might consider that the occasion required, he would have embraced him next moment, had not two of the attendant nobles moved forward hastily to protect the person of him who was sacred both as priest and monarch from further sacrilege.

"My brother," Montezuma said, "will have the honour of conducting you to the accommodation I have arranged."

He turned as he spoke, and re-entered his litter. As he did so, the Spanish trumpets sounded a bold advance. The strange sound might be taken as tribute or defiance by those who heard. Downcast eyes lifted again to the steelclad cavaliers. Even the trumpet-flourish could not deaden the strange sound of steel-shod hooves on the concrete pavement, or the rumble of the wheels of the gun-carriages— themselves a miracle of movement to those who had never seen or imagined a wheel before.

But while Mexican eyes gazed, with mingled admiration, wonder, and fear, at the advancing Spaniards, they looked at that which was an equal enigma to them.

They knew that they were in the midst of a great lake, on the floor of which must be the foundations of all they saw. But there was no suggestion of instability, or even of space being a restraining consideration. The broad street stretched straight ahead for several miles, and there was the firmness of concrete beneath their feet. The red stone houses had flat parapeted roofs, which were seldom of a height of more than one story. But many of them were spacious—sprawling rather than compact, and some had wide gardens around them to serve the Aztec need of perpetual flowers. Only the occasional temples were lofty—pyramids that rose to an altar-crest of continual flame.

There was no suggestion that the city was not built on solid earth—it might, indeed, have been laid out on a specious plain, where acreage was of no account—except that some of the narrow side streets showed glimpses of water instead of stone; canals came up to the main thoroughfare on either side, and sometimes passed under bridges beneath their feet.

There was a very wide open space in the centre of the city, beside which rose the great pyramidal temple with which only that which had been stormed at Cholula could be compared. And opposite to it there was a range of buildings of great extent, with spacious courtyards around them, which the Spaniards were invited to enter.

As Cortéz did so, he saw that Montezuma was standing there to receive him. As he dismounted, the Emperor said: "This was my father's palace. It is now unoccupied, and is for you to use as you will. You will need rest, having come so far, by so steep a way."

As he spoke, he placed a rich chain of jewels and goldsmiths' work round the neck of his guest. If that were the etiquette among Eastern kings, he would not fail in the courtesy which the occasion required. So he had said, and a chain had been very quickly found.

"I will return in the evening," he said, "for there is much of which we shall wish to talk."

Meanwhile the long files of the Spanish army were entering through the palace gates, pausing only to allow outward passage for the royal palanquin, and its attendant nobles.

Cortéz looked round at the ample courtyard: he looked at the surrounding wall, which was high and thick. Alvarado said: "We should be secure here, though an army were round the gate."

"Yes," his Commander replied, "we could stay and starve! But could we fight our way out? Will you tell me that?"

"So, if the need should come, I should see you do," was the confident and diplomatic reply, but it did not change the look of careful calculation with which Cortéz surveyed the scene.

"Pedro," he said, "I will have every man or woman who came with us, to the last porter or camp-follower, within these walls, and none shall go out except by a written order from you. Will you see to that? Diego, will you see what dispositions for their reception can best be made? Bernal, you must find a sound roof for the horses. They must come before men, for they are of more value. Mesa, will you place the guns at such angles as will be best for a good defence?"

He turned to Marina, who had been standing beside him in a waiting silence: "You have something that I should hear?"

"It is only that you may stay here for this day at least, and not starve. There is a steward here, who says that there will be shelter within the walls for all you bring, and food for eight thousand mouths is near to come.

"For ourselves, there is banquet laid in the central palace, where they will expect you to make abode."

"Then we will go there, and select rooms, that the baggage may be brought in."

They realised the extent of the accommodation the palace provided as they walked to a central building which was conspicuous as the only one which had a second story.

Here they came to the luxuries of tapestried walls, soft-matted floors, and furniture of scented woods, finely carved. The bed chambers had the low padded floor-mattresses which were universal in that land, but their canopies, of featherwork or embroidered cotton, were such as only nobles could hope to own. And there were flowers—everywhere flowers. But these were no more, an Aztec would have said, than is indispensable to any civilised men.

Alone with Marina (excepting only for the attendance of an Aztec slave, of which a number had been provided for their comfort, and who would certainly have no knowledge of the Spanish tongue), in the bedchamber which he had selected for their own use, he spoke the doubt which was most prominent in his mind.

"I have told Pedro," he said, "that all men shall be confined within these walls, unless they have written exits from him. There will be grumbling at that; but it is the way of peace. I meant it more for the Tlascalans than for those of my own land, for these men are their bitter foes. Or, at least, they were; and it would be ill for us if that enmity should be overcome."

"You have less than a sure trust that they will be loyal to you?"

"I have little doubt. But a little doubt is too much to have. Are you sure yourself? You have seen falsehood before which was hidden from us."

"I think they will be loyal so long as they are sure that they are not doubted by you."

"Well, they should see that now! I have kept my own men ever apart (as I did at Cholula) until today. But this is a new thing to have them within one wall. If they should be bought at a great price, is it not what this Montezuma might be tempted to do? And we could be massacred in the night!"

"I should say it is a small risk, they hating each other as they do, and the more you show you trust them, the less it is. But I will be wary to watch and hear."

"Well, it is a risk we must take, and you are right that it should be done in a bold way. But I have a doubt that I did wisely to bring them here."

CHAPTER FORTY-SIX: EXTREMES MEET

In the evening, Montezuma came again, as had been arranged. When Cortéz heard that he was approaching with about a dozen of the greatest of the tributary kings and nobles who supported his throne, he summoned the same number of his own officers to attend himself, and when Montezuma was seated, and his companions remained standing around him, the officers of Cortéz grouped themselves in the same way.

Emperor and Commander faced one another, seated on cushions either side of a small low sandalwood table, with Marina between, and their supporting groups stood behind them for two hours in respectful silence. But the time did not seem long to them—they were too intent to listen to what was said.

Montezuma had come to learn. His questions were worded with great politeness, but they were of a probing quality.

The Emperor's first questions were addressed to Marina herself, though he had the courtesy to ask permission for what he did.

"Will you ask your lord's consent that you should tell me of whom and how long you come to be where you are?"

Cortéz said, when he heard this: "Tell him what you will, and you may add that you are assured that what you now do has the high favour of God."

She answered Montezuma without embarrassment, and with little reserve. When she had been a heiress in her own right, she would have thought it a wonder beyond belief that she should be talking freely with him who was the whole world's lord, both as priest and King, and whom the highest nobles approached with unsandalled feet.

Since then she had endured the indignities of a purchased slave, and now she had become one concerning whom the Emperor had an enquiring mind.

He asked: "You are Aztec born?"

"Yes."

"Where?"

"In the northeast of this country."

"You could be more explicit."

"It would be beneath your regard."

"You were well taught?"

"I was in the sacred college for several years."

"And how came you into the Spaniards' hands?"

"I was presented to them as a slave, having been sold to a Tabascan noble, who gave me to them."

"So I knew. You are one who speaks truth without waste of words. Are you loyal to these men, or your own land? Or do you think to be both?"

"I am my lord's wife."

"That answers much, but not all. Are they friends at heart to us, or malign foes?"

"They are foes to some of our gods."

"I know that. Have you cast your faith?"

"When I was at the College, there was a priestess who taught me much of Quetzalcoatl, a god I loved."

"You think this to be he, or to come from him?"

"It is a natural thought. Do they not come from the Eastern Sea?"

"It is that which our priests deny with one voice, though they see them come with lightnings, and other most godlike powers. Knowing them as you must, do you say they are civilised men?"

"They have some cruel and savage ways, but they have others which are better than ours. They think us to be less civilised than themselves."

"That is absurd. They have cruel habits, and they are seldom quite clean. Even you have not taught them the use of flowers. Perhaps there may be men of better customs in their own land. Their King may not have sent us the best he had."

"It is of that I am less than sure."

"So am I. Yet, if Quetzalcoatl—"

He broke off, aware that he was going beyond questioning of fact, to speculations which it might be foolish to speak aloud, where his own nobles could hear, and understand a doubt which the priests condemned, but which had been torturing his own mind, and weakening his decisions from the day which he had first heard that the Spanish ships were anchoring off the shore. And Marina showed that she had been infected by the same doubt.

For Quetzalcoatl had been a benign god (if god he were) or a godlike man who had taught faith of a Christlike kind in earlier centuries, before the Aztecs invaded the land. It was for his worship that the first temple had been built, before it had been imagined that blood must be shed at a god's feet.

He taught mercy and faith, and (men said) he had not died, but had entered a boat which had sailed out into the shoreless sea, after saying that he would return on a far day, with redemptive power. And he had been a white, bearded man, as these strangers were. Montezuma broke off, to say, as one who recalls the present need to a wandering mind: "But your lord waits. Will you ask him with what purpose he has come to this distant land, and if he would ask more from one who has given much, as it has been pleasure to do?"

After that, the talk went on for two hours, Marina interpreting well, as both sides believed, though each must take on trust that which, from its nature, could not be proved.

The Aztecs heard Montezuma's questions, and then, after she had talked with Cortéz in a strange tongue, the reply she gave in their own.

The Spaniards waited in turn, heard her talk to Montezuma in strange words, and then heard another question in Spanish from her. Both sides could only hope that she interpreted correctly, and that they were making their meaning clear. It was not an unusual position when men of different nations confer, except in the fact that she was the only one in the whole land who could use both tongues. No one could check what was said.

She might be telling the Aztecs how to break in during the night, aware that it would be impossible for the Spaniards to understand her treachery, or for anyone to inform them thereof.

What was happening was that the Aztec Emperor, in his courteous, dignified, remote way, was making questions to which replies which would be both polite and correct were not always easy to give.

He would know the distance that divided Spain from his own land, its size and population, the status of the Spaniards when at home—were they blood-relations to the King? Did they assist him to rule? Why, precisely had they been sent at this time? How soon did they propose to return? And would others come?

Cortéz replied with much detail, and an appearance of frankness. In fact, he aimed to tell as much truth as the occasion would bear.

He said his monarch was very great, and must be considered first in the whole world. He picked his servants with wisdom, employing each in that for which he was best suited. He himself had been chosen for this mission, for which he must humbly suppose that he was more fit than others.

Its object was to make the acquaintance and friendship of Montezuma, and, above all, to bring knowledge of the True Faith, by which alone men could come to God.

Montezuma, putting the question of religion aside, said that he accepted the assurances he received. He had always been reluctant to doubt, and had sent gifts from time to time to demonstrate his goodwill. But he had been misinformed. He had been told that the Spaniards attacked those they met, killing them with lightning in most cruel ways. But now he had seen them, he could realise how much he had been misled.

Cortéz replied that it was true that the powers of thunder and lightning were his, but they could be used for purposes of peaceful honour, as well as death.

It was thus that his guns would speak that night, harming none, but firing a salute of honour to the Emperor, which he was anxious should not be misunderstood.

Montezuma accepted Marina's assurance about that, showing an impassive face to an honour which he might not welcome, but recognising the sincerity of her assurance that there would be thunder and lightning without harm to any. What greater evidence could there be, she adroitly asked, of goodwill than that the lightning should show itself as lying harmless and tamed at the Emperor's feet?

He made no answer to that. But said, with grave condescension: "It is a most fortunate and marvellous chance that all went as it did—so that you came to your lord when it was essential that he should have speech with those of our world."

"Yes," she said, "there have been many chances alike to that. For Christ is a potent God."

He rose, asking that he might be told the names of the Spanish officers, and the appointments which were theirs. At this time there were four—León de Velásquez, Alvarado, and the two younger men who had proved their worth, Sandoval and Ordaz, who were nearest to their leader's confidence, and in the greatest authority under him; but, to the Aztecs who heard the occupations of each, it was Mesa, who controlled the lightning that left the guns, and Bernal Díaz, who ruled the horses, who were regarded as holding the highest ranks.

As the Emperor left, he mentioned, as a matter of small account, that he had brought some gifts which would be found in the outer courtyard.

Cortéz asked if he might wait on him in his palace next morning, for which permission was readily granted.

When Montezuma had re-entered his palanquin, the gifts were inspected. They had not been brought in, because they could not have been accommodated in an interior space. There were new garments for all who followed the banner of Spain. Even for the hated Tlascalans there were six thousand tunics of quilted cotton from the military storehouses of the city. And there were gold chains for the Spaniards, their greed for that metal being an idiosyncrasy that Montezuma never forgot. Surely, if munificence could prevail—!

At a later hour, the eight cannon thundered the promised salute. Their flashes lit the darkness, terrifying the crowds that still thronged in the great square, which the black powder filled with sulphurous smoke.

But Cortéz had kept his word. No one was hurt. And by that forbearance he had demonstrated his power more than if he had strewn the square with a hundred dead. Even the lightning was tamed by him, so that, without his permission, it dared not kill.

CHAPTER FORTY-SEVEN: PEACE OR SWORD

After a day of toil, Cortéz slept well in the canopied palace bed, his arm holding one who was more wakeful than he, for her conversation with Montezuma, and her renewed contacts with her own people, had raised many contending thoughts, and speculations as to what the future would bring.

It was not merely that she was unsure of what tolerable issue there could be from the contest of races and faiths which she saw to be nearing a decisive hour. She was uncertain of what she would wish it to be.

The thought that these white strangers from the unknown were those whose coming had been foretold had been prominent in her mind from the hour when she had first seen the great vessels, with folded wings, riding at anchor beside the shore. It had been supported by the fanatic determination of their leader—more uncompromising even than that of Father Olmedo—to establish the Faith he brought, and to overthrow the worship of those gods who had been brought into the land by her own Aztec ancestors, long after the departure of Quetzalcoatl, and which had overlaid the simplicity of the faith he taught, with elaborate ritual, and sacrifices which he certainly would not have approved.

The slaying of human victims, however mitigated by an atmosphere of music and flowers, and by the belief that their present pain would be rewarded by endless bliss, is so repulsive to normal minds that it may tend to obscure the fact that the Aztec religion had fundamental similarities to that of the Catholic Church, which Marina had now been taught to prefer.

They both worshipped one supreme, omnipotent, omniscient, spiritual Deity, of whom no image was made. Some of their prayers to him were of a spirit and wording which might have won prominent positions in a Christian prayer book. While there was no suggestion of Trinitarian doctrine, there was the Christlike, semi-godlike figure of Quetzalcoatl, whose teachings were closely similar to the moral standards of Christianity. The difference was in the bloody ritual which had been introduced by the worshippers of inferior deities, recognised as subordinate, but whose sacrifices had now become the universally dominant feature of religious worship throughout the land. Against which, it might be partially argued, there was nothing in the Aztec religions, at their worst, to compare with the idea that the supreme God would keep alive, in eternal torment, those who had opposed His will.

Even in their religious practices and ceremonies there were extraordinary similarities, suggestive of a common origin at some prehistoric period. That of infant baptism into the church was almost identical; and confessions (with two important deviations) could win priestly absolutions in the same way. The deviations were that a man might not confess twice to the same manner of sin, and that absolution would win immunity from the penalties of civil law. (How could man punish that which had been pardoned by God?) This might have resulted in prompt and frequent resort to confession, but for the qualification that it must be followed by abstention from the same species of sin, which caused prudent men to delay it till the autumn of life, when it could be done comprehensively, and they could act with sufficient subsequent circumspection to assure their post-mortem welfare.

Marina did not doubt or regret. She did not doubt that she had a more potent Deity, and a better faith. She particularly liked its major novelty, which was the worship of the Mother of God. She would have welcomed the adoption of Christianity throughout the land. But she could not imagine that it would occur in a speedy and peaceful manner. Popular superstitions were too deeply rooted, vested interests were too strong for that. Montezuma himself might find it beyond his power.

Yet she saw that Cortéz was determined to bring it about, and she had learnt that, though pliant in method, he was inflexible in resolution. She could only wonder and fear what the end would be.

In the morning, accompanied only by Marina and ten of his principal officers, and preceded by court officials with golden wands clearing the way, Cortéz set out on foot to cover the short distance to the palace of Montezuma.

It was of the same structure, and built of the same red stone as his father's palace, and it sprawled over a huge space in the same way. But it was fronted with red marble, more beautiful, and far more costly than the red stone which was in general use, it being obtained from a quarry near the shore of the lake; it was of even greater—far greater—extent; it was surrounded by well-kept gardens with many fountains, and pleasant groves; and it was alive with the coming and going of princes and nobles, courtiers and suitors, tradesmen and servitors, such as must always be in attendance upon the monarch of a great realm.

The Spaniards, martially clad rather in steel than silk, but unweaponed, except for the swords which they always wore, were led through a low-ceiled but very spacious anteroom, crowded with those who had petitions for Montezuma, or business with the officers of the court, but they were allowed precedence over all, and conducted without delay to the Emperor's presence.

He sat on the low cushions which were customary to all whose dignity did not allow them to be acquainted with a bare floor, in a room which was smaller than that through which they had passed, but more ornate in its appointments. He had with him his brother and nephew, with three others as richly dressed, by which they showed that they were all of the royal blood. The nobles who entered with Cortéz paused at the threshold, to put off their sandals, and to take coarse overalls from waiting slaves, with which they covered their own attires.

Montezuma was gracious: "You have slept well? You have had every comfort that you require?"

Cortéz replied with the appreciation which he had good reason to feel; but he came at once to the object of his visit: he had requested this audience for the urgent purpose of acquainting the Emperor with the True Faith, that he might find salvation, not only for his own soul, but for a whole nation to whom his example would not be lost.

He watched Marina interpret this announcement to one who received it with a noncommittal politeness, and went on to a detailed exposition of the theological basis of Catholic Faith, and then to assertion of the literal nature of the Genesis parable of the creation of man, ending with an exhortation that Montezuma would accept the Faith, and win Divine favour by establishing the Cross in his heathen land.

To this audacious proposal, urged with the sincerity of one who believed that he was the instrument of God for the conversion of heathen men, and interpreted by one who had already accepted this Faith, and could present it with knowledge of where it harmonised or clashed with the beliefs of her own land, Montezuma returned a temperate but uncompromising reply.

"There are," he said, "many beliefs which we have in common. We believe in a supreme spiritual Deity. We have similar traditions concerning the creation of man. We have very similar moral codes. We practice baptism and confession alike. We are alike in having subordinate manlike gods, though they are not yours. There should be a basis of understanding, of toleration here. But I cannot be false to our own gods, who have been very faithful to us, and raised us to supremacy over many lands."

His thoughts went beyond what he spoke aloud. He knew that even he would be powerless to persuade his nation to such a course. But that would have been foolish to say. Were his own lips to deny the accepted delusion that he had absolute power?

Cortéz replied with what he considered to be moderation, in repudiation of a monstrous blasphemy. He was glad that the Emperor recognised the degree to which God had been gracious in revealing Himself to the Western World. But the so-called gods that were worshipped in Aztec temples could not be compared with Christ, or the Mother of Christ. They were demons, leading those who trusted them to the dreadful gates of eternal hell. Did not the bloody sacrifices which they required demonstrate what they were?

Even as Marina rendered this reply, correctly in substance, but in far less offensive phrasing than Cortéz had used in his own tongue, it was a challenge which no Aztec could be expected to hear without resentment and repudiation. Those who stood beside their seated monarch, being the greatest men in the empire except himself, were only partially successful in maintaining the impassive demeanour which the etiquette of the occasion required, while Montezuma replied, with somewhat colder courtesy than before, that it was beyond serious consideration that he should repudiate the gods of his fathers, of whose worship he was now the head priest, and whose protection had brought him to where he was.

"Cannot," he finally asked Marina, "Malintzin"—(which was the title he always gave to Cortéz)—"cannot he see that he asks that which is much beyond reason or possibility, as if I were to require him to abandon the faith which is dear to him?"

"I will tell him that," she replied, "but it is the custom of human sacrifices which revolts his mind, to a degree which is not easy to understand."

"Yet, be that as it may, it is a custom that will not change. You can tell him, also, that we consider that, in this way of dealing with those we defeat in war, we show a civilisation, a humanity, and a sense of practical values, superior to those which his people have.

"They maim, and wound, and leave their victims squirming about in ways, and to an extent, which we should be most reluctant to do.

"And there are two things that you may add. We do not eat those of our own kin, preferring to consume them with fire; and I have been debating a law which would entirely prohibit the slaughter of private slaves, but there are complications involved, and I would do justice to all."

Still with the same aloof dignity, he watched Marina convey in the unknown tongue the substance of what he said. He saw the anger that came to Malintzin's eyes, and he thought that Marina argued to bring him to reason, or a more placable mood. It was no surprise, when she turned to him, and said: "It is a matter on which my lord cannot give way, for he would incur the anger of his own God. Who would wish to do that? But he will talk of it at another time."

There was a slight stir when she had said this, as though men relaxed, in the belief that the audience was done, but Montezuma motioned with an imperative hand.

"I have more to say.

"I know that there was a white God who left this land in the ancient times, taking the way of the Western sea, and telling men that he would return at a later age. I can believe (though I have had reason to doubt at times) that Malintzin and his companions are of the same blood, or are sent by others who are.

"I would live at peace with the great King who has sent them here. And to that end I will pay an annual tribute of gold to exalt his name. Let Malintzin rest here in peace for what time he will, before he returns to his own land.

"More than that. I will do the will of his King, in all things I may, as though I were vassal to him. But there is one thing of which he should think well. Every chain has its own strength. If it be strained too far, it will break apart."

As he said these last words, his impassive dignity failed. To the surprise of all, and the consternation of those of his own house, his voice broke, and men saw tears in his eyes.

Recovering himself while Marina transmitted what he had said, he rose from his seat of cushions. "There are gifts," he said, in his usual remote voice, "for those who have come here." So there were. Bernal Díaz, standing back among officers who regarded themselves as of more account, being better born than he, yet had two heavy collars of solid gold. He said to Marina, as they passed out: "Doña, we could have all, if he would let them run loose in their heathen mode." She was unsure whether he grumbled, or simply said what he saw to be fact, in his blunt way.

She answered, from a confused mind: "Do your horses run loose, or do you require of them more than that?

Meanwhile, Montezuma was saying to his brother: "You think me weak. But I am a priest first, and then King. I will hold our faith though the skies fall."

"You are King," was the answer he got. "You must take your way. But is it wrong if I think of our house's crest?"

There was no easy answer to that, for their crest was a mountain eagle, holding its prey in its claws.

As brother and nephew went out, the young prince of Tezcuco said: "It would be better if he would take either road in a settled way, but he stands at gaze where they divide."

"So it is. But we should sharpen swords. For their hour will come."

Chapter Forty-Eight:
Cortéz Sees Beauty and Strength

"You are unsure of mind," Marina said, watching Cortéz pace the length of their own room. "I will tell you this. You have come to that which you may break, but it will not bend."

He looked down to where she still lay on the low bed. "Yes, I am unsure. And I should call you right, as you mostly are. The next move must be mine, and I cannot tell what it should be.

"Are we trapped? I can do this first. I can feel the bars of the cage."

He sent a message to Montezuma, asking if he were free to wander about the city; and received reply: "Malintzin may go where he will." This was modified in the next hour by another message saying that he might go where he would, excepting the Great Temple; but if he wished to visit that, and would say when, Montezuma would meet him there. He was also told that the Emperor's care had provided police, who would not obstruct his movements, but would guard his safety wherever he might go.

These were both capable of diverse interpretations, but Marina was not disposed to take either in a sinister way.

That Montezuma should wish to be present when Cortéz visited the very centre of the faith of which he was the Spiritual Head, was surely natural. At the best, it was a gesture of exceptional courtesy. At the worst, it might be the result of fear that some act of violence might be attempted, such as had been reported from Cempoalla and Cholula.

The escort of police was almost certainly intended as a protection against a population of uncertain temper. If it sounded strangely to Cortéz's ears, it was mainly because there was no organised police in the Europe of his day. He had come in that, as in some other details, to a more advanced civilisation than that which he had previously known. Here the police were ubiquitous, quiet, efficient, unobtrusive. In the markets, they had a magisterial authority, settling disputes where they occurred. It was a community in which breaches of law had been almost entirely eliminated by certainty of detection and severity of punishment—a community in which the imposition of continual fines for repetitions of the same offence would have been considered to be of an almost insane futility. If road-hogs or prostitutes be public evils, they would have said, their activities should be stopped, or they should be eliminated; it is best to have an effectual law, or no law at all.

It was, in fact, very improbable that there would be any unauthorised interference with the Spaniards, had no police escort been provided. It was absolutely certain that, if they were present, their authority would not be defied. But what might their secret instructions be? It was a risk which must be run, in a position in which it was essential to maintain a demeanour of confident strength.

Cortéz rode out next morning, accompanied by Marina, and three of the four cavaliers who were now his constant companions, leaving Alvarado in control till he should return.

The little party moved at a walking pace, both that they might have leisure to see what they passed, and to avoid terrorising a population crowding streets which, excepting the main avenue, were often so narrow that they must ride in single file, as was also the case when they came to canals which had no more than a narrow breadth of pavement beside them.

Amazement at the extent and solidity of this lake-surrounded city was modified by observing that it was not entirely built on piles. There were great areas where the buildings rose on piles of a height which allowed canoes to be paddled beneath them, much of the merchandise traffic of the city being carried on in this way. But there were others which had solid ground for their immediate support. The fact was that the centre of the lake, which, though of very wide extent, was rarely more than a few feet deep, had been originally broken by a cluster of small islands, which had been the basis from which the great city grew.

It was of more interest to the Spaniards to observe that not only the main causeways, but many other of the canal-crossed streets were broken by drawbridges, the destruction of which would make movement difficult.

They also discovered that, in addition to the great causeway by which they had reached the city from the south, and which went on through it, and then crossed the lake again to the northern shore, there was another at right angles to it, of similar magnitude and construction, which stretched for two miles to the western shore of the lake, leading to where the city of Tezcuco lay, beyond wooded hills, and to the red hill of Chapoltepec, the site of the garden palace of Montezuma, and of a fountain so affluent that it supplied all the requirements of México (Tezcuco lake being salty) through two six-foot pipes carried on a great dyke to the city.

That evening Cortéz discussed with the little band of his trusted friends the implications of what they had seen, and how splendid the prize would be, if they could win it for God and Spain.

They had surveyed the centre of a civilisation which was, in many features, more advanced than that of Western Europe. A city nine miles in circumference, the streets of which, wide and narrow alike, were kept far cleaner than were the interiors of most European homes. A city without factories or shops, without slums. As at Tlascala and Cholula, whatever industries it had were handicrafts, carried on in private houses. In place of shops, it had a great square (three times the size of that at Salamanca, they made their guess), where a market was held every fifth day. They had seen its bare expanse. They could see its activity on the next day.

They had seen gardens and palaces, zoological collections, aviaries, aquariums, fountains and flowers—always profusion of flowers.

It would have been an Elysium of culture and heavenly peace, but for its central pyramid—the redstone temple, with its crest of undying fire, and its courtyard pens, where captives fattened for the monstrous sacrifices of its Sacred Days.

"I will not rest," Cortéz said, "till that temple is crowned with the Cross of Christ."

"You will not rest long here," Alvarado, who had joined them, replied, "either for evil or good. The men grumble and fret. They are too closely confined. They say you have got your gold. For what do you linger now?"

Cortéz made no reply. Was there no one (unless Marina) to share his dream?

CHAPTER FORTY-NINE: MART

Marina said next morning that which Alvarado had hinted the night before. She had been talking to the Tlascalan leaders, and they had said plainly that their troops would not consent to be held for a longer time in the narrow confines of the palace courtyards. Immense in themselves they might be. But what is a great space for a palace court may be a close jail for eight thousand men.

"Were we not told that even the gentlest beasts of the wild may become savage if they be too closely confined?"

She repeated wisdom which they had had from one of the keepers of the zoological pens, which they had visited on the previous day. He had been giving reasons for the large spaces the captured animals had, and for the efforts that were made to reproduce conditions which were native to them. However much he might have been right or wrong, they were opportune words to remember now.

Cortéz said: "So it may be. But to let them loose is a great risk. I may be bustled before the hour."

He paced up and down the room, as his way was in private irresolute moods, in a frowning perplexity, such as only Marina would ever see. Then he said: "It must be risked. Your garlands are well enough. Let them be. Will you go now, and tell the Tlascalans they can let their men out, three hundred at once, for what time they will, but, the shorter it be, the sooner will the gate be wide for the next lot. They must go in threes, neither more nor less, having no arms but a knife. They must leave the women alone—"

She interposed: "They will understand that." (Did he think those of this civilised land to be of such manners as she had seen once or twice that a Spanish soldier could be?)

He went on: "They must pay for anything they may buy, to the seller's content, be it less or more. If they make disturbance, they will learn that a rope chokes. Send to Alvarado a word that I would see him in the outer chamber at once."

"I suppose," Marina said, "we must make friends, or else go."

It had a sensible sound; but that Aztecs and Tlascalans would become friends was a wild hope.

Alvarado came, but with some delay. He said: "I have been riding out for a short time, but found that I must take a quiet pace, for the streets are full. I should say the canoes on the lake are a hundred score. All men move to the Square."

Cortéz frowned at that. Alvarado had no explicit instruction not to go out, but it was implied. And he knew that, though the confident reckless valour of the blond-haired giant was a constant support to him, and an inspiration to less resolute men, he had an arrogance of manner—and of action at times—from which trouble might most easily spring.

He said: "I will visit the market today with all the cavaliers, and two hundred spearmen in ranks of three, straightly arrayed. They can fall out and disperse, rank by rank, in the market-square, but must be alert to return if the trumpet call." He added more detailed instructions. "You will let it be known," he ended, "that there will be the same freedom for all, allowing only that a garrison must always remain here, and that there must be crews for the guns. We shall move out in an hour's time."

So they did, the cavaliers riding two by two, and the narrow ranks that followed finding themselves too broad at times for the busy crowd amidst which they moved, though it all faced in the same direction as they. For this fifth-day market was not only attended by the citizens of México, but by many thousands who came from the garden cities that lay on the outer shores of the lake, and beyond the hills. And merchandise came from the mainland also, in canoes that had been thick on the lake since the sun rose, and were still moving along the canals, and beneath the houses to reach the market square and augment its stocks.

This square, which had been vacant on the previous day, was now crowded with a gaily-coloured, lively, chaffering crowd, moving among many booths of jewellery, pottery, garments, furniture, tools, weapons, food and flowers. The alcoves surrounding the square were also occupied, many with less portable goods, and some by merchants of building materials, metals, and other wares which could not be displayed in bulk, but offered by samples of distant stocks.

The Spaniards' disciplined ranks moved slowly through crowds which closed round them in curiosity, shrank timidly away, or met them with blank, inscrutable stares.

They noticed that those among whom they moved, customers and tradesmen alike, were of a standard of material culture superior to anything they had seen in other Western cities—and far in advance of that of a European market. Not that they made such comparison. To them, these people, dress as they might, were still heathen, and therefore barbarian, fit scarcely to lick the steel-shod feet of a Christian man. Only Father Olmedo, had he been there, might have looked with wiser and more tolerant eyes.

Yet appearances could not entirely fail to impress. These people might not change their raiment four times a day, as their Emperor was reputed to do. But their gaily embroidered cotton tunics, and tasselled sashes, had an appearance of being worn for no more than the last hour. Their featherwork cloaks, of which more were seen now that days were becoming cool, had as bright an aspect of vivid colouring as those that were displayed in the drapers' booths. And there were flowers everywhere: on the women's heads, and around their necks, and festooning the structure of every booth. To the Aztec shoppers they were so commonplace, so obvious, as to be scarcely perceived: they looked through them to the wares which they half concealed. They did not notice the deliciously scented air; they would only have been roused to attention had they been deprived of the fragrance of flowers. The Spaniards would not have noticed that; they were conscious of the exotic atmosphere, half with pleasure, and half with aversion. Was it natural for Christian men?

Cortéz said: "Let the men fall out now, rank by rank, from the rear first, in a gradual way."

It was wisely planned. He could halt now as he would, without creating a long block between the booths of the crowded square.

He kept the group of twelve horses together—himself and Marina, and ten steel-clad cavaliers, moving two and two through the thronged aisles. He had little desire to buy, all his requirements, by Montezuma's munificence, having been well supplied; but when they came to a refreshment booth, of which there were many, he was glad to pause to drain a cup of hot chocolate, which he had learned to like (with cotton, tobacco, and maize, it was the New World's gift to the Old, for which it was to be recompensed with horses, gunpowder, and steel, and the Christian Cross); and when he saw strange or beautiful fabrics, he was curious to gain explanations of what they were. For the Aztecs, although, or because, they had avoided the tyranny of the machine, the shadow of which was already menacing European civilisation, were expert and patient at demonstrating the beauty of the work which can be done by human fingers, guided by human brains. There were soft flexible garments of fur, not on its original skin, but every hair of which had been plucked and woven; there were feather garments made in the same way, from the stripped web, by which means colours could be combined more subtly, though not with more flashing beauty, than they had shone on the tropic jewels from which they came. At this time of year, such garments found ready sale. There was chaffering as to price, where each was an individual creation, but all was done in an orderly, restrained way—perhaps the more so, because there was a corner of the square where assessors sat, to resolve disputes, and with powers of punishment of any offender who might be brought before them by the quietly efficient police, which could be drastic, prompt, and without appeal.

They moved on to the quarter of the square where fruits and many strange vegetables were sold by numbers or basket measures (scales not being used), and watched payment being made in the coinage of tin discs, bird-quills of gold-dust, and bags of cocoa beans.

The time passed as they watched, till Cortéz glanced up at a sun which was now descending the autumn sky. "Bernal," he said, "sound the recall."

Rapidly the ranks reassembled—for who would wish to be left behind among these people who spoke in a strange tongue?—and they marched back, past the barracks where the royal guards were housed, to the number, it was said, of ten thousand men, past the great central temple, which Cortéz had resolved to visit on the next day, and so to the precarious safety of their own walls.

CHAPTER FIFTY: SHRINE

Montezuma received a message next morning, saying that Cortéz would appreciate permission to visit the temple, and replied that he would be there to receive him at noon.

He had had another restless, unhappy night, while his wives murmured at his neglect. Through previous years he had had the loneliness that is the penalty of supreme power, but he had the counsel and support of his kin, even though past events had reduced their power, and exalted his. Brother and nephew had been loyal and potent allies while he had extended his empire beyond the bounds that previous rulers had sought to do. And though Ixtlilxochitl was sulking still, it was at a distance from which it could be disregarded with ease.

But now he knew that both brother and nephew disapproved of the reluctant favour which he had shown to these strange invaders, and—worst of all—he was not sure that they were wrong.

Three months ago, he had been nearest to God Himself. He had been God-on-earth to the known world. He had learnt to give, as a god gives. He had learnt the deep wisdom of the beatitude which he had not heard: "*It is more blessed to give than receive.*" He had given like God, given to all.

He knew that the complicated palace accounts were kept with scrupulous accuracy. The piled books of picture-writing in the treasury contained records that none could doubt. But these records were largely concerned with the realisations of what he gave, and their distribution among the palace officials.

When these Spaniards had vexed his peace, he had sent gifts, supposing that they would avert any trouble from them. As they still advanced, his gifts had increased. He had bid higher and higher as they approached; but never highly enough. And he had tried (or it had been tried with his connivance, and in his name) to destroy them, both by force and fraud. But that had failed also. Lastly, there had been the events at Vera Cruz, about which it had been unpleasant to think, because they had been at his orders, and at a time when he had been assuring the Spaniards of his goodwill. The treachery contemplated at Cholula might seem worse to an impartial judgement, but it had not been so directly his, nor had he been so directly involved, for the Aztec troops had remained still. It was true that had only been because Cortéz had restrained those who might have given them instructions to move. Did he guess that? But there was the fact that they had not moved. And also (because of that?) that the plot had failed. There was difference there. But he was glad that he had ordered the destruction of the Spaniard's head.

And both these treacheries—the one whole failure, the other less than success—had been advised by the priests, who would not admit that these men were of Quetzalcoatl's blood. Were they right about that? But he was not obliged to listen to them. He was himself the Chief Priest. Was it not for him to decide? And these strangers, who could not be duped, whom the lightning obeyed, were most godlike men. (But they were primitive savages also: that must be allowed by a fair mind.)

What was this new religion they preached? Much of it sounded well enough. Much of it was what he had learnt himself in the Sacred College. But there was one point to which they always returned: that of human sacrifices. They could not leave it alone. They talked as though it were the most important practice of the Aztec faith. Which was absurd. It was an integral part. One which would be very hard (for obvious reasons) to abolish, but that did make it central of all.

Should it really excite such horror?

War was natural to man. It had always been.

It was surely natural to these Spaniards, who had landed with lethal weapons, such as had not been seen or imagined before, which they had been ruthless to use.

To make thunder and lightning their tame allies, and use them to strew a field of battle with writhing men—was it more civilised, more humane, than the practice of capturing your enemies while they were still entire, lodging them comfortably, feeding them well, and slaughtering them in a manner which was swift and exact?

Even the victim chosen for the great annual festival (who might be of their own race) had much cause for content, and little of which to complain. Was there not actual competition for that sanguinary honour? He would be approved and admired by the whole nation, as one without blemish from head to heel. For long months he would live a life of luxury and regard. A girl could hope for no higher honour than to be permitted to share his bed.

When the day of sacrifice should come, he would be led to death, applauded by all, on a flower-strewn way.

From that death, he would ascend to Heaven, his sacrifice having assured him of everlasting bliss. Had it not been bought at a light price?

Anyway, one thing was sure. The people would not surrender their faith at the Spaniard's call. Even he could not command them in that.

After receiving the message from Cortéz with his usual impassive dignity, and sending affirmative response, he took a cup of frothlike chocolate from a golden goblet by the medium of a tortoiseshell spoon, and then without the usual interval for relaxation and entertainment, he retired to his dressing-rooms, and assumed the ceremonial robes of the priestly office which he had been taught to consider a higher dignity than that of the Emperor of the known world, which, until three months before, he had not doubted himself to be.

He ordered that his palanquin should be brought to the palace door, and proceeded to the temple in sufficient time to receive the Spaniards, and to give previous directions to the priests and other attendants as to their deportment towards their heretic and unwelcome guests.

Cortéz, entering through the main gateway at the head of his cavaliers, and a score of footmen who would guard the horses while he ascended the temple, was conscious of the vastness of the sacred precincts, but his first care must be for the horse he rode, the polished stone of the pavement being of such smoothness that steelshod hooves must take steps which were cautious and slow.

He said abruptly: "Halt! They must not see us distressed thus. We will dismount, and walk." He thought: "If they had determined on our massacre here, how worse than useless the horses would be." He walked on with Marina, Father Olmedo, and eight of his captains, aware of the weight of the armour they had not thought it prudent to leave behind.

Before them rose the great temple, solid, foursquare, flat-topped. It was ascended by a flight of steps, which wound round it four times. As each circuit was completed, there was a receding terrace, of the breadth of the steps, and the final platform was therefore of less area than the base of the pyramid to the extent of three such contractions.

The nobles whose shoulders had bent to bear their monarch up the weary climb were now waiting with others, at his orders, to bear the Spaniards in the same way, but Cortéz refused the proposal, when Marina explained it to him. "Tell them," he said, in his smiling way, "that a Spaniard is never tired."

Nor did he show that he was, as he mounted the long ascent, being conscious that he was open to the gaze of the whole city that lay beneath, and thinking with content of how brightly the sunlight must be reflected from the steel basinet and back-and-breast-plates he wore; so that he could repeat the smiling boast to Montezuma when they came out of the great platform that had no canopy but the sky. And though Father Olmedo was somewhat short of breath—well, is it not the weapons of the spirit that priests prefer? And his lungs had always proved sufficient to use them well.

Cortéz looked round on a wide platform of polished stone. He saw two three-storied towers at the far corners, built of stone and of carved and gilded wood. In the centre of the wide space was an altar. At a distance of twenty paces from it was a huge snakeskin drum. Before each of the towers was a pillar on which burnt an undying fire.

Montezuma stood alone, except for a black-robed, long-haired priest, with bright fanatical eyes. The Emperor had sent his attendants down the stairs for the service for which they were not required, and its refusal had left them uncertain of whether they should ascend again, or remain below. In this doubt, they remained.

The priest was next to Montezuma in titular, and above him in real authority in the church. He was its actual head. His long black robe was collared with rubies, and embroidered with the plumage of scarlet birds. It had stains, suggestive of recent blood.

Montezuma did not lead the way to the altar, or to the enigmatic towers. He directed the eyes of his guests elsewhere, and found them willing to stray.

They looked down on the great enclosure which, in its mile-wide girth, contained four similar but smaller temples, on each of which burnt the eternal fires. A wide range of lower buildings, set in gardens and groves, was pointed out by Montezuma as the Sacred College, where the youth of the aristocracy was assembled from all parts of the Aztec land for education in languages, picture-writing, science, and art. Separating the boys, who went to advanced astronomy, mathematics, and the science of war: and the girls to embroidery, weaving, cooking, and household management. All were taught religion, a high standard of ethics, cleanliness, chastity, and the dignity of restrained, disciplined life.

Marina, translating, added: "I was there myself for more than five years—until little more than a year ago. I was asked to remain as a votaress, but declined. I should like to call on the Head Priestess, who taught me much."

Cortéz said: "So you may. What is the use of that huge drum?"

"It was to call the people together at a great need, such as there would be if foemen should come through the hills. It was sounded more than once in the old days, but is useless now. I do not suppose it will ever be heard again."

But she must turn back to Montezuma, who was pointing out the priests' dwellings; the pleasant grove-enclosed houses where distinguished visitors were accommodated; the great storehouses, arsenals, and museums, within the girth of the great wall. There was one range of buildings only to which he did not refer—that of the human stock-pens, at the further side of the seminaries, from which eight victims had been selected at dawn for the anniversary of the Aztec triumph, and slaughtered before a message from Montezuma had caused a hurried clearance to be made for this unwelcome visit.

Passing silently over those sinister roofs, he looked further out. From their great height, the whole city could be seen, its wide central streets, its gardens and parks, its temples and palaces, its three-score thousand private residences. And, further out, they could see the three great causeways that connected it with the mainland, and the extent of Tezcuco lake.

They could see the lake of Chalco further away, the wooded hills of Chapoltepec, and Montezuma's summer palace thereon; the city of Tezcuco, only partly hidden, at their great height, by the intervening ridge; and, far around and beyond, the autumn richness of the great Mexican plain, stretching on all sides to its surrounding mountains, crowned with black volcanic smoke or unmelting snow.

Exclamations of wonder, and words of praise, were translated by Marina to the satisfaction of the monarch whose dominion was so strangely threatened by these ambiguous invaders. He said to the high priest, who watched with grim disapproval: "Have I not done well? Is it not as I said it would be? Here only can they see the extent and quality of my central power."

His reply was a low mutter, not being meant for Marina's ears: "I suppose they may yet come in another way."

She caught nothing of that, for she was following Cortéz, who turned abruptly round, and was now walking towards the central altar.

It was a solid block of black jasper, with a convex surface, on which a man or woman could be stretched, with the spread limbs fastened to metal rings. It was a position which raised the belly conveniently, so that the officiating priest could make an incision in it with the knife in his right hand, and his left, almost in the same instant, could be thrust upward to reach the heart, and pull it out.

It was, in fact, a most expeditious method of slaughtering, and may have been an easier death than most men are destined to meet, but that did not lessen the repulsion of those by whom its foul significance was perceived.

Emperor and priest, now standing somewhat behind could not mistake the meaning of the comment, or the curses, of the white men, though they could not understand the exclamation of Cortéz to Father Olmedo: "Father, this is beyond the endurance of Christian men. I will require now that they cast their devils away, and consent to the erection of the True Cross, where all men can look up to a true belief. I will require their consent, lest we cast them downward to death, as we are well able to do."

"And for how long," Father Olmedo replied, "would the cross remain here, or our lives endure? You must learn to win them by other ways."

His words were of an evident wisdom, and gained the sullen approval of those who were accustomed to give him obedience on matters of faith; but the little band of cavaliers were in no amiable mood as Cortéz said to Marina: "Ask that we may inspect the towers, for we would see all."

Montezuma hesitated, as he had reason to do; but Cortéz was already moving toward that at the northwest corner, without waiting for his reply, and his sense of dignity caused him to consent to that which might otherwise have been taken against his will.

Clinging desperately to his dignity, and to the avoidance of open quarrel, he acknowledged the sense of tension by saying to Marina: "It is needless to ask me. You know enough. You can explain."

By that means he at least secured that the venomously angry priest at his side would know nothing of what was said.

To a point, Marina, knowing more of the minds of those to whom she spoke, made a better job of it than he would be likely to do. But she had never been on that elevation before, nor spoken to one who had. She only vaguely knew what to expect.

"This tower," she said, as they approached, "is sacred to Tezcatlipoca. It is he who created men. He is second only to the Unseen, of Whom no image is ever made. He is righteous and benign. He rewards mercy and truth, after death, with enduring days."

As she spoke, they entered the temple door, finding the light dim to eyes that had been enduring the sun. Dimly they saw the image of the god, black as ebony, but with a shield of dazzling light.

"That," Marina explained, "is a mirror to him, through which he sees all that men do, to the world's end."

Bernal interrupted her, in his blunt way: "It has a stench like a slaughterhouse, whatever gods it contains."

As they became used to the light, they saw some reason for that. Before the statue lay five hearts, on a golden dish.

Ordaz exclaimed: "By the fiend! They are hearts of men."

"It is a good guess," Bernal agreed; "and that they were alive at this dawn."

They were all in the chamber now, filling its narrow space.

Father Olmedo, grave and pale, said: "We have seen enough. Shall we not go?"

But Cortéz said: "I would know the whole."

Next moment, he was crossing the platform, Marina, who was aware both of the passion which moved the white men, and of the way in which Emperor and Priest were being ignored, found that she must hasten to keep his side.

"The other temple is that of the God of War—the God of the Aztecs, who has made them first in the world. I should guess that there will be nothing there that you will be eager to see."

"I will see all."

As Cortéz pushed open the door, there was a sound of voices, of scurrying feet, and of the climbing of stairs.

They saw the War-God's image, grotesquely foul, magnificent with jewels, a glittering serpent around his waist. There was a golden bow in his right hand, and arrows were in his left. Round his neck was a chain of gold and silver, moulded to the shapes of the hearts of men.

There was a dish before him such as had been seen in the other chapel, on which were three similar hearts; for even the Aztecs, worshipping their own particular deity, could not render him the same degree of honour as that which was paid to the Creator of men.

But the stench of the slaughter house, that Bernal had professed to detect at the other shrine, was unmistakable now. Cortéz pushed up the stairs, and its cause was clear.

The fact was that Montezuma's intimation that the Spaniards would soon be visiting the temple had come at a most inopportune time. The custom of taking prisoners of war, rather than killing on the battlefield, with the ultimate ceremonial slaughter of the captives, had grown in recent years to a monstrous extent, and it is doubtful how far this was the result of the war of conquest which had become almost continual, or how far the demand for such victims had stimulated the adventure of further wars. But there were still many days when the altar was clear and bare, and the inspection might have taken place with no more than inferential evidence of the practices which prevailed. But this had been a holy day, on which sacrifice must be made.

The Emperor's instructions that such evidences must, as far as possible, be removed before the Spaniards would arrive, had given little time for the necessary adjustments to be made. The officiating priests had retired into the War-God's tower, into which they had not supposed that they would be followed, but where, partly as precaution, and partly as customary routine, they had conveyed tools and bodies, and other evidences of their occupation during earlier hours.

The cleansing of the altar itself and the surrounding floor had only been completed after Montezuma's arrival, and, in the upper rooms of the War-God's tower, the evidences went far beyond anything that could be hidden or cleared away, even had the inclinations of the priests been more willingly turned in that direction.

Cortéz, at the head of the first stair, looked on a sight that was loathsome beyond detailed description: he looked on three priests in black, bloodstained gowns, of whom two drew back fearfully, and one, in a mood of irresolute defiance, laid his hand on a copper axe.

Cortéz saw the motion, and his own hand went to his sword, at which the two frightened priests bolted incontinently up a ladder stair to a second-story loft, and the third, after one moment of indecision, followed them, as the sword flashed clear of its sheath. He escaped with no more than a pricked buttock, and Cortéz, without sheathing his sword, went down in a mood of the blackest wrath, which was partly directed against himself, for he was conscious that he had been near to loss of self-control on which he had been able to depend, till then, at whatever crisis he had been fated to meet.

The impulse to kill that foul slaughterer of his fellowmen had been of an overmastering intensity. It was only as the upward thrust had been made that he had restrained the inclination to give it a fatal force. And it would have been hard to defend or excuse, even to his own men.

Whatever it might be justifiable or expedient to do for the suppression of a devilish custom, no one could say that it would be sane procedure to ask permission to inspect a temple where rites were practised of which he already knew, and there to slay one of its inferior priests, without exceptional cause.

He said to those among whom he descended: "You should go up. You should all see for yourselves." At which some ascended, and others remained below.

He said to Marina, who went out on to the platform with him, moved from her usual restraint to put a restraining hand on his arm: "Tell him that this must cease. We will have the Cross here, though we be opposed by all the forces of Hell!"

He was facing Montezuma now, with the priest still at his side. The priest's face was distorted by a rage equal to that of the man he confronted. Montezuma was pale, but still calm, in his dignified way.

Marina said urgently: "Hernán, will you not put up your sword?"

Cortéz looked down on it. He had not been conscious that it was still bare in his hand. He saw that the last inch of its point was red. He said, not wholly without confusion of face: "Yes. So I will. But, if I do so, you must tell him what I will have. You must be very plain."

She asked: "Have I failed you yet?"

She saw the sword drop back into its scabbard of crimson velvet. She said to Montezuma, who had shown no symptoms of fear, though he and the priest were alone on that high space with a dozen armed and evidently angry men: "My lord wishes me to make it plain that the sacrifices of men are a matter which he will not endure. He will not rest till the Cross of Christ is raised here, for all men to see." She added, in a different tone, making it clear that they were her own words: "It is that on which peace depends."

Montezuma's paleness had gone. He had the self-control that he had never been so near to losing since the day when he had been called to the throne from his lowly task on those temple steps. He saw that, the priest having heard Marina's reply, the time for decision had come.

He replied coldly: "You will tell your lord that I would not have invited him to this holy place had I anticipated that such sacrilege would result. He can go now, but I must remain, to expiate by prayers and penance the insults which I have allowed." Marina translated this to one who had now achieved the self-mastery which the responsibility of his position required.

He said: "You can reply that I regret that what I did was in the wrong way. It is an incident which he may be generous to forget."

She might translate that as she pleased.

He saw that Montezuma heard it coldly, took formal leave, and led his officers down the long descent of the pyramid.

CHAPTER FIFTY-ONE: THE BOLDER WAY?

During the next three days, there was an increasing murmur of dissatisfaction among the Spanish adventurers. They had reached the capital city. Cortéz had interviewed its Emperor, as he had always declared his resolution to do. They were laden with costly spoils. Indeed, with far more than their own hands would have been able to bear away. (But they had been provided with porters for that.) What more was there to see or do? They were impatient to go.

There was still an aspect of peace. Indeed, a request to Montezuma that he should give permission for one of the larger rooms of his father's palace to be converted into a Christian chapel, had received a cordially worded consent.

That had been quickly done, and mass could now be celebrated in any weather, which all Christian men could attend.

But the conversion of the room had led to a revelation which Montezuma could not have foreseen when he gave consent.

Bernal came to Cortéz, when the work was half done. He said: "We have stripped the walls of tapestries which would have been unfitting for eyes of prayer, and have exposed something which you should see."

It proved to be no more than some fresh plastering of the wall, which had the shape of a door. There was no menace in that. But it was very fresh. It must have been done immediately before the Spaniards had been allowed in. Why? Cortéz liked to know. He said briefly: "Break it through, and let me hear of what is beyond."

It was a very short time before he was told. Alvarado came now. He said: "I had not thought that there was so much wealth in the world. You must come and see. It is for you to dispose."

Cortéz was soon looking at treasures piled in a disorderly way, as though jewels and gold were of too little worth to be counted, or even piled ranged. There was a kingdom's revenue in gold cups and platters alone.

It was easy to guess what had occurred. The palace had been stripped of its costliest contents before it had been opened to alien guests.

Even so, it was an inadequate explanation. There must have been treasure harboured there before that.

Alvarado said: "Shall it be hauled out, that the scriveners may take account, or is there a first tribute for those who find?"

Cortéz looked at him in a way which was infrequent, but which the blond giant, despite his reckless courage, had found hard to endure with a bold front, once or twice before that.

"Are we thieves? You will have it plastered up as it was before. I would hang the best man I have should he touch but one golden chain."

No one would be first to question a decision so firmly expressed, for all men knew that they had a commander who seldom threatened, but who kept his word in an inflexible way. But there were sullen faces among those who bent to unwelcome toil.

An hour later, Alvarado asked: "If we may not take when the chance is ours, why do we linger here?"

"As to that," Cortéz replied, "you may summon a council of whom you will, so that it be not more than twenty in all. If there be grumblers, let them appear. But I have not said they are wrong. Let it be tomorrow, at prime of day."

That night Cortéz paced the floor of his room till a late hour. He knew that he had brought matters to a point at which they could not remain. He must move forward or back. And he had an idea—audacious, and which, should it fail, would be regarded as having been foolish beyond belief. And there would be no retreat. If it were tried, he must risk all, life and reputation alike. He would have been a failure for God and Spain. A name for the mockery of the future days.

And he could go back now—he was almost sure he could do that—with a great tale and a great spoil, and perhaps to triumph over all at a later time.

Marina watched him from their low bed, of which the cushioned depths were no more than a foot from the matted floor. It was a mood she knew, from which would evolve some implacable decision for the next day.

She was silent for a long time, regarding him with grave considering eyes. Then she raised herself on one hand, showing a breast and shoulder of golden brown in a deliberate way. She asked: "Will you not come? You must be fit for this council at the full light. I have seen that you vanquish all when you have spent the night as God had meant you to do."

He looked at her with blank eyes that changed to laughter as he replied: "And what may be this meaning of God which you know so well?"

"It is love and sleep," she answered, with a quick response of laughter in her dark eyes. "Will you tell me you do not know?"

"I will tell you much better things. But how shall I win elsewhere, being so quickly defeated by you?"

"Do you call it that?" She smiled, as she watched him flinging a gay doublet aside. "I should say you come to win, as you always do."

She moved backward toward the wall, making space which would not be vacant long. They would sport, she resolved, but it should all be done in a quick way. It was sleep that he needed now.

CHAPTER FIFTY-TWO: SECRET PLAN

There were twenty officers of the little army who came to the chamber of council, where they must be content to sit on low stools, or on cushions upon the floor, in the Aztec mode. More than that number had felt that they had a right to be included, and there had been necessity for Alvarado to exercise more diplomacy than he was accustomed to use. Commands must, he said, be vigilantly maintained, and could all those of the greatest trust be apart, for perhaps long hours, in an inner room? It would not be reasonable to propose.

Marina was there also, which she had not expected or wished. Cortéz had said: "There may be questions raised as to what can be wisely done, on which you could advise as no other would be able, for you know their ways as we never shall."

When they were seated, he was brief and blunt: "Comrades, we cannot stay doing nothing here, until Montezuma, it is easy to think, would grow tired of feeding not only us, but six thousand Tlascalans whom he had no reason to love. I would have your counsel of what may be best to do."

"The question is," Alvarado said; "Shall we go back by day in an open style, or by stealth in the night hours?"

His words raised long debate, to which Cortéz listened without giving sign of his thoughts.

Mesa, whose sole thought was that the artillery should not be lost, was in favour of a sudden move in the night hours. He proposed that they should escape by the western causeway, and then circuit the lake. "But even that one," he said, "is two miles in length, and we are trapped rats if the bridges be broken down."

Bernal Díaz, with the horses upon his mind, said the same. "Though," he allowed, "if they were stripped of gear, they could swim. And the lake is not deep. It could be waded by them for the most part on the way we came. But I know not what its depth may be on the western side."

Diego said that they should march boldly out, after announcing what they would do. "Would they attack us then," he asked, with a sound reason, "who now leave us alone? They would be blithe-hearted to see us go."

Salvador gave him support. He said: "If we go by night, we show both distrust and fear. It would not be return, but flight. We should be asking for attack on every mile of the backward way."

Mesa did not dispute that, but yet held to his own view. "Get me clear of dyke and bridge, and the guns will blast a way through the densest rank they can muster to cross our path."

León de Velásquez had become as silent as Cortéz while this debate went on, until it was shown that the two views had about equal support; but when he spoke it was with decisive effect.

He said: "I can hear reason from all, but you waste words. I will tell you why. You could not go in a secret wise, either by night or day. Even if we presume that we are not closely watched (and to think that is to allow that there is little reason for stealth, and much weight in the other scale), we have yet to ask ourselves how long it would take for horses, and guns, and from eight to nine thousand men, many laden with gear and spoil, to file out through the gateway here. I will not ask how long it would be before the last files would have left the dyke.

"I do not say that the cavaliers might not flee along the dyke at a hot pace before obstruction would raise its head (that is, if the barrier gates should be forced with ease, which those may forecast who are sanguine of mind), but if the whole should go without riot of strife—well, it would show that it could have been so done, and much better done, in the daylight hours."

"You mean," Cortéz said, speaking for the first time, "that, if we go, at whatever hour, there is hazard to face which we cannot miss?"

"So I think. For bridges can soon be raised, or be broken down, and there are few streets that they could not cut in that way. Besides that, could we make defence when we should be spread out on a two-mile dyke? Could we use horses, or the guns?

"At the least, they would vex our rear, and there would be many bowmen in their canoes who would send shafts into those who would be crowded upon the dyke. If we should be stopped midway by a broken gap—well, it is easy to guess how we should fare.

"León is right in that. We should go at hazard either by night or day. If that be so, then were daylight best, both for itself, and for the aspect which it will have. So, having resolved that, we must ask ourselves, should we stay or go?"

That was not what the debate had been, but they could not see him as changing ground, for, until then, he had said nothing at all. He had let them talk as they would in their own ways, and now, when the more cautious among them had been additionally discouraged by condemnation of the hope that they might fade quietly away in the night hours, the question was put to them in a new form: "Should we go or stay?"

Alvarado asked: "Did you not tell us that we could not stay, for our welcome could not endure?"

"I said we could not stay idle here. I invited counsel from all."

"Will you tell us what we could do to our lasting gain?"

Cortéz looked on those who sat around, his eyes dwelling on them, one by one, while they waited in silence, easy or tense, as their natures were. They knew their leader well enough to expect some unguessed audacious proposal from him, while he weighed them one by one in a cautious scale. If one only should speak, and the tale spread, it would be ruin for all, even though it should be abandoned in the next hour. Well, it was a risk he must take; and he thought it small. He said: "We might remain with quiet minds if Montezuma were hostage here."

It was so casually said that its audacious implications were not instantly realised by all who heard.

León was the first to speak, he being one who listened to all with the cool alertness which few things could surprise, and no crisis could overbear. He asked quietly: "Would you practice by force or fraud, or do you think to win his consent, in a reasoned way? Have you a plan formed?"

"I would not practice by fraud; nor would I have violence done, which might be our loss. We may be adroit to persuade. But I will tell you the cause we have.

"I had word from Vera Cruz, before marching here. You know that, but I told none of the news I had. You must have wondered that I sent de Giado back with ten men, including two crossbowmen, whom I grudged most. It was an evil tale, which I told to none at that time, we being busy in other ways. I have hoped for better news, but it has not come.

"This is what I heard: a message came to Escalante from a cacique some distance away. It said that he was a foe to Montezuma, and wished to visit Vera Cruz, that he might make a good treaty against the Aztec power. But he was intimidated by the fact that, to do this, he must traverse territory the inhabitants of which, though friendly to us, were foes to him. He asked Escalante to send Spaniards who would assure his peaceful passage.

"Escalante believed this: he sent four. Two of these returned. They said the plea was a lying trap, from which they had come free by speedy flight. But their comrades were slain.

"After that fighting broke out. Vera Cruz sustained hard attack. Though it stood (to the day when the message left), eight of our comrades, including Escalante himself, were lost.

"Captives told that the treachery was on the direct orders of Montezuma himself, apart from which there would have been no thought to entice our comrades to death, or contest our power.

"It is left a doubt whether Vera Cruz stands today, or whether our one ship has fled to we know not where. But we may suppose it to stand, or these Aztecs would have faced us in a more resolute mood."

Alvarado frowned as he asked in bold reproach: "You have held this back?"

"I would have held it longer, waiting for further report. But I think it wrong that you should plan retreat without knowing that you might arrive at a bare beach, and a burning town."

Alvarado became silent, being unsure what it would be wisdom to do. His choice was the bolder way, but he was unwilling to give Cortéz instant support in his resentment against having been treated without earlier confidence.

In the pause, León de Velásquez spoke with a different tone: "I have lost a good friend, and we have all lost a comrade of trust and worth. As to Montezuma, you may plan as you please, and will have my voice. For I should say we must stand firmly, and here is a possible plan."

Diego gave quick assent. It was gay adventure to him.

Mesa did not show that he heard. He had had no heart for the causeway retreat, whether by night or day. He was already considering how he could place his guns, without aspect of threat, so that they would cover the street between the two palaces.

As to Bernal, everyone knew that he would follow what his Captain might rule, but he had a contented smile, for the risk to his horses would be less by this later plan.

Sandoval did not dissent. He looked round the seated group with appraising eyes. "If naught," he said, "be spoken outside these walls—"

Cortéz took up his word: "It is a plan which may only succeed if it be unguessed. But without that—or if there should be act or word to make Montezuma alert—we shall be failures to God and Spain, and our own lives a light loss. But I should say that who might betray us by careless words, or a loose trust, would be assured not only of his own death, but of the damnation of Hell."

There was a murmur of assent; and, after that, they debated what should be done on the next day.

CHAPTER FIFTY-THREE: THE GREAT HAZARD

Marina said: "It is so far well. The messengers have returned, bringing word that the Emperor will be pleased to receive you at noon. He will have a gift for you of a new kind, which he thinks you will not despise. No, I have no guess of what it will be. Being of a new kind, it cannot be gold! I should say there is no suspicion at all."

The prudence of what had seemed to be a hazardous course became evident as those who had received full confidence did their various parts. The Tlascalans were not informed of the plot, nor asked to deviate in any way from their usual routine; but the Spanish soldiers were paraded at prime of day, and a larger number than was customary at one time were given permission to go into the town, three by three, with instructions that they must return not later than one hour after noon, thereby assuring that the street would have many little groups of Spaniards moving toward the gate at what might be a critical time.

A somewhat stronger guard than usual was detailed to support Cortéz and his attendant cavaliers; and these were somewhat more numerous, and more completely armed than they had been previously; but the differences were not sufficient to arouse suspicion— certainly not to suggest the incredible audacity which had been conceived in the Spanish commander's mind, and received a detailed development as he had paced his room during the night hours, while Marina slept.

Montezuma was in a gracious mood. Like Cortéz, he had made plans. After months of fatal irresolution, a chaos of mind which had increased as the necessity for decision had become more acute, he had now decided that the wisest policy was to establish friendship on a secure and permanent basis, which he considered (as had the Tlascalans, and was common policy among the monarchs of the Old World) could best be attained by a marriage bond. He would give one of his own daughters to Cortéz.

This did not imply any intention of accepting the Christian Faith (except by the girl herself, who would naturally do so). He had already assured his indignant colleague in the high priesthood that he would not support any attack upon the national religion. Indeed, it was not a matter of practical politics. He knew that even he would be impotent to shake the traditional worship of the God of War, by whose support the Aztec nation had become supreme in its own world.

But, apart from that, he had resolved to establish a basis of friendship, such as would put aside, perhaps forever, the threat that lay in the dreadful weapons the Spaniards controlled. If his thought went further, to an ultimate possibility that weapons of lightning and tempered steel might come into the hands of his own troops, and extend his empire to the far north, and southward through tropic lands, was it not his duty to plan providently for the welfare of those he ruled?

But he had put thoughts of treachery and massacre definitely aside. He had given orders to burn or bury the Spaniard's head.

Having these intentions, he had decided to receive the Spaniards in absolute privacy, the method of communication through Marina rendering it otherwise inevitable that everything said on both sides would become publicly known. He could not even pick up a paintbrush and write an idea for only the Spanish Commander's eyes. He was dealing with men so barbarous that they could not read! The plainest picture might have no meaning for them.

The steelshod Spaniards came quietly across the thickly-matted floor. They were more completely armed than usual, but there was not enough difference to draw attention to that. Even Cortéz had worn a steel basinet, rather than his wide-plumed hat, on many occasions since they had entered this potentially hostile city.

When Montezuma said that he wished to talk in private, and his attendants faded soundlessly away, it could be perceived by devout hearts that the saints were active to aid the courageous servants of God.

Montezuma was on his usual richly-coloured cushions, half seated and half reclined. A low table was before him, about a foot high, as those of México were.

He invited Cortéz to sit on the further side, with Marina between them. Five steelclad Spaniards stood behind Cortéz, but Montezuma saw no menace in that. The thought of personal insecurity did not enter his mind.

He spoke his purpose at once: "You will tell your lord that I wish to bind our friendship with an unbreakable cord. My daughters are of a fine quality, for their mothers are picked from the best of the whole land. There are three now fit for marriage, from whom he may take his choice."

Marina translated this without comment, but it seemed to her to contain a better hope than lay in the wild errand on which they came.

It was so utterly unexpected, so contrary to the programme he had designed for the future days, that even Cortéz was brought to a moment's silence before he framed his reply.

Then he said: "You will thank the Emperor for an offer which is gracious beyond my deserts, and would be an honour even to my master, the Spanish King; but you must add that it is one which it is beyond my power to accept, because I am already married to a wife in my own land."

It was Marina's turn to pause now. For an instant, her eyes showed the bewilderment of her mind. If Cortéz could not marry Montezuma's daughter because he had a wife in another land, what about his marriage to her?

It sounded nonsense, because marriage, to her and to Montezuma, was not a ceremony, but a fact. Cortéz might have a wife in his own land. That was no less than a natural probability. And (to her certain knowledge, being herself) he had one in México. Should he marry Montezuma's daughter, he would have two in México: three in all. That would not be a matter for argument: it would be physical fact. To say that he couldn't have two or three wives was not even a clever lie. Everyone knew he could. Therefore it had the sound to her of an unmeaning insolent jest, and she supposed that Montezuma would take it in the same way.

The idea of a difference between wives and mistresses was an insult to women which had not entered the Aztec mind. There might of course (in theory) be infidelities, adulteries, illicit intercourses, but they were not approved; and, as it seemed logical to the Aztec mind that things which were disapproved should not happen, the punishment for such transgressions was death, with the consequence that they did not occur. (There were some distinctions as to the relative rights of the children of an emperor's wives, implying gradations of honour, but that did not imply any moral gulf, such as that which divided wives from mistresses by European standards.)

She asked: "I am to say that?"

He mistook the wonder in her voice. Did she think him foolish not to accept so golden an offer of peace, even though it would mean putting her aside, as he would obviously have to do? But he had no intention of that. He answered: "You will say it with all the courtesy that your language allows, but it is the only possible reply that I am able to give."

She made no further protest, having learnt that there was method in what he did, and supposing the form of the reply to have some motive beyond her guessing, explanation of which must await a more suitable time.

She said: "If I were sure that I know what you would have me say!" And turned to Montezuma, and to the use of the Aztec tongue: "My lord says that he is prostrated by the offer of that which is so greatly beyond his worth, and which would be an honour even to his master, the Spanish King. It is his sorrow that he cannot accept the privilege that your gracious recognition of his inadequate merits would bestow, because he has left a wife in his own land."

Montezuma had a great pride, which would often prevail when courage would have been inadequate for his support. It was not often that those around him (except when he was alone with his closest kin) could tell what his feelings were; and, apart from that, there was a long moment during which bewilderment hindered thought. Then he asked: "Will you tell me what may be the meaning of that?"

"I cannot say beyond this—that it is an offer he cannot accept, but which he wishes to decline with recognition of the honour it would have been."

Cortéz was aware of the tones, though not the substance of what was said. Desiring to make his decision clear, he interposed with an explanation which he might have given earlier. He said: "Will you say that the Christian Faith does not permit that a man may have more than one wife?"

Marina repeated this in a mechanical way. She said: "My lord says that a Christian may not have more than one wife."

Montezuma flushed with an anger he could no longer control. He exclaimed: "But it is clear that he has two now. Does he make my offer a jest? Tell him that we will talk more on another day."

It was evident dismissal, and his hand was reaching toward the gong which would have called his attendants, when it was arrested by the sharp authority of the exclamation which he heard in a strange tongue, and Marina's quick translation: "No, not that!" And then: "There is more which must be said now in a private way."

Montezuma controlled himself by an effort to the remote dignity which was his habitual shield. He said: "Tell your lord that I can give him but a short time, but that I will hear what he is anxious to say."

After that he listened to Cortéz's angry Spanish, and was aware of a mood which the Spanish Commander had not previously shown to himself. He judged that what was to be translated would not be pleasant to hear, and clothed himself in advance in his armour of self-control, but he had no preconception of the strain which it would have to bear.

Marina turned to him to say, in less discourteous words than those of the original tongue: "My lord has complaint to make of that which has lately occurred at his camp by the seashore. It is not a matter which can be put lightly aside. He has heard that good men of his were lured by a lying tale into the power of those by whom they were cruelly slain. His captain was killed in the fighting those murders bred. Captives say that these things were done on direct orders from you, and, indeed, it is hard to think that such deeds would be, except that your approval were sure."

"You can assure him," Montezuma replied, with outward calmness, "that if such things have been done, they have been without my authority, and against my will. The offer I have just made is sure proof that I desire friendship to be firmly founded, and well secured."

"My lord says that he does not doubt that your intention is such, but, if that be so, the culprits surely will not be left immune?"

Montezuma struck the gong three loud and rapid blows, and a high noble entered at once, clad in the sackcloth that the etiquette of the court required.

"Tezo," the Emperor said, addressing one to whom his lightest word was implacable law, "you will hasten at once to the Eastern coast, to where Quauhpopaca rules, and bring him here with such others as companioned him in contrivance against the soldiers of Spain. If they do not come of their own will, all who are faithful to me must be their foes in the next hour, and you will raise force to bring them with fettered hands. Here is a warrant, that all will heed."

He drew a signet-ring from his finger, bearing the royal eagle with its prey in its claws, it being a sign that none other would dare to carry without his explicit authority. From the moment that Tezo put it on his finger, his word became as potent as that of Montezuma himself, to whom alone he must render account of what he might order or do.

He went out, and Montezuma said with dignified gravity: "Malintzin may be assured that justice shall be done. Let him be satisfied upon that, and we will talk of the offer I made on another day."

But it seemed that this assurance was not to be received with a brief assent. Montezuma, reclining with an expressionless face, was aware that Cortéz was instructing Marina at length as to what she should say next, and being met with queries from her, to which he gave further lengthy replies.

When it seemed that she was thoroughly informed, she turned to the Emperor, and was able to sustain an audacious argument without the delay of intervening translations, and fresh instructions for her replies.

"My lord says that he is well content with what you have done, and does not doubt your friendship and faith, either to him or to his distant King, but he has officers who are less assured, and who are bitter at the loss of those who were slain in a very treacherous way. He proposes that you should reside with him in your father's palace until the conclusion of this affair, which would be accepted by all as assurance that your accord has such foundations as will not fail."

Those who watched saw blank astonishment, followed by indignation hardly controlled, and then by a pallor of fear on the Emperor's face.

They heard a reply that was angry and curt, and saw that Marina met it with placating, reasoning words. She was saying: "But that is not the intention at all. You would be as free as you are here. You would hold the same state. Your servants would be as free both to come and go."

"It is an insult on which we cannot debate. It is that which my people would not endure. It is intolerable even to think."

"My lord feared that you might take it thus, in the wrong way. But surely you can reside in what palace you may prefer? Your people do not dictate that."

It was an argument with which she had been adroitly armed, and might, under different circumstances, have had plausibility. But Montezuma was not seeking to be convinced, nor could he entertain the prospect (monstrous to him from whatever angle) quite as he would have done had he not been conscious that his vacillating mind was not entirely free from knowledge of, or consequent responsibility for, the treacheries either of Cholula or Vera Cruz. Certainly, any fate which might have overwhelmed these aggressive strangers would have had approval from him.

Yet, so great had been his indecision, his protestations of friendship had not been entirely insincere, nor had his munificence been dictated entirely by fear.

But here was a proposal on which he felt that it would be insane—intolerable—to give way; and as Marina continued an argument on which she had been instructed that Cortéz would have his will, by fair means or whatever violence it might require, he offered at last to surrender two of his own children—a boy and girl—as hostages for the satisfaction which the Spaniards required.

That was a proposition which must be put to Cortéz, and one, she may have felt, which he might accept, as giving him a large measure of the security at which he aimed. But he instructed her to refuse it absolutely, though still in a polite and argumentative way.

She said: "My lord recognises that you offer much, even beyond that which he would have thought it seemly to ask; but yet it would not have the aspect that he desires, for hostages are given by those who are held in doubt, who would not be trusted without a pledge.

"What he seeks is that you should come to the palace where he is set, both as being free to make use of that which is yours, and as one who visits a friend. When you do that, all men will see that Aztec and Spaniard are one, and the foundations of concord will be secure."

It was a specious argument, and one in which Cortéz may have been little less than sincere. Had he been assured that Montezuma would keep faith with him, he would not have provoked strife, and would certainly have honoured any bargain he might have made—always with one fundamental, fatal qualification, that he was resolved to establish Christianity among a people who were not disposed to abandon their own faith. But that, he would have said, was his duty to God, and of infinite advantage to heathen men. It was a matter on which he had no option at all.

But, were the argument faulty or sound, Montezuma was not willing to consider it with an open mind. He had no intention of leaving the dignities and comforts of his own palace for this dubious alternative, for any argument that mental ingenuity could devise. So the debate went on abortively between Marina and him; she using all the dialectical weapons with which Cortéz had armed her mind, with such added persuasions as her own intelligence could provide, and Montezuma rejecting them in an immovable way.

The time seemed longer to those who listened because Marina was conducting an untranslated argument, as she had been instructed to do. There were murmurs of impatience from the steelclad cavaliers who stood idly round, and were all aware that they had taken a hazard at which it would be certain ruin to fail. They culminated in an outburst from Velásquez. He said: "Are we to stay here for a second hour? Perhaps while an army gathers outside the gates? Let him come with good heart or ill, or else let our swords make a quick end."

There may have been calculation in this protest, for León was not without caution or self-control, but, be that as it may, it brought crisis, for his voice was loud with impatience, and held contempt.

Montezuma, striving without full success for the cool dignity which his position required, asked: "What was it he said?"

Marina thought frankness best. "He threatened violence, if there be longer delay. They were not the words of my lord."

Montezuma considered that he was alone with six impatient and resolute men. The idea of violence to his own person might seem a monstrous improbability, but it could not be put entirely aside. The memory of Cortéz's inflexible determination to reach the capital came to his mind, and there was no comfort in that. He saw also that the Spaniards had brought the issue to a point from which they might think that they could not safely retreat. He said: "You know these men as I cannot do. If I consent, will their pledges stand?"

"I have not known my lord to break his word, or to act in a treacherous way."

"I must have more. You are of my race. You may think of that. And you are trusted in all. You give what you will of their words to me, and you shape mine to them. Do you pledge your faith to one who is still Emperor to you that, if I should change abode, I shall be undiminished in freedom and in my state?"

"That was pledged at the first." But then she turned to Cortéz to say: "He is of a disposition to give assent. But he had asked assurance from me that I am certain in my own mind that his honour will not be less, nor his freedom to rule; and that his servants may come and go as they do now. Shall I go too far, if I pledge that?"

"Not at all. For it is how I mean it to be. It shall be no more than a change of palace from which to rule."

Marina translated: "You may take my lord's word without fear. It is truly meant."

Montezuma made no reply, but he touched the gong once, which brought a noble menial into the room. "Have my litter prepared," he said, "with full attendance of state. I go to visit my friends."

Did the words or the voice sound strangely to him who heard? He bowed obedience, giving no sign of thought. But he may have spoken afterwards in a way that provoked doubt, for, as the litter was borne the short distance from palace to palace, with escorting Spaniards before and behind, a crowd had already gathered, blocking the road, among whom a murmur of consternation and amazement spread, rising to a note of anger, as the mounted cavaliers pressed forward to clear the way.

The crowd thickened at every step, and its obstruction increased. The green-plumed palanquin swayed and lurched.

Cortéz saw Alvarado pull out his sword. He said sharply: "Do not use violence, if patience can make a way." And then to Marina, whose bay stallion was at his side: "What does this shouting mean?"

"There is a cry that you have taken Montezuma by force."

"You can contradict that."

"I can try."

She saw that the position was critical. It looked impossible that peace should not be broken. Soldiers were coming out at a run from the barrack gates. Should spears once begin to fly— She raised her voice to its highest pitch: "You mistake all. The Emperor goes in peace at his own will. May he not visit his friends?"

Those who were nearest heard. They made some effort to withdraw from under the horses' heads, but the crowd was now too dense and too fiercely roused for their efforts to have much avail. It pressed forward on those who attempted to open way.

It was Montezuma himself who preserved the peace. He rose from the palanquin, and called to a crowd that quietened into awe as they saw him descend to the common street: "What is the meaning of this? Do you bar my way? Shall I not visit my guests if I will? Or shall I ask leave of you?"

There was prudence in what he did, for the Spaniards could easily have killed him before rescue could reach his side. But his motive may have been less simple than that. Pride forbade that he should appear to have been kidnapped against his will, and rescued by a promiscuous mob—he who was Lord of the World they knew, and High Priest of their God of War. Having accepted the position, he saw that it required to be carried through to a different success from that.

The crowd did not disperse, but it became irresolute. It gave sullen reluctant way, and Montezuma's glittering, green-plumed palanquin entered the gates of his father's palace.

CHAPTER FIFTY-FOUR: THE PRICE OF TREACHERY

Cortéz kept his pledged word to the full, as honour required, and it may have been politic to do.

There was ample space in the great palace for Montezuma to continue the elaborate ceremonies that his dignity had required in the past, and he selected what suites he would for his wives and nobles to share. He lived in the same manner, had the same attendance, and gave audiences as before. The Spaniards treated him with the ceremonious respect which had been accorded to him in his own palace. If he did not go abroad, it could not therefore be said that he was subject to constraint, for he was too prudent to risk denial. But there were strong guards at the palace gates, both front and rear. Sixty men at each, in eight-hour relays of twenty, at either gate.

So it was for two short Aztec weeks, until Quauhpopaca arrived.

He came in his litter, as his importance required, free of chains, or any physical restraint, having his son with him, and fifteen of those whose authority had been closest to his.

Cortéz examined them at once, with Montezuma's consent, but not in his presence. Montezuma had received them previously, and may have given them instructions as to what they should say.

Marina was, as usual, the sole inevitable channel of communication.

With some fencing, they admitted the facts, which were, indeed, very difficult to deny, or to clothe in a decent dress. But they said that Montezuma had had no knowledge of what they did. They had assumed an approval which they now knew that they would not have had.

Cortéz said that they had pleaded guilty to a crime for which they must certainly die.

Quauhpopaca may have expected this when he saw the Spaniards to be so securely established, but there were others who certainly did not. There was a clamour of cries that what they had done had been at the Emperor's orders, for which they could not be blamed. Finally, every man of them, including Quauhpopaca, agreed that this was the truth, which loyalty to Montezuma had led them to deny previously.

Cortéz believed that he had the truth at last, and Marina agreed. But he did not therefore change his judgement, for which there were those who blamed him in later days, which may have arisen from confusion of thought. For what had been done had not been a legitimate operation of war. It had been a murderous treachery in the guise of peace, when there had been no semblance of hostility from Vera Cruz, or assertion of warlike purpose from them. There has been no country, and no time, where it had been held that those who do such deeds, being caught, may escape reprisal by pleading that they acted under higher authority. Even spies do not expect to gain immunity by that simple plea, and the offence of these men was of a worse kind.

It may be objected that all the seventeen may not have been of an equal guilt, but it does not appear that any of them set up the defence that they had not been willing parties to what occurred, and it may be concluded that Tezo had made his selection well.

It must be observed also that the end which the Spaniards had suffered—that of being killed and eaten by those who had lured them into their power—was particularly loathesome to their comrades, who dreaded their liability to the same fate far more than that of being killed in battle in what they considered to be a more orthodox way.

When this is added to the consideration that they were now reduced to less than three hundred white men, surrounded by millions of cannibals who were all potential foes, it may be agreed that there was occasion for an emphatic demonstration of the peril of such a meal.

Cortéz had shown the clemency of his disposition at Cholula, and on numerous other occasions: it would have been treason to those who trusted him to have shown it now.

The convicted men were publicly burned, enduring their fate with stoic fortitude in the sight of a silent, sullen, bewildered crowd. Did the Emperor really approve? Had these men acted against his will? No man knew. Since the trial had begun, it had been given out that Montezuma would give audience to none till judgement should be complete. None of his own race went in to him, and armed Spaniards guarded his door.

But he had not been left entirely alone, and there was good reason why his condition should not be known to those of his own race.

Cortéz had entered his room without ceremony, with Marina, and Christóval de Olid at his side. He had charged him harshly with being responsible for the murders. He had ordered de Olid to put fetters upon his ankles, as he reclined on his usual cushions. Marina had given a plain warning: "He will kill you, if you resist," which she knew that de Olid would have called it pleasure to do.

Turning abruptly from one who had become speechless with mingled anger and shame and fear. Cortéz left the dishonest monarch to the misery of his own thoughts. Why had he not taken his brother's counsel, and met the strangers with open, continuous war? Many thousands might have perished, but it was certain that they would never have come to the sight of Tezcuco's lake, and all men would have approved what he did.

Or why had he not accepted Cacama's contrary advice, and received them with sincerity as welcome friends, till they should prove themselves to be unworthy of such a word?

He had vacillated between contrary policies, with this degradation for his reward. And what was he to expect on the next day?

CHAPTER FIFTY-FIVE: RELEASE OF SHACKLES

Cortéz came into the Emperor's room, as the ashes cooled in México's central square. Only Marina was with him. He knelt down, and removed the fetters.

Marina said: "My lord wishes me to tell you with what sorrow he subjected you to this shame. But, after the confessions which were made, the feeling among the comrades of those who died was so bitter against yourself that you were in danger of their fatal assault, had he not acted in such a way. But now that the tempest of wrath has cooled, and the ashes of those who died (which are still blowing about the square) are a sure warning of the fate of such as defy our God, all may be forgotten, and you may unite with him for the building of a new day."

"You believe this in truth, or is it what you are told to say?"

"It is both. I would not say that my lord might not have prevailed against those who are accustomed to do his will, for I have seen him to do so before now, when it has been harder to expect. But, in a matter in which the peril was yours and not his, he chose the safe way. Now that they have watched execution done, their minds may be diverted to other things."

Montezuma rose with some stiffness of limbs, and his eyes, as they encountered those of the man who had asserted his mastery by so humiliating a method, held a resigned melancholy, but no other indications of what he thought. Cortéz met them with the friendly smile which was always easy to him, being the reflection of his most natural mood. He said: "Tell him that his own people know nothing of what has occurred, and will hear nothing from us. They will see, by the executions, that we are sure friends, and distrusts can be put aside from this hour."

It was a singular basis on which to build better relations than had previously prevailed, but, with the event concluding thus, Cortéz might tell himself that he had handled it well. That Montezuma had had some measure of responsibility for the treachery at Vera Cruz is a certain thing. Indeed, with the absolute authority that he had, it is not reasonable to suppose that a local cacique would have attempted such an enterprise without assurance that its success would be approved—or would have sent him the head of a dead man. The incident might, under the military usages of the day, have justified Cortéz in putting Montezuma on trial, and executing him if the charges were sustained. But there were two objections to this— that of honour, because Montezuma had entered the palace under a pledge that his safety would be secure; and that of expediency, for, while he remained there, he might be of more use to the Spaniards alive than dead.

But he had gone through some hours, while he lay fettered, during which he must have had little hope that his life would last beyond the next day; and the reaction left him with a sense of the clemency of the Spaniards, as well as of their confident power. To Cortéz, personally, he came, whether logically or not, to have a much friendlier regard than before. He knew in his own mind that he was not guiltless of what had occurred. He judged that Cortéz had come to the same opinion. That being so, it could not be denied that he had shown forbearance in what he did. Did not the whole event support the conclusion that these men were those whose godlike coming had been foretold?

Beyond that, it seemed to show that, if he should ally himself to the Spaniards in a genuine way, his safety would be secure, and his personal dignities would remain.

When Cortéz had parted from him, with the same formalities of respect which he had used on earlier occasions, Montezuma summoned one of his obsequious suite, and announced that, now that those who had shown enmity to the Spaniards had met the fate that their deeds deserved, he would hold audiences again.

Once more high nobles stood before him in menial garb, once more he delivered judgements that dealt prosperity or ruin, life or death, from Pacific to Atlantic coasts, once more he was served with a meal that included every delicacy which the land could offer, on dishes which would become the perquisites of inferior men, once more he was entertained by jester and juggler as night approached. Then he ordered that he should be joined by one of his inferior wives, who would not venture to ask her lord why his ankles were as they were.

CHAPTER FIFTY-SIX: PRECARIOUS POWER

"Gonzalo, Cortéz said. "I have a mission for you which you may not like, but which I cannot longer trust to a lesser man."

Sandoval recognised that this opening had a dubious sound, but he answered readily: "I am at your service for what you will."

"So I was sure you would be. I am recalling de Grado, of whose conduct I have complaints, and appointing you commander at Vera Cruz.

"You may think that this will deprive you of honour here, as perhaps it may, but you will not go to a command which will be sterile of hazard or call for valour—and the discretion which I know you have.

"It is the refuge to which we must fall back should we be reversed here (as I do not count that we shall), and it is the watchtower from which you will first descry the sails of those (as I dread more) who may come not to strengthen us, but to put us aside, making our gain theirs.

"We will talk more on those matters before you go. But there is one charge on which there must not be a day lost. I purpose that we shall build two brigantines here, to control the lake, and free us from the menace that the causeways are. You must send here enough of canvas and cordage, of nuts and bolts, of tools and gear, which were brought ashore when the hulls burnt; and Martín tells me that he can build us two vessels which it will be pleasure to see."

Martín López had worked in a shipman's yard. Cortéz did not think him to be one who would undertake more than he would be able to do; and there were three objects in this design. One was to obtain command of the lake, and a sure way of retreat from the city, should there be occasion for such a flight; the second was to impress the Aztecs with a visual evidence of the superiority of the European; the third was to find occupation for idle men.

Having made these dispositions, Cortéz waited upon Montezuma, to obtain his assent to the felling, around the shores of the lake, of the timber which would be required for the two projected vessels.

He prefaced this by introducing the subject, of the Emperor's return to his own palace. It might have been confidently supposed that Montezuma would desire this, while the Spaniards would regard it as a hazard they must scheme to delay. But the fact was precisely opposite. Cortéz, with one of those audacities which punctuated the caution of his procedures, had decided that the position could not be indefinitely prolonged, and that it was politic that the proposal for Montezuma's return to his own palace should come from him, rather than be ultimately agreed in a grudging way. He had decided that it would be policy to assume that the lesson of the executions would be conclusive to Aztec minds, and that peaceful relations could now be maintained if all were done in a friendly confident way.

So it might have been, but that will never be known, for Montezuma made the surprising reply that he was comfortable where he was, and would prefer to remain. He realised that the Spaniards were friends, as he had become to them. His father's palace was large enough for themselves, and him. He knew that they would soon be on their return journey, and till then he would remain with them.

He was influenced in this decision by a confusion of motives, such as had betrayed him before. Perhaps his sense of dignity was the strongest of these. To go back because he was permitted to do so—told to do so might be an easy interpretation—would be derogatory in itself, and emphasise the fact that he had not come in a voluntary way. But if it became evident that he still made his residence in his father's palace, while going freely abroad, as he would be able to do, would it not confirm the evidence of that dramatic moment when he had descended from his litter to forbid the rescue which loyal subjects designed?

Next, he had arrived at a decision to accept the friendship which Cortéz had so consistently offered. And, if he did that, was there danger in remaining? The danger had been and gone, with the executions that lit the square.

Finally, he was uneasily aware of a danger, vague but real, which might be actually increased by a return to his own palace. Reports had been brought to him that his closest relatives, brother and nephew, after himself the most powerful lords in the land, had come to the same mind that the Spaniards must be destroyed or expelled. If he should return, would he not be vexed by, or implicated in their intrigues? Forced to join them in hostilities of doubtful wisdom, or perhaps thrust aside—superseded—even murdered—because he refused to bend to the common will?

He assured Marina that he enjoyed the society of the Spaniards too much to remove himself while they were there; and when the request for timber was made, he gave ready assent. When had he refused anything in his power to give? It would be an additional pleasure to see how the floating houses were built. He would select the timber himself, that there should be assurance that its quality would be good.

It was an attitude which is not incapable of diplomatic defence, from whatever angle, but it ignored one latent factor which would not remain permanently quiet—the stubborn loyalty of the Aztecs to their own religion, and the belief of the Spaniards that its overthrow was a duty they owed to God.

So Montezuma remained at the palace, going abroad now as he would. He made friends of the Spaniards, high and low, by his habit of munificent gifts, and by acquainting himself with the name and rank of every officer that they had. He watched their military exercises, he learnt their customs. He provided exhibitions of native sports for their entertainment. When a Spanish soldier was caught pilfering one of his golden vessels, he interceded with Cortéz for his pardon. When the personal deference which Cortéz always observed and enjoined towards him was grossly outraged by a common soldier, and Cortéz ordered that the man should hang for his disobedience, the sentence was reduced to a flogging at his request.

So, with surface smoothness, the weeks passed, while the two brigantines were swiftly built by the labour of many hands. They were small vessels, but the larger of them had four falconets mounted upon its decks, only the heavier guns now being left in Meza's control; they gave the Spaniards a sense of added security, offering an alternative to the long narrow lake-washed causeways for the removal of horses, artillery and stores, if it should become necessary to withdraw from a hostile city; and their spread of canvas was a marvel to Aztec eyes.

Montezuma, reclining upon a cushioned deck under gay awnings, was a willing guest of the Spanish Commander when they sailed across the great lake, and landed to hunt game in the royal forest.

Beyond the lake, beyond the hills, in Tezcuco's palace, Cacama, cursing his uncle's weakness, plotted the destruction of the hated foreigners, and either rescue or a similar fate for the Emperor who was so unequal to the assertion of his own position—but which he meant may not have been clear even to his own mind.

Chapter Fifty-Seven: Surrender

The winter passed, and the fresh green came to Tezcuco's woods, which the folly of a later generation would change to the desolation of an arid land.

Much happened during three months, which had brought Cortéz to a position of almost incredible power.

The intrigues of Cacama, the one man of courage and ability to reverse the position, had been communicated to Montezuma by those whose loyalty to himself overrode their dislike or dread of the foreign intruders. He himself had been betrayed into his uncle's hands, with the caciques who had shared his plans.

Charged with treason by Montezuma, he had met the position boldly, denouncing the invaders and his uncle's weakness. He had expected death, but he and his companions had found that, by the intercession of Cortéz, they were to experience nothing worse than a dignified confinement, while Montezuma placed a younger brother, Cuicuitzea, upon Tezcuco's throne.

Cortéz had seen that the most serious danger had been removed, and though the event had demonstrated how deep was the sense of personal loyalty for their monarch among the Aztecs, there had appeared to be little peril, or even advantage, in this while he continued to favour the Spaniards and shower favour upon them.

Were they still greedy for gold? The sealed treasure chamber in the palace was opened by Montezuma's orders, and much that Cortéz had refused to seize before became theirs by a royal gift.

Were they curious as to the source of the metal for which they longed? An expedition was guided three hundred miles to where they could see the gold being washed from the sand of the river beds.

Was Cortéz interested in agriculture? He received a grant of fertile land in the name of his Spanish King, which he stocked in the Mexican way, and commenced to farm with all the successful energy which had made him rich in his Cuban days.

Did he lament that the harbour at Vera Cruz was not protected on every side? Maps of the coast were produced, and a mission half Spanish, half Aztec, was sent to survey the coast for two hundred miles.

With a few score Spaniards only, made more numerous, but not strengthened, by their retinue of wives and servants, Cortéz had come to a power rivalling or exceeding that of the Emperor—and he had determined to risk all by demanding that its precedence should be publicly recognised. He proposed to Montezuma that he should make a ceremonious recognition of the supremacy of the Spanish Crown.

The audacity of this request may appear to be no more astonishing than the fact that it was not rejected with indignation. But this appearance is reduced on close examination of the position as it must have appeared to Aztec eyes, whether with challenging anger, as with Cacama; or with hatred controlled by fear; or with hesitation by Montezuma, who of all men had most to lose, and most therefore to save by surrender, if resistance would prove to no avail.

It was true that the dominating position of Cortéz had been obtained with the support of no more than a few hundred men, and about a dozen each of guns and horses. It was certain, as Montezuma's brother had argued from the first to last, that they could have been destroyed by sustained and united effort.

It was apparent, if the position were closely analysed, that the Spanish successes had been dependent upon Montezuma's irresolution, and the support of native states which had been hostile to, though they were no match for, the Aztec power. But the Spaniards had succeeded. Through discords and vacillations, the inflexible purpose of Cortéz had thrust on as a spear goes to the heart.

There was the ascendancy of a moral confidence here, which might be supposed to have had a solid foundation on which to build. By this time, a large proportion of the Spaniards, including almost all the officers, had taken Tlascalan or Mexican wives. The barriers of language had weakened, and, in many instances, had broken down. The Spanish page whom Cortéz had given to Montezuma, who had become closely attached to his new master, had become fluent in the Aztec tongue. The great distant Empire of Spain had become a conversational reality. It might be less than the imaginations engendered by Spanish boasts. It might be more. But it was correctly realised as a very formidable potential menace. If a few hundred Spaniards had come in an amazing self-confidence, which had been justified by its results, what would a hundred thousand be able to do?

Montezuma recognised Cortéz to be a man of uncompromising assertions, but he had found that a pledged word would be kept. With reluctance however bitter, with whatever reservations may have been known only to his own mind, he decided that the humiliation must be endured. He summoned his nobles, his military leaders, his tributary kings, from the farthest limits of his dominions, to a great conference, at which he exerted his authority for its own destruction.

He addressed those over whom he had an absolute authority, both as priest and King. He said that the ancient prophecy was fulfilled. The messengers of the long-departed god had returned, as He had foretold that they would. They represented an invincible power, to which allegiance was due. He himself had accepted this. As they were faithful to him, he required them to swear fealty to the Spanish Crown.

The degree of amazement with which this declaration was heard depended largely upon the distance from which his auditors had come, but it must have been unwelcome to all. Yet there was none who refused.

They saw their supreme Lord moved by an emotion he could not subdue as he made an announcement that was practically abdication from a position of authority wider and more absolute than that of his ancestors, and which had rarely been equalled in the records of men.

They were moved to kindred emotion as they took the required oath, and there were tears of sympathy in the eyes of the Spaniards who watched the ceremony.

That night Cortéz sat down to commence a long letter to Charles V. He did not know what might have happened to the envoys whom he had sent to Madrid more than six months before. They might have reached their destinations, or their small vessel might have been sunk in tempestuous seas. They might have been true or false to him. If they had been true (on which he confidently relied), they might not have prevailed. His authority might have been confirmed or revoked. There might be one on the way to supersede him now. With a mandate that he could not resist. But nothing could alter the amazing triumph of what had been done by himself alone. He could report that he had won an Empire for God and Spain.

CHAPTER FIFTY-EIGHT: DIVISION OF SPOIL

Cortéz had finished his letter to Charles V on an earlier day. There were figures, not letters, before him now. He had been seated for several hours with Ávila, and his three most reliable scriveners, while Alvarado and Meza had been superintending the weighing of gold in a larger room.

"Well," Ávila said, "you may exclaim as you will, but that is how it works out. Figures will not give way. If Alvarado confirm the weights, as I think he will, and the valuations of other articles stand, there will be eighty-three pesos for every man."

"It cannot stand thus," Cortéz replied. "If it seem to me beyond belief, what will be its aspect to them? It is a thing they will not endure."

"Then you must divide it in other ways."

"And will you say how we can do that? We will leave it now. You shall all be here at tomorrow's prime, and we will approach it anew."

They got up to go. The three scriveners had no pleasure in their looks, for, while they could not dispute figures at which they had done much to arrive, they were among those who would come off worst, and the disappointment, after their dreams of wealth, was proving hard to endure.

These were the facts. The total wealth was immense. The gold alone, which was now being melted down into ingots for ease of transportation, was equivalent to about a million English pounds.

Wrought silver, in cups and plate, weighed five hundred marks. Ornaments and jewellery, valued article by article, in endless-seeming lists, totalled more than five hundred thousand ducats of gold.

Featherwork and embroidery could be valued at what they would, but it was of great bulk, and its quality was the best that the land produced.

But a fifth of all was the legal property of the Spanish Crown: there could be no pruning of that. And a fifth was due to Cortéz, by an equally recognised law. On the remaining three-fifths there were huge preferential claims, which could not be ignored.

There were the sums due to those who had financed the venture at its inception, and the proportions of ultimate profits which had been agreed. Accounts had been very scrupulously kept, and the consequent obligations had been worked out with care, and could not be changed.

There was the long-dated bond which Cortéz had given to Sedeño, when he had seized the cargo of wheat, and the vessel in which it was.

Obligations had been largely increased when the fleet was burned.

The officers did not expect to rival their general's share, but they also had custom for their support in substantial claims, or special agreements to be observed.

There were the men at Vera Cruz to be remembered, the two envoys who had gone to Madrid, and their crew.

The crossbowmen and arquebusiers were entitled to twice what the spearmen received. When it came to them, it worked out at eighty-three pesos a head. Mathematics could not be moved by impatient words.

Marina saw Cortéz walk the room that night, as he would do when he had a problem he could not solve at a better hour, and was less concerned than amused.

She said: "I should ask what they can do with the gold. They have all they need. I should call it useless to them. Louise says she has been told that it will buy women in your land, to be put to a lustful use. I should say it is false talk; and it is certain that it could only be true of those who have very barbarous ways. And, anyway, they are not there! They can have wives here, if they will, as they mostly do.

"But that you should be perturbed about this! You can make them believe black to be white, if you will. I have seen it done. Can you not convince them that black is what it is? It would be hard to believe. If you will lie down, we will pass the night in a better way."

So they did; but in the morning he must go to the figures again, and when they had worked for two hours, and revised values, and reduced claims to a level which would ill content those who must be told at a later day, they had increased the spearmen's due to one hundred pesos, and a small fraction beyond, where it must stay. Cortéz said he would tell the men, which it was certain that no one else would be willing to do.

But he found there would be no occasion to go to them. Rumours spread. Perhaps the scriveners had talked. Men came to him, with bitter or incredulous cries. Some said they were being robbed. Others that they were not perturbed, because they did not believe. They knew Cortéz too well. They had seen the wealth, and they knew that they would not be cheated by him.

Cortéz said: "I will talk to all at one time. Let assembly be made, and you may be well assured that what is just will be done."

A man said: "So we believe. But you can end our doubt in one word. There are some who say we shall have each one hundred pesos, or at most two. If you will say it is a false tale—"

"I will say nothing until I am speaking to all," he answered, seeing the sullen anger of those who had waited for his reply, and was then aware that men were looking aside, and that they began to run to a place where there was a clashing of swords. He turned to see León de Velásquez in mortal dual with Mexía, the treasurer for the Spanish King.

The Government in Madrid did not leave its claim of twenty per centum upon the gross profits which its explorers made to the dubious prospect that honest loyalty would prevail over private greed. Every major expedition was accompanied by an officer responsible only to the Spanish Treasury, who watched its interests, and received its due.

So far, Mexía had no cause for complaint. Far from that, he had been able to report the liberality with which the whole of the earlier accumulation of treasure had been surrendered to his disposal, without legitimate deductions. But that did not dispose of his duty to secure his due percentage on this occasion, and he had already conceded more than he had felt it easy to do.

Had the spoil been all in precious metals, the division would not have been difficult. Even goldsmith's work has a value which is not beyond fair assessment by expert eyes. But cloaks and headgear of strange materials and workmanship are of a more disputable worth. Who shall assess the value of a toque of feather webbing, brilliant in its intricate colouring, which may have taken a year to make, as few craftswomen, even in Cholula, would have been able to do, and which must have required contributions from the plumages of five hundred birds?

And spoils of this category could not be divided among the men. They were only interested in gold. Almost the whole had been allotted either to his Royal Master, or to Cortéz himself, and this morning Mexía had given grudging assents while such articles had been written up, in some cases, to double their first valuation. It had been hard for him to resist. He remembered the previous generosity to the Crown; he saw the present difficulty: he watched Cortéz, quill in hand, writing up the values of his own share, and slashing his claim for gold, in the same way.

He had agreed. But it left him ill-content, and aware that he might be criticised in consequence, even penalised, by those who would be less sympathetic to difficulties from which they were more remote.

In this mood he made an accusation against León which he did not meet in a logical way. He said it was a foul lie, and drew out his sword.

León, as we know, was a near relative of his namesake, the Cuban Governor. He had preferred to follow Cortéz, when choice had to be made, but it had left him with special obligations, as the financial representative of his kinsman, and others, who had invested large sums in the enterprise. He may have felt that his political defection increased this responsibility. Only satisfactory financial results could justify the course he had taken.

However this may have been, Mexía's accusation was that he had been seen to smuggle some pieces of gold plate into the Cuban appropriation in an illegitimate manner. Accepting León's method of agreement, he had drawn his own weapon, and swords met.

Fortunately for themselves, they were both good swordsmen, and the duel prolonged itself sufficiently for Cortéz to reach the scene.

He saw two men who fought with fury. There was blood on their swords. Blood on the ground. But neither had yet taken a deadly wound.

He drew his own sword. He struck up theirs, thrusting himself between them with less risk than there must have been for a lesser man.

There was no smile on his lips now. He said: "Torment of hell! Would you ruin all? Do I lead babes?" He said to Bernal, he being the officer nearest at hand: "Put these brawlers under close arrest, till I have more leisure than now. They will have time to cool, and to lick their wounds."

He went back to the waiting men.

"Comrades," he said, as his breath returned, "you have heard the truth, though it might have been told in a better way. For those of you who use powder or bolt, there will be two hundred pesos of gold to be taken now; and for the spearmen half that amount as the custom is. Can you blame me for that? The calculations are not mine. Do you blame me that I take a fifth of all, so that I may become far richer than you? I will tell you this. I have given bonds for much. There are stores and ships for which I am pledged to pay. And I have not taken my share wholly in gold, as it will be given to you. But if I had much, is it not by a custom I did not make, and of which you all know?"

"It is mine of right. But I am not here to seek gold. If any one of you be less than content, let him come to me, and say how much more he should justly have. When I have summed my debts, the remainder is yours to take.

"And I will tell you this. If you bicker now, it is your own throats that you are being active to cut. Have we made an end here, or have we come near to ruling the land? Are its mines emptied, its craftsmen dead?

"Be content with that which is justly yours, and those who are loyal now may reap much more on a later day. Payments will be made to all at the third hour after noon. And I suppose that by sunset half of you will have diced it away."

The last word was shrewdly added, for he knew that many of the more turbulent of the spearmen were so addicted to gambling that the prospect of instant gold would be irresistible, little or much, when the idea was put into their minds.

He turned from men among whom there were still many who scowled and murmured, and was confronted by Ávila and Alvarado, in more agreement than they would frequently be.

"Three hours after noon?" Alvarado exclaimed. "Why did you say that? It is an impossible thing."

"Pedro is right in that," Ávila agreed. "There is too much to be done."

"Yet you must. Get Diego's help, with every man you can trust well. Do you not see that each hour is an added risk, till the gold be in the men's hands? What shall you propose to do, if they use violence to take what they think to be due to them? Shall we destroy ourselves, and bring all to naught, being surrounded by watchful foes?"

He went on to interview Mexía, and hear what he had to say, to which he answered: "If it were all true, and I must not judge, not having heard León thereon, was it not a matter that you should have brought to me? Are our foes so few that we must reduce ourselves with our own swords? You may go free if I have your sworn word that you will not contend again."

"I would have you know," Mexía replied, "that I was not the first to draw. Seeing a bare sword at my throat, what would you have had me do?"

"I believe that you were not the first to draw, but you made a charge which some would think should be met in that way, concerning which I have told you I will not judge. Nor will you find that León will draw on you again, for I shall send him away. If you think the Crown may have been wronged, you may take what you will from my own share."

"That," Mexía replied, "I would not do, for you give too much. You will have no more trouble from me."

Cortéz went on to the tent where León fumed with anger, as he bandaged a throbbing arm. He met the eyes of a Commander who did not look to be in a merciful mood, and who spoke without waiting to hear what he might urge in his own defence.

"León," he said, "we had discord before, which I had put out of my mind. I had made you a trusted friend, and what reward do I get? How would it have been told in Madrid, if the Crown's treasurer had been slain in defence of his Master's right? No, I do not ask you to make retort about that. Be it right or wrong, it would have been the same colour to those who watch us across the seas. I have Mexía's pledge that there will be no more trouble from him. And I am about to tell you that from which you will see that there will be no more trouble for you. You are not to stay here. I had report yesterday from those whom I sent to the coast to make survey, but I was too busied to talk of it then. They have found good anchorage far southward of Vera Cruz. We will build a city there which may become the port of the New World. I will trust you for this. You will march at tomorrow's dawn with a hundred and fifty men, being nearly half of those I have that are worth trust. You will have your own horse, and another, lest it should fail, and your own choice of a cavalier to be companion to you. I give you the greatest trust that I can, for I am assured that you will not fail."

He grasped León's uninjured hand, and turned away, without waiting for the thanks of an astonished man.

CHAPTER FIFTY-NINE: THE FINAL CHALLENGE

Cortéz considered fearlessly a position which had become one of moral rather than material power. Now that León had gone, he had scarcely more than two hundred Spaniards under his immediate control, including some who were hurt or sick. He still had the artillery, and most of the horses, with which to make a display of power.

Many of the Tlascalans had left. Most of the porters had been paid off. For others could be found, if the need should arise. He had given León of the best men he had, and many had taken their wives with them, and there had been a miscellaneous retinue of servants and others, making more than three hundred, without counting the four hundred porters who bore their gear. It had looked more like a procession to found a colony than to build a fort, which, indeed, it was. There would be children to augment their numbers before summer would come. No one had thought of the possibility that they might be setting out for a destination they might not reach. It was a march of a few days through a friendly land.

Cortéz might have no more than two hundred men of his own race for his support, but he was the representative of the distant King who had been publicly accepted as overlord of the whole realm. His anxiety now was less for the position he held than that it might not be confirmed by Madrid. In spite of all he had done, he knew that there would be voices that would urge that the man who conquers is not adapted for civil rule. He might expect to be re-called, with fair words, and a title, and perhaps the grant of an estate in his own land, while a courtier of plausible speech, who had learned how kings can be flattered or amused, would be sent out to take the place he had won for Spain.

Well, before that could be, he had one thing—the greatest of all—which he could do for God, and which he must no longer neglect.

He put this to Father Olmedo, and found him more disposed to listen than he had been on an earlier day. The abominations of the Aztec religion were now practised in all the temples of the city, and the Spaniards, now moving freely among them, were sickened by what they saw. They both knew that, by sheer audacity of demand, he had already obtained almost incredible political gains. Was he to attempt less for the cause of God? And now that the overlordship of Spain had been accepted by Montezuma, had they not become responsible for the abominations which they did not forbid?

But they agreed that there should be some moderation in their demand. They would not require that Christianity should entirely supersede the national religion, for which they recognised that even Montezuma's command might not avail. They would ask for that which was in his power to grant, and would do no more than put the Christian Faith where it ought to be in any land that had accepted the overlordship of Spain.

If the great pyramid should be given over to Christian worship, the lesser temples might still be used for the worship of Aztec gods, provided only that the savage custom of human sacrifices should be abolished.

This was to be put to Montezuma for the formality of his consent, which Cortéz did not doubt that he could obtain.

He had at this time arrived at a strange intimacy with the Aztec monarch, with whom he could now converse to a considerable extent in a language which blended the Spanish tongue with a profusion of Aztec words. His union with Marina had done much to acquaint him with Aztec habits of thought, and her position with him had often enabled Montezuma to gain assurances and understandings which would otherwise have been hard to reach, while her conversations had done much to convey her own confidence in the power and integrity of him whom she had learned both to trust and love.

And Montezuma, at this time, had become a most lonely man. His previous eminence had been lonely enough, surrounded, as one in his position must always be, by those who approached him without equality of status, or independence of spoken thought. But, since he had yielded to Spanish claims, he had become doubly lonely as he had lost confidence in the respect, if not equally in the affection of those of his own race, to whom he was now neither admittedly equal nor securely eminent.

Paradoxically, it was the Spaniards who had contrived his fall, and it was among them that he felt that his position was most secure.

Cortéz asked: "Should you say he will grant this?"

Marina answered with more doubt than he had expected to hear: "You have done so much! Is it I who shall forecast a limit to your success?"

"But, if you speak your thought, it is here I may be expected to fail?"

"If I speak my thought I say no more than that I do not know. There may be some things that even Montezuma may be unable to do. But we have a very great God."

"That is a sure word."

They went into the audience with Montezuma for which Cortéz had made request, for such etiquette was still strictly observed.

The sad dignity of the Emperor's face brightened as they came in. He asked: "What would Malintzin have now from one whom it is ever pleasure to give?"

"Tell him, Marina .You can put it better than I."

Marina said: "It is the temple worship, about which there has been discussion before. We have an omnipotent God, and He dislikes the worship of these gods who are less than He. He also dislikes the sacrifices of living men, even on altars that are not His. Most of all, He is wrath that He has no temple worthy to show to all men how great He is."

Montezuma looked at her with apprehensive eyes: "To what do you lead when you say this?"

"Perhaps to less than you may forebode. Till the people be better taught in our Christian ways, we do not ask that they be compelled to the worship of One Whom they do not know. If the great pyramid be made the temple of the true God, men may still worship what gods they will in the others throughout the city; so; only, that human sacrifices be denied. It is a request which allows much."

Montezuma said, with more decision in his voice than would often be heard these days: "It is an impossible thing. It could not be done. If I ask it, I ruin all the peace which we have been careful to build. And I cannot ask it! Am I not the High Priest of the Faith you would bring to dust? Nor, if I should, would my word prevail. Does not Malintzin understand that, if I should whisper a word—or if any evil should come to me—he would not have a friend in the Aztec lands?— That there would not be a man's hand in which a weapon would not be raised? When I say this, I do not threaten, I warn. Tell him that I counsel that this attempt be not made, and that it is the voice of a friend."

Cortéz did not understand all that was said, but sufficient for him to appreciate both the intensity and the quality of the opposition which he must meet. He began to speak to Montezuma directly, arguing in his persuasive way in the hybrid tongue that they were now accustomed to use. So, for some time, it went on. They talked directly, while Marina interpolated, defined, explained, or argued, as they appealed to her, or allowed her, to do.

In the end, compromise came. Montezuma was to see the priests of the Great Pyramid, and to urge their assent to a portion of the building being allocated for Christian worship. Cortéz would undertake to advise *his* priests, that that would be the utmost which they could hope to obtain as yet in a peaceful way. They could continue to learn the Aztec tongue, and to preach the religion of Christ to all who had disposition to hear.

This being agreed, the War God's attendants sullenly removed their images and altar from one of the larger temples that stood on the flat roof of the great pyramid, and Christian priests arrived to cleanse and dedicate it to their satisfaction, and erect their own altar, with its symbol of sacrifice, and its image of the Mother of God.

Soon there was a procession of the little Spanish army, with their wives, and such of their attendants as had accepted the Christian Faith, led by Father Olmedo and Díaz, and with the cross lifted triumphantly in the van, moving from palace to pyramid between silent crowds of Aztecs, whose gay garments and flower-crowned heads did not disguise the sullen anger and amazement with which they watched this bold invasion by an alien faith of the very citadel of the religion which was the foundation and inspiration of their national life.

To the Spaniards, this celebration of Mass in a chapel from which the devils had been expelled was but one forward step in a crusade of salvation which must not cease until the whole nation had been rescued from the perdition in which they dwelt. The Aztec priests looked at it in the same, or rather in the opposite way. To them also it was a battle to the death, which they did not intend to lose.

CHAPTER SIXTY: SHADOW OF LOSS

There was a soldier stationed on guard at the entrance to the Christian chapel. The position had been given to an elderly man who was unfit for more active affairs. But he was one who had been diligent in learning the Aztec tongue. He reported conversation he overheard. Both priests and people regarded the use of the chapel for Christian worship as an intolerable sacrilege, which could not endure. They talked freely of a coming day when the Spaniards would provide nourishment for Aztec bellies. One of them, not supposing that he understood, had jeered at him, as being likely to make a tough meal.

Cortéz did not think it wise to increase the chapel guard, as though apprehensive of trouble, but he substituted a more vigorous and fully armed man, and one who could blow a trumpet note if there should be any attempt to desecrate sacred things.

It was noticed that the chief priests made several visits to Montezuma, accompanied by some of the principal Aztec nobles. They had long conferences; and it was a significant fact that Montezuma did not allow the Spanish page, whom he now usually kept at his side, to be present on these occasions.

Aztec wives of Spanish soldiers became nervously alert to a sinister atmosphere which increased around them. They heard talk in the market which led them to warn their husbands against going out alone.

Cortéz saw dark clouds rise in a sky which he had supposed to have become clear. He determined to have a conference with Montezuma to define the position, and his own attitude thereto; but Montezuma was quicker than he. He requested that he should attend him on matters which would not wait.

Cortéz showed consciousness of the altered atmosphere in taking with him not only Marina, but Alvarado, Ávila, Ordaz, and Olid. He was received with a reserved dignity reminiscent of earlier days—the armour with which Montezuma had always protected his natural diffidence from the observation of lesser men.

It was another sign of deterioration in their relations that there was now no attempt at direct conversation. Montezuma addressed himself to Marina, using his own tongue exclusively, and Cortéz replied in Spanish in the same way.

The Emperor said: "You may tell Malintzin that all is happening of which I warned him when he refused to be guided by me. The people whom I rule have endured much. They have even allowed that their own country should accept the supremacy of a King they have never seen, and who reigns in a distant land. That was a matter of most importance to me, and if I called it well, they could not resist. But to insult their gods, and the religion through which they have become great, is to create foes for yourselves in every home in the land.

"Now the War-God's priests have made proclamation of that which he has threatened to them. They will desert the city unless the sacrilege in the Great Pyramid be quickly ended. You must tell him, beyond this, that a feeling has now been raised which I cannot alter, or long control. All men ask when you will go. It is for your safety I speak, having made you friends. For if I should lift a finger to show assent, the whole nation would rise, and your deaths would be beyond my power to prevent."

Marina translated this, which Cortéz heard without visible emotion, or being quick to reply. It was evident that he was threatened with a general hostility, which he was ill-prepared to meet, his forces, inadequate at the best, being separated as they now were. He judged that the storm might be stilled, for the moment at least, by abandoning the use of the chapel in the Great Pyramid. But, even if that should be tolerable in itself, what would be the position on the next day, the safety of his little army depending so largely on the prestige which he had gained?

It was true that Montezuma was in his power, but it was not clear that he could base effective action on that. Indeed, any report of further indignity or restraint might be a signal to rouse offence. And it appeared that Montezuma was dealing straightly with them. He could have spoken the secret word which would have set the whole country ablaze, and still professed that it was wholly against his will.

Marina was soon translating a quiet reply: "My lord says that he thanks you for a warning which is clearly that of a friend, but he is not greatly perturbed, not only as having behind him the power of Spain, but knowing that those who should insult his God would be asking for death.

"But it seems to him that there is little cause for your priests to fret, the time being near when he will be leaving the land.

"Only, he would not do it as one who flees, and if he should, he would be delayed at the coast, for dearth of ships. If he should go thus, he would have no choice but to ask that you should go with him, to show that your favour is not withdrawn.

"But is there need or reason for that? Ships are soon built, if there be abundance of willing hands, as was shown with the brigantines. If you will give orders that sufficient labour and timber shall be supplied, the ships shall be built with speed, and he will return to his own land."

Montezuma saw satisfaction in this proposal, not only for himself, but as a basis of likely peace. He said that he would supply all the material and men that the work required, and he would let his command be widely proclaimed that the Spaniards should be treated with honour till they should go.

In both these matters he kept his word. It was seen next day, with popular satisfaction, that about a dozen Spaniards, including Martín López, left the city, in company with a number of those who had gained some experience by assisting in the building of the brigantines. Montezuma sent for the priests and nobles who had interviewed him before, and persuaded them that it would be a most dangerous folly to molest those whose power had been learnt already at a great cost, and who were now preparing to go at their own will.

For the moment, his counsel prevailed. The priests ceased to incite the people; they advised patient endurance of that which would soon be done. But the Spaniards, now reduced to little more than two hundred fighting men, with much encumbrance of women and gear, had lost something of their previous confidence. Cortéz alone continued to think and plan with a steady mind. He sent a secret instruction to López that his previous orders to build the new ships in haste need not be taken too literally. They must be constructed with care, not disregarding the dangers of stormy seas. In the palace, he increased vigilance. Sentries were doubled. Arms were to be kept at hand during sleeping hours.

And then, passed rapidly through the hands of native runners, a letter came from Vera Cruz.

Sandoval wrote: *"There are sixteen ships on the southward coast. They have landed a thousand men, with many horses, and guns. What shall I do?"*

CHAPTER SIXTY-ONE: NARVÁEZ

Cortéz read Sandoval's letter as he was about to visit Montezuma, at the Emperor's request. It prepared him for what he heard.

Montezuma handed a picture-writing to Marina. He said: "There will be no need for the building of ships. Tell Malintzin that they have come to him."

Marina passed the picture on, but she knew that Cortéz was unable to read. She said: "What it tells is that sixteen ships have anchored on the coast, at the place where you had your ships first. They appear to be awaiting you there. About nine hundred of them have come ashore. They have eighty horses, one hundred and fifty crossbows, and eighty arquebuses. They have landed nine cannon and are still bringing them from the ships."

Cortéz said: "Tell him that I am grateful for the blessing of God, under whose protection he will now know that I am."

He went back to his own quarters, and let the coming of this new fleet be known, at which his soldiers rejoiced. He did not rebuke them for that, nor suggest a doubt. But he wrote at once to Sandoval: "Do not accept the authority of any who does not come with a commission direct from Madrid. Subject to our King, I am Governor here. You must hold your walls, and refer them to me."

He called a Council, to which he said: "It may be that those whom I sent have reached Madrid, and that we have reinforcements from Spain. If so, they will have orders which we are bound to obey, whether they confirm my position, or cast it down.

"But I do not expect this. I think the time to be too short. I should say that it is from Cuba they come, and they may assert that which we must deny. We shall soon know."

Three days later he had another letter from Sandoval, at which he frowned, and then laughed.

He called to Bernal: "Take two horses out on to the road from the east, and you will meet a priest and a notary bound on to the backs of porters, as though they were sacks of merchandise. That is Gonzalo's work, and I would not say but that he has done well. But you must bring them along the causeway in a more dignified style."

He had learnt that he had conflict to face, and been quick to see that it would not add to his security for Aztecs to perceive that those who had landed were not his friends.

He received the two men with courtesy and apologies for the indignities they had sustained. He said: "Gonzalo de Sandoval is young. You must make allowance for that. And, as I understand from him, you asked him to betray his trust to myself, which was wrong to do."

Father Guevera, a rather plump, rosy, black-eyed man, who was the senior member of the deputation which had been treated with such contumely, answered: "We did nothing beyond what our instructions were, we being the emissaries of the Lord-General de Narváez, who has been appointed Governor of this land."

"I must ask you by whom such an appointment had been made. But I will say first that such a claim should have been presented only to me. Should my loyal officers be suborned before I have knowledge of what is set up? But I do not say that you should have been so roughly bestowed. You must believe my regret. For this is sure—we must not quarrel among ourselves, being surrounded by watchful foes.

"You shall be refreshed, and shall then tell me your tale, and you may be well assured that all will be done thereafter to the honour of God and Spain."

With this pacific assurance, very different from the reception they had had from Sandoval when they had proposed to him that he should transfer his allegiance, they went to meat, after being given water to cleanse themselves from the dirt of their ignominious journey; and, while they ate, Cortéz sent a letter, by the running post of the land, to order León de Velásquez to abandon the enterprise on which he had set out, and march to Cholula, to which further orders would be sent.

After that, some hours passed during which Guevera was alone with Cortéz, and being closely questioned by him.

This is the tale that he told:

When the Governor of Cuba had heard the tale that was brought to him by the man who deserted from the ship which Cortéz had sent to Spain, he was roused to a condition of extreme cupidity by hearing of the wealth and extent of the newly-discovered land, and to an almost uncontrollable fury by the fact that Cortéz had ignored him, and sent treasure and information direct to Spain.

He was, of course, primarily responsible for the position which had arisen. Had he parted with Cortéz on cordial terms, few things can be more certain than that he would have been treated in a very different way. But there was no consolation in that.

It was just at this time that he received dispatches from Madrid that extended his authority to seek and administer additional territories—on which the terms of his appointment had been deficient before.

With this encouragement, he resolved to organise an expedition which would have authority from him to take over control in the new lands, and with sufficient strength to enforce its will, if Cortéz should have temerity to resist.

He looked round for a suitable commander for the expedition. He could not find another Hernando Cortéz, and may scarcely have wished to do so. But he fixed his mind on one who had been closely associated with him in the conquest of Cuba, and subsequently in the government of the colony.

In that conquest Narváez had gained a reputation for rather brutal efficiency. He had some military reputation. He was of a self-confident, even arrogant disposition, which de Velásquez considered would be particularly appropriate for the occasion. Cortéz would find that he had to deal with one whom he could neither intimidate nor cajole.

The expedition had taken some months to prepare, but when it sailed it was of a strength to justify that delay. It consisted of eighteen vessels (two of the smaller ones were destined to sink before sighting the Mexican coast), and nearly a thousand men, besides the seamen who manned the fleet. Its armament had been reported very accurately in the first report which Montezuma received. It far surpassed the greatest strength that Cortéz had ever had.

Word of its preparation had reached the Government, known as the Royal Andienea, at St. Domingo, which was the central Spanish authority in the Western World, and had some rather vague rights of general control, in the absence of direct orders from Spain.

This tribunal was alarmed. It cared little for the rights of Cortéz or Velásquez, but much for the interests of the Spanish Crown. It was obvious that, if a second expedition were sent, it should be in support, rather than in opposition of that which was already engaged in an operation of evident magnitude. They sent one of their number, a man named Ayllón, to expostulate with de Velásquez, and control the purpose of the expedition.

Finding the Cuban Governor in no mood for moderation, he urged that, while it might be natural for him to wish to assert his authority, and perhaps legitimate for him to do so, he should give de Narváez instructions not to quarrel with Cortéz, but, if he were insubordinate, to cooperate with him, and refer the dispute to Madrid.

Having less than a satisfactory reply to this proposal, he decided to accompany de Narváez, and observe, and perhaps influence, what might occur.

De Narváez sailed early in March. So eager had been the desire to exploit the fabulous riches of the newly discovered lands that the expedition included an actual majority of Cuba's principal citizens. The Governor's secretary, Duero, who had been a particular friend of Cortéz, largely instrumental in securing his commission, and of vital assistance in warning him of the risk of it being revoked, was among them; and so also were many, including the treasurer, Bermúdez, who had known him in quieter days.

The voyage was slow against adverse winds. There was a storm in which two of the smaller vessels were lost. There was a long pause on the coast of Yucatán, where Cortéz had landed before. It was late in April when the fleet cast anchor at San Juan de Utua, and were received by a single Spaniard.—the sole guardian of the place which Cortéz had occupied before sailing northward to found the city of Vera Cruz.

This man gave Narváez a full account of the events which had occurred since Montejo and Puerto-Carrero had left. It was a tale of amazing hazards taken and successes hard to believe. It did not diminish the invader's confidence in the mandate with which he came, or his ability to enforce it; but it showed that his reward might exceed his most sanguine dreams.

He learnt that the small forces of his opponent were scattered, and his first action was to endeavour to detach their allegiance. He did not anticipate any difficulty with León de Velásquez, who was so close a relative of the Cuban Governor, and had joined the previous expedition to represent his interest. He sent a friendly letter to him, announcing that he had been appointed to the Supreme Command, and asking him to join him at Cempoalla, to which he was proceeding at once. The letter assumed rather than argued—León was to do the obvious thing.

He learnt that Sandoval was at Vera Cruz, with about sixty men, including some who were sick. He sent Guevera, with a letter announcing that he had authority to supersede Cortéz, and requiring submission. He relied not only upon the warrant he had from the Governor of Cuba, but upon the report which his envoy would give of the overwhelming force at his command, to secure either willing or reluctant obedience. And why should Gonzalo de Sandoval care whom his Supreme Commander might be, so long as his own position should not be lost?

But Guevera came to barred gates, and to meet a man who was in no mood to listen to him. Sandoval had sent his sick men to the care of friendly allies. He had prepared to defend his walls from attacks of whatever strength.

He read the letter that Guevera handed to him, and he replied; "There is already a Captain-General in this land, who is responsible only to Spain. I should recommend you to yield to him, or you will meet the fate that the lawless earn. I can recognise no other orders except those of Madrid, which you have not got, or you would have told me at first."

Guevera said: "You ignore facts. Your men are two score or three. There are a thousand not far away. If you resist him who is now ruler of all the land, you will hang, as a rebel should. If I return with such a reply you will have bought a sure death."

Gonzalo laughed, as one seeing a joke. He said: "Do you think that? Well, there is a gallows here, which is not for me. It is for any who may be traitor to my own lord; but it is one I do not think I shall have occasion to use. If you return? But why do you think you should do that? You are going another way."

He called for porters, and ordered that priest and notary should be bound securely upon their backs, and be delivered to Cortéz, as, three days later, they were.

That was the tale that Cortéz heard, and he thought it bad enough, but that it might have been worse.

He said: "I have won this land for Spain, and it is to Spain that my account will be made. But I am not a quarrelsome man; and, if I were, I would not be willing to quarrel now, for, if Narváez and I contend, we may lose all. Would the Aztecs remain still, when they shall see our swords become red with our own blood? I will write a letter to Narváez, which you shall take, proposing that we shall be comrades in arms in a Christian way, and we will cast down the demon-worship that fouls this land, as I tell you frankly that alone I have not been able to do. You shall join Father Olmedo, whom you will have known before, and Father Díaz—yes, so I supposed—and they will tell you much which you will be glad to know."

Having put him into the charge of his brother priests, Cortéz called a council of those whom he could trust well, and put the position to them.

He said: "I have laid my worst fear aside, which was that they might have some mandate from Spain. For though I was of a settled mind that this expedition was not from there (knowing how long preparation must be), I was in doubt lest a letter might have arrived from Madrid which would have given them better right than they had hoped to have when their plans were made.

"As to that, what I have learnt is that Montejo put into a North Cuban port (as he was forbidden to do) and, though he made no communication to St. Jago himself, a man deserted, so all was told that we had done to that time, together with the fact that we were ignoring Cuba, and sending directly to Spain.

"As to what Puerto-Carrero and Montejo may have done for us there, we have still to learn. There has been time enough for word to arrive, but we know that the methods of Courts are slow. On that all depends at the last, should we triumph here. But I have good hope that they will not entirely fail, unless they have floundered in stormy seas.

"Now we have Narváez with whom to deal. I have offered peace, which I would always prefer. And, with the menace around us now, it is wooing death for us to bicker among ourselves. But, should he reject the hand which I have extended to him, will you say what it will be most prudent for us to do?"

Alvarado said: "You have offered peace. What can you do more?"

"I can give place to him, if you will."

"Cinders of hell! Would you do that?"

"I would not serve under him. I could go home."

Olid scowled: "He is no more than a strutting pig. He is not one for us to fear."

That was unfair to a rather arrogant man, with whom Olid had had a difference in earlier days.

"There is none," Ordaz said, "but will stand with you. They will not be so mad as to start strife, we being placed as we are; but, if they do, we must hold our ground. You would say the same?"

He turned to Ávila, as one who might be slower than others to speak, but whose word might be decisive for all.

Ávila said: "We are not babes to be scared by a loud word. I should say the men would stand even against their own kin. But I was wondering what León will do."

Cortéz said: "We must suppose that he will do as he should, having had his orders from me."

"If we suppose that, we are more than four hundred men, and it is said that there are nine hundred of them. We are near to half, and we may be better practised in arms. I should say we must draw to one head, and await what they will do."

"That is a good counsel," Cortéz said, "but you may see that it is hard to contrive, unless we leave here, to which we might not return. And if we assemble here, we must abandon Vera Cruz, it being too weak to be left standing alone, and Narváez would be free to make allies through the whole breadth of the land, which it would be easy for him to do. Could he not say that he is the Aztecs' friend, and Montezuma would be rescued by him, and their freedom saved? We must think of something better than that."

"Which you will be equal to do," Ávila replied; "for if we are fewer, we know that we are the better led."

Cortéz saw that his captains were of no mind to allow Narváez to take his place, as he had supposed, but desired to test. He said: "Well, we will look for peace, for which we will be active to work. I will send Father Olmedo among them, for he has the wit which the occasion requires. And, if all fail, we will take counsel again."

They rose in a sanguine mood. Cortéz thought, though he did not say: "If I could have another nine hundred men, there is not much which I should be unequal to do. But how shall I come to that?"

It was not an easy question, even for him. And what would León be doing now? It was clear that he could wreck all, if he would.

He sat down to compose a letter of conciliation for Guevera to bear. He pointed out the obvious fact that they could unite and be very strong, or clash in a strife from which even the victor would emerge in a draggled way. Beyond that, such a conflict would be certain to encourage the Aztecs to rise against them. He had won ascendancy over the whole country, but it was still a precarious victory, won less by physical force than by the prestige that he had established for the Spanish Crown, which would be largely diminished by signs of discord between themselves. Could they not become brothers-in-arms, with the understanding that he would accept a second place at any time when there should come a mandate to that effect from Madrid?"

It was a reasonable appeal, but it ignored absolutely that demand for surrender which Narváez made. It did not argue or deny. It put it aside without words.

Three days later, Narváez, now established in Cempoalla, and having explained to an astonished cacique that Cortéz was a rebel of no account, and he the true representative of the Spanish Crown, saw Guevera's return from a place to which he had not been sent.

He heard what his experience had been, and was naturally wroth at the demonstration of Sandoval's contempt; nor was he much better pleased by the friendly reception that his envoy had had in México, which, with some presents of value that Cortéz had bestowed upon him, and some talk he had heard, inclined Guevera to speak of those by whom he had been entertained in the wrong way.

Narváez broke the seal of the letter, and, with doubtful wisdom, read it aloud, amid the derisive cries of those around him. "There are some," he said, "who know when they have lost, and others who must be taught in a painful way."

The licentiate, Ayllón, had heard the letter read, and he looked at it differently. He not only argued with Narváez, he talked to others, endeavouring to persuade them that the offer which Cortéz had made should not be put so lightly aside.

Narváez saw a danger here which he resolved he would not endure. He could spare a ship. He considered that his own commission was from the Governor of Cuba. If Velásquez had exceeded his authority, the blame would be on him, not on the one to whom he had given that which was not his. The position of the Royal Audience at St. Domingo in such a matter as this might be the substance of a lawyers' dispute. It would ultimately depend upon the caprice of Madrid. But if Ayllón were ever at his side, making protests, he might not be able to shield himself behind his Cuban commission—especially if events should be adverse to him. Also, such protests must discourage his troops, even if no worse than that.

He told Ayllón he was sending him back to St. Jago. He could go with dignity, or in shackles, as he might prefer. Ayllón said he would go on his own feet. So he did; but, when the little vessel was out at sea, he had a talk with the captain, who agreed with him that they should avoid St. Jago, and tie up at St. Domingo quay, from which place a letter could be sent to Madrid, which the Cuban Governor could not control.

Narváez was unconcerned by that which he did not know, but he had a fresh occasion for wrath two days later, when Father Olmedo appeared with another letter. It was much the same as the last, but was now presented by one who gave it oral support, with the argumentative eloquence that his vocation required.

Praise of Cortéz was not to be endured silently, with his officers round. He replied with emphasis that, if his authority were further defied, he would deal with him as a traitor must expect. His chief captain, Salvatierra, added, thinking he made a good jest: "Tell him I will fry his ears for my morning meal, if he cannot use them to save themselves."

Father Olmedo looked at him as one who was about to speak, but was silent, and turned away.

He had other letters to deliver—one for Duero among them; and one for Ayllón, which he must tear up, for it was not intended for other eyes. He mixed with the troops, confirming the accounts which Guevera had given of the wealth which was to be seen in the hands of the Spanish troops, where he had seen men dicing for collars of solid gold, and of the popularity of their leader. He would soon have formed a party favourable to Cortéz, even among those whose mission it was to procure his ruin, had not Narváez, who was alert to such a danger, decided that he should be put under restraint; which he changed to an order for his expulsion, on Duero's representation that it would be unwise to offend the Church in a needless way.

After this, for a moment, the event paused.

Narváez remained at Cempoalla, active in intrigue, but judging correctly that he would embarrass Cortéz more by that apparent inactivity than by an immediate advance.

Cortéz would have agreed upon that. It was satisfactory to know that his officers thought him to be a better general than his opponent, but that had to be proved, which might not be easy to do.

If Narváez advanced upon him, he had a clear plan. He had been careful, since his letter had been dispatched, to say nothing to imply hostility to the invaders, let others guess as they would, that being beyond his control. But if Narváez advanced, he would converge upon him with all his forces at such a spot as would give him advantage of ground.

He was free from one anxiety, which he had scarcely admitted to his own mind, though he knew it to be that on which others held anxious debate—the test had come, and León had proved loyal to him. He had, indeed, heard of the coming of the strange ships before the letters either of Cortéz or Narváez had reached his hands, and had turned instantly to march back to Cortéz's support. Now he had been directed to Cholula, to await further instructions there.

If he were to march onto Narváez's flank, and Gonzalo come up behind, and Cortéz meet the advance with frontal attack—it was a matter of timing which might not fail. And it could be where absence from México City need not be long. And there would be no need to disclose to Aztec ears whether their purpose were hostile or not, till the moment of conflict should come. Indeed, it might still be possible for discretion to prevail at the last hour.

But if it should be necessary to go to Cempoalla, there would be no choosing of ground for him. It would be he who would have the long march, leaving México far away, which it might not be easy to enter again.

But Narváez saw all this as clearly as he. He had a different policy. He made loud proclamation that Cortéz was an enemy to be rooted out. He promised much to those who would assist him in this. Sandoval sent reports that Narváez was gaining strength. Should he continue at Vera Cruz, where the position became more menacing every day?

Cortéz saw that he must move. Narváez had won the first trick of the desperate game, as they both knew.

CHAPTER SIXTY-TWO: ORDER FOR SPEARS

While Cortéz waited for a movement which his foe was too shrewd to make, he had not omitted any precaution within his power.

He had considered the eighty horses Narváez had brought, which he did not like. It meant that his footmen might be subjected to a charge of mailed and mounted men which could not be met with an unbroken front—and, if a line of infantry broke its rank when exposed to a cavalry charge, it was the end. All the battle experience of the day was conclusive on that. He considered how the difficulty could be overcome. He knew of all the methods taught by the military schools of the day—the alternate pike and bow, with a changing rank if the arrows should not stay the charge—the bold English experiment of eliminating the pikes entirely, so that the arrow-volleys would be doubled in strength, which had failed at Bannockburn, but succeeded on other fields—and he had been taught that the crossbow was deadlier than the English weapon, of which he was not sure; but if that were so, it was no avail to him. His crossbows were too few, and it was a weapon which could not be easily made.

He recalled the Swiss method of meeting cavalry with a line of lances of such length that a second line could be advanced over kneeling men. That was obsolescent now, but it might still be the right one for him. He enquired whether such weapons could be obtained in the New World, and had an affirmative reply, such as he could scarcely have hoped to hear.

Far to the southeast, not yet subdued by the Aztecs, and bitterly hostile to them, there dwelt a tribe known as the Chinantla, who fought with a very long double-pronged spear, a curious weapon, but which might answer his present need. The Chinantlans had, in fact, already sent a privy messenger to him, offering their support if he should quarrel with Montezuma. How now should he procure these weapons for his own use?

Marina said that was a simple matter. He must approach the merchants. They would quote a price and date. He would pay cash in advance, and could rely upon the bargain being exactly kept. The fact that the Chinantlans were at war with the Aztecs would not affect the matter. The merchants went everywhere. Anyway, if they said they could procure them, it would be punctually done. The merchant guild never broke its word.

So it proved to be. A price was quoted which Cortéz thought to be excessively high, but Marina advised again that it would be useless to discuss that. The merchants never bargained. They quoted, and men could order or not as they would.

It was a method of business offensive to a mind which had been legally trained, but he was one who ever put the essential first, as when he had had bought meat with a gold chain in St. Jago during the night. He said: "I will do as you advise. But tell me this. What remedy shall I have if the spears do not arrive?"

Marina replied: "But there is no danger of that! The merchants do not undertake what they cannot perform."

He was not wholly convinced. He said: "They must be omniscient men," with some sarcasm in his voice.

It was a word which Marina did not understand, but she was not troubled by that. He had wanted the spears, and she had told him how they could be obtained. She put fresh flowers in her hair.

CHAPTER SIXTY-THREE: CHALLENGE

Cortéz said to Alvarado: "Pedro, I shall march out at tomorrow's dawn in a sudden way, taking no more than seventy men, and leaving twice that number with you, for you will have the women to guard, and all the treasure and stores. Also, the Aztecs must not have cause to think that we are leaving the city, or that I am marching to give Narváez battle. Let them wonder and doubt. I shall leave you half the horses, and all the guns. I shall take porters enough to carry such things as we must have, but no more than that. And the porters must be a choice of most active men, for I shall move faster than they will expect me to do."

"Why should I stay here? I would rather go."

"Because I must have one here in whom I can wholly trust. And you are he whom the Aztecs respect next to myself, or perhaps more. We have heard Louise upon that! Do they not call you the sun?"

"Well, they will find it to be a hot sun, if they should make trouble while you are away."

Cortéz was not sure that he liked this reply. He had a doubt whether he had made a good choice. But what else was he to do? Alvarado was a bold, confident man, with a presence and manner that had impressed on the Aztec imagination. He would be more likely to command respect than one of a less colourful kind. And who else could he spare among the few who would be put in such a position without jealousies being aroused?

Apart from that, the fact that Alvarado would remain would tend to reduce the significance of his own departure. Where so much rested on prestige being maintained, this was an argument which could not be put lightly aside.

He went on: "I shall be away, as I suppose, but a short time. Either I shall come to accord (as I seek ever to do), or I shall bring all to a head in a quick way, and resolve it by bout of swords. I do not only say this as an order to you, it is what I ask as a friend, that you will be gentle in all you do; and that, if a sharp issue may arise (as it may, beyond your power to prevent), that you will aim to delay it till I am back with a fuller force than I can leave now."

Alvarado said little to that. He looked as one who has received a rebuke which he had not earned, and Cortéz turned the talk in his smiling way to matters in which he could give praise in sincere words. He had done what he could, and must leave the issue to God and his patron saints, of whose help he had little cause to complain till this hour.

But he spoke to Marina apart, saying: "It is the first time that I go where I am not dependent on you, and where it would be foolish for you to come, even if you were not with child, as we know you are. But there is one thing I say, which I know you will tell to none, but which it will be well for you to know.

"If I come back (as I think to do—have you known me fail?), it will be with more men than I have now, and we may look for a sure peace. But I shall not come back in another way. I should not be lackey to a man who had been less than I in another land, and who would reap that which he did not sow—as he could never have done. But though Narváez fail (as I think he will), I may still die. And if I do, I have no mind that my work shall fail. Pedro is a man of much worth, but there are some things that he could not do. León will be the man who should take my place, which Pedro would not lightly endure. That is one reason of weight why I design that, at such a pass, León should have most of the men at his call, and Pedro should not be there.

"On this, I intend that León shall know my will, and Diego, Gonzalo, and Ávila, but only they. As to Olid, it is best that nothing be said, for he has a loose tongue in his cups. But you should know what my will is, and that I shall tell León to guard you well."

Marina listened to this in a grave, but untroubled way. She said: "You think of all. But I suppose this Narváez (of whom there is much talk on the market days) is not equal to you. I will tell Louise that Pedro is to be kept quiet; but no more than that, for she is very loyal to him."

Cortéz went next morning, as he had said, and the watchful Aztecs observed that most of the Spaniards remained behind, and that the cannon showed at the gates and over the walls, as before. They did not know what it might mean, which was how Cortéz meant it to be. But they saw that Montezuma accompanied him until the southern causeway was reached, and that they parted with an embrace in the Spanish style, such as no Aztec would have ventured to ask or give.

They watched with scowling or puzzled eyes. What did it all mean? And were the hated foreigners really intending to go?

CHAPTER SIXTY-FOUR: OFFER OF TERMS

Cortéz had come to within fifty miles of Cempoalla, from which Narváez still showed no disposition to move. He had been joined by León, and by most of the men who had been stationed in Vera Cruz. These last had included several who had deserted from Narváez. They were not so many, and their quality might not be much. The reasons for their change of allegiance may not have borne investigation in some instances, but they were a welcome sign of what must be hoped for in a larger degree.

At Cholula, to which place Cortéz had ordered that the lances should be delivered, he found that they had punctually arrived, and were in the charge of an officer, Tobillos, who he had sent forward to take them over. He paused there for no more than a single day, that the troops might take some exercise in the use of a weapon which was twice the length of that which they were accustomed to use, and to marshal the combined ranks in their final form.

He had no more than five horses with him. A show of cavalry was beyond possibility. But he picked sixty of his best men, with whom he included Ordaz, de Ávila, and the two younger brothers of Alvarado. He gave Gonzalo command of this force, knowing that de Ávila would take it well, though he was the older man. He directed them to have but one object before their minds—to capture Narváez, dead or alive. "It is the end of this conflict," he said, "that we must aim. We do not seek that our fellow Christians should feel our swords. Go for Narváez alone, and smite only at those who retard your way."

He chose another twenty to be at his own disposal, to wait events; and he placed the remainder, being somewhat less than two hundred men, under the command of Olid, a solid and capable, rather than an inspiring leader, with orders that, when the assault should be made (for it was his forecast that Narváez would not leave the protection of city walls), they should seek first to silence the artillery of the enemy, having none of their own with which to make distant offence.

Having made these dispositions, he resolved to march more slowly on the last stages, that his men, who were feeling the heat of the lower lands to which they had now returned, might be fresh when they should arrive.

Considering the absence of artillery on his side, the disparity of forces, and particularly the threat of his opponent's cavalry, he was now disposed to a night attack rather than to depend upon the lances which he had obtained at so great a cost; but he did not move at all on that day, for a deputation arrived from Narváez showing that his opponent was alert to his movements, and bringing fresh proposals.

They came, with an introductory letter, from the lips of his friend Duero, and they were more reasonable than before, though not such as he was likely to entertain.

"You cannot alter," Duero reasoned, "the fact that the commission you hold is one that Velásquez gave. That which he did, he can revoke. So he has done; and the legal right is with Narváez, though it may be bitter for you. But I have urged upon him that you have done much for the glory of Spain, and for the advantage of Velásquez himself and it will be to his lasting shame if you should be treated in a base way.

"I have also told him that, even though you should submit (as I think you must), you and he would not work together thereafter—it would be beyond hope.

"Having urged him thus, I have brought him to consent to the utmost which you can expect him to do. He will place sufficient ships at your disposal, both for yourself and all who may not be willing to take service with him. You will leave with honour, taking with you all the gains you have made, which will not be tallied; and you may sail to what port you will."

"You speak," Cortéz replied, "with a friend's voice, and with the heart of a friend, as I am willing to think. But I am not here in the name of Cuba, but that of Spain, and I will give place to none, unless the warrant of Spain be his."

"If you call me friend," Duero said, "it is a true word. And, because it is, I will not ask whether any warrant from Spain may be in your own hands. But I will ask you to look at facts. We have three men to your one, or it may be four, and there are four score cavaliers thereamong. They are well appointed and armed, as it would be too much to say that yours are. I have seen notched weapons and threadbare coats, even though a chain of gold may be round the neck. I should say that there are not a hundred breastplates of steel among the whole of the force you have."

"They are more than that. And there is a better thing. There is the will to assert our right. Will you tell me why the men who come with Narváez should risk death, or a lost limb, that he may rule them here rather than I, who more rightly should? Or why they should risk all (being beset by a million foes) of the gains which are now ours because Velásquez is an angry man? And I will add this: when you say we could depart with our gains untallied, I know it is friendly meant, but I do not take it in that way. I have kept account of every ounce of gold we have won, and it has been apportioned as exactly as though I were a Baltic merchant rather than a soldier of Spain.

"Velásquez put his gold into this venture, and you may be sure that his portion is laid aside, and has been reckoned as it would had he been more friendly to me. You also have a venture herein, about which I will tell you this. When you gave me the hint which enabled me to set sail from St. Jago Bay before I could be restrained, I doubled the profit that you should have. I do not say this to bribe you now. You can see it writ in my own hand, and that the larger gain has been set down to your name. It is not with me now, for I left the treasure at México City, and the accounts therewith. But if you ever get to that place, you will find that I do not lie."

"I know well that you would not lie, and, for my part, I am not one to be bribed. But it was nobly done, and I thank you well."

So they talked for a long time. They argued over the question of whether the extent of what Cortéz had done, or the voting of the Assembly at Vera Cruz, had gone beyond the jurisdiction of Cuba's Governor, and they both knew that it was a matter that would have to be resolved in Madrid at last, and by policy rather than point of law. But the practical issue was that Cortéz and Narváez were face to face, and Madrid was far.

Duero went at last, seeing that Cortéz would not be moved. He said he could not blow hot and cold, and had done all he could to avert strife; but they parted after the manner of friends.

CHAPTER SIXTY-FIVE: THE BATTLE OF CEMPOALLA

"You say," Narváez asked, in an incredulous tone, "that he refuses the prospect of going off with his spoils, and a whole skin, and that he will attack me here? Has he any horses at all?"

"I saw five."

"And he knows that we have eighty cavaliers, who could ride him down, even if we had not more than eight hundred of other ranks? What are his guns, of which we have nigh a score?"

Duero answered: "I saw none. But I will say that his men have a very cheerful resolute look. He is not one to be put aside in a light way."

"Am I one to do that? He comes here of my will. It is what I have forced him to do. But I did not think him to be so mad that he would insist on his own loss. How soon could he be here?"

"I should say by late tonight, or tomorrow noon."

"Well, he should be met on the open ground, where our horses must prevail. I will leave nothing to chance."

It was noon when he said this. Duero had just arrived. There was rain in the streets, and a high wind. Narváez would not be deterred by that. He marched out from the gates. He arrayed his troops. He advanced against a tempest of rain. Three miles out he came to a wide stream, which was called the River of Canoes. It could be forded on finer days, but it was in flood now. There was no sign that Cortéz approached.

Narváez said: "We cannot stay here. It will be dusk now before we can get back. He will be camped in such weather as this."

But he was not slack in conduct of war. He sent forty of his cavaliers up stream. "You must ride westward," he said, "till you come where the stream could be passed, even in such weather as this. And, if you see them, ride them down as they come ashore. Yes, you must be out for this night. I will risk naught."

He rode back to Cempoalla by tracks that were now deep in mud, and the rain did not ease. Half a mile from the city, he left two sentries, who must be wet through the night. It was plain that there would be nothing to fear till the next day, but he would risk naught.

As the dusk closed, the little army of Cortéz came to the bank of the River of Canoes. They were a weary and draggled crowd. The stream was now too deep to ford, and still the rain fell. They ate what food they had, which was not much.

Cortéz rode up the stream, seeking a ford. Through blinding torrents of rain he found a place where it could be ridden, but for footmen it was a very perilous passage.

He said: "This is where the spears will avail." He gave an order that all must cross as they best could.

With the long lances on which to lean, they entered the rushing flood. There were loose stones under foot. They held on to one another, the water washing their shoulders at times. The five horsemen did what they could, standing in the midflood, to succour those who might have been swept away. In the end, the flood-soaked ranks were arrayed on the further bank. Only two men had been lost. The long spears might be thanked for that. It was the only use they were destined to be.

The rain still fell as they advanced. Underfoot, the mud sucked. They came to a wayside cross, which had been erected by some of themselves, when they first entered the land. They halted here, and the two priests were busy with those who, on Cortéz's example, would make confession before going to deadly strife. The porters, and most of the baggage, had been left on the further bank, but they stripped themselves now of everything but the weapons they bore, finding such cover for their gear as the bushes gave. Even the horses were left haltered here, for it was on silence that they relied.

They moved so quietly that they were close on the two sentries before their coming had been perceived. One man watched. He ran, and was pursued in vain. One slept, and was caught.

Olid took on interrogation of him. How were the sleeping quarters of the army disposed? When he remained silent, a noose was thrown round his neck. Still he would not speak, and what might have followed will not be known, for the voice of Cortéz came out of the darkness. "He is a true man. Let him go." He added: "We must move with speed now, for silence will not avail."

Yet they went as quietly as they could, coming to the suburbs of the city, and to unguarded gates. It was said afterwards that the sentry who fled had brought a tale that was not quickly believed.

Narváez did not control the city gates, which he would have said there was no occasion to do. He camped in the main temple, as the Spaniards generally did. But the temples of Cempoalla were not as large as those of Cholula or México, and Narváez had a numerous following. He was in the main temple, lodged at the flattened, pyramid-top, and his troops were partly there, and partly in smaller temples, not far away.

The soldiers of Cortéz advanced along a silent street, keeping close to the houses on either side, lest they should be suddenly exposed to artillery fire. Then a trumpet sounded. In a moment the city waked.

Fortunately, though the sentry had refused to speak, Cortéz had had earlier intelligence of how his foes lay, which had not been changed. As the trumpet sounded, Sandoval and his companions, abandoning stealth, raced for the temple where Narváez was lodged.

A cannon fired, and then another. No one knew where the shots went, least of all those by whom they were discharged. Cortéz, his sword out, stumbled over a dead man, recovered himself, and with his rallying cry of *Espiritu Santo!* was the first of those who drove the thin rank of the gun crews backward, and made the guns theirs.

While the confusion raged in the streets, with more noise than blood, Sandoval's party were mounting the steps which ran round the outside of the pyramid. Arquebuses were firing at them from the platform above. Crossbow bolts whizzed downward. A wounded man came to his knees. Another fell, with a wild shriek, from the unrailed steps to the court below. But they gained the platform. Narváez was there. He was armed, with a group of his immediate companions around him. They fought stoutly, but the order which had been given caused all the attack to centre upon himself. He took and gave wounds. A man died at his side. Then a sword point found his left eye. Helped and guarded by his friends, the anguished man retreated into the temple building from which he had come. Its door closed. For a moment, the strife paused.

Then a torch was thrown on the thatched roof of the building. Heat and smoke forced those within to open the door. Cries of "Narváez is taken, Narváez is dead" rose through the night. The injured man was half carried, half dragged down the temple steps.

The soldiers in the other two temples had not come out at all. They were summoned to surrender, with the information that their leader was captured, and that their own cannon were now pointed toward their gate. They had no heart to fight under such conditions, nor would it have been clear what they would have been fighting for.

When morning came, Cortéz was in a chair of state, wearing a rich mantle which had been captured from his rival's wardrobe. One by one the soldiers of Narváez came before him, formally laid down their arms, swore loyalty to him as civil and military commander of the Aztec lands, and received them again.

The wounded general was also brought. "You have much cause," he said, "to thank Fortune for what has chanced."

"I have been well-fortuned at many times; but this is no more than a petty thing," was the cold reply. But he gave orders that there should be care for his rival's wounds.

Salvatierra came also. There were chains for him. He had been in command at one of the lesser temples. He said that he had been incapacitated by sudden illness. He talked no more of the grilling of ears.

"There are eleven dead on their side, "Ordaz reported," and five on ours. There are many hurt, but most of them will do well enough."

Cortéz asked who their own dead were. There was none of his that he did not know. He thanked the saints that it was no worse.

He had trouble enough in the next hour. His new followers complained that their horses were taken, their fair doublets had been stolen by ragged men. Was that how new comrades should be received, who had always been friends at heart, and had made hardly any resistance at all?

Cortéz ordered that everything should be restored.

After that Father Olmedo and de Ávila came to him together. They were a formidable deputation from outraged men. Was there to be no reward for victory hardly achieved? Did he think first of his foes, or of those who were faithful to him?

"Father," he said, "I had thought you to be a man of wit. Can you not still babes without coming to me? Do I need to say—or is it wise that it should be said—that we are in the hands of these men, rather than they in ours, they being of the number they are? We must make them are true friends, and not conquered foes. Shall we not have the whole land divided, if we do that?"

He took the surrender of the forty horsemen who had been left out in the night. He began to plan sending troops this way and that, so that new quarrels should not breed between well-furnished and ragged men. He let it be known that those who fought for him would be rewarded from his own purse.

And then a runner came, with a scroll that Alvarado had signed. It said: "Come with your utmost speed, or we are undone. The brigantines are burnt. The Aztecs are round our walls, of which one had been undermined. Some are dead, and the wounded are many."

"Gonzalo," he said, "I will send Rodrigo to Vera Cruz, with five score of men, but you must come with me. We march for México in two hours from now. Those who are not ready must come behind, and the sick and wounded be left here."

He did not leave in two hours, finding much which must be done, and reflecting that those who ride may overtake footmen. But within two hours a runner was on the México road, with a letter to Alvarado, telling him that the vanguard of his relief was already clear of the city gate.

By the noon of the next day, all had left, even the long procession of porters, excepting only that two score had been left in charge of wounded and sundry stores, with instructions to retire to the shore, where the fleet lay, and await further instructions there.

CHAPTER SIXTY-SIX: RETURN TO MÉXICO

They had left Cempoalla with abundant food, freely supplied. For the first days, they found friendship and eager trade in the fertile land. But as they advanced to that which was higher, bleaker, and more sparely peopled, they lacked sufficient food, and even water at times. The army, with its great train of porters, was much more numerous than they had been with whom Cortéz had ascended that road before, and there were nearly a hundred horses to be watered and fed.

He sent word forward to Tlascala, by mounted men, asking that provisions should be prepared, with some doubt (though not much) as to what their reception would be.

But there proved to be no reason for fear. There was abundance waiting to meet their need.

When he had passed through on the previous week, he had enlisted some Tlascalan troops, who had followed him for a short distance, and then deserted so rapidly, when they had realised that they might be required to fight against other Spaniards, that he had sent the remainder back with a jesting word.

But now, when he asked if they would be willing to march against Aztec foes, there was instant response. He left Tlascala with two thousand of their best troops at his rear.

It was an encouragement that his men required, for, as they crossed the last sierra, and descended into the Mexican plain (which he had thought it prudent to do by a more northerly road, so that he came on those who had seen no Spaniards before), he found that he was met everywhere with sullen looks, and that supplies were grudgingly given.

The road he had now taken entered Tezcuco city, where Montezuma had replaced Cacama by his younger brother, who was supposed to be complaisant to the Spanish connection. But he was said to be away; and they met hostile glances from the few who moved in the empty streets.

What had happened in México?

Passing through Tezcuco, they crossed the intervening hills, and looked down on Tezcuco lake, with México in its midst.

The city itself showed no change from this distant view, but there was a strange absence of boats on the lake, and the caution of Cortéz caused him to turn south along the lake shore, so approaching the causeway by which he had first entered the city. He still had no assurance that the Spanish flag continued to fly there, and he proposed to enter, if at all, from an unexpected direction.

But as the army moved along the lake shore a canoe came from the city quay. It brought a message from Montezuma, and a letter from Alvarado.

Montezuma said that he wished Malintzin to know that whatever trouble there had been had not originated with him, and Alvarado wrote that active attacks had ceased, and been followed by passive siege; but he had no doubt, now that Cortéz had returned with so great a strength, that all would be well.

Cortéz said: "Let the trumpets sound," and, as the notes of martial defiance shrilled over the water, there was an answering discharge of cannon from the beleaguered garrison.

With no opposition at all, the army traversed the long causeway, and the silence of the central street. The whole city appeared to be deserted. Only, it was observed that there were gaps in the side streets, where bridges had been removed.

Now they came to the palace gates, and the greetings of those who had had doubts of whether they would ever see them again.

CHAPTER SIXTY-SEVEN: SUSPENSE

Cortéz took Marina apart. He said: "I would hear all, as I can have it only from you."

"I would have written to you," she replied, "only I had to remind myself that you are unable to read. I will tell you what I know, which is less than all, for there are some things of which I am unsure.

"After you had gone, there were deputations both to Montezuma and Alvarado concerning the Great Feast, which is held in spring when the moon is full—it is Whitsuntide in our Church.

"It is a great feast, to which many thousands come from all parts of the land. It is very gay, not of death but flowers, but there is a central sacrifice, for which a willing victim had been prepared.

"As our chapel is now in the midst of where the celebrations will be, they asked that we should not use it for that time, which they said the people would not endure.

"Alvarado would not agree to that. He said it was our Feastday, as well as theirs; and to withdraw would be to dishonour our God. He proposed that they should begin their feast on the next day, to which (as Montezuma warned him) they would not consent.

"In the end, Alvarado gave way to this point, that we would not go to our chapel on that day, but would hold Mass here, providing only that they should have no human sacrifice. There was more argument after that. You will say he was right. But they asked, was it any business of ours? They did not tell us how we should celebrate our Mass. If the Feast were not held in the usual way, they said that there would be riots, in which not one, but many lives would be spent. Was there sense in that?

"And then, when the quarrel was bitter, and Montezuma said we were rousing a fury he could not hold, Alvarado suddenly gave way. He said that we would have the Mass here (as we did), and that they must serve devils in their own way, which he had not strength to prevent.

"He says now that he had heard that there was a plot to kill us all when the city had become full, and that arms for that use were being stored in the houses near. I do not know about that. He did not have it from me."

"You do not believe it?"

"I did not say that. I do not know. But Alvarado says that from that time he had resolved that, to save our lives, he must deal with it in another way.

"There was to be a dance on the first day, as the custom is, which the greatest nobles would attend, and no others but they. There would, of course, be women there. Alvarado asked that they should be unarmed, in proof that the great assembly was not hostile to us, and this was agreed.

"When the dance was on, he went suddenly with a hundred armed men with swords and pikes. They closed the doors, and they killed all who were there. Six hundred of the greatest nobles—they are all dead.

"After that, riot broke out, and they assailed us from every side. When it seemed that we could not longer endure, Montezuma spoke from the wall. He said his own life would be lost if they did not desist, which he commanded them to do. So they held back, but they have watched us closely, both front and rear, so that none may go out, unless with their consent, or pricing his life low, and they have allowed us neither water nor food.

"We still have some food, but we could not have endured had there not been digging within the walls (for it is an island on which we stand) and discovery of a fresh water spring, for which a saint has to be thanked."

Cortéz said: "Well, it is an ill tale, very clearly told. I left the wrong man. He has ruined all."

He went to Alvarado, and heard the same tale, boldly put by the blond giant, though in a sulky way, as he saw that it was not being well received.

Cortéz asked, at the end: "Did I not tell you to lie still? Have you done that?"

"Did you tell us to lie flat, and be all slain? They had planned our deaths. Being first, as I was, I lopped off the head of the treason which they designed. However bad things may have been, they would have been worse had all their leaders remained alive."

"It is hard to say. They are bad enough now. But for what you did, there might have been no insurrection at all."

"Or we might have been all dead, and you on the outside of the lake, and to what end it would be hard for you to say. At Cholula, when you were faced by a like peril, did you not...."

"It was far from like. Those whom we trapped were warriors with concealed arms who designed our deaths."

"Would you have let Montezuma free?"

"You know that I would not. Why do you ask that?"

"Because I think it was on that that the event turned. When they first talked of this feast, they asked that he should be there, as the custom was, he being their priest and King. When I declined, they saw that he was a prisoner here, and one whom we could not trust to go free."

Cortéz turned away without further words. He had a black anger, hard to control. He felt that Alvarado had failed him in the way which he had feared. Certainly, he would not have himself ordered that massacre of unarmed, unsuspecting men. But he saw also that a position of extreme difficulty had been made almost impossible by the advent of the Great Feast.

It was, indeed, one which could not have endured. Crisis had been averted before by his undertaking to go, and by the project of building the ships which he would require. But that had been interrupted by the coming of Narváez. And did he mean to go now? Certainly it would be a poor prospect to offer to the new recruits he had gained. They looked for further successes, and rich rewards. They had already been disconcerted (as some of them did not conceal) by finding tension and hostility where they had been led to believe that Cortéz controlled all in a regal way. If he should propose returning to Cuba at once, he was not sure that even his authority would endure.

Yet, with the feeling which now prevailed, could he hope to restore any tolerable position, if it should be realised by the Aztecs that he intended to stay? Could the anomalous position of Montezuma continue? Could he ever trust him to resume his freedom, and remain loyal to the curious unnatural alliance that now prevailed? Debating these things in an anxious mind, he even had a doubt of whether it might not have been better to accept the offer which Narváez had made. If he had returned to Cuba or Spain, with reputation of full success, and loaded with spoil, and Narváez had afterwards come to wreck (as he thought he would), might it not have been a later triumph for him? Might he not have come back with a great fleet, and all the support of Madrid, to recover the rich prize he had won for Spain?

Well, it was idle to think of that. He had the friendship of Tlascala, and others who had no love for the Aztec rule. He had a far larger company of those of his own race than he had found sufficient before. His artillery was more than doubled. His store of powder renewed. His horses were ninety, instead of ten. The Aztecs had not dared to oppose him, as he had marched in, uniting his forces. Probably, opposition would cease, now that they saw how great was his augmented power. Why should forethoughts of disaster invade his mind, such as he was not accustomed to have? But there was one matter that would not wait. Gathered within the wide courtyard that enclosed the vast straggling buildings of the palace, even after the majority of the porters had been dismissed, there were little fewer than ten thousand mouths to be fed—and provisions were very low.

Since the massacre, the fifth-day markets had not been held. No food had been openly brought into the city. Would they now be resumed? This would be a crucial indication of the Aztec attitude. It would also be of vital moment to those who could not be fed for another week without further supplies.

He asked Marina on which day the market would next be held in the normal course, and learnt that it should be in three days' time.

"We can endure till then," he said, "but I must know what to expect. Alvarado says they will not hold another market till we are gone. He had that from Louise."

"Louise would not learn much in a direct way, though she might get it from those who can. I will enquire."

Cortéz saw reason in that. Louise was a Tlascalan, which Aztecs did not forget. Half their grievance against the Spaniards was their introduction of the hated Tlascalans into the city.

Marina went out alone. She came back with a poor report. She said: "They do not know, as I think. If they do, they will not say. They wait orders from the priests, who have won control. All the great nobles are dead, including some who were friendly to us."

"I must see Montezuma on this. You shall come with me."

So he did in the next hour. Montezuma said little. He was morose, with more than his usual reserve. He said he had no wish for the market to remain closed. Would he order that it should be resumed? He was evidently reluctant to do so. He said it would be better to wait, and see what would happen. It could not be kept closed permanently. In the end, he gave a reluctant promise to intervene.

He then changed the subject to enquire when Malintzin would be leaving. He assumed, the difficulty about the ships being over, that he would be anxious to go. He hinted that, if that should be made clear, obstructions might become less.

It was now Cortéz who gave evasive replies. He was anxious to know that the agreement already made would not be broken. If he should return to his own King, he must not take a report which would prove untrue.

Montezuma was roused by that to a flicker of anger. He said: "If there were some who plotted (which is more than I know) they are all dead. Would you have them die twice?"

Hearing this, Cortéz retorted: "Tell him I will not discuss what is past. Have the market open, and all may end in a good way."

He went at that, with a confident mien, but a great doubt in his heart. Marina said: "It is not that he wishes the market to remain closed. He will take the way of peace, if he can. But he is in doubt of whether he will be obeyed, which he is reluctant to put to proof. The nobles whom he could trust are all dead."

Cortéz muttered a curse, which was for Alvarado's door. But then he thought: "If it is the priests with whom I shall contend now, I shall overcome. Do I doubt God? Do I call their devils as strong as He?"

But Montezuma was not in doubt. He was in despair. It was true that he feared that his orders might not be obeyed. He had not heard that there were any who openly challenged his authority. But he knew that orders were being given by others than he. He did not even know with whom they originated. He looked both to right and left, and could see no hope for himself at all.

CHAPTER SIXTY-EIGHT: SIEGE

The desperation of his position led Montezuma to make a proposal which he would otherwise have been unlikely to do. He had sent out servants whom he could trust, with instructions in regard to the opening of the market, and they had come back disconcerted by the fact that they could contact no one with clear authority to deal with the matter. The fact was that the city was in such disorder, and of such a temper, that the market might be said to have shut itself. Montezuma sent a message that he would like to confer with Malintzin again.

He now proposed that his brother should be offered freedom, if he should consent to accept a delegated authority, and use it in such a way that peace could be restored.

"Would he do that?" Cortéz asked with some natural scepticism, but yet being very willing to explore any possibility which might bring food to his gates.

Marina answered at once: "Should he give his word, it would be honestly done. You could expect that."

"Well, let him be brought here."

So it was done. There was conversation all of which only Marina could understand, with one who yet spoke in a bold way, as a prince should, but who was evidently prepared to make a bargain for his liberty, if honour would not be lost.

He made conditions—qualifications—in the end, he had not promised much, but there was some confidence to be gained from the fact that he would pledge nothing in a rash way.

He professed no friendship for the Spaniards, nor would he forecast any comfort for them while they should remain in the land. He thought division was now too deep. But, if his liberty were to be conditioned upon the reopening of the market, he would arrange that, unless it should prove beyond his power, and afterwards he might endeavour to arrange for the Spaniards to have a peaceful exit, which they would speedily make if they would be advised by him.

Cortéz said: "We may gain much. We risk less. Let him go."

Cuitlahua went, and there is no reason to doubt that he would have kept his word; but he found that the priests had taken control. He could lead the people to crush those against whom they were now roused to an untamable wrath, or he could stand aside, as he would. It was as simple as that. He was heir to the Crown, by Mexican custom, if Montezuma should die; but, till then, he had no status at all, unless it should be by the goodwill of the priests, who had now gained practical control. Faced by this position, he elected to act as the heir to a shaking throne might be expected to do. Certainly, he was under no obligation either to the Spaniards or Montezuma, beyond that conditional promise, which he found himself unable to keep. He turned his thoughts to the military problems of how the Spaniards could be expelled or destroyed, which he did not think to be impossible.

Meanwhile, Cortéz, waiting to see whether the market would be busy again when its day should come, and, cautious that no previous incident should jeopardise the event, had given strict orders that no one should pass out of the gates except by his own permission. But on the evening before the day which would demonstrate what the future would be likely to be, he wrote a letter to Rodrigo, his new commander of Vera Cruz, informing him that he was again established in México, and that the hostilities which had threatened Alvarado had ceased as he had approached the city.

He wrote confidently. Evidently, the event might have been worse. He chose a Tlascalan messenger whom he could trust, and told him to leave at dawn.

So the man did, but he returned quickly. He had been felled by a slung stone, and his shoulder was badly hurt. But, before he had had that plain hint to return, he had gone far enough to observe that it would have been difficult to leave the city. Bridges were up in all directions. The causeway gates were guarded and closed.

Most sinister of all was the strange silence of the city, the empty streets.

Hearing this, there could be no surprise that the market square (part of which could be overlooked from the palace roof) was deserted.

It was a position which obviously could not continue without development. Cortéz said: "Let all men stand to arms till the noon hour. If nothing happens by then, I will ride out, and survey the city. In palace or temple there must be those who can hear plain words, and give plain reply, when we shall know what must be done."

It was clear that they could not remain there without food, for which, if all were consumed without choice, there might be meagre fare for three days, but not more. But there proved to be no need to ride out to ascertain what was meant. When noon came, there was riot of noise and conflict around the whole extent of the vast courtyard, where a great army, regardless of its own losses, strove to scale the low stone wall, and were met by less numerous, but better armed, and desperate men.

The assault continued for several hours, and was of a ferocity which the Spaniards had not previously encountered, even when they had met the Tlascalan army.

The palace courtyard had been elaborately prepared against such an attack. The artillery had been mounted where it could be used with most deadly effect. The walls had been pierced for the arquebusiers to fire at such angles as would be most effective against those who might advance in the open street. The low towers which rose from the wall at short intervals had Tlascalan garrisons of selected marksmen with stone and arrow. Groups of cavalry were alert to ride down any who might be successful in scaling the wall.

But, in fact, the horsemen had no cause to lower their lances on this first day of siege.

The Aztecs, advancing with deafening whistles, had suffered such losses from the artillery before they could reach the wall as would have been sufficient for the defeat of most European armies. But they had not faltered. Many had gained the comparative shelter of the wall, and there, supported by volleys of stone and arrows discharged from the flat terraces of surrounding buildings, they had driven their lances between the stones, to make supports on which they could climb.

But as their heads, often grotesquely helmeted in imitation of an eagle or beast of prey, had appeared over the parapet, a thousand Spanish swords had been bare to meet them, and many times that number of Tlascalans, with hearts as bold and weapons equal to those of their opponents, had been eager to throw them back.

Later, there was an abortive effort to batter down a part of the wall, and, when that failed, a new form of attack was tried, by which persistence had a more substantial reward.

The main palace buildings (though, except at their centre, without a second floor) were of such extent that they had given ample accommodation to the few hundreds of Cortéz's original following, and space for the state which Montezuma required, and for his very numerous retinue. Even beyond these, and much storeroom space, they had now given harbourage to many hundreds above the original total, with no more difficulties than were unavoidable where adjustments had to be made, with some jealousies between old claimants and new, and some grumbling at the extent of Montezuma's apportionment.

But there had never been sufficient accommodation within the walls for the Tlascalan troops, nor had they made claim upon it. For the advantage of being within the same area as their Spanish allies, they had been content to camp in the courtyards and garden grounds which were contained in the mile-wide wall.

As the months had passed without certainty of when they would return to their own land, they had increased their comfort by the erection of extensive buildings, mainly of wood, which were, in many places, not far from the girdling wall. On these buildings, the Aztecs now rained volleys of arrows to which flaming rags were attached. Fires started, and spread. Water was not available (it had become far scarcer even than food). Soon it was clear that all the buildings must be consumed, with much of their contents, which could not be removed with sufficient speed. The palace buildings were mainly of stone, but did not wholly escape.

Assisted by the confusion that this conflagration caused, fresh assaults were made on the wall, and, at one point, it was broken down. Aztecs poured through the breach, and there was sanguinary fighting before they were forced back, and sufficient artillery brought to bear on the gap.

Evening came to exhausted men, of whom some must toil to repair the wall during the night, while the Aztecs rested from strife.

CHAPTER SIXTY-NINE: SALLY

Cortéz called his captains together when darkness came.

He said: "They have suffered much, and our losses are not large; but if we allow this to go on, I should say they will bear us down at the last, being the great host that they are, and indifferent to their own deaths, as we have seen them to be.

"Besides that, our food will not endure."

There were some who wondered what he might mean. How could the assault be stayed, if the Aztecs could endure their deaths?

But Olid, who was not always quickest of wit, said at once: "So it is. We must get to horse."

He was one who would do nothing on his own feet, if a horse could be found, and so the idea in his leader's mind was apparent at once to him.

Cortéz said: "That is what we must do. We must sally out, with all the force we have. We must ride them down. We must not let them think that we need a wall."

Bernal Díaz, whose horses were ninety now, got up at that word. He had heard enough. He went to give such orders as would have all (except Marina's bay stallion, which was always reserved for her) fit to file out through the gate when the dawn should come.

When he had gone, there was some debate, but soon all were agreed. The wall was no use to them.

The dawn came, and there was no doubt that many Aztecs were ready to die.

With some care to avoid such ground as the guns could take, but not overmuch, even of that, all the surrounding streets, and the great square, were gay with banners, and bright with bronze, and the featherwork that their leaders wore. They had removed the wounded and dead of the night before, and all was closely arrayed for the strife of another day.

Cortéz, looking out from a tower on the wall, but already in cavalier arms, said: "They are more dense than yesterday, and the further streets appear to be crowded alike. Well, it will be harder for them to run, as they soon will." He descended to mount his horse, but, before the trumpets sounded advance, the shrill whistles of their foes were a deafening evidence of their intention to assault again.

It was a disastrous moment for them, for as they advanced toward the walls against deadly volleys from all the weapons the defenders possessed, the palace gates were thrown wide, and more than fourscore of mail-clad cavaliers charged upon them.

They had no defensive armour that would avail against the long Spanish lances, set firmly in their rests, driven with all the force of the rushing charger, and the deadly aim of the guiding hand; they had no weapons which would avail against tested steel. Their habit of hacking rather than thrusting—of capture rather than slaughter—diminished the effectual use of what strength they had.

Dense ranks, already somewhat disordered in their advance by the heavy fire directed upon them, and treading pavement already slippery with their comrades' blood, were borne back by the weight of the charge, and were soon struggling to get clear of that deadly front where the lances slew.

Cortéz had been right when he had foretold that the slaughter would be worse because men would be unable to fly.

As broken lances were cast aside, swords came out, and took as heavy a toll from what had become a refluent mob, which was seeking only to escape those who were tireless to slay.

And, behind the horsemen, the Spanish infantry came, and the Tlascalans were pouring out of the gates in their rear.

Down the great main street the Aztec regiments were driven in a wild confusion of slaughter which might well have had decisive results, if they had not been commanded by one who had forethought and skill in the waging of war. But, in the midst of the street, the Spaniards came to a place where they must rein their horses before a barricade which they could not leap. It was a solid rampart of earth and of heavy stones, behind which the Aztecs rallied, and bent their bows.

Cortéz, breathing hard, with a reddened sword, for he had been ever first of the first rank, with Alvarado emulous at his side, called for cannon to be dragged into the street, from either side of which heavy stones were now being hurled from the platforms of the houses, while Spaniards and Tlascalans forced entrance into them, both to stop the nuisance, and to plunder them of the water and food which they were likely to have.

Cannon breached the barrier, and the advance was resumed, but now against a less surprised and more resolute foe. The Spaniards found themselves engaged in a widespread battle, which was continually successful, but without finality, and became the weaker the further it spread. There were barriers everywhere. Every side-street must divert some of their force, or be a danger upon their flank.

"Fire the houses when they are stripped," Cortéz commanded, and the area of the spreading advance became dense with smoke, as the read-walls of the houses burst into flame, between stone pillars, and beneath platforms of stone and wood. Few were constructed so that even their shells could stand when the work of the flames was done. On the side, at least, from which the sally had been made, it was certain that there would be less cover for their foes on the next day.

So the fight went on until evening came. There had been a great slaughter of the Aztecs. Several hundreds of houses, with their contents, had been destroyed. Some useful plunder had been found, though not enough, even of food, to supply the full needs of the day.

But the Aztec resistance had not ceased. They were still shooting from every unburnt house, and from every street. They were still numberless, and still ready to die.

Cortéz reined a weary horse, and surveyed a scene of confusion and blood which must be ended for that day. He said: "Let the trumpets sound the retreat," and as the signal shrilled through the din, and men turned thereat, no one wishing to be last through the gates, the Aztecs surged forward from every side.

The streets rang with renewed strife. The cavaliers, divided for the purpose into bands of ten or twelve, urged tired horses to charge anew, that the footmen should not be too closely pressed.

They knew that, if a man should be dragged from his horse, or the horse should fall, it would be likely capture for him, with the prospect of death on the altar, after a manner of which they had far more horror than of what they considered to be a more natural end on the field of strife.

Cortéz, on the extreme rear of retreat, looking right and left, as a captain should, saw that which caused him to use his spurs in a sudden way.

Down a side street, he saw Duero, dragged from a horse that stood uncertainly, disregarded by a group of Aztecs who were struggling to bear the disarmed cavalier away.

The Cortéz charger, roused by a sharpness of spurs that it seldom felt, and wearily gallant in obedience to his riders will, came with thundering hooves down the concrete street. The loud cry of his rider, *St. Jago!*, was the last sound that an Aztec heard as a sword swept down. Wrenched clear of a cloven head, it thrust into the throat of another man, and then cut air as it missed one who had dodged aside.

Cortéz swung round to catch the reins of Duero's horse. "Are you hurt?" He cried. "Can you mount? Then we will not wait."

They rode off with a rush of Aztecs upon their rear, and found that there were others now at the head of the street who must be ridden through, and cast off, as they struggled, reckless of their own lives, to pull the cavaliers down.

They met Ordaz and others, who had become aware that their leader was left behind. But he was in safety now.

Cortéz said: "Well, I owed you a debt I am glad to pay, as I had not supposed that I ever should."

"You are ever one to pay well," Duero replied.

They went in together to cleanse the dust of the day.

CHAPTER SEVENTY: MONTEZUMA MUST INTERCEDE

Marina said: "There is dirt enough; but more blood. What have you done?"

"As to that, I was done to. But it bled well at the time. I did not think it would have started again."

They looked at a deep cut in the palm of his left hand. A torn gauntlet lay on the floor, where he had cast it aside. He said: "There were three at me at once, and one would have cut my side had I not held his blade in a strong grasp. But the gauntlet failed at the strain."

"Yet you came through," she said. "It is ever you find a way. But tomorrow you must not go to the front of war. You must nurse this."

"For a hurt to a left hand? Have you not seen that I have two? But when you call me one who will find a way, I ask myself can I do it now? For I call us trapped, and I cannot tell how we shall come free. And you may observe that I am not alone when I think that."

He alluded to a noise that came from the street, and penetrated even through the palace walls. The Aztecs did not fight in the dark hours, but that was no reason why they should not keep their foes awake chanting forecasts, which the Tlascalans, at least, would find it easy to understand.

Actually, Cortéz, who knew more of the Aztec tongue than he was in the habit of showing, also understood, as did many other Spaniards, who would have been content to understand less. For the Aztecs agreed with the opinion which Cortéz had formed as to the significance of the days events. He might sally out again, and burn more houses, and kill ten for one, but it would not alter the end.

So they thought, and so they chanted songs about the triumph which their god was about to know; and of Christians and Tlascalans who, though they might be getting thin now, could be fattened for the right day. There was no reticence in their songs. Bellies were slit; living hearts were torn out; offal was burnt. They were not cheerful songs to the ears of those who were most concerned.

Marina said, without showing a disturbed mind: "They sing now, when they might do better to sleep. But I suppose many of them will be dead by tomorrow noon. They should think of that. Why do you not ask Montezuma to send them away?"

"Do you think he would?"

"It could be asked."

"I will think of that."

So he did, during the night, while he lay awake with a throbbing hand, but thinking little of that, he having so much else to resolve. Perhaps Montezuma might. But there would be terms. If he should leave México now, as a beaten man. It would be better than to be overwhelmed here. But not much.

Morning came, and Marina was persistent with her idea. She said: "If you are too busy in other ways, I could go to him alone, if you would tell me what I should say. He might be glad to bring this to an end."

"So he might. But we will leave it for now."

He went out. He came back in two hours, or perhaps three. He called for Marina, and, after a time, she came. She said: "I did not look for you at this hour. I was dressing wounds. How is your hand?"

"It is well enough. But we do no good. We have had a hundred inside the wall. They are all dead now. But, if it should happen again, it might end in another way. You can do what you will, and promise the least you can."

"You leave me freedom for that?"

"There is none whom I trust more."

"I will do what I can."

She went to Montezuma's room, and was admitted at once. They talked long, and she as patient and adroit to persuade, but she came away, having failed.

She said: "He is a man from whom the courage has gone, and I think, the desire for life. He has lost faith alike in himself and you. He says you might promise to go, but you would change when the need was past. He will do nothing now but wait what the end may be."

There was debate about this among the captains in the next hour. They had come to agree that Montezuma's intervention was the best hope that they had. Olid said it had been done in the wrong way. Let him try, and he would make the dog howl, unless he should jump as he was told.

He wanted Marina to go with him, that he might try his own methods, which she said at once that she would not do. Montezuma would not yield to such threats. They would throw away any chance that they still had.

Cortéz was less sure of that. He stood in doubt. Marina did not wish either to give way, or oppose his will. She said: "If Father Olmedo would also come? He can persuade, as few may."

That was agreed. Montezuma, reclining by untasted food, lifted listless eyes to receive Marina with the priest, for whom he had some respect, and the Captain of the Guard, whom he disliked, and would have found it easy to fear.

He supposed what they would ask, and was resolved that he would not yield. He had yielded so many times—and it had brought him to this.

Yet yield he did in the end, not supposing that it would be for the last time, and that without Olid, standing scowling by, having spoken a word.

For Father Olmedo had convinced him that, if he would persuade his people to give them a free exit, the Spaniards would really go.

He rose confidently at last. He ordered that his most royal robes should be brought. He said: "It will bring all to a good end. For they must listen to me."

An hour later he went to the wall, over which arrows flew. He was not daunted by them, for he was not a coward, though he had shown himself to be an irresolute man.

He wore imperial robes, splendid in white and blue, and imposed gold. He was diademed with a tiara in which great emeralds shone. Spanish officers mingled with the nobles that were his obsequious train. As he appeared, the tumult died, so instantly, so absolutely, that the silence was more impressive than sound.

His voice, low but very clear, addressing people, many of whom were now on their knees, with the quiet authority that they had been accustomed to hear. He said it was his will that they should disperse, and that the Spaniards would then go home, and all would be well.

Confident in his power over those who had always been subject to do his will, he called the Spaniards his friends, which may have been an unfortunate word. But there was no doubt that he had control of the majority there, no doubt that he would have been obeyed in the next hour.

But there was a small minority of a different mood. A murmur broke out when he called them friends. And one man slung a stone, with too good an aim. The next moment Spanish shields were round him on every side. But Montezuma lay on the ground.

His nobles bore him back to his own room, where they ministered to a head wound which did not look to be of a fatal kind.

In the street outside, those who had seen their Emperor fall had instantly fled. It was silent and empty now.

Had the appeal failed?

CHAPTER SEVENTY-ONE: THE FIGHT FOR THE PYRAMID

The temples which were built at two of the corners of the platform at the top of the great pyramid overlooked, from their great height, a large part of the palace courtyard, and it had occurred to the high priest, who had watched the swaying conflict with calculating vindictive eyes, that the distance was not too great for the flight of an arrow from a strong bow, if it should be sufficiently bent. He offered the use of the temples for this purpose to Cuitlahua, who thought it good.

Arrows from this direction had begun to fall in the courtyard, and had been one of the deciding considerations, when Cortéz had called for Montezuma's intervention.

In the pause of darkness, when evening came, he considered what should be done on the next day. He was building a *manta*, from his own design, of which he had great hopes, but it would not be ready for two further days, at the best. There was another thing which must, and could, be done at once, if the morning should bring resumption of strife.

He required an officer who would be sufficient for the event, and whom he could spare, without too great a regret, if he should not return, which must be recognised as possible, if not more than that.

"Escobar," he said, "you have not yet had a separate command, but I will give you one now; and if you bring it to a good end, there will be others in later days.

"You have seen that arrows fall from the temple towers, and you know that there were four wounded (and one is dead) before darkness came, though we left the courtyard on that side as bare as our defence would allow. I cannot let that endure for another day.

"I will give you a hundred of our own men, and as many Tlascalans as you may desire to be a guard in your rear, and you shall sally out in a sudden way.

"When you arrive at the temple steps, you will see that there can be no more recruits for those who will be above. You can mount and slay, and the steps can be held meanwhile at the foot by a small guard, if they be well-armed and resolute men.

"You can burn the temples, and their archers will have no more cover from which to shoot."

Escobar listened to this, and he thought that it might be as simple as it was made to sound, or it might not. If the lower steps could be held with such ease, why should not the higher ones be held by their foes in the same way? There were other questions which might occur to a cautious mind, but he knew that there would be the same answer for all—that an Aztec would be no match for a Spaniard, even without the body armour which many had. He said nothing, and Cortéz went on: "You will move out at the dawn, or as soon thereafter as it shall appear that Montezuma's appeal has failed, which we will not conclude without proof, for a stone can be slung by one man."

Escobar thanked his Commander. He went to make such preparations as the occasion would need. And when morning came, as it was clear that the besiegers had no intention of peace, he sallied out, as his orders were, fought his way across to the Great Pyramid courtyard, and about halfway to the foot of the steps which ascended around it. By that time his men were encompassed by foes to such density that they made slow progress, though their swords might be proving that steel is better than bronze. Aztecs died, but not in a quiet or consenting way. They gave wounds. Most of all, they tried, three or four to one, to pull Spaniards down, and drag them away. Men were in terror of that, knowing what their fate would be. Cries for rescue sounded from right and left. It seemed to Escobar that they were becoming a disorderly mob, moving in no certain direction. He had a fear that they might struggle there till they would be gradually separated and overwhelmed. He looked up at the pyramid, with the unrailed steps winding round it, four or five times, being nearly a mile in length before reaching the top. He saw many faces, far above him, which looked over the edge of the top, watching the strife. Could they hope to climb that length of stair, against the shower of missiles and stones they might expect to meet, and then overcome those who would crowd above them, to fling them down? And if they should so far prevail, would they be able to fight their way back through those who would have collected in augmented numbers below?

A man may be personally brave, and yet unfit for the responsibility of command. He may be less resolute for others than for himself. Escobar thought: "I am responsible for a hundred lives. It is a vain attempt, and, if I do not give the word to retreat, they will all die."

A trumpeter was close behind him, where it was his duty to be. Escobar turned to him: "Sound the retreat."

The man, who had his sword bare, with his instrument slung from a shoulder sash, looked surprised. But he put up his sword, and blew a loud note, at which men paused and reversed.

It proved to be harder to go back than it had been to advance, and the Tlascalans were now in front. Escobar put himself at the rear, where it was now the greatest danger to be.

As he got through a gate which was moving to close, and a cannon was discharged through the narrowing gap, so that he felt the heat of the blast, Cortéz met him.

Escobar said: "We did all we could; but it proved to be an impossible thing."

"How could you know that? You should have been on the platform by now. How many men have you lost?"

It appeared that of the Spaniards there were four missing and many hurt.

Cortéz said: "You must try again. You shall have fresh men."

He thought: "It has got to be done; and if Escobar fail now, he will be useless for future days."

Escobar said nothing. He felt that he was unjustly blamed. Well, he could die! He would not sound the retreat again.

Many of those who had been with him volunteered for a second attempt, but this Cortéz did not allow.

Escobar started out with a different hundred, and this time no retreat was sounded. They got further, almost to the foot of the steps, but they were forced back, as it seemed, without order given, and this time there had been many deaths.

Cortéz said: "I was wrong. You are not to be blamed. I will go myself, with such a force as will more avail."

He ordered an hour's delay, that the Aztecs should think he had accepted defeat. He went to his own room to make preparation, while the derisive whistling of triumphant foes was deafening from the street.

Marina said: "You cannot go, having no more than one hand."

"No," he laughed, "that would be foolish to try. You shall bind a buckler upon my arm. I shall be more guarded than is my wont, for the buckler will not be slung aside."

"And you will tell me how you will hold the rein?"

"As to that, you must watch and see."

She said no more, but was active to bind the buckler to his arm in the best way, and so that the hand should not be exposed.

At the hour's end, the gate was flung wide again, and he rode out at the head of three hundred men, of whom thirty were cavaliers. By surprise and speed, and the advantage of mounted men, they made better progress than before, and so large a force of Tlascalans came at their rear that they held the whole of the road, from gate to gate, which it was well that they were sufficient to do, for when the horses entered the Temple courtyard, they found (as had been in that of Montezuma's palace on an earlier day) that it was too highly polished for the horses to move thereon, and they must be sent back, which was successfully done, though the Aztecs fought hard to reach them from either side.

Headed by the dismounted cavaliers, they having more defensive armour than many of the footsoldiers possessed, the three hundred Spaniards fought their way to the foot of the steps, where Cortéz ordered that a dozen arquebusiers, brought for that purpose in the midst of the swordsmen, should be stationed, with an outer ring of Tlascalan warriors to protect them the while they fired.

Cortéz, with a bare sword and a bucklered arm, led the way up the steps, with Ordaz and Alvarado beside him. As the ascent began, the Aztecs who had pressed attack on those who remained below withdrew not merely for a clear space, but to the outside of the wall, a manoeuvre which was understood when a rain of huge stones and other missiles began to descend upon the climbers, some of which struck the lower terraces, rebounded far out into the courtyard, and leapt in flying fragments therefrom.

It was a menace which was ineffectual at first, there being the practical difficulty that there were four terraces below the final platform—one each at the points at which the steps completed a circuit of the pyramid, and to reach the climbers it was necessary for the assailants to be on the terrace immediately above them. Even then, it was not easy to wound those who kept close to the wall, unless bowmen and slingers should lean far out from the unfenced platform above them.

Estimating the danger which must be faced, without possibility of reprisal for the whole of that mile-long climb, Cortéz hesitated between considerations of speed and safety—should he order that men should advance in single file, close to the wall, or five abreast, as the width of the steps would allow? He saw objections to both. Single file would be very slow, and disadvantageous if there should be resistance as each terrace were reached—five abreast would mean an extreme hazard for the outmost, who might not only be injured by a descending missile, but overbalanced, and hurled to death over the fenceless edge.

"Ranks of three," he called. He took his own place at the outmost front, and set a pace which others might find hard to maintain, and which he must be content to slacken before the summit should be approached. But then he saw that a close formation would make it more certain that the missiles would find a victim. He sent an order backward that the advance should be made with many gaps, which could be closed up at the last.

For the next twenty minutes the climbers were most aware of silence and of suspense. They mounted to the great height they must reach at last, in a still air, beneath the light of a summer sky. They had a wide view of the city, the many towers of which were below them now. They saw the lake's extent, and the wooded hills that enclosed it, still in the green habit of spring. They looked more directly down on the streets and the great square, crowded with Aztec warriors, who stood motionless, with upturned faces. They saw those of their own part, in the palace courtyard, watching in the same motionless way.

The noise of the falling stones did not break the silence so much as make them aware of how deep it was.

Once a great block of wood struck the head of a man in the outmost file. He staggered blindly, clutched for support which was not there, and fell over the edge. The derisive whistle of Aztec triumph sounded from ten thousand lips as he crashed to death on the concrete pavement below.

The worst peril came when they reached the last lap of each of the five circuits of the pyramid, where stones need not be dropped from the edge of the terrace, but could be rolled directly down. Had the garrison had the time to make more extensive preparation for this form of defence, the ascent could not have been made without heavy loss, if at all.

But the idea that such an attack would be made had not occurred to them till a few hours before, and after that they had supposed that it had been abandoned. Only an urgent order from Cuitlahua, who was not one to underestimate the quality of his opponents, had caused the measure of preparation which had been made.

So with too many wounded, left to crawl backward, or lying upon the steps, but with few deaths, the assailants came to the final height, and a dense rank of Aztec warriors around the head of the stair.

Cortéz, bringing down the man immediately before him with a fatal thrust, pushed sideways, to give those behind freedom to advance, and, as he did so, he was grappled by two, who would have thrown him over the edge. For a moment, they swayed perilously. Striking outward with the buckler which was bound to his left arm, he threw one from him so that he fell to death, but he would have followed the same way, but for the grip of his right arm on his second foe, who pulled backward to save himself. Next moment a rescue came from those who pressed upward behind him, and he could stoop to pick up fallen sword.

There were six hundred Aztecs on that airy platform. They were more than twice the number of the Spaniards, but they were no match for them, man for man, so that they could hold their ground at the head of the steps; and, after that, it was only a matter of time before the last one would be chased into the temple buildings, and despatched by merciless swords.

It was a struggle without thought of quarter or possibility of flight, in which all, of one side or other, must die; and the Aztecs, so cornered, fought desperately, though with weapons which were unequal to those they met.

The sun was approaching the height of noon when Cortéz gazed round on a wide platform which was now strewn with six hundred of Aztec dead, and nearly fifty Spaniards, while there were few of those who remained who were not busy in relieving their own or their comrades' wounds.

Only the High Priest, and two of his stints caught skulking in an upper room of the War-God's temple, remained alive, being regarded as captives too valuable to slay.

The Spaniards had been angered, but had no cause for surprise, to find that their own chapel had been desecrated, and its images removed, for which they could now take revenge in a more spectacular way.

The great statue of the War God was dragged from its temple, and hurled over the side of the platform. Bounding from the highest flight of steps, it fell clear to the ground below, where it smashed to fragments, while a cry of mingled rage and horror rose from ten thousand worshippers who watched a desecration which they were powerless to stay.

After that, they must watch the two temples become pillars of smoke and flame which could be seen for many miles beyond lake and hills, the death-pyre of a faith that was near its end.

The Spaniards, wounded and exhausted, but exulting at the greatness of their success, descended to march back without further opposition from dispirited foes.

CHAPTER SEVENTY-TWO: PARLEY

Some provisions had been obtained from the temple buildings, but they were utterly inadequate for larders which had become almost bare, and from which many thousands must be fed.

To meet this urgent need, and to strike fresh terror into foes whom he hoped to have disheartened by the events of the day, Cortéz ordered that there should be an extensive sally during the dark hours, when he knew that the Aztecs were not accustomed to fight.

It was a further success, much plunder being taken, many Aztecs killed, and several hundred houses and other buildings being set on fire, after they had been stripped of everything which was valuable to Spanish or Tlascalan eyes.

He had left the control of this operation to León, having need of rest too urgent to be denied.

He rose next morning to hear report of what had occurred, and to consider how best he could exploit the success which he had gained.

"They should see by now," he said to Marina, "that their god was no more than a wooden log. They should be ready for the True Faith, and we may be near the dawn of a better day."

"Do you think that?" She replied, her mind divided between her confidence in him (and in the God Who had become hers), and what sounded almost senseless to her.

"Am I wrong? You know them better than I."

"What has become of the images which they took from our own chapel? We may guess what they will have done with them. But should our Faith be less because our God did not protect them?"

Cortéz saw reason here, though he had a reluctant mind. Not admitting that there was any reality beyond the image of the War God which had been fashioned by human hands, it was hard for him to see that his worshippers would not look at it in the same way.

He asked, with less assurance in his voice than before: "Should you not say they will be in a more amenable mood, after what they have seen us do?"

"No. I should have said less. But you may judge better than I."

"I must hope I do. I propose to call for a parley, at which I shall offer to leave without doing more damage to them, if they will supply our needs. I shall want you to help in that with persuasive words."

"As, of course, I shall."

"And Montezuma may aid us to the same end. I suppose that he would now be glad for us to go."

"We shall get nothing from him. His wives say that he is determined to die."

"Why should he do that? He may be free in two day's time, if we have our will."

"Well, so it is. He has had shames that he does not try to forget."

"Not from me. I have given him all the honour I might, without failure to God and Spain."

Marina did not discuss that. She said: "You will wish a message sent? I will see to that. They may consent to talk, if no more."

So it appeared that they would. A truce was made for three hours, during which Cuitlahua himself would come to talk with Cortéz beneath the wall, at the place where Montezuma had fallen two days before.

When he appeared, Cortéz mounted the wall, with Marina at his side, and some of his captains also. They wore steel, as it was prudent to do, remembering what had occurred before, and velvet and silk therewith, gay clothes enough from Narváez's stores having replaced those which had been soiled and torn beyond simple repair. They wished to show a bold flaunt, as it may also have been prudent to do.

Cuitlahua came in his own habit of war, and in a litter so richly gemmed, and so haughty in its green plumage of war, that there could be little to change if he should come to Montezuma's estate, which he might think to have become very probable now.

He alighted from the litter, after attendant nobles had brushed the ground, and seeing that those with whom he would speak were already there, he said to Marina at once: "I have come to hear whatever petition Malintzin may wish to make. He cannot expect much, for the altars will not be wholly denied, but there may be some measure of mercy for beaten men."

"It is not to ask or grant mercy that we are here," Marina replied, she having been fully instructed as to what she should be first to say. "You have seen that your god is fallen, your soldiers slain, your houses plundered and burned. Do you wish for more?

"For Montezuma's sake there may still be peace, if you will return to peacable ways. But if you persist in rebellion both against Montezuma and Spain, you will see your city in ashes, with few alive to mourn what you have been persistent to cast away."

It was a bold attempt, which may have been wisely tried, being the only chance that there was, but it was destined to fail.

Cuitlahua had been consistent throughout in advice, which was now determination, that the Spaniards should be destroyed, at whatever cost.

He answered: "You will tell your lord that we are not blind to the ruin which he has wrought, but let his eyes be as open as ours. If we destroy one Spaniard for a thousand that he may slay, we shall prevail, as we are resolved to do. Let him look at the ranks of those who are round him now. Do they seem less numerous than they were? Let him count his own. Is it not already somewhat shorter to do?

"Beyond that, we know that water is scarce, and food gone. *And the bridges are broken down.* We look on those who are penned for sacrifice, though the days of fattening lie ahead."

While Marina translated this, Cuitlahua showed the inflexibility of his purpose by turning back to his litter. Marina was quick to ask: "Shall I recall him? Is there more to be said?"

But Cortéz answered: "No. Let the dog go," the contemptuous words being intended more for those on the inside of the wall than as an instruction to her.

He went in to hold council with those who had been with him from the first, and had earned his trust, but while they debated a problem they could not solve, Duero was at the door. He had come, he said, at the request of many of Narváez's men, who were united in their opinion as to what should be done. They must (and as for themselves they were resolved that they would) leave the city without further delay, whatever loss of life and treasure it might involve.

Cortéz said: "Duero, you are one I trust, as we both know. I will tell you what is in my own mind, and you can repeat much or little, as you think best.

"The men of Narváez are more numerous than those who may be more loyal to me, but we are all in the same boat, which is near to wreck. It is near to wreck because Narváez brought discord, where unity would have meant triumph for all. Now we can quarrel again, if we will; and, if we do, we shall make that wreck sure.

"I do not say they are wrong—that is what we are weighing now—but it would be making disaster sure, and we may yet think of a better plan. We will try the *mantas* tomorrow, and there will be another trouble for the Aztecs to overcome."

Duero went back, and justified the confidence that Cortéz felt both in his integrity and his tongue. For the moment, discord was still, and all men waited to see what their commander would be able to do.

CHAPTER SEVENTY-THREE: RETREAT

"If we go," Cortéz had said, "it is Tacuba causeway that we must choose, for it is no more than two miles in length. And, if we go that way, we must pass down the central street. Let us secure that first, which must become ours whether we go or stay, and they can guess which our choice will be."

To achieve this, he relied mainly on the three *mantas* which he had been building. These were a military machine which had been often used in the wars of the Old World, and which he had adapted to his own need. They were two-storied wooden structures, mounted on rollers, their sides being pierced for arquebusiers, and having platforms at each side of the upper storey, raised by ropes, and which could be let down to form bridges by which the flat roofs of the houses could be attacked.

They rolled out at the next dawn, drawn by ropes which Tlascalans pulled. They turned along the central avenue, and the Aztecs fled from volleys of bullets fired at leisure with careful aim, to which they could make no reply.

From time to time, as they advanced, the bridges were let down, and houses from which trouble came were cleared, and then plundered by the troops who advanced in the rear of the machines.

It was a successful experiment until they came to the first of seven bridges which divided them from the Tacuba causeway, and found that it had been entirely removed. It was unfortunate that there was a building at the roadside here, too high, and of such structure, that the platforms of the mantas did not avail for its attack; and before the danger was appreciated, and the ropes could be reversed to drag the mantas backward, some large stones were dislodged from its flat roof, and one crashed on to a timber structure which had not been constructed to resist such an impact. The roof collapsed, and there were injuries to those within.

Cortéz resolved that the mantas should not go further from their base. They had done well till then. Let it so remain. He would proceed now by other means. The clumsy structures were dragged back. The gap where the bridge had been was already being filled. Stones and timber, rubbish of whatever sort, was being thrown by many hands into the shallow water of the canal. Soon the gap had been roughly filled to the road's height. There was a surface across which the rollers of the mantas certainly could not have passed. But the horses could. Cavalry charged along a street which the Aztecs had not thought that they would be able to reach. The first obstacle had been overcome.

Cortéz now resolved to deal with the six remaining gaps in the same way, although Aztec opposition increased. While each gap was filled, they attacked the workers with stones and arrows, even though it exposed themselves to heavier losses from deadlier volleys. As each gap was bridged they fled before cavalry lances against which they could not contend, to renew resistance at the next gap.

The whole day, and the next, were occupied in this struggle. By the afternoon of the second day, every casual crossing was strongly held by detachments of mingled Spaniards and Tlascalans who had not attacked during the dark hours of the previous night.

And as the garrisoning of the last bridge was being arranged, a word came to Cortéz that the Aztecs were at the palace gate, desiring to discuss the peace they had rejected before. He rode back at the head of the three score cavaliers who had been operating with him, with more joy in his heart than he would have been willing for his enemies to have guessed. For he had been near to resolve that the only remaining hope was to evacuate the city by the causeway during the night hours, and it was a bitter choice that offered a very doubtful release.

He found that Cuitlahua had not come himself, but had sent a deputation with whom Marina had already been in conversation.

When he arrived, she said: "They profess that they are now anxious that the slaughter shall cease, and we can have a free passage, if we will leave tomorrow, and undertake to go back to the ships. If we consent, we are to release the three priests we are holding, in token that peace is made, and they will then send provisions, so that we may set off at dawn."

"You think this is in good faith?"

"How can I say? They are strangers to me. But it is what you wish, as I think."

"So it is. We have come to that. Was nothing said about Montezuma's release?"

"Nothing." She added, in a lower voice: "He is dead."

"Which is known to few?"

"Yes. It was in the last hour."

He saw that that made his position weaker even than it had been before. "Was nothing said as to the treasure we shall be able to take away? Of porters we may require?"

"Only that the priests are to take word of the number of porters, who will be here at dawn."

"Very well. We will let the priests go."

So he did, and went in to a needed meal; but he was roused from that by a clamour without, and by one who burst in upon him, with a cry: "The Aztecs are fighting. They have cut off some of our men. It is said they have the bridges again."

He saw that it was a trick, by which they had got the priests free, and led him to withdraw the cavaliers before the protection of night had come. He rose wrathfully: "That may not be beyond repair."

Soon, with trumpets sounding the charge, the cavalry were pouring out through the gate, and clearing the way to where Alvarado fought a losing action to defend three bridges where he had been cut off, and one of which was already in Aztec hands.

There followed an hour of wild confused fighting, in which the mailed cavaliers cleared portions of the contested street into which the Aztecs would swarm again as soon as the tails of their chargers were disappearing toward the next disputed bridge.

Over one of these, the Spaniards had thrown a wooden bridge, which the Aztecs had partly demolished, but not so that Cortéz, in advance of the troop he led, did not venture to ride over it safely, and use his sword to good purpose upon those who would have completed its destruction.

He had already been the example and inspiration of those he led, and now that the work of restoration was nearly done and it was evident that the Spaniards would again be in possession of the whole street when the protection of darkness would be theirs, he rode too far, and too desperately from his supports. He chased those of whom the hindmost were his to slay; he swung to take in the rear those who still sought to demolish the bridge. He saw five flee as his sword came down on the sixth, where neck and shoulder joined, with a fatal force. He saw that he was alone, and that Tlascalans on the other side of the bridge were signalling him to return. So he would have done, but the next thing of which he became aware was that, while he had been chasing those who fled first, those who remained had carried demolition too far for a charger to cross the loosened planks that remained. He heard the shrill derisive whistles of foes who observed his isolation, and were now closing upon him in numbers that would be certain to pull him down at the last, however heavy the price should be.

Could he leap the gap? It was a poor chance, and must require that he should first ride back into the press of swarming foes. There was a moment during which the great charger was turning amidst those who assailed it with hacking blades, or caught at housing or reins, indifferent to its rider's descending sword. Then it broke clear, felt the sharp impulse of spurs that were seldom used, and knew what it had to do. One of the hind hooves slipped on the broken edge as its leap was made, but the other held, and it scrambled to firmer ground.

Cortéz rode into a courtyard where a rumour that he was dead had caused consternation a few minutes before. He got down wearily from a weary and wounded horse. "Bernal," he said, "see that he be well fed, though the others may go somewhat short, for today he has served me well. And let the wound on his counter be dressed with care."

CHAPTER SEVENTY-FOUR: THE NIGHT OF SORROW

Cortéz returned to his interrupted meal an angry as well as physically exhausted man. He knew he had been fooled. He knew that there was no longer any doubt that the city must be left—or rather that it must be left if that should prove possible, which was a very different matter. He knew that there was constant debate both among captains and common men, as to whether the attempt could be better made by night or by day. He was inclined to favour the night, largely because it was not the custom of the Aztecs to fight in hours of darkness. He knew that there were strong arguments in the opposite scale, the fact being that it must be a desperate hazard, whether by night or day. But, as he ate, a thought came. *Why not tonight?*—with such suddenness that no word could go in advance to Aztec ears? It was true that he was a weary man. So were the horses. So was everyone. But the Aztecs would be weary too. Life is a great stake. Surely, for one night, they could resist the exhaustion of wearied limbs. To his audacious imagination, it seemed the one chance of success.

"Marina," he said, "I know the feeling among my own men. Botello is swaying them. But would the Tlascalans move in the night? I am less than sure."

Botello was a soldier who studied stars. He had made some prophecies which had proved true. He had said that they would escape in the night, but that it would be the time of his own death.

Marina said: "They will do what you direct. They think you are next to god. I mean theirs. There are few of them who will leave their faith."

"Then we shall be leaving tonight."

"Tonight! But you are too worn."

"I am well enough. It is the horses that are not fresh."

"Well, you can have mine. It has not been out."

"I cannot do that. Though you might not lose much by the exchange." He knew that the heart of the one he had ridden that day would not fail while its life remained.

"But I shall not ride. Can I do that while the other women will walk, both of my race and your own?"

"But you are now next to myself. It is an honour that is your due."

That was well meant, but it could be taken the wrong way.

She answered: "Do you think I had no honour before? I was born to a great house. There were two of my near kin among those Alvarado slew."

She had not mentioned that before. He knew that the six hundred had been the greatest in the whole land. He saw another aspect of her position. He said: "It was hard for you."

She put that serenely aside. "It is not so to those of a clear mind."

He reverted to the previous question: "You may walk, if you are resolved. It is not certain that the horses can be got through."

She thought: "If they could not, we should all die," but it was not useful to say. She asked: "Montezuma, and those who serve him, will be left here?"

Yes, there was the dead King to be considered, and those who might betray them too soon. He asked: "You know one of his wives?"

"She is my cousin."

"She would listen to you?"

"Yes."

"I saw Montezuma this morning. He said then that he should not live. He did not doubt that Spain would rule this land in the end. He asked me to take charge of three of his children who are now here, and to intercede with our own King that they should have honour in recompense for what he has done for us.

"I promised that with goodwill. Now, you shall let his wives know that my word shall be kept, if I live, and that will largely depend upon their silence, and that of those who are with them in the next hours. I could shut them up, but I think this may be the better way.

"You will tell them to prepare Montezuma's body to be returned to his own palace with honour, so that his people may deal with it as they will. They will be kept busy preparing for that.

"When we have moved out, they can raise alarm if they will, as it would be natural for them to do. At that time, it can do no harm."

"You think that we cannot get clear before sound of alarm?"

"I do not think Cuitlahua to be an infant in war. He will have a watch. I hope to be far out before they can make danger for us. I will take your horse, for there may be occasions for me to move with speed, and it is now best the conditioned of all we have."

The suddenness of the projected exodus would have produced disastrous confusion, had not Cortéz had plans prepared with such detailed care that complete orders could be issued and each man know what his place and duty would be in the next hour.

Now that the obstacles in the main street had been overcome, the greatest danger lay in the gaps in the causeway which it had been decided to use—one at each end, and one in the middle—from which it was known that the bridges had been removed.

Even though some men might be able to swim, or the water might not be too deep for a horse to ford, it was certain that they could not be passed unbridged by baggage and guns, and there would be little hope for footmen who bore their arms and all the impedimenta that they would need the next day. But this difficulty had been faced, and it might be hoped that it had been overcome. A wooden platform had been built, suitable to be laid across the sloping sides of the gap where a bridge had been, and this was to be entrusted to an officer named Magarino, who had forty soldiers under his command. His orders were to go in the van of the advance, with a screen of cavalry moving ahead, the platform being dragged on rollers till they should come to the first gap, where it would be laid, and they would wait till the whole army had passed, after which they would take it up and bear it to the next gap, when the army would go forward again.

The night was dark, and there was the doubtful advantage of steady rain when, at the stroke of midnight, the gates were opened, and the perilous exit began.

Sandoval led an advance guard of about twenty horsemen—Ordaz and de Lugo among them, the platform, drawn by a troop of Tlascalans, and protected by its two score of Spanish footmen, moving closely behind.

Every man had permission to take the share of treasure which had been allotted to him, or the chance of the dice had won, and there were few who did not wear chains or collars or belts of gold. Beyond that, they had been allowed to burden themselves at their own risks, and with warning that they were going a way on which those who travelled lightest would be the most likely to reach their goal.

Behind the platform, two hundred Spanish foot-soldiers followed, with ten times that number of Tlascalans, and after them, guarding women, treasure, baggage, and the heavier artillery, Cortéz himself with the hundred trusted soldiers who were his own guard. The Captain of the Guard, de Olid, was there; with de Morla, and de Ávila, attached personally to himself, which they could not resent, while those most fitted for independent action were at front or rear.

Among the baggage, the King's Treasurer, and his assistants, were in charge of the royal fifth, which they would not leave. And in the midst, with the women, were the three children of Montezuma, and some prisoners of importance, including Cacama, with whom Cortéz had a hope of making some bargain, now that Montezuma was dead.

After them came the main force of the Tlascalans, and finally the main body of Spaniards, both horse and foot, entrusted jointly to Alvarado and León de Velásquez, with the major part of the artillery, which might be effectual for defence, if there should be pursuit on the straight course of the causeway.

The rain-soaked ranks moved down the deserted street as silently as the chargers' hooves and the lumbering guns would allow. Hope of quiet escape rose to its height as the advance guard rode up to where the causeway began. They looked down upon the water where the first bridge had been removed, and reined aside for the platform to be brought forward. Certainly the causeway was not defended, except by that open space which they had made provision to span.

They did not know that a sentry patrol was approaching from the cross street that was the city boundary, nor did it know of them, through the darkness and rain, till it was less than twenty yards away. Then a whistle shrilled through the night, and in an instant, as it seemed, the whole city became alive.

As the platform was hurriedly thrust into its place, the great drum on the pyramid, which had been left undamaged when the temples were burned, sounded the warning beat which was only beaten at times of national crisis or calamity and could be heard far outward beyond the lake.

The platform sank firmly into its place. Sandoval rode over it alone, found it to be safe, and shouted for his troop to follow.

Men were hurrying now—faster for the noises that increase from the city streets.

As Ordaz (reined aside to watch the vanguard crossing the bridge, as was his part to do) saw the last of his Tlascalans cross the bridge, and Cortéz, on Marina's bay stallion, rode up, firing sounded in the street behind, showing that attack had begun.

Cortéz said: "You should go ahead. I will wait here."

As the guns appeared, he had two of them pulled out of the line. They would be useless for the main street, which was crowded by those of their own part, but, swung right and left, they could be death to any who should come by the margins of the lake.

He watched treasure, women, and prisoners approaching the bridge, while the noise of fighting increased behind them, and then his attention was drawn to a sound of many paddles upon the lake.

Dimly, through the still-falling rain, he could see that the water, on both sides of the causeway, was covered by hundreds of canoes, from which flights of stones and arrows were now raining upon those who hurried along it. Well, there could be no effectual answer to that but to hasten on.

As the women appeared, with a protecting file of his own guard upon either side, he rode on to the causeway beside them. He still bore his buckler strapped to his left arm, though the hand could now be used well enough, and he turned it to give what small protection it might to those who were not armoured against the missiles which were now falling thickly upon them.

As they advanced, the ferocity of the attack increased. Canoes grounded upon the causeway's side, and their crews clambered up endeavouring, in contempt of their own lives, to drag down those who would be borne to a dreadful death.

He had seen the thousands of canoes that would be on the lake during the market days, but he had not supposed there were so many as now appeared out of the night, with cries that were deafening, to far ahead where the vanguard rode, and showers of missiles so blindly aimed that many must have vexed their friends on the further side.

There was as yet no attempt to land on the causeway where the women were. The orderly files of soldiers on either side were not near the brink, and the lances of the occasional cavaliers who rode, as he was doing, on their outside, were a menace too deadly to be ignored.

But further back, the Tlascalans, in less orderly array, were hurrying on in a crowd that covered the causeway's breadth, and they were being vexed by bold attacks from the water, which they did not turn to repulse, but tried to shake off and avoid without ceasing to advance, which was not easy to do.

Cortéz swung his horse round. He rode back. He reined when to go further would have been to ride the Tlascalans down. There he sat, while they crowded past him. All, while they passed, would be safe at least at this spot.

Further back, perhaps twenty yards, he saw several canoes ground, and their crews climb. The Tlascalans, shrinking inward as they advanced, gave him the needed space. He charged forward, his lance transfixing one, and casting him off into the lake. He thrust down, staving in a canoe. He put the lance aside, it being too long to avail against those who were round him now. His sword was a thrusting death. The Tlascalans hurried on, scarcely aware of the help they had.

The gaps where the bridges had been were a mile apart, the causeway being two miles in length. The army (including women and other camp followers), in spite of its losses in recent fighting, still numbered more than eight thousand. With its guns and other impedimenta it occupied most of the first mile, when the vanguard halted, and sent back an urgent word for the platform to be passed forward.

It would not, in any event, have been a simple matter to convey it for the necessary mile along a causeway crowded with men, and the guns and baggage which were theirs, but, in fact, it was a problem which did not arise.

Forty men toiled in vain to raise a platform which had become fixed too firmly by the prolonged weight which it had borne, while the rearguard protected them on the landward side, and cannon, now retreated from the gap, fired on the canoes.

The mile-long line, now halted in front, continued to press forward until it could crowd no more. Aware of its dilemma, the exultant Aztecs increased the ferocity of their attacks.

The noise of conflict, the derisive whistling of the assailants, the cries of men wounded or overcome, who were dragged down to the canoes, rose into the darkness, from that inferno of dreadful strife.

Sandoval, after waiting for half an hour for a platform which did not come, received a message which, while not final in its wording, made the position clear enough for him to take an instant decision.

The Aztec canoes were now swarming behind and before. Their missiles were an unrelenting merciless hail. Many of them had clambered on to the further causeway, and confronted him from the other side of the deadly gap. Around his feet were the dead—horses and men—who had fallen during that half-hour's wait. He said: "Throw all you can into the gap. We must fill it up. Now who will swim over with me?"

He did not say that he himself was unable to swim. He spurred his horse into the water.

It leapt gallantly down, but found no foothold. The water there may have been eight feet deep. Opposite was a sheer wall which no horse could scale, even had there been no foes leaning, with brandished weapons, over the brink.

Slipping from the saddle, with an arm round the charger's neck, he directed it to the open lake. The sides of the causeway sloped. There was a better prospect of mounting there. As he did this, he saw that the bows of half a dozen canoes were directed toward him, so that a poor chance, as he thought, had become none.

But as he got clear of the gap he was surprised to feel the horse rising out of the flood. The fact was that the lake (everywhere shallow) was of not more than four feet depth in that part, and had been artificially deepened beneath the bridge.

The sloping side of the causeway was difficult, but not impossible, for a horse to scramble up, with the encouragement of one beside it whose hand strained on the rein. Ordaz, and others who had swum the ditch, mounted beside him. The Aztecs, never equal to facing the swords of steelclad cavaliers, gave ground as they appeared. With the encouragement of their example, there were others who followed in the same way, while everything of bulk, even dead horses and men, even boxes of ammunition and ingots of gold, were brought up and flung into the ditch, so that there might, as there was at last, be a passage in shallow water for human feet.

But before this was done the struggle along the first half of the causeway had increased in its intensity. The tortured files surged forward slowly, harassed and diminished on either flank by attacks from the water that became bolder each moment, and deadlier in their results.

CHAPTER SEVENTY-FIVE: RESCUE

The long column, in what seemed to be its death agony, revealed the extremities of human nature, from height to depth, as some fought blindly forward, indifferent to the deaths of comrades, or of who might be trampled beneath their feet, while others still thought first of succouring the wounded and shielding the weak.

It became difficult afterwards to say what the movements of Cortéz had been, for, when dawn came to a scene of desolation and death, he was remembered as having been everywhere that the need was most.

The women recalled that when they who remained alive had come to the half-filled gap, they had seen him, almost saddle-deep in the flood, his page, de Salazar, and de Morla, beside him, defying the Aztec canoes, and ferrying those of them who were faint or wounded, in his arms, to the further causeway.

Those who, following Sandoval and his companions, reached to sight of such safety as could be hoped from the solid land, and found the third flooded gap had to be crossed as the others had been (but with nothing now to be tumbled to fill it up), remembered that he had been there, with the same confident directing voice, the same strong aid as before.

But de Salazar was no longer beside him then. The Aztecs had pulled him down. And it was at that time, as the first grey uncertainty of dawn gave a doubtful sight of the mist-covered waters, that word was brought that the last survivors had passed the central gap.

Was Pedro among them? Cortéz had asked. Was León safe? And when he had the reply that nothing was known of them—that it was supposed that the rearward cavaliers had perished, with the forty who had had charge of the platform, he had said a word to de Morla at his side, and the two had ridden backward, followed by half a dozen others whose horses were still able to make some pace, though it was not much.

They made the best speed they might along the half of the causeway which was still obstructed by a slow-moving throng of wounded and wearied men, which the Aztecs—themselves inevitably exhausted by the strife of the long night hours—had almost ceased to molest. They came to the central gap, or what had been a gap once, but was now half filled with debris, including the bodies of many slain, with a cannon-muzzle protruding upwards between the stiff legs of a dead horse, and beyond it, to a causeway that was now deserted except for the dead, the dying, the scattered treasures they had ceased to value, and many Aztecs who prowled among them, to plunder that which had been the spoil of conquest before.

Cortéz drew his rein. Through the mist and the grey beginnings of dawn he could see that the water was still thickly covered with Aztec canoes. He could not tell how strongly the causeway itself was occupied by those who were plundering now, but whose weapons were near their hands. To ride further back was to invite the fate of those, horses, and women and men, whose broken bodies were scattered thickly before him now. And it might be too late—it almost certainly was too late—to avail.

De Morla said: "I hear distant sound. Shall we go on?"

"I hear nothing. I would not throw good lives away for a vain hope."

Then there came the noise of a cannon shot through the mist. He used his spurs at that, rousing the exhausted horse to an effort which carried him forward beyond the capacity of his companions to keep his side.

The forty men whose duty had been to raise the platform and bring it forward had toiled in vain till many of them were dead, and there were few who would not have had the excuse of a wound to claim the succour of others at a possible time. The cavaliers under Velásquez and Alvarado had remained for their protection, with some gunners, and Tlascalans whose duty it had been to hand the platform along.

When Alvarado reluctantly gave the order to abandon a labour which had become hopeless, there was a strong force of Aztecs upon the causeway dividing them from their comrades' retiring rear. In the darkness, they could not see how dense or how deep it might prove to be, but they dare not use their two cannon in that direction, knowing that the shots might go on to destroy their friends. They used them only to protect their retreating rear, while the cavaliers led the slow advance, now obstructed by active foes, and which must, at the best, be at the pace of weary and wounded men, some of whom were cumbered by disabled comrades whom they were reluctant to abandon to certain death.

Slowly and stubbornly they advanced, resisted in front, and assailed upon either flank by flying missiles and those who scrambled up from the canoes. While the horses endured, they made gradual advance, but as, one by one, they were lamed, or exhausted by many wounds, the advance lessened, and ceased. There came a time when even the long swords of dismounted cavaliers were unequal to holding back the pressure of those who regarded them as their certain prey.

Alvarado alone, conspicuous even on foot by his giant stature, and the great mane of his yellow hair, was so dreaded by those he faced that they gave way before his repute as much as from the thrusts of a tireless sword. His efforts could not secure a steady advance, but they swayed forward at times, and were then borne backward a greater way. Even to him, there was no doubt now of what the end must be. They could delay death. But the thought of rescue did not enter his mind. Then there was the sound of disturbance some distance away, at the rear of their thronging foes. He heard *"St. Jago"* above the din. It was a war cry and voice he knew. He saw swords flash through the mist. He saw the six great steeds break through ranks that fled or were rolled down the causeway's side. Cortéz waved his sword in greeting. He shouted: "The way to safety is short." He swung his steed round, and his five comrades did the same, charging forward again. But he did not go far ahead. The rescued remnant came on.

So, at a decreasing pace, never being brought to an absolute halt again, they fought their way onward to the central gap, but not without further loss. They were in sight of it, the mist having thinned, and daylight widening around them, when de Morla's horse fell with a broken foreleg, throwing his rider forward among his foes. He fell heavily, and there was a flurry of strife while his comrades strove for his rescue, and Aztec hands were eager to drag him away.

They were driven off him at last, more than one having lost his life through his lust to capture a victim for the altar of his dishonoured god; but those who would have raised him found that de Morla was dead, and, when they knew that, they must hurry forward, still uncertain of how death came to a gallant knight.

The five horsemen who remained plunged into the lake when the gap was reached, to protect it on either side, while weary and wounded men climbed down and waded ankle-deep over the debris that choked its depth. Alvarado guarded their rear with a sword that few Aztecs were bold to face, but they hung back a few yards at the last, concerting among themselves that they would have him when he must turn and descend and flounder with no one to guard his rear.

It was a danger to which he was not blind, nor were the cavaliers who now saw that the last of the living remnant had dragged their wounded up to such safety as the causeway gave. Cortéz shouted something to him he did not hear, for he was stooping to the ground where lay the long lance of a cavalier who must have laid it aside during the night for a sword which would be better avail. He picked it up, and ran backward for a few paces, his astonished foes giving way before the long weapon, and the unexpected advance. But he did not aim it at them. Having gained the distance he required, he turned, and running back, used the lance as a jumping-pole, and leapt over the gap.

There were a hundred, Spaniards and Tlascalans, who saw it done, and bore witness to it in later days. The Aztecs said the same. Such witness is hard to doubt. But Bernal Díaz did doubt it, or perhaps doubt may be an inadequate word. He was a mile away at the time, being one of those who had passed the last gap, but he wrote in later years, and said it was a tale which he had never believed, because he had seen the gap, and it was of a width which could not be leapt by a mortal man.

As to ourselves, we cannot even discover what its width was. The lake has dried, and the causeway exists no more. But Alvarado and those who had witnessed his escape agreed that it had been done in that way, and that they invented the tale or deluded themselves may be regarded as greater improbabilities than that he leapt a gap, with his life at stake, of a width which we do not know.

CHAPTER SEVENTY-SIX: RESIDUE

After the shore was gained, the Aztecs made no further pursuit. There was rich spoil to be gathered in, and they themselves were mostly weary men.

Those who crossed the last gap, after they had seen Cortéz and his companions ride back into the mist, threw themselves down exhausted upon the ground, wandered aimlessly about, or gave slow obedience to the efforts of Sandoval and Ordaz to muster them in the ranks they knew.

In the minds of these two, the ablest of his remaining captains, there was the same doubt: "Would their leader return alive? And, if he did not, what, without his sanguine courage, his genius for organisation, would they be able to save?

But it was a doubt which was soon done. Unpursued since the passing of the central gap, the rescued remnant of the rearguard advanced slowly along the final mile of the causeway. But Cortéz had come at a faster pace. His eyes, hard with resolution, surveyed the thin ranks of those who remained alive. They sought the women, and next moment he alighted at Marina's side.

"You are safe," he asked, "and unhurt?"

"Yes, she said, as though the night had been passed in a quiet way. "I was guarded well."

That was true. It had been shrewd wisdom on his part which had placed her as companion to Louise, for he knew that the Tlascalan princess would be guarded by those of her own race, more for whom she was than as Alvarado's wife, and that Marina was in a double protection while she was at Louise's side.

"And I still live," he said, his tired eyes even now attempting a smile, "which is thanks to Roland, if not to you."

Roland was the bay stallion of hers, which he had ridden throughout the night. His own charger might have been equal of spirit, but he had been a tired horse when the day was done.

He added: "We must make count of those who remain. Alvarado tells me León is dead."

"But you have saved him?"

"Yes. And it may be a hundred more. León was killed while they still toiled to get the platform raised. There is none whom I should be more loth to lose, for he kept faith when many would have taken Narváez's part. And de Morla went down, which was the death of a gallant man."

"They say that Montezuma's children cannot be found, nor those in whose charge they were. And Cacama is gone."

"So he would do. He will be back with his own people by now, to make more trouble for us."

That was a natural conclusion, but it was not true. Neither Cacama nor Montezuma's children, nor those who had been detailed to guard them, were ever heard of again. With six thousand others, Spaniards, Aztecs, and Tlascalans, they had gone to death in the night.

Ávila rode slowly up as they talked, on a halting steed. He asked: "Will you have them camp here, or go further on? Even those who are not hurt are near the end of their strength. If they lie, they will sleep long."

They were in a pleasant woodland area on the lake shore, with scattered houses among the trees. Before them was Tacuba, a small residential city at this time. It had a great past, but it had become less at this day.

Cortéz said: "They must go on through the city, and to the hills. You may say that those can stay here who are willing to die. The horses must not be ridden longer. They must be led. Bernal—is he safe? That is well. Bernal will agree about that. I can see that Alvarado is here now. You can stay with him to drive the rear, and I will go to the front."

He rode on, giving directions as he advanced that the few horses that remained should be treated with care. Those who had ridden during the night should be equal to walking now. His own horse was the only one that had been in stall during the previous day.

Hungry, footsore, dejected, wondering that they were not further pursued, the mingled rabble of Tlascalans and Spaniards straggled through the silent streets of Tacuba, the inhabitants of which gave no sign of life, and there was no inclination to challenge its silence by invading the houses, even for food.

Cortéz rode on with a new thought in his mind. Men would remember afterwards that his constant question had been: "Have you seen Martín? Is López safe?" Until he came on the boat-builder, sitting on a wayside porch, and twisting a soiled rag round an injured knee. They might be no more than a flying rout, but their commander was already planning ahead.

Coming clear of the city streets, they saw, to the left, and some distance ahead, a low hill, the extent of which was covered by one of those extensive temple or barrack buildings which were a conspicuous feature of the whole country, and some of which had already been convenient for their accommodation.

Cortéz, riding to the front of the long straggling line of fugitives, directed them towards it, but as they approached they saw that there were armed soldiers about its gates, and it was a sign of the exhaustion of those who led that they halted thereat, or moved with a hesitation that showed no eagerness to be in the front of the advance.

Perhaps no more critical moment than this had come since the little fleet of the invaders had cast anchor at Vera Cruz. It was to be decided by the resolution of the one who had no lack of faith, even now, in himself or them.

"Ordaz," Cortéz cried to the cavalier he could trust who was next in sight, "you must try the horses again. Let those mount them who have a whole lance. Sandoval, can the arquebusiers be drawn to one head?"

They were now at a definite halt, but it was one out of which order would come—and with it realisation of the losses they had sustained. Of the eighty horses there had been on the last day, there were now twenty-four, including that which Marina was used to ride. The arquebusiers were not arrayed, because there was not one whose clumsy weapon and tripod had not been lost. Cortéz knew already that the artillery had been left behind; he realised now that, even if any ammunition remained, the use of powder was done. Seven crossbowmen still had weapons that they were able to wind, and there was a sheaf of bolts that a Tlascalan had carried stubbornly throughout the night.

In the end, an advance of those who were hardiest to endure was made with an appearance of strength. The crossbowmen in the centre had ten cavaliers on either side, and beyond them a hundred swordsmen to right and left, with a strong force of Tlascalans in their support. They approached walls from which arrows flew till they were near gates which were not closed, when the nuisance ceased; and, as they entered, the garrison, being fewer than they, fled from an exit on the far side.

"Sandoval," Cortéz ordered, "you will see that all entrances be secured. Ávila, will you have search made for what food there may be, and see that all have a fair share. There will surely be a well here. I will take count of the force that we yet have."

He called a scrivener who had come through the night, and still had the tools of his trade. He stood at his Commander's side by the gate, and took record of those who came through, Spaniards and allies. Had the astrologer been right? Would it have been worse had it been tried in the daylight hours? He had, at least, been right as to his own fate, for he was not to be seen now.

Well, most of the captains had come through. There was some consolation in that. And he had saved Alvarado (though de Morla had been the price). And Martín López still lived.

He considered that (in spite of the losses among the rearguard) a disproportionate number of his veterans had survived. The losses had been greater among the men that Narváez had brought. Well, he had warned them not to burden themselves with that fatal gold!

Then he thought of what the fate of those would be who had been captured alive, as he knew that so many had. Men who were cleaning and binding wounds which kept them awake said afterwards that they saw their Commander weep on the temple steps.

But that could not have been for long, for he was soon at the side of Ávila, asking what food had been found, and making such dispositions as the occasion required.

CHAPTER SEVENTY-SEVEN: OTUMBA

Women (who had not toiled and fought through the previous day, whatever their night had been) volunteered to watch while men slept, but there was no occasion to call alarm. The exhausted Aztecs made no pursuit.

"You will wake me," Cortéz had said, before he had allowed sleep to come to his own eyes, "two hours before darkness," and this Marina had promised to do.

When she did, he sent urgently for his captains to come to a counsel for which she would be required, for he must consort a plan with his Tlascalan allies. He asked: "Can we trust them in this reverse?"

"But of course," she answered. Did he not understand that the marriages of their princesses had secured that, whether for evil or good? She had always wondered that he had not established peace with the Aztecs, when Montezuma had offered it, in the same way. She still did not understand his refusal, as its implications affected herself, though she had doubts which were not always easy to still.

Now she must be a medium of communication between those who had half learnt each other's tongue, lest mistake be made. But it was a short counsel where all were agreed that Tlascala must be their goal, and that they should go by such route as the Tlascalans advised.

Nor was there much debate as to when it would be. After darkness fell, by which time some litters had been made for the lame and sick, they moved out by a northern road, which they would not be expected to take, having lit fires to delude any who might watch into supposing that they remained in the temple during the night.

For seven days after that they fled, through a hostile land, from which fear had gone, and only hatred remained. They must stay to search for food which they could not buy, and which violence could not lightly procure for such numbers as theirs. They must move with the caution bred of knowledge that those who straggled would not return. The most they would know further of them would be the cry of a captured man.

But they had not been opposed in force, and Cortéz had the memory of one good meal, when their foes had killed a horse they could not carry away, and it had been eaten so thoroughly that its hide could not be found.

And when a rumour came that he was not destined to reach Tlascala without opposition, he had not hurried on, but had deliberately rested his weary troops for a whole day, with no activity but the incessant foraging for food, so that it was not until the morning of the Eighth of July that they climbed the high sierra that bounded Otumba's plain, and could look across it to the sanctuary of Tlascala's territory, a short day's march away.

But their eyes, as they looked ahead, were not drawn to that distant hope, nor did they regard the ancient pyramids, covered and obscured by the luxuriant vegetation of the valley, which were the enigmatic memorial of a nameless race which had disappeared without trace before the Aztecs entered the land. What they saw was an array of white, cotton-uniformed regiments, with gaily coloured headdresses and banners, and green-plumed leaders, brilliant with feather cloaks, and bright with bronze-tipped spears.

It was a host the extent of which may have been known to its Aztec leaders, but there is no remaining record of that. One who guessed on that panorama of war said afterwards that it was not less than two hundred thousand men. There were much less than three thousand of those who looked down upon them. Was it worth while to attempt count of their foes? One thing was sure: there was no safety except within the girdle of the Tlascalan hills. They must go forward, or die.

There was no artillery now. There were no firearms at all. The seven crossbows would be a derision to the great army that faced them now.

There were twenty cavaliers, with lances enough. Ten on each flank, as they came to the lower ground, and the front of battle was extended to meet their foes.

Cortéz sat again on his own horse. Marina did not ride. Her bay stallion was burdened with baggage now. So was another horse whose rider had taken a wound which refused to heal.

The absence of the porters on whom they had come to rely had been a great hardship for fleeing men. It was true that most of the treasure, the guns, the ammunition, tools and spare weapons, and clothes, and all the impedimenta which is essential to those who move in a homeless way, had been left behind. But such things as they still had of weapons and clothes, of food and plunder, must be carried on their own backs.

Now all but weapons must be cast into a common pile, and left unguarded. That was the order that Cortéz gave, and which had been strictly enforced. They might all die, in which case their need of it would be done. They might break through their foes, and be unable to return, in which case they would be living but naked men. Or they might—if imagination would run so wild—drive that great host from the plain, and have leisure to sort out what they had cast into one pile.

Cortéz looked down on that far-spread host, and thought: "It is the end. Men have trusted me, and I have led them to death. But if it end thus, it shall not be because I have failed to do what I yet can."

He had been an ill man during the last week. His hand healed well enough, but it had become clear that it had two fingers which would be of no further use. And he had a wound on the head, of which only Marina knew. It had not bled. He had taken a heavy blow on the casque. His skull, if not fractured, must have been badly bruised. It had ached so that he slept ill. But such things would be forgotten now. The next two hours must be a time of triumph or certain death.

He rose in his stirrups to call to all who could hear: "Comrades, Tlascala is near ahead. We can cut them through. Go forward for God and Spain!"

He was answered by a great shout from the moving men, to which the Tlascalans added the shrill whistle that mocked their foes. But next moment these cries were drowned in the defiant sound that rose from the confronting host, a whistle that did not cease till they were so near that the arrows began to fly.

The Spaniards quickened their pace at that, but, before they clashed, the cavaliers rode into the Aztec front. From the right flank, Alvarado and his companions swung leftward, breaking into and along the front of those to whom the steel-clad cavaliers were a menace they could not meet. And, at the same moment, Sandoval, with his company, rode from the left, making a somewhat wider curve, and bringing wild confusion to those immediately behind those among whom Alvarado slew.

The troops reined up in each others' places, breathing their horses for a repetition of that disconcerting attack, and as they did so the footmen, now at a run, closed with the Aztecs' disordered front.

It gave way before them. Spanish swords slew freely among those who were slowest in that retreat. The cavaliers repeated their charges across the front of the shaken foe.

Rapidly, for a time, Spaniards and Tlascalans advanced over the plain.

But they found that they were surrounded by an ocean of thronging foes. That which opened in front was closing upon their rear. And it was far more difficult for the retreating rear to maintain defence than for the van to advance. The more progress that was made, the more rapidly must the rear retreat from exultant foes. Soon the cavaliers must transfer their attention to its defence. Deprived of their support, the advance slackened, and ceased.

After a time, a renewed effort was made. Stirred to desperation by the peril in which they stood, they surged forward again. They gained ground that was slightly higher than that by which it was surrounded. A mere knoll, which gave them little advantage, unless it were in a fuller sight of the extent of surrounding foes, and the distance of the hills where their safety lay.

Cortéz saw that they were not merely brought to a halt, they were becoming more congested, were being slowly driven inward from every side. There could only be one end to that.

With Sandoval, and three other cavaliers who were still resolute to resist their fate, he charged the Aztec ranks in an effort to get the front moving again, and had an almost fatal success. The Aztecs gave way before them. Some died. It seemed that they could go forward as far as they would. But the footmen had not followed. The Aztec ranks closed behind them. Their whistles rose in a derisive blast. None too soon, the little group of horsemen swung round to return, and that movement was a signal for the Aztecs, careless of their own lives, to press round from every side.

They got back. The footmen opened their ranks, and closed them when they had ridden through. Cortéz came to ground at Marina's side. She asked: "You are badly hurt? You can do no more." Blood flowed from his head, where he had taken a second wound.

He answered: "We can win yet. But I must have Roland. This horse is done."

That was plain. The great charger stood breathing hard, with its head down. It was bleeding from several wounds.

None could guess what he would do, but they heard the hope in his voice. Hastily the baggage was tumbled from Roland's back. Saddle and harness were changed.

A young cavalier, Juan de Salamanca, who had ridden in with him, was at his side.

"Juan," he said, "get Alvarado here, and Olid, and any others who yet have a good horse. Tell them we stake all on a winning throw."

Cihuaca, a cousin of the new Emperor, who had the greatest reputation among the generals of the Aztec armies, was in command of the great host which had been assembled for the destruction of the hated Spaniards. His litter, brilliant with featherwork, and precious metal, and floating plumes, might have vied with that of the Emperor himself. His rank was shown by a short staff attached to his own back, from which a banner of golden net rose behind his head.

He did not approach the scene of conflict closely, which it would have been foolish to do, although the young nobles round him formed a guard on which to rely.

Rising in his litter, he had seen the last outbreak of the dreaded cavaliers, and its retreat. He saw that it had not enabled the Spanish front to move forward at all. The meaning of that was plain. He said: "It is near the end."

They told him: "Malintzin was badly hurt in the head, and his horse was not far from death."

He answered: "I do not wish him to die. He must be alive for sacrifice at the Great Feast. It is only so that the War-God's anger can be appeased. Do they come out again?"

So it seemed that they did. Rising in his litter, he could see that the cavaliers were in somewhat greater force than before. He saw that Cortéz was there. He knew the great ostrich plume which he wore clasped in the casque. Part of it had been shorn away, but it was still conspicuous, no other feathers of its colour being worn upon either side.

Cihuaca watched the progress of the cavaliers with calculating eyes. It was clear that his own footmen were giving way. He had expected that. He thought that the cavaliers made more rapid progress than before. He said: "They are mad. They will not return. They come out too far." He watched for the moment when they would rein round, and his troops would close upon them both behind and before, as they had orders to do. That was when they would come to grief. He sent a reminder that Cortéz must be captured alive. He could see them more plainly now. They were coming straight towards him, as they had done from the first. But he was not alarmed. He was not one to have nervous doubts. He said: "Let our men be told that they come too far. They must now be stayed."

But they were not stayed. The war cry *"St. Jago"* could be heard over the din. He saw the little band of cavaliers now driving among those who were unprepared to resist this dreaded onslaught of mounted men. He saw their swords rise and fall, as they smote at those who were slowest to yield them way, as most did. He saw his own nobles drawing hesitant weapons, and then that they were ridden down, or were retreating to right and left. Now Cortéz was here. The charger struck the side of the litter, which turned over as Cihuaca leaned on its further side, twisting to avoid a blade which missed his neck, but went in under a shoulder blade at the next thrust. Juan de Salamanca leapt from his horse. His sword made an end of a wounded man. He rose with the golden banner of net held in a gauntlet that streamed with blood. He handed it to Cortéz, who held it aloft. The cry: "Cihuaca is dead," rose in a long wail which reached the ears of Tlascalans who understood.

There was nothing for them to do now but to slay on the rear of a flying foe.

CHAPTER SEVENTY-EIGHT: TLASCALA'S CHOICE

It was no blind impulse of vengeance which led Cortéz to direct pursuit. He knew that the Aztec strength remained, and, if it should be rallied, the battle might yet be lost. So the Tlascalans were urged to put slaughter first, and let plunder wait till a later hour, and the wearied horses continued to ride down the fugitives, and to break up any attempt to gather to a fresh head of offence.

There were some who would have preferred to go on at once to the friendly hills; but it might have proved a poor policy had the unmolested Aztecs assembled again. And the distance was great for a day that was near its noon, and the baggage would have been left behind.

Cautious in his audacities, Cortéz had a question ever in his mind of how the Tlascalans, who had been both foes and friends, would receive those who had become fugitives from the Aztec power.

Now he thought: "If we enter Tlascala without baggage or spoil, even though the Aztecs may not rally to vex our rear, or surround us again (as I think they might), we should still have an aspect of flight, and be suppliants for a bounty we might not get. Today's risk may well be tomorrow's gain."

So he pressed pursuit in relentless mood, camped on the knoll where the last stand had been made, and gathered as much spoil as two dozen horses and many hundreds of human backs were equal to bear away.

They moved out without molestation at the next dawn. Cortéz had a bandaged head, but he made nothing of that, and, indeed, there were too many busy with their own hurts for it to cause much remark. Only it might have been noticed that he kept Roland for his own use, when the horses were required for the spoil, and those who knew him might have judged much from that.

They had cause to approve the rigour of the pursuit on the last day (some who were present put the Aztec slain at twenty thousand, which we may believe if we will) when they saw that they were still followed for the first miles by skirmishing crowds, so that there was a doubt of whether the horses must be mounted again. But these did not venture a near approach, and disappeared at the boundary of Tlascalan land.

The burdened army, heavy with plunder, and slack with wounds, did not reach Tlascala that day. They halted at a smaller city twelve miles short of the capital, where they found they were welcomed well.

They were provided with ample food: they responded with many gifts from their recent spoils. They remained there, glad to rest and to dress their wounds, for the following two days. Then they were visited by the elderly Maxixcatzin and the younger Xicotencatl, with a number of other representative Tlascalan citizens. They came not to criticise but to praise. It was a marvel that, for so many months, the Spaniards had defied the whole strength of the Aztec empire, and that its army at the last had proved too weak to prevent their return.

Finding that his recent experiences were interpreted in this satisfactory manner, Cortéz lost no more time in completing the journey to the Tlascalan capital, where he became the guest of Maxixcatzin, who had been from the first his consistent friend. The rest of the Spaniards were hospitably received in the quarter of the city over which Maxixcatzin presided. The Tlascalans scattered to their own homes.

For some weeks the Spaniards rested, recovering strength, and healing sickness and wounds. They debated among themselves what the future could be, and a decision grew in which Cortéz could have no voice, for he lay at the threshold of death. The will relaxed that had sustained him through anxiety, toil and wounds, and he learnt what his weakness was.

The wound in his head became inflamed, and it was found that it contained a piece of broken bone, which must be removed. Fever followed, and such weakness that men must doubt what the end would be.

Meanwhile there were discouraging reports. The Spaniards who, in confidence of their established prestige, had been scattered over the land, would never be seen again. A party of twelve who had been ordered to join Cortéz at México had been massacred to the last man. Worse than that, a party of nearly fifty from Vera Cruz (including some sick men left at Tlascala by Cortéz three weeks before) on the way to México, with a great quantity of treasure, had been entirely destroyed.

Only from Vera Cruz was the news good. The settlement was safe, the Totonacs still friendly, peace prevailed, the way of return to Cuba was not cut off.

For the weeks that Cortéz lay ill, men were content to wait in the comfort and security to which they had come. But by when it became known that he was rising again, some were impatient, and all were willing to move.

There were some who wished to see their Commander, to obtain assent to their own plans, which they did not doubt that it would be easy to do. But they found that Marina had an opinion on that, which she would not change.

What, she asked, would be the purpose of that? Till he could move, it was clear that nothing could be done. When he should be recovered, he could decide what would be best. "Does he," she might have added (but was too polite), "require opinions from you?"

So it followed that, two days later, as he sat looking out on Maxixcatzin's garden of summer flowers, he received a letter which she could not prevent, and he read thus:

> "We, the undersigned, being loyal to Spain and you, are somewhat troubled in mind, knowing that the treasure which had been won has been largely lost, and fearing that you may feel that it would be dishonour to return to Cuba with no recompense either for those whose stakes were in your own expedition, or in that which followed.
>
> "We therefore wish to give you assurance, as being among those who will be returning without reward, that we hold that, from first to last, you did all that was within human power, and more than most would have had valour or wisdom to bring to pass, as, we believe, will be lightly agreed, even among those who are brought to loss.
>
> "And now we hold, in the strait to which we are brought, there is but one thing to be done, in which, without dishonour, you may concur.
>
> "The artillery and all firearms having been lost, with most of the horses and ourselves, and we who remain alive being sick or weakened with many wounds, there is but one hope that remains, which is that we should march to Vera Cruz while it yet stands; for if it fall we are lost indeed, which would

bring joy to our foes, but no honour to God or Spain."

This petition was signed by an actual majority of the Spanish troops, and their signatures were attested by the Royal Notary, giving the document an appearance of deliberation which could not be disregarded. The signature of Duero—a tested friend—headed the list. He noticed other names that he was sorry to see, but took some satisfaction from the fact that there were many more of Narváez's party than of his own veterans, and that those of Pedro de Alvarado and Gonzalo were not there. Neither was that of Olid, the Captain of the Guard, and he was not one whom he had ever been able to call a friend, there was some satisfaction in that.

He saw also that the request was not made in a disloyal tone, and that it was one which most men, whether ruled by prudence, policy, or military science, would approve. It was even open to the construction of having been done out of consideration for him. Seeing that he would be bound to retreat, they had provided him with a document which would make the announcement less bitter, and which would support him when explanation must be made to St. Domingo and Madrid. Perhaps Duero had thought of that! It would be consistent with the usual workings of the secretarial mind.

Well, he would make it no ground of quarrel with him. He would quarrel with none. But he had no intention of such retreat. He knew that, at any moment, he might be ruined by a word from Madrid. (Had Puerto-Carrero been sunk in Atlantic storm?) He might be overwhelmed by his Aztec foes. He might be ruined; but it must be done by others. He would not ruin himself.

Marina was at his side as he read this. He cast it down in her sight, but she had not yet learned to read in the Spanish style. (Why did they not write with a paintbrush, setting out their thoughts in a way that was simple and plain?) She did not think he was unendurably vexed.

He said, after a time of silence: "Will you let it be known that I wish all Spanish men to assemble tomorrow at prime in the courtyard here, when I shall have something to say?"

Even to her he gave no hint of what it would be. Let them wait in doubt.

CHAPTER SEVENTY-NINE: TURNING POINT

The Spaniards who assembled in the courtyard when morning came were fewer than three hundred men. It was still much less than a year since Cortéz had cast anchor on the Mexican coast, and not one in four of those who had been with him then, or had come later, was now alive, and able to bear the weapons of war.

From the hour when he had received the letter, he had avoided seeing even those on whose loyalty he could most surely rely, for he was resolved that his own purpose should not be known before that moment when he could speak at the same time equally and to all.

They saw a man who was thinner than he had been, and still weak from illness, but one whose mind was buoyant, whose resolution was fixed. Since that fragment of broken bone had been removed, the maddening pain that had hindered thought had ceased, and he knew now that he would be physically fit for that which he believed it was his mission from God to do.

He heard the murmur of welcome that his appearance roused, and looked round with his ready smile on those who were plainly anxious as to what they should hear from him. He judged that there were many whose minds were fixed on returning to Cuba while life remained. But he thought that it would be hard for them to object to what he was going to say.

"Comrades," he began, "I understand that most of you are agreed that it will be prudent to return to Cuba, and, of your kindness, you tell me that you will be content with a tale of failure, for which I shall not be blamed.

"Well, we are agreed there, for success or failure must be unsure till the last dice are flung, which has yet to be.

"But I will first tell you two things, so that you may not be kept in doubt while you hear others I have to say.

"First, all may return who will. They may set out to Vera Cruz at their own time. They may take due share of all that we still have. They shall go with the godspeed of those of us who remain, whether they be many or few.

"Second, I shall not go myself, seeing no compulsion thereto, and being bound in honour not to go for a less cause.

"There are some of you (if not all) who are not bound in the same way. They may each do as they will. But we have allies to whom I am pledged. Shall we leave them naked to Aztec wrath? You may say that the Tlascalans held their own before, and may do so again. But there are Totonacs also, and others who have been friendly to us.

"And you must see that we should not go as defeated men. Who fled from Otumba plain a few weeks ago? Was it they or we?

"We have won triumphs such as (we being few) have been scarcely matched in the annals of Christian men. That was by the favour of God, in Whose name we fight. Shall we abandon His high crusade, not being driven thereto, but by weakness of Faith in Him? By His design (as we may not doubt) we have brought His faith to a heathen land. Shall we have the honour therefor which our wounds deserve, or shall we be known as those who shrank from the first reverse—or rather, and worse than that, as those who ran from a place where we lie safe, unmolested by beaten foes?

"Will you leave a land to which others will surely come to win the honour and take the wealth which your merit deserves to have?

"As for myself, I have taken hold of this heathen land in the name of Spain. So I have made report to Madrid, and decision will come from there to which all loyal Spaniards will yield consent. It may replace me by one of better worth, or it may confirm me as I now am. Should it do this, shall it be found that I am not here?

"I have said, all may go who will. They will have neither hindrance nor condemnation from me, but I stay here though there be no more than five or ten of a like mind—and I think, there may be more who will have first regard for the cause of God and for the honour of Spain."

He looked round, as he finished, as though inviting reply, and a cheer broke out of sufficient volume to show that there were many of whom he could count among those who had not signed the petition, and perhaps some others who had been swayed by passionate words.

The meeting now dispersed into argumentative or quarrelling groups, those who wished to go being no better content because the decision to which they had listened gave them no logical cause for complaint. Could they argue that because they wished to return, they should be able to compel others to do so? It would be absurd. But that did not alter the fact that they had little heart for leaving Tlascalan allies and Tlascalan walls to march to the coast in greatly diminished numbers, leaving their best and boldest (and all the horses) behind, as they would have to do. Might they not thus be inviting the very fate they would be active to fly?

But the inclination to withdraw was too strong, too obstinate, and too sure of the strength of its arguments, to abandon its purpose without further effort.

In the evening, Bermúdez and Duero came to Cortéz, as a deputation from other men.

"Hernán," Duero said, "you know me for a true friend, and though Bermúdez, if he return now, must go back with an ill tale, he has shown friendship for you in past days, nor has he changed.

"We understand how you feel, and that you are unwilling to see that which others do not mistake. When we drew up that petition (in which we do not hide that we were largely concerned), there were two things of which no mention was made. We thought that they must be known to you, but, however that might be, they are of the sort which should not be passed about in a public way.

"The one is that we have a duty to Cuba, and Cuba's Governor, to which we cannot be blind, and which weighs with us in the decision to which we have come.

"You must regard that your expedition was fitted out at His Excellency's cost, and our own, and that of almost every Cuban cavalier of estate, and that that of Narváez was financed in the same way.

"You had a large stake also. We know that. And, as Commander, you stood to gain most largely in percentage thereto.

"Well, the treasure you had gained was to be some compensation for these claims, and we observed that you apportioned it in a liberal way.

"But that treasure is lost. Suppose that you remain here, and are confirmed as Governor by our King. You may gain honour and wealth, as you think, though it may look to most to be a poor hope as you are placed now. But will there be return of treasure to those of Cuba whose jeopard made possible what has been done? It is our view that we should return home at once, and that His Excellency should be informed of all that has chanced, and refit the ships if he be of that mind, appointing what captain he will, though we (and many others) would urge your claims."

"Is it the loss of the treasure which would have repaid Velásquez and others of Cuba which has caused you to change?"

"We do not say we have changed," Bermúdez was quick to reply. "That is a change of which we must make account, even though there be none in ourselves. And it touches that which, as Cuba's treasurer, is my especial concern."

"So it does. If I give you my bond that such claims shall be straightly met, before my own be discharged, will it turn the scale?"

"I do not say it would do that, for it is no more than another weight in one which tips to the beam, but it would be useful to have. It might make His Excellency your friend for a future day. But there is the second matter which we have not mentioned before. You say we are safe here, with our Tlascalan allies. So it would be pleasure to think. But there is talk that there are many who look on us with friendless eyes, as having brought a great loss to the land; of some thousands slain, by which there is mourning in many homes; and it is said that they are words that Xicotencatl is glad to hear."

"You mean the younger?"

"Yes. We mean he who opposed, and, it is said, might have destroyed you before. Have you thought that he may be waiting his time?"

"I have thought many things. Have you thought that his father is very friendly to us, and his daughter is Alvarado's wife?"

"He would not be the first," Duero said, "to think that his father's wit to be less than his. And, if I have the tale right, it was not by his will that Louise was wed."

So the argument went on till the hour was late, for none was willing either to quarrel or to give way; but, in the end, Cortéz, having given the promised bond, wrung from them a reluctant pledge that they would not be in haste to lead others toward the coast, which was of doubtful worth, for they both wished to be gone, thinking that the hazard was now too high; and it is by such pledges that friendship cools.

Yet they would have been loth to go without the support of Cortéz, and the best of the cavaliers. They felt that he constrained them to their probable deaths, beyond what wisdom or equity would allow.

They left him less concerned as to what they would be likely to do, than at the doubt that they had raised concerning how far Tlascalan friendship would endure the strain of profitless days. He had had reports already of individual rudeness to those who may themselves have given cause for offence, and he had issued orders to warn and restrain his men.

He knew that the feeding of so many while he had lain ill must have been a burden on the city, for which payment had not been made—and the means of payment were becoming difficult to contrive. There might be discontent about that.

But he was most concerned at the suggestion that the younger Xicotencatl might be ill-disposed, which, from past experiences, it was easy to think.

He asked Marina about that, and found that, if it were so, it was outside her knowledge; but he recalled how closely she had been waiting upon himself, and felt that there was the less assurance in that. He was more contented by the opinion she gave that, while the four rulers of the city were friendly, even the younger Xicotencatl could do little harm.

But next morning it appeared that the question of Tlascalan friendship was to be resolved in a quick way, for an Aztec deputation appeared, consisting of six nobles, bearing a letter of friendship from Cuitlahua, with a present of salt and other commodities difficult to get by ordinary commercial channels. He offered peaceful alliance, such as there had never been since the Aztecs came from the Northern lands. There was only one condition—that there should be unity in exterminating the white strangers, or driving them back to the ocean from which they came.

The deputation was received by the four elders in public. Their proposals received polite attention. They were told that they would be considered, and a reply given the next day. They retired; and the Council went into private session to debate what the reply should be.

It was the etiquette of the debate that the younger members should speak first, and Xicotencatl, ignoring his father's feebly restraining hand, leapt eagerly to his feet.

"This is surely not a matter," he said, "on which there can be debate, except as to the measure by which we should proceed to rid ourselves of these foreign foes, who have brought disaster to every land to which they have come, whether in friendly or hostile guise.

"Are we not offered the peace which we have been unable to win in generations of bitter war? Are not the Aztecs nearer of blood than these strangers who have the skins of monkeys rather than men? Are they not of our customs and of our faith? Do not these white men dishonour the gods even of those who are in friendly alliance with them? Have we not made an unnatural bond in the hope that it would enable us to put an end to the Aztec war? Has it done that? Or has it led to five thousand casualties to our best troops, with the war no nearer its end than before?

"Now we are offered all we had hoped to gain, with little cost to ourselves, or perhaps none—"

He would not have ceased, had he not been interrupted by the general applause of the younger members of the Council, and, it was seen that his father had risen at his side, and had constrained him to resume his seat.

"You have heard many questions asked, which I will answer in fewer words. The sight of the old may wane, but it is still the sight that can see far. Were the Aztecs ever our friends? Are they friends now, or are they moved by a great fear? Were the fear gone, would they still be friends? I should say not. And you may prove that by a bitter road, when it will be too late to repent."

He sat down, being one who would rarely speak more than a few words, but men had learnt that they were such as should be heeded with care; and, as he did so, Maxixcatzin rose, being next in seniority to himself, though of a more vigorous frame. He had been a firm friend of Cortéz from the day when they had first come to accord, and he now made it clear that he was not one whom adversity would defect.

He said: "You have heard the voice of one who made war at an earlier day against strangers who came in peace, who were foes of our foes, and who sought no more than to pass through our land in a friendly way. He pressed that war beyond our direction or our desire. It is of those who died therein of whom he should think, for their deaths were no gain to us. He asked many questions, to which I will add one, and you will find that to answer this is to answer all. Against whom did we fight at Otumba a month ago, having on that field little more than two thousand men, and by whom was it held and won?"

"It was won," the younger Xicotencatl answered in heat, "not by ourselves, as you well know, but by these strangers who mock our gods, and bring ruin upon our land."

There was the silence of consternation throughout the chamber as this was said, for the etiquette of the Council was that its younger members might speak at first, if they would, but it was with the Elders that decision lay, and it was the part of others to be silent when their judgements had been pronounced. But Maxixcatzin did not appear to observe this, and made a reasoned reply.

"If they are so powerful as you imply, we should be the more foolish to quarrel with them, to content those who have ever been foes to us.

"If you believe in your own faith, does it not teach that such strangers will come, and will prevail in a godlike way? And if that be false, it must follow that we have a religion on which we cannot rely, and that which they urge upon us may be the one which we should prefer.

"And when you assess their power you must remember that their nation is not here. There must be many—there may be a great host—whom their King could send, now that they have discovered our land, armed with weapons of steel, and the lightnings we cannot face."

His opponent answered, still with the patriotic passion that put convention aside: "So there may be; and it may be the end of our civilisation and of our race. But shall we therefore submit to that which is still unproved? Shall we defeat ourselves, striking less than we might, and not in the first hour? Had you heeded me, we should have given no aid to these foreign men, who have no love for us, or our ways; and they would have died alike on Aztec altars and on those of our own land. Had we—"

But the tide of his passion was not destined to rise to its final height, for the wrath of the older man had now mounted to an equal degree, and custom was on his side. He rose before the astonished Council, and laid an old but still vigorous hand on the shoulder of the indignant soldier, pushing one who, even in that emotional extremity, had too much respect to resist, toward the entrance of the room.

"Have you," he asked sternly, "forgotten the respect which our laws require, as well as the honour which keeps friendship through days of storm? Have you no thought that other methods of meeting these strangers, even though all that you fear were true, may be better than those of weapons of war?"

As he spoke, he thrust his unresisting opponent out of the Council Room, and, in the atmosphere that the incident had produced, there was unanimous agreement among those who remained that the Aztec proposals should be refused.

But the opportunity to do this in a formal way did not occur, for, by whatever channel, sufficient information of the result of the meeting reached the envoys to cause them to decide that they could not be gone too soon, and they fled during the night.

CHAPTER EIGHTY: PRELUDE TO POWER

"The low tide has turned," Cortéz said, as he reflected on the flight of the Aztec envoys, and all it must have meant to him had they been received in a different way. "But there must be swift action to reap our gain, or it will not last."

Marina knew little of tides, and this somewhat involved metaphor may not have been clear to her. She replied cheerfully: "Louise says that you will have nothing to fear while the elders are on your side."

This was important in its implication that, however strongly he might feel, Louise's father would not assert his authority with the army against that of the Council; but it did not alter the fact that he represented a hostile group of uncertain strength, who might become stronger if the Spaniards should remain idly quartered upon the city.

Cortéz turned his mind to the fate of the twelve Spaniards who had been massacred in one party when the news of his flight from México had spread through a relieved and astonished land.

This had been the action of a small aggressive tribe, the Tepeacans, who were nearly of Aztec blood, and had given allegiance to them. They had been accustomed to make war on the Tlascalans as often as they could rely upon active Aztec support, but fear of the Spaniards had caused them, after the Tlascalan alliance, to make submission to Cortéz. Then, believing that Aztec supremacy would survive, they had returned to their old allegiance, and proved their sincerity in that merciless slaughter of captured foes.

That was when they heard of the Night of Sorrow, and before the Aztec defeat on Otumba's plain. Now Cortéz sent a deputation to them, offering forgiveness if they would again submit to the authority of Castile. It was a magnanimous offer—if he were in a position to chastise them, which they did not believe.

There is no doubt that it was sincerely meant to this extent that, had they accepted the opportunity of submission, he would have kept faith with them. But he did not expect, and may not have wished, them to do so, while its rejection would justify retribution if they should afterwards be subdued.

What he got was a contemptuous message that the pots in which the twelve had stewed were now ready for further meat, and it would save trouble if more Spaniards would come to them.

Having anticipated such a reply, Cortéz was ready for instant action. Ignoring what he knew the feelings of the younger Xicotencatl to be, he had invited his co-operation, which could scarcely have been refused, for the Tepeacans were his country's continual foes. Together they marched out, at a speed which they hoped might surprise their foes. But they were met by those who were as vigorous and alert as themselves.

They had scarcely entered the Tepeacan country before they were encountered on well-chosen ground. Tall maize obstructed the little band of cavaliers on whom Cortéz mainly relied: their enemies hid in it, and struck upward at the horses above their heads. The battle ended in repulse rather than defeat, and must be fought over again two days later, but this time much nearer to Tepeaca, and with more decisive result. The city surrendered, with a province which had a population of not less than a hundred thousand. It was the conditional submission of a conquered foe, and was received with the clemency which was natural to Cortéz, and may have been politic also to show. But neither in policy nor in justice could the massacre of Spanish soldiers be regarded lightly. No one was executed, but all who were connected with the event were branded with a hot iron in a way that they could not remove, and were sold as slaves, the proceeds of a successful action being the foundation of a new fund, from which the royal fifth was reserved, and the balance divided between Spaniards and Tlascalans, with recognition of the old claims which Bermúdez had urged.

It was a success which, while not great in itself, was a warning that the Spaniards did not regard themselves as a disheartened or beaten force, and that none could harm one of their race, however isolated he might be, without fear of vengeance in later days.

To Cuitlahua also it was a warning he did not fail to observe. He was busy during these days in repairing the ruins of México, fortifying its frontiers, raising larger armies, and drawing scattered forces together. He was retarded in some directions by the insubordination of conquered provinces who were still unsure whether they had more to hope from Spanish than to fear from Aztec power. He cajoled, he threatened, he bribed. On both sides there were preparations for a struggle which neither felt strong enough to commence at once.

Cortéz did not return to Tlascala. He sent for the remainder of his forces, with the women, and what baggage they had, to join him at Tepeaca, where he established himself with more independence than he could feel while relying upon the hospitality of his Tlascalan allies.

Conscious of the necessity of keeping his little army actively and successfully occupied he looked next to the southwest, where a city stood which had no love for the Aztecs, but was occupied by them, having a large garrison, and a position of natural strength.

It had mountains behind it, and deep, steep-sided rivers, which descended from them protecting it on each side from its flanking hills. It could be approached only by the valley at the head of which it lay, and was defended on this front by a high wall of solid stone which stretched from river to river.

The Aztec armies had stormed it some years before, and its inhabitants had lost hope of any freedom in future days until they heard the strange tale of the White Man who had the thunders in his control. Now that he was established in Tepeaca, which was little more than thirty miles away, they sent a secret mission to him, promising that there should be insurrection within the city, if he should assault it without. Cortéz thought: "If the Aztecs could storm that wall, it should not be beyond the capture of Spanish swords."

But he was reluctant to go himself, remembering what had happened in México while he was away, and seeing that he must leave

Alvarado in charge, or offend him by a different choice. He saw also that it would be a delicate matter to make choice between him and Sandoval, as leader of such an expedition, and his thoughts turned to an alternative by which neither could feel aggrieved.

Christóval de Olid, the Captain of the Guard, held an office which could be said to be higher or lower than that of the other cavaliers on whom Cortéz most largely relied. He was of noble family. His duties did not call for inspiration, but were always efficiently performed. He was one who could control men, which he did by a harder discipline than Cortéz might have employed. He was a good chessplayer, and a student of war.

He was not one of whom Cortéz had found it possible to make a friend. When they diced, as he and his captains would often do, should they be weary of chess in the quiet hours, he was known to play an unsmiling game, and, if he lost, it might be in a surly way. But, more often, he won; and his mood might appear little better for that.

Cortéz often won. Men said he had devils' luck. But, lose or gain, it would all be done in a smiling way, and his other captains would be more or less of a like mood. But Christóval de Olid had been cast from a different mould.

So that choice was made, and the bow-legged cavalier rode away on his first separate command, with no other horsemen (for what use would they be to storm a wall which was said to be more than twenty feet high?), but having two hundred Spanish footmen (including most of those who had been of Narváez's party—for was it not best to give occupation to them?) and six hundred Tlascalans who had learned to cooperate with Spanish tactics.

Such an expedition could not set out in a secret way, nor could it move at the pace of the runners by whom news was spread throughout the Mexican land. But its destination was not disclosed, and when it marched out, it was not on the direct road for its destination, but at an angle between that and the Cholula road, that town lying upon its right. This would make slower approach and increase surprise.

So it did, or at least surprise, which had consequences which it would have been hard to foretell.

Cortéz saw them go, and in the next hour had news of another kind which it was no pleasure to hear.

When Narváez's fleet had anchored, and his army had gone ashore, a sick negro had been landed among them, to whom no one gave much regard. Was it likely they should? But in the next week he had died of the smallpox.

Even for that, the excitement would not be much. Men did die of smallpox in the Europe of that day, and the habit had been taken into the New World. But, for the most part, they lived. Many had it who did not die. Very many had become immune. It was a tolerable curse.

But to the Mexicans it was a new contact for which their bodies had no technique of resistance. It spread like a forest fire.

Those who fled before it were often too late to save themselves, but equipped to plant it in a fresh place.

Now it had come to Tlascala, where there was panic and many deaths. Maxixcatzin had contracted it. He had sent a letter (which Marina must read), saying that he wished to embrace the Christian Faith before he died, as he expected to do. Father Olmedo hurried to Tlascala. He could give the advice of experience in resisting the epidemic; but his first concern was for the eternal welfare of those who were near to die.

Cortéz gave orders by which traffic with Tlascala was reduced and controlled. He could do no more. He waited news of Olid, for it was vital that he should not be repulsed. After deduction of those who had gone with him, the remaining Spaniards were few. Cortéz must rely once more on prestige rather than present strength in the city which had been faithless before.

Then he had a report which he found hard to believe. Olid had turned aside to Cholula, where he had no business to be. On the next day, the mystery was resolved. Olid brought prisoners to him, with a queer tale, having taken them with no battle at all.

The secret of his destination had been most carefully kept. He himself had not been told what it would be until the morning on which he had marched. Only Marina, on whom Cortéz must ever depend, both for her own knowledge, and that which she could obtain from others, had been in his confidence until then.

But the movements of the Spaniards were incessantly observed, and to many who were conscious of hostile acts or intentions during those days when it had been reported that they were destroyed, it was a matter of watchful fear.

This being so, Olid's oblique march, which appeared to aim at no probable destination, had occasioned a widespread doubt, in which Cholula had shared.

Obviously, if it were a mission of vengeance on which he came, it was better to be one of the avengers than one who suffered his wrath. Almost from the first hour, he was embarrassed by those who came, with native arms in their hands, offering to give him support.

On the second day, when the route which he had been ordered to take brought him nearest to Cholula, he was met by a regiment of over a thousand men from that city, who had been sent, they said, by its rulers to join his ranks.

At this, suspicion rose. He had already accepted recruits to a total exceeding his Tlascalan contingent.

He remembered Cholula's previous treachery. He concluded that they were there to fall upon him when he should be engaged with a frontal foe.

Had his suspicion been correct, it could have been said that he acted in a bold and successful way. He marched on Cholula, arrested its principal citizens, accused them of this meditated treachery, rejected their astonished protests, and brought them back to Tepeaca, for Cortéz to pronounce judgement upon their guilt.

But Cortéz must observe that he made accusation of which their was no proof. He interviewed indignant caciques who protested that they had done nothing disloyal to him from the moment when he had reformed the government of their city, and placed them in authority. He now knew enough of their language to understand much that was said, but must still rely upon Marina for his own side of the conversation, and for elucidation of much that would otherwise have been less than clear. Even more, he relied upon her opinions as to the sincerity of those he examined, who were, more or less, of her own race, her own land, and her own habits of thought.

In this case, she was not long in doubt. She said with conviction that they were innocent men. She had a private conversation with the cacique whose child she had aided, and whose wife had become her friend, and was then more entirely sure of that which she had not doubted before.

Cortéz observed that Olid's accusation, in one detail, had a defect of logic. The Cholulans had not known the object of the expedition, and could not therefore have concerted plans with those against whom it was directed. Had they thought themselves to be its object, it was not clear that they would have gained advantage by that which they were alleged to have done. Their levies might have been better used in another way, at a later hour.

In the end, he released the captives, with apologies for what had been done, and gifts which would have been more liberal in more affluent days.

It left Olid sullenly wroth, declining to submit that he had been wrong. Cortéz learnt again that officers who do well under control may be unfit for separate command. Now he was unwilling to send Olid again, or to disgrace him further by replacing him with one of those whom he should have chosen at first. He discussed the difficulty with Ávila, and received advice confirming his own inclination. At what ever risk, he must now go himself, taking such force as would ensure that he should not fail.

"You say that I should leave our women, our sick, and what treasure we still have, with no protection at all?"

"I say that their protection will lie in the fact that you are not forty miles away; and I say that you, and therefore themselves, are safer if you do not divide your strength. Let me stay with them, and I shall show that I do not urge a course by which the hazard will not be mine."

Cortéz felt that he had had sound advice from one who was ever of good counsel, and quiet courage, though he might lack the adventurous sanguine spirit of Ordaz, Sandoval's gift of leadership, or Alvarado's stature and strength.

He told Marina what he had resolved, and found her to be of the same mind. "They will be more greatly impressed," she said, "by your confidence in leaving us thus, than if you should provide a guard of a hundred men; and those extra men, who would be insufficient to guard us here, might be vital to you."

"You say 'us'. I did not mean that you should remain."

"Yet I think I should. And there are others who will be well enough for any need you are likely to have. Juan can speak much of their tongues now, and you do not use him at all."

"So it may be. Yet I still do not see why you should remain here."

"Am I useful in war? Isabella would be more potent than I! But when you leave me, they will see that you are very sure of how strongly you stand. And it will give a like confidence to those of our own part, which they must be equal to show."

He saw again that he was having good counsel, though it was less to his liking than that he had had from Ávila; and it was ever his way, if he took a risk, to prefer the course by which the stake is highest, but the hazard of failure least. He said: "So it shall be," and in the next minute was issuing orders for those who must be quickly arrayed.

He marched with all his strength at the next morn, but before that he had evil news. Smallpox raged in Tlascala now; and Maxixcatzin was dead.

CHAPTER EIGHTY-ONE: RENEWAL OF STRENGTH

The Mexican garrison did not entangle itself in the town. It had a camp far above it, to the rear, where the mountains rose. It had a smaller, but sufficient force in the town, the headquarters of which were in the city temple, which was of the customary construction; and its mission was to guard the great wall, which was the only side on which there could be hostile assault.

So it might have done, had there not been insurrection within the town, and an armed rabble upon its rear. Threatened thus, it abandoned the wall, and took refuge in the temple, with the Spaniards storming upon the gates.

Before the main body of the garrison could arrive, the temple was stormed, and its defenders scattered or slain.

The Aztec garrison, said by some to number thirty thousand men, were by this time in the upper suburbs of the town, in which fierce fighting developed. They were met by the Tlascalans and other allies—including the thousand Cholulans whose first appearance had been so dubiously received—and Cortéz had cause for satisfaction in the large number of these levies whom he had allowed to accompany him.

Reinforced by the Spaniards, after the capture of the temple, they slowly drove back the Aztecs, who now fought amid blazing streets, for one side or other—it was never clear which—had set fire to the town.

Forced backward from these blazing suburbs, they were charged by the Spanish cavaliers when on clearer ground, and, few as these horsemen had now become, they were still able to turn the tide of battle against Aztecs who had heard talk of their invincible strength, but had not seen them before.

The refluent strife moved up the narrowing distance between precipitous mountain heights, its pace only controlled by the steepness of the ascent. The Aztecs fled to their camp, which was on a wide plateau above the gorge, still closely pursued by their eager, vindictive foes. Killing Aztecs was a pleasure which neither the townspeople nor the Cholulans had had till now. Even the heat, which became oppressive as the sun mounted to noon, could not abate the ardour of those who slew.

There was rich spoil in the camp, including many slaves of the army lords, but Cortéz, impatient even to make division of this, resolved on an instant march to another Aztec stronghold—an irrigated valley among the mountains, where they had a garrison in control of a prosperous town in the midst of a fertile land. Here again a sharp short fight was followed by absolute victory. The fleeing Aztecs tried vainly to secure safety by flight over river bridges which they demolished when they were crossed. Their pursuers waded or swam through the shallow flood, and pursuit and slaughter were not relaxed.

Cortéz returned to Tepeaca with his reputation restored, and loaded with spoils. Hearing that the energetic generalship of Cuitlahua had interposed a levy of growing strength between him and his base at Vera Cruz, he promptly despatched Sandoval, with a strong mixed force, to destroy it, which he was equal to do.

Within a fortnight Cortéz had gained the willing or unwilling loyalty of all the various tribes and cities between Tepeaca and the Atlantic coast; and for the most part it had become loyalty of a willing kind, for what could they want better than a leader who could relieve them of the hated Aztec yoke, and who was just in his dealings, and liberal in sharing the spoils that his conquests brought?

He had acted with the energy which he had rightly thought that the occasion required. He did not suppose that Cuitlahua was either unaware of what he was doing, or slack in his own preparations for further war. But in this he had a respite on which he could not have relied. The scourge which was decimating his Tlascalan friends had passed on to México, and Cuitlahua was dead.

And meanwhile he had augmented his own strength in a way on which he also would not have relied, though it was also the result of the operation of very natural laws.

The way to the Gulf of México during the past year had been like a one-way street. Apart from the vessel which Cortéz had sent to Spain several months before, none had sailed eastward, and, apart from the deserter from that ship, no one had taken any news to Cuba of the course of Mexican events, either good or bad.

Velásquez, having sent Narváez to displace Cortéz, and not doubting that he would have done it successfully, sent him a further vessel with a cargo of supplementary stores. Its commander was allowed to land before being acquainted with the true state of affairs, and was then persuaded without difficulty that it had become his duty, as it was his inclination, to support the ascendant power.

A second vessel from the same source, and loaded in a like way, had the same experience, with the same result.

And meanwhile Cortéz had made his plans for retrieving his position in the Mexican capital, with his usual audacity of conception, and detailed care.

One thing was sure. He had had enough of causeways. He would assault México by obtaining control of the lake, and that would require larger vessels than the canoes which abounded upon its waters.

He took counsel with Martín López, and it was decided to build thirteen brigantines, such as had been constructed before, but this time they were to be made in sections in Tlascala, from materials brought from the fleet at Vera Cruz, and transported overland to México, where they would be put together at the lake-side. They would not be large vessels, and must be of shallow draught, for many parts of the lake were not deep. But it was a bold conception, which, when he put it to Duero and Bermúdez, had a mad sound.

So he may have meant it to have, for he had concluded that those who would prefer to go home had become few, and he would be more than willing to see them go. So he offered this again, and in so cordial a manner that they saw the way of return to be open to them without penalty or deprivation.

Those who now elected to return rather than attempt the capture of the city from which they had made disastrous retreat were not more than would be sufficient to form the meagre crew of a small ship, and one of those that the Cuban Governor had sent (its own crew being of more adventurous mind) could be used in this way.

The fainthearted few were sent back with their share of the spoil, and that due to the Cuban Governor and Spanish Crown. They had some gifts of goodwill, beyond that. Alvarado escorted them down to the coast, giving them his jesting contempt, which they did not like.

They could not say that Cortéz had not treated them well, but it may be according to the nature of men that, from that moment, they ceased to be friendly to him.

Now he did not content himself with the limited Tlascalan aid. He knew how great the struggle must be. He sought to raise an army of every man in the wide land who hated the Aztec name—and they were not few.

And at this time he gained some further Spanish recruits, whom he had no cause to expect.

The tale of a land of jewels and gold which could be invaded with ease had spread from the mouth of that one deserter through the West Indian settlement, and the Governor of Jamaica had been another to send ships down the one-way street. He sent three, with orders to avoid Cortéz, proceeding northward along the coast, and landing where they could operate in a free void.

So they did, and the result became known when two of them cast anchor at Vera Cruz, and appealed for aid.

They had landed where they were told, been heavily attacked, and defeated with serious losses. Retreating from a coast that they could not hold, they had been caught in a storm, and one vessel had sunk. Many who survived were wounded, and more were sick, and food had become scarce.

Cortéz ordered that they should be hospitably received. Their sick and wounded were nursed ashore. It was a natural sequel that they should enlist with him. What else could they have done?

And after that, a Spanish vessel sailed into Vera Cruz, with a merchant captain who had a cargo of munitions which he had taken to Cuba, where he had supposed that his market would be. But when he had entered St. Jago bay, he had heard the tale of the New World, and concluded that Narváez or Cortéz—it mattered nothing to him which it might be—would give him a better price. He was right about that. He found more market than he had expected to have, for Cortéz bought the ship also, and, as the price was good (and his crew, in any event, would have deserted him for the new service which offered), he was well content.

But while preparations went on, with an aspect of bustle and growing strength, Cortéz had an anxiety the cause of which he mentioned to none, for it would have been foolish to make it public among his own men, and it came from the side of his life which Marina could never know.

The captain of the first store ship that Velásquez had sent had been the bearer of a letter addressed to Narváez, which Cortéz had read and put away in a secret place.

It was signed by Fouseca the Bishop of Burgos, who was President of the Royal Council of the Indies, the supreme Spanish authority on all Colonial affairs, and who, during many past years, had been, not merely President, but the active authority in its control.

He was a man of industry, and had shown great ability in controlling these conquests, so rich and so remote, and the turbulent adventurers by whom they must be first obtained, and who (he considered, with some reason upon his side) must afterwards be replaced by more pacific and amenable men. He was also, by the malice of circumstance, a personal friend of the Cuban Governor.

The letter was simply an instruction to Narváez to arrest Cortéz, if he had not already done so, and send him for trial to Spain.

This letter left much to the imagination, but its implications were clear. Velásquez must have protested to Spain that Cortéz had acted in defiance of his authority, and had obtained a hearing for this complaint.

Of the mission which Cortéz himself had sent to the Spanish Court, he was still without any information. They might have perished at sea. They had certainly not brought matters to an issue favourable to himself.

He considered that, now that he had allowed Duero and his companions to return to Cuba, they would make report of all that had happened in México in their own way, and he would prefer it to be in his. He would also prefer that his version of events should go direct to the Spanish King.

He sent four of his largest ships to St. Domingo, with empty holds, and enough gold to purchase cargoes of the munitions of which he was most in need. With them he sent a long letter to the Royal Audience there, narrating the great things he had done for Spain, and those which he intended to do. That was the supreme authority in the Indies, and had the final word until instructions should come from Spain.

He sent also a much longer letter to be forwarded to Charles V, in which he narrated in detail all that he had done, and petitioned for the Royal support against the obstruction he had sustained.

It was destined to be printed in Seville during the coming year, and to amaze Europe with its contents.

He made his intention of sending this letter known, though not its immediate cause, and when it went it was accompanied by a petition which was signed by all the officers and men who were available at the time. Its theme was their confidence in himself, and a valid argument that the oppositions of Velásquez and Narváez had been detrimental to the success of the enterprise, and therefore to the interests of the Spanish Crown.

CHAPTER EIGHTY-TWO: AGAIN TO MÉXICO

It was the middle of December 1520, nearly six months after that disastrous midsummer night when the long causeway of Tezcuco Lake had been scattered with Spanish dead, and now Tlascala was loud with music, and gay with flowers. It made festival for the coming of Cortéz, who had left Tepeaca to make Tlascala his base for the campaign which he was about to wage against the centre of Aztec power.

He had left about three score Spaniards at Tepeaca—men who through sickness or wounds might prove unequal to the hardship of war—and had formed them into a civic group of permanent residents. They were to found a Spanish colony, to be called Segula, for he no longer disguised or doubted that he would make the Spaniard supreme and permanent in the land. But those who had been friendly to him had not found him to be unjust in his dealings or oppressive in his demands. The orator who met him now, with words of praise in the city's name, called him the Deliverer of the Land.

It was the easier to forget the Night of Sorrow because he had come back to a strength which was little less than had been his when he had marched through México's silent streets to the causeway where most would die.

Now he rode at the head of two score cavaliers, with Marina, still on her great bay stallion, upon his right.

After them came four score arquebusiers, a group of crossbowmen, and nine pieces of artillery, taken from the incoming ships. (He was short of powder, but there might be a way by which that could be overcome.)

After them came the women, who had become a numerous following, with a few children already among them. Some were in litters, as a mark of respect to high rank, of which Louise was one; but most came on foot, which, by Mexican or Tlascalan standards, was no insult to them. They stepped as lightly as they wore their garlands of tropic flowers.

Behind them came the Spanish infantry, twenty-three score in all, advancing in ranks of five and files of four. Most of them were now armed with the long two-bladed spear—the one native weapon which Cortéz had thought worthy of adoption; and that being one which was only favoured in one remote province, by those who were México's foes. But it was as swordsmen that they were dreaded most, and that weapon was borne by all.

Last came the burdened porters, their numbers showing that the Spaniards had again become prosperous men, and their position in an unguarded rear, that they were among friends whom they did not doubt.

Indeed, there could be no cause. Xicotencatl had adopted the Christian Faith. His son showed no discontent, commanding that part of the Tlascalan army which was under his control in conformity with the Spanish plans. He had even become docile to learn and practice their science of war, and use the training and tactics he had learnt from them. If he still held to the old faith, and would have been glad to redden his sandals in Spanish blood, he concealed his thoughts.

Maxixcatzin had also become a Christian before he died, and his heir, a boy of twelve, proved to be willing to be baptized, as a condition of being confirmed by Cortéz in the inheritance which was his, and knighted by him (despite his youth) in evidence of his allegiance to Spain.

It was the old religion now which must be practised by sufferance, and a diminished ritual, the wisdom of Father Olmedo restraining any more active effort to stamp it out. Shorn of its horror of human sacrifices, and without the support which repressive measures would surely have roused, it was left to the gradual decay that contempt will bring. A disparaged wargod cannot expect that many will continue to serve his shrine.

Meditating on the advance which had been made by the Christian Faith, and the many who had already been saved thereby from eternal woe, Cortéz resolved to set clearly before his soldiers the high purpose for which they fought, and what the conduct of such crusaders should be.

Protesting first that his own purpose was, before all, to uproot the idols that fouled the land, and bring heathen men to saving faith in the True God, he required that all should keep this ever before their minds, apart from which their presence there was without moral support, and their acquisitions were thievish gains.

They must remember next that the Mexican Emperor had admitted the overlordship of Spain, and it was their mission now to subdue, in their monarch's name, those who had become rebels against his right.

Engaged in these causes they must:

(1) *Avoid oaths, which dishonour God.*

(2) *Avoid gaming, except in forms and to degrees which he would prescribe, lest a pastime became a vice.*

(3) *Avoid quarrelling and brawling among themselves; and, in particular, the practice of duelling, which might be permissible under different conditions, but now wasted strength which should be expended on heathen men.*

(4) *Avoid indiscipline on the field of battle, and in particular the fault of charging without orders, from which confusion might arise, and defeat follow. Consequences of such conduct might be so serious that this must be regarded as a grave, and, on the part of a captain, a capital crime.*

(5) *Avoid private booty. Anything taken on the field, or in more private ways, must have the approval of the appropriate officer, and if licensed, must be surrendered to the common stock. The penalty of*

infringement of this edict would be death, and no mercy would be allowed.

Experience was to show that these edicts would be strictly enforced. The last, in particular, was essential if they were not to become a looting terror to the people among whom they moved, until general detestation would bring them to the ruin which they would deserve.

It was not long before two porters were caught plundering an Aztec home, and were hanged for the offence. A Spanish soldier, convicted of similar misconduct, was also hanged, though he was cut down while some life remained.

It was an evidence both of the good discipline that prevailed in the Spanish ranks, and of the difference between European and Mexican standards of conduct, that Cortéz did not consider it necessary to deal with the relations of his troops with the women of foes or friends.

These ordinances were publicly proclaimed on the 26th of December, when men rested at ease, and in a mood of goodwill, after the celebrations of the previous day.

On the 27th Cortéz reviewed the ranks of the allies, which had now risen to the huge total of 110,000, or, if we include 40,000 porters (necessary in a land where beasts of burden were unknown) to 150,000 men.

Next day, he marched out, taking the whole of his Spanish troops, 5,000 Tlascalans, and 5,000 selected from the levies of the provinces. He judged that it would be difficult, if not impossible, to provision a larger force, as they penetrated the high passes that gave entrance to the Mexican plain. The main army was to wait instructions. The brigantines, which made good progress, but were not yet complete, were to follow as soon as they were ready.

He took the hard road he already knew, with a different reason from that which had led him to choose it on the first occasion. He remembered that Ordaz had proved that the active volcano that overlooked it could be scaled, even to the edge of its crater of fire. He needed sulphur for the manufacture of powder, and meant to obtain it there.

So he did; but when he weighed the result against the toil and danger it had required, he decided that it would be better to import his powder at future times.

Chapter Eighty-Three: The Stage Is Set

After the death of Montezuma, Cuitlahua reigned for four months before he died from the foul disease that the Eastern barbarians brought to a healthier land.

During that time he had expelled the Spaniards from México, and after finding it impossible to complete their destruction at Otumba, he had commenced, with great vigour, to rebuild the ruins of the damaged city, to repair its broken bridges, and to organise the defence of the land. He strengthened alliances, he gave privileges to discontented provinces, he threatened, persuaded, cajoled in a score of ways. He used the arguments of race and religion. He did much which was not easy to do; for the wealth which Montezuma had distributed with generosity had been accumulated in harsher ways.

When he died, the choice of his successor was debated under the shadow of fear. But there was little doubt of what the choice would be.

Montezuma had a nephew, Guatemozín, who had married his eldest daughter, and was now twenty-five. He had a hatred of the Spaniards founded on religious and racial passions, surpassing even that of his predecessor. He was a soldier by profession, and had a reputation of boldness and of success. It was he who had organised and led the canoe-attacks upon the causeway on the Nigh of Sorrow, which had been so deadly in their results.

He was elected unanimously, and issuing energetic orders within an hour.

The long pause which followed had enabled Cortéz to consolidate and increase his strength, but he had not misled himself into supposing it to be a sign of weakness or procrastination. He recognised and respected a strategy which he could not prevent.

Guatemozín had said: "It has never been easy to attack the Tlascalans within the circuit of their own hills. Why should we go to them? Let them come to us. It is what they must do in the end, if we lie still. Let them have the long march, the climb into the clouds. Let them fight far from their own base, where food will be hard to obtain for a sieging host. México shall be the bait for a trap which they will enter to die."

So he and Cortéz prepared for the same end, and he showed a thoroughness which Cortéz could not have excelled.

Before Cortéz marched out of Tlascala, the civil population of México had been entirely evacuated. The whole country was under arms. Through the width of the land there was no one who did not know that a captured Spaniard would fetch a fantastic price. A fat Tlascalan would not be despised by the Aztec god; but those who could trap a Spaniard would become honoured and wealthy men.

The route which Cortéz, lured by his need for sulphur, had chosen, had been hard before, but it was harder and colder now.

Harder, because not the approach alone, but the whole length of the rough precipitous way had been hollowed or piled, blocked with boulders, and obstructed with fallen trees. So the other ways would have been found to be. Guatemozín was thorough in all he did.

Colder, because it was January now, and the snow-line was far lower than when they had climbed that mountain barrier before. They were faced with sleet and most bitter winds. To the Tlascalans, few of whom had been in the first invasion, it was a new experience, which they were not clothed and not constituted to meet; and to the Spaniards, not ignorant of cold in their own land, it was a change from the warmth of the lower slopes, too sudden to be lightly sustained.

It was no pleasure to halt, under such conditions, for long hours during which comrades toiled to clear and smooth an ascent which must be made possible for the feet of horses, the dragging of heavy guns, and the weary climbing of burdened men.

Cortéz had cause for content that he had not adventured a larger force on this preliminary penetration of his enemy's territory. He did not doubt that he would be able to repulse attack, for all the best of his strength was here; but it might have been fatal to be cumbered with numbers now.

He was glad when they came to the turning road that he remembered riding when he had not known what it was soon to show. Now he looked down again on the fertility of the Mexican plain, on its forests and shining lakes, its orchards and garden grounds, its cities and fertile fields, its towers and temples that could be seen at that height, and in that clear air, for so many leagues, till the distant mountain barrier closed them in.

There was no visible change, no sign of all the human effort and agony of the intervening days, no sign that disturbance again menaced that peaceful scene—except that, on distant hills, there was a sudden flicker of fire. And then others, further away. Warning beacons of his approach he could not doubt them to be. He had an opponent who did not sleep.

They marched down with freer steps, those who were new to the sight of that great plain, stretched out at a mountain's height, being roused to awe or cupidity, or a little daunted by what they saw.

They marched on till they came to a ravine, and a broken bridge, which they must repair. Some arrows fell among them here, but those who sent them knew the range and accuracy of firearms too well to continue within arrow range. They drew bows, and were slipping away as the arrows fell.

The bridge having been repaired, two parties of cavaliers, under Sandoval and Diego, were sent forward, right and left, to reconnoitre the ground. They came onto small bodies of footmen, who may have been the advance guards of larger forces. They charged these, and, when they refused to stand, pursued them, and rode them down. After that, the advance continued without opposition, the tactics of spreading out the dreaded cavalry being effectual in keeping the bowmen away.

Soon, the opposing forces disappeared entirely, and the march continued without further incident through a fertile country in which the population did not appear.

When night came they had reached Coatepec, in and around which they camped with the precautions necessary to those who enter a hostile land. They had arrived within ten miles of Tezcuco, which Cortéz proposed to make his headquarters while organising his attack upon the capital city, but he had spoken of this purpose to none until he was in the privacy of his own room, when he said abruptly: "If we enter Tezcuco tomorrow, how should you say that Coanaca will behave?"

To understand this question it is necessary to observe the complicated loyalties and disloyalties of the royal house of Tezcuco, both to Aztec and Spaniard, going back to a period before Cortéz came.

At that time Cacama had been established by Montezuma as Tezcuco's prince, and in authority over the lower and more fertile portion of the province which bore its name, but his succession had been disputed by a half-brother, Ixtlilxochitl, whose claim had been compromised by giving him the higher and more distant region. But he had not been contented with this settlement, and had sent a secret mission to Cortéz, soliciting his aid in obtaining what he regarded as his just inheritance, which had had no immediate result.

This prince had been affected from birth by a prophecy that he would join the foes of his country to its destruction, and his father had been urged to kill him at birth, which he had refused to do. As a young boy, he had been of so turbulent a character that some of the ruling nobles, remembering the prophecy, had resolved upon his death. But they were not sufficiently expeditious or secret in this design. It came to the boy's ears, and, in a mood of natural resentment, and with a characteristic reaction, he enlisted the aid of some juvenile colleagues, entered their homes, and put them to the death they had intended for him. He was still watchful for an opportunity to assert his claim.

When Cacama opposed Cortéz, and was imprisoned, Montezuma nominated a younger brother, Cuicuitzea, to take his place, but this young prince, being regarded as a Spanish nominee, was afraid for his life when the Spaniards were expelled from México, and fled to their protection.

In his absence, Cuitlahua had given the throne to a third brother, Coanaca, who professed a bitter enmity to the foreign invaders.

Cacama disappeared on the Night of Sorrow, and was doubtless dead. Cuicuitzea had ventured back secretly to Tezcuco, with Ixtlilxochitl, lord of the further province, watching events with unfriendly acquisitive eyes.

There was no reason to expect a friendly reception from Coanaca now, and Cortéz could not have been surprised by Marina's reply: "How can I tell? He is a prince of whom little was said when I was in the Sacred College, and heard the gossip that came over the lake. No one thought at that time that he would come to a place of power. He cannot be much older than I. But I should say that he will be hostile to you, unless he be subdued by a great fear."

That was the reason for hope. Tezcuco, being built on the lake shore, had not the protection the waters gave. México might feel secure, but Tezcuco could not be defended unless Cortéz were defeated in open, immediate battle, which there was no present sign that the Aztecs would array.

It was possible that Coanaca would endeavour to avoid his dilemma by an insincere profession of amity, but he could have the less hope of this being believed or accepted because he had been directly responsible for the massacre of the forty-five Spaniards who had been approaching México on the day following that on which Cortéz had fled from that city by another route.

They had been overcome to a man, being too confident to maintain a vigilant watch. Some, who had been captured alive, had been sacrificed on the re-erected altar of the Mexican wargod. Now their arms hung as trophies upon the walls of temples throughout the land. This was not a matter which could have been forgotten, or could be lightly condoned.

To Cortéz there could be no alternative now but to go forward with a front of confidence until the event should prove what Coanaca would choose to do.

He breakfasted next morning with his captains, giving them detailed orders of the dispositions which he desired in the event of his entrance to the city being seriously resisted, but while he did so he was interrupted by word that a deputation from Coanaca was at the door, with a yellow flag, the significance of which Marina must explain, when she saw that it was not understood.

The white flag is recognised by the whole world. It has a meaning, simple to understand. But the flag of gold, unrecognised in the Old World, was of equally definite significance in the New. It was a sign of friendship and high regard. It might be rejected, as a flag of truce is equally likely to be, but it gave a similar immunity to those who used it in their approach.

There was a fine point of ethical probity here, which might not arise, but one which, should it do so, Cortéz would be likely to resolve in a generous way. Did it give immunity to those who relied upon its protection against those who did not recognise its convention?

Cortéz said: "Well, we will hear what they have to say. There are three? Show them in here. You need not all go. Space will avail."

The three men came in, and their leader was as voluble to Marina as was natural to the dignified Aztec manner. She said: "They protest that they come as friends. Coanaca desires that you accept the hospitality of Tezcuco, but that you do not enter till tomorrow noon, as they have preparations to make, that they may receive you in the right way."

If this approach was welcome, Cortéz did not allow it to appear in voice or manner, or the substance of his reply: "Tell them that forty-five Spaniards are dead, which is our reason that we are here. Will they make answer to that?"

"They say that all was done by the order of Cuitlahua, who is now dead. It was against Coanaca's wish, but is he equal to oppose that which the Aztec Emperor may require?"

"If he is not prepared for that, how can he hope to be friends with us? The men who died were convoying a great treasure. Have they brought that back in evidence that their protestations have more substance than words?"

"They say that Cuitlahua had it all. Nothing remained."

"Tell them that I accept Coanaca's offer, and if it be made in good faith, they have nothing to fear. But I cannot delay till tomorrow noon. I must move with more haste than that. We are marching now."

The reply was disconcerting to those who heard. They were plainly protesting, and it could be seen that Marina put these protests aside without even troubling Cortéz with their translation. What she said was: "When my lord has resolved, it is foolish to argue more. If you go with speed, your palanquins may arrive somewhat sooner than we, and give Coanaca a warning of our approach."

They went with faces that they sought to make void of expression, but their discontent could not be wholly concealed.

Cortéz asked: "How do you read that? Do they distrust us, or do they plot evil which needs delay?"

"How can I tell?" She answered. "But it must be well that we move at once, it being disconcerting to them."

So they did, marching with all the care that is required in a hostile land, and entering the suburbs before noon, where they were met by those who said they had been instructed to lead to the accommodation which had been provided—the palace of Nezahualpilli, the predecessor of Montezuma, and the greatest Emperor that the land had known.

It was much alike to that other deserted ancestral palace that had been occupied in México, and, though not so large, was more than ample for the accommodation of the little army of Spaniards, with their women and personal servants, horses, artillery, and baggage, which they would have been reluctant to leave outside its protecting walls.

So far so good; but what had been difficult to understand had been the silence and emptiness of the streets through which they had come. Tezcuco was not a city of busy traffic and narrow streets. It was a resort of most wealthy men, a place of gardens and orchards, festooned with flowers. But even in such a setting they had expected signs of the movements of men. It would have been no more than a normal experience had the roadsides been crowded by those who welcomed them, with garlands of flowers for the horses' necks.

Well, timidity might explain that. They had good reason to doubt how Cortéz might feel to them. If they remained quiet in their houses, it might be no more than a sign of a very proper sense of the enormity of what they had done.

But when the central streets were seen to be as empty and bare, wonder increased, and a natural doubt of what it might mean. Immediately that the whole of the Spanish force (the native allies remained outside the city) was settled within the palace, the artillery posted, and the gates secured, Cortéz ordered a strong party to sally out, ascend to the upper platform of the central temple, and report on what they might be able to see.

Sandoval led them, and came back with an explanation both of the solitude which had been observed, and of the request that their entrance should be delayed. The roads from Tezcuco over the hills to the lake shore were gaily coloured by crowds of fugitives showing burdened backs.

The undying fire had still burned on the temple platform (they had quenched it now), and evidences of recent human sacrifice had not been entirely obliterated, though there were signs of the attempt. Some entrails had been overlooked. They had come on a Spanish spear—which would be useless to Aztec eyes.

Cortéz listened to that which he had been expecting to hear, and he was instant to act.

"Christóval," he said, "you will take twenty cavaliers—their horses are harnessed now—and ride at once to the lake shore. The fugitives will not fight, and you will harm none who will be docile to you. You seek Coanaca, and only he. You may be too late, but bring him back if you can. Alvarado, you will tell the Tlascalans they must enter the city, and occupy the houses that have been left. But there must be no violence or spoil. You must be plain on that. We seek friends. There must be barricades in the streets."

Alvarado knew enough Tlascalan now to give such orders as these. He had learnt from Louise.

Cortéz went on: "Marina, I shall need your aid for a proclamation that must be made in the Aztec tongue. Men must know that, if they stay here, their lives will be theirs, and their goods secure."

So they were to find it to be, but not all who fled would see the contents of their homes again. For it proved hard to restrain the Tlascalans from the plunder of empty houses, and some public buildings were looted, and a library burned (which was seen to be a great loss at a later day) before order was fully made.

And then Sandoval came back with no gain. Coanaca had been seen, but he was in a canoe too far off for pursuit.

CHAPTER EIGHTY-FOUR: TEZCUCO

Coanaca having fled. Cortéz sought another occupant for a vacant throne. He found a young man of the royal family, who was an unfortunate choice, except in one respect. He would do what he was told. He was no trouble. He was of no account. In a few months he was dead.

When the Tezcucans heard of the election of this youth by the citizens who had remained in their homes, and accepted Spanish authority, and that lives and property were secure, many of them came back. Some were to be trusted, some not. But it was a great gain that the hostile prince of Tezcuco was in exile, and that the province, without resistance, had, nominally at least, accepted the overlordship of Spain.

No doubt Ixtlilxochitl thought that the vacated throne should have been his. But he showed no sign of resentment at that. There was no doubt in his mind on one point. He was the enemy of Coanaca, and friend of all who were unfriendly to him.

Cortéz met him, heard of the enterprising energy for which he was already renowned, and determined to give him something to do.

There was a small stream that ran through the suburbs of the city, curved round the opposing hill, and entered Tezcuco Lake. Cortéz walked with him to its grassy, tree-shaded bank, Marina between them. He asked: "He has heard of the two ships I built, which the Aztecs burned?"

Marina said: "He both knew and saw. He says they were a marvel to Aztec eyes."

"Tell him I build more. They will be brought here. I will have them safe when they are not active upon the lake. I will deepen this stream till it is equal to take their draught. Will he get me labour for that? Will he take control, so that the canal may be called by his name in the days to be?"

Marina translated this, and the young man's eyes lightened with joy. Cortéz noticed that he expressed no surprise at the audacity of the idea, no doubt of its possibility. He was clearly one who welcomed the call to action, of whatever kind.

Marina said: "If you will let him know the depth and width which you will require, and of the docks which must be built to hold so many vessels at once, he will undertake that you shall have all that you require at an early hour. He says that it will be joy to labour for such as you, and he can see Coanaca pleading for life at your feet at no distant day."

The length of the little stream was less than two miles. Having no machinery, vehicles, or beasts of burden, to undertake great engineering operations by manual labour was natural to the Aztec mind. Within a week eight thousand men were labouring to dig the canal, and to provide docks within the city, for which a portion of the wide loveliness of the exotic pleasure gardens of the old palace was to be destroyed.

This must take time; and the building of the brigantines was not complete. But military operations were not therefore delayed.

The lake of Tezcuco had no outlet. It was a very large expanse of water, shallow and salt. The freshwater lake of Chalco was divided from it by a long strip of land, in some places less than a mile in breadth. Chalco Lake was several feet lower, and there were places were dykes had been built to prevent the flooding of this separating isthmus on which the pleasure city of Iztepalapan stood, at the termination of one of the great causeways which connected México with the shore. It was built partly on solid ground, and partly on piles in the reeded Chalco shallows.

This city was about twenty miles from Tezcuco, taking the road along the lake shore and the isthmus. Cortéz decided to capture it. Though covering a great space, it was of no more than fifty thousand inhabitants. With it in his possession, he would then attack the more distant city of Chalco, on the southern side of that lake.

He undertook the first of these enterprises himself, having kept the secret of his intention privately to his own mind. He marched within an hour of the dawn, at the head of eighteen cavaliers, two hundred Spanish footmen, and over three thousand Tlascalans. He took no artillery, relying upon speed and surprise.

But Guatemozín was an opponent who did not drowse, and the enterprise ended in a way that Cortéz had not foreseen.

Fifteen miles had been covered by now, only one halt having been allowed, and they were at the narrowest part of the isthmus, when they found themselves opposed by an Aztec army with which they were quickly engaged. It fought desperately, but the narrowness of the ground was not to its advantage. Superior numbers could not be brought into action, and, under such condition, Spanish superiority in equipment was sure to prevail.

The Aztecs were driven back, until retreat became rout.

Soon Spaniards and Tlascalans were entering a city from which its inhabitants fled in canoes which darkened the waters of its bordering lakes.

Chaos, spoil, and massacre followed. Many of the inhabitants had been unable to flee, and the Tlascalans broke into their houses, and slew them, young and old, without restraint or exception. Cortéz strove without success to control an event for which he was largely responsible, through interference with customs of warfare which had been repugnant to him.

Six months earlier, the Tlascalans would have collected a sufficient number of prisoners to satisfy the requirements of their altars and appetites, and would have led them away in a civilised manner, to be efficiently slaughtered at later dates.

Now, being forbidden to do that, they took (to them) the natural alternative of the immediate killing of frantic victims, in more savage, uncertain, unseemly ways. The Aztecs were hated enemies. Should they leave boys alive to become men? Or girls to breed further foes? It was silly to think.

The Aztecs would not have approved being led off for sacrifice. They would have disliked it intensely. But they would have said that it was obviously preferable to what was happening now. It showed the degeneration of those who ally themselves with uncivilised men.

As dusk came, the murderous Tlascalan activities were lessened, not only by the efforts of Cortéz, but by the fact that, like the Spaniards, they were loaded with costly spoils. The sunset paled, and the darkening waters of the two lakes were lit by the reflection of many fires, until the Spanish efforts to control them and bring order to the captured city, were rudely interrupted as they became aware that the water was rising around their feet.

Careless of what destruction it might cause to the half-looted city, or of the consequences to its remaining inhabitants, the Aztecs had opened a dyke through which the waters of the higher lake, before entering the city, had already cut off the Spanish retreat.

It was evidence of the ruthless spirit with which the new Aztec Emperor would war against those who, he saw clearly, would destroy him unless he could be the destruction of them. On both sides, the hard incidence of war was eliminating the first older, weaker, protagonists, and giving a final prominence to Guatemozín, Coanaca, and Xicotencatl—younger, more resolute, and more ruthless men.

But the Spaniards had no time for such abstract reflections now. Trumpets shrilled through the dusk, calling the scattered, loaded looters to retreat while there might yet be time.

The cavaliers, leading the way through a darkening flood, capriciously lit by reflecting fires, could demonstrate that the depth of water was not yet up to their horses' bellies. The burdened infantrymen splashed and stumbled behind.

But as they approached the place at which the dyke had been opened, the water not only became deeper, it poured into the lower lake in a fierce current against which footing became hard to sustain. In absolute darkness now, it was not a question of saving loot, but themselves, that engaged their minds.

Clear of the water at last, men struggled on, drenched and cold in a bitter wind, and fortunate if they had retained weapons to repel attacks which were now made by canoes from the lakes.

As daylight came, there were still many stragglers who had not regained the security of the last inland mile of the Tezcuco road. To those who remembered the long fight for life along the causeway of the Night of Sorrow, it was a repetition of the disaster of a kindred kind, though, when the roll was called, those of the Spaniards who would not answer again were fewer than had been feared. The losses among the Tlascalans, to whom the condition had been more alien, had been heavier, but even these were light in comparison with the many thousands of the inhabitants of Iztepalapan who had perished.

To Cortéz, it had an aspect of disaster, until he realised how it appeared to others. To the Aztecs, and to their many half-hostile half-reluctant vassal cities, it was the destruction of the famous pleasure-city of previous kings that was significant of the terror attached to the name of Spain.

Its consequences were immediate in approaches, some openly and some very secretly made, from cities which desired to be freed from the Aztec yoke, and did not look far enough ahead to ask who would be their lords on a later day.

Even from Chalco, which he had designed to be the object of his next assault, there was a secret message. Marina said: "I have talked to a man of Chalco in the market, who will be here after dark and desires to say more tonight, when he will make excuse to come as one bringing merchandise I have bought. It may be best that I see him, and that none can say he has sought converse with you."

"You think this important?"

"It may be no more than to discover what you intend, which I should say with truth that I do not know. It may be nothing, or much."

"And you will discover which, as I do not doubt."

"So you will think till I fail." A smile lit the normal gravity of her eyes. At this time, they understood each other well, and were in closest accord.

After dark, the man came, and spoke to Marina apart. He said he had been sent by two young caciques, who shared the government of the city, and who would welcome Cortéz, if he could expel the Aztec garrison. They would undertake that the populace would cooperate. Their price was that the city should not be sacked.

"What," Cortéz said, "did you answer to that?"

"I told him that you were ever clement to those who were friendly to you, and that he could go back, telling them to await the time of deliverance, and then to act as was proposed; but to be very secret till then, lest suspicion should rouse too soon."

"It was wisely said. But I had already resolved that Chalco should be the next to fall. I will trust Gonzalo for that."

He knew Sandoval to be discreet in civil, as he was skilful in military operations. He preferred not to go himself, for the absence involved would be too long. His present difficulty was to maintain successful operations until the canal should be completed, and the vessels arrive, without separating his small army too far for too long a time.

He was afraid to accept or even acknowledge offers of submission or pleas for help which now came to him from subject cities in many parts of the land who saw a chance of throwing off the Aztec yoke, for they all asked for military aid, or assurances of protection that he was unable to give.

His intention was delayed for two days by a sharp struggle for the possession of ripening crops of maize on the lake side. Intent on its acquisition, the Aztecs came across the lake in canoes at the dawn of a day when it was scarcely fit to cut, thinking it better to secure it in that condition than not at all, but they were defeated after a strife that was stubbornly waged, and the corn was reaped and carried into Tezcuco granaries.

Following this, Sandoval set out on a march to Chalco, which was at the eastern end of the lake of that name. He had most of the cavaliers, and every footman that Cortéz could dare send, with the most part of the Tlascalans. He moved rapidly, but the Aztecs were too alert for that to avail. As he neared the city, he was opposed by a large Aztec army, which relied on fields of uncut maize to obstruct the cavaliers, and provide ambush for its own troops.

These tactics were so far successful that Sandoval had some loss and a first repulse, but he succeeded at last in driving them from the field of their own choice; and after that he found that his task was done, for the Aztec garrison fled from a city that opened its gates to receive the Spaniards with music and many flowers.

The two young caciques who had invited Spanish assistance accompanied Sandoval back to Tezcuco. They explained to Cortéz that their father, before his recent death, had expressed a conviction that the Spaniards were sent from God, and enjoined them to make accord.

But to their request for alliance, he could only, in their own interests, give a cautious reply. The fact was that their own attitude had embarrassed rather than helped him. He could have taken and spoiled the town, giving other watchful Aztec vassal cities a further evidence of his power. But he could not supply a garrison to replace that which the Aztec had withdrawn, and might send in again on the next day. He could only tell these friendly suitors to go back and wait circumspectly till he should be able to give them the protection that they required.

CHAPTER EIGHTY-FIVE:
THE COMING OF THE BRIGANTINES

Hernando Cortéz thanked God aloud. He thanked St. Jago also, who, from the day when the loosening of a stone under Doña Carella's bedroom window had saved him from sailing in Ovando's squadron, he had regarded as a reliable saint, and one who took interest in his affairs.

There were two excellent causes for this cheerful and grateful mood.

First, he had had a letter from Vera Cruz, telling that his mission to Hispaniola had borne a crop of the right kind.

His ship had come back loaded with stores, and with two others following in its wake. They bore two hundred volunteers, and four score horses to recruit his thin ranks at these most critical hours. They also brought Señor Julián Alderete, delegated to act as treasurer for the Spanish Crown, to supervise the division of spoil which it was now recognised at St. Jago might become very large.

Cortéz did not mind this. Always aiming at equity or generosity in such distributions, he preferred that a royal representative of high standing should be present to see what was done. He was more interested to learn that there was no letter from Madrid of the wrong kind, though there was evidence that the Church had become alert to the importance of what was happening, in the appearance of a Dominican friar, who had travelled with the letter-carrier, in haste to commence his mission, which he intended to be lucrative both to his order, and to himself. He had a large stock of indulgences, papally signed, by which men who fought heathens were allowed to commit various sins in return for sufficient gold. He was to find that Father Olmedo would receive him in a curt way, and, which was much worse, when he made confession to him (for even such as he must confess at times), he was refused absolution except upon terms which he could not endure. He told himself (with some truth) that Father Olmedo was unfairly prejudiced against Dominican friars.

The second reason for which St. Jago deserved praise was that the brigantines were finished at last. Thirteen of them had been put together, and tried afloat. They were now being dismantled, that they might be transported on human shoulders over the mountain roads.

While they were being built, the Tlascalans had been assembling their strength. They were now a nation in arms. There could be no final victory for Spain while México remained secure in its four-mile moat, and while supplies could be sent to it from any point on a coastline which was too long to guard. Cortéz and Guatemozín, were alike in observing that. Guatemozín held back his full weight of offensive strength. He said: "Come here, if you can." Cortéz saw that, even if the bold device of the brigantines should avail, he would need a large army for such a siege. He had asked the Tlascalans for twenty thousand men, who were to come with the ships, so that there should be no lack of protection for them. Yet that left him less than content. He told Sandoval to march to Tlascala at once, with fifteen cavaliers and ten score footmen, taking the route through Zoltepec, the place where the massacre of the forty-five had occurred, and punish any who could be proved to have been directly concerned.

"You will need an interpreter," he said, "having two tongues with which to contend" (for Sandoval, who was frugal of his own, had not been quick to comprehend alien words), "and Marina is not now to be spared. But I have a Tlascalan who will suffice."

Sandoval was not surprised at this decision, for apart from the fact that Cortéz was always unwilling to part with Marina, there was the fact of her pregnancy, which was a reason that only she would have been puzzled to hear.

Ignorant of the traditions of the Old World, the production of children had been accepted by Aztec women as deserving of no particular sympathy, and requiring little consideration. She had seen something of a different attitude in the Spanish camp, and had been particularly repelled by the fact that women would allow—and, indeed, expect—the presence of others when their children were born. Surely, of all times in her life, that was the one when a woman would prefer to be alone! But she had observed all with the unprotesting reserve that was the normal quality of her race. She must not forget that they were not of a civilised kind. And, perhaps, even among Spaniards, there were noblewomen who would act in a more dignified way.

Sandoval lost no time. He set out on the next day, and was at Zoltepec as quickly as footmen, followed by loaded porters, could be expected to move; but the news of his coming had gone ahead, and he entered an empty town.

Yet the warning had been so short, the guilt-prompted flight so instant, that there had been no time to remove the evidences of what they had done.

The temple-trophies included tanned hides both of his horses and men, and the preserved heads of several Spaniards, those who had perpetrated the massacre having been allowed to retain that portion of the evidences of victory, the remainder of which had been distributed to many cities to demonstrate that the Spaniards were not of invincible strength.

The prison in which the victims had been confined while awaiting death was also found, with a charcoal inscription upon the wall which had no meaning to Aztec eyes: *Here the unhappy Juan Juste was imprisoned with many comrades.*

It was well for the people of Zoltepec that those who saw these things could not fall upon them in the first bitterness of indignation.

As it was, Sandoval sent his cavaliers out on a brief search for the fugitives. They came back with several citizens of the little town, of a status which rendered it at least probable that they had been complicit to what had occurred. Sandoval sent them to Tezcuco for judgement, where Cortéz ordered that they should be branded, and sold to slavery. Afterwards, a deputation came to him from the town, with the familiar plea for forgiveness because they had acted reluctantly under Aztec pressure. Collectively, it could have been little, if any, truth. But of each individual, how could he be equally sure? Or judge what his part had been?

Rather than risk further punishment of men who were just possibly innocent, Cortéz said he accepted their protests, and let them go.

Sandoval did not go all the way to Tlascala city. As he crossed the boundary of the republic, he met the great host of those who, having been assembled for war, had become too impatient to await his arrival. The component parts of the thirteen vessels were now on porters' backs in the midst of an army of far more than the twenty thousand for whom Cortéz had asked.

Sandoval was annoyed at this. He thought that orders should be exactly obeyed. Numbers may be too many as well as too few. Questions of accommodation and feeding arise. He said that the excessive levies must be sent back, at which the Tlascalan general felt an annoyance he did not scruple to show.

When the march recommenced, he had a further grievance in the fact that the little force of Spaniards were in the van. He said that his place had always been there, as the dignity of his position required.

Sandoval was always a man of a few words. He would not alter his disposition, but he told Jerónimo to placate him with the idea that the rear was the more dangerous post. He would himself join the irate general there, in support of this opinion.

It is possible that the interpreter was not as clear or convincing in his translations as Marina would have been. The general professed a new grievance, that he was not trusted to control the point of danger alone. Sandoval rode back to the van.

Lengthening itself to several miles on the narrow mountainous road, the great army, with its central thousands of fantastically burdened porters, toiled and stumbled upward. It was a hard climb for all, and most difficult for such burdened men. It was the fourth day from when they had met that saw them enter Tezcuco between cheering, flower-flinging crowds, and before that they had learnt that Sandoval had done wisely to send back those he did, for it had become necessary to rule that the porters should have precedence of food that was near to fail.

It had been the first of January when Cortéz had entered Tezcuco. March was ending, and the canal was nearly finished, as Martín López and his trained assistants supervised the reception of the piles of timber, canvas, cordage, and metal which were intended to become the fleet of an inland lake.

Not only had the canal been cut, but a large basin and quays, where the ships could ultimately be moored within the security of the city, approached completion.

Cortéz was well pleased both by the ability and energy that Ixtlilxochitl displayed in the provision of this channel of communication with the lake, and, as the weakling who had been his temporary puppet on the Tezcucan throne suddenly died, he offered him that which had been refused by Montezuma—the combined throne of the whole Tezcucan land. It was accepted with eagerness, and, as Ixtlilxochitl was a very popular prince, and he thereby became the unalterable enemy of Coanaca, it won over the whole of the Tezcucan branch of the Aztec race to the Spanish interest. It was a political victory of the first magnitude. Now at last, the wild adventure took on an aspect of possibility. But Cortéz did not therefore disguise from himself that hazards, and possible disasters, still lay ominously ahead.

CHAPTER EIGHTY-SIX: OPERATIONS AROUND THE LAKE

Martín López stood with a mallet in his hand, for he was not one who directed work which he did not share. He said: "In three weeks, if all go smoothly, as now it should—"

Cortéz thought: "Call it four, and I should be glad to think it no more than that." But he was not one to discourage the optimism of those who worked hard and well. He said: "You can have that time, for I shall be away for two weeks, if not three; and if the masts are stepped by that time, I shall thank your skill."

He marched out next morning with the greatest army he had yet led, though at times there had been more of the swords of Spain. He had three hundred of his own footmen, fifty cavaliers, twenty thousand Tlascalans, and five thousand of other levies, including Tezcucans, on whom he could call now that its prince was his ally.

He marched to the north, having told no one, not even Marina, what his intentions were, but did not advance many miles before he was met by an Aztec army, so vigilantly was he watched, and so pertinaciously opposed. The noise of his artillery could be heard for over an hour, and then ceased. Evidently, he went ahead. The policy of the Aztec Emperor appeared to be to harass continuously, relying upon his troops to equal the Tlascalans, and accounting it sufficient success if an occasional Spaniard were captured, or slain, or maimed, at whatever cost. Does the baited boar escape at the last because more than one dog may die?

For the next fourteen days nothing more was heard of the army's progress. It was clear that it was not operating on the Tezcuco side of the lake, but nothing was known of it beyond that. Martín rose early and worked till darkness came, hoping that the two weeks might be three, if not four; but on the fifteenth day the army returned, leading slaves, and loaded with spoil.

Cortéz answered Sandoval's greeting (he had left him in charge, taking Olid and Alvarado) with a cheerful optimism that yet made light of what he had been able to do: "Yes, there are fallen towns, and we have seen the backs of men who were fast to fly. But we have seen also how great is the Aztec strength, which we must overcome, or all will be naught at last."

He passed on to Marina, leaving his captains to boast as they would of the exploits of fourteen days, during which their swords had been in their hands more than their sheaths. There he became explicit in recitation of routes and cities which would be familiar to her.

He had made a wide loop, following, but many miles away, the north shore of the lake. He had fought three pitched battles with those whose purpose may have been to delay rather than to destroy. He had come to the smaller lake of Xaltocan, where the smaller town of that name imitated the capital city in being built on piles in the lake, and reached by shorter causeways of the same kind. He thought that this should not be beyond his strength to subdue, and, in the end, so he had done, taking great spoil. But this had been through the treachery of one who had shown a way through the lake which was not more than three feet deep, by which his infantry had waded into the town; and before that he had looked defeat in the eyes, having tried to force the main dyke, and come to a pass too much like that of the Night of Sorrow to be recollected with a serene mind.

After a restless night attending to the many wounded and burying dead comrades and allies, he had moved out early the next day. Weighed down by spoil and slowed by prisoners, he had continued his sweep through the hurriedly emptied towns of Cuauhtitlan and Tenayuca—which they had named 'City of the Serpents' because of the prayer houses' large stone carvings—whilst derision was whistled from the safety of nearby hills.

From the City of the Serpents he had moved on to take stategicaly important Tacuba. During this time his army had been subjected to almost ceaseless attacks, though mostly of a skirmishing kind designed to wound the horses, and each day Cortéz had ridden out at the head of his cavaliers, to teach caution to those who sought less formidable foes. But on the second occasion the lesson of caution had been his to learn, at a cost which had been too nearly that of his life to be remembered without chagrin.

A weak Aztec force, facing him with less resolution than they were accustomed to show, had been encountered near the approach to the great dyke, the first bridge of which had not been demolished. He had with him about a dozen of his hardiest comrades, and though the Aztecs were twenty or thirty times as numerous as themselves, they did not hesitate to charge those who instantly broke and ran. They fled towards and along the dyke, running so fast that it might be thought that they had been chosen for that ability (as in fact they had), and the horsemen pursued them, slaying some; but most kept ahead, or plunged into the waters on either side.

They were not less than a quarter of a mile out on the dyke, in this hot pursuit, when Cortéz looked round and back. "Volante," he said to the trumpeter who was also his standard-bearer, and whose duty it was to be next to his side, "sound the retreat."

The sharp note of recall shrilled over the water, far beyond the little band around him, or still riding ahead, for whom it was meant; and it was answered by a louder, more challenging sound—the derisive war-whistle that came from thousands of Aztec throats.

Those who ran turned back at the sound. They rushed at the cavaliers, who were now showing their horses' tails, with a reckless disregard of what might happen to themselves. On either side of the dyke canoes swarmed, and their occupants clamoured up the side. The horsemen made little progress to evade these attacks upon flank and rear, for they were confronted by foes who had advanced as far as themselves, and now crowded the dyke.

The chargers trampled, their riders slew. But it seemed that the Aztecs had orders to stand their ground at whatever cost, which they did not shrink to obey. One of them, having a Spanish sword lashed to a pole, by which means he had made for himself a long pike, thrust at Volante's horse. It came down, and rolled over, screaming in death. Volante was thrown off. He rolled down the sloping side of the dyke. Those who could have killed him with ease preferred living prey. Many hands dragged him into a canoe. He was a powerful man, and, with the strength of desperation, he struggled, so that the canoe overturned.

Drenched, and swordless, he struggled upward, flinging off one who clung to his arm, while the sword of Cortéz, thrusting downward, entered between the shoulders of another who clutched his throat.

"You are unhurt?" Cortéz found time to ask. Volante ignored the question in his reply. His trumpet was gone, but he held out the flag, which had been clutched in his left hand throughout the struggle.

"You must mount behind me," Cortéz answered the wordless reply, "being swordless now." They both understood that it was the flag which must not be risked in the hands of a dismounted weaponless man.

Volante vaulted on to the charger's back, while his captain smote at those who were closing around him. Cortéz used the spurs as he rarely would. Two of his cavaliers were swinging round to his support. After a hard flurry of strife, the little group were together again, and fighting backward foot by foot along the causeway which they had ridden at such headlong speed.

In the end, and aided by a Tlascalan attack on the Aztec rear, they broke free of the trap, leaving a trail of dead to show how far they had ridden out, but there was not one who had escaped wounds, and their horses had suffered more than themselves, which Bernal thought to be the more serious thing, as perhaps it was.

Cortéz, showing Marina a long cut on the inside of his left arm, which was no more than four days old, said, with less inconsequence than appeared: "I will have Ávila and the other captains to dine with us tonight, and you must be there, for I shall say something that all must hear."

She agreed to this with her accustomed serenity, but it was still a strange custom to her that men and women should eat at the same board. And stranger still were the high table and chairs which Cortéz had had made for his use. It was clear to him that he could not squat on the floor in the undignified Aztec way, and it was a wonder to her that anyone should endure the discomfort of chairs, after having been shown how meals could be taken in a more civilised style.

He went on to tell her how, when he had marched out of Tacuba on the next day, the Aztecs appeared to have regarded it as a gesture of flight, and had harassed the army with such persistence upon its rear that he had felt it necessary to assert his supremacy by the ruse of leaving a strong force of cavalry concealed in a wooded place. They let the pursuers pass them, and then followed. As the Aztecs worried the Tlascalan rear, it turned fiercely upon them, and, at the same time, they became aware of the horsemen who assailed them behind. They broke in panic flight, and were then ridden down and slaughtered to an extent which left them no heart to continue the nuisance they had begun.

The fortnight's campaign had certainly not been unsuccessful, but it had shown how formidable was the opposition which had still to be overcome.

Cortéz met his captains, both those who had gone with him and those who had remained in Tezcuco, at the evening meal, and said little while he listened to the conversation of men who were relaxed from the strains and vigilance of the past weeks, and had much to tell to those whose time had been passed in a quieter way.

They were comrades in whose loyalty he had reason to trust. He was one who won loyalty, being loyal himself. There was no one there for whom he would not have risked his life as a casual thing. They were men he loved, and in whom he had a confident pride. But no two men are alike, and it was his business to know with exactness how far each could be trusted, and in what ways. So he would listen, and learn.

"Comrades," he said, when the meal was done, and the attendants withdrawn, "I was near to death when I rode out too far on the dyke, as you all know. I was nigh caught in a simple trap. It was not the first time that I have been hardly beset, it being a risk that we all take. But it caused me to think that, should I come to a quick end, there must be one of you who will take my place, which it is my right to select, and I should wish that it should be settled without debate. What I now ask is that you shall all swear that whom I name shall be accepted without demur. I ask you to do this in St. Jago's name on the Cross of God.

"I shall not say now whom it will be, but I shall write the name for Marina (who cannot read) to keep in a privy way, and produce, you being assembled as you are now, should I be missing or dead."

Marina said: "I should tell you that I am learning to write in your way."

"Are you that? Well, it will be of much use. But the scroll shall be sealed, that my will may be known to none."

He looked at men who gazed at one another with the same question in every mind. Alvarado, the blond giant at his right hand, was the one who, more than others, might feel that the position would be rightfully his. His experience went back before the date of this expedition. He was probably the one whom the Aztecs most greatly feared. There was none more formidable nor fearless in bouts of strife. He had been left in delegated authority once before, and though the result had been disastrous, he did not admit that indiscretion had been the cause. His brothers were men of worth, but they were eclipsed by himself. They were less successfully cast from the same mould.

Ávila, at Cortéz left hand, was a quieter, less spectacular man. He seemed more naturally engaged with a quill than a sword. But all he did was efficient. None could say that he was backward or unskilful as a cavalier, or, indeed, in any relation of life. He might do much in a quiet, unflurried way. He was, of all, most difficult to assess. Was Cortéz thinking of him?

Christóval de Olid, Captain of the Guard? Probably no one thought that the choice would fall upon him. And he was one whom others would be most reluctant to serve. Yet he was a good cavalier. Resolute in a dark hour. Nothing could be said definitely in his dispraise, except that he was morose. None could credit him with a kind deed, or a jesting word. He would not be a good choice, if only because he was not liked. But none would be more likely to resent that another should be preferred.

Gonzalo de Sandoval must have been guessed by some. He had been trusted on many occasions, and had not failed. Also, he came from Medellín, Cortéz's home town. They had known each other in youth, though Gonzalo had been the much younger boy. That was the reason why some might resent his choice. He was much younger than they. And there is a wide difference between being trusted with a specific mission, and being placed in entire control.

Youth, too, might be disqualification for Diego de Ordaz, climber of volcanic heights, fearless and adventurous, and with the same smiling attitude to those around him which made Cortéz popular, not only with his captains, but all he led.

Or it might be that there would be a surprise choice, that would not be any of these. There were a dozen around the board.

But what ever it might be hoped or thought, there could be no hesitation now, no refusal to swear. The oaths were made, and that night the sealed script was in Marina's hand, and hidden safely away.

Cortéz said: "So you learn to write?"

"So I must, if you will not understand mine."

"Little can be said by pictures, however skilful you be."

Marina answered with her usual consenting gravity: "So I know that it seems to you."

She thought that a few pictorial strokes will tell more, and more vividly, than can be expected from many words. But if he would not see that, she would go his way.

They were both right, and both wrong.

CHAPTER EIGHTY-SEVEN: RELIEF OF CHALCO

The brigantines were not ready. Martín López and his comrades toiled, and the work was visibly being advanced, but the fact was that they had of necessity been so thoroughly broken up to enable them to be transported after the first test—and that test had been little more than a demonstration that hulls would float—that there was much to be done over again, and much in final furnishing and equipment which had not been attempted before. Martín allowed reluctantly that there might still be two weeks to wait, if not three, before the vessels would be fit to operate on the lake.

This made it less important that the Tlascalans wanted to go home, and could not be refused. That which had been a preliminary foray to Cortéz had been a major campaign to them. They had fought battles; they had sacked towns; they had taken a great spoil. They had suffered casualties also, far more numerous absolutely, and perhaps relatively, than those of the Spaniards.

They would return, but they required a break for rest, for boasting, and for distribution of spoils.

They had been gone for two days, during which there had been no greater excitement than a third attempt to set fire to the brigantines, which was a constant danger (there still being many citizens of the town who hated Spaniards, and who regarded Coanaca as their lawful prince, and with whom the Aztecs were in constant communication), when a letter came from the lords of Chalco, which Cortéz was, of course, unable to read.

To Marina, to whom he passed it, it was so simple, so obvious, that even her previous experience of his obtuseness to picture-writing did not prevent wonder now. Its single meaning was so clear, and it was so difficult, if not impossible, to interpret it in another way! She said: "They tell you that the Aztecs are gathering against their city. There are four regiments already assembled six miles away. They ask you to go there, and as swiftly as eagles fly."

"Which I shall not do, having few but Tezcucans, and my own Spaniards now. I will not divide my force, nor can I abandon the ships. There are several places which have professed allegiance to me which are not too far from Chalco to give aid. You must write letters to them."

So it was done. Marina got her paintbrushes. She sat down at the queer high table. She asked: "Shall I command? Shall I threaten or plead?"

"You will just tell them what I require to be done. Chalco must have their support."

The letters, with one to Chalco, were soon done, and despatched. But Cortéz was not easy in mind. He considered that Chalco was, for him, an essential town. Even when his letters had produced replies which (Marina said) made it clear that Chalco was receiving the assistance he had required, he had anxiety which was justified when a deputation from Chalco appeared. They desired an instant interview, and, on this being granted, he heard, from Marina's lips, that they had felt their position to be so precarious, their need so urgent, that they had not trusted to the reply of a picture scroll, but had come in person to plead for help without which their city might be a ruin before the end of the five-day week.

The fact was that Guatemozín had recognised the strength of the game that Cortéz had decided to play, and had replied with the same card. He was concentrating his forces, outside México City, upon one selected victim. If Cortéz thought that México could be left until he had subdued inferior cities, the Aztec Emperor would treat Tezcuco in the same way until those who had made it their ally should be brought to dust.

If he were to act at all, he could not be too abrupt, either for his own safety, or for Chalco's relief. He would send Sandoval at once, so that his intention would only be known for an hour before the expedition departed. And the shorter would be the time for the Aztecs to molest him before its return.

He told the envoys that they could go back with the assurance that sufficient would be done for Chalco's relief, though he would not say what or where it would be. They went ill-content with this vague reply, which was the best they could get.

They were not back in their litters before Sandoval had been summoned, and told: "You march in two hours from now. You must strike at once in such a way that Chalco will be relieved. You must not return till you have done that, unless you have a summons from me. But, when it is done, you will not lose a moment in your return, for it may be a ruse to divide my strength, and it may be here that the blow will fall. I will not constrain you with more directions as to what you shall do, for I have found you to be wise in the ways of war, and it can be best judged when you are there. I cannot spare many cavaliers, but you shall have twenty horses, and three hundred of other sorts."

Sandoval was always a man of few words, and there was no time to be wasted in talking now. Within three hours he was on the Chalco road with the force that Cortéz had given him, and the porters and camp-followers that such movements required. He would have liked more cavaliers, but thought that he would do well enough.

As he rode, he made plans. He did not go to Chalco, but turned on to a more southerly road. It had been said that Huaxtepec, in a mountain region six miles to the south, was one of the places where the Aztecs gathered. If he were to finish this matter with speed, he must not wait for them to attack Chalco (which they might never do), he must strike directly at them. Also, he could attack them in detail by this method, reversing their own design.

The operation was justified both by its difficulty and its success. The Aztecs met him some miles outside the city, choosing their own ground, on which it was difficult for cavalry to act decisively, being obstructed by bushes and low cover, where men might lurk and stab upward at the horses, before they were seen. An attempt to charge a fluctuant foe under such circumstances had no success. One cavalier was severely wounded. Two horses died.

Sandoval ordered them to the rear. His footmen moved forward. The Aztecs must meet them, or let them through.

A stubborn battle followed, ending, as such conflicts usually did, in Aztec retreat. But Sandoval decided to defer the attack on the city to the next day. For the moment, he thought he had had enough.

The Aztecs thought differently. Reinforced from the city, they attacked again, as the camp fires were being lit. The second battle was severe, but not long. This time Sandoval did not pause. His wearied men pressed hard upon those who fled. They followed them into a city which its inhabitants had already left. They chased them through it, and out. They spent the night amid the luxuries of an opulent city from which those who fled in haste had been unable to take much away.

Sandoval made his quarters, as his status required, in the residence of the city's lord, who was not a king, but to call his house a palace would not be wrong. It had pleasure gardens, beautifully planted, that were nearly six miles in circumference.

Sandoval paused here for two days, leaving the Aztecs to guess what he would do next, and resting his men. When he moved, it was again in a direction which would not be a probable guess.

Jacapichtla was six miles away to the east. It was on an abrupt height, approached only by precipitous paths, or a sheer climb. He heard that a large Aztec force was garrisoned there, and he considered that it was the kind of place that only footmen could reach. It was in them that his strength lay.

He marched at dawn, and came, in two hours, to the base of more formidable precipices than he had expected to see. The first assault he ordered did not succeed. Some were crushed by downflung rocks; others thought it well to retreat while their limbs were whole. Wounded or whole, those who lived were agreed that it could not be done.

Sandoval had good reason for not making the attempt himself. He had a knee that had been badly bruised in the battle of three days before, and it moved stiffly. But he ignored that. He said: "This is clearly a matter for cavaliers."

Those whose lances had been meant for a guard to the half-deserted camp were ordered to dismount, and to follow him. He said: "All shall come, both of horse and foot, and my orders are that no men retire till the summit be reached and won. If they do, they may choose a leader more of their own kind, for I shall not be there."

Spreading widely, to make a less certain mark, the little army started upward again, Sandoval, and the cavaliers leading the way.

Arrows met them, of which most were shot too far out to avail, the angle of discharge being acute. Slung stones were a greater danger. Great rocks, that bounced and splintered and bounced again, were the most dreadful to face.

There was some cover at first, but, as they neared the summit, the gradient became less steep, and the danger more. Men were crushed and maimed. Stricken men fell, clutching the air. Still their comrades climbed on.

A huge rock fell past Sandoval, grazing his head. He put up his hand, which came away dripping blood from a torn scalp. He felt dizzy. He thought: "If I faint, I must fall to death." He climbed on.

The moment came when he heard a shout *"St. Jago!"* over his head, and then other voices responded with the same cry. Strife was being waged by those who had climbed better than he.

Soon he was at their side. They had gained a plateau on which there had once been a small town, but which had become a fort, garrisoned with two thousand troops who opposed them now.

They were nearly ten to one, but Sandoval knew that Aztec weapons in Aztec hands could never protect their owners from the pikes and swords of the Old World. He drew his men together, and wheeled them round so that the Aztecs soon had their backs to the precipice he had climbed. Being placed thus, they learnt that numbers did not avail.

They were slaughtered in heaps. They were thrown to death from the cliff edge. Clambering down, they were followed by those who risked limbs and lives that they should gain more occasions to slay. A stream at the cliff foot was so polluted with blood that none could drink from it during the next hour.

Sandoval considered that if the Aztecs had been intending to attack Chalco, he had given them other subjects for thought. He heard that the Chalcans had been reinforced by those whom Cortéz had asked to come to their aid. His own losses were not light, and there were many wounded requiring care. He had driven them hard, and he now marched them back to Tezcuco in haste, having little doubt (in which he was right) that he would be there before the Aztecs would have taken advantage of the division of Spanish force. He thought he had done well, and may have expected praise, which he might have heard, had not his report to Cortéz been interrupted by the information that a deputation from Chalco was at the gate.

Cortéz looked surprised, as he well might. He asked: "What do they want now?"

Sandoval said: "That is more than I am able to say."

"But, having left their city, it may be two days before they must have set out—?"

"Have I not made it plain? I have not been there at all."

Cortéz said to Marina: "See them. Tell me why they are bleating now."

He turned back to Sandoval as she went out: "Am I mad? Or did I hear aright? Did you say you have not been to Chalco at all?"

"So I said. I attacked the Aztecs in their own lairs."

He began to tell what he had done, without boastful words, which were not his use, making it sound less than it was. Before he had told all, Marina returned. She said: "They will have it that you have sent no relief, and they say that, when they left, the Aztecs were closing round them on every side."

Cortéz said to Sandoval: "Do you hear that? Was my order that you should relieve Chalco, or go elsewhere?"

"You told me to deal so that I could return here in a short hour."

"When your task was done. Did I say before that? Will you tell me it is done, after that which we have both heard?"

Sandoval said shortly: "If it is not, it shall be done now."

He turned abruptly, and left the room.

Then the Chalco delegation were shown in.

Cortéz felt an irritating uncertainty as to the justice of what he had done. He was conscious that he had been in a mood of exasperation before Sandoval had appeared. He had just learnt that only two of the brigantines, which he had regarded as requiring no more than a few hours of further work, could be completed without sending to the coast for certain bolts which might not be there. There had been losses, it seemed, for which no one could be certainly blamed. Enemy theft was a possible explanation, though beyond proof.

Now he said curtly to Marina: "Tell them that there is no occasion to come pestering here time after time. What I promise, I do. Let them hasten back, if they would be there as soon as those who are on the way."

Marina translated this fairly enough, but without the tone which gave sting to the words. The deputation withdrew, feeling rebuked, but satisfied, that the required aid would not be delayed.

Sandoval meanwhile had called on wearied astonished men to set out again along the road by which they had just returned. Some grumbled, as it was natural to do. But it was proof of their confidence both in Cortéz and himself that they answered the call in a very prompt and resolute way.

The envoys had not set out on their return for more than an hour when Sandoval, at the head of his little band of cavaliers (for whom two fresh horses had been provided, and among whom Bernal Díaz, indignant that two should have been lost, had himself taken the place of the wounded man), took the same road, followed by as many footmen as were not too exhausted by toil and wounds to re-join their places in the files.

Sandoval marched to the limit of the strength they had, and came at last to a place where he was no longer required, for the men of Chalco, strengthened by those whom Cortéz had called to their aid, and heartened by the tale of slaughter which had come from Jacapichtla, had encountered the Aztecs outside their city and ef-fected what, for the moment at least, was decisive defeat.

Once more, Sandoval lost no time. "Comrades," he said, "It is less toil to march than to fight. We will return to Tezcuco again, and this time we may perhaps be permitted to stay."

Those who heard this said in a bitter tone, and at greater length than his words would often be, knew that something was wrong, as some had already guessed. They marched back to Tezcuco, where the first that Cortéz heard was that Sandoval had dispersed them to their own quarters, for he went to his without making report of what he had done.

But now Cortéz was in a cooler mood, and he had been more fully informed. He said: "So he sulks? I will go to him."

Marina said: "He has reason to be displeased. He had done well."

"So I think."

He went out, seeking Sandoval, whom he found with Bernal ar-guing over a lame horse, on the treatment of which they did not wholly agree. Others stood round.

Cortéz said: "I was wrong. I was vexed about other things. Will you forgive?"

CHAPTER EIGHTY-EIGHT: BEYOND THE LAKES

The troubles of Chalco were not over. Or, at least, that was an opinion that Chalco had, and about which it would not be still.

Chalco's citizens (with those of some other towns) had inflicted defeat on the Aztecs, to their own lasting surprise. After that, surely they could expect to be left alone?

But the Aztecs looked at it differently. Defeats from the Span-iards they expected to have, counting against them a single Spaniard captured for sacrifice, a horse crippled or slain.

But to be repulsed by their own vassals, and in the centre of their opulent power, was an indignity they could not lightly endure. There came another letter from Chalco, at which Marina glanced, and said: "What is it now? It is the same as before. There is only one thing that they ever say."

Cortéz said: "I will go myself."

It scarcely varied what he had intended to do. The ships could not be ready for two weeks or perhaps more. He planned to go south, as he had gone west. He would complete the circuit of the lakes, and give a lesson to all that it was more perilous to support the Aztecs than him.

A large number of Tlascalans had now returned. In addition to the Tezcucans who supported Ixtlilxochitl, he had now levied an army from the mountainous region which he had always ruled.

Cortéz could leave a sufficient garrison for the protection of city and ships, and yet take a larger force than that with which Sandoval had operated. He arrayed three hundred footmen, and thirty cavaliers, still preferring to leave behind most of his mounted men. They would be no more than the essential spearhead of a large native army which he was welding into a formidable force, confident in his leadership and themselves.

Leaving Sandoval in command at Tezcuco, he marched straight to Chalco, which he reached on the same day. It was the Fifth of April 1521, which was one of sultry oppressive heat, even at the great height of the Mexican plain.

He called a conference there of the leaders of the allied troops, and all caciques who were loyal to him, and near enough to attend. He told them that he intended to go beyond the plain and down the sierras, as far as Cuernavaca, which he proposed to subdue. It was an Aztec garrisoned city, which dominated the lower land.

Marina explained this, and there was lively debate thereon. She was soon busy translating from several tongues.

Cortéz asked: "What do they discuss?"

"They say it is a rough way, and it will be hard to pass through the hills."

"So you told me before. Tell them that is why I brought footmen rather than horses. Do they doubt that it can be done?"

"They doubt nothing after what Sandoval did. And they say you will have the advantage of surprise, for, even after that, it is more than they will expect you to try. They want you to know that the hilltops may be strongly held, above narrow defiles."

Cortéz saw that these men, knowing more than he, would have regarded it as a wildcat enterprise, but for their confidence in himself. He said to Marina: "You shall go back. Others can do all I require."

She answered: "No. I will come with you."

She thought: "He may learn words, but he is not of their blood, or their ways. He cannot read thoughts, or what a silence may mean."

The council broke up in a cheerful resolute mood, no one having dissented from what was proposed, or rather stated to them, but Cortéz had a feeling of gravity, which he must not expose. That which he had regarded as no more than a preliminary to his main operation was evidently of a different complexion to those who knew the conditions which must be faced.

He marched at the next dawn, and when evening came he was in a black mood, having learnt to accept defeat and move on, leaving it unavenged. He had had victory also, but that was no more than routine. It might have contented those he led, or diverted their minds, but it was no cancellation to him of that which had occurred at the earlier hour.

Also, there was tomorrow to consider, which threatened the same experience without compensation to blot it out.

He had ordered that camp should be made where there was an interval in the wild heights. There was a scattered grove of mulberry trees, and two small streams which, before the whole army had quenched its thirst, had become muddy, and nearly dry. He said to himself: "I brought too many men. There was no wisdom in that." So he had said, for a different reason, earlier in the day. Then the long array of his native allies, with the porters which all movements required, had congested a narrow pass, making it easy for those above to inflict casualties with arrows and falling rocks.

One who was there, writing of it after many years, would say that it was the greatest army he had yet had. That was not true. But so he thought. In those narrow passes it had seemed more.

Cortéz had thought the casualties he had suffered to be too serious to be left unavenged. "Corral," he had said to a gallant man. "Will you dislodge those hounds, and plant the flag of Castile where they are whistling defiance now?"

Corral was willing to essay that. With a mixed force of Spaniards and Tlascalans he had started the climb.

Two hours later, he stood before Cortéz, a wounded man making report. The flag of Castile was gone. It had not been taken by Aztec hands but struck by a boulder which had borne it away, by which he had narrowly escaped death. There were eight Spaniards dead: there was none who had come back who could not show the evidence of a wound. It was greater loss than a major engagement would be certain to cause. And it had been necessary to accept defeat, and march on.

After that, they had been opposed by an army on more open ground, and this had been broken and chased, with little loss to themselves. That was well, but not well enough. And now, when he looked the way which he purposed to go, he saw narrow defiles ahead, and steep fortressed heights from which death would descend. There was nothing more certain than that. What was he to do?

The men, who were bivouacking around him, were cheerful and free from care. They diced, they sang, they cleaned soiled velvet, they sharpened swords. Some of them had taken spoil from a flying foe. Besides Marina, there was no woman to make discord in all the camp, for they had known that they would march on a rough way. And even Don Juan Xamarillo, of whom it was a jest that he confused her in his mind with the Madonna of God, knew that she would never give him a wanton look. The grave pleasure of her own amativeness was for Cortéz alone. She had eyes only for him; and, besides, wandering levities were not for those who had been taught for six years in the Sacred College, and knew that which Aztec law and female dignity were at one to require.

But Cortéz did not gamble, or sing, or jest. He looked at the mountains before him with anxious eyes. *If any man would be first among you, let him be the servant of all.* There is no profounder wisdom than that.

He went into his tent, to be watched by Marina with eyes in which trouble was not allowed to appear. She asked, as the silence lengthened. "Things go ill?"

"It seems we must still go forward by narrow paths, with our foemen entrenched above."

"It is only that? You will find a way. You have a strong God."

Yes. He must take comfort in that.

CHAPTER EIGHTY-NINE: THE WAY OF THE AIR

There were two hills closely ahead, with most precipitous sides, but walled and flattened upon their summits, making them forts of a height which could not have been erected by human hands.

Cortéz had made brief demonstrations against them before camping, his thought being that he would be more secure if they should be occupied during the night by men friendly to him.

But he had not found them to be vacant, easy to scale, or lightly held. He had desisted from their attack, lest he should have two defeats on one day.

With dawn, he must decide whether he would assault them again, or march between them, in which event he knew that the long train of his array would be subject to constant battery from above, for the hours that its transit would require, to which it could make no reply.

After more hesitation than he allowed to appear, he ordered that assaults should be made.

None can say what would have occurred had the Aztecs maintained their positions of the previous day, but they had made a movement during the night which had an aspect of prudence, but was to be fatal to them.

The higher of the two eminences was also much the smaller, and its garrison, doubting their own strength, had abandoned it, and joined their companions on the wider but inferior height.

As soon as Cortéz learnt that the one ascent met with no resistance, he halted the other, to allow time to secure the crest of the higher hill. When this had been done, and arquebusiers and crossbowmen had ascended, the Spanish flag was displayed, and, at that sign, the assault of the height on which the Aztecs were concentrated began.

When they exposed themselves, to rain volleys of stone and shafts on the climbers, they found that they themselves were exposed to a deadlier hail, and realising that, under such conditions, they could not make a prolonged resistance, they had discretion to yield while terms could be obtained. Cortéz, himself ascending the height, found that it had a broad summit which could not otherwise be reached, and which was occupied by buildings amounting to a small town.

He gave orders that these, and their inhabitants, should not be molested, and told them to let it be known through the land that those who remained quietly within their own dwellings would be secure; but towns which resisted would be sacked, and deserted ones would be burned.

Encouraged by this success, the march continued, meeting less opposition than before, and halting at Huaxtepec, to be met with welcoming crowds. Still continuing to penetrate the barrier of the southern sierras, and burning several minor towns from which the hostile inhabitants had fled, they came, on the ninth day, by an abrupt descent, to more tropical regions. All day they clambered down mountain paths so steep that the cavaliers must dismount and lead their horses with care; and as the short twilight came they saw the city of Cuernavaca, the largest and richest below the sierras on this side of the upland plain, and one of the few that were loyal by inclination rather than fear to the Aztec cause.

This was the most southerly point to which Cortéz had planned to come. The reduction of this great city was to be the terror-striking culmination of what would otherwise be an audacious but barren raid.

And now it became evident that its capture would not be easy, and might be impossible. The army halted when they were so close that they could see the people who moved in its streets, and who were level with them. It had not even a protecting wall.

But they could not cross that last fifty yards, for there was a deep sheer-sided rent in the rock, a canyon into which it would be difficult to descend, and surely impossible to mount against any active resistance on the opposite side.

Cortéz and Alvarado walked together to look over the edge of the ravine, ignoring the arrows which were discharged from the shelter of the buildings on the opposite side. What was steel armour for, if not to enable them to disregard such an annoyance as that?

They looked down an unclimbable wall of sheer rock, to a riot of vegetation almost hiding the stream below. It was a hothouse of green steaming fertility.

The further side of the chasm was slightly less perpendicular, and there was a rough path winding down it, by which the inhabitants of the town doubtless took toll of the affluent growth below.

"There must be means of crossing," Alvarado said reasonably. "We must find a way."

Diego de Ordaz went along the edge of the ravine. He passed the remains of two bridges, which had been broken down, on which he sent back report. He saw that the stream widened, the depth of the ravine slightly declined, but he came to no point where a crossing could be reasonably essayed. It was a nameless Tlascalan who proposed the audacious plan by which that which could not be done below might be attempted above.

The bank down which the explorers moved was heavily wooded. Great trees stretched their high branches over the ravine. There was one that leaned far out, and its skyward boughs touched those of one on the further side.

The man said: "We could cross there, if you will."

Diego looked up. It was a great height. There would be the depth of the ravine below, into which no man could fall and live. At that height the meeting boughs looked more fragile than they actually were. He asked: "You could do that? May I see it done?

The man laid down his bow. He cast off his coat. Agile as a monkey, he went up the tree.

While Diego watched him, he thought. If such crossing were possible, it could only be while there would be no opposition—by instant surprise. He had with him about thirty Spaniards, and four score Tlascalans. He saw the man swing on an outward bough. Then his feet were on another a yard below. It was a branch of the other tree. He waved and shouted. He was asking, should he go on? Diego signalled him to descend on the other side. He said: "Is there one among you who cannot climb?"

The question was met by a moment's silence, its implications being obscure. Then one man said, with a laugh: "I can climb a flight of stairs. I would not go beyond that."

Emboldened by the sound of another voice, one said: "I cannot climb, for I go dizzy at any height."

So they saved their lives.

Diego said to the first: "You will return with report of what you will see us do, and ask for instant support. Say that I am attacking the town." He said to the second: "You will remain here, that there may be no debate as to where we have crossed. Others will soon arrive, to whom you will report what you may see us do." He thought: "or be done to," which it would not have been useful to say.

He said: "Comrades, you will follow me, if you can. But the Tlascalans will come first."

There was prudence in that, for he was more confident in their climbing capacities than in those of his own race. Let an example be set—and avoidance of that which might make his men less godlike to native eyes.

There could be no discarding of armour or weapons now. They must climb equipped. Adjusting his sword-belt as best he could, he went up the tree. The Tlascalans followed. They climbed with confidence, they crossed with apparent ease in the windy height. Most of them had gone over when the first accident occurred. A man slipped and fell. Those who watched saw him fall past them, turning in the air. He disappeared through the tops of the trees in the gorge. Far below though it was, they could hear the impact of body and yielding boughs.

After the Tlascalans, the Spaniards followed with no apparent reluctance, though there must have been some among them who felt that they went to death by a dreadful way. There were some who owed their lives to comrades of greater skill, or of better heart. There were two who fell.

So far, there had been no opposition. Evidently, their foes had not foreseen the possibility of crossing by such a way.

Diego arrayed his men. Twenty-six Spaniards, seventy-nine Tlascalans. No firearms. No cavaliers.

Reinforcements might soon arrive by the same path. But it was not his disposition to wait for them. He went on to attack the town.

CHAPTER NINETY: HUAXTEPEC

Cortéz heard of the broken bridges, and at once went to inspect them.

At the most, they might not be entirely destroyed. At the least, they would show the best places for bridges to be.

He found some hope in the one which faced the more central part of the city. There was a wide gap to be repaired, but the demolition was not complete. It had been too hurriedly done.

He set those to work who were best provided with defensive armour. That was its penalty. To have good back-and-breasts was to be placed where the arrows fell.

They came thickly now, glancing from steel, sinking deeply into padded coats, quivering in broken woodwork. But the work went rapidly on, while wounded men stumbled or were carried away, and the dead had less attention than that.

Cortéz listened to the second message that Ordaz sent, and gave directions that more Tlascalans should go by the same road. But it was the bridge on which he relied, by which horses could cross. He urged on the work. Soon there were distant cries, telling that Diego was there. And, whatever might be happening to him, his arrival had immediate effect, for the arrows ceased. Freed from this nuisance, the work proceeded at better pace. Soon there was a yard's breadth of strong planking crossing the abyss. Would the horses face that?

It seemed that some wouldn't, but some would. And some, which shied at first, would follow others. Soon, with the encouragement of ropes stretched on each side, the whole army, including the loaded porters, was streaming across.

After that, they found that there was no fighting to do.

Diego's force had been small, but the surprise great. It had produced confusion, and while his men chased, and slew those who made no orderly opposition, either by order or common panic, men began to abandon the town.

Those who took the hazard of the narrow bridge, found that they were not to be further vexed by hazard of strife; they were free to loot, which, for a time Cortéz allowed.

But, after that, there was the usual white-flag deputation from the city's rulers, with the usual plea for mercy, on the usual dubious ground that they had acted under Aztec coercion, and would willingly abandon that servitude for allegiance to Spain.

Cortéz, while reserving belief in these professions, saw that it was politic to accept them as genuine. Apart from that, he hated destructions and waste, and was always eager for excuse to exercise his authority for its restraint.

Trumpets recalled the plunderers to their ranks, and proclamation was made that the city had passed into the protection of Spain. It had lost much which would remain in the hands of those who had taken spoil. One quarter was in flames which could not easily be put out. But, even so, the prompt clemency which was shown to those who submitted, beyond the customs either of the Old World or the New, was regarded as further evidence of the merciful disposition of Spain, and inclined other cities in this divided land to place themselves under the same protection.

After resting for two days in the surrendered city, the homeward march began in a confidence which gave inadequate recognition both to logical consequences and natural facts.

CHAPTER NINETY-ONE: THE FIELD OF FLOWERS

Cortéz planned to return northward by a more easterly route than he had yet used. He would recross the mountain barrier by a pass he had not penetrated before, and return to Tezcuco by way of a garden city, known as Xochimilco—"the field of flowers"—which he did not doubt that he could subdue.

As to natural facts, he had to learn that the new route was not only steep and rough, but an arid, waterless way, on which he had cause to regret the number of those he led. Food became short, and water entirely failed. All suffered, many fainted, and became a burden to others, some died.

Emerging to the sight of a part of the Mexican plain which was new to him, and which surpassed in luxuriance anything which he had seen before in this land, Cortéz was soon to learn the logical consequences of his strategy. Guatemozín had been unable, when he set out, to guess where he would go. But his return to Tezcuco was not in doubt. Troops were massed at the best strategic points to molest his return.

Entirely indifferent to that of which he was only partly informed, he went on through a land of flowers, approaching Xochimilco in no haste, being disposed to rest and refresh his men after the toil and privations they had endured.

"The Field of Flowers" (a literal translation of the city's name) was scarcely twelve miles from México City. It also was built on the waters. It had the beauty, the luxury, of the capital city on a smaller scale.

It may excite wonder or even incredulity, that there should have been so many opulent cities, with numerous populations, and more evidences of the pursuit of pleasure than toil, not merely on this central Mexican plain, but within a few leagues of the capital, thickly clustering round the borders of the great lakes, or projecting upon them, or upon the smaller lakes to southward that completed the group.

But the fact was that the whole subcontinent gave its support to this favoured region; every garrisoned city throughout the land paid its tribute to the central authority, making luxury of a life which, in any event, in that equable climate, that fertile land, would have been one of affluent ease.

Xochimilco, like México, was built out on a lake. Its name was an allusion to the floating gardens that surrounded it. In every respect, though on a smaller scale, it was like the capital city. The lake on which it stood was smaller, its causeways were shorter, its population was less. Its subjection should be no more than an experimental prelude to that of the capital. So Cortéz thought, and so (with qualifications) it proved to be.

His approach to the city was disputed by an Aztec army far larger than he had expected to meet, and its resistance was of unexpected obstinacy. When it was so far defeated, or thrust aside, that he arrived on the lake shore, he ordered that his slender force of cavalry should continue to operate against it, to hinder its reformation, and turned to consider the causeway which lay before him.

Its length was not more than three hundred yards, its surface breadth about six. It lay vacant before him. There were no canoes on the lake. But he could see that, at the city end of the causeway, a bridge had been removed, and, beyond that, a wooden palisade erected. Behind this lay the city, in which low, one-story private residences surrounded the occasional high flat-platformed temples, on which burned the undying fires of devotion to México's various deities, but primarily (as it was everywhere), to the ferocious god who, in return for offerings of human blood, would lead her to conquering war.

Doubting whether he would encounter fierce resistance, or enter a deserted city, and aware that repulse would be a discouraging prelude to the attack on México, which he intended to begin at once on returning to Tezcuco, he resolved to lead the assault himself.

He ordered that twenty Spaniards should be in the van, followed by one hundred Tlascalans, and then others in the same order and proportions, until the Spaniards should be exhausted, and the remaining Tlascalans would follow (their numbers being much greater than five to one). Then he rode forward, conspicuous as the first, and the only mounted man, the flag of Castile following closely behind.

There was no sign of life from the barricade until more than half the length of the causeway had been passed. Then the arrows came. It was a signal to rouse his walking pace to a gallop, and the men behind him began to run. He was more concerned for his horse than himself, he wearing armour of proof; but the stallion also had frontal armour of tested steel, excepting for its legs, which would not be easy to hit.

The destruction of the bridge left a gap too wide for a burdened charger to leap, even had there not been the obstacle of the barricade, but it was Cortéz's intention to risk the depth of the lake—to wade, or, if must be, swim.

The charger slid perilously down the sloping side of the dyke. He stood in three feet of water. There was no obstacle here.

The Spaniards plunged after him. In two minutes they were behind the barricade, and mounting the causeway from either side. With the advantage of position, the Aztecs made some resistance, which gave way as the number of their assailants increased. Then they had fled through the city, closely pursued. Many escaped in canoes. Many reached another causeway (there were three in all) and so gained the mainland, where there was more trouble for them, for their flight took them where cavaliers rode back from the slaughter of fleeing men, and weary horses must be spurred to a new effort, the nature and purpose of which they were learning to understand.

So far so good. A city abandoned by its civilian population had been occupied with far less effort than might have been feared, the hard fighting having been at its approach. But it was not over yet. Even previous experiences did not incline Cortéz to the degree of caution which this occasion required.

He saw a rush of Aztec warriors approaching along the third causeway. He saw that the lake had become dark with canoes approaching on either side. He thought (rightly) that this unexpected attack could be repulsed most easily while it must advance on a narrow front of no more than the causeway's breadth. He knew that, man against man, the Aztecs would never hold their ground before Spanish swords, and that even Tlascalans, with new confidence added to ancient hate, would be likely to drive them back.

Yet the Aztecs could not be lightly esteemed. He respected their numbers, their discipline, their sombre willingness (when they were so ordered) to die.

Now he called to those who were scattering to plunder a taken city to gather for further strife. The trumpet shrilled its most urgent call. At the sound, the derisive whistle of the assailants answered from lake and dyke.

Those who were nearest, Tlascalans and Spaniards, came running at the trumpet's call to join the group of those who were appointed to keep his side.

Not counting how few they were, he rode on to the dyke, and they advanced around him. Few they might be, but yet enough for his purpose, if, as he rightly supposed, the Aztecs must recoil when they met on that narrow front.

So they did. They made little resistance before they ran, for it was what they had been ordered to do. And as they ran, the canoes paddled to the side of the dyke and clambered upon it.

As Cortéz rode down men who fell beneath trampling hooves, or felt the thrust of a reddened sword a sudden memory vexed his mind. Had he not done this before?—at Tacuba, and been near to capture or death? At the memory, he drew rein, and looked back, though it seemed needless to do, for he was surely not in a position in which he could be heavily attacked from the rear. Yet what he saw was that the causeway was densely crowded with Aztec warriors who were concealed in the surrounding houses. In fact, he was caught in almost the exact trap which had been sprung on him before.

The loss of every man who had been allocated to this design—the loss of the city itself—would have seemed to Guatemozín to be matters of small account beside the capture of the Spanish Commander, alive or dead, though it was his preference to have him alive.

Again the Spanish trumpet call sounded urgent appeal. It would be heard in the city, where it would call overwhelming rescue for those who were now hardly beset. The little group of Spaniards and Tlascalans who, a moment before, had been exultantly pursuing a flying foe, closed their ranks, and began the backward flight. It was not far. No miracle had rendered the Aztecs equal to facing the

Spanish swords. They fought, and were slain. But there was the difference now that they did not give way. They came on, though it might be only to die.

Cortéz reared his charger, bringing the iron hooves down on those who were most forward, while his sword thrust—and thrust. They had been crowded on to the very edge of the dyke. Perhaps one of the charger's feet slipped over the edge—perhaps it flinched from a wound, of which it took more than one. From whatever cause, it came to the ground. Next moment it had regained its feet, but it was riderless now. Cortéz was on the ground. An Aztec sword struck his casque with such force that he became dizzy, and only dimly aware that he was being dragged away. A Tlascalan leapt to the rescue. That was more than he could achieve, but the vigour of his intervention gained the moment's delay on which life depended. Then Spanish swords flashed over the spot from which Cortéz was now struggling to rise.

He was still alive, and without serious wound. Next moment, he was on his charger again. But the peril had been more extreme even than at Tacuba. He had been saved only by the desire to take him alive, that he might be sacrificed to the god he had blasphemed, in a ritual way.

In a few further moments, the danger was over. Reinforcements had arrived. Those Aztecs who were not slain escaped by leaping into the lake, and clambering into canoes that sometimes overturned in the shallow water, and were righted again.

Next day Cortéz asked the Tlascalan who saved his life to come forward that he might be rewarded in an adequate way, but there was no response.

Had he died subsequently? If he were living, he would not speak.

CHAPTER NINETY-TWO: RETURN TO TEZCUCO

The twilight came, none too soon for those who found that a routed enemy could return, and was resolved to do so, even though it were only to be routed afresh. Indeed, was routed a fitting word?

The whole army and its followers had entered the city now, but the Aztecs were round them on every side, like an elastic band, which would expand to pressure, but contract as the pressure lessened. The dispositions and movements of the Aztecs were of such fluidity that their numbers were hard to guess, but they were certainly in great strength. Had Guatemozín decided to make this the decisive battle, before Cortéz could unite his strength? He thought it unlikely, but was sufficiently alert to the possibility to send a letter to Sandoval, asking him to use a strong cavalry force at dawn to clear the Tezcuco road, and after that to act at his own discretion, with the object of uniting their forces.

It was not quite the way in which he would have wished to end three weeks of (till then) uninterrupted success, but facts had to be faced. He had resolved to capture the Field of Flowers, and he had done. But he had not expected to be besieged within it, in anxiety as to how his forces could be safely disposed through the night hours.

He asked himself, did he exaggerate the danger of the position? Had his nerve failed, because he had so very nearly become a captive, to be reserved for degrading death?

He gave orders for the crossbowmen to be so stationed that they could repulse attack at the dawn (if there should be respite till then), and was told that the bolts were nearly done.

He lost patience at that. He said: "But we brought bolt-heads enough. Why, in Heaven's name, have not bolts been made to suffice our needs?"

There was no excuse beyond the fact that many had been expended during the day, and, being so nearly back, it had not been thought that there would be shortage.

But excuses, good or bad, would not avail. There were bolt heads enough, and, having them, bolts are not hard to make. Men must work through the night.

In the end, Cortéz decided to concentrate his forces within the main temple. Its courtyard was large, as they always were. But not equal to the palace grounds in which he had been besieged in México.

Otherwise, there was an unpleasant similarity. It was all too much like the same thing on a smaller scale. Or, again, had he lost his nerve? The causeway was much shorter, and he was not encumbered with cannon and baggage and women now.

Marina, the only woman there, was unperturbed. He could always rely on that. Her concern was for her horse, which he had ridden. She said: "Bernal tells me that Roland is too much hurt to be used again for some days. You hope Sandoval will be prompt to move? Can you doubt that? But will he find any with whom to fight?"

Her own thoughts were on the horse which she was no longer allowed to ride. She was with child. She must be borne in a litter now. Cortéz had said that riding was unsafe for pregnant women. Well, he should know. He certainly knew more about horses than she. But she had learned to like riding. And it was a thought which would not have occurred to her.

So they spent a wakeful watchful night in crowded discomfort, in the city which it had seemed triumph to take, and were attacked at dawn upon every side. The fighting that followed was longer and more stubborn even than that which had preceded entry into the city. Driven from the streets, the Aztecs contested the main causeway. When the whole length of that was captured, and the Spanish-Tlascalan army deployed on the mainland, strife resumed with fresh fury there. But its result had never been in serious doubt. The Tlascalans, man for man, had always been equal, and were now somewhat to be preferred, to their Aztec foes. Wherever the Spaniards operated, by firing of ball and bolt, by charging of steel-clad cavaliers, or by footmen with pike and sword, the scale tipped, and the Aztecs were slaughtered unless they fled.

The black doubt which had been on their leader's mind as the night had fallen had dispersed with the dawn. But when the causeway had been passed, he regretted that the letter to Sandoval had been sent, and despatched another to say that there was no occasion to operate beyond Cojohuacan, a city which lay about halfway between them, and which, if it should show hostility, he intended to subdue as he passed.

By midday the Aztecs' losses had become so heavy that they could not sustain further attacks. They had become a widely scattered rout, harried by the cavaliers with a vigour which left little hope that they could reform.

It had an aspect of final victory, darkened only by the fact that, in the extremity of the struggle, the Aztecs had taken a substantial number of prisoners, including four Spaniards. To the Tlascalans, these losses were no more than the unavoidable toll of war. They looked on them as those of the Old World looked on the deaths which are a certain feature of sustained battle. But to the Spaniards it had a different aspect. Death on the battlefield was an honourable jeopardy which they expected to face. But to be captured for public slaughter on the altars of heathen gods was a horror of which they could not endure to think. The fate of the four men cast a shadow over the little army, which was only partly lifted when Cortéz caused proclamation to be made that the town was abandoned to spoil. Let the men have some immediate recompense for the peril and hardships they had endured! And let those who had made such stubborn resistance, and then fled the town, learn that there was a penalty to be paid. Before he marched out on the next day he set fire to the town.

It was only six miles to Cojohuacan, from which it was found that the population had fled, which was no occasion for wrath, the army being so loaded with the spoil of Xochimilco that it was in no condition to defend itself without laying down more than it would have been willing to lose.

But the silence of the town confirmed a statement made by more than one of the prisoners who had been questioned separately on the previous day. They had said that it was not the policy of the Mexican Emperor to bring the Spaniards to decisive battle, but to exhaust them by continual skirmishing, while awaiting their own attack upon the capital city, which, he thought, would bring the conflict to a position which would be advantageous to him. The armies which he had so far used, large though they might be, were not, they said, even a major part of those which he was assembling for the destruction of his foes.

This statement, corresponding with the policy which Cortéz would himself have adopted in a similar position, and which he had already decided to be that which he had to meet, was confirmed by the silence of the city into which they now entered. Would it have been abandoned thus, unless for a deliberate policy of delay?

Opposition appeared to have subsided, and Cortéz, always instant to adapt his tactics to change of circumstance, decided to avoid the appearance of being harried back to his own lair, by halting in the deserted city during the following day, and then visiting Tacuba instead of taking the direct Tezcuco road.

This decision was not disastrous, but it is certain that it would not have been taken had its consequences been foreseen. As the army turned off the direct road, attacks recommenced. Aztec archers worried its flanks. Raiding parties were a nuisance upon its rear. It may have been that the weight of spoil which decreased its aggressive mobility was the provoking cause of these persistent assaults.

They were met by utilising every available porter, and assembling them in the centre of the march; and by a series of sweeping movements of the little band of cavaliers, to ride down those who were boldest in vexation of flank and rear.

Several times this was gallantly and successfully done, until it was attempted too boldly at last, and two of the cavaliers were cut off, dismounted, and captured.

They were not two who had been most prominent in places of honour, but they had been in close attendance upon Cortéz. He had regarded them as personal friends. When he heard that they were missing, he broke into wrathful reproaches of those who had failed to save them, for the injustice of which he had expressed regret at a later hour. He even proposed to ride out to an impossible rescue, and was restrained with difficulty from that quixotic folly.

In a depression from which his companions were powerless to rouse him, he continued the march to Tacuba, and on arriving there proceeded to ascend its central temple-pyramid, from the height of which he could survey the twin lakes, and the capital city which he planned to conquer.

It had been a scene of bitter fighting before, culminating in the disaster of the Night of Sorrow, when he had led the exhausted, struggling survivors through the streets that were immediately beneath him now. Since his return, there had been fierce fighting everywhere around, for the many miles that he was able to view. But it was still a land of flowers—a land that was instant in hiding the wounds of war. To those who thought of its ghastly religious rituals, it was a land of blood. To those who thought first of their Christian Faith, and did not question its creed, it bore the curse of a heathen land.

But to those who looked with unprejudiced eyes (yet who was there who could look thus?), it was a land of high civilisation, of simple industry, of many gracious customs and lovely arts—above all other distinctions, a land of flowers.

It was true also that its affluent prosperity was founded upon the exploitation of many peoples, extending to distant lands. But this did not appear, nor could it be said that it was a matter with which the Spaniards were directly concerned. Yet that fact had been decisive in its result. The sinister inventions of the Old World, the horror of explosive powder, the keenness of tempered steel, the terror of mounted men, the inspiration of a fanatic faith, the genius of one of the greatest leaders the world had known, could not have availed against a contented, united land. Whatever might have been subsequent, the few hundred Spaniards that Cortéz led could have made little impression upon the united millions they would have met, nor is it probable that attempt would have been made.

From the great height at which he stood, turning his back upon Chalco Lake, he looked down on the garden city which he controlled, and out upon the wide waters of Tezcuco Lake, alive with canoes, and lovely with floating islands of flowers, with, stretching out from immediately beneath him, the long causeway on which so many had died on the midsummer Night of Sorrow of the previous year.

He saw the great city of the waters, with its many temple platforms on which flickered undying fires, and on the highest of which some, if not all, of the six who had been captured during the last week were certainly doomed to die.

He saw the great wooded circle of the lake shore. Its palaces. Its garden cities. The long hill behind which his headquarters at Tezcuco lay. He looked, for, and thought he saw, the course of the widened stream, coming out from behind the hill, on which the brigantines were to sail.

The two Alvarados and Ordaz were at his side.

"Pedro," he said, with a sudden burst of emotion, astonishing those who heard, "why has God cursed me to bring desolation here?"

Alvarado was incapable of responding to such a mood.

"Oh," he said, "you will give the dogs what they deserve. I expect we shall be equal to that. I should say that you would be cursed if you fail, as you will not do."

But he wondered what such words from his leader could mean. Had being so nearly captured—or the fate of his companions—affected his mind? He wondered as he often did, what was the name so closely guarded by Marina, who could not read. He supposed it to be his. He thought it to be his right. He supposed, but was not sure. He was teaching Louise to read. Could she get sight of it from Marina by any wile? He knew that there were few things that his Tlascalan wife would not attempt at a word from him. The young Sandoval was so much in favour now. And Ávila. No, he could not be sure.

His glance followed the line of the causeway. Far out, he saw where he had leapt in the night. It was bridged now. Certainly, it had been a wonderful leap. He shook back the great mane of his yellow hair. Even the Aztecs thought of him with respect and fear. Did they not call him The Sun?

Cortéz was a tall man, but, as they stood together, it was apparent that Alvarado was three inches taller than he. Certainly the place ought to be his.

CHAPTER NINETY-THREE: TREASON

Ávila sat alone with Cortéz at the noon of the next day. There had been a triumphant return. The population of the city had given a great welcome of music and countless flowers. There had been the good news that the ships were ready. Three of them had been tested for a short distance upon the lake. The time for decisive action had surely come.

Ávila mended a quill.

He had been occupied with the record of casualties during the three weeks' raid, and they were not light. Indeed, looking to what must be ahead, their arithmetic was ominous of defeat. He did not remark on that. He said quietly, without looking up: "Hernán, if you will be guided by a friend's voice, you will not walk alone when the light fails."

Cortéz looked surprised. Then he said: "You think there may be traitors within the town? So there must be. But do I go among them alone?"

"I meant more than that. There are those of our own race whom I do not trust. There is much discontent. Gonzalo will tell you the same."

Cortéz was unmoved. He said: "So there always is when men are idle. They must talk. They cannot dice all the day. Now they will have something to do."

Ávila said no more than: "Well, you will find that Gonzalo will tell you the same."

Cortéz doubted that. He thought that Sandoval was a younger, bolder, more sanguine man; and he was always frugal of words. But when they met, he also had something to say.

"While you have been away there has been much talk. They think you cannot be turned, that you will go on till they all die."

"Are there many who think that?"

"I should say most."

"Do they see that we always win? That we have the high favour of God, and many saints?"

"They count deaths. Every time we win; there are but fewer remaining alive. They say we have done enough both for God and Spain. We should go home with the spoil we have."

"You would not say that there are not many who are loyal to me?"

"There are many, but most of them think the same."

"And you also?"

"I suppose you know me better than that."

"Yes. I should not have asked. Well, I will give them something to do." He thought: "There will be no trouble when I have roused them with lofty words."

He went to look at the brigantines.

Men who turn audacious dreams into incredible fact are not careless in the details of what they do.

Cortéz had a sleepless imagination that explored possibilities, either to embrace or avert. But he had not thought of the danger of being assassinated by one of his own men, of whom he would have said confidently that, though they might curse or abuse, as soldiers will, there were very few who were not loyal at heart to him, as he was to them.

Yet, when he reflected upon it, he could see that it was the one way out—and the only one—for any who felt that he was now being driven to certain death, with the prospect that it might be of a particularly repulsive kind.

Even timidity might think it to be the less dangerous course. And, if he were dead—suppose it were not by a comrade's knife— suppose he had been dragged away at Xochimilco during the last week—and the men met, and, ignoring his nomination, elected their own leader, might they not vote for, and constrain him, to take them home? Or, if they should accept his nomination, might they not make it a condition that that should be done?

He did not think that all were of so faint a heart that they would not be willing to go on. He had a confidence in those whom he had made his closest comrades. Even Olid, who might have no love for him, had a stubborn fibre which would not be pliant to fainthearted arguments. Yet he was not sure that any of them would obtain general support for continuation of a campaign which had the conquest of a continent for its goal. Was it really so wild a dream?

He could not deny that it would seem so to many minds. But, to him, the question simply did not arise. It was God's matter rather than his, and one with which God would surely be able to deal. He had to deal with each danger, to overcome each difficulty, as it arose. It would be faithless to look beyond that. But this idea of assassination had been a serious one to both Ávila and Sandoval— fundamentally different men. He would be failing in his duty if he did not take precautions, having been warned. There was that shirt of Milan mail, which he seldom wore because it was rather tight in more places than one.

With these thoughts in his mind, he paused a moment to watch a man who was inserting a bolt where it might do little good, but where its absence would have occasioned remark. Such things were being done now—the last touches before the whole fleet would be warped down to the lake.

The man said, in a low voice, and without raising eyes from his work: "Excellency, if I come to you at the noon hour, can I be admitted without demur, and see you alone, it being told to none that I come, or I might not be there, for it is a matter of life and death."

Cortéz asked: "Meaning mine or yours?" And was sorry next moment that it had been said, seeing fear in the man's eyes, and not knowing how much of warning he might have given. He added, in a different tone: "You do not talk as one who is scared by a small thing. Come at noon, and I may put you in better heart."

When noon was near, he called Bernal Díaz, and said to him: "There will be a man enquiring for me who is small and dark, and somewhat marked with the pox. Also, he is short of the lobe of his right ear. Watch for him, and lead him to me, I shall be alone."

He thought it likely that the man had some petty grievance to bring before him: Some act of tyranny or injustice of which to complain, and that there was no more in it than that. He did not think that there would be any violence attempted against himself. A man would hardly make appointment for that! But he was prepared for whatever development there might be, and the fact that he decided to see him alone shows that he was aware of possibilities which he did not define.

Bernal brought the man in a casual way, and retired at once, having been roused to no curiosity by so small an event, and recognising him as one of little account, who was more use as fitter for Martín López than in the vanguard of war.

Cortéz sat at the table which he had had made for his own use, and the man stood before him. He seemed reluctant to speak, twisting a soiled cap of padded cotton between his hands.

Cortéz looked at him with the friendly smile on which his leadership was so largely founded. He did not know the name of every Spaniard he led, but it was not often he failed to give men a sense of intimacy—of being comrades in a great cause. Now he said: "Well, Guiseppe, what is it you want to say?"

"If I tell you that your life is not safe, shall you blame me for that?"

Cortéz showed no sign of his thoughts. He answered, as though unsurprised: "No. I am not so foolish as that. But my life is never safe. Tell me of the danger that threatens now."

"It is Villafana," Guiseppe said. "They plot to kill you tomorrow, when you are together at meat."

"Why should Villafana wish to do that?"

"We were afraid that you would lead us to death, and that we could save our lives in no other way."

Cortéz gave no sign that he noticed the intruding plurals, expressed or implied, in these answers. He asked: "Who is with Villafana in this?"

"There are many."

"How many is that?"

"I do not know. But there is a paper on which it is written out."

Cortéz knew that conspirators do sometimes hang themselves, or each other, through the folly of written words, yet it still had an improbable sound. He asked quietly: "Why should he do that?"

"There is the name of the office that each will hold."

"Of which one is yours?"

"No. They would say that I am not fit. Those who have no other reward are to have three ounces of gold; but it is to escape death that men agree, not for the gold."

"Who besides myself are to be killed?"

The man gave names. Eleven in all. Cortéz heard those of his principal officers with the satisfaction of knowing that they could not be involved. He asked: "Does Villafana think to take command? Could he sail to a Spanish port where he would not hang?"

"Señor Verdigo is to be asked to take the command."

"To which he assents?"

"He is not to know until—until you will all be dead."

Cortéz saw that the plot had been shrewdly planned, which Guiseppe could not be likely to have invented. Francisco Verdigo was an officer of some ability, and a near relative of the Governor of Cuba. He was not one who would be likely to be engaged in such a conspiracy himself. But, if he were invited to take control when all the present leaders were dead, he might consent, and, if he should return to Cuba with a great spoil, and a tale of how Cortéz had been assassinated because he would otherwise have brought all to ruin— well, it was that which Velásquez would be pleased to believe. It might easily win pardon for all, if Verdigo, innocent himself, should undertake its defence.

He said: "You will remain here for a short time. You have nothing to fear. You have done rightly to come to me."

He went out, and summoned Alvarado, Olid, Ávila, Diego and one or two more, to whom Guiseppe repeated his tale.

Cortéz gave no time for its discussion. He thought action could not be too speedy for the safety of threatened men, and he looked, as his way was, even further than that.

He said: "I think we should hear what Villafana may have to say. Olid, you bring four of the guard; they should be enough."

They went together to where Villafana was lodged in a first-floor room. They entered without ceremony, and found him sitting with four companions. They saw five frightened men, one of whom fingered a sword, which he did not draw.

Cortéz said courteously: "I have a word to speak to Señor Villafana alone. Gentlemen, will you retire?"

The four rose at once. They had the aspect of men who had heard something they did not expect, and were glad to go.

Cortéz said: "I do not ask you to confess. You may have a priest, if you will."

Villafana made a sudden movement, cramming a paper into his mouth. Cortéz leapt at him. There was a moment's struggle, and the paper was in his own pouch.

The sudden flurry had roused Cortéz's companions to his assistance. Villafana was now held beyond possibility of escape.

Cortéz said: "Find a cord. I need a noose for his neck." He said to him: "I do not wish you to speak, either to accuse others or to defend yourself. If you remain silent, you may have time to confess, for which a priest will be fetched. If you speak, you will hang at once."

The man made no answer, and Cortéz sent to Father Diego to confess one who was about to die.

An hour later, those who passed could see him hanging from the window of his own room, at which some wondered, and some feared.

Cortéz retired to his own room. He denied himself to all but Marina. He paced restlessly in a great doubt. At times his hand went to his doublet, where the list lay, and was then withdrawn.

He had not read it, but he had seen several of the names at the top. They were men he had trusted, men he could not spare. Yet they were of those who had agreed to his murder, and that of the officers who were closest to him, whose places they had conspired to take.

Beyond that, it had been evident that it was a long list.

At last, he went out. He sought Alvarado, to whom he said: "You will give orders that all Spaniards are to assemble at dawn in the central square. None is to be excused except he have explicit orders from you, for duties which cannot be put aside. I shall have that to say which all men should hear."

He retired again, and was still vexed between desire to know, and thoughts of a better kind.

Then Marina said: "You will have no sleep if you fret thus. I cannot read Spanish words. Give it to me. You will sleep when you know that it is destroyed."

"It is good counsel," he said, and drew out the list, which he gave to her with averted eyes.

She took it away, and returned in a short time. "It is gone," she said, "where it will not be seen again."

After that, he slept well.

CHAPTER NINETY-FOUR: NO CAUSE FOR FEAR

The army assembled at dawn, with secret terror in many minds. Few, even of the conspirators, knew more than that the body of Villafana swung on a short rope above those who passed in a busy street. But this had been enough to turn to more personal considerations the thoughts of those who had pledged themselves to assist in the assassinations which were to take place at the time of the midday meal. Beyond these, there were more than two score who knew that their names were on a list which had been—but where was it now?

Cortéz looked round on silent ranks, and was careful that his glance should not rest on any in what might seem to the guilty to be a significant way. He said: "Comrades, there must be few here who do not know that Villafana is dead. He was hanged because he had lost his faith. He forgot God. He thought him to be unequal for our support, though we trust in Him. Well, you see God's answer to that, as I suppose that he knows it now. I will say no more about him. I must talk to you about greater things. I will say no more except this. He had accomplices. That we know. But we do not know who they were, He made no confession to me. You may say that he was too quickly hanged. But I will say this. If any man have a grievance against me, or against the service to God and Spain which I require him to do, let him step forward now, and say what it is, and I will be patient in my reply."

He paused, as though waiting for such protests to be made, though it had become an unlikely thing, for to speak in that way now would be to suggest sympathy with those who had plotted his death. There was silence for a long moment, and then someone cheered, and in an instant he was joined by others, and then by all, in a deafening volume of sound, that rose again and again, as though reluctant to die, and in which those may have been loudest whose names were on the list that Marina had been unable to read.

When it died at last, he went on: "We are assembled now, for the last time, until we unite in triumph within the citadel of our conquered foes, as I doubt not that it is the divine purpose that we shall do. In two days from now, you will march out for the siege of México, which we shall encompass both by water and land. Already our foes must have become aware of the great armies that are moving to our support, so that there is nothing revealed to them when I tell you that fifty thousand Tlascalans are crossing the mountains now.

"Tomorrow, we launch our fleet; and we march ourselves on the next day. If there be any here who is faint of heart, let him step forward now, and he shall be returned by the next convoy to the coast, and put on the next ship that shall sail for a safer land."

There was no response to this offer, which also might seem to be of a dubious safety, for, if one should step forward now, might it not be held for evidence that he had given Villafana support? And, when no one did, were they not committed in honour and reason to go forward together in loyal comradeship and obedience?

Cortéz watched the motionless ranks of the men on whom he depended, both for loyalty and stoutness of heart, and was well content.

But when he sat with Ávila at a later hour, he had another trouble with which to deal. The ships, which were ready now, were to be launched on the next day, and they must have crews.

Ávila had a list of seamen who were willing to work the ships, and they were not half enough.

He had another list of men who were, he thought, suitable for such work, which most of them had refused to do. In some cases there was no doubt of their capacity, or of the fact that they had done such work at previous times, but there was a distinction that must be drawn.

A large proportion of the men who followed the banner of Cortéz were esteemed to be of gentle birth in their own land. Many were of substance, and had a financial stake in the expedition. More were the younger sons of noble families, who had their own fortunes to make. Many were gentlemen—hidalgos—by legal status, having the rights, and being bound by the customs, appertaining thereto.

A hidalgo might act as a captain of his own ship. He might, without disparagement, hire himself as captain of a ship that he did not own. But he was not expected to soil his hands, or the gay clothes he would wear. In times of peril or stress he might, in fact, do what occasion required, as many had on the ships that had come from St. Domingo or St. Jago to Vera Cruz; but there was a vital difference between doing such things at a time of need, and taking them as an obligation of service.

Was a hidalgo of Spain to put himself in such a position that men could jest subsequently: "Did you say he was a companion of Cortéz? That he was one of that band of gentlemen-adventurers through whom México fell? Well, he heaved anchors, he hoisted sails, he scrubbed decks, he was a sailor on one of the brigantines."

It seemed that there were many whom Ávila had thought suitable—some perhaps on no better argument than that they had come from a coastal town—who had been emphatic in calling the proposal an insult they would not endure. He mentioned Sedeño, whose grain ship Cortéz had seized and then bought when he had sailed from St. Jago in haste, without taking in sufficient supplies. Sedeño had joined the expedition through Cortéz's persuasive words, and had been a quiet, efficient, uncomplaining man, doing his part without pushing to the front, or falling behind the rear. He had said, with such an oath as had not been heard from him before, that he would not do such work to save Ávila from the damnation of hell.

Cortéz said: "Should he not have been one of the captains, having been one before?"

But it appeared that, though there must be thirteen captains for the little ships, there were still more—more than twice the number—who competed for those positions. They had been filled before the question of Sedeño had arisen. Could one of them be asked to give way to him? Ávila thought not, and Cortéz agreed.

He said: "I will talk to him myself." He thought that he might agree to act as mate, with a promise of the first captaincy that should fall vacant. But that was not certain, and to how many could he offer such bait as that?

He sent a messenger to bring Sedeño to him, and the man came back with a tale that was disconcerting to hear. He could not contact him because he was at a meeting which was being held in a building which had been barred from within. He had learnt nothing of its purpose, but had been told that it had been convened by Quinones and Xamarillo, and that there were a large number—certainly more than a hundred—attending it. They were mainly the artillerymen, the crossbowmen, and arquebusiers: those who were entitled to more than a swordsman's pay.

Cortéz frowned at this news. He saw that it might mean one of two things, each of which would be serious, though in opposite ways. It might be that discontent was not stilled. Men who might not (though they might) have been parties to a plan for his own murder, might yet be unwilling to follow him further in the wild adventure that he proposed. He knew that the losses of the last three weeks had been relatively heavier than he had experienced before, even apart from the disastrous horror of the six who had been captured alive. It could be asserted, with arithmetical logic, that such losses would destroy them all while many Aztecs would remain. And there was something else he should not forget. The artillery men had been in a mood of bitter protest ever since he had ordered that each brigantine was to have a falconet mounted upon its poop; for many of them must lose their occupations thereby.

But the meeting might not be occasioned by cowardice or discontent. It might mean that there was a determination that those who had conspired with Villafana should not escape. And to reopen that, with the certainty that trials and executions must follow, would be an ill of another kind, and perhaps worse.

Would that create the atmosphere in which such a venture should be begun? Would it be a good tale for the Tlascalans to hear?

He said: "I will go myself. They will not deny entrance to me."

Ávila said: "Are you sure? Would it not be well to know more?" He was one who thought that, when in doubt, there is prudence in sitting still.

Cortéz said: "Pedro may know what it means. He should have been here before now." And, as he spoke, Alvarado entered the room.

He heard the tale, but was not greatly impressed, though it had been kept from him till then. He said: "Quinones and Xamarillo are men to trust. I should wait and see."

Cortéz allowed that they were men he trusted—or would have done twenty-four hours before.

Alvarado added: "Quinones is one whom it would be foolish to doubt, and for Xamarillo—well, you could ask Marina's opinion of him."

It was said as a jest, but Cortéz was not sure how it was meant, which he did not like. He said: "So I will."

Marina was near at call. He told her of the meeting behind closed doors, and by whom it had been convened. He said: "We all know these men, or we thought we did. Can you guess what they are doing now?"

"No," she said. "You should do that better than I. But Juan will do nothing faithless to you. He would know I should not be pleased."

To her mind, it was simple as that.

Without knowing why he so resolved, Cortéz determined, as he heard her reply, that he would have patience to learn what it might mean, and he was confirmed in the wisdom of this when she added: "But I can tell you one thing. Bernal is there. You can judge something from that."

Actually, he would not have arrived before the meeting was broken up, for it was no more than a few minutes later that Quinones and Xamarillo were at the door. They said they had been deputed to put a proposal before him.

He asked: "Would you see me alone?" He thought there might be wisdom in that.

Quinones smiled. "No. We have nothing private to say. We have that to ask that we beg you not to refuse, lest we end in a common wreck. We wish to form a guard whose use will be to shield you both in battle and from the danger of private foes."

Cortéz asked: "Am I so weak that I need that? Have I been insufficient to this hour for my own defence?"

"We thank the Virgin and all saints that you still live. But you take risks by which you tempt the mercy of God, and which, if I may say it without offence, are treason to us. We are in this venture because we have faith in you. Are we to have faith at last in no more than a dead man?"

"I have not been careless to guard my life."

"Should you say that of your peril in México's streets? Or when you rode back to Alvarado's rescue, when León and Morla died? Or when you rescued Duero? Or at Xochimilco, a few days ago? And now it seems that there may be private perils with which to deal."

"You will consider that there is already a guard, which is Olid's rule."

"But we would that you should have one of a more personal kind."

"You put it so that I cannot lightly refuse."

Alvarado said: "It is what all will approve."

And on that it was agreed that there should be eight men appointed to guard him both by night and day, and that Quinones and Xamarillo, one or other, should always be in control. Which was somewhat modified at a later hour, when it was found that Ávila had put Xamarillo down for the command of one of the brigantines, which he was unwilling to change, Xamarillo having been a ship's captain before.

CHAPTER NINETY-FIVE: DISPOSITIONS FOR SIEGE

The canal had been a great work, which few Tezcucans except Ixtlilxochitl would have undertaken, and carried through. For many weeks it had been the toil of eight thousand men. It was thirty feet wide, and twelve deep. It had been found necessary to construct locks at three points. It was barricaded for all its length.

The brigantines were two-masted vessels, as their name implies, with a foremast square-rigged, and a mainmast rigged fore-and-aft. They were of shallow draught, as the depth of the lake required, and of such size as would just allow of their passage down the canal, taking crews and stores on board when they had been warped down to the lake. They were fully decked, and each had a swivel-mounted falconet on the poop.

When at last they were launched, and their sails spread, it was found that twelve of them were all that their builders had hoped. But the last, for which materials had been scant and bad, was slower in movement, and very sluggish to answer its helm. A sailing fleet, which must move, at the best, at the wind's will, should be made to dance alike to one tune. It was sent back to the dock. But the twelve were thought to be of a strength with which no canoes could contend. They should control the lake, or, at least, the portion of it, from causeway to causeway, in which they lay.

Besides that, they were the justification of one of the most audacious conceptions which even the mind of Cortéz had ever had, one which must have been ridiculed as absurdity had it failed, but which had now become an evidence both of the height of militant civilisation against which the Aztecs must contend, and of the implacable purpose that was driving the Spaniards on.

From the high platform of the great temple pyramid, Guatemozín and Coanaca, standing side by side, watched the ships, one by one, emerge from the canal. They saw their sails rise. They saw them manoeuvre, swanlike in the bright sunshine of an April day. Guatemozín said: "I will have the six Spaniards slaughtered here at tomorrow noon, where all men may see the fate of those who provoke our gods. They shall be quartered, that a Spaniard's limb may be sent to twenty-four temples throughout the land."

Meanwhile Cortéz watched the little fleet as emulous captains steered new commands into their appointed places, in a line that now tacked or wore against a westerly breeze, gaining the coherence on which the fighting value of a fleet of sail so largely depends.

They had been his companion, even at the dawn that had followed the Night of Sorrow, when all others would have said that there had been final defeat, and they would do well to escape with their own lives from the countless exulting foe. Was it not then that his first question to Bernal had been: "Does Martín live?"

Now he did not boast of his own design. He gave Martín López the praise. And it was surely his due. To build such boats from the residue of much larger vessels, without other metal or cordage, and by the hands of unpractised men, was a feat which few would have essayed, and still fewer would have brought to success.

He gave Martín the praise. But, as he did so, it was transferred to a Higher Power. For one who saw that triumphant sight burst into song, and next moment *Te Deum laudamus* rose from five hundred throats, and was carried across the lake to the ears of the watching

Emperor, and to those of the captured Spaniards who, stripped already of their clothes, like six beasts in a pen, the mockery of those who threw food on a filthy floor, were to be slaughtered on the next day. And next moment the chant was taken up by one of the doomed men, whose spirit refused to die, and his example inspired his comrades to the same height. It came to the ears of astonished priests, whose bitter hatred was disturbed by a pulse of fear.

Leaving the crowd of watchers upon the shore, Cortéz had hurried back to Tezcuco to deal with the endless detail which must be resolved if he were to march on the next day.

He found Ávila busily occupied with dispositions which only awaited his approval before the necessary orders would be issued, and Marina with him, her paintbrush ready for the production of written orders to their allies.

He said to Ávila first: "I have silenced the discontent among those who are on the ships by an order which we must have publicly displayed. It is that aboard each vessel there will be twenty-five men, of whom, under their captain, there will be twelve who work them, and be of their rank ashore. The second twelve will be for fighting the vessels, or for landing parties at need. Every seven days they will be reversed, so that it can be said of none that he was with me here as less than a fighting man."

Ávila said: "It was shrewdly thought." He picked up a quill, to give wording of a good sound, at which he excelled. But Cortéz said: "That can wait. Bernal tells me that the sound horses are eighty-seven. We shall march in three separate ways. You will allot twenty cavaliers to each array, and there will be nine horses for each, beyond that, for the officers' use, or for any purpose for which they may be needed at sudden call. They will not be used for burden of spoil. You will make clear order on that. It is for warfare their use must be. To what does the powder amount?"

"There is half a ton."

"It must be portioned and used with care. The three heavy guns must be one for each. And what of the falconets remain will be fairly shared."

They went on into detailed calculations of available men and equipment, providing for the safety of Tezcuco, and the equipment of three armies which were to assault the Aztec capital from different points.

The defence of Tezcuco, as the base from which the fleet would operate, and where the women, the sick, the wounded, and much treasure and equipment must remain, was to be entrusted to Ixtlilxochitl, with his Tezcucan levies. Besides them, the three hundred Spaniards allotted to work and fight the fleet would be available for support.

"I," Cortéz said, "Shall command the ships, though there may be times when I shall be absent at other posts. Alvarado will occupy Tacuba. Olid will operate from Cojohuacan; Sandoval from Chalco. The Tlascalans will be divided equally between Pedro and Christóval—twenty-five thousand to each. Gonzalo must rely upon the levies from the other nations, who are ordered to Chalco direct. I hope that they may be as numerous and as good. You will be in charge here, when I am away. Diego will be with me."

He went on to make exact appointment of his slender Spanish resources, which could be no more than spearheads to the native armies which were being assembled, in the new confidence which his presence gave, to challenge the Aztec tyranny.

After deducting the three hundred men that the fleet required, and allowing for the twenty cavaliers which each of the three armies would have, there remained about five hundred in sufficiently robust condition to take the field. These included one hundred and eighteen arquebusiers and crossbowmen, who, with the remaining spearmen, were divided into three equal divisions, so that each army—if it could reasonably be dignified by the name—would consist of about one hundred and ninety Spaniards.

CHAPTER NINETY-SIX: THE LAST TLASCALAN

Next morning the Tlascalans arrived—fifty thousand under the joint commands of Xicotencatl and Chichemecatl—the general who had been easily willing to take affront from Sandoval when he had been bringing the brigantines from Tlascala.

After being welcomed and reviewed, they were ordered to march ahead round the southern shore of the lake, to be followed by the Spaniards on the next day. They left with flaunting feathers and beating drums, under the banner of the wide-winged eagle by which Tlascala defied her foes.

Watching the dense ranks, and observing their buoyant mien, Cortéz could feel a natural confidence in the great enterprise to which he had set his hand. He who had fled on the Night of Sorrow, with the loss of artillery and baggage, and a large proportion of the army he then controlled, had come back in another guise—and the final laughter might yet be his.

The flower-pelted Tlascalans went, and the Spaniards, few in numbers, but terrible in what they were—they who were sheathed in steel, who controlled great beasts, who could command the lightning like a tame dog, and who were feared most of all for the omnipotence of their foreign God—prepared to leave at the next noon; but it was an hour before that when Marina sought the Spanish Commander, and said: "Hernán, I must speak to you apart."

"Is it urgent?" He asked, with more impatience than he would often show to her. "I am busy with matters that will not wait."

"Should I have asked, if it were not?"

"Will you let it stand till they have left? You know that I shall not ride today?"

"As you will. But I will tell you this. Xicotencatl has gone home."

Cortéz stared at her with uncomprehending eyes. "Gone home?" He asked. "Where? Do you mean he has returned to Tlascala? And Why?"

"It is not a short tale."

"And how has it come to you?"

"From Louise."

He was already walking beside her to their private rooms as these words were exchanged. His first thought was that the two Tlascalan generals had quarrelled, which would not occasion surprise, for it had been seen that Chichemecatl was a quarrelsome man. Perhaps it had been imprudent to let them march away together, but it would only have been one day before they would have reached Tacuba, and parted there. Surely, for one day!

But it was not that at all.

"It began with something that happened here yesterday," Marina said. "There was a quarrel between one of our soldiers, and a Tlascalan officer, who is cousin to Xicotencatl, and the Tlascalan was badly hurt."

"But I had given orders—! What was the quarrel about?"

"I know nothing of that. Alvarado knew. He told all to Louise, but it was not then expected to lead to this. Alvarado thought you must hang the man, if you should know, after what you had sworn, which he did not wish."

"Alvarado should leave such matters to me. And it is because of this that Xicotencatl has gone home?"

"I should not say that it is as simple as that. Louise says, that by his own will, he had never come."

"Had you her leave to say this to me?"

"She would not have said that which she would keep from your ears. But she wished you to know. She fears that he may lead the way to his own death. I have promised that you will send such as may prevail on him to return."

"I must know more. Can you get Louise now?"

"She is waiting near."

When she came, Cortéz said: "You have done well to let me know this, of which I might have heard in a worse way. Why has he gone?"

"I suppose it is true that he was annoyed at his cousin's wound, and that he who (as he thought) had been in the wrong should go free. But it is also true that he came with an ill will."

"Are there many who have gone back with him?"

"As I have the tale, his own regiment, and certain officers (it may be no more than a score or at most two) who are friends to him. I should guess that they are not more than a thousand in all. But there may be others who are more fully informed."

"Will you say why you tell me this?"

"Could it be hid? I would have effort made to persuade him to better ways."

"You can paint letters?"

It was a question to her as though he had asked a Spanish lady if she could read, but she answered with the impassive gravity of her race: "Yes. I can do that."

"Then will you send him that to which he may give more heed, coming from you, than if it were from one less closely akin, and Marina shall write for me. You must have it ready in the next hour, for the sooner it be in his hand, the less folly he may have done."

Louise answered: "So it shall be." She added: "You are kind," including both Cortéz and Marina in a glance of gratitude which restrained tears. She turned to go, and then paused irresolutely.

Marina said: "You were wise to speak."

Louise asked: "It will be without flaunt of force?" It was said in the Tlascalan tongue, and Marina translated its meaning, as she was practised to do.

"She thinks that he may be more likely to change his will if it be asked in a quiet way."

"She asks much. But it is how I mean it to be."

Louise went, and Marina sat down to paint the letter which would be dictated to her.

Cortéz asked: "If a general desert his army in the field, what is the penalty in your land, or in Tlascala, if you know that?"

Marina looked her surprise. Could there be question of that? "It is death, of course. It is treason of the worst kind."

"So that he cannot expect to come free, unless he can persuade Tlascala to break with us?"

"It is how it looks."

Marina sat before the stretched cloth, with the paintbrushes at her hand, but he was slow to begin. He said at last: "We must keep faith with Louise."

"So I knew you would."

But he was still slow to dictate. He remembered how fiercely Xicotencatl had opposed his first entry into Tlascala. How he had resisted those who would have made peace. How he had kept back his country's envoys, while he had sent spies into the Spanish camp. After that, he had appeared to give frank acceptance to a position he could not control. But he had probably still kept the doubt in his heart.

As to which, could it be said that he was wrong? If he differed from the other rulers of his nation, might it not be that he saw farther than they?

Now he might think that the blood of his nation would be shed to overthrow their traditional foes, which had a good sound; but, if they should succeed in that, would they not find that they had exchanged enemies which had been hard to resist for that which there would be no hope to resist at all?

If he felt so, it would be hard to say he was wrong, even though Cortéz knew that any bargain he made would be fairly kept, so long and so far as it should continue to be in his power—and even in that, there was the qualification that he was resolved to establish the Christian Faith.

Looking at it fairly, he did not greatly blame, but that generosity did not disguise fact. Tlascala was at war with the Aztecs by its government's decision, and in alliance with him. There could be no justification for one of its generals to act in a contrary spirit, persuading comrades to leave the field.

There was another aspect of this matter. Having gone so far, must he not try to go farther? And Xicotencatl was very popular, especially among the Otombis, and those of his own house. And where would the Spaniards be now, if they should suddenly lose those who had been their most loyal and most potent allies? If two of his armies should each suddenly decline from just less than twenty-six thousand, to less than a thousand men?

"Well," he said, "Louise may be right that we should be wise to coo. But it will not be done twice. And I must be plain as to the peril in which he stands, lest he have cause for complaint on a later day. You shall write this:

"I am told that you have left your command, and withdrawn men from the field, which is hard to believe; but if you, or your kinsmen, have been abused, it was without knowledge of mine. If you will now return your men to Tacuba, where they should be, and come to Tezcuco yourself, there shall be justice done, and no word said of what may have been too hastily thought. And I offer much when I say this, for treason is that for which there is but one penalty known. It is what I could not offer a second time, and I do it now because you are one whom I have considered a gallant friend."

He watched Marina, now using her brushes with practised speed, and asked: "So you like that?"

"It has a good end."

"You would say that is all?"

"I do not say you could write in another way. But it will not avail."

"You are sure of that?"

"Louise's may."

"So we must hope. For the ground sways where we thought it firm."

Within the hour the two letters were despatched by ordinary runners, which was certainly the speediest and may have been the most diplomatic method.

At a later hour, there came a letter from Alvarado, reporting the defection of the Tlascalan general, on receipt of which Cortéz despatched a deputation with instructions (unless they should find him to be already returning to his duty) to repeat the offer of amnesty which he would have received previously in a more picturesque form. They were to warn him, as a final effort, that his action was one of treason both to his own countrymen and the Spanish King, and that he must be prepared to meet the consequences of what he did.

They had not returned when there was a further disquieting report from Tacuba. There had been a quarrel between Alvarado's and Olid's men regarding the quarters which they should occupy, which had been referred to the two commanders for decision. But that had only raised the level of the dispute. Each had taken the side of his own men. Angry words had been followed by the drawing of swords, and a violent duel had been prevented only by the interposition of their inferior officers.

"Are we," Cortéz said bitterly, "to be ruined by our own folly? Doing to ourselves that which the Aztecs would find too hard?"

He sent letters of cold rebuke, and the same wording, to the two officers, with instructions that Olid was not to go forward immediately, but that their combined forces should attack the northern causeway.

It had not been his original plan, and it may not have been wise in itself, but there was the overriding consideration that the Tlascalan army should be committed to action before the defection of Xicotencatl could have done further mischief. Suppose that he should prevail upon the Tlascalan Senate to recall them, and make peace with México, for which they could scarcely hope for a more favourable time?

The quarrel which might have had disastrous consequences arose from the order in which the troops had arrived at Tacuba. First there had been nearly fifty thousand Tlascalans, who had naturally taken for themselves the most convenient camping-ground. Next, and slightly in advance of Alvarado's column, there had been that of Olid, which was to continue its march on the next day. It accommodated itself in remaining buildings to which the troops of Alvarado considered that, as they were to be permanently there, they should have had the first claim. But the dispute would have been easily adjusted or overruled by sympathetic commanders. The real trouble was in the arrogance of Alvarado, and the sullen jealousy of Olid, who thought, not without a partial justification, that less capable men were frequently preferred to himself. It was his disadvantage that, though he was expert in military science, a most capable cavalier, and cool when moments of crisis came, he was not one whom it was easy to like or trust.

Having disposed of this annoyance, Cortéz had not long to wait before the deputation returned. It had been composed of Spaniards, Tlascalans, and Tezcucans, partly to approach Xicotencatl from every angle, and partly to overcome the language difficulty, Cortéz having been unwilling to allow Marina to leave him on so uncertain a mission.

Now they came back to report an absolute failure. They had been met with confident assertion of the wisdom of the course he had taken and assurance of the support he would receive. He was now back in his own province of Titcala, and preparing to urge his view upon the Senate at Tlascala. Contemning the Spanish members of the delegation, or relying upon their inability to understand what was said in the Tlascalan tongue, he had urged their colleagues to abandon their alliance, and join the Aztecs for the destruction of the invaders.

"Diego," Cortéz said, when he heard this, "I have done all I could to save him from himself, and to avert a danger that we must face. It is he or we. You will ride in the next hour, with every horse that is still here—it should be thirty in all—and bring him in, dead or alive. And if he be alive, as I should prefer, he will hang in the next hour. Marina, you will tell Louise that I have done the utmost I could, he being father to her."

Marina said: "You have done too much. She will see that."

Had he done too much? Had he delayed till too late an hour? It would soon be known.

Cortéz turned next to Marina, for her brushes to give further aid. She could write to the Senate at Tlascala in a way that they could best understand. He dictated:

"He is traitor to you and me. He seeks to throw us down, which would bring the Aztecs about your gates in the next hour. I have no quarrel with you. You have kept faith. So will I. But he shall hang on a gallows I build here, relieving you from that which you might be reluctant to do."

Cortéz looked at the letter before it went. He had said much to her, and it seemed short. Marina explained that what was a sentence in words could often be expressed by a single symbol. It was a much simpler method than writing words, and one by which meanings could be more exactly conveyed.

He found it hard to believe that. He said: "So it may seem to you. But there must be much in the written word which you have no symbol to match."

So it may have been, and it is now beyond proof, for the Spaniards in later years were to demonstrate their barbarism by destroying such writings in a huge bonfire that would blacken the skies over Tezcuco square. But she may not have been as far wrong as may be carelessly thought. She had been taught several thousands of arbitrary symbols, which were known to all educated people, and were readily memorised through association of ideas. And these could be varied in many ways. A parrot might mean a quarrel, or dissension of any kind. But there would be many variations. It might be red, green, yellow, or blue, its wings might be lifted or closed, its beak might be open or shut, it might be lying dead on its back. Anyone who could read would know at once what these differences, and a score of others, would mean. Marina learnt to write in the Spanish style, which she thought clumsy and dull. But Cortéz did not learn to write as she did, though it had the advantage of not being limited to a particular language, so that it was understood as far as civilisation extended in the New World. In fact, it was an art that no Spaniard would ever learn, which was no credit to them.

Ordaz was back on the next day. He brought his captive in a litter, shackled both hands and feet. A number of his adherents followed, loyalty leading them into a danger they might have missed.

Xicotencatl was brought before Cortéz. He may have been a frightened man, but anger was all he showed.

Cortéz saw how he was brought, and knew that one of the most perilous episodes of his life had been overcome. He looked on a man whom he had honestly tried to save, and who could never be trusted again.

Xicotencatl looked at him with defiant hatred, and said things which Marina did not translate. But she gave the words of Cortéz to him: "My lord says that the gallows wait. There is nothing that it would be useful for him to say."

So it did. Cortéz had had it erected before Ordaz returned. He had seen that the impression of what he did would be doubled if it were done as though it were doubtless to his own mind.

Those who had followed the Tlascalan warrior, regardless of their own risk, were allowed to go safely away. They begged for the garments of the dead man, which they were allowed to have, and they tore up to be cherished as sacred relics of one who had died for a land he loved. Patriot or traitor? He had been both. And they too often have the sound of a single word.

CHAPTER NINETY-SEVEN: THE FIRST ASSAULTS

From the deserted city of Tacuba, the combined armies of Alvarado and Olid attempted to force their way into México along the great dyke by which, on the Night of Sorrow, they had made their disastrous flight.

It should not have been attempted, and it failed, as it was certain to do.

It was true that their combined armies totalled more than fifty thousand men. But what gain was there in that? Their front could be no more than the dyke's breadth, and, so far as they might force their way along it, they would be subjected to attack from the water on both sides, from thousands of canoes which had been bulwarked to give protection to the archers they carried.

By stubborn valour the first gap in the causeway was won and bridged. Beyond that, time after time, advances were made and were driven back. The longer the advance, the more precarious would be the position that valour won. And the causeway was not easy to the horses, for most of its length, as it once had been. It was not a thoroughfare now, but gapped or barricaded with piles of stone at short intervals, for all the miles of its length.

Cursing Alvarado, to whom he erroneously attributed his detention to take part in that vain attempt, Olid moved on to his own station.

All of which report to Cortéz could boast was that the fresh water supply, which was carried in two-foot pipes by a narrow dyke, had been severed, so that all the drinking water the city would get from that day must be carried by canoes from a shore which would be patrolled by a watchful foe.

Meanwhile Cortéz, the moment that he was relieved of the fear of treachery from his essential allies, had ordered Sandoval to march southward, join the native levies which had been sustained to assemble at Chalco, and proceed from there to the attack of Iztepalapan, which was again occupied by an Aztec garrison.

He had planned to support this attack (the city being half on land, and half on piles in the lake) with the brigantines, and he carried out this plan to the extent of reaching the southern shore of the lake, where he landed at an isolated rock, which the Aztecs used as a signal beacon.

This he stormed, and destroyed the garrison, but astonished some Aztec women and children, whom he captured there, by telling them to go free.

From here he would have sailed on to Iztepalapan, but was withheld by the wind's caprice.

His sails hung idle in a still air, while he must watch the assembling of innumerable canoes converging upon him.

Their paddles paused while they were still out of range of his guns, either because they hesitated to attack, or were awaiting the coming of other boats, by which their strength was augmented continually.

Whether they would have attacked at last, had the calm continued, cannot be known, though the possibility of converging upon one end of the immobile fleet must have been apparent, but, as they appeared to have gained their maximum strength, a wind came from the land. It freshened even before the little fleet had taken sufficient advantage of it to range themselves with the breadth of front which their plan of battle required. It enabled them, when they had done this, to advance upon the canoes with a speed at which no desperation of paddle-plying would enable them to flee. They looked up to the white-winged monsters that swooped upon them, as sparrows beneath the remorseless talons of birds of prey. The sharp bows struck them, throwing them aside, swamped or overturned, or bearing them down to the drowning water beneath their keels.

Men struggled in water which was deeper here than at the northern end of the lake, and appealed for aid in vain to those whose first concern was for their own lives, which they were expecting to lose.

The twelve ships drove through the crowded fleet of canoes, augmenting terror and destruction by firing ahead and down upon the water beneath their sides.

When they had driven through the entire fleet, they put up their helms and turned into the chaos behind them, to ensure the destruction of any canoes which might have avoided the common fate.

It was an action that demonstrated the power of the brigantines beyond further challenge. It would have placed Cortéz in undisputed possession of the whole lake, but for the obstacles of the dykes.

The principal of these were the great southern dyke by which the Spaniards had first entered the city, which ran due north, being continued by the wide central avenue, and then, going straight ahead, there was the northern dyke by which they had fled on the Night of Sorrow.

In addition to these, there was a dyke which approached the southern dyke approximately at right-angles, and joined it about a mile and a half outside the city.

The point of junction was one of those places where the lake shallowed, and there had been a group of islets there, on which buildings had been erected, and then others on piles in the water between them, until a small town had developed, the inhabitants of which made an assured living by abstracting salt from the lake.

This place was called Xoloc. The point where the dykes met had been widened and strengthened with heavy gates, and two towers of a height that could not be easily stormed. Cortéz knew what degree of resistance they would be likely to make, having observed them with care when he had marched along the southern causeway on his first entrance to México, when the gates had been opened to let him through, and the causeway beyond had been crowded by Aztec nobles who received him with obeisance and flowers.

Now he thought to test its strength by landing from the brigantines on the causeway north of the towers, and so taking them in the rear.

He found them to be garrisoned, but not heavily. Being surrounded, and menaced by the artillery of the fleet, their resistance was short. They were glad to yield on terms which allowed them to continue to live.

With scarcely a wound to lick, he found himself in possession of this point of primary strategic importance, and swiftly revised his dispositions for attacking the city, which now appeared to be a prize which would not be difficult to secure.

He decided to make Xoloc his headquarters. It placed the southern end of the great dyke—more than half its length—securely in his possession. It gave him equal control of the western-side dyke which had its junction here.

He sent an order to Sandoval not to remain at Iztepalapan, but to continue along the lake shore until he came to Cojohuacan, which was at the landward end of the side dyke, and to occupy that position. He sent another to Olid, to continue his advance around the northern shore of the lake, and to come down its western side with half his force, and join his at Xoloc. With fifty of Sandoval's men added to these, and those who had been landed from the fleet, he felt that he would have a force strong enough to hold it against any attack. He landed some of the heavier guns from the fleet, and pointed them along the remaining length of the causeway, toward the city. Looking northward in the direction to which their muzzles were turned, and backward upon a lake which was scattered with the wreckage of the canoes, it was natural to feel that the great city was near to fall. Awaiting the arrival of the reinforcements he had ordered, he planned a simultaneous assault, both from north and south, and that Sandoval, with the remainder of his division, should join Alvarado for that purpose. By these successive dispositions, he contrived the separating of Alvarado and Olid, without reflection on either. Olid would be with himself. Sandoval would not quarrel with Alvarado, and was the one whom he could trust, beyond any other, for the combination of valour and discretion which bring such enterprises to a good end.

Within a week, these preparations were complete, and the assault was made.

CHAPTER NINETY-EIGHT: INCURSION

Cortéz said: "We must leave the horses. The causeway is too barricaded, and the water too deep for us to ride through, as we did when we escaped on the northern side. But we will use the cannon to clear the way."

So it was tried, and the cannon blasts were of sufficient avail to clear the causeway as far as the next obstacle, but this was a wide gap with deep water therein, and beyond that, a wall of such solid stone that the battering did not greatly reduce its bulk.

When it was judged that the guns had done all they could (or that the expense of powder was beyond reason for what it did), Cortéz, with such cavaliers as had full body-armour advanced on foot, and were followed by other men.

The brigantines, luffing into a light wind, protected them on their right, but, on the western side, the Aztec canoes, having nothing to fear, were a nuisance hard to endure.

Seeing that this would be a continual menace, unless it were dealt with in the one effectual way, Cortéz halted the advance while a breach was made in the dyke, of sufficient depth for the two smallest brigantines to be warped through, at the sight of which the canoes fled in frantic haste for the safety of the city canals, where the water would be too shallow for pursuit.

Freed from this irritation, the operation of occupying the causeway proceeded with the inexorable repetition of a process to which the Aztecs could find no effectual reply.

The ships sailed past the barricaded gaps, using their guns the while, and landed men behind them. Those who held their ground were cut off, and could only escape final destruction by jumping into the lake—a method of retreat which was unattractive now that the canoes had been driven away.

The cavaliers, following their leader's example, then swam the gap and clambered up the undefended barricade.

After them, a numerous body of Tlascalans would hurl the stone of the barricade into the water, continuing this operation, if necessary, even to dislodging those of the causeway, until they had levelled a rough passage for the guns over the gap, and they would be dragged forward, for the next barrier to be attacked in the same way, to the same result.

So they won at last to the city itself, and halted again at the southern end of the Great Avenue, till the cannon could be brought up. Then they fought their way forward, where the barriers were not so strong nor the gaps so wide or so deep, but where they could have no further aid from the brigantines, and must endure the added danger of stones and other missiles descending upon them from the flat-roofed buildings on either side.

But these altered conditions were met by new tactics as effectual as those which had been used before.

A strong force of Tlascalans was ordered to fire the buildings on either side.

The cannon were brought up, and proved sufficient to breach barriers which were not of the solidity of those which had been erected upon the causeway.

The houses might be built of stone, but their appointments and furnishings were inflammable. Smoke rose from them, one by one, as the Tlascalans advanced, and their inhabitants fled.

Slowly but inexorably, hour by hour, filling up every chasm they crossed, the invaders advanced until they came to the central square, around the huge extent of which were grouped the great temple pyramid, the palace of Montezuma, and the older palace which had once been the prison from which they burst at so great a cost.

The Aztec army, retreating before the Spanish advance, and with a natural desire to avoid the direct line of the avenue which the cannon swept, were largely congregated in the square, and now withdrawing to the shelter of the side-streets, but some of them, actuated by desire to defend the most sacred place, or desiring the advantage its structure gave, were retiring to the temple pyramid, and Cortéz saw the opportunity which prompt action might bring to a good success.

He had not the advantage a saddle gives, but his lifted sword pointed to the temple gates, as his voice strove with the din: "Forward, comrades. Give them no time to array."

He ran forward, careless of who else might be quick to follow, but Quinones with his companions were now his unfailing guard. They were close around him as he reached the still-open gates, with the most part of the infantry at their heels.

The Aztecs were allowed no time to rally on the high platform. They were too closely pursued up the stairs that wound round the outside of the pyramid. The sight of that high-raised altar of sacrifice where their comrades had died roused the Spaniards to a merciless fury that gave no quarter to priest or warrior. Even Cortéz, cornering a priest whose garments were stained with what must surely have been the blood of his fellows, forgot the principle that he was constant to urge upon rougher men, and flung him screaming over the edge, his body bouncing from stair to stair, until it smashed upon the concrete pavement below.

A new effigy of the Aztec wargod was tumbled down, and plundered of jewels and golden mask in the sight of thousands of upward-gazing Aztecs, who were roused to fanatic fury by what they saw.

Cortéz, looking down, saw that a refluent tide of Aztec warriors was now sweeping across the square, by which the Tlascalans were borne back, if they did not flee.

He saw that the guns had now been brought up the Avenue, and were being swung round to command the square. But would there be time to bring them into operation before the tide of battle would overwhelm them? And could they be used earlier, while the square was crowded by a confusion of friends and foes?

"Comrades," he called, "Volante—Guzmán—blow the retreat." As the trumpet sounded, he was already descending the steps at a pace which others found hard to match.

As it was, they came out into the square amidst thronging foes—men who might be slighter than they, and inferior both in protective armour and offensive weapons, but who had become reckless of their own lives in fanatic hatred of these men who abused their gods. Careless of their own lives, they crowded upon them, so that the little company of Spaniards, struggling to retreat to the Avenue, sometimes lacked freedom to use their swords.

Holding together with the dreadful knowledge that to be separated was to be doomed to repulsive death, stabbing outward on every side to break the pressure of hateful foes, they were carried past the abandoned guns, to where there should have been safety in the Central Avenue amidst the denser Tlascalan ranks. But these ranks were already breaking before the Aztec ferocity. Where the Spaniards should have reached a place of safety, their coming, in obvious retreat, increased panic among wavering ranks.

But the threat of decisive retreat was gone when the noise of horses was heard, and Diego rode out from a side street at the head of the twenty cavaliers who had followed to take their part in the conflict as soon as the causeway had been rendered fit for them to traverse.

Their charge drove the Aztecs back sufficiently for their comrades to rally, and recover the abandoned guns. But Cortéz would risk no further advance. The sun was already low in the evening sky. If the first day's attack had enabled him to reach to the very heart of the city, how many more could it endure?

He rode back, well content; but even while he did so, Guatemozín was issuing orders to nullify during the night that which had been gained in the day.

The young Mexican Emperor had not taken up residence in Montezuma's palace. He had neither time nor present inclination for elaborate ceremonial, for exotic meals, for wives and jugglers, for changing raiment four times a day. Let such things wait till he had cleansed the land of the strange plague that had come from the Eastern Sea.

He was lodged in a house, spacious enough, in the northwest of the city, in its least vulnerable part, and he was saying there: "Men must not wait till the light return. They must clear the gap. They must build new barriers. They must restore all as before."

Knowing that his orders would be obeyed by ten thousand hands, he turned to discuss a plan to entice the brigantines to their own destruction. It was simple, but might avail.

CHAPTER NINETY-NINE: REPULSE

The following days brought access of strength to the Spaniards from several directions, and offers of surrender from cities which had previously been potential, if not actual foes. Levies also arrived which Ixtlilxochitl had raised in his more distant Tezcucan provinces, amounting to 50,000 men, who were distributed among the three armies. It was evident that, however it might be regarded in the Aztec capital, the penetration which had been made was regarded by those who watched as forecasting its fall.

Cortéz looked at it in that way, and sent an offer of merciful terms, if it would surrender, which received a derisive reply.

He then planned to make a further attack on the same lines as before, but with a corresponding advance from the northern side, and that these inroads should be continued, day by day, till the end should come.

So far, Alvarado had not made such spectacular progress as his Commander. Indeed, since his first disastrous attack upon the northern causeway, he had not advanced far enough even to make contact with its landward end. It would be suggested in later days that he had shown less energy than Cortéz in these attempts. But the comparison is unfair. Cortéz had the great advantage of having established himself at the causeway junction of Xoloc, and if it be said that Alvarado had seized no corresponding position, the reply is that there was no such position to seize.

Neither had he had the support of the brigantines.

He was confronted, or rather surrounded, by a very large Aztec army, which could either fall back into the open country, or retire into México City by the causeway which it protected.

Even Tacuba, though he had occupied it at times, he had found that he could not hold.

What he had been able to do was to keep his opponents fully occupied during the day that Cortéz raided the city, so that no succour had come from them.

Now, with augmented forces, he fought his way to the causeway's head, and succeeded in establishing himself there, so that the Aztec army with which he had to deal was divided into two portions, of which one retreated onto the dyke, with the city as its base, and the other was in the open country, with a rear which might either provide supplies and recruits, or from which further foes might appear—which had become approximately equal probabilities, now that the whole country was in a chaos of changing allegiances and confused policies which altered from day to day as men watched the conflict, and guessed what its end would be.

Now Alvarado must face both ways, prepared for attack on the landward side, which would be certain to come at the time which would be most unwelcome to him, and holding the head of the causeway against those who swarmed upon it, to block penetration into the city.

Regarding the causeway as of no more breadth than forty Spaniards should be able to maintain against sudden attack, he detailed a hundred and twenty for this purpose, divided into three companies, each of which undertook the duty of watchfulness for an eight-hour period, the others lying closely in reserve. It would have been a more pleasant duty had the weather been kind. But it was the season of rain, and winds were cold. It was especially miserable for those who must watch through the night, perhaps with the ache of a wound which had been taken before the bandage was off the last. For it was the method of Aztec fighting to give many wounds for one death.

Even the cavaliers, who had the protection of steel (against which must be set the fact that they were ever in the front rank) were continually nursing the wounds they took from arrows or hacking swords. It was last week that Sandoval had found it a labour to get to horse, owing to a wound in the thigh; and next week, when he would have orders from Cortéz to give Alvarado support, he would have three to urge, should he be of the disposition to make excuse.

On the day that Cortéz made his next attack on the city, Alvarado advanced along the northern causeway for all its length. He penetrated into the northeastern suburbs, and though he did not effect a junction with his comrades who came in from the south, he kept so large a portion of the Aztecs busy with bitter strife that he had no small part in the success, which he knew was won when he saw a great pillar of flame-lit smoke arise from the central square.

Cortéz had fought his way again to the city's heart, and had set fire to the old palace from which, a year before, in the short pause of unquiet peace, he and Montezuma had ruled the land.

He meant mercy in ordering that. He had sent another message to Guatemozín proposing peace, and had no reply. He said: "Must I lay the whole city flat before they will see the folly of what they do? Perhaps, if some of their public buildings go, they will understand that they have no strength to resist, and make terms before I have scorched them out of ten thousand homes."

He burnt more than that. The great aviaries which adjoined Montezuma's palace, being built entirely of wood, could be easily fired. The birds, a collection of many thousands from the limits of the known World of the West, were released. Condors, sea-eagles and hawks, soared with harsh screams into a sky where they were pursued by the rising smoke, while smaller birds, of the brilliance those countries bred, scattered over the lake, and found refuge in the wooded country beyond.

Thinking that this would be too plain a lesson to be disregarded, he ordered that Montezuma's palace should not be touched, and would have been content to withdraw as the day waned.

But these fresh evidences of inflexible will were not received in the mood he had hoped to see. Wild fury roused the Aztecs to such assaults as must be met with a firm front, and when, at last, as twilight neared, the trumpets sounded retreat, it must be with the Aztecs still worrying flank and rear.

In this conflict, Ixtlilxochitl was engaged with his Tezcucan levies, and was the target on which the Aztecs concentrated their most scurrilous abuse, and their lust to kill. It was a natural attitude toward one who, they considered, had put personal ambition before patriotism. But his reaction was no comfort to them. Derisive whistles were answered by his troops with others of like contempt. He himself led the charge which met the Aztecs in a fury equal to theirs. It was his sword which found their leader's throat, inflicting a fatal wound.

Cortéz wrote to Marina that night, in a script which she must spell out with care, or ask Father Olmedo's aid: "The palace burned, and it was a waste most hateful to see. But what can I do? It is as though the devil they worship has made them mad, and they will not stint till they are all dead, and the city a blackened ash. St. Pedro send us a better end!"

But, during the four days that followed, he must ask himself whether he had not been too sanguine when he had talked of a beaten foe.

It was not only that, so far as they must withdraw for safety during the night hours, the Aztecs were instant to pile barriers, and clear gaps anew; it was that there was now ceaseless, systematic attack upon his forces that protected the three causeways at their landward ends. At Tacuba, at Cojohuacan, at Iztepalapan, they would fight during long hours with Aztec armies, that suffered more than they could inflict, till it seemed that they could endure no more, which may have been true; but, when they withdrew, it was not to allow the victors a time of rest. Other banners would be seen to advance, other Aztec regiments would continue the relentless attack.

And meanwhile there was an incident on the lake which was hard to bear.

However bitter or indecisive the land fighting might continue to be, it seemed that mastery on the water was so complete that it could never be challenged again. And when Pedro Barba, the captain of one of the smaller brigantines, who, with a companion vessel, was patrolling the lake at dawn, to prevent food or water being smuggled into the city, saw four large canoes that were some distance out from the shore, he gave chase at once.

The canoes appeared to become aware of their danger at the same instant. Paddling frantically, they turned for the shore. Captain Barba put his helm over, and followed.

The light was bad. There was squally rain. The wind (which came in gusts) was from the southwest. The canoes might just escape. Or they might not.

The lake shallowed gradually. There were wide reedbeds into which the canoes might retire. Indeed, some could be seen hiding among them now.

Captain Barba did not fear them. Why should he? But he would run no risks. He sounded continually, the while he endeavoured to steer his ship between the canoes and the reeded shore. There was ten feet of water beneath him—much more than he drew—when his consort, which was a short distance behind, struck some underwater obstacle, and swung round, pounding against its side. As it did this, the boom of its for-and-aft mainsail swept across its deck, and it heeled over, out of control.

He heard shouts from the leaning deck. He saw men clambering to the shrouds. But then he lost sight and thought of what his consort's difficulties might be, for his own ship stuck an obstacle which it seemed to be dragging beneath its keel. Overhead, a spar snapped. There was the loud crack of a bursting sail. Then there was some other underwater obstacle jarring its starboard side.

He shouted orders for the anchor to be dropped—for sails to be taken in, and, as he did so, became aware that scores of canoes were paddling swiftly out of the reeds and converging upon him.

Seeing that, he called to the men who were about to cast the bower anchor over the side to let it be. He saw that, with twenty-one men aboard (which were all he had) both to work and to fight the ship, mobility was his one chance. He took the helm in his own hands.

Under persuasion of helm, and well-handled sails, the ship came clear of whatever gripped it below, just as the canoes were at its side. He rammed two. He put the ship before the wind, and ran on for half a cable's length, with no thought but to come clear of what he now saw to have been a well-baited trap.

So he might have done, had not his consort been in a worse plight than he, being tightly held, and having a smaller crew.

So he went to her aid, and was soon jammed again amidst piles that the Aztecs had driven deeply into the lake bottom (being work that they undertook well) and which rose near to the surface of the shallow flood.

There they lay, side by side, their two falconets, being all the guns they had, blazing from their poops, and every man, letting the ships fend for themselves, fighting to beat back the hordes of Aztecs who strove to board.

In the end, the smaller vessel suddenly came clear, a pile breaking beneath it, and it escaped with those who were then alive of its own crew, and seven from Captain Barba's ship who passed from deck to deck with a cable's aid. Besides that, there were two who swam underwater, and so escaped. But both captains were killed, and Barba was a loss to regret, for he had been captain of the crossbowmen before he had volunteered for a seaman's post, and he was one on whom his fellows had learnt to lean.

There were sixteen Spanish men lost (taking no count of wounds) by this sleight, and the brigantine which was caught was hauled ashore, and then burnt, the sight of which was cheering to Aztec hearts, and encouraged doubtful allies.

CHAPTER ONE HUNDRED: COUNSEL

Cortéz heard a plan that he was not sure that he liked, but which he would not lightly condemn, for there was reason in what was said.

Alderete, the Royal Treasurer, put it to him, and he was one who had not been slack in service, even when his office would have exempted him from the hazards and hardships of lesser men. He had a buoyant and chivalrous spirit which made pastime of the implications of war. And, besides this, there was an angle from which he could argue with a special right to be heard, and which was also one on which most men would be inclined to agree.

Cortéz said: "We will have Council on this," which would be likely to mean (as Alderete knew) that he would get his own way, even though he might seem to be overruled, and he had a doubt that it would not be his; but it was not a decision he could oppose.

Actually, Cortéz had a cautious rather than a resolved mind, and though he contrived (as his habit was) that some should be absent from the Council whose presence he did not desire, it was rather, in this instance, because he knew they would have opinions already fixed, or would have no wisdom to offer, than because they would oppose a decided way.

Alvarado would agree with Alderete before his argument could be fully said. Everyone would know that. Let him stay in command on the northern shore, from which he could not be spared. He would see the reason for that! But Sandoval, who would be equally audacious, but in the more cautious way that Cortéz approved, might have an opinion to offer which it would be prudent to hear, though he was the much younger man.

And Olid could come. His opinion would be as certain as that of Alvarado, and would be the same. But it was of small account, because no one would listen to him—indeed, there were those who would only require to hear him to take a contrary view. And he would be certain to sulk if he were not called, let the reason be what it might. And it was true that all the distant posts of hazard around the lake, liable to sudden attack, could not be left without men of valour and discretion in their control.

Cortéz had made his headquarters at this time in the guardroom at Xoloc, where the two causeways met. It was ill adapted for all his needs, but it was a post of advantage he would not lose. It gave him direct contact with the landward ends of the two dykes, while he was as near to Alvarado (by water) as it was possible for him to be.

It was in fact, a room that would hold thirty men (as it did); for the junction of the dykes was a wide well-fortified post, and even beyond that, where the single dyke ran on northward to the city, it was so broad that it had been possible to build huts on both sides, sufficient for the shelter of Cortéz's own Spaniards, and their women and attendants—more than two thousand in all.

This had been an essential provision, if the Spaniards were to remain in strength at the junction of the storm-beaten dykes during the season of rain, and it had given much-needed occupation to some of the huge native armies which had come to join what they now thought to be the winning side.

Cortéz estimated the total of these to be not less than one hundred and fifty thousand. They were difficult to control and supply. They were far more than could be effectually used against the lake-surrounded city. Many of them were ill-armed. Many were of dubious loyalty. Few would be willing to meet the Aztecs on equal terms, unless some Spaniards were in the van.

It was impossible to ascertain how the numbers of the Aztec armies compared. Probably they were more numerous. Most of the civil inhabitants of México had been evacuated, and it was now crowded with troops, who must be watered and fed by canoes that slipped hazardously across in the night. Other armies lay on the outside of the besiegers' camps, which centred round the causeway heads.

Cortéz, who was well aware of the difference between numbers and strength, would have been glad to select the better half of his supporting hordes, and to send the rest home; but suppose that should lead to discontents and desertion? Suppose that those he dismissed should be resentful, and go to strengthen his foes?

Now he looked round on thirty men each of whom had proved himself in the hard tests of preceding days. He saw men who were boldly expectant of hearing some final plan for the capture of the city, into the heart of which they had already raided successfully, and he had none to propose himself—at least, none of a spectacular kind. And they were to hear one which he did not like.

"Comrades," he said, "an operation has been proposed to me by which it is thought that resistance could be brought to a quick end. It is Señor Alderete's design, and you will agree that he is one whose counsel should not be lightly dismissed. But I have not called you here to assent to that which is already resolved. I ask you all to think well, and to consider what is now in debate. I will ask Señor Alderete to give it you in his own words, that it may be put in the best way."

Men did not know how to take this, which was how he meant it to be. They looked to him for guidance he would not give. He was in doubt, and, perhaps for the first time since he had sighted Tezcuco's shore, he had called a counsel which would have a loose rein.

Whatever Alderete may have thought of this method, it was a procedure of which he could not complain. He rose at once, and his words were lucid and brief. He said: "We may all be agreed that we are near the end of this war. It is not only our own judgement, we can see that those who look on—even those who have been in alliance with Guatemozín—regard him now as a fallen man, and seek peace with us.

"Yet he is of stubborn temper, and his surrender delays, while we raid the city, and return therefrom with no better result than that we have slain some, and some of ourselves are slain, and another street (or perhaps two) is a burnt-out shell.

"Can we not do something that will make it plain, even to him, that the end has come, and that he should submit to those who will be clement in their success?

"What avail is it to advance at morn, if we withdraw when the night is near?"

He paused a moment, looking to observe how his argument was received, and saw that there were some to whom it was a matter of frowning doubt. There had already been much debate as to whether it would be well to seize one of the major buildings within the city, palace or temple, and establish a permanent station there. But the memory of how they had been besieged in such quarters a year before, supported by observation of the pertinacity with which the Aztecs rebuilt their barriers and hollowed their chasms anew, had not brought this idea to a general popularity, and Alderete was quick to show that he had a different, and (he argued) a more feasible plan.

"Have you thought," he went on, "that Tlateloco—the great marketplace—is of an extent on which an army could camp, and that its booths would be sufficient to give shelter for a numerous host? Why should we not occupy that with an army of our allies, with whom we could maintain contacts both from north and south? We should split the city's defenders into two camps, with consequent confusions which are unsure, but easy to guess; and we could operate from that central position in what direction we would, making the permanent defence of the city a hopeless dream."

León de Ávila said: "It has the sound of a good plan, if we be of the strength it needs, both to win and to hold. It must hinge on that."

Sandoval said, but with more doubt in his voice than his words held: "We drive into the heart of the city, and then return. Why should we not win to the market-square?"

"It is not quite the same thing, as we all know," de Tapia objected to that. "We have reached the central square from the south, though not yet from the north; but we go by the broad central avenue. The market must be reached by smaller streets, and is further away."

"It is not further away from the north," Sandoval remarked, but his voice was still rather that of one who considered but did not urge.

They all knew where it lay—to the northwest of the central square from which it must be approached by one street of half a mile's length, which was a minor causeway, with a canal on each side, or by smaller streets which were so narrow that they would be hard to pass if the roofs on either side should be held by an active foe.

Alderete was one who would not be lightly foiled in debate. No one, unless he were both suave and adroit in verbal conflict, would have won to the place he held. He did not doubt that the most part of those who were present would be disposed to support his proposal or any other which would be likely to bring the war to a quick end. But he saw now that those whose opinions were of most weight were cool, if no worse than that. If they should sway others to the same doubt—? He had an argument in reserve which he did not longer delay.

He said: "There is not only loss of time, and abortive expense of blood, in the slow course which we now take, there is loss of the spoil. We conquer street by street, but, as we go forward, we burn. There will be no city at last, and we shall be victors with empty hands."

That was an argument which was natural, which it might even be said that it was duty, for him to urge, he being there to safeguard the Royal fifth, and to go back with a fifth of nought would be a poor boast, both for Cortéz and him. But it was one which appealed to all, and it was a fact that whatever wealth the city might contain (and they had reason for thinking that it must be immense) was not coming to them.

They had fought their way to the Central Square, and their allies had fired and plundered the houses on either side, but they had said that they had found little to share. That might be true, but there was no consolation therein.

What they wanted was that Guatemozín should plead for terms, to which reply could be made that the city would be spared (and his own life) if he would pay a ransom of such amount as would recompense them for all their toils. But they saw him as a man who was beaten, but would not yield.

Cortéz, watching silently, judged that the proposal would have general assent, and he could not be sure that it might not be the best, as well as the speediest way. It remained for him to order it so that it should come to a good end.

CHAPTER ONE HUNDRED ONE: DISASTER

"Alderete," Cortéz said, as the Council dispersed in the buoyant mood that the prospect of action roused, "we will go forward at dawn, for we shall need all the daylight hours, and much will depend upon no word of what we intend having gone about; and you shall lead the main force, for the honour is rightly yours. But there shall be other advances made, upon either hand, which will relieve you, and though this must be along narrow streets, I suppose they may be ill prepared for defence. But if you are to succeed, you will need to make every step secure, that you be not cut off, which we know our foes to be constant to try."

He said much on this, planning with the cautious detail which was habit to him; and at the next twilight of dawn the Spanish army advanced from Xoloc at its utmost strength, up to the Central Square of the city. To that point, it was on ground which it had made its own on previous occasions: beyond, it was to enter part of the city which had not been penetrated since the disastrous flight of the previous summer.

Simultaneously, the northern army, controlled jointly by Sandoval and Alvarado, advanced down the causeway from Tacuba, supported by the fire of the brigantines, to attempt to reach the market place from that direction. The native armies were to deploy behind both advances, as rapidly as their breadth of advance along the causeways allowed; and all available canoes were used to support the advances by operating in the city canals.

The southern army met little opposition until it arrived opposite to the Central Square, and the ashes of the Old Palace which it had burned previously. It was evident that the Pyramid Temple, and Montezuma's palace on the other side of the Square, were very strongly held, but they were ignored now.

Alderete, with the main body of Spaniards, commenced to force his way up the main street which, running in a northwesterly direction, led to the Market; and Cortéz, with a smaller force, adventured the penetration of narrower streets to the right; while a similar body, led by Tapia, and one of Pedro's brothers, Jorge de Alvarado, made a similar attempt on the leftward side.

As they advanced, they heard the distant guns of the brigantines, proclaiming that their comrades advanced from the northern shore.

Cortéz went forward on foot, the narrow, canal-cut streets not being adapted for cavalry operations. Those who were now his perpetual guard, however, had his horse a short distance behind, that it might be available at a sharp need. The main body of the cavaliers remained in reserve at the entrance to the Central Square, Tlascalan and Tezcucan regiments pouring by them on either side.

Cortéz moved cautiously, having no obstacles in his rear. The streets behind him were occupied by Tlascalan warriors. He could have advanced more rapidly, if he would. But he reflected that Alderete would have a more difficult task in protecting his rear along the main street, and he did not wish to outdistance him.

He heard the guns of the brigantines more loudly. He judged the Alvarado and Sandoval were clear of their causeway, and in the northern suburbs now. Everything went well.

A canoe-borne messenger came. He had a short scrawl from Alderete: "We are in sight of the Market Square, having been only lightly opposed. Tapia is even further ahead. They seem to be too much surprised to resist, or their heart is gone."

As he read it, Diego who was at his side, noticed that he turned pale, either with anger or fear, but when he spoke, it was calmly enough, though his words had a disquieting sound. "Guzmán, halt the advance. Could Alderete be so quickly advanced, if he had guarded his rear, as I warned him to do? I must see this for myself, for I have a doubt that they lure us on."

He took a narrow left-hand way, between silent houses beneath which the canoes could move, and soon came to the street along which Alderete had passed ahead. It had canals, wide and deep, on each side of a causeway which was of a breadth of ten yards. The causeway was not of solid concrete, as was the Main Avenue. It was a mere dyke of earth, with strengthened sides. In these days of rain, and having been trampled by many feet, it was a quagmire of mud. He looked ahead, and saw a gap six yards wide, with deep water below. Beyond that was a dense throng of Aztec soldiers, who had withdrawn somewhat at his approach. There were signs of conflict around. It was a simple guess that whatever force of Tlascalans had been left with instructions to repair the gap, it had not been in their power to do. In fact, some had fled backward to find the safety of comrades who were coming up behind: while others were carried off in Aztec canoes to the dismal end that their captives were fated to know.

"Fill it instantly," Cortéz urged. "Break down the sides of the dyke. Throw in what you will." But even as he spoke he was aware of confused sounds ahead which he did not like. And, next moment, there was the measured thud of the great drum from the Temple Pyramid, at which signal, as though they rose from the earth, Aztecs were leaping upon them from every side. Their mocking whistles rose to a volume of sound that, for a moment, silenced even the noises of strife and flight which told that Alderete's force was retreating toward the gap which he had been careless to leave.

A scene of wild confusion followed, difficult for those who experienced it to remember clearly, even if they were fortunate enough to survive.

Cortéz held his ground, his example inspiring those around him to an equal fortitude. Some timbers, the remains of a barricade which Alderete had broken down, were flung abortively into the flood, while, from their canoes, crowding the canal, the Aztecs assailed them from either side, while a shouting, struggling crowd, in which Tlascalans, Aztecs and Spaniards were wildly mingled, swept towards them, and, by its own impetus, bore many over the edge. But the Aztecs fell to be pulled to safety by rescuing hands, while others, even if they could swim, were fortunate indeed if they were not dragged into an Aztec canoe.

The horror did not end until a dry way could be trodden over the bodies of those who died, and meanwhile, far backward along the dyke, the Aztecs were dragging victims down to the water on either side.

Cortéz, with a little group of like-minded companions, held his ground on the edge of the gap, one hand stretched to rescue the most he could, and one with a ready sword for any Aztec whose lust for victims might bring him within its range.

The gap filled, and the crowd of fugitives passed them, while the cry of "Malintzin!" showed that the Aztecs had recognised him, of whom they now thought they could make a prey.

A sword, thrust upward from the side of the dyke, cut his left leg under the knee, bringing him to the ground. There was a rush of foes to seize him, and of friends for his support. The sword of one of his sworn guard, de Olea, cut off a grasping arm, and went through the body of another, before he died of his own wounds. A Tlascalan chieftain, whose name does not survive, killed three of those who were dragging him over the side of the dyke. Quinones, plunging into the water, beside him, succeeded in raising him up. A page, bringing up his horse, was wounded in the throat, so that it broke free. Guzmán caught its bridle, and held it while others helped their wounded leader into the saddle, but, as he did this, and the eyes of others were turned a moment away, his feet were seized, and he was dragged down the dyke, and too swiftly borne away for any rescue to avail.

On horseback, and no longer disabled by the laming wound, Cortéz refused to retreat. "Not," he said, "till the last man has come clear," but Quinones heard an order he would not heed. "Your life," he said, "is much to us, though it may be nothing to you." Pulling on the bridle that he still held, he forced his general to move with the moving crowd. And, as he did so, there was a shout of triumph above the din, for the ensign-bearer, Corral, who had borne the Spanish flag throughout at his leader's side, having been caught in Aztec hands, and seeming lost, had broken free, and outstretched hands had drawn him to safety when hope seemed gone, with the torn flag still in his hands, at which a howl of baffled fury answered the Christian cheer.

Falling back upon advancing reserves, and covered by a charge of cavalry as they gained the Central Square, the remnant of the Spanish army made some front of defiance, and the pursuing Aztecs were halted at last, and even obliged to scatter when artillery fire was directed upon them. But the victory had been clearly theirs, and it was accentuated with a fresh dread, when two Spanish heads were thrown on to the ground amid cries that they were those of Sandoval and 'the Sun', which was Alvarado's Mexican name.

Cortéz turned pale again when he heard these cries, but he recovered himself at once. "It is," he said, "a most likely lie. Could you get through," he asked de Tapia, "by the western causeway, and learn how they have fared, and tell them how it has gone with us?"

Tapia said his horse should be equal to that.

Cortéz seemed to have forgotten his wound. He toiled to restore order and confidence among those who might be liable at any moment to further attack. So Sandoval found him when he appeared in the afternoon.

He had ridden in the reverse direction, by the way that de Tapia had taken, but he had seen nothing of him. He said the Aztecs were everywhere. He showed three arrow wounds in proof of that, but they were not deep.

Why had he ventured to come? He had been anxious to know what had occurred. The Aztecs had tried the same trick with them. They had shown what they said was 'Malintzin's' head. He had not believed, but had wished to assure himself. How had they fared? They had fought their way nearly to the Market Place before the sounding of the great drum. After that, they had kept up the attack, though they knew matters had gone wrong, thinking that pressure upon their comrades might be relieved.

But, at last they had been so heavily assailed that they had been forced to retreat, and their losses had not been light.

Later, there was news that de Tapia had ridden through, though he also had wounds to show.

Meanwhile, Cortéz had at last been persuaded to dismount, and to have his wound washed and bound. He lay exhausted both in body and mind, but he would not rest till he knew all.

"I must have a list," he said to de Ávila, "of every man who has gone. I must know whom I have lost."

"If you will lie still," de Ávila replied, "you shall know all, but it will not be learnt in an hour."

He said he would see Sandoval alone before he should return.

He said to him: "I do not know how long I shall lie here, but it is on you that I must rely. Today was lost because men will not be cautious, even when they are admonished and warned. And Alvarado is of that kind. You must watch, lest he ruin all."

He talked to him as though he were brother or son, which came in part of the confidence that Gonzalo had earned, and in part of the fact that they came from the same village in Spain, and from the same school, though Hernando had left as Gonzalo entered its doors, being nearly ten years younger than he.

The sun was still at some height (for defeat had come before noon) when de Ávila came with the full tale of the missing, who were no better (or worse) than dead. Guzmán was only one among sixty-two Spanish names. The Tlascalan captives could not yet be told with exact accuracy. They were probably not less than five hundred. Two guns had been left behind. Seven horses were dead.

But the full bitterness of the day was in its last hours, when the great drum on the platform of the Temple Pyramid was beaten again, and the Spaniards, looking out, and wondering what it might mean, were not too distant to see the procession that moved round the pyramid, as it ascended the outer stairs.

They saw six naked men—three white-skinned Spaniards among them—driven up to the altar. They saw them slaughtered there, and their bodies thrown contemptuously to the crowds below, who would banquet on whatever each was able to bear away.

It was a sight that might be continued for many days.

CHAPTER ONE HUNDRED TWO: THE EIGHT DAYS

The Spaniards on the northern causeway could gaze on that clear though distant spectacle of their comrades being brought to ignominious death (they were actually nearer than those at Xoloc to the scene of sacrifice), with no distraction of mind; but those who held their position with Cortéz on the opposite side could give less heed to their comrades' death, for the drum that sounded for their sacrifice appeared to be regarded also as a signal for the Aztec forces that faced them to renew assault, which they did with reckless ferocious courage, as though the intoxication of victory had left them regardless of reason for life.

They gained little by that, for the Spaniards, now withdrawn to the causeway's head, met them with blasts of artillery fire which tore lanes of unsightly death through their crowded ranks. Indeed, it seemed only to demonstrate that the weapons of the Spaniards had not lost their potency, and that those who thought that their sun was setting might still have something unwelcome to learn.

But, in fact, Cortéz, impotently listening, counted each discharge, as though it were a bell that was tolling doom. For the truth was that the powder was nearly done.

It was known to few—to those only on whom he could most surely depend. Mendes knew it, of course. But he was at Tacuba, with Alvarado, or the guns would have been served in a more frugal way. Diego knew it, and was at the side of his leader's couch proposing that he should make another expedition to the volcano. It had been an unspoken reason inclining Cortéz to agree to the plan which had brought them to the edge of disaster now.

But the powder was not quite done, and the guns sounded until the Aztecs grew weary of dying to no purpose at all, unless it were to provide food for those who remained alive. For it had come to that. Starvation was at their door, which even victory did not at once relieve.

It had not been the Aztec custom to eat their own kin. What civilised man would? They cremated equally those who died of disease or were killed in war. But it was now two days since Guatemozín had issued a reluctant order that there should be cremation only of organs which it would be repulsive to eat, whether taken from friend or foe. Spaniards, or any other savages, might; but were Aztec habits to be degraded to theirs? So, a month ago, it would have been said with contemptuous lips; but hunger rules in a very tyrannous way. In Mexican kitchens they were eating lizards and rats. They would not be quick to throw a Spanish liver away. It might come to tripe, if the siege should last for another week.

But of such things there was little fear, for in the morning there was proclamation by the High Priest of that which the War God had told to him. Within eight days the Spaniards would be entirely destroyed.

Knowing this, Guatemozín acted with energy, and in a merciful mood. He sent the heads of Spaniards and horses, with which he was well supplied, to all the principal cities which had revolted from him; and letters therewith. The letters told of the defeat the Spaniards had suffered; they told of the divine revelation of their imminent doom; they offered unconditional pardon to those who would return to their allegiance within the time.

Cortéz heard the tale of the eight days, and it brought the first smile to his lips that men had seen since Guzmán had been drawn into an Aztec canoe. He said: "That is the kind of blunder that a false priest will be likely to make." He gave orders that all men should remain in the strength of their own camps, only the brigantines patrolling the lake both by night and day to keep provisions from starving men—and also to seize what they could for their own use, for food did not come as freely from the country round as it had done before, nor could it be as safely fetched. But he did not smile on the second day, when he was told how many of his allies—even Tlascalans—had slipped away during the night.

It was at the noon of that day that Marina came. She had been at Tezcuco during the last weeks, it being one of those times when civilised women thought that men could not be too far away. But now she rode in with a strong guard that Sandoval had supplied, and there was a baby upon her back.

She had not come to show that, supposing that Hernán's mind would be on more immediately important matters, but she thought that he would have need of her, in which she was not wrong. When you have a husband who cannot write—!

He realised, with some wonder in his own mind, how much added confidence her arrival brought. Not that she minimised the danger in which they stood. But she looked at it with quiet eyes. She was grave and cool.

Before the night many letters had been painted, to follow the flying men, and to be sent to doubtful allies. They all said the same thing: *Wait for eight days, and watch the prophecy fail.* It sounded a discreet proposal, but then Guatemozín had put it another way.

They discussed these allies, one by one, she aiding conjecture with all the knowledge she had; and, while they talked, the guns thundered from the causeway's head, and from the brigantines, and also at times on the shoreward side, for the Aztecs did not long cease from attack, they also being aware of the passing hours.

It was agreed that, in most cases, though allies might desert, they would not be actively hostile in the next week. They would be impulsed only by fear. They would withdraw, and expect the Aztecs to be contented with that.

It was agreed also that the impulse must ultimately depend upon the extent to which the Tlascalans and Tezcucans continued support, of both of whom they had moderate hopes, though many Tlascalans were gone, and many more would go during the next night. They agreed that Chichemecatl would not be moved by any Aztec argument, whether promise or threat. He was a proud and obstinate man, difficult to persuade or control, but he hated the Aztecs, he had spoken of Xicotencatl's defection with contempt, and approved his execution. There might be satisfaction now that he was not of a pliable kind.

Then there was the bond formed by the Tlascalan marriages. "You should have had one of the princesses yourself," Marina said gravely. "I told you so then. You can see it now. But you could not? You may know what you mean, but I never shall. It has no sense. Louise? Oh, Pedro had good fortune with her. She is sharpening a Spanish sword! She told me to do the same, but I said it is with a brush that I can be useful to you."

Then there was Ixtlilxochitl: It was agreed that there could be reliance on him. The Aztecs hated him too deeply for his defection. They would never forgive. Also, they had his rival among them, waiting to resume the Tezcucan throne. But it did not follow that the whole nation would be loyal. The probabilities were the other way.

Probably, more than on all else, the attitudes of these peoples would depend upon their opinions of who would prevail. And it was difficult to blame them greatly for that.

Well, they had done all they could. Cortéz said: "You will ride back before darkness comes?"

"I had thought that I should stay here."

"Bringing a child to the midst of war?"

"I should say it is safest here."

He saw implications in that of a heartening kind.

Safer for the moment it might be. She was in the very citadel of his strength: approachable only by one or other of the strongly defended causeways, with the choice of two by which to escape if one should be lost, and with the brigantines also at call. She might reasonably prefer that to residence in Tezcuco, where Spaniards were now few, and they had agreed that the loyalty of its inhabitants was unsure.

But that was a short view. If the Spaniards were to be over-whelmed, that was about the last spot that prudence would choose. And, if she were caught there, there was perhaps no one in the Western World, woman or man, excepting Cortéz himself, who would be more certain to provide a central dish at an Emperor's feast.

But at Tezcuco she would be free to go or stay. She could take refuge where she would. And there were still remote lands that could give asylum to those who fled from the Aztec power.

Cortéz said: "Well, it will be pleasure to have you here. But I suppose you will need flowers."

"I spoke to Sandoval of that. I supposed you would have none. They should be here now."

So they were. As many as twenty porters could bear, waiting without.

She looked at them, and at the extent of the rooms which had to be rendered habitable, with some natural discontent. They could render first aid, but no more than that. She thought dispassionately of how difficult it is to educate adult savages into decent ways. They professed to contemn her civilisation, but even a victim destined for sacrifice in the next hour would not be deprived of flowers. They were not as brutal as that.

"There is one thing which I must not omit," she said, when she had given instructions for the flowers to be festooned in economical ways. "I must thank Juan for his part in saving your life." For he had been active (being ashore from his brigantine) at the critical time.

Cortéz laughed at that. He said: "Well, so you should. It was for you it was done."

"So I suppose."

He was amused that Xamarillo should risk his life to save that of a successful rival. He was amused also that the position held no amusement for her.

Much as she had learnt of Spanish customs, and habits of thought, she would have been surprised had she known what went on in the minds of the two men who, each in his own way, were devoted to her.

Cortéz did not doubt her, either in love or faith. But, had she been attracted by Xamarillo, he would not have thought it unnatural, nor even as a cause of quarrel with her. It would have been Juan with whom, at such a crisis, a man of honour must deal, killing him (if he could) in a set way; after which Marina would presumably renew her loyalty to one who had demonstrated that he was the better man.

As to Juan, he had the selfless passion which seeks the good of the one loved, even to its own loss. While Marina desired Cortéz to live, it must be a first object to guard his life. Nor did he think (nor, indeed, would he consciously have desired) to seduce her from that allegiance. Indeed, such infidelity would have reduced her attraction, which was based on a respect which he would have given to very few of his own countrywomen, and which it is a mere statement of fact to say that few of them would have claimed or valued.

Was he therefore hopeless that his devotion would ever come to a blissful end? That might be too much to conclude. Love can endure on a faint hope, but to have that is a desperate need.

Military leaders may die, even though there be special efforts for their protection, and that is especially true of those who adventure their own lives on the front of war. Dimly, other possibilities appeared.

Chapter One Hundred Three: Shadow of Doom

The eight days passed and, at Xoloc, the flag of Castile still flew.

The Spaniards had confined themselves, for that time, to defensive fighting, which had been severe, but had caused more losses to their opponents than to themselves.

This had been mere prudence, after the prophecy which had been made, for their control of the causeways gave them a strongly defensible position; and, though loss of time had its own problems for them, those of the Aztecs were more acute. Starvation had become to them a very menacing foe, and may have been the argument which led the priests to forecast success at too early a day. They may have thought to arouse hope, to strengthen fortitude, or to incite effort. But, from whatever cause, they had blundered, and would be weakened by that mistake.

The Spaniards had their own problems of penury also, in the failure of powder, which became too acute to hide, for, during the last three days, it had been imperative to ration its use.

Only the brigantines, patrolling during the nights, were allowed to use it without restraint, and it would be seldom that an hour of darkness would pass without the sound of firing upon the lake.

Many boats must have got through, for a canoe can be paddled very silently, and is far less visible in a poor light than is a ship with a spread of sail that obscures the stars; and paddles can be used in a windless hour. The perimeter of the lake was far too great for the shores to be effectually patrolled, and parts of them were held entirely by the Aztecs during these days of restraint.

It was on the eightth night that Cortéz showed the agitation of mind which Marina had known before, though she could not now guess its cause, as it had usually been easy to do.

She had placed the child with a nurse in a near room, and returned to her natural couch. She said: "Have you made it a habit now to spend the night in this way, or is it because I am here that your pillow will have no dent?"

He gave a laughing answer to that, but then added bitterly: "Am I cursed of God that I must ever bring disaster and death to men? And destruction of precious things? I am one to build, not to break."

His mind went back to the Cuban days when he had made his farm a model which few could match; when he had imported cattle from England as well as from Andalusian pastures; when he had been diligent to study new methods of cultivation to win the service of unfamiliar soils. That was work to endure! But this that he now designed— His thought was broken by Marina's voice, which rejected his mood.

"Well, you have not broken me yet, though I know not what may be to come. But I shall die of cold, if I lie longer alone. Will you weep for that?"

He said: "I know not what I shall do. I am tempted much."

But she was adroit not to ask explanation then. She said: "If you do not know, then you must take knowledge from me."

After that, he forgot his doubt till sleep came.

And in the morning there was much to divert his mind. There was the news that most of the Tlascalans were back in camp, with a true tale that they had never gone to their own land. They had actually marched as far as the battlefield of Otumba, where Cortéz had once before confounded those who thought him a ruined man. It was a place to inspire doubt. And they had had a doubt of another kind. Would Tlascala receive them in the right way? They remembered Xicotencatl's fate. Certainly they could not all be hanged. But some might. It was mere prudence to halt, and watch the event, which would soon be clear. Eight days is not long.

Well, they had to find out how Cortéz would treat them now; and he thought they could wait.

But there were two letters from further away which might deal with more urgent affairs. They were such as Marina must read. She said: "This is from Cuernavaca. They call for aid, being suddenly threatened with chastisement by Guatemozín's allies."

"And I suppose the other may be of the same sort?"

"It is much the same, but from those who are still further away: and I should guess, who have done little for you."

"That may not be easy to say. Gonzalo," he went on to Sandoval, who had been taking instructions from him as to expedition for sulphur which must be fetched from the crater's mouth, "you must do nothing more with Diego for the next hour. These are matters for which even the powder may stand await."

Sandoval looked doubtful at that. He was seldom quick of speech, and least of all in debate of any orders he might receive, but he asked: "Shall we do well to further divide our strength, being no more than we now are?"

"Yes. I should say that is why we must. If we doubt ourselves, shall we be trusted by other men? But it shall be done most largely by our allies."

If these risks were to be taken at all, it was evident that they were reduced by speed. Within the next two hours, forces were arrayed which would march before darkness came, Sandoval and Tapia each leaving with an army having a spearhead of five or six score Spaniards, and as many thousand native troops, selected as being most naturally antipathetic to those they were required to subdue. The returned Tlascalans found that they would incur no penalty beyond the burden of this adventure, to which they could not object, for the more distant plaint had come from a remote Otombic tribe, being of a race who were their country's closest allies.

With each party there went a single cannon, and enough powder to fire it twice, which might be sufficient argument to those who did not know what its limits were.

It was while Cortéz had ridden the causeway to Cojohuacan to see the repentant Tlascalans there, and decide how many of them should go (his knee-wound having now healed sufficiently for him to walk a few steps, beyond which he would trust to a horse's back), that a runner came from Vera Cruz, who, being directed to Xoloc, naturally approached it from Iztepalapan, by the southern causeway, missing him thereby, so that the letter first came to Marina's hands.

She opened it at once, knowing that, in such matters, he held no secrets from her, but she found much of it hard to read, in spite of her diligence at this time in studying to write in the Spanish way.

She understood that a ship had come, which meant, almost certainly she supposed, that there was at last the word from the Spanish King, dreaded or hoped, and so long and inexplicably delayed, which would cast down or confirm, but she could make nothing of that. And there was a name, de León, which came twice, and might allude to the dead man who had been the Cuban Governor's repre-

sentative, and Hernando's friend. But that was unsure, for she knew
León to be a common name in the Spaniard's tongue, being that of a
great beast which even they were unable to tame.

Also, there was an allusion to sending powder, but there was little wonder in that, as she knew a letter had been sent to Vera Cruz,
asking that four-fifths of what they had should be sent, whether little
or much.

"Hernán," she said, as he came in, "there is a letter from Vera
Cruz."

"Brought by whom?"

"By a runner. Not by one of your own men."

"Then it is a matter of haste."

"There is a ship come."

He had it in his hand by this time, and saw at a glance that the
news was good, though it left aside that which was his best hope and
his greatest fear.

Ponce de León had sent another ship to the Florida coast, with
further stores for the support of his expedition, and like those that
had come before, it had blundered into México Bay.

Whether by reason (as it now was), or more forcible arguments,
which Cavallero did not trouble to say, he had unloaded the ship,
and enlisted those it bore to augment his numbers at Vera Cruz.
Knowing the urgent need of powder, he was sending most of that
which he had obtained from this source in charge of a convoy which
would start in the next hour.

A schedule would follow of much else that the ship contained
which it would be pleasure to have.

Cortéz said: "It is well. We shall have the powder we need."

"There is no word from Spain?"

"No. The ship comes from another port, and was not destined
for us."

He looked troubled now, as he often would when that doubt entered his mind. Nothing from Spain. Had a ship sunk? That might be
the most likely explanation. But the day must come which would
either ruin him or confirm his power.

The two expeditions marched away, and the diminished ranks
of the Spaniards remained on the defensive, with the support of the
augmented armies of their allies, and enduring attacks from those
who were still aggressive and truculent foes.

So it was for the next two days, during which Cortéz gave no
sign of any plans he might have for resuming the siege. Men said
that he was waiting for the powder to arrive, or for those he had sent
on the two punitive expeditions to return, but there was silence from

him, and only Marina knew how long he paced the room in the night.

And then, on the third morning, Captain Holguín, who commanded one of the swiftest of the brigantines, reported the capture of a canoe during the night which contained the freshly severed heads of one Spaniard, and six Tlascalans, and the staler foot of a horse, which were evidently being sent ashore to be distributed through the land, in the way that Guatemozín was regularly doing now, and as the number of his prisoners would enable him to continue for weeks to come.

Cortéz looked at the heads. He saw that of de Guzmán, who had been faithful servant, companion, and friend. He said: "It was I who brought him to death."

"That," de Ávila answered, "is not reason to say. It was his duty to guard your life, and, what he did for you, you would have done for him at a like need."

"That is not what I mean," Cortéz answered. "We should not have been there. For I knew of a better way, which I would not use."

He turned away, as one wishing to avoid further words. He went to his own room, to continue a report which he wrote from day to day for the Spanish King, not knowing whether it would ever come to his sight.

Now he added: "I am resolved on that which I should have practised before, for it is the one way by which the war may be brought to a quick end. I was reluctant, it being a city of palaces and gardens, such as the whole world may not contain elsewhere. But these heathen men are of a most obstinate kind, and I lose lives, which are more than stones."

By the next morning, there was satisfaction in the Spanish camp, and joy among their allies, for they had orders which they could understand, and the native armies foresaw the ruin of Aztec power, beyond any previous anticipation that they had had.

From north and south, at either end of the Central Avenue, strong forces deployed from the causeway heads, but only advanced sufficiently far to protect the numerous bodies of various nationalities which came behind them, whose hoes were more prominent than their swords. The ground over which they spread had already been so far wasted that its canals were half choked with rubble, and its dwellings were hillocks of tumbled stones. But destruction was to be complete and orderly now. The ruined houses supplied materials from which the canals were entirely filled; where they had been, the pavements would become a smooth surface of morticed stone. The thousands who whistled pleasure over their willing toil were not given a set extent of ground which must be cleared. They were to spread outward and onward from day to day, doing as much as they could. But behind them there must be such level smoothness that the cavaliers could ride over it without fear of a stumbling hoof.

So it was done for the first day and the second, the Aztecs not comprehending what was meant, and awaiting further advance, which would enable them to strike back, as they had done before. But when they surveyed the ground from which the Spaniards retired as the twilight came, and observed that it was so thoroughly smoothed that it was vain to hope that its obstacles could be raised or hollowed again, comprehension came to them, developing to a great fury, or a great fear.

Unless they should yield, their whole city was to be steadily, methodically, entirely destroyed.

Next day, the extending ranks of those who protected the labourers were subjected to fierce and prolonged assaults.

But these were sustained only at a great cost. The powder, despatched immediately after the runner who brought news of it, had now arrived. Cavaliers could operate upon open ground. To issue from the labyrinth of ruins, gardens, breaches, barricades and canals, was to invite death, which Spaniards, Tlascalans, Tezcucans, and a dozen other revolting nations, were very willing to deal.

Yet some would not suffer more than they would be first to give, and the spirit of resistance did not decline. Rather it leapt to a fiercer, more virulent flame.

So it was for some days, and then, having demonstrated what such destruction would mean, Cortéz ordered that the demolition should cease, while he sent a deputation to Guatemozín, promising such terms of peace as seemed, in the position in which he now was, almost insanity to decline.

For this purpose, three Aztec prisoners of gentle birth were released, and consented to bear the message, although with some reluctance, for the Mexican Emperor had made proclamation that any man who mentioned surrender should be executed.

"But this," Marina urged upon them, when she had interpreted the proposed terms, "is not surrender which is required, but a treatied peace, and you will be messengers only. You are not pledged to advocate what you bear."

They could see that, and must hope that Guatemozín's sight would be equally clear. They may have been moved also by what Marina said of herself, it not having been spoken to her. "As I see it," she said, "you may call yourselves very fortunate men, for you go free. If you refuse, and you be given to the Tlascalans for their next meal, would you have cause for complaint? Even the clemency of my lord finds it hard to restrain his allies from eating Aztecs while the Aztecs are eating them, and while we must watch deaths each day on the pyramid which all men see."

They could not deny that, and in the end they consented to go, and with a pledge that the proposed terms should be fairly urged. They said themselves that they were good, but that Guatemozín was not one who was quick to bend.

That might be; but it is fair to observe that he did not threaten them with punishment for coming thus. He listened with care, and called a Counsel of priest and lord, to whom the offer was put.

It was simply this: he was to acknowledge the overlordship of Spain, and his own position would be confirmed. There were to be no penalties: no reprisals. The 'rebellion' of the Aztecs was to be forgiven, their persons were to be unmolested, their property confirmed to themselves. They were to observe, when they considered so fair an offer, that their own allies had deserted them, that they were isolated and starving. Did not Guatemozín see that he could save his people's lives, and the wealth and loveliness of his city, in no other possible way?

It is certain, and was demonstrated by his subsequent conduct, that Guatemozín was bitterly unwilling to make peace with the Spaniards on any terms. He desired their extermination, and was reluctant to admit that he could not secure that result—an obduracy which had been increased by his recent success, and the knowledge of the many still-living prisoners that his cages held. But it is also certain that he listened to these proposals with some measure of patience, and it is improbable that he would have rejected them had his counsellors been united for their acceptance, as it appears that some of them were.

But the attitude of the priests was uncompromising in its hostility, which was logical, even in desperation, for they judged correctly that Cortéz would have no mercy for their religion, or for themselves.

Their pens still held some hundreds of prisoners, who were being slaughtered, up to a dozen a day, to give encouragement to their own warriors, and to provide extra rations of meat for those who were already suffering more from starvation than Spanish swords.

Were these spoils of successful war to be surrendered? Were their gods to be cast down again, and the hated Christian worship established in temples consecrated to them?

The High Priest spoke with the hate and fury of a vicious, cruel, frightened, and baffled man.

The eight-day prophecy had been a gamble of desperation, but it had almost succeeded. On the fourth day, as desertion increased, it had seemed certain that it would; and he still thought, and had been fearless to say to Guatemozín, that it would have been so, had military attack been urged with greater vehemence during the days that followed.

Now he mocked with derisive eloquence those who would accept the overlordship of a king they had never seen, of whose existence they had no proof, or who would place their trust in a Spaniard's word.

"Montezuma" he said, "was a friend to them. Is he reigning securely now? We know that they long for gold with a strange greed, being savages in that, as in all. Montezuma gave it to them till his treasuries became bare. Did they do him honour for that? Give them all the gold you yet have, and they will throw your gods to dust on the next day.

"Have you forgotten the six hundred nobles who were basely slain, having no thought of enmity in their hearts, and no arms in their hands? Such will be the fate of all who place their trust in a Spaniard's word.

"Do you envy those who exult now, as they toil with axes and spades to destroy our temples and homes, lacking wit to see that they will have double toil to build them again, whether as our slaves or the slaves of Spain?

"I will tell you this, that you may know how greatly your god had wrought, and that it was through the failure of your own faith that a Spaniard remains alive. In those days their guns were without food, and the lightning had left their mouths.

"New food had now been brought from the sea, and they have become active again. Had you had courage to go ahead, you would have found them as dumb as those which we captured in the Great Square. It was not the Wargod who failed. It was your valour, and faith in him."

He paused at this point to look round upon men who were silenced by this, which they were disposed to believe, for those who brought the powder from the coast, being harried by many foes, had left some powder behind, in such a way that it had spoken with the same voice as the guns, by which three had died. And, since it had reached the Spanish camp, the guns had become vocal again.

He would have said more, but the Emperor interposed: "It is enough, for there is wisdom in what you say. We will die, or release our land. And he who falters will gain nothing by that, for he will come to a quicker end.

"Let it be proclaimed that each man, be he high or low, and each woman alike, must have but one thought from this hour—to kill Spaniards before they die."

CHAPTER ONE HUNDRED FOUR: AN EMPIRE ENDS

For two days the camps of the besiegers remained quiet, waiting for an answer which did not come.

Judgement and desire combined in their Commander's mind to assure him that so fair an offer would not be refused, and the cessation of Aztec attacks confirmed belief that it was not rejected without debate.

But when the answer came, at the third dawn, it was in the form of an attack which, reckless of its own losses, stormed up to the causeway heads, and, for long hours, confined the Spaniards to those narrow fronts, and even drove them, at times, some distance backward along the dykes; while, at their distant bases, and along the shores of the lake, the noise of conflict showed that the Aztecs beyond the city were making concerted attacks, where dispositions were more equal for them.

It was long past noon when the Aztecs bore off the last of their countless dead, and withdrew from the area where the demolition had been completed, so that there was no shelter for them; and, as they did so, the Spanish forces, closely upon their heels, re-occupied it, and, pressing further forward, renewed protection for those who followed with axe and spade.

Sheltered now by their own threatened buildings, the Aztecs turned upon their pursuers, and it was only in the rear of a further strife that the work of demolition could be continued; but it was beyond their power to prevent that which went on until darkness came.

It had been the supreme effort, and for the next three weeks, though the resolution of its defenders was not reduced, the work of the city's destruction went on through the daylight hours.

These days were all of the same pattern, though darkening for the Aztecs from hour to hour.

The two expeditions returned, having chastised those who had thought that the day of the Spaniard was done.

Day by day, fresh thousands of recruits volunteered for the welcome toil of demolishing the city that had been built upon their oppression. Day by day, both from north and south, palace and temple fell, trees were felled, and pleasure gardens were trampled down, so that the flattened areas spread, on to which the Aztecs could not venture without being the unprotected victims of ball and bolt, and of the cavalry charges which were almost equally dreaded. Day by day, the bitter fighting went on, both on the contracting margin of city buildings, and round the great camps that protected the causeways at their shoreward ends. And night by night the brigantines, and a host of canoes, ceaselessly patrolled the lake, to sink or capture such as might attempt to take food to the starving city.

But day by day there was gradual change. Resistance did not cease, but it steadily weakened. The speed of the demolition increased. Attacks upon the shore camps were less frequent, and less resolutely sustained.

And day by day the pressure of starvation within the city was more acute. It fell first, and most severely, as was natural, upon the non-combatants: most of all upon the women and children who, daily with each advance of their enemies, were crowded into narrower and more squalid quarters. To mitigate this misery, and perhaps to encourage a spirit of surrender, Cortéz gave orders that those who surrendered should be kindly treated, and promptly fed. But, even so, there were few who were attracted by the clemency. On the Aztec side at least it had become literally a war to the death, to which they were resigned, if it could not be won.

They were dependant for water now, as the rains ceased, almost entirely upon deep wells which had been sunk in those parts of the city which had been built upon island ground. It was brackish, and would have been rejected as unfit for consumption in normal times. But it was far better than that of the lake, which, having no outlet, was intensely salty.

For food, there is no doubt that they depended more and more upon human flesh, and, when prisoners were exhausted, and others could not be taken, they overcame their aversion to the use of their own dead in this manner, so that it could be said that when the Spaniards killed them they were providing food through which resistance could be prolonged.

And, in spite of all the influence which could be exercised by the Spaniards, and those of other races who had adopted the Christian Faith, and desired that its customs should be observed, there is no doubt that the large armies of their allies subsisted to some extent on the same diet; but with the qualification that they did no more than consume enemies who had been killed in conflict. They had ceased to capture prisoners for that purpose, in deference to Spanish objections, and, beyond that, their proceedings, however repugnant to European standards, might have been impolitic to oppose, and impossible to prevent.

As the demolitions continued, and approached, both from north and south, the marketplace which had been previously found impossible to reach, it became a frequent experience to find that captured buildings would contain those who were sick or wounded, or too weakened by starvation to flee. The orders of Cortéz that such wretches should be kindly treated were observed by the Spaniards, and some of their allies, who rescued many; but there were others in whom the spirit of hatred burned with too fierce a flame. To them, the Aztecs were vermin to be exterminated, and there were cases where buildings were allowed to burn above those who were too weakened to crawl away.

But while the Spaniards often found these buildings to contain those whom they did not seek, they were baffled by the absence of that which they had expected to find.

Some spoil, usually of bulky nature, there certainly was, but mainly such as was more desirable to Tlascalans or Tezcucans than Spanish eyes. Of precious stones, or gold, either in bulk or with the value that cunning workmanship gives, there was nothing found. Dying Aztecs, with such venom as snakes will spit, would jeer at the disappointment of the white men, and foretell that such riches would forever elude their search.

But there was a presumption that portable treasure was being withdrawn before them, and accumulating in the ever-lessening area that remained unconquered, which disposed the invaders to increase the ardour of their attacks.

By this time, the larger part of the city had become a flattened wilderness, to a degree which would have been impossible but for the canals, which provided ditches into which the stones could be cast which fire refused to consume. Even those areas which had been entirely under water, the buildings being erected on piles, and canoe-traffic having been carried on beneath them, had become no more than shallow depressions, the depth of the water—usually not more than two or three feet—having been filled up with the stones and timbers of the houses which had been above, and surrounding debris.

When he had seen that this work was being performed with less thoroughness than he required, Cortéz had himself not merely directed operations, but put his own shoulder to the work, giving example, though still with a limping leg, of the right lifting and disposal of stone and beam.

So it came to be, at the beginning of the fourth week of this process of demolition, that the southern army, almost within sight of the Market Square, but seriously hindered by a broad canal which the Aztecs had fortified as a final resistance line, saw a dense column of smoke less than half a mile ahead, which told them that their emulous comrades from the north had stormed and fired the major temple in that part of the city—only second to the central pyramid—to which the chief priests had transferred their ritual ceremonies and sacrifices, since they had been expelled from their headquarters by the Spanish advance.

It was a forecast of final victory, stimulating additional effort from weary men, and warning them that no more than a few hours might pass before Alvarado would be in the Market Square which was the objective for which they had agreed to compete.

Cortéz, regardless of arrows that he thought his armour should be equal to meet, rode himself to the brink of this last obstacle, to decide what should be done.

Running from northeast to southwest, the canal formed a broad moat beyond which the Aztecs had erected barriers too strong to be pierced by anything less than the shots of his heavier guns—and shortage of powder was again becoming acute.

If he should wait long enough, he supposed that Alvarado might attack the position in the rear. But he was averse from this course, both as a matter of prestige, and because he did not know what opposition Alvarado might still have to meet. One thing was certain: if he should remain still, the Aztecs could employ larger forces against Alvarado's advance. Every argument supported the policy of forcing the passage, but the desperation with which the Aztecs would fight for what was apparently their last ditch was beyond doubt, and he did not delude himself that it would be easy to do.

He said: "There is only one way. The canal must be filled up."

It was a colossal labour to undertake beneath the volleys of stones and arrows that the Aztecs would direct upon it. But the labourers were ordered to the front, excluding all, however willing, who were not wearing well-padded coats and headdresses, and behind them the arquebusiers were ranged, their clumsy tripod-mounted weapons pointed upon the edge of the barricade, and their matches ready, so that they could take quick aim at any heads that should be exposed by the slingers and archers which it concealed.

It was work at which there was no inclination to lag. Logs were borne or rolled, and stones were dragged, by those who knew that each moment they might suffer broken bone or disabling bruise from a hard-slung stone, or that an arrow might transfix hand to log, or enter mouth or eye with fatal effect.

So the canal was filled in at last, at whatever cost, and cannon blasted a breach in the barricade, at a place where there was sufficient open ground beyond for the cavaliers to operate, and after that the work of demolition proceeded as before, until the hour came when Cortéz and Alvarado met in a street in which the dust of demolition was still obscuring the sun. There were still warrens of small crowded houses to right and left that the Aztecs held, but seven-eights of the city was a flattened desolation on which its enemies moved at will.

That afternoon Cortéz rode into the Market Square, which Alvarado had already entered without opposition. Its great extent was bare, and its surrounding booths were empty. Life—crowded life—stirred in the houses beyond but did not emerge. Was the war done?

The next day gave the answer to that. The remaining buildings, and whatever else might be theirs, still sheltered an Aztec army of fanatical valour, which would not admit defeat.

Simultaneously from every door, from every street and alley, a rush of warriors invaded the square. For a time, those who had occupied it were driven backward, not without loss, by the impetuosity of the assault. Rallying, and reinforced, they recovered ground; but it was only after two hours of the fiercest and most sanguinary fighting the war had known, that the Square was recovered, and the Aztec army thrust back rather than routed, into the streets and alleys from which it came.

After that, there was a pause of three days, which meant less to the victors than those who skulked and starved in the crowded houses in which the scent of flowers had been changed for the stenches of disease and corruption.

The previous trouble had recurred. Powder—used too freely in blasting the Great Pyramid (with the double object of destroying the centre of the Aztec religion and providing material for filling up the canals)—was again short.

But whatever Guatemozín might think or plan, and however many of his race might still be faithful to him, it was evident to those who looked on that he had suffered absolute and final defeat. Almost every day now there were deputations of submission from distant cities whose dialects Marina must endeavour to understand, or letters which she would find more easy to read.

Every day extended the domains of a Spanish King, who might know much or little of what was being done in his name.

CHAPTER ONE HUNDRED FIVE: CATAPULT

Alvarado said: "I should not wait for that. I should smoke them out."

Cortéz answered: "But if we wait, I hope it may not be used. They must see sense. They are starving now. We may yet save what is left."

They were talking about a catapult which one of the men who had arrived in the last ship, and come up from the coast with the powder, said he knew how to make.

His name was Sotelo. He was one who had the prestige of having been in the Italian wars. A professional soldier. Not an amateur, as most of Cortéz's comrades were. A condottiere. One of those men who owned his horse and weapons, and would hire himself, and perhaps a few followers, by yearly contract to a military leader—a contract which would contain proper clauses, not only assuring him of liberal wages, but compensation for wounds or damage that he or his horse might sustain, and a suitable bonus for any fighting that had to be done. And, of course, his Leader would make a contract with some wealthy Italian state, that would make his own profit secure. It was all done in a safe, solid way. There had been security there.

Sotelo had left Italy for reasons best known to himself, and had been drawn by the lure of the New World; but now he was not sure that he liked the conditions to which he had come. He had asked for a contract, and got one of a kind, and all men told him that Hernando Cortéz would keep his bond. But the terms were too loose for him. He was one who liked to know not only where he was, but where he would be on the next day.

When he had been in the Mantuan campaign, he had seen a catapult set up, and been one who had helped to work it. It had interested him, for he had a mechanical mind. He felt sure he could successfully superintend the making of one of a similar kind.

There was a platform in the midst of the Square on which jugglers and acrobats would perform—not on market days, but on festival occasions, when the whole space around it would be cleared of stall and booth, and half the city could see the show, if it would. Sotelo saw that this platform was solid stone, and he thought it would be an excellent position for the erection of the machine.

He had asked whether he could have an interview with his Commander, and was told that there would be no difficulty about that. Anyone could.

Cortéz was in a tent, erected on the barren ground where a city had been. It protected him from the sun of a hot day. He was dicing with some of his captains, which he would do more shrewdly than most, but all in a laughing way, as he played all games, even chess, seeming careless of whether he might win or lose, but preferring a hard bout. A man who played poorly, that his Commander might win, would have found that he ploughed in a barren field.

Cortéz pushed a stake which was on the board before him into a common heap. He said: "I pay forfeit for leaving the game." He got up at once, and left the tent, to see Sotelo without.

He listened, and his eyes lit. It was an idea he liked. It would save powder. It gave him excuse to pause while the machine would be made. It might lead to a better end than he had expected to reach during the last days, while the obstinacy of the Aztecs had continued beyond anything that it had been reasonable to expect. It might save many lives.

Having had the idea approved, and his assurance that he could build the catapult accepted more readily than he had forecast, Sotelo asked what his remuneration would be.

Cortéz said that he could leave that to him with a quiet mind.

But that was a way that he did not like. He asked, could he not have a written contract? Cortéz laughed: "So you can, but you will get less."

In the end, he got a contract which assured him of a large sum, if the machine would throw a stone of specified weight for two hundred yards, or else more. Otherwise, he got nothing at all. He argued about that, but Cortéz (when he was provoked to it) had a lawyer's mind. He asked for a guarantee that he would not be losing time, and expending labour and material to no avail. The main gamble was his. Sotelo had enough sense to see that he would gain nothing by saying more.

So the catapult was built, and meanwhile the strife stayed, and the Aztecs starved.

They still got some provisions smuggled over the lake during the night, but not much, and at a great cost, for the waterfront on which they could be landed was now so much restricted that the brigantines patrolling during the night had an easy task.

The Aztecs, in their confined area, were not only suffering from wounds, starvation, and sickness. They, of whom their enemies had said that their streets were cleaner than the interiors of Spanish houses, were living in squalor and filth, and many in flowerless rooms.

One of the brigantines had run down three canoes, and had captured two, loaded with food. They had evidently sacrificed themselves that the third might escape. The wind had brought the scent of honeysuckle and roses from that. At all costs, to the last hour, the decencies of private life must be maintained in the Emperor's rooms. The Aztec civilisation, mangled by the deadlier weapons of European savagery, was dying hard.

The day came when the catapult was complete. It was now recognised that Sotelo had knowledge of the construction of such machines. It was a huge complicated affair, but for some days there had been a growing confidence that he had not promised more than he could perform.

Now those who watched were assembled on the side of the Square which should be dangerless, even if the great stone should not be projected for the full distance required.

They saw the spring wound, the lever pulled. The stone rose straight into the air. It was projected to a great height, the machine proving itself as powerful as had been guaranteed. But when it fell, as it must at last, it descended precisely upon the spot from which it had risen. It smashed the machine.

Wiping blood, those who worked it were amazed that their lives had escaped the scattered fragments of iron and wood.

A great shout of laughter rose from those who watched, the event bringing a degree of ridicule upon Sotelo which may have been beyond what he deserved. But he could not demonstrate that, the catapult being shattered beyond repair.

The watching Aztecs wondered what new devilry it might be, and what the laughter might mean.

CHAPTER ONE HUNDRED SIX: CHAOS

Men might jest at the way in which the catapult had destroyed itself, but to Cortéz it was not a matter at which to jape.

Those who expected that instant orders would be issued to renew the process of demolition waited in vain during the remainder of the day on which the catastrophe had occurred, and Marina had experience, which was not new to her, of a consort who paced the room during the night hours.

But this time it was not for so long as it had often been in the past.

After a short time, he said abruptly, but not as though speaking to her: "There is one way, and it must be tried. It must be tried. I suppose it will accord with the high counsels of God, even though it should come to a poor end."

Then he turned, and looked down on her, where she lay, and asked: "Will they give respect to a flag of truce, or are they too hateful for that?"

"How can I tell? I suppose it would be observed. It is Guatemozín who will not yield. I have told you he never will."

"So you have. And a city has been destroyed. Must it go on?"

"Have I blamed you for that? You have done all that forbearance could, as I know you will."

He could not say that there had been any lack of loyalty from her, as she had watched him destroy the city which had been hers, and which had held the most of wealth and beauty her world had known.

She had sympathised: she had understood. But in these days she had ceased to smile.

He said: "Well, I will make accord, if I can. It may be that the day has come when they will cease to listen to him."

When he said in the morning that he would approach the Aztecs with a flag of truce, he found little support. Alvarado said: "You waste time, while those die who are faithful to you. Would you have the plague? I tell you that there is no cure but fire."

There was reason in what he said, for, while the catapult had been built, the wind had changed to the west, and had borne an evil stench to the besieger's camps, and there were more sickening of fevers than might have been killed in strife had they fought without pause.

Olid said the same. Why should they risk themselves among these eaters of human flesh, in a pestilent town?

Cortéz said: "I shall need ten cavaliers who will ride with me. But I compel no one to come. I suppose I shall not go short."

Then he got to horse, having ordered that a flag of truce should go before him, instead of that of Castile. He had Marina at his left hand, and ten riding behind, having found that some must be refused, for there were more who were of a disposition to come, of whom Alvarado was one. But Olid did not appear.

He entered an alley so narrow that, though they rode it in single file, they would have been endangered by rocks tipped from above, and they saw some that were poised to fall, but none did, and the houses remained silent and closed. But there were dead or dying bodies, over which the horses were timid to tread; some that had the distorted faces which fevers cause, and some showing starvation's bones, and some both. There was uncleansed filth also, such as had not been seen in an Aztec city before.

Then they came out to a wider street, and saw a group of soldiers, who disappeared, getting into boats, and so away by a canal.

Cortéz reined here, and grouped his retinue in a better way. He said: "We will remain here for two hours, if none comes."

So they sat with their lances raised, the chargers very still, as they knew that such occasions required; and when they had waited about an hour they were aware of those who approached in a peaceful way.

There were three Aztecs of some degree, though not of the first rank, being the Governor of the Market Square, and two others who had local rule in that quarter.

Cortéz told Marina what he would have her say, which he knew she would, but he must wait while there was much said, too rapid for him to grasp, though he now knew many words of the Aztec tongue, and which was more than she had had from him.

At the last, she said: "I have prevailed that they will intercede with Guatemozín, which at first they were reluctant to do, saying that it would not avail. We are to wait here for a short while, if you will consent."

"Tell them I will wait till the noon hour, and it is the last hope they will have."

They went at that, and came back in less time than had been agreed. Their words were good enough, but they did not look as those will who are well content.

Marina said: "What they say is that they have prevailed upon Guatemozín to meet you at noon tomorrow, in the Great Square, so that peace may be made at last."

She made the best of what had been said, for she judged that the Emperor had given a blank refusal to the proposal of an immediate interview, and a very dubious consent to the later suggestion, which had not originated with him. She judged that they were making a desperate effort to save the remainder of their city from useless destruction, and they should have no lack of support from her.

But when she was alone with Cortéz, she said: "Hernán, I would not have you deceived. Guatemozín may come, or he may not. But there are those who will make him face facts, if they can."

"So I supposed. Or should we say that there are those who will keep us quiet till he have escaped, to raise up strife which may be a curse for this land for long years to come?"

"He may try that, as we know. But he should have done it before."

There was no more that it was useful to say. The meeting having been agreed, preparations for the Emperor's reception must be made.

The central platform in the Square, from which the wreck of the catapult had been removed, was spread with matting, and cushions on which the royal guest could recline. Low tables, such as he was accustomed to use, were provided, and, as the hour of meeting approached, spread with such a meal as even he would not be likely to scorn.

But, when the time came, he did not. The same three who had been seen on the previous day made apologetic appearance. They said that Guatemozín was ill.

Cortéz received this statement with more courtesy than it deserved. He offered food, which they were very willing to eat. He urged them, for his own sake, to try to bring Guatemozín to a different mood.

They went, promising to do this, and soon returned, saying that the Emperor had been persuaded by the messages he had received. He would come himself at the next noon.

"Well," Cortéz said to Marina, "tell them that he must, for it is the last chance he will have."

Next morning he was prepared either for peace or war, but resolved that he would not be longer befooled, about which men were beginning to jest.

The central platform was draped and furnished as before. Spanish soldiers were drawn up in the Square. The allies, diplomatically kept out of sight, were a little further away. They had orders to remain still unless the trumpets should sound advance, when they had instructions as to what they should do.

Noon came, but no one appeared from the Aztec streets, not even the envoys who had come on the previous day. Cortéz waited for a further hour, and then let the trumpets sound.

There was to be no further attempt at slow demolition. From what he had seen on the previous day, he judged that the Aztecs would no longer be in condition to oppose a general advance.

He had given emphatic instructions that there should be no violence to noncombatants, nor should mercy be refused to those who were willing to yield, and he had placed Spanish observers among the allied troops to ensure that these instructions were obeyed.

So it might have been if no resistance had been made, but the fact was that Guatemozín had roused the remnant of his subjects to a final frenzy; and, among those who had strength to stand, noncombatants would have been hard to find.

Spaniards and Tezcucans had scarcely entered the narrow streets before their advance was obstructed by what may best be described as an armed and resolute rabble, while missiles descended upon them from flat roofs and terraces on either side.

Through the hot afternoon the streets became a chaos of fire and strife, of plunder and blood, through which the invaders forced their disordered way.

Among the Spaniards, although taunted by mocking cries about the gold they would never get, the orders of Cortéz prevailed, and those who yielded were spared, and even succoured, so far as conditions allowed; but among the vastly superior numbers of the allies, the observers he had placed were too few to do much more than to record excesses which they could not restrain.

They saw wholesale massacres of young and old, of sick, wounded, or starving wretches who were too weak to crawl away from the butchery which approached; they saw the wanton firing of buildings from which no resistance was offered, and which often contained those who might be dying, but were not dead.

The streak of sombre cruelty which ran through the character of all the Mexican races, now excited both by past grievances and present triumph, was exhibited here at its worst, and, for every act of mercy or clemency which Cortéz could inspire among those around him, there were a hundred brutalities which he did not see, and could not prevent.

As the sun declined, there were still many streets unoccupied, and the frantic futility of resistance had not abated when the trumpets sounded retreat.

The victorious armies withdrew for the evening revelry appropriate to an hour of triumph, but their leader, adding his usual nightly paragraph to the report which was meant for the eyes of the Spanish King, was in a different mood. *Their cries broke my heart*, he wrote, describing the slaughter of helpless wretches which had been beyond his control.

Putting aside the fibrous Mexican paper on which he wrote, he said to Marina: "You must come with me tomorrow. I will stop this slaughter, if reason can. And you can talk to them in the right way."

"I will do all I can. But they are asking for that which they need not have," she answered, speaking calmly because she saw how much his mind was disturbed.

Then he sent to Sandoval.

"Gonzalo," he said, "I am placing you in charge of the brigantines. If they do not yield tomorrow in an orderly way, we must continue our advance, and, as we do so, I suppose that many will seek to flee by way of the lake, for which their canoes are in thousands on the canals that remain, and along the shore.

"I want you to patrol the lake tomorrow from the Northern to the Western Causeway. They may spread out to that extent as they flee, but cannot cross them, for I shall have them too strongly held. With the eleven vessels that you will have, you should be hard to avoid."

Sandoval asked, in his slow speech, and without sign of his thoughts: "Am I to sink all?"

"You are to sink none. You will observe all, and let them go, except Guatemozín alone. You will seize him, being careful that he come to no harm, and bring him to me."

"This is all as the winds allow."

"If it continue as it now is, it will be fairly abeam. You can tack and wear as you will."

Sandoval still had a worried look. He said: "He will be disguised. Can I inspect all as they hurry past?

"Eleven ships can do much. He has three swift piraguas. He may use them."

Sandoval had the same hope, though he had been slower to speak. The royal piraguas could be picked out in a moment, among a hundred canoes. Sandoval hoped that Guatemozín might rely on their speed, if he should attempt flight, though he thought he would be a fool if he did.

He knew it would be a far surer way to sink all the canoes they could, though he did not wish to do that. He saw clearly, in a slow shrewd mind, that the time had come when a captive Emperor would be useful to have.

Going out, he met Alvarado, told him of the instructions he had received, and found that he was not alone in his thoughts.

"Keep him alive with care!" He exclaimed. "You should be practised to watch him drown. You can tell Hernán that it was what you could not prevent. He would take it from you. But I suppose you may spoil all."

Alvarado went on whistling, undistressed by the prospect which he so lightly foretold, and Sandoval went his own way, to call the captains of the brigantines together, and give them the instructions that the position required, which must be done by five or six, for half of them were patrolling the lake now.

He thought that Alvarado was right, and that his Commander's heart was outrunning his brain, but he knew himself well enough not to doubt that the instructions he had received would be closely obeyed, and he knew that Cortéz had chosen him for that certainty.

But perhaps the Divine Wisdom would still the wind.

CHAPTER ONE HUNDRED SEVEN: GUATEMOZÍN

The next day came, and again the soldiers of Spain and her allies were marshalled, and then held back, like leashed hounds, while Cortéz, with Marina's support, obdured magistrates who could only say that they would enquire the Emperor's will, and then return to falter from unwilling lips a defiant reply.

So the advance through the tortured city began again, with the difference that it must now traverse streets which had been scorched with fire and strewn with death on the previous day.

And again there was the weak frenzied resistance of the half starved and the hopeless, still blindly loyal to an Emperor who would not yield, and impulsed by a hatred of their opponents surpassing the ordinary extremities of human passion.

Again there was the inexorable advance against resistance that could do no more than delay, and as those Aztecs who remained alive were crowded into constantly decreasing space between their foes and the shore, they took to the water, as Cortéz had rightly judged that they would be certain to do. He had been equally right in supposing that Guatemozín, having to choose at last between captivity, death, or flight, would choose the last, and take the only way that remained. But he did not guess what his plan would be.

Ruthless in sacrifice of those who were devoted to him, as he had already shown himself to be in prolonging a vain defence, he ordered that all the canoes, after taking aboard such soldiers as still remained of a fighting worth, should put out at the same time, and attack the brigantines, both with arrows, and by attempting to board.

He could not hope that such assaults would avail to capture the vessels, but he relied upon them to cause sufficient embarrassment to enable him to escape, if his time for the attempt should be wisely chosen.

He would have had a better prospect of success had not the wind freshened during the morning, and shifted toward the southeast. If there were intervention of Heaven here, it was contrary to that which Alvarado would have approved.

The long-stretched line of the brigantines, with topsails reefed, close-hauled to the rising wind, were just going about, when several hundred canoes shot out at once from two miles of opposing shore. The sailing vessels had no choice to pursue or to let them go. The orders Cortéz had given did not apply to canoes which converged upon each, twenty to one. They must fight or fly. Naturally, they elected to fight.

Powder was not yet so short that they were unable to serve their guns. The lake was soon loud with cannon-fire, and dark with wisps of sulphurous smoke drifting toward the further shore.

Some canoes were sunk by these discharges; some were rammed. Others came close enough for their arrows to have some effect. The helmsmen must steer with care, if they would not have hordes of Aztecs climbing aboard.

None of them may have been in great danger, but they were closely engaged.

Captain Holguín was stationed at the northern end of the line, because his vessel, the *San Salvador*, was the fastest in the fleet, and the widest stretch of water to be guarded was there.

His lookout saw three very large canoes which had been creeping along under the shadows of the pile-built houses which were the city's northwestern extremity, strike outward in a west-northwest direction toward the further shore of the lake.

It was a manoeuvre which gave them a substantial start, and had there been no more wind than the northeastern breeze of the previous day, they would have made certain escape.

But the wind was now almost dead east, and Guatemozín, sitting in the stern of the largest boat, in his green-plumed war-helmet, and golden armour, with a gilt buckler upon his knee, saw the *San Salvador* shake out its topsail, break through the gnat-like group of canoes by which it was pestered, and come down the wind at a pace which it was no pleasure to watch.

But even then the three boats might have escaped, had not Guatemozín made an unsound deduction, which seemed logic to him.

He had watched the fleet on the lake. He had actually been on board one of the two brigantines which Cortéz had first built, when Montezuma had been entertained upon it. He knew that they depended upon the wind, and he underrated their capacity to adapt it to their own requirements. He ordered that the canoes should take a northerly course, which was to a more distant part of the shore, but which (he supposed) would reduce the speed of pursuit to a far greater degree.

By when he had learnt his mistake, and reverted to the direct course, he had lost much of the advantage which he had had, and he saw that he was in a desperate strait.

He was additionally troubled by the fact that the two other boats were proving to be slightly faster than his. He had ordered that his own should be manned by the best paddlers, but such difference (which was not much: they were all good men) was more than offset by the fact that his own was more heavily loaded with treasures with which he would not readily part.

When he realised this, he ordered them to slacken effort sufficiently for him to keep ahead, and when he saw that, even if he should require them to allow themselves to be taken, it might not avail for his own escape, he told them to separate, so that the pursuer would be baffled of two thirds of his prey, and he might have good hope that his own boat would be one to escape.

Captain Holguín, steering his own ship, watched these successive tricks with shrewd calculating eyes. He was one of the few real sea-captains that the fleet contained, more Dutch than Spanish, and not one to be easily taken in. What he feared most was that the water might shallow toward the shore, so that he would have to abandon pursuit. Well, even then he had a good gunner aboard. But he knew what his orders were, and he thought he could bring in a live catch.

He saw Sandoval's vessel coming up fast on the port quarter, and was well content to calculate that it would be too late to do more than provide an audience for the final scene.

He watched, with a sailor's admiration, the speed and regularity with which the canoes were paddled, content that his spread of canvas in the ever-freshening wind was beyond the competition of mortal muscles.

He was unperturbed when they separated, for he had already formed his opinion of which one had the Emperor on board. As he closed upon it, he knew that the prize was won.

Drawing alongside, he looked down upon a crowded vessel, the occupants of which were more numerous than those on his own deck. But it was one that a twist of his wheel would have rammed and sunk; and the falconet that was trained upon it would have made it a shambles in thirty seconds.

Captain Holguín would have known the man who rose from the stern, even without the indication of the green-plumed helmet. He said: "I am Guatemozín. I am Malintzin's prisoner. Take me to him." His voice had the reserved dignity which was common to those of Montezuma's race.

Captain Holguín did not understand Aztec, nor did the Emperor understand the Dutch in which he felt it appropriate to reply. But the position was clear.

The Emperor climbed to the *San Salvador's* deck. Signs were sufficient to give consent or command for his retinue to follow. There were more than twenty of these, besides the crew, who remained, and were allowed to paddle away. They included several women, among whom was a young girl, a daughter of Montezuma, whom Guatemozín had made his wife. Coanaca also was there.

Captain Holguín, tacking into the wind, surveyed a lake on which the confusion of conflict ceased. The Emperor's capture had put an instant end to the war.

The canoes ceased their futile attacks upon vessels which were larger, better armed, and (in that wind) more mobile than they. Some put back to the city: most, being unpursued, fled to the further shore.

Captain Holguín found that he had a companion in Sandoval's vessel, which followed tack after tack with the closeness of a twin sister, while Sandoval demanded, in a voice which had the wind's help, that the prisoners should be handed over to him. He said (with truth) that Cortéz had given him the task of bringing them in, with the command of the fleet.

Captain Holguín, in a gruff voice which was more accustomed to such exchanges, invoked the law of the sea, by which the spoil (and surely a rich reward!) was entirely his.

Sandoval knew little about sea law, and cared less, but he knew what his orders had been, and that he was in command of the fleet for that day. He expected his own orders to be obeyed.

Neither was an eloquent man, and Holguín's profanity had the disadvantage of being in the Dutch tongue, to which, in moments of mental stress, he was inclined to revert.

Sandoval ceased these abortive exchanges, observing that he could not assert his authority until the prisoners should be put ashore.

There was no place at which this could be done nearer than the city end of the southern causeway, and, when they lay side by side at the wharf there, Sandoval found there was to be a further difficulty which he had not foreseen. Captain Holguín was alert as to the position which would arise if he should put his prisoners out on to the dock. He said they should remain on his own deck until he had instructions for their disposal from Cortéz himself.

So, with a swivel-mounted falconet trained inward upon them, the prisoners remained grouped on the deck, unable to exchange speech with those around them, or to make more than a poor guess as to what their fate was likely to be.

For the next hour they remained there, as though their conqueror were too much occupied with more important concerns to give heed to them.

Guatemozín, planning in the night hours to escape to the remoter mountains where he might be able to maintain a guerrilla war, had seen the possibility of capture, and wondered what might be the worst it could mean for him.

He had imagined many indignities, many deprivations from the amenities of luxurious life, even torture or death, to be faced with the stoicism of his race. But not this. Not that his surrender would be treated as a matter of small account, to be disregarded among more important affairs.

With no protection from the sun's heat as the sails were furled, the group waited upon the deck.

Montezuma's daughter sat on a coiled rope.

CHAPTER ONE HUNDRED EIGHT: HOW THE NIGHT FELL

The word that Guatemozín was in Spanish hands spread through the streets which had not yet been occupied by the invaders, and, as it did so, the last flickers of resistance suddenly died.

Cortéz, watching all from the highest temple platform that remained on the edge of the undemolished remnant of the city, when this was reported to him, sent instant messages, right and left, to restrain the allied armies from further slaughter. He ordered also that there was to be no opposition to those who might still seek to flee over the lake.

He knew that the captives must be landed nearly three miles away, and was prepared for some delay, but when Sandoval did not appear with his prisoners as promptly as he had expected, he sent a cavalier to enquire the cause; and this messenger had scarcely left when one from Sandoval appeared, with explanation of the delay.

At this, he sent Diego with a curt order that Guatemozín was to be brought to him at once, without further indignities, and that he would deal with the dispute between the two officers at a later hour.

He ordered that the platform should be carpeted in the Mexican style, and a meal provided. He sent to Marina to join him.

By when these preparations were completed, Ordaz reappeared, with a company of infantry, and the Mexican Emperor in their midst.

As he was led up the temple steps, Cortéz advanced to meet him, with an outstretched hand. It was a gesture of magnanimity, but it implied that European gestures would now prevail.

"He says," Marina interpreted, "that he is in your hands by the fortune of war, and you must do with him what you will."

"Tell him that the war was waged by him, which I did not desire. If he will now be faithful to Spain, he will have nothing to fear from me."

Guatemozín inclined his head when he heard that, which might mean little or much. Cortéz added: "But where is his wife, and Coanaca, and others of whom I heard?"

"He says that he supposes that they are still on the ship."

Cortéz swore at that, as he seldom would. He asked Diego, and found it to be true: Captain Holguín had obeyed a command he dare not ignore in a very literal and minimal way.

He gained nothing by that, having to obey one of more explicit wording in the next hour. The prisoners, including Guatemozín's wife (for whom, on Cortéz's urgent orders, a litter had been quickly obtained) were to be sent at once.

Meanwhile the meal was delayed. Guatemozín found himself disregarded again, while his captor dealt with a hundred urgencies, issuing orders the purport of which could be partially understood, and partially guessed.

And when the other prisoners were brought in, there was more of haste than speech, for twilight was near, and there was a prospect of rain, the wind having become a gale, and the sky black with hurrying clouds.

Sandoval had come by this time, having relinquished control of a fleet which had done much for the Spanish cause, but might never have occasion to fight again.

Cortéz said: "Let Holguín be for this night! I do not say he was wholly wrong, but he could have asked in a better way. The prisoners will be in your charge. You will conduct them to Cojohuacan and that with haste, for a storm is near. Have Guatemozín's palanquin fetched. I will come myself when I have dealt with some matters here, for this is not a place in which to remain."

In fact, as the conflict died, men became more fully aware of the horrors which had been, and of those which were round them now.

Two cavaliers would write afterwards that it was impossible to pass through the narrow streets without treading on heaps of those who might or might not be dead.

Men became conscious that the air was fetid to breathe, and that it was laden with a continual murmur of woe.

As darkness fell, the rain came.

All troops had, by this time, been withdrawn from streets in which the Aztecs still crowded and crawled, except a small guard of such as Cortéz could trust not to cause further misery, though they might be impotent to relieve that within their sight.

Cortéz said: "I will ride to Cojohuacan tonight, though the heavens fall. But there should be a litter for you."

Marina laughed: "Am I one to fear rain?"

They mounted horses which were standing await, and rode back to the Great Avenue; and, as they did so, the storm broke.

The wind had fallen. The rain came straightly down, a solid flood in which the horses waded and splashed. The lightning was round them on every side. The deafening thunder was overhead.

It was such a storm as Cortéz had never known, and Marina but once.

It brought the thirsting Aztecs out of their houses to be soaked, and to lap it up. If they could not walk, they could crawl. It was life to them.

And it cleansed streets which had been cumbered with dead, and covered with filth and blood.

When morning came, the water was foul and red for two miles of the lake shore. The Aztec Empire was washed away.

Cortéz supped at midnight in one of the pleasure palaces of Cojohuacan. They had ridden to Xoloc, and then westward, nearly six miles of causeway in all, while they must trust their horses more than themselves to avoid the lake, in the black intervals that the lightning left.

They had obtained dry garments of sundry sorts.

Now he sat with Marina, de Ávila, and Sandoval, and Father Olmedo was at his right hand. They were those among whom he would talk with little reserve.

Now he was saying: "Father, I have caused much evil, which I lament; but I suppose that I have done well. For I have brought a whole people to God."

Men would call him bigot in later days, but his fault was no more than that he believed what the Church taught.

That is not a matter of dogma or of opinion. It is simple mathematical fact.

If the earthly lives of a nation be brought to misery, and one man be saved from eternal torment, there is an incalculable but enormous gain.

The mathematics of Europe were not equal to those of the civilisation which it had destroyed, but they were sufficient for proving that.

CHAPTER ONE HUNDRED NINE: GOLD

The order which Cortéz issued next morning was one of humanity, but also demonstrated his supreme confidence in the triumph that he had won.

The Aztec armies were not required to surrender, nor even to lay down their arms. Their existence was simply ignored. All who remained alive in the ruined streets, combatants included, could leave the city—were, indeed, required to do so within three days, which was a preliminary measure of sanitation, in view of the condition to which it had been reduced.

They could go where they would; they could take with them whatever possessions they were able to bear away.

Only, under penalty of death, they were not to remove without permission gold or silver, wrought jewellery, or precious stones.

On the second and third days there was an inquisition as to this being done, but nothing of importance was found.

Gold is heavy, and its uses are few. Those who had no better means of conveyance than their own backs naturally preferred articles of greater value.

But by the dawn of the second day the mystery of the missing gold was in all men's mouths.

Of its existence there could be no doubt. Apart from the treasures of kings and princes, it had been as common in every Aztec home as was iron in Madrid.

Yet the whole quantity which had been obtained since the first residences at the head of the southern causeway had been sacked amounted to so little that the soldiers of Narváez, who had come in anticipation of sharing fantastic wealth, contemptuously refused to accept their shares.

Some remembered the taunts that the Aztecs had flung at them during the last days of the siege. They believed the gold to have been cleverly hidden, and clamoured for the Aztec leaders to be coerced into revealing it.

Others accused Cortéz of having concealed it for his own profit. There may not have been many who could have believed this, but a few can make an unpleasant stench, especially when they resort to such methods of attack as lampoons scrawled on the walls.

The allegation became serious when it was supported by the King's Treasurer. Alderete had been an unpopular man since he had successfully advocated the attack on the Market Square which he had unsuccessfully led. The sixty-two Spaniards who had been sacrificed on Aztec altars had not been without friends. Men said that, but for the rescuing action that Cortéz took, the losses would have been much higher than that. Many felt that it was no praise to Alderete that they had not themselves fallen into the hands of the priests. Alderete said, on the contrary, that had Cortéz continued his own advance, the operation would have been successful. There was no proving of that, but it was not widely believed.

Alderete may have been sincere in his accusation, though it is hard to credit. Everyway, it was to his own gain. He was showing zeal for his master, the Spanish King. He was advocating the cause of the common soldier, for all must go short, if the gold could not be found.

Cortéz had interrogated Guatemozín about this on the first day, and, getting no satisfaction from him, he had ordered that there should be examination of whatever might be removed from the city, and diligent search among the houses that yet remained.

When both of these searches proved abortive, he had Guatemozín fetched before him again.

"Will you tell him," Cortéz said, "that it is useless for him to profess that he will now be loyal to Spain, while he is silent on that which I ask, and he surely knows. The war is done. With no gain to himself, why should he still seek to do evil to us?"

Guatemozín said he did no evil at all. He simply did not tell that which he did not know.

Marina did what she could, using all arguments that reason or policy might suggest. She said: "Can I tell my lord that? The gold would not have been so largely removed without orders from you."

That was a fact, as they both knew. He fenced with it, adroitly enough: "Can he not understand that I was occupied with larger concerns? We do not value gold as the Spaniards do."

"Then you could do much for them, which would cost you less."

He made no answer to that, his eyes becoming remote, as though he had ceased to hear. Did she think he wished to do "Much for them"?

Training, policy, and passion contended to vary his reactions to what she said.

It was his habit to hide his thoughts, to be remote and aloof. It was his policy to persuade, if he could, that he was indifferent as to whether the Spaniards should get the gold, and genuinely ignorant as to where it could be. But, under all, passion stirred, with loathing for these men who had brought him from height to depth, with the ruin of all his race—except the traitress who could be as aloof as himself.

There was one joy left—to watch the baffled fury of these savages, with their crude and senseless admiration for yellow metal, which would be impossible to a civilised man. Certainly he would not tell them—even if he could tell anything now which would be useful to them, about which he was less than sure.

Alvarado, who had asked to be present, said impatiently: "Cannot you see that we waste time? Make the yellow dog jump! You will find it the quickest way."

Guatemozín understood the tone, and perhaps something of the meaning, of this outburst. He looked at Alvarado with a remote dignity until, for a second, their eyes met, and those of the blond giant fell before a contempt so great that, for a moment, it even put hatred aside.

Cortéz saw that no progress was being made. He wished that Alvarado had not been there. He was not passionless himself, but, when he had a great purpose to gain, he could subordinate all else to the cold judgement of what would achieve his end. And, at that, Marina (as he had often observed) was even more adroit than himself.

He said: "Can you make him understand that this is a matter I cannot leave? Soon or late, I must know where the gold is. Tell him that I desire accord, such as will leave him with a great place in the land. But, if he will not speak, he will lose all. Nor could I promise that his own person will be immune."

Marina put this in her own way. She said: "My lord would have you know that this is a matter he cannot leave; but, if you will help him in this, you may still be a great power in the land.

"You should know that he is one who will have his way, be it soon or late. But, if he give you a pledge, you will stand secure."

Guatemozín replied wearily: "Must it be said many times? Can I tell you that which I do not know?"

She said: "You will do no more at this time."

"Tell him," Cortéz replied, "that he should think well. Tomorrow we will talk again."

So they did. But they gained nothing thereby: and after that Marina adventured a flank attack. She saw his wife, Tecuichpo, Montezuma's daughter, a girl scarcely mature, and would have persuaded her, for her own ultimate welfare, as well as that of her husband, to counsel Guatemozín to yield. But she had only failure of which to tell.

The girl had character, intellect, and beauty. In later years, when the wife of a hidalgo of Spain, she would do much for her country's peace; but she said now that she had no influence over her husband, nor did he give confidences to her. It was clear that, though they might be physically married, they were mental strangers.

Marina said: "I have done no good for the purpose on which I went, and no harm. She will say nothing to him. I have comforted tears."

Cortéz said: "Then I must let others make their attempt, who have less mercy than I. I am blamed by all. It is not reason that we should be thwarted thus."

Marina asked: "Shall you cut off his feet?" Remembering that which had once been threatened before.

"No, we shall not need to do that. But we shall find methods to make him speak."

Among those who had been taken captive, there was Tacuba's lord, who was said to be a weak man. It was thought (with reason) that he was likely to know what had been done with the city's gold, and it was suggested that, under threat of torture, he would be more likely than Guatemozín to speak.

Olid said: "Let me deal with them, and you will know all in the next hour."

Alvarado said much the same.

Cortéz put it to Ávila, as a thing which he was most reluctant to do, thinking that he would have his support. Ávila looked doubtful. He said at last: "Well, it would be their own choice."

There was a sound of reason in that.

Sandoval looked at it in much the same way. He pointed out that, if they remained silent under torture, it would mean that they enjoyed thwarting the Spaniards more than they disliked being hurt.

Cortéz was in a state of indecision such as would rarely vex him for long unless it were when his ideals of conduct conflicted with the normal standards of his time, to which he was expected to conform.

When he would pace the room in the night, he would be working toward a decision which required that many factors should be assessed.

Now he had an instinctive dislike to the proposal that men should be tortured to obtain gold. Should he order on behalf of others that which he certainly would not do for his own gain—though it was largely his own gain which would result?

Also, he had legalistic doubts which would not have entered into Olid's mind, and which Alvarado would have laughed away.

Would such action conflict with the words he had spoken when he accepted Guatemozín's surrender? Was the disposal of the gold *before* that surrender a matter of legitimate complaint, whatever it might have been?

On the other hand, he saw that there was cause for the bitter disappointment that displayed itself in sulky argument, or offensive scrawls upon wall and door. The men he led had toiled and fought, they had abandoned ease and risked life, almost everyone could show the scar of a wound, and he had promised them a reward which had been almost within their grasp. Was it to be lost through the spiteful obduracy of a man against whom he declined to enforce their will?

And he was not asked to do anything beyond what was the legal custom of every civilised land. Could he question that torture was a legal necessity? Justice required truth, and how else, in many cases, could truth be obtained?

It was not usual, in the Western Europe he knew, to apply torture with the bestial barbarities which would be shamelessly practised by European tyrannies four centuries later. Rather, it could be compared (though cruder in its applications) with the police practices of some twentieth-century American States. The aim was to obtain confessions before any permanent injury would be done. Even a mere sight of the instruments of torture would often have the required effect.

But it was a matter on which abstract argument did not suffice. Many people eat mutton who would be unwilling to kill a sheep.

He was accustomed to impose his will upon less resolute men. Now the resolution was theirs, the wavering his, and the result was equally sure.

He said at last: "Let them be warned that, unless they will tell what they surely know by tomorrow noon, they will be forced thereto in a way which I have been reluctant to use."

When the noon came, and they would not speak, he said to Alvarado: "You must do this in your own way. But what do you intend?"

Alvarado laughed. "There are ways, even if we have not got a good rack. There are two thumbscrews Narváez brought. (He may have meant them for you!) We will treat them in the same way, and see which will be first to squeal."

Cortéz thought there would be little doubt about that, on which point he was right, for when, half an hour later, he sent a message after Alvarado that he was to do no more, whether he had succeeded or not, the position was that Guatemozín had endured torture in stubborn silence, only broken to express contempt at his companion's weakness. But the lord of Tacuba had said, at the second turn of the screw, that the gold had all been thrown into the lake. And though the screw had had some extra turns after that, it had only produced squealing protests that he could say no more, for that was all that he knew.

That was no more than had been guessed already, and now being confirmed, and seeming to be all the guidance they would be likely to have, it was decided that the lake must be dredged, which the fleet, having no more fighting to face, could be adapted to do.

Cortéz saw advantage in the fact that this might be quick to succeed, but must be much slower to fail, the lake, though much of it was very shallow, being many miles extent; and, meanwhile, men's minds could be diverted to better sources of wealth, the whole country having become theirs.

Dredging and diving went on for two months, and brought up little but mud. There were some oddments of gold, but that was a natural thing, it being so commonly used.

The most important discovery was that of a great sundial of solid gold, which had been thrown into a pond in Guatemozín's own grounds.

It is certain that an enormous quantity of jewellery and precious metals must have been successfully hidden or removed, though it has never been found.

It may be suggested, as the most probable explanation, that Guatemozín ordered that, as the inhabitants withdrew from their threatened dwellings, they should cast such articles into the canals. It would have pleased his bitter humour to observe the invaders, as they filled them up, toiling to bury that which they sought to gain.

CHAPTER ONE HUNDRED TEN: DOUBTS

It was the night of the 13th day of August 1521 when Cortéz rode with Marina on the long causeways through the blackness of storm and rain to the luxurious comfort of the Cojohuacan palace, where he might sleep (if sleep he could) in the knowledge that he had won an empire for God and Spain.

It had been the 18th of November 1518 when he had sailed like a fugitive from St. Jago's harbour.

Looking back, as he did now, it seemed incredible that it should have been so short a time. His mind went back to his wife, his farm, the herd that he had bred from imported cattle, which had been so great a success. How were they doing now? He had been obliged to leave all in charge of Juan, who would do his best for his sister's sake, but his best might not be much.

He had not supposed that he would be away more than four months, or at most six. How much of what had happened was known in Cuba now? Did they know little, or all? Did they think him dead? What could they have concluded when they heard nothing from Narváez? When even the ship which had followed him, bearing additional stores, did not return? Would Catalina think he was dead? And, for how long would she be faithful to him? Even if she knew he lived— Well, he did not know that he would blame her greatly for that. Would he greatly care? He would, of course, behave as the honour of a hidalgo of Spain required, if infidelity should be revealed. But he would prefer not to know. The fact was that he had always been fond of his wife, as he was still. And he had no doubt that she was of him.

But, faithful or faithless, it would all be in a casual way. Would she have married him had she known that she would be left for nearly three years? Without other consolation? He thought not. She was one who considered that celibacy should be avoided with care. An attractive woman. Particularly for the night hours. She would never be more—or should we say less—than that.

His mind went on to greater matters. With the resources of Spain to support him, he did not doubt that he could weld the whole country into a great empire from sea to sea. Or even without. He could make it Christian within three years. Or perhaps less. How much had been done in two! But Spain could ruin him, utterly, and at once. She might not ruin all he had done, but she could place others in control. The edict might be on the way now.

Could he resist that? Could he found his own empire, ignoring Spain? Probably he could, if she remained quiet. Against such an armada as it was in her power to send? Probably not. But the thought did not even enter his mind. What he did was for God and Spain.

One thing was certain. The enigmatic silence of the last year could not endure. It would certainly end itself, even if it were not effectually ended by him, as it was obvious that it must be. He must send another vessel at once, ignoring Cuba, to St. Domingo, and then to Spain. And what a tale it would have to tell!

Loaded with spoils—for that which the Aztecs had hidden or cast away would have been regarded as of small value by them, and those things which were much had less value to Spanish eyes—the armies of the allies hurried away to spread the news of the utter ruin of the nation which, for three centuries, had controlled the land. But the tidings had not waited for them.

Almost at once, while Cortéz was grappling with the first problems of administration, to create a new order out of the chaos which he had caused, there was an embassy from Mechoachan at his gates. This kingdom lay on the Pacific coast to the north, beyond the severity of the Aztec yoke.

The envoys watched an exhibition of horsemanship. They gazed with wonder at the strange beasts and their steelclad riders. They heard the thunder of guns, which could slay at will, but had been ordered to be harmless to them. But they were most impressed by the sight of the flattened plain which had been a royal city three months before.

They did not propose peace, and offer friendship on equal terms. They asked for the protection of Spain. They went back with Spanish companions, to whom they had undertaken to show the resources of their own land, and to guide them to Californian gold.

Within a few weeks, Martín López would be there, building ships to explore the Pacific coast, for, as Cortéz would write to the Spanish Court, this must surely be the ocean by which the spice islands of the East could be reached—but how far away?

Others came with similar submissions, while Sandoval and Alvarado marched in different directions to overawe those parts of the country which had been most active in support of Guatemozín throughout the siege.

They came back with reports of a land fertile and lovely and rich in mines, in which no spirit of resistance remained.

With this miracle of success to report, there should not be any doubt that there would be praise and gratitude and confirmation of power from the King whose dominions had been extended so greatly without his exertion, or even knowledge of what was being done in the name of Spain.

CHAPTER ONE HUNDRED ELEVEN:
WHAT HAD HAPPENED IN SPAIN

To understand the position in Madrid, it is necessary to go back to the time when, in July 1519, Montejo and Puerto-Carrero had sailed on the first mission that Cortéz dispatched to Spain.

It was already known that, contrary to instructions, they had put in at Marien, on the north coast of Cuba, and that a deserter had crossed the island to St. Jago, the expedition of Narváez being a direct consequence.

Beyond that, Cortéz knew nothing of what had happened to them.

But, in fact, they had done well.

Outsailing two warships which Velásquez had dispatched to seize them, they touched at the Azores, as was the invariable custom on these voyages, and arrived safely at St. Lucan, about three months later.

They had early evidence of the extremity of the opposition they would encounter. Immediately that their arrival was known—and the news they brought, and the treasures they bore, stirred the country to a general excitement—an emissary of Velásquez, acting on information already supplied by him, swore an information against them at Seville, alleging that they were rebels to the Governor of Cuba, and traitors to Spain.

He did not, of course, obtain judgement on this unsupported assertion, but he was successful in obtaining an *ex parte* order, by which the ship and all that it contained were arrested until the case could be tried.

The officers of the law boarded the ship, and the envoys found that they were unable to remove even their own possessions, or a remittance of gold which Cortéz had made to his father.

In this dilemma, they went first to Medellín, explained the position to his parents, and obtained the support of Martín Cortéz, who agreed to accompany them to the Royal Court, to present their credentials, and seek redress.

But this could not be easily or quickly done. The Spanish King had just become Emperor of Germany also, which he regarded as the more important position.

He came to Spain of necessity, but he was in a hurry to get away. He was holding Court at Compostella, in the far north, and even there he could not be found. He had gone to visit his mother at Tordesillas.

It was March 1520, six months after they had landed, and nine since they had sailed from Vera Cruz, when they saw the man who was now the most powerful in the world, as Holy Roman Emperor and King of Spain.

The treasure which Cortéz had sent addressed to him, had been released by the Seville Law Court, and had just arrived.

Up to this time, the Spanish Colonial Empire had consisted of fertile islands of wide extent, offering great agricultural opportunities, and inhabited by primitive peoples, who could easily be coerced into performing the labour by which their masters profited, with the blessing of Christianity for their reward.

The weight of gold which was now unpacked was evidence of wealth in more dazzling form; the intricate jewellers' work proclaimed a civilisation such as had not been imagined before.

The envoys found themselves the centre of congratulatory excitement, and might easily have succeeded in their mission, had they not been opposed by one who could not be lightly ignored.

The difficult administration of these distant colonies was in the hands of a body known as the Royal Council of the Indies, and its President, de Fonseca, Bishop of Burgos, was a man of such industry and administrative capacity, that, for some years past, he had practically been the Board.

He was friendly with the Governor of Cuba, and a marriage between their respective families was already arranged. He received an account from Velásquez of his grievances against Cortéz, which he did not hesitate to believe.

Informed of this opposition, and pressed with affairs which he considered to be of greater urgency, if not importance, the Emperor postponed his decision until the last moment, and finally sailed from Corunna without giving Cortéz's envoys more satisfaction than an order that sufficient of their property should be released to enable them to pay the costs of the voyage.

Meanwhile, Fonseca received a further letter from Velásquez, informing him of the expedition which he was preparing under Narváez to chastise the culprit, whereat he felt that matters might be left to take their natural course, without further interference from him.

When the further letter which Cortéz had written to the Emperor from Segora in October 1520 (which was not immediately dispatched, owing to the loss of the vessel in which it was first intended to send it) came to Fonseca's knowledge, he determined to bring the matter to a decisive issue.

He may have been wrong in the course which he persuaded the King to take; and a man, having conquered a great and wealthy country, it may be said almost single-handed, to lay it at his sovereign's feet, would not normally expect to be rewarded in such a way. But, to be fair to all, we must appreciate Bishop Fonseca's position, and the difficulties with which he had to contend.

These colonies of the New World came to his country by no right but that of conquest, which was usually a matter of naked violence, without provocation or decent excuse. The protests of Christian men (and there were many, to the honour of Christianity, and of the Catholic Church) were met by the argument that, if the bodies of these barbarians were brought into servitude, their souls were saved from eternal hell, and it was one to which, beliefs being what they were, it was hard to reply.

But the men by whom these conquests were made, often brutal and unused to civil administration, were apt to have a very liberal view of the value of what they had done. Some of them had encountered little opposition, and displayed little ability. Narváez (for instance) might have fallen to a low level under the harder test of European warfare. In the interests of humanity and good civil government, it was Fonseca's constant difficulty to get such men out of the way, without injustice to themselves, when their use was done.

Cortéz himself had experienced the same difficulty with Olid and Alvarado, in finding that they could not be trusted to act with good judgement and equity, if they should be entrusted with separate commands, and meet with positions for which their instructions did not provide.

CHAPTER ONE HUNDRED TWELVE: MISSION TO SPAIN

The war being over, Cortéz followed the report written during the previous autumn, that had been delayed in transit, by a further one, which he completed and despatched in April 1521, in charge of de Ávila and Quinones, men on whose loyalty he could rely, and who would not be uncouth when introduced to a foreign court.

He sent a great treasure therewith. He sent specimens of maize, tobacco, coffee, and cocoa—of many strange and valuable products of the new land.

He also sent rich and curious presents to various individuals whom he had known, and to the principal churches in Spain.

The envoys carried a supporting letter, bearing many signatures, petitioning that Cortéz should be confirmed in authority over the rich territory that he had won.

Their ship called at St. Domingo, where the news it gave cause for many helms to be turned to a westerly course, and many Spaniards from the Islands to hasten to join the service of Cortéz, where there were now so many rich appointments to be obtained.

It went on to the Azores, where it must put up for a few days, for men to be rested ashore, and fresh water and stores to be taken in. When it sailed, Ávila was alone in his mission, for there had been a tavern quarrel in which Quinones had taken a fatal wound.

It sailed on until it was pursued by a ship which showed the French flag. The French at this time took little interest in the New World, and when they did so, it would be northward of México Bay. But they were at war with Spain, and it was an armed French privateer which now sent a shot across the bows of the Spanish ship, as a signal to lay to.

The French captain knew the Spanish flag from whatever quarter of the world it might come. The Spanish captain surrendered, having, as he considered, no choice, let de Ávila rail as he would. When his ship cast anchor, it was not at Casablanca, but Bordeaux.

The captain of the privateer had become rich beyond his wildest dreams from his share of the spoil, most of which must go to the French King, who, in due course, would gaze at such wealth as even he had not seen before.

With this plunder to count and weigh, letters were not matters of great concern. Ávila could not secure his own freedom, but his papers were not taken, his purse was not robbed. It was not long after he had landed that he found means to send his letters to Spain, for which he paid well. There would come a day when they would be in the hands of the Regent of Spain. But they would arrive late, and much was happening in the meantime.

Five weeks before, the Spanish Regent had put his signature to a document which was then countersigned by Bishop Fonseca, who controlled Spain's colonial world.

It appointed a commission with many powers. It was to investigate, among other matters, why Narváez had sent Ayllón back. But its main purpose was to enquire into the dispute between Cortéz and the Governor of Cuba, with power to suspend his authority, and, at its discretion, to arrest him, and seize his property until (based upon the report it would make) there should be a final judgement from Spain.

It is a curios evidence of the international status of the Roman Church at that period that the French monarch, while retaining all else that Cortéz had sent, as the legitimate spoils of war, released his gifts to Spanish churches, which ultimately reached their destinations.

CHAPTER ONE HUNDRED THIRTEEN:
COMING OF CATALINA

"Gonzalo," Cortéz said, "there is a runner here from the coast, with word that my wife has come. She must be met with the honour her rank requires. You shall start at once, taking a better horse for her than they may have at the coast, and other things she may need, and a fitting guard. You should meet her before she will come to the rougher ways."

Sandoval said bluntly: "Doña Marina will know of this?"

"She has always known."

Sandoval said no more. He was never one of a fluent tongue.

Cortéz saw Marina in the next hour. He said: "There is a runner arrived. He brings word that a ship from Cuba is in."

Marina answered: "There should be news that you will be glad to have. There is nothing wrong?"

"Not at all. My wife has come. She should be here in four days from now."

"She will be welcomed by all."

There was silence until she asked: "You do not doubt that? There is more that you wish to say?"

"I was thinking of you. I must make arrangements for where you will be."

Marina looked puzzled at that. But, underneath, there was a doubt which she would not show. She said: "You vex yourself without cause. Women arrange such matters among themselves. You will find that all will be done in a good way."

She saw that he was disconcerted by this reply, which confirmed her doubt.

Was jealousy, that meanest of human vices, to wreck her life again, as it had done three years earlier? And why should he assume that his wife should be of so low a type? Would she think of herself alone, disregarding him? There was no marriage in that!"

She added tonelessly: "What would you have me do?"

"There is a house on the further side of the square. The one with three fountains in its garden upon the left. It is rich in the flowers you love. I will have it furnished for you in the right way. You will still be near, as my interpreter ought to be."

There was a moment of silence after that. Her eyes were expressionless, baffling even him. Then she said: "You are always kind."

He thought that she was taking it well. He would not say anything disloyal to Catalina, but he had his own grief, as he hoped that she might be able to guess.

She met Sandoval in the next hour. She knew where he was going, and why. Everyone did.

She said: "You go to meet Doña Catalina? She will need a good horse on the mountain paths."

"I am providing for that."

"You must take Roland for her."

Sandoval looked his surprise. "There are others. Why should I do that?"

"He is used to a woman's hand. I will send him to you."

He was going away when she called him back. "Gonzalo, you will make no mention of me. Hernán must do that."

Sandoval also thought that she was taking it well, but that she might be wrong as to what Cortéz would do. Would he mention her to his wife? And why should he?

When Bernal sent the horses that would be required, Sandoval saw that Marina's stallion was there, which could only be through instructions from her.

He left and travelled with speed, as he was accustomed to do, and met Doña Catalina's train as it ascended the lower slopes of the cordilleras.

He saw a woman with large dark eyes in a face that was thin and white, with a petulant mouth. She was of the kind who have a youthful attraction which quickly fades. She was twenty-eight, and looked ten years older. Also, she looked ill.

He soon learned that she was so, on her own assertion. She had asthma. He learnt nothing definitely, beyond that.

They travelled slowly, for she often complained of fatigue. She complained of everything. In the next five days he said little, and heard much.

Hernán should have come to her at the coast. She should not have been forced to travel in this barbarous land. If he had not known she was coming, he should have come at once when he knew she had landed. She had not waited for that? That was because the officers had been rude. They had said they were sure that he could not come. That was nonsense. If Hernán wished, he would always contrive a way.

He should not have left her three years ago. It was a silly, dangerous thing to do. And he had treated Diego badly. Everyone said that. Isabella had explained it to her. But now she was going to take him home, and Diego had promised to forgive him if she did that.

She expressed sympathy for Gonzalo, he having wasted three youthful years in this savage land. Would he not prefer a wife, and a home, and a settled life?

When he told her that he had a Tlascalan wife, she professed to understand something he had not meant. There was no need to put it politely to her. She knew what men were. She expected Hernán had not been faithful to her. She implied that she was unconcerned about that: that 'native' women did not count as competitors with a real wife.

When he tried to explain that he was really married, she put it lightly aside. A youthful folly, to be excused. Doubtless Father Olmedo would find a way to release him.

By this time he would have ceased to argue, even had he been of a more voluble kind. He observed her petulant reaction to every deviation from her accustomed routine. He recognised that she had an inflexible mind.

Cortéz met her as she rode into Cojohuacan. He had had a runner stationed to give him notice of her approach. He lifted her down from her horse with a warm embrace. If he noticed any change, he gave no sign.

She said: "Oh, Hernán, why did you do it?" But it was in the tone of one condoning a past offence. Was it not her mission to take him home?

Cortéz eyes went to the horse. He said: "You took Roland!" And there was a faint surprise in his voice.

Sandoval said: "So I was instructed to do."

Cortéz said nothing to that. He took his wife to a house which had been very carefully prepared for her comfort, though she found many omissions of which to complain.

He was tender and patient. She was a happy woman for that night, and looked younger on the next day.

She had told him more than once that she was going to take him home. Looking at his maimed hand, and the scars on body and head, could he doubt the wisdom of that?

He did not argue this, but put it aside, in his smiling way. He had a small matter on his mind concerning a capital city to be rebuilt. Should it be on the old site, in the midst of a salty lake, or should Tacuba be preferred, on the lake shore? Or even Chalco, on the shore of the freshwater lake which was to the south? They would ride together, and she should advise him on this.

She said: "Well, if the sun would not be too hot—"

He was interrupted by being told that a deputation had come from a tribe on the northward Atlantic coast. He would need Marina to talk to them. Actually, it proved not to be as simple as that. A Totonac had to be found, to whom she could talk, and who would understand them.

When they had gone, Marina asked: "Can you spare me for four days, or it may be six?"

"May I ask why?"

"I have a thought to visit my own home."

"Then so it must be. You can do what you will there, and it will have approval from me."

He thought again that she was taking it well.

CHAPTER ONE HUNDRED FOURTEEN:
MARINA TAKES COUNSEL

Next morning Marina left for Pamalla. Whatever she might do in consequence, she intended to learn the truth. But she was only partially successful in that.

She rode herself, taking the child with her in a litter, with a young nurse. She found her remote home, its garden peace unruffled by the devastation of war that had wrecked so much of the land.

She found her brother there, as he would not have been, at his present age, in more normal days. He had the change of three years of growth, but that was no disguise to her. She had changed less, but he gazed at her with doubting incredulous eyes, for had his sister not been cremated three years before?

Recognition being established, he said that his mother would be away for some days. He told what he knew, with details that were convincing as to their mother's part in the matter, though leaving much unexplained.

She told him not to let his mother know that he had seen her, but to be easy in mind as to the inheritance which he had assumed to be his.

She stayed for two days, having taught him in that time to lose his fear of the horse on which she had come, and even, greatly daring, to climb on to his back.

She left with the old affection renewed, and assured that her mother would not be told either by him, or by the servants who may have seen or guessed things which her brother had not imagined at the time when he had been told of his sister's death, and to whom the truth might therefore be plainer than it was to them.

Marina rode back, having learnt much, but nothing to guide her in a decision which she felt had to be made.

When she met Cortéz again (whom she neither avoided nor sought), she told him how she found her own home, and how much it had confirmed what she had supposed before.

She was friendly even to familiarity, but with no reference to a closer bond, past or to be.

He felt grateful for reticence and discretion, the impulse of which left him in a doubt which might have distressed him had he not been overwhelmed by more urgent, if not more important, affairs. For he had now decided that the new city should stand on the site of the old, even though the lake must be drained.

He had proposed to Father Olmedo that a cathedral in honour of St. Francis should be built on the site of the Great Pyramid Temple, and that the Aztec gods should be put to a good use by being broken up for foundation rubble, and the reverend Father had thought it a good idea.

Cortéz turned his mind to consider how the labour could be procured by which a new city should be instantly built, and of a magnificence to succeed the old. Without machinery. Without beasts of burden. Solely by human hands.

Well, it would put Guatemozín to a further test, which he was anxious to do.

Meanwhile, Father Olmedo's pleasant dreams of cedar and stone, of a cathedral that should surpass most of those in the Old World, were interrupted by a servant who said that Doña Marina would like to have an interview with him, which he did not welcome, but his office would not let him turn down.

He thought he knew why she had come, but he might be wrong. She had been visiting her home, as she had told him before she went. He had hoped it might be in connection with that. He asked: "You found your home untouched by the war?"

"Yes. I found all well. But my mother was away. I am not aiming to speak of that. Father, am I Hernando's wife, or will you say where I stand?"

"You are not his wife, as you should know. Did he not tell you he had a wife in Cuba when first you met?"

"Yes. I do not object to that. I ask, what am I to him?"

"You have been his mistress, as all know."

"I have been his wife for more than two years."

"By Aztec law perhaps; but not his."

"I am not speaking of law, but fact."

"You have been united in a bond the church does not approve."

"Why was this not said before now?"

"Did you ask?"

"Should I be expected to doubt that all was done in a Christian way?"

Father Olmedo was not quick to reply. A priest may have a great advantage in the fact that he hears confessions from more than one, and, however confidential they may be, he cannot exclude the knowledge of them from his own mind, even if he should so desire. But they may introduce complications also.

He heard Cortéz's confessions, and knew thereby both the nobilities of his character, and the weakness against which he strove.

He heard confessions from Marina also, but they were occasional and meagre. She was liable to tell him that she had not consciously sinned, which is not the expected attitude of one who is described as a penitent, in anticipation of wrongdoing to be revealed.

He had told her once that arrogance was itself a sin, but had recognised, after a characteristically briefly worded duel, that the accusation could not be sustained.

She had given him matter for contemplation by her contention that a god should be obeyed. If you broke his law and were forgiven, and went straightway to break it again, what could you expect? Especially from one who dealt with those who did not respect Him with the very maximum of unpleasantness.

On the other hand, if you made an honest effort to conform to laws which were often far from clear to yourself, what more could He expect?

Father Olmedo, a man of culture, of much knowledge of human nature, and of a broad humanity, recognised that allowances must be made for those who were converts of another race, from a different creed.

He recognised also that the religion which had been taught to Marina had a basic similarity to the Christian Faith, and that its deviations, while not to be accepted by him, might be worth some consideration by those who controlled the teachings and policies of his own Church. That was, of course, putting aside the gross evil of ritual cannibalism, which had been introduced by the Aztecs, overlaying and obscuring a more ancient and purer faith: a faith which, from its spiritual vitality, still persisted, as, by an analogy which would not have entered his mind, Christianity persisted in spite of being burdened with the grotesque horror of eternal torment.

The relations which had existed between Cortéz and Marina were not approved, but were condoned by the Church. Cortéz was allowed to cancel their irregularity by donation and penance. In the case of Marina, he had considered that, while she was not conscious of sin, there could be no condemnation for her. And he may have been restrained, more than he would have been willing to recognise, by the certainty that she would have ended at once, at any cost, an intimacy which she would know to be contrary to the law of God.

As he was silent, she spoke again: "I was taught that a woman should be the wife of one man, and should be entirely loyal to him. If any did less than that, she would be killed, which was not the worst, for her kindred were shamed. I have not known of one being killed, for our laws are obeyed, being few, and the penalties being enough to secure that.

"A man might have more than one wife, though few did. But the obligation would be the same.

"I am not now bound by that law. Our faith is gone. I am Christian now. But I will not be less than I was. I will not change to a law that I do not keep."

It was a speech, from her, of unusual length, and Father Olmedo understood that it was not carelessly said. She was resolved to find out what had been wrong, and that it should come to a quick end. He moved with caution on a path the end of which was not easy to see.

"I have heard," he said, "that, among your own people, all wives were not alike. Did not Montezuma have children who could not become heirs to the throne?"

"So he did. But there was no confusion in that. They were wives who were not of our noble blood. But their honour stood. Is it against my child that a difference is made?"

"Not by Hernán's will. You may be certain of that. And his wife has none. But there is a Christian law that a man can have only one wife, and that her children must be preferred. He could not alter that if he would. But it is fair to him to observe that when he told you he had a wife, he supposed that all this would be understood."

"Have I spoken against him? But I must know. Now his wife is here, am I cast aside? Am I to be hidden from her? Will he seek to return to me in a quiet way, after a time?"

"I cannot say what he will do. It is a position which the Church cannot approve, though it may be lenient to the weakness of men. But I should say that his affection for you is very great."

"Have I doubted that? It is my honour that is unsure."

She went at that, having learnt all that she wished, which she had guessed before, but was not pleased to know.

After that, she sought Xamarillo, and had a long conversation with him. It ended with an appeal from him, which she rejected with a quiet finality. "That could not be. It takes too long to forget."

CHAPTER ONE HUNDRED FIFTEEN: WARRANT OF ARREST

The warrant which had been issued in Madrid in April 1521, for the apprehension of Cortéz, and of his alleged offences, was forwarded to St. Domingo for execution, the name of Christóval de Tapia being inserted as the commissioner who was to execute it.

By the time it arrived at Hispaniola, sufficient was known of the progress which Cortéz had made toward the complete conquest of México to make it a very formidable undertaking for a peace-loving man, which Tapia was reputed to be.

His official position at St. Domingo was that of inspector of gold foundries, for which integrity was more important than more militant qualities.

His selection is evidence that Fonseca desired the enquiry to be equitably conducted. His character, on other grounds, caused him to be deliberate, if not dilatory, in executing a warrant which he could not have liked, and may not have approved.

Indeed, to say that he executed it may be doing more than justice to him. As the months passed, he found a ship which landed him a Vera Cruz in December, where he showed his warrant to Cavallero, and that very capable officer subjected it to a scrutiny which resulted in the decision that it was not in the requisite legal form. His best course would be to wait at Vera Cruz, while the document should be submitted to Cortéz, and his decision obtained upon it.

This was the more to be recommended because the commissioner, being an elderly peace-loving man, had brought with him the carriage and team of horses with which he was accustomed to travel, and it was necessary to advise him that they would be unsuitable for the mountain paths which he would have to take.

Having agreed to this, he soon had the satisfaction of receiving a very friendly letter from Cortéz, regretting that the road was so hard and rough. He was anxious that the charges which had been made against him (which were entirely false) should be investigated, and the appointment of de Tapia for that purpose was most welcome to him. As the commissioner could not come to México, he would endeavour to come to Vera Cruz.

Finally, he offered to purchase the carriage and horses at a very high price, so that the expense of taking them back need not be incurred.

De Tapia replied that he would await him at Vera Cruz, and put the offer to purchase his equipage aside.

A week later he had another letter from Cortéz. It appeared that when he had announced his intention of coming to Vera Cruz, it had aroused such strong and general protests that he had been obliged to put the project, for the moment, aside. Perhaps, at a later date, when the country had become more settled than it was now—

De Tapia considered this to be most probably a diplomatic excuse. The protests might have been inspired by Cortéz himself! But, having a cool judicial mind, even if it were so, he was not sure that Cortéz was wrong.

He knew far more of the circumstances, and of the protagonists, than was evident to those in Madrid. He did not think that the conquest would collapse because Cortéz should come to Vera Cruz. But if he should attempt his arrest, and to seize his property, the consequences would be incalculable. Even if Cortéz's supporters should remain passive, the effect among these people, so recently subdued, of seeing their conqueror degraded, and the Spaniards quarrelling among themselves, might be such that all would be permanently lost, or, at least, have to be done over again. In fact, he had been given an impossible mission, and so he must make report.

He wrote to Cortéz accepting his reason for delay, but saying that his own health would not allow him to remain longer at Vera Cruz. He would accept the offer to purchase his equipage.

He went back to St. Domingo, and reported that the apprehension of Cortéz was impracticable, and would be most dangerous to the interests of the Spanish Crown.

CHAPTER ONE HUNDRED SIXTEEN: DEATH OF CATALINA

Hernando looked on the face of a dead woman, with grief and regret, beneath which was a relief that would not enter his conscious thought.

Catalina, whom he had seduced (or, if we prefer truth, who had seduced him) ten years ago, and whom he had married from a chivalrous feeling that it was her wish—Catalina was dead.

He had given her six years of happiness in Cuba, three years of unavoidable separation, and now three months here—months of happiness and pride, as she had begun to realise the great place he had gained, and even ceased to worry him to return to Cuba, though she always complained that the climate would be fatal to her. But who could have foreseen that? Everyone had said that she gained strength. Certainly some of the vivacity which made commonplace talk attractive had been recovered in voice and eyes. And then—the doctor, bleeding her assiduously, had called it a fever upon the lungs—she had been dead in three days.

She had loved him with such depth as her nature had, and he had made her all the return she required in his smiling way. Her passions had not been strong: they had been weakly controlled.

He had not expected—certainly he had not counted upon—her death. He did not think now (though he knew) that it would leave him free to marry into almost any of the great houses in Spain. And with such a marriage, no one would venture to intrigue against his position as ruler in the New World. He would have an impregnable power.

And he would be free to go reproachless to where he would. He did not intend to remain here. When a new order should be established throughout the land, and Christianity made secure, he would take a fleet to explore the farther ocean, until he should come upon the spice islands of Cathay. Or lead an expedition to the vast forested lands which lay southward of Yucatán. Need he rest, being young as he was, because he had won this great land? There might be still greater things that he could accomplish for God and Spain. It was Marina he would require. She might not avail as interpreter. Such distant languages would surely be strange to her. But it was not as an interpreter that she came to mind, but as lover, comrade, and counsellor both by night and day.

She was still beside him at need, with knowledge that had averted more than one error in the new administration that his conquest required. But there was a distance between them that, for different reasons, neither had attempted to lessen.

Well, it must be ended now. But not too quickly, too evidently in sight of others, lest it should be said that he was glad of Catalina's death, and to return to her. Catalina's honour must not be lessened by that.

CHAPTER ONE HUNDRED SEVENTEEN:
INQUEST IN EUROPE

It was only a few days after Catalina's death that trouble came from a new quarter. Far to the northeast, a turbulent people, dwelling in the valley of the Panoco, who had never accepted the Aztec yoke, had thought that there should be advantage to themselves in the fall of that predatory power. They took to their arms, and began to overrun what they considered to have become an abandoned land.

It was an illusion that did not last. Cortéz marched instantly against them, their reputation being sufficiently formidable to cause him to go himself with a powerful army, which proved to be none too many for what had to be done.

After defeat in one hard-fought battle, the Panoches gathered anew, and victory must be won again. In the end, they yielded, and gave sudden consent to the overlordship of Spain.

He returned from what he regarded as finished work to hear almost at once that insurrection had broken out, with the massacre of several hundred of those whom he had left behind to control the land. The menace to a nearby Spanish settlement, established at San Esteven, called for instant action. But his absence from the rebuilding capital had been long enough for much confusion to result. Rather than leave again, he sent Sandoval, with a larger force than before. Sandoval did his work thoroughly, as his way was. The natural difficulties of the country, and the ferocity of those he encountered, made it one of the most difficult of the missions of the kind which he had brought to final success. But so he did, arresting and executing four hundred of those most actively implicated in the massacre, with a severity which the circumstances required.

Cortéz meanwhile had decided that, though he could not again absent himself from the control of civil administration, he must find suitable occupation for those of his older comrades who were ill adapted for places of responsibility in a peaceful state.

He was settling all he could on the land, giving generous grants to those who were prepared to undertake its cultivation. He was encouraging those who were now being brought by every available vessel from the older West Indian settlements, with a similar liberality; to which he attached a condition that wives who had been left behind should be brought (assisted, if necessary, by a grant in aid) within eighteen months, on pain of forfeiture of allotted lands. Those who were unmarried were to provide themselves with wives within the same period, or the same penalty would be incurred. It was a provision which did much to procure the stability of the new state. It led to many marriages between Spaniards and Aztec women of good status, blending the interests of the two nations in the best possible way.

But, as King David had been embarrassed by old comrades of his Adullam days, so he found that there were many for whom he must provide who had no aptitude for agricultural life.

A large, well-organised army, under the command of Alvarado, was sent southward to explore the country in that direction. It went on, under its impetuous leadership, to win Guatemala for Spain.

Sailors who had been employed to man the brigantines, now sailed northward from Vera Cruz to explore the Florida coast, in the natural hope that there might be an opening to the Pacific.

Others were held in readiness to man the vessels that were being built on the Pacific coast, but when the bitter news came that that half-built fleet had been destroyed by fire, they were added to another maritime expedition, which was to sail southward to explore the coast beyond Yucatán, and, after landing a military force under Olid, which was to endeavour to penetrate Honduras from the coast, to continue a further search for the strait which it was (not unreasonably) hoped to find, either to north or south.

As energetic, as daring, as circumspect in peaceful construction, as he had been in the sharper hazards of war, Cortéz watched a wide realm develop, and a new city grow, in many ways more ornate and more beautiful than the old.

And meanwhile, at the court of Charles V, the greatness of his achievement had reached the consciousness of an astonished court, and the battle which was as critical for him as the worst that he had hardly won upon Mexican soil had reached an intensity which could not endure.

Bishop Fonseca had committed himself to an opinion that he would not change, and the great weight of his authority, and all the influence and resources of the department which he controlled, were directed to persuade the King that Hernando Cortéz, however bold or fortunate he might have been in operations of war, was destitute both of the character and qualities which the control and development of a great province required.

Let him not be condemned unheard, although his lawless, overbearing ways had roused protests from the day he slipped out of St. Jago harbour with the knowledge that his commission had been revoked. Let him be brought to Madrid, and most fairly tried—his conduct even condoned and rewarded (though it had not been beyond criticism), as that of a bold, successful adventurer ought to be, when he had brought gain to the Crown. But do not leave him to undertake the art of government, which, by training and character alike, he was unsuited to do.

To support his case, though it had meant delay, Fonseca had fetched de Tapia from Hispaniola, gaining less than he had expected thereby, for de Tapia had reflected the prevailing St. Domingo opinion that Velásquez's treatment of Cortéz had not been to the advantage of Spain. But de Tapia had been frustrated in his mission, and it could be urged that it had been in a spirit of contempt, not only of him, but of the King in whose name he went.

Also, Narváez was there. He had been treated kindly by Cortéz, and his return to Spain facilitated, in a spirit of magnanimity, which may have been contemptuous of anything he would be likely to do. But he was an active and bitter foe.

More surprisingly, Duero also was there. Having been friendly to Cortéz through long years during which he had been in the employment of the Cuban Governor, he had found, on returning to St.

Jago, that he must decide definitely where his allegiance lay; for Velásquez commissioned him to go to Madrid as his personal advocate there. And Duero, under whatever persuasion, forgot what had once occurred in a Mexican street, and agreed to go.

Having done so, he cannot be blamed that he was faithful to what he had undertaken, and his words may have had more weight than would those of a more virulent man.

But the advocacy was not all on one side. Martín Cortéz was not a lawyer. He was a country gentleman, and a retired infantry captain, but he was at Madrid, conducting his son's case with a moderation, ability, and persistence, that made it easy to see from whom Hernando's ability came.

He was supported by a less interested and more powerful advocate in the Duke of Béjar, who had put Cortéz's case, on more than one occasion, strongly before the King.

Their efforts had already resulted in an order being issued forbidding Bishop Fonseca to interfere further in any matter in which Cortéz was concerned. This had been obtained from the Regent, and had been a bitter rebuff, but it really amounted to little more than an interim injunction, requiring that the position should not be further prejudiced, and may have been actuated more by anxiety not to impede activities which were to the advantage of Spain, than by any opinion of the merit of past disputes.

In July 1522, Charles V returned to Spain, his Spanish Regent having become head of the Church and removed to Rome. Charles acted with wisdom and promptitude. He did not attempt to judge issue himself. He appointed a Commission with the Grand Chancellor of Naples in the Chair, to enquire into the accusations against Hernando Cortéz, and report to him thereon.

The indictment which was submitted to this tribunal was formidable in the number, the nature, and the particularity, of the charges which it contained, and the amount of supporting evidence which it could produce.

The charges (more lengthily stated, as is the way of lawyers in every land) were these:

1. That he had seized a fleet which the Governor of Cuba had provided and fitted out, which he had afterwards caused to be destroyed.

2. That he had subsequently usurped the authority of the Crown, professing to act in the name of the Spanish King, when he had no license therefor.

3. That he had resisted Narváez, with violence and bloodshed, in contempt of the legal commission which had been issued to supersede him.

4. That he had enriched himself by misappropriation of wealth which should have been surrendered to the Spanish Treasury.

5. That, in his greed for gold, he had treated the natives of México with cruelty detrimental to the good name of Spain, and, in particular, that he had put the Aztec Emperor to torture, in the hope that he would obtain knowledge of further treasure thereby.

6. That he had treated de Tapia with the same contumely as Narváez, even though he bore a commission signed by the Regent of Spain.

7. That he was, even then, using the treasure which should have been remitted to Madrid for the building of a city at a wasteful cost, for his own aggrandisement, rather than for the glory of Spain.

The reply which was put in on Cortéz's behalf answered these charges in detail, and with much supporting evidence.

They read:

1. That the fleet was not the personal property of the Cuban Governor. Accounts would be submitted to prove that two-thirds of the cost had been defrayed by Cortéz personally, or been covered by his guarantees.

2. That the license held by Velásquez at the time of the sailing of the fleet allowed him to trade but not to colonise. Consequently, he could not delegate an authority which he did not have. When colonisation became necessary in the interests of the Crown, the most regular course possible under the circumstances was followed by applying at once to Madrid direct for approval of what was done.

3. That, for reasons stated in the previous paragraph, the commission of Narváez was bad. The illegal action of the Governor of Cuba in issuing it had been rightly resisted. It had been the direct cause of the expulsion from México, with the loss of a vast treasure, and hundreds of Spanish lives.

4. This was so far from the truth that he had consistently remitted more than the percentage due to the crown, largely at his personal cost.

5. That he had not only avoided cruelty himself, but had constantly enjoined a contrary policy upon his followers. It was the Royal Commissioner, Alderete, who had demanded the torture of Guatemozín. He had permitted it with reluctance, and it had been stopped by his intervention.

6. That he had treated de Tapia with all the consideration that the circumstances allowed. Had he repeated the error of leaving México, the tragedy which resulted from his seeking Narváez might have happened again. He was not responsible for the fact that the condition of de Tapia's health did not enable him to wait till the journey could be safely made, or to come to him.

7. That the rebuilding of the capital was necessary in itself, and for the glory of Spain. It was being financed in such a way that it would be no charge on the Spanish Treasury.

The hearing of evidence brought by both sides to support or rebut the charges, and the legal arguments that followed, occupied several days.

The friends of Cortéz did not content themselves with denial, they made counter-charges of equal gravity, and which could be more easily sustained.

They said that Cortéz, while rendering service to Spain, had been obstructed by those who had put their own personal interests and jealousies before that major consideration.

They urged also the greatness of that service, the great wealth it had won, the extension at once of the domain of Christianity and the Spanish realm.

The commissioners addressed those who listened with inscrutable faces, and asked questions at times which gave no indication of what they thought.

They closed the hearing, saying only that they would make report to the King.

CHAPTER ONE HUNDRED EIGHTEEN: HEIGHT OF NOON

A warship sailed into St. Jago harbour, flying the Royal Standard of Spain. It bore a letter for Velásquez, signed by the King himself, directing him that his differences with Cortéz were matters for the civil courts, in which he could bring any action that he desired.

It did more than deliver that. There was a flourish of trumpets in the market square, and proclamation read to the crowd it drew, that all loyal Spaniards were required to assist and support Hernando Cortéz, by royal warrant, Governor, Captain-General, and Chief Justice of New Spain.

Diego de Velásquez did not die of the shock. He died some months later. Men said it was of a broken heart. But he was a grossly fat man, and other organs may have been more concerned.

He was a futile rather than an evil man. One who had gained an easy reputation by conquering those who had no power to resist, and been rewarded by a position for which he was unfit. Bishop Fonseca (had he not got down on the wrong side of the fence) might have used him as a better text for an argument which was largely sound.

The ship sailed on to Vera Cruz, where it delivered a number of sealed packets to be taken to México City. Those who handled them observed that they were addressed to Cortéz as Governor, and saw good meaning in that.

The documents, which could confirm or ruin all that Cortéz had achieved in three years of incredible hardship and peril, were delivered to him on a morning which had already brought sufficient trouble to vex and engage his mind.

He was at the fort that he had built on the Tezcuco side of the lake, which he had intended for an impregnable stronghold, and begun immediately after the war had ended. It was where the brigantines had been launched, and it included a dockyard which had been constructed for them.

It was only on this day that he had been able to mount the guns—seventy in all—for which its walls were designed. That itself was an evidence of the hostility of those from whom he should have had the promptest support. He had ordered them from Spain, and, owing to Fonseca's obstruction, they had not come. Now he had surmounted that difficulty. The few guns first taken from the fleet had been supplemented by several dozen which he had had cast in an alloy of tin and bronze, from a foundry that he had set up. He had been left without powder also, and it had been necessary for Ordaz to lead another expedition to the volcano's mouth. He made balls of stone.

But these difficulties had been overcome, however ominous their necessity might have been. There was satisfaction in seeing the guns being dragged by scores of yellow half-naked figures up to the platforms where their carriages stood await.

But he had had a rebuff on the previous day, when, after waiting longer than he could have been expected to do, he had attempted to resume the old relations with Marina, and been quietly repulsed. Not unexpectedly. He had waited so long because he had felt that there was a barrier between them which, for all her friendliness, he could not surmount. He saw Xamarillo, once captain of one of the brigantines, and now admiral of the little fleet, crossing the courtyard below. Could it be he who caused this impalpable barrier to arise? Instinct said that it was, but reason argued that there was no sign of intimacy between them, and Marina was not one to do things in a furtive way. She was much occupied with her child now, and in a friendship with Guatemozín's wife—a lonely, tearful girl, but one who made no complaint, accepting her position and its obligations in the highest Aztec way. But Guatemozín must be a poor husband to have. He still said, if he spoke at all, that he was faithful to Spain. But who would believe that? If it were genuinely so, would he not say where the hidden gold could be found, even though it should be at a price? Cortéz kept him constantly at his side, distrusting what he might otherwise do. He watched the building of the new city with expressionless eyes.

But it was not Marina who was on Cortéz's mind now. He had had tidings in the last hour that called (he thought) for action which must not be delayed, and which must be reported to Madrid whatever harm it might do to him.

The fleet he sent southward had landed Olid on the Honduras coast, and had gone further, searching the shoreline for a strait which it could not find, because it was not there. It had returned as stores failed, and put in for water at the place where Olid landed.

It found that he had gone a short distance inland, and, after some skirmishing with those who had never seen a white man, had come to terms with them, and built a fort over which a flag flew. But it was not that of Castile. It was one of his own devise. He was not taking that land for Spain. He had decided that, being so remote, it was one of which he could be a very suitable king.

Cortéz saw the inscription upon the heavily sealed packet, and his heart beat with a great hope. He broke it open to find his appointment to the high offices designated was signed by the Emperor himself, and what had been done was not in a niggardly way. His power was absolute. He could appoint what military or civil officers he would; he could expel anyone from the country in the interests of order and peace. He could draw a salary from the national revenues suitable to the positions which had become his.

And there was much else of the right kind.

There was a personal letter from Charles V, giving praise and thanks, and foretelling further rewards. There was a similar letter to be read to the troops: there were honours to be distributed among them. There were rewards to be paid to the principal officers, and instructions that all who had done good service should have liberal grants of land. An application he had sent in while his wife lived, asking that Marina should be granted possession of a house which he had planned to build in the new city for her, together with estates in her own province in compensation for those of which she had been robbed, was endorsed and sealed with the royal assent.

Chapter One Hundred Nineteen: Pause

That which a king grants he can also revoke. Cortéz recognised that. But while his commission stood he had an immense power, either for evil or good. And it was a power which, though it might be granted by Charles V, had come to him in his own right. It was a position which Charles could not have given to any, had it not first been created by him. On such foundation he should be able to stand secure. And Christóval de Olid had thought that he could defy him, and be a traitor to Spain.

Considering how this had arisen, he told himself that he was not free from blame. He had been anxious to find occupation for those of his followers who were turbulent, quarrelsome, discontent, who would be least likely to make good settlers upon the land. Had he sought to provide Olid with those who would support him in that criminal escapade, he would have made almost identical choice. He had not thought of the possibility of such a development, but ought he not to have done so? Did not the incident condone much that Fonseca had done, or refused to do?

Now he considered whom he should send to deal with Olid in the right way. He would have gone himself, but it was a long way to Honduras, and such an absence at such a time—no, there must be others who would be equal to this, and who he could better spare. But he hesitated to send one of those who had been Olid's companions in arms. Neither friendship nor antipathy must have any place in that which it would be a duty to do.

So he came to think of Francisco de Las Casas, a kinsman who had recently joined him from Spain. He thought him to be a man to trust, and one who would deal with the matter in an efficient, impartial way.

Within a week, Las Casas was on the march to the coast with a sufficient force to overcome any resistance that Olid would be likely to make; within a fortnight two ships had been provided to convey them to Honduras. Cortéz put the matter out of his mind. He had dealt with that.

It was the less likely to engage his thoughts during succeeding months because he had occasion to learn during that period that his enemies, though defeated, were still alive, and with power to harm.

The report that the Commission of Enquiry had made had been entirely favourable to himself. Acting upon it, Charles V had given him his support in a liberal way. But when a man against whom such charges had been made was placed in a position of almost absolute authority, was it not the duty of the Indian Council to watch what he did, and impose such checks as their authority would allow?

So they thought, and did. They appointed officials to oversee the revenues of the new land, which may have been reasonable. But such oversight may be exercised in different ways. Cortéz had to deal with much interference and criticism, ignorant or malicious. He had to deal with expostulatory correspondence from the Indian Council, which must have been founded on adverse reports which they had made. He realised that they did not consider themselves to be his subordinates, or even his colleagues. They were there to criticise and spy.

He found relief in developing the resources of a land to which he had given peace such as, in its recorded history, it had never had; and in labouring to establish the Christian Faith, with more success than he could reasonably expect. He wrote to the Emperor himself, imploring that priests should be sent out to preach the new faith, of a quality to command respect. The Aztec priests had conformed to the requirements of their religion, knowing that transgression would be punished with certain death. The people simply would not understand teaching which went beyond the practice of those who taught.

In response to this request, he was sent twelve Franciscan friars, whose lives of simple righteousness conformed to the teaching their lips proclaimed.

To establish their authority, he rode to meet them, dismounted, and, before an astonished native populace, knelt to kiss the ragged hem of the garment that Father Martín of Valencia wore.

Within a few years of the destruction of the old city, a Franciscan convent would rise on the site of the aviaries of Montezuma, emphasising the principal difference between the cities of the old race and the new—there would be more stone now, and higher buildings—and fewer flowers.

Within a year, in spite of the solace of these activities, and the successful establishment of many centres of European settlement throughout the land, he was so greatly vexed by the annoyances that came from Madrid that he resolved to return to Spain, and put the matter before the Emperor himself, as his most powerful advocate, the Duke of Béjar, had advised him to do.

He had another purpose in this—to seek a wife of his own degree.

He was not false to Marina in this, which it may be said, of his own will, he would never have been. He recognised that he had made an error of approach in first endeavouring to resume their relations on their old footing, and, after that repulse, spoke of the marriage that it had become possible to offer.

But she had refused it with the quiet finality which he knew too well for much hope to remain. Yet it dies hard, and explanation he felt he was entitled to have.

"Do you tell me," he said, "that your feelings have changed because I went back to my wife, as I was in honour obliged to do; or that you blame me for what happened before, when, by my conscience" (which she knew to be an oath which he would use when he was deeply moved and sincere), "when I told you I had a wife I thought you would have understood more than it seems you did."

"No," she replied, "I have not spoken of my feelings at all."

"But now that I ask?"

She was silent for some time, debating to herself the wisdom of saying more, but at last she answered: "Will you believe when I say that I am not free, as I then was?"

"You have wed another?"

"No."

"But you so intend?"

"I said he must give me time to forget."

"Which you have not done?"

"Must I answer that? Could I tell that your wife would die?"

So it was. And she held to that which he could not shake. She had pledged herself to Xamarillo when she should have had time to forget, and no sophistry of argument would turn her from the obligation that promise held.

He had seen little of her after that, the need for an interpreter being less, and more being available at a need. And if he thought now of the women of his own land, should he have blame for that?

She went about her own quiet affairs, with the reserved dignity of the aristocracy of her race; and their paths were such that they seldom met.

For the most part of a year there had been no news from Honduras. But now there was a rumour that Las Casas had not got to Olid at all: he had come to wreck. One of his ships, it was said, had been sunk in a tropic storm. One had been shattered on the rocks of a hostile coast. That was the tale. It was confirmed in part by floating wreckage which another vessel had found.

Well, a third expedition must be sent. And that thought brought another, at which Cortéz leapt to his feet, and began to pace the floor in the old way. Why should he not go himself? Why should he not go overland, as should have been done before? Why should he not explore the resources of the wild forests between the settled country and Honduras? Here they baited him in petty irritating ways which he found hard to endure. Why should he not reply by giving another empire to God and Spain? Even spite and jealousy could not say that he was misusing funds, or misruling this land, if he were hundreds of miles away.

Before the next dawn his resolution was made. He would not return to Spain, or remain here. He would go landward to Honduras, and deal with Olid according to what he should find when he got there.

CHAPTER ONE HUNDRED TWENTY:
AN IMPOSSIBLE PLAN

To consider in detail the idea of marching to Honduras was to realise the changes that even two years can make, when the routines of life are also radically altered.

Cortéz saw that he must take men he could trust, for loyalty, for valour, and for willingness to fight Spaniards, if Olid should be supported by other renegades like himself. For the last requirement, it might be well to take those who had recently come to the land, to whom those with Olid would be unknown.

Indeed, he could hardly help doing that. So many of his old comrades were scattered, and those whom he had sent with Las Casas had been picked in the very way he was seeking to do now, making them harder to find.

Even of captains, he could not make a ready choice. Some of those he could best trust he had sent to Europe. Whether they had got there or not, they were lost to him. Alvarado was in Guatemala. Others (such as Bernal) had been settled on distant farms. Sandoval remained. He could trust him.

So he sent for Sandoval, and told him of his design. Sandoval said little, as his way was. But he asked: "You will not leave Guatemozín here?"

Cortéz saw that, when they thought of Guatemozín, their minds agreed. He had not thought about him before, but now he said: "No, he must come with us; and that rogue of Tacuba as well."

The Tacuban chief had been Guatemozín's constant companion since they had surrendered to Captain Holguín together. They were alike in their attitude of silent patient watchfulness, impossible to condemn, but sinister to those who had to endure it. The danger from them might diminish as the foundations of the new order were firmly laid, and the number of Spanish settlers increased, but it still remained a fact that those who looked upon Guatemozín as their natural lord were many millions, and that the Spaniards must be counted in hundreds only. It was he—probably he only—who could rouse a spirit of insurrection, and it was certain that a word from him at any moment would raise a flame of revolt, with the massacre of many Spanish families who were now scattered over the land.

Cortéz might (as he estimated) be absent for three months, or perhaps four, and he had learnt already that there could be much trouble, even in less time than that.

"I shall take, "he said, "a large force, such as will make resistance vain, for I will avoid strife, if I can; and I will take Tlascalans for the most part, whom I can trust, but some Spaniards I must have, for the Tlascalans might refuse to fight without them, nor would I have it said that they had defeated Spaniards unaided by us, which I might have to ask them to do."

Sandoval went out to enlist men, and consult those who knew more than he of the equipment that would be required, and Cortéz busied himself with the arrangements for the absence that he designed.

It was several hours later that Sandoval returned. He said: "No one is willing to go overland. They say it cannot be done."

Cortéz remembered that Marina had told him that, which had caused him to use the sea, but it could not be said that the results had been good.

He asked: "Why is that?"

"They say it is a land where no man can live. It is all rivers and swamps. We should starve."

"Then we must take food. Rivers can be bridged. We shall find a way. On what captains can you depend?"

"I have none as yet."

"Xamarillo would not refuse."

"But he did."

Xamarillo was one of the few of his old captains who was still in the city. He had taken oversight of the building of the new houses in the Spanish quarter, and was a prominent member of a municipal council which Cortéz had set up.

He had not altered his resolve that he would have Marina at last. He remained in the city, but he had seen little of her. He gave her time to forget, as he had promised to do.

But relenting at last, she had promised to marry him before the end of the year. It was October now. Was it likely that he would go to Honduras, from which he was told that it would be many months before men would return—if they ever should?

Cortéz said: "It is unlike him to decline. He is one to whom ventures call. But I will have none who is unwilling to go."

They discussed other names.

Meanwhile, Xamarillo had gone to Marina, and told her of the request that had been made, and which it had vexed him to decline. Perhaps, he thought—

But she heard him with incredulous eyes. "He cannot go overland," she said. "I told him that once before."

Xamarillo did not agree. "If his mind be fixed, he will find a way."

She accepted that, frowning in thought over the difficulties which she knew must be faced, and possibilities by which they might be overcome.

"They must be chosen," she said, "who are young and strong, and of spirits that will not quail. The Tabascans may give counsel and help, if we talk to them in the right way."

He was puzzled that she should regard the proposal as of so desperate a nature. He supposed that there was some native superstition to be overcome. But it was the 'we' which was of moment to him.

He asked: "Why do you say 'we'? You would not be there. And I have told Gonzalo that I shall not go. I had your promise in mind."

"Which will be kept. But we will talk of that at a later time. We shall both go. Hernán may need us now as he never did. But perhaps I can persuade him to reason yet."

In the next hour she went to see Cortéz, and found that an interview was not easy to get. He was in a new palace now, which had been built to his own design, which was more after the style of Seville than those which had been familiar to her.

He was not one who would parade power, or be distant to those with whom he had been familiar before, but there were those around him by whom she was little known, and he had given orders that he was not to be disturbed by any for whom he had not enquired.

She might have been foiled, had not Sandoval met her as he was coming out.

He said: "Yes. He has said he will see none. But that would not be meant for you. Montejo, will you show Doña Marina in?"

He spoke to one whose beard was ungrown, who had come to follow his father's way. He wondered that Hernán and Marina did not accord. Now that Catalina was dead, it would be to the country's advantage, and surely theirs.

She found Cortéz bending over some maps that had been found for him, which were not easy to read. He said: "You have come at the right time. They have found me maps of the country beyond our own. Or at least, that is what they say they are. They are more like pictures to me. I suppose they will have a meaning for you."

"So they will. But you cannot go to Honduras overland. They will show that."

"But I think I shall. I have always hated the sea. And I would learn what the land is like, which may be advantage to us."

She looked at the maps. It was a wonder that they had survived. She knew that all the riches of her civilisation were being destroyed in a way that was the more ruthless because it was undesigned. How could the products of barbarians be of value to civilised men? (Excepting, of course, the gold.)

Marina looked at the maps. She learnt little. She said: "It is a thought. There are rivers traced, but most of it is vacant land. The merchants shun it, for there is no one with whom to trade."

"But they would go there, if there were?"

"Yes." She allowed that. "But it is a land where you cannot live. There is no food."

The map told her that, which she knew before. It gave all else as surmise. It was an impenetrable, impossible land.

Well, Hernán had done such things before. Now, he was not defying men, but the gods of the land, who are much stronger than they. But he—she altered her thought to 'we'—had some very strong gods.

She said: "The Tabascans may tell us more."

"They may find us a guide."

"So they may. But I think not. No one crosses that land. But we may have some counsel from them."

"You speak as though you were coming so far with me?"

"I go as far as you, if you will. Do you refuse that? You will need such as are loyal to you."

"I will decline no aid of the right kind. But do you call it a woman's way?"

"I call it mine. And it may be safer than here. What shall you do with Guatemozín?"

"He is coming with me."

"That is wise. Then Tecuichpo may come too?"

"Is that also wise?"

"You may say that she will be companion for me. And she can ride well."

"Have you taught her that?"

"I have taught her much. She is of our faith now, and she is loyal to you. Guatemozín cannot object to that. But he does not confide in her. Will you tell me who will be going of those I know?"

"It is too soon to say. Xamarillo has refused."

"Which he regretted. You can count surely on him."

"He is one whom I shall be happy to have."

He still thought that the difficulties of the march were being exaggerated beyond reason, and was the more curious to survey this unoccupied land, which was so dreaded by those who, it appeared, had never ventured therein.

He reckoned that it should be a matter of not more than three weeks or perhaps four from when he would leave the known Mexican land to when he would reach that part of Honduras where Olid was supposed to be. But call it five—call it six—he would still be back within three or four months. Surely all that he had done could not be wrecked in so short a time.

Rivers and swamps? Was there not an implication of forest lands? And could not many trees be felled with speed, if there were enough axes and enough labour at hand?

It was foolish to say that he should not take a large force because it could not be fed. Every man could bear his own food. And the more there were, the more quickly natural obstacles would be overcome.

Besides, he had a plan. He knew that the rivers he would have to cross must be those that flowed northward through the Tabascan land. He would not march in a straight line, but making an inland curve, by which means he would encounter them nearer to their sources, where they could not be of much depth. How often before had he found a way when others had seen nothing but the obstacle to be overcome?

He was largely wrong, as is easy to see now that every mile of that dismal land has been measured and mapped. But he would not have come to the high place he now held had he allowed difficulties to defeat him without a test. And the thing had to be done. Olid must not continue to be an example of how easy it was to contemn the authority of the parent land. And would it be more likely to be accomplished if he should send another, and remain here? Few men would think that.

He marched during the next week, and the quality of the little army was the best he had ever led.

There were no more than eighty cavaliers, but they had the best horses the land contained.

There were a few score Spaniards on foot, men who had proved in past campaigns that they could march well. There were nearly two thousand of other races, picked for endurance and strength, and so diverse that it seemed there could be no fear of any general insubordination. There were Tlascalans, Aztecs, Totonacs, even a few Cholulans, and small bodies of half a dozen other of the nations that had been restive under the Aztec yoke. And there were a thousand porters, picked with an equal care.

Guatemozín rode at Cortéz's right hand, no one knowing whether it was with a willing mind. His wife had said she would not remain behind, and rode with Marina in the midst of the cavaliers. Many of these had come recently to the land, the young Montejo among them. They were drawn by the lure of the unknown, and the glamour of their leader's name.

They rode eastward, but taking a more southerly course than that by which Cortéz had first invaded the land. They made good progress, and the eighty cavaliers became five score as they were joined by veterans who had taken farms in the fertile lands, and who could not resist the invitation their general gave.

Bernal Díaz was one of these. He grumbled long afterwards that he had not wanted to leave his farm, but that Cortéz's command could not be disobeyed. This was nonsense, for many others remained, and Cortéz was not one to conscript an unwilling man.

Grumbling to himself that it was an act of a fool. Bernal mounted a well-groomed horse, and fell into the shining ranks of the cavaliers.

They stopped for two days at Huazacualco. Cortéz had no wish to tire them before the more strenuous part of the march should begin, and there was a property dispute here of some magnitude, with which he had undertaken to deal himself, when he should be passing the spot.

The allocation of extensive farms to some thousands of Spaniards had not involved hardship to others, because there was so large an amount of state land which could be distributed in that way. But the trouble had been that the Record Office in México had been entirely destroyed during the siege.

This office had contained pictorial charts of the whole country, so far as it had been under Aztec control. By a system of duplication, similar charts were held locally in each centre of administration, thereby rendering it very difficult for forgery to succeed, or error to occur.

This difficulty appeared to be overcome, for immediate needs, by the discovery of what should have been a complete and accurate record of Government lands still existing as a Taxation Exemption Schedule which had escaped the general destruction.

The trouble was that the destruction of the Record Office and its contents had become widely known, and temptation to alter the local charts, so that government lands were, more or less, absorbed by other estates, had become irresistible to many, who may have felt that they had no moral obligation to leave them for the benefit of the conquering power.

Consequently, there were frequent difficulties with settlers who arrived to take up grants of land which the local records now showed as being portions of private estates, most of which were doubtless adjusted without prolonged difficulty, because those who had trespassed would not dare to contest the matter to the point at which investigation might be fatal (literally by Aztec law) to themselves.

But there was a district in Coatzacualco which was exceptional in the obstinacy of the disputes which had arisen, and with complications which suggested that there might actually be errors in the only chart which the central government possessed, and Cortéz had said that, as it would be no great deviation from his route, he would investigate the issue himself.

Marina had not heard of this, being no longer so closely in his counsels as in earlier times, but she saw that the route they were taking would go very near to her own home, and debated in a doubtful mind whether she should use the occasion to see her mother.

But when they made camp on the night before they would reach that district, Cortéz came to her with a request that she would act in her old part of interpreter on the next day.

It was a fertile, well-wooded, well-watered land, with scattered houses and farms. At that time of year, most of the little army were content to camp under the trees in the open air, but Guatemozín was entertained in the residence of an Aztec aristocrat who doubtless regarded it as a welcome honour to have him and Montezuma's daughter under his roof, even in their fallen estate—and Guatemozín's aspect was not that of a fallen man.

Marina, owing to her friendship with Tecuichpo, and they being the only two women who had had the hardihood to join the expedition, shared his hospitality.

Cortéz was introduced to a large, low-ceiled room, scented with abundant flowers, and ornately furnished in the Aztec manner, in which he found Marina alone.

In the new México city which he was building, chairs and tables were of European design, the Aztec carpenters having taken readily to such constructions, but here he must either stand, or recline on cushions (as he preferred to do), and take the chocolate that was offered to him from a table no more than nine inches high.

He said: "I shall hold an enquiry tomorrow, at which I should be glad for you to interpret for me. It concerns the accuracy of this map, which I should make a guess that you can read better than I, though I have studied it well."

He passed over to her what would have looked to European eyes a slim book, with thin-polished cedar-wood covers, but when she opened it, it had the construction of a concertina, and its material was of aloe-cloth, more durable than paper, and softer, glossier and thinner than parchment could be prepared.

To Cortéz, the brightly painted contents, which could be widely spread, or opened at a single page, were more like a picture than a map, but every colour and line had a simple meaning for her.

As she spread it, she said: "Do you know that part of these are my own lands?"

He thought she alluded to the estates which he had secured for her in that province, and which had been ratified by Madrid. "No," he said. "They are not distant from here, but I should have said they are to the east, by five leagues or ten."

"I meant those which my mother holds."

He was surprised, as he well might be. He said: "No. There is a schedule of ownership on the last three pages, with references to the parts of the map to which they pertain, but they have meant little to me."

She smiled. "You will never read. But it is my brother's name that is here, with our mother's as having charge of his right, as it would be expected to be."

"Is there anything you would have me do?"

"No," she said indifferently. "You will do justice, I know. Could I ask more than that, or else less? But is my mother greatly concerned?"

"I am not entirely clear, but should say not. I am calling on all who hold lands that are painted there to assemble tomorrow. Do you challenge the record as it stands?"

"No. You will let it stand as it is."

They went on to discuss the limits of the crown lands as they were shown on the map, and as he understood that they were in dispute, and she was able to give him some help which he might have got, of such integrity, in no other way; but it was not much, for, in the old days, they were matters of which she had not taken much heed.

He left her not ill-content, and resolving what she should do on the next day.

But events did not happen as she had forecast (as they seldom will).

The assembly was in the open air. Cortéz sat on a raised platform, under a great tree, and she must be next to him.

He had ten cavaliers on each hand, sitting motionless, with their lances raised; for he knew that nothing else would impress the assembling crowd so much, as a gesture of invincible power.

There were other guards and attendants on foot, and there were two scribes, Spanish and Mexican, who could write or paint swiftly, so that the evidence could be recorded in ways that would be baffling to none.

There were about sixty called, who were allowed to sit on the ground, or on stools that their slaves had brought, and a great crowd standing around.

The witnesses were called up to give evidence, one by one, the Spanish settlers being taken first.

Those who were seated were some distance away, and the sight of Marina's mother was not good. But Marina saw her, with her brother beside her, and he recognised Marina almost at once.

"Mother," he said, in excitement, "there is Marina," at which she had a great fear, for she did not think her to be dead, as she had made others believe, but in a distant land.

"Nonsense," she said, "Marina is dead."

"Oh no," he said, with a confidence for which he had more cause than she knew, "she is there," and he pointed to where she sat.

His mother looked, and saw one who still dressed in the Aztec way, and as only one of high rank could have been permitted to do. She thought her to be like Marina, the flowers in her hair being those of her daughter's choice, and being arranged in her way, and the collar of featherwork, in which blue prevailed, was such as she would have chosen to wear. But she was talking familiarly with the strange lord who had shown more than a mortal's power, and become possessed of the whole civilised world, as she knew it to be. It was absurd to suppose that Marina, whom she had sold for a slave, could have come to so great a height.

But the idea vexed and frightened. Memories came which she was accustomed to exclude from her mind. She watched Marina with short-sighted eyes, and the fear grew.

Then her name was called. She had only to go up to the platform taking her own chart for comparison with the record of the local office, and of that which Cortéz had brought, and to have her own re-signed by the notary. She had nothing to fear. She had not been foolish enough to join in the grab of the crown lands, and she had no reason to doubt that the three charts would agree.

Actually, it was because this was anticipated that she was called so early. Those records which would not be challenged were being checked first, so that the innocent would be free to leave.

But as she left her place a sudden fear rose. Suppose that *were* Marina, marvellously come to a place of power, and naturally seeking revenge? If Marina were known to be alive, her declaration would be false, and she was being invited to commit a capital crime.

With trembling knees she had almost reached the platform, when she heard her daughter's voice, which she could not doubt. It said: "Yes, they accord. There is a grove where the stream bends—the yellow line to the southeast—" Then she knew that she was trapped. Her daughter could have been brought there for no other purpose than to be confronted with her, as she was in the act of claiming the land which was not hers.

In a blind panic she turned, and as she ran back towards where she had left the boy sitting, she screamed: "It was a plot—a plot. But I did not sign."

And then the hand of a Spanish guard was an iron grip on her arm. He was drawing her toward the platform when Marina stood in their way. She said: "Juan, there is no occasion for that," and the man, who had known her place beside his commander in earlier days, loosed the arm he held.

Marina said: "Mother, would you wrong me a second time?" She loosed a brooch from her throat, in which a golden snake twisted round a Californian pearl of great beauty and size. She pinned it to the front of her mother's embroidered cloak. She put an arm round her, drawing her gently toward the platform. She said: "The estate is yours. The notary will confirm your right."

CHAPTER ONE HUNDRED TWENTY-ONE:
THE PRICE OF TREASON

It was nearly four months later that the little army camped on a slight elevation, a mere groundswell in a wide depression which was no worse than damp, while all around for many miles, was perpetual slime.

They had had good days, when they had moved forward from five to ten miles, and bad ones when they had done less than one. For many days they squelched through pathless swamps where, every half-mile or less, there would be a sluggish river, too deep to wade, over which a bridge must be built, strong enough for guns to be dragged, and horses ridden.

They had come on occasional villages which had received them with friendly hospitality, and had spared what food they could from their own slender resources, which, for such an army, was next to none.

They had come on others, the flimsy huts of which had risen in flames on their approach, while the hostile and frightened inhabitants had fled into the surrounding forest.

They had learnt much of edible roots, and other unsatisfying foods which could be sought in the wilderness, and by which life might be prolonged in a bloodless way.

For the last four weeks they had come, at somewhat better pace than before, through an interminable forest of cedars—such a forest as the Northern Hemisphere would be unlikely to match, and only the Amazon valley in the New World could exceed. Those who climbed the highest trees would see nothing in all directions but far miles of interminable forest tops beneath the blue dome of sub-tropic sky, or a heaven of low black clouds from which would burst a deluge of thunderous rain.

Below, the cedar boles grew so closely, the dark foliage was so dense, that the men who pushed ahead on a pathless way could not always see the soil that their feet disturbed.

But now there was some change, if no improvement; there was more air around, and swampier ground below. They camped, sharing, not without bitter grumbling, the meagre rations that, even on a starvation basis, were almost done, with the knowledge that they could go no further ahead on the next day, for their path was crossed by a river that was broad and deep, far beyond anything that had been encountered before.

Cortéz, a sick man now, driven on by the inflexible purpose that it seemed only death would have power to weaken, said there was only one way by which the crossing could be made. They must construct a floating bridge. There were murmurs among weary, half-starved Spaniards at this. They did not propose a better plan. They said it could not be done. And they said, further, that they were being led every day into a deeper wilderness, to more certain death. Let them turn back or aside, for there was an obstacle here which could not be crossed.

Cortéz heard a deputation who urged these views upon him, to which he merely replied that the bridge would be built, but not by unwilling hands. He sent at once for the chiefs of the various native contingents, and explained what he required. Not having heard of the discontent in the Spanish camp, they gave willing assent to what, indeed, was the only hope that they had, for, while they faced their greatest obstacle, it was also to be their last.

The axes flashed, and the trees fell, and were cut to the shapes required. At the end of four days there was a solid floating bridge which would endure for many years, and be a marvel to all who saw.

Cortéz, now writing, night by night, a diary which would become another letter to the Spanish King, recorded that more than a thousand trees had been felled, each supplying a beam of not less than sixty feet, which had been dragged to the river side, and securely fixed, till a bridge had been constructed by which men and horses could pass to the further side.

For the first day, there had been few Spaniards among those who toiled. Cortéz had brought Mexican jugglers and mummers to give entertainment to the army at the end of monotonous days. He ordered that the Spaniards should be entertained by them, while the Mexicans worked, which had the effect he had hoped to see, and, by the second day, there were few Spaniards who were not helping the work.

The two women would have helped also had they not been fully occupied by essential tasks that they were more fitted to do: Cortéz, worn with illness (but who was not?) put his hands to the dragging-ropes, reminding men of how they had seen him shouldering beams on the first day after he had given orders to fill in the México City canals: even the porters, breaking lifelong trade union rules, which had been religion to them, were active, with muscular bodies, to fell and haul.

The bridge was finished, its end resting securely on the swamp of the further side. The cavaliers led the way over a structure that had ceased to sway in the sluggish current. They came to the further side, and plunged into a depth of slush. They sank fetlock deep, and then deeper in places, as they struggled toward the thickets of dryer ground.

Don Xamarillo rode by Marina's side. They were wedded now. She had kept her word when December came, not allowing the conditions to which they were reduced to furnish excuse for further delay. How much she had forgotten was best known to her own reticent mind, but she looked serenely content in spite of the sharpness of feature starvation gave at that time; and that she was pleasure to her Castilian bridegroom was apparent to all.

Now her horse sank deeper than most. Xamarillo, his own horse drawing its feet with difficulty from the thick slime, reached to her bridle, and pulled at it in vain. Others were not in much better case.

Those who had struggled to higher ground hewed great branches which they cast round the floundered horses. These would provide a platform by which the riders would be rescued, even if horses, now girth-deep in glutinous mud, could not be saved. But, in the end, they all were; the same industry that had built the bridge, crushed down leaves and boughs into the swamp until it became firm enough for footmen to cross, and, at last, for the cannon to be dragged over without mishap. And then they came to fields of pepper and maize, and could guess that the worst of their toils were done.

That night Xamarillo came to Cortéz, with a request that he could talk in a private way. With some inward curiosity as to what it might mean, Cortéz agreed, and was soon listening to that which he had not expected to hear.

"The man," Xamarillo said, "is in our tent now, and Marina fears that it might be observed if he should leave, which might be danger for him, and in other ways; but she will send him, or come herself, if you think it too great a thing to be dealt with while it is only hearsay from me."

"Why should I think that? You are one I trust." But though he said this, he stood as one in mental debate. Then he asked: "She is quite sure? I have not known her to warn me without a need."

"She thinks it to be a tale that none would invent. You can see reason in that. The man himself is not one she would trust."

"Bring him here in an hour's time. There will be no need to be private by that time. And I shall need Marina."

When he had gone, Cortéz sent for de Ordaz. He said: "Diego, I have that for you to do in which you should be discreet, for we probe a tale which may be little or much. You will go to where Guatemozín is lodged, and bring him here, saying no more than that I wish to see him on an urgent affair; but (if he should ask) you do not know what it is. If he should refuse or defer, you will bring him straightaway, whether dead or alive, knowing that, either way, I should be content. You will take with you no more than two, for I would have no aspect of arrest; and, if he be willing to come, let them fall behind.

"And you will send others to bring the lord of Tacuba in a like way."

They were at this time in a fertile and friendly land, to the inhabitants of which the Aztecs were no more than a distant name.

They had no wish to contend with strangers who sought to pass through their land in a friendly way, and to pay for fodder and food.

There were houses scattered about, good and large, in one of which Cortéz was lodged, its owners having withdrawn, but left service for him.

The room in which he was seated was broad and low, and furnished very nearly to the Aztec style, though with fewer flowers.

Preferring, in the European style, to be raised above the floor, Cortéz had had his own trestle-table of cedar set up, with a carved and polished chair of the same wood.

He had a guard stationed about the doors, which he ordered to be increased. He sent for Bernal Díaz, and ordered him to go round to the Spanish encampments, and to some Tlascalans whom he could trust, and stir them to be alert for a sudden call, though it would be what they must not expect.

Guatemozín was slow to come. The lord of Tacuba arrived first, and was required to wait in another room.

Then Marina came, with Xamarillo, and an Aztec with a scarred lip which gave him a sinister expression his character may not have deserved.

Cortéz said in Spanish: "I will question him myself, and you will observe whether his replies conform to what he has said before."

The man's eyes flickered uncertainly between them, as though he feared what might be said in that foreign tongue, and then Cortéz addressed him in Aztec, of which he had learned much, though he feared to be without Marina when dealing with public affairs. He said: "I hear that you have brought a tale of treason, as it was your duty to do. If you speak truth, you have nothing to fear. You may have reward. You shall repeat it to me."

"Lord, I meant no wrong. It was a plan of which I should not have thought. But I was afraid."

Cortéz saw that he was not destined to hear the tale in a straightforward manner, as it had been given to him before. But he must check its obliquities with what he had already heard. He asked: "You have been afraid for how long?"

There was an implication here at which the man blinked again. But the truth had to be told. He said: "It was before we entered the great wood."

"That was a month ago. And why has nothing been done for so long?"

"It was designed for a time when you should be bogged or trapped, or when Spaniards should be scattered about. But when we came suddenly to a fertile land, there was word passed among us that no better time would be likely to come, and that the darkness must be our friend."

"Do you say that a time is chosen?"

"We were told to be alert for tomorrow night."

But at this point, he was ordered to stand back, and the examination ceased, for Guatemozín had come.

Diego explained the delay. "I was told that he was unwell, and had retired early. He must not be disturbed. I had to insist that he should be roused, and then that he should consent to come, and to wait his time. But I was not refused, so I did not think you would wish me to act in a violent way."

"You have done well. I will have him in. You will remain with him, with your two men, and Montejo also. You will all be alert, listening to what is said, and watching his reaction thereto."

Guatemozín came in.

He was dressed in the rich colours that his nobility allowed him to wear, and they were unsoiled by any hardship through which they had come. Unlike his victor, he had kept himself aloof from manual toil. He had been borne in his litter, as he had come now.

But he was without attendants. He was not invited to sit. Cortéz looked up coldly at one who stood in emotionless dignity, but whose state was gone.

Cortéz said: "You have planned to kill me tomorrow night?"

It was so said that it might be taken as a question, or a mere assertion of fact.

"There has been such talk," Guatemozín answered with equal coldness, "but it has been discouraged by me."

"It is what none would attempt without approval from you."

"Has attempt been made?"

"By your own statement you know of those who propose my death, and said nothing thereon."

"Could you expect that?"

"I expect your pledged allegiance to Spain."

Guatemozín made no answer to that, and Cortéz asked nothing more. He had an admission far beyond anything he had expected to get. He must weigh it against what others might have to say.

He said: "I must hold you in restraint until this has been probed to the root." He ordered that he should be detained under a strong guard, and Tacuba's lord was brought in.

His answers were much the same, though they were given differently. He trembled and whined. Such proposals had been made, but both Guatemozín and he had declined to give them support. He had no scruple to mention names of whom he said were the guilty men.

Arrests and inquisition went on through the night.

In four cases there was absolute vehement denial of complicity in, or any knowledge of the plot. The others were alike in admitting knowledge, but they said it was Guatemozín's plan, which they had declined to support.

It was clear that some lied, or else all, but who could be sure where the truth lay?

Cortéz told Marina that which tortured his mind. He said: "If Guatemozín contrived this plot, he should hang, and I should have one danger the less. I know him to be a most implacable foe, and of his guilt I am almost sure.

"But I would not do injustice, even though he be a constant danger to Spain: Will you tell me what you think?"

"I am not sure."

"There is his wife, and she is friendly to you. I would believe her."

Marina frowned over that. She did not think that Tecuichpo would be taken into confidence in such a matter. Also, she *was* his wife, however distantly held. Could she be asked to betray?

But, after a time of silence, she said: "You should have the truth. I will try."

She saw Tecuichpo in the early morning, and then said: "It was a surprise to her. She would say nothing. She said she would enquire of those in whom she had trust. She has the list of all those you have detained."

Cortéz said: "She is Montezuma's daughter, and loved by all. She will be told if she ask in the right way."

Later, Marina saw her again. She came back with what sounded a poor tale, but, being considered well, it meant more.

She said: "I have learnt this. There may have been a plot, which she will not assert or deny. But she has marked four names on the list, who, she is sure, are innocent men. They are loyal to you, and, if there were such a plot, it would not have been confided to them. She would not have you condemn innocent men."

They were the same four who had protested their ignorance. Cortéz ordered that they should be released at once, and given positions of trust.

Considering what had—and had not—been said, he saw that he had had confirmation of much, but not all.

He said: "You have done well. You shall ask her no more."

"So I had resolved."

"There shall be public trial of all."

So there was. It went on for two days. Everyone concerned, high and low, made the same admission, the same defence.

They had been approached regarding a plot which they had declined to support.

Guatemozín, after a few words, refused to answer further questions. His attitude was contemptuously aloof.

It was a question of who were to be believed, and how much, where much lying was probable, and some certain.

Cortéz considered that it was most improbable that such a plot would have grown to implicate so many, if it had been discouraged by Guatemozín, from whom it was not hidden. He considered also that it was improbable that those who looked up to Guatemozín as their natural lord would be unanimous in bringing such an accusation against him, if it were not true, even to improve their own positions.

He considered also that his wife, after enquiring from those who would be likely to be truthful to her, had declined to do more than to rescue four innocent men, and so, by implication, condemn the rest.

In the end, he condemned Guatemozín, the lord of Tacuba, and one other, to hang, and let the rest go free, as having been incited by them.

It was a merciful judgement, in that it condemned three only, where a more wholesale execution would have been considered both legally justifiable and politically wise, by most rulers of most nations, in that and in other days. And, in coming to that decision, he had earnestly sought the truth. But it left him morose, and self-questioning of the justice of what he had done.

He was not free from the criticism of others also, some of whom would not have been concerned at the hanging of three men, or of thirty, on such evidence, had they been of a nameless kind. It was the position of Guatemozín which caused the attention to be concentrated upon him from which sympathy springs.

He had come from high birth, and a place of power, to a shameful end, and there was tragedy here which was written boldly for all to see.

He had been the Spaniards' stubborn unyielding foe, and his resistance, after it had become clear that it could not avail, had caused the destruction of a beautiful and opulent city, which Cortéz strove to avert; and he had sacrificed the lives of thousands of his own people vainly to that same obduracy. In the end, he had accepted the overlordship of Spain, but he had, even then, refused to disclose where the city's treasures had been hidden or cast away.

Cortéz had always recognised that he would be likely to take advantage of any moment of weakness to have revenge; but he would not condemn or confine him for that which he had not done. The fact was that two men of inflexible wills had clashed, and one or other must, soon or late, have been overthrown with all that was at stake between them. There is certainly no reason to think that Guatemozín would have treated his opponent with equal clemency had their position been reversed. For Cortéz, at any time, under any conditions, to have come into his power, would have meant death on the sacrificial block, with rejoicing and mockery at his end.

For his widow also, it had been a position of tragedy, which, as with Marina, nobility of character overcame.

She was destined to happy marriage with one of the conquering race, and her name may be linked with that of Marina as having done much to reconcile her own people with them, in the spirit of the religion she had adopted.

CHAPTER ONE HUNDRED TWENTY-TWO: THE FATE OF OLID

The three condemned men were hanged on one tree, Guatemozín maintaining the same dignified aloofness throughout, as though he were a distinguished spectator of his own death, the lord of Tacuba protesting that he had been unjustly condemned and entreating mercy until the moment that the rope constricted his throat, and the third culprit being merely hanged, with no more ceremony or record than a nameless man should expect to have; and Bernal Díaz looked on, and wrote of it, forty years later, that he could never be sure that Guatemozín was guilty, and thought he should not have been hanged. But he did not appear to have considered the fate of the other two to have been of any great importance, or to have worried his mind as to whether they were guilty or not.

He noticed that Cortéz (for whom he had a great admiration and regard, in a soldier's critical grumbling way) was troubled in mind, and that the signs of ill-health were more pronounced than before. But the little army moved on the next day to a thriving and friendly city, which traded over a wide area to west and south, but not in the direction of México. Pathless forest and swamp had been both obstacle and protection toward the north, and they did not consider the Spaniards either as potential foes, or having removed any menace from them.

But they warned them that, though the worst might have been passed, there was still a long and arduous wilderness to be overcome, before they would see the ocean from Honduras. And so they found it to be.

Turning southeastwards, they were soon to learn that nature's weapons were more than one. Forest and swamp were forgotten words, but stoney heights and mountain torrents could form barriers no less formidable than they.

A time came when the little army halted, its hardships past, within a few miles of the Spanish settlement it had reached by so hard a way, and sent forward its scouts to determine what the conditions would be with which it would have to deal.

But before that time arrived it had lost many, horses and men, who had been unequal to the hardships they had endured, or the acrobatic feats which mountain climbing and torrent crossing required, with no better incentives than ceaseless rain.

There had been times when half a mile a day was the best progress for which they could hope. Rushing mountain rivers cannot be crossed by a floating bridge. A tree trunk pushed outward from rock to rock, even if one side had been laboriously flattened, is a poor method of transit for horse and man, where a slip will mean certain death in the whirling cauldron below.

One by one, sixty-eight horses had died, or been left behind. More than once, when man and horse rolled together down the mountain side, the man had been rescued with broken limbs, and could not be left. Those whose own footing was hard to keep must increase their peril to bear him on.

There were thirty horses that survived, but there was no need for Bernal's opinion that it would be three months before they would be fit for service again. Anyone could see that.

Cortéz said: "Diego, I must have sure report. You shall go yourself, and take Montejo, whom none of our old comrades would know. He has quick wits, and might make some contact without disclosing that we are here."

It was shrewdly planned, but matters did not go in that way.

The two men advanced cautiously through covering woods. They observed a settlement near the coast. Skirting it, they came to a shore on which long Atlantic rollers were driven by an easterly wind. They knew that the homes to which they might never return lay beyond the immensity of that dreaded perilous sea.

They saw a man who fished for they knew not what, following a receding tide.

Diego recognised one who had once been a friend to him, and by whom Olid had been disliked. He did not think he would betray him. He walked boldly out.

The man, supposing them to be neighbours, took little notice till they were close to him. Then he heard Diego's voice, and looked, and asked, in a tone of wonder, by what means they could have arrived there. He looked toward an inlet along the coast, where two small ships lay at anchor, expecting, with a vain hope, that they had become three. He asked: "How did you get here?"

Diego followed his eyes. He answered: "No. We came overland."

The man stared at that. But there was only one question which could be of much moment to him. He asked: "Do you bring food?"

"No. We starve."

"Then you have come to the wrong place. Are you only two?"

"We are two thousand, or nearer three."

"Am I mad? Or it may be you."

"Pedro, if you will come this way, I will make it clear."

He turned aside to the trees from which he had come, for they had been walking toward some timber huts that were near the shore, and he knew not who might be there.

Pedro followed without further words till Diego spread a faded and tattered cloak on a fallen tree (for the rains had not wholly ceased) and told him all that was to be said on his side, at the end of which Pedro said: "It is nigh to an incredible tale, and that which there is only one (as we both know) who would have been equal to do; but it is one at which the world will laugh for long years to come," and his own laughter broke out, at which they would have been more displeased had they not felt that there must be a reason they could not guess.

Diego said: "We have had no spirit to jest. Why should men make a mock of us?"

"Because it has all been done for just nothing at all. Olid is dead."

"How was that?"

"Las Casas cut off his head."

"But we were told that his ships were lost."

"So they were. But one was wrecked on the shore, and he swam. He joined us, and, after a time, he showed us that we were fools, and should come to a bad end doing that by which only Olid could gain. Besides, Olid did not know how to rule, and, by that time, his friends were few.

"So we fettered him while he slept, and gave him a fair trial, and there was a verdict that was signed by all. And after that we cut off his head, and could hear our own voices again, which had not been easy till then, for he struggled and howled. It was like killing a pig."

"It is good hearing for us, who thought that we might have to fight with our friends."

"It was really the only thing to be done. For there is another settlement down the coast, and they had heard that we were here. And, besides that, we had found that we could not live on the land, and our stores were low. We had to send a ship to Cuba for aid, which should have been back before now.

"You will be welcome, of course, but, as for food, we are starving men."

CHAPTER ONE HUNDRED TWENTY-THREE: NITO

Diego came back to the waiting camp with news which was good and bad.

Spanish men were blithe that they would not be embroiled with their own kin; but it was a bitter hearing to those who starved that they had come at last to an empty land.

Cortéz said that he would ride ahead, and consult with Las Casas as to what could now be done. He wished to learn the worst, and make his own decision, before others would hear; for the tale which Diego had brought had a desperate sound.

He knew that the thousands for whom he must provide might be ill-fed for two more days, or perhaps three.

After that, could they take whatever might remain in the hands of men who were not in much better case, and whose most (they being but a few score) could make little difference to them?

So he took Diego, and the two best horses there were, and rode into a village which showed that strenuous work had been done, as did the cleared fields around, and the half-grown crops.

He could not say that he was not welcomed well, but he heard a poor tale. The climate was bad, the land swampy, and infested with poisonous snakes, and insects that (being more numerous) were nearly as bad. Some had died of fevers, and others had only survived in a weak state. Even the Indians they had brought with them found the climate hard to sustain.

He said: "You have had a lean time; and so have we in a diverse way. But why do you stay here, if it be so hopeless a spot? You should explore further south, for which your three ships should avail."

They said: "You mean two."

"I mean three; for we saw them as we rode over the higher land. There were two that rode with bare masts, and one that was furling sails."

Las Casas leapt to his feet. "Then our ship is in."

In the next moment he had become one of many who ran to the little harbour which was a mile, or more, from where they had cleared and built. But they knew, before they got to the harbour side, that their present troubles were done.

They knew that *The Ark of God* would have brought food enough even for the thousands who had so unexpectedly appeared to share it.

Cortéz saw his most desperate problem relieved, but the position was still one which was not simple to solve.

He was responsible for three thousand Indians of various nations and lands, whom he had led a thousand miles, more or less, from their homes, and who would be little likely to welcome permission to return by the way they came, now that they knew what its hardships were.

In any case, it was useless to think of that, for he lacked the food, without which it would be a venture of certain death. Even at the best, they had learnt that no porters could bear enough for so long, so arduous, and so barren a way.

Neither did he see how ships could be assembled to take them home by the long voyage around Yucatán.

He could take ship himself, and it was the obvious thing for him to do, having been already absent from México far longer than he had intended, or it was prudent to be. But he was reluctant to go, leaving those who relied on his leadership marooned there; and averse also from returning after so long a time with a record of nothing done.

Beyond these hesitations, he had a feeling of distaste for the life he had been leading as Governor of the great land he had won for Spain.

He had conquered it, as few others would have been likely to do: he had brought it to civil order with equal success. His reward was that he was worried, obstructed, and slandered by smaller men, whom he must treat with an ever watchful discretion, regarding not only how things were, but how, three or four thousand miles away, they could be represented to be.

He had come to Honduras with sufficient cause. He could defend that. But he knew that, in his heart, he had *wanted* to get away.

And beyond all, he was sick and exhausted. He had good reason to rest; and, so, for a time, he did.

But rest with him would resemble energetic enterprises of other men.

Not waiting for the *Ark of God* to refit, he despatched one of the other vessels to Cuba, to bring further stores, proportionate to those who must now be fed, and including many things which the infant colony might require, and which only he could finance.

He sent out four exploring parties into the interior in different directions, with instructions to survey the land, and examine its resources with exhaustive care.

He then sailed with the other two vessels, southward along the coast, visiting the Spanish settlement at Truxillo, of which he had heard, and seeking some limit to the land which would enable men to sail into the further ocean, and become a supreme justification of all that had, so far, been so abortively done.

He could not succeed in that, for the land, as we know, went on until it encountered Antarctic seas; but he gathered much information about the country which would be called Nicaragua at a later time, and was planning its exploration, when a ship, which had sailed from Vera Cruz without anyone concerned informing the central government in México City of what it did, brought him a letter which turned his mind back to those things which he would prefer to forget.

It was written by one of the officials, Zuazo, to whom he had delegated authority during his absence from México, and who had remained faithful to him.

This is what he read:

> "*My honoured lord,*
>
> *I write this in the hope that it will arrive safely at Honduras, and that, when it shall do so, you will be there, and have taken control, as I cannot doubt that you will have been able to do.*
>
> *If it reach you, I ask that you will return in haste, for what is Honduras to the great empire that your absence will cast away?*
>
> *You had scarcely left when we were at issues one with another, each man seeking his own rather than to administer justice and truth. But there was some*

order and restraint while it was supposed that you would soon be with us again.

But when some months had passed, and you did not return, there came a report from Tabasco that you, and the whole army, had perished in a land of swamps, which you had been warned not to attempt to cross.

At first, this was not believed, but, as the months passed, and no word came either by land or sea, it had a more probable sound, and when we had certain word that you had not reached Honduras (Las Casas having dealt with Olid there without aid from you, as you will know, if you get this it was agreed by most that it must be true, which I still doubt, and I am sending this [with the good aid of the Commander at Vera Cruz] in the hope that you are still live.)

But a day came when your death was proclaimed, and a great funeral held, after which your estate was seized, it being said that it would be spent on masses to save your soul (as some was), and much was taken, which it was said you owed to the state.

The property of others who are with you has been dealt with in a like way.

The Aztec population is so hardly used that it is near to rebel, the system of requisitioned labour, which you restrained and controlled, being now so harshly applied that they are worse off than slaves would have been by their ancient law.

The Franciscan friars that you had from Madrid have gone home, where they say they will make report, with what result we can only guess.

If the Aztecs rise now, it may be the end, for many Spaniards would join with them; but if you get this I suppose you will soon be here."

There was more than this, but all in the same vein.

He read, and reacted at once as he was likely to do. There was one ship in the harbour, and within an hour it had orders to get ready to sail.

The next day it put out to sea, bearing him and as many of his companions as its accommodation allowed.

But a week later it struggled back, having been struck by a tropic storm, which it had done well to survive.

Being refitted, it sailed again, and once more, dismasted and waterlogged, it limped back to the Nito quay.

For the moment, perhaps for the first, perhaps for the only, time in his life, and under the depression of a slow fever which did not mend, he accepted defeat.

The next vessel put out to sea, and succeeded in casting anchor at Vera Cruz, but this time he was not on board. It bore only a letter to assure his friends that he was not dead, and hoped to see them again.

After the ship had sailed, he ordered that there should be public prayers that the will of Heaven might be disclosed, and, as he led the procession to the Church, it was said that he had the look of a dying man.

Rendered despondent by a malady which the climate did nothing to cure, and which would have been better diagnosed at a later day, he asked himself, without bitterness: Was his work done? Was Heaven's mandate withdrawn?

It was not of his nature to turn his thoughts to a life of ease; he would go on, if he could; otherwise he would be contented to die.

And then Sandoval came to him, with word which he could not decline, and may have been contented, to hear. He was the one man whom Cortéz could wholly trust, the one who was entirely devoted to him. The one who shared the memories of their childhood home. Who was so much the younger that Cortéz, in affectionate moments, would call him son. Who spoke little, rarely initiating a plan, but would take all orders, however difficult, without argument or complaint, and had never failed to bring them to full success.

In his slow lisping speech, he assumed rather than said that they would sail together for México as soon as the ship could be equipped for another voyage; and he implied, in a confident way, that such return would make everything simple and smooth. More subtly (if subtlety it were) he made casual allusions to the abuses suffered by their friends which must continue till his return; and the injustices threatened or inflicted upon the native population, and in a proposal that the exemption from labour requisition which Cortéz had obtained for the Tlascalans by Royal Order from Madrid should be withdrawn, which would certainly be resisted, and probably, in its ultimate consequence, lead to bloodshed and rebellion throughout the land.

Cortéz listened wearily. He said little, and that in despondent words. But he made preparations to go. The remaining Spaniards (apart from those who were making the new colony their unattractive home) arranged to return with him. They were no more than a score now—those who had been most closely attached to himself; and passages were then offered (as on every outgoing ship) to such Mexicans as would dare the perils of unfamiliar ocean, rather than remain, separated longer from home and friends, in a place where even food was precarious to obtain, or dare the thousand miles of barren precipice, forest, and swamps, which must be traversed if they would adventure the landward way.

Some parties, after prolonged hesitation, had done this already, preferring it to the unknown dangers of the sea (by means of which their large numbers could only return gradually, at the best) or to separation from their homes being indefinitely prolonged.

They could not do this, if they would, without the consent of the colony, for it must provide them with as much food as they could carry, to its own deficiency, but less certainly to its loss, for it put a limit, however onerous, to what they must provide, against the indefiniteness of what might be required before it would be possible for all of them to go by sea.

So the twice-baffled *Ark of God* put to sea again with a crowded deck, and this time it completed its voyage, though that was not until the lapse of many weeks, for it was driven by the stress of weather far off its course, and found shelter in a Cuban harbour, where it remained for some weeks, before it sailed again to cast anchor at last upon the Mexican coast.

Cortéz landed quietly. He was glad to be back on that soil which he had won with such heroic effort, such tireless service to what he believed to be the high causes of God and Spain. He had a feeling of having come home to a place of rest. But he was in no haste to resume the life of controversy and intrigue which he had left with relief, if it would be unfair to say he had fled.

He had brought no horses upon the ship, and he went on foot until he reached a settlement of Spaniards about fifteen miles from the coast, which he had named Medellín, being that of the village where he was born.

The weather was hot, for it was nearing the end of May, and the walk wearied him, to a degree that was strange and new.

He came to the sight of men who had been his close companions two years before, and was so changed by illness and fatigue that they wondered whether it could be he.

But from that point there was no more walking for him: there was no more returning to México in a quiet way.

The news of his death, definitely announced several months earlier, had been widely believed. The control of a country that had been in a condition of hard transition, politically immature, had passed to smaller, meaner, less magnanimous men.

The news that he was alive, and had returned, spread with such rapidity that he rode next day, mile by mile, along roads that were lined with cheering, delirious crowds, and strewn with continual flowers.

Tabascans, Totonacs, Cholulans, Aztecs, and men of other tribes whose armies he had defeated, whose cities he had subdued, came as he went on, from hundreds of miles on either side of his route, to welcome him whom they had known to be courageous, clement, tolerant, generous, and just. He had been inflexible on one point only—the establishment of the Christian Faith, and the destruction of other gods, and his moderation on what to him were inferior issues, had emphasised this immobility, and done much to convince reluctant minds that he spoke with the voice of God.

Seldom if ever in the history of human civilisation has there been tribute paid to an alien conqueror so spontaneous, so eager, and so extreme.

Even music, which was of religious significance to the Aztec mind, and seldom, if ever used for secular festivities, either public or private, was loud to greet him as he entered Tlascala, and again as he approached the capital city which he had destroyed, and recreated.

The belief in his death, and the darkening shadow of an inferior standard of government, cruel and rapacious, which had quickly followed, had caused men to appraise him with clearer sight than they would have otherwise had.

CHAPTER ONE HUNDRED TWENTY-FOUR: MADRID MOVES

Cortéz returned to his own palace to resume, though for six weeks only, the great power he had held before, but with the added knowledge, which he could have gained in no other way, that he reigned secure in the hearts of men.

He knew that, to almost all, Spaniards and Aztecs alike, his return was an occasion of joy, though there must be a few who would be waiting his vengeance in a great fear.

Even for one who had loyal and loving friends, to return among them after a year during which they had not doubted that he was dead might produce confusions, and disappointments hard to endure. And these men had been his envious competitors, his intriguing foes. They had tried, even while he had been among them, to reap the harvest that he had won; they had tried to overset his method of government for that which they believed would be more profitable for themselves, and more appropriate for a conquering race.

He had to find that most of his property had been sold, and had passed—much of it beyond recovery—into their hands. The proceeds of part of it had been remitted to Madrid, with a false report that discovery had been made after his death that he had misappropriated that which was due to the Crown.

They had enriched themselves, and invited Madrid to conclude that they had a standard of honour above his own.

What was the Spanish Government to believe?

But he did nothing against those who had acted thus. They were punished by no more than their own fears, in a short suspense.

He did little to recover his own property, though he found that much of that which remained was surrendered to him in a hurried way.

His friends even reproached his weakness in doing no more to assert his right, and to punish those who had abused the trust he had left with them. But he was reluctant to use his power for personal ends.

His own two homes—the palace he had built in México, and the garden retreat in Cojohuacan, had been little disturbed, mainly owing to the exertions of Xamarillo and Marina on their return. He had thanks for them, and rewards for all who had been faithful in difficult days. He reported to Madrid how powerfully the influences of Tecuichpo and Marina, and some of the Tlascalan princesses, had been used to prevent rebellion among those of their own races. (Louise had no part in this, for she was with Alvarado in Guatemala, where they were winning a new land for Spain, by means which Cortéz would not have used, but without Olid's folly, in trying to be independent of their source of power).

Health and energy were rapidly resuming in a better climate, and under more favourable conditions of life, when, within six weeks of his return, the news came that a delegate of the Spanish Government had arrived at Vera Cruz, with temporary authority to take the control of the administration entirely into his own hands.

This action, though it doubtless had its roots in the intrigues of Cortéz's enemies, who were still jealously active in Madrid, does not appear to have been either unreasonable in itself, or directly hostile to him.

The home government—always irregularly and very slowly informed of what was happening in these new lands, over which it had such vague and doubtful control—had been told that Cortéz had misappropriated its revenues; they had been told that he wasted the country's wealth in gigantic schemes for his personal aggrandisement; even the popularity which he had won among the conquered races by an equity on which they had found that they could rely was turned into an accusation against him—he was making friends of them so that he could have their support in throwing off the yoke of Spain. It had also been reported definitely that he was dead.

Was it wonderful that it was decided to send a man of carefully chosen character and integrity to find out what was really happening, and with authority to take such measures as the occasion required?

Ponce de León came to México not knowing whether Cortéz were alive, but, to meet that contingency, he brought a personal letter from the Spanish King, assuring him that the intention was not to attack, but to vindicate him from persistent calumnies. Cortéz received him in a friendly spirit, and assisted him in his investigation.

There was no reason to doubt that a report would have resulted which would have led to the confirmation of the authority which Cortéz had previously held, but, after a few weeks, de León fell ill of a malignant fever, and in a few days he was dead.

Before he died, he transferred his authority (with doubtful legality though with Cortéz's consent) to a man who was of amiable rather than forceful character, from whom there was little danger that any trouble would come, but unfortunately he was not young. A few months later he was also dead, and before *he* died he had followed precedent and delegated his authority to the Royal Treasurer Estrade, who had schemed to obtain it from him, being one of Cortéz's most virulent foes.

Estrade studied his much-transferred commission, and decided that it gave him authority to rule the land as he would, which he proceeded to do. A delegation of Spaniards, Aztecs, and Tlascalans waited on Cortéz, urging him to take action, which would have their support, whatever it might be.

He answered that he had already sent a letter to Spain asking that Estrade should be removed. He would do nothing without the authority of Madrid. That meant waiting for four months, or it might be six, while Estrade might do as his nature was. For that time, Cortéz used his influence to the utmost to prevent any lawless action. It was that influence which made it possible for his rival to rule.

The answer came from Madrid as quickly as it was likely to do, but it was no pleasure to read. It simply confirmed Estrade's authority.

It had not quite the significance which appeared, for the Spanish King had decided to send out a Court of Enquiry to dispose finally of these vexatious disputes. It was already preparing for embarkation, under the imposing title of the Royal Audience of New Spain. There would have been little point (and some aspect of pre-judgement) in superseding Estrade immediately before its arrival. It was instructed also (with ambiguous intention) to advise, or even insist, that Cortéz should return to Spain while its enquiries were carried on. What would have happened, had this been known, it is vain to guess.

Cortéz took the reply he received to mean that his enemies were again being credited at Madrid, and decided what he would do. Estrade came to a similar conclusion, considered the game was won, and acted accordingly.

A man was brought before him charged with being implicated in a small matter, impossible to judge at this distance of time, but when he learnt that he belonged to Sandoval's household, he ordered that he should lose a hand.

Sandoval hurried to Cortéz. Indignation almost conquered his lisp. "Will you allow this? He asked. "Is there no limit to what we must endure from this upstart clerk?"

Cortéz picked up his hat. He said: "Do you think me one to desert my friends? He shall not lose his hand. You can be easy on that."

He walked over to the palace where Estrade now ruled. He was told that he was in his room alone, and pushed open his door.

"Estrade," he said, "you go too far. Do you know that, but for me, your life would not be safe for an hour? The man shall not lose his hand, though the skies fall."

Estrade tried to reply in a bold way, though his cheek paled. He said: "Do you think you are still Governor here? You have appealed to Spain, and you know what the answer was. There is nothing more you can do."

Cortéz answered in the smiling way which had become less frequent than it once was: "Oh, but I know what I shall do, which you may not like. But I am not talking of that. The subject is a man's hand. I ask you to let it stay where it is, as a small favour to me, which, if the occasion should come, I should well repay. You should think of that."

"And my answer is that I will neither be threatened nor bribed. But there cannot be two rulers here. I must order you to leave the city by tomorrow noon, and to keep out till you have my leave to return."

Cortéz considered this, and was still smiling when he replied: "If I do that, and let it be known that I am obedient to you, is the sentence quashed?"

Estrade thought that he was offered much at a low price. He would feel freer if Cortéz were further away. He asked: "You will go in peace, plotting no vexation to me?"

"Yes. I will do that."

"Then I will send the man to you tonight; and you will be gone by tomorrow noon?"

"So I will." Cortéz put a white-plumed hat back on his head and walked out. He had the air of having engaged in a skirmish that had been easily won.

When he told Sandoval, he met with surprise, at which he smiled more than before. He said: "It is to Cojohuacan that I go by tomorrow noon; and you can join me there as soon as you will. But we shall go further than that. We shall go to Spain."

CHAPTER ONE HUNDRED TWENTY-FIVE:
RETURN TO SPAIN

Estrade heard that which he did not like. There were two ships at Vera Cruz which Cortéz was equipping in an opulent way. Indeed, he was sending so much of his treasure on board that it raised a doubt that as to whether he meant to return. There was some comfort in that, but there might have been more had he not reflected that Cortéz at the Court of Madrid might make much trouble for him.

But the months passed, and his departure delayed. He was planning a campaign of vindication, and he prepared all with the careful detail that had preluded his most audacious exploits of other sorts.

He was at Vera Cruz now, and while there he heard of the Commission which had been appointed, but it did not arrive. Men of the station and quality who had been chosen did not hurry in those days to cross the world on a mission from which they would not quickly return. They had their own affairs to adjust.

Cortéz did not change his purpose for that, nor because the ship which brought the news also brought that of his father's death, which was both grief and loss, for Martín Cortéz had been both agent and advocate for his famous son, patient, indefatigable, adroit.

He had two of the finest sailing vessels which could be procured in those days, and they would not sail with empty cabins or empty holds, nor without good means of defence, if they should meet with pirates after they left the Azores, as they would be quite likely to do.

Sandoval was going with him, and taking his wife. And other Mexicans and Aztecs were preparing to take the long voyage to the unknown land, a son of Montezuma among them, and a son of Maxixcatzin. And so were de Tapia, and Montejo, and others who still remained of the old captains, or who had joined him in later days.

And he was gathering specimens of animals and the most brilliant birds, and of the natural products of the land, which would be marvels in Spain; and featherwork and jewellery, showing its crafts, and minerals, showing its wealth. And he was taking jugglers and mummers that every feature of Aztec civilisation might be displayed.

Estrade decided that he had gone too far. A reconciliation would be better than that. He appealed to the Church's aid. The Bishop of Tlascala appeared at Vera Cruz before the ships were ready to sail.

He was a patient negotiator, and he tried hard, believing that he worked in the cause of peace, as it was his Christian duty to do.

Cortéz was also patient, but there was no change in his smiling reply. His resolution was made. His preparations had gone too far. Estrade could put his case before the Royal Audience which was now on the way—or he could resign, which it might be wisdom to do.

Estrade got no comfort from that advice, and Cortéz, after waiting for a time, that he might have a fair wind and a steady keel for those who had never before encountered the open sea, started on what was to be a wind-favoured voyage, until he cast anchor in the little harbour of Palos in the early summer of 1528—twenty-four years after he had left his native land with Quintero's fleet. He was forty-three at this time, and thanking St. Peter (his patron saint) for the blessing of health restored.

Yet the shadow of death was over the little port as it stirred to animation and wonder at the strangeness and opulence of those who landed, with brown-skinned lords and princesses in rich outlandish garments and golden collars and flashing gems, and such store of treasure, and unknown beasts, and bright-plumaged birds, as they had not thought that the world contained, until they proved to be too much for the quay, and must be sheltered in a mean inn, and other buildings throughout the town, while transit was collected to start them on the road to Seville.

It was the port at which Columbus had landed thirty-five years before with news of the Western World. It was of more importance than it would be in later times, but it had no adequate accommodation for those who were landing now, and Cortéz moved forward at once to the convent of St. Rabida, as Columbus had done before him, but he left Sandoval behind, who said he felt unwell, and would follow on the next day.

But the next day he did not arrive. There was a message from him that he was ill. He would follow when he could. Cortéz went back. It was not his way to leave a comrade at need, whether through illness, or in the hazards of war.

He was one who gained the loyalties of many friends, but he was to lose the most faithful, the most entirely devoted, and, in many aspects, the most capable, here. In a few days Sandoval was dead.

He was thirty-one, having lived, for the last ten years, a life of constant peril and ceaseless toil. He was the only one of the captains sharing the great adventure who could show the scars of more wounds than their leader himself. Men would say that he died from exhaustion, having done more than human nature should be called upon to endure.

But against that there is the fact that he had just had the restful benefit of a long sea voyage. Sudden deaths were not infrequent at that time, from ill-defined 'fevers', which were insufficiently understood.

Anyway, he was dead. And Cortéz, having remained at his side, prolonged delay for his burial, and paid the priests with an open hand that there should be many prayers for his soul's peace on its new adventure, and went on, with a friend the less, through a land which had now had time to become aware of his presence, and was stirring to excitement at what it heard.

Even apart from this initial delay, Cortéz moved with a slowness which must have been deliberate, he being one who planned hazards with detailed care.

He buried his friend in the convent cemetery at La Rabida, where he still lies, and while he halted there, a young man named Pizarro claimed the hospitality which was not refused by a House of God. He said that he was on the way to the Court to petition the King for aid in exploring the New Land below the equator, of which he had much to tell, and much to learn from these veterans of conquest, whom he was to emulate in an almost equally brilliant, though on an inferior moral plane.

Leaving there, the bizarre procession advanced inland to the castle of the Duke of Medina Sidonia, who entertained it in his semi-regal way, and enquired of Cortéz why, being affluent in other possessions, he was so ill supplied with horses that even some of the noble Tlascalan women must go on foot, as a Spanish lady would not be allowed to do.

"There is," Cortéz replied, "a simple reason in the fact that they come from a land where (though some litters are used) walking is not held to be an ignoble mode. But, beyond that, it would be the act of a fool to bring horses from the New World, to which they are hard to transport, and where we need many more than we have. There is much wealth to be made by those who will be most forward to breed them there, for which it is a suitable land. My own horse? Yes, I brought that. He is a bay stallion I would not leave, not knowing certainly that I should return.

"I gave him once to a dear friend, but, when the occasion for his use became less, she preferred to return him to me."

The Duke looked faintly surprised. "She? I should not have called him a woman's horse."

"He was one that she rode with ease. She did most things well."

The Duke noticed that he spoke in a past tense, and that there was sadness in his voice easy to hear. He said: "I should not have asked? She is dead?"

"She is not dead. She is the wife of Don Xamarillo, whose kinsmen I think you know. She is one I lost, though I loved her well. It may have been my fault. I am not sure."

The Duke saw that he had raised a memory of that which his guest would be better pleased to forget. He said: "Well, we can amend the lack of horses for those who prefer to ride. My stables have those that they can spare."

After that, he wrote to his friend, the Duke de Béjar, saying: "He is unwed, and should be consoled. He is also one whom it is a pleasure to know. You should contrive that Juana shall see him without restrain. He is one for whom she would sell her soul, if he could be hers in no other way."

When he left, after a stay of some days, there were six Arabian mares awaiting him to use as he would: "When you return to your Western rule," the Duke said, as though he spoke of a settled thing, "you may find them useful to have."

Cortéz went on to Guadaloupe, where he stayed for ten days, having been gratified to find that the King's orders had provided accommodation for him, and being greeted in such a manner by the nobility there as to strengthen his determination to move slowly, and let rumour and expectation work to their full effect.

At Toledo, he was met by his correspondent and powerful advocate, the Duke de Béjar, with a group of lesser nobles, in the midst of a deliriously cheering crowd.

He went on to be received by the King himself, not as one against whom accusation had to be examined and weighed before acquittal (even if confidently anticipated) but as the conqueror of a vast land, who had done all (as in fact he had) for the glory of God and Spain.

The fact was that his return had itself pleaded his cause, as all the documents and figures which he had brought would have been unequal to do. He had thought that he could argue his innocence and loyalty in personal session before the King, as no letters or paid advocacy would, but he found that they had become arguments that no one wanted to hear.

All the accusations that had been made, all the evidences that had been offered in their support, interested the Crown primarily from one angle: "Did they raise a doubt as to whether, when he had made his own position secure, he would renounce allegiance to Spain, obliging it to lose the prize, or to embark upon a distant, precarious and most costly war?"

And the mere fact of his voluntary return had answered that fear in the most conclusive way possible. He was no longer one to be challenged in any way. He was to be feted, honoured, and praised.

The Royal Audience which, by this time, had arrived in México, saw it in the same way. They had come prepared for all contingencies. They had power to direct him to return home, and to enforce their will by violence, if necessary, should he refuse. (Though how they would have had the means of doing so, under such circumstances, may not be easy to see.)

But to find on their arrival that he had already gone, was to find that their work was done before it began.

Yet the enquiry must be held, and Estrade's party, seeing it in the same way, though with reluctant eyes, shifted their ground, and accused him of a variety of civil and political crimes.

He had not only defrauded the King's revenues (that accusation, at least, could stand!), he had murdered his wife. He had murdered Ponce de León. He had murdered his successor. Why he had not murdered Estrade did not appear.

The Royal Audience took down the evidence which was tendered in support of these picturesque charges. It prepared a report of a hundred pages thereon, which, in a year's time, arrived at the law courts of Seville, where it seems that it was silently filed.

But meanwhile, by simply remaining in Spain, he had risen beyond their reach.

In the early part of 1530, having been more than eighteen months in his native land, Cortéz sailed again for México, and, after a prolonged pause at St. Domingo, landed on the 5th July, 1530 at Vera Cruz.

He had the high title of Marquess of the Valley. He had the high office of Captain-General of New Spain and the Southern Sea. He had the grant of an enormous area of the most fertile land in México.

He had, in Juana, a young, beautiful, noble, most loyal wife.

He brought his mother to rejoice in the acclamations with which his return was greeted by Spaniards and Mexicans alike.

He brought horses, cattle, and sheep to be settled in the new world, and many plants and seeds, that he might found a paradise where all that was best in the two worlds he knew could be felicitously combined.

There may have been few, among the myriads of forgotten men, who have striven with such inflexible purpose, through such continual hazard, to achieve some improbable end. It is certain that there have been very few who have come to a triumph so high, and a felicity so complete.

CHAPTER ONE HUNDRED TWENTY-SEVEN: THE FALL OF NIGHT

The records of human weakness show that, for supreme triumph, there is no sequel surpassing that of immediate death. But the fate of Wolfe or Nelson is a climax that comes to few.

To most there must be ordeals of idle prosperity, or the shadows of meaner days. They may sink into ignoble vices: they may watch their fames lessening hour by hour, till they fade from the recognitions of men. There are many paths they may take, either of honour or shame, but they must all lead downwards from the height which they had been lonely to win.

Hernando Cortéz died in the village of Castilleja on a December day of 1547. He had abandoned hope of life two months before, when he had signed his will in Seville, and removed to a quietude where he was less likely to be disturbed.

He was sixty-three. Seventeen years had passed since México had risen hysterically to greet his triumphant return.

Circumstances had brought him to Spain, while Juana remained in charge of their Mexican home, but his son Martín, a boy of fifteen, was with him, doing all of consolation that was possible, in a spirit of admiration and final love.

When he signed his will, he felt that he had closed the chapter of his worldly affairs. It was a document of many pages, covering many complex matters, with clarity and characteristic care.

In Spain, his friend the Duke of Medina Sidonia, and two other nobles, were to be his executors. In México, his wife was to act, with the co-operation of the Bishop of Toledo, and two other prelates.

He set out the principle on which he had levied ground rents from the Mexican estates which had been awarded to him.

They had previously belonged to the Aztec Government, and he had been scrupulous not to exact more than the tenants had paid to it. He wished this limitation to be continued, and if it should be found in any instance that it had not been observed, excess payment was to be returned.

He attached a list of the agents he employed on his various properties, and requested that they should not be superseded. They were good men, whom he had chosen with care, and they understood the spirit in which he wished his properties to be controlled.

He provided, with careful but liberal discrimination, for children and dependants, endowed the hospital he had founded in México City, and provided for the foundation, in his own favourite Cojohuacan, of a convent, and a training college for missionary priests. He entailed the remainder of his property upon his young son, Martín, who would succeed to his own title of Marquess.

Finally, he put a moral issue before his executors and his heirs—was it right for a Christian man to own Indian slaves?

"Since," he wrote, "this is a disputed question, I require my son Martín and his heirs to spare no effort to resolve it exactly, for their consciences will be involved no less deeply than mine has been."

Having disposed of these matters with the finality which his condition required, he could turn his mind, during the last weeks, while he wasted away from the cancer which his doctors' treatment could do little to alleviate, and nothing to cure, to regard the recollections of eventful life with satisfaction, or with regret.

His thoughts moved forward from the almost forgotten years when he had been farming in Cuba, with bold experiments in cultivation, importing cattle that his father procured, and making happiness for a passionately-loving, barren, maddeningly incompetent wife, to the time of planning and hope, when he had been bargaining, buying, mortgaging, staking all he had, for the fixed purpose of exploring an unknown land—the quarrel with Velásquez—the flight of unready ships at the break of dawn—to a day when he had been talking with Montezuma, half in Aztec and half in Spanish, reclining on the sunlit deck of a brigantine, with Marina beside them, and the boom of the mainsail creaking above their heads. They were in Montezuma's room now, with a sense of urgency and suspense, while Aztec hordes raged round the palace walls, and she was talking to him. He wondered what she could be saying for so long without referring to him. But he had never doubted her from the first. She had been loyal, although aloof. In some ways, of several women his life had known, she had been closest to him. Need he have lost her? It was she who had drawn apart. Of her own will, but surely not of her own desire. Had she not said that she had needed time to forget?

He saw that what had divided them at the last was the gulf that there had always been. The alien civilisations. The different standards of noble living. He had destroyed her civilisation. He had done much evil. Yet he supposed that he had done well, for he had brought a whole people to God. His thoughts went to Juana, waiting for him in the sun-drenched loveliness of their Mexican home. It was about now that she would be gladdened by the letter announcing that he was leaving Seville—on the way to her.

It was a few hours after that letter had been sent that the pain had become suddenly worse, and he had known that he should never see her again.

But it was best so. Why should her last memory of him be that of an ageing man, with a haggard face, and all the flesh gone from his bones? She, who had always worshipped him as a demigod. But she would have their son. Martín would go back to her. Marina had a son Martín too, of whom he had seen less, but reports were good. He had provided for him in his will. Juana would deal with that. It was how she would wish it to be. And for others also. There was nothing hidden from her.

His thoughts were now on the later years—after the triumphant return to México, when most men would have been content to rest, or rather to live in quiet activities, administering their estates.

But that would have been the end of his life to him, before the darkness need fall, as it fell now. He had continued an adventurous life. Not merely to be, but to do. And men would say that he had bitterly failed; as, at times, he had.

But he did not look at it that way.

He knew that his life ebbed to its last hour. His sight had become dim. But he could feel Martín's fingers twined in those of his own wasted hand. And, by the great blessing of God, as he had become weaker, the pain had gone.

"Martín," he said, "you will tell her that there is no occasion to grieve. We shall meet in a better place." His thoughts wandered again. He was on the deck of the first ship that had ever penetrated into the Californian gulf, which would be known forever after as the Sea of Cortéz to Spanish ears. There was a storm coming from the east, and he was tacking to get what distance he could from the peril of a lee shore on his larboard bow. His thoughts moved forward to a more recent event, when he had joined the expedition against Algiers, and the Admiral's ship, on which he had sailed, had been wrecked on the African coast. Martín had been with him, a boy of ten, and they had both swum safely to shore through a night of storm. Martín had always been with him since then. He had tried to teach him the mode of dangerous living where honour lies, and he did not think he had failed. But his thoughts wandered back to the Pacific shores which he had done so much to explore. When he could not go himself he had sent Ulloa, with three ships, to continue the work. A most gallant and able man. He had explored the Californian peninsula on its outer side, sailing far north, to prove that it was the mainland, and that there was a great continent there. He had sent one ship back with the record of what he had done, and gone on—where?—with the other two. He had gone further into the unknown, and not been heard of again. God rest his soul! But there was little doubt that he had arrived at a good end. He had been faithful to God and Spain.

ABOUT THE AUTHOR

SYDNEY FOWLER WRIGHT (1874-1965) penned over seventy volumes of science fiction, fantasy, classic mysteries, historical novels, poetry, and non-fiction, many of them being published by the Borgo Press Imprint of Wildside Press.